Craving 1985 Collection

Kirsten S. Blacketer

CRAVING 1985 COLLECTION

When I Found You

Can't Fight This Feeling

She Gives Love a Bad Name

Owner of a Lonely Heart

Just What I Needed

Published by BlackShip Press

Cover Art by V. Miller Artist

First Print, October 2025

Print ISBN: 9781966905196

Dedication

For those who lived through the 1980s and the 2020s.
We felt the sting of the present and longed for a taste of nostalgia.
This is for you.

Also dedicated to the following gents:
Val Kilmer
Kevin Costner
Adam Driver
Sebastian Stan

Thanks for the inspiration.

Content Warnings

These books touch on some heavy issues.
If a book that addresses topics like parental death, abuse, domestic abuse, PTSD, murder, thoughts of suicide, and sex are something you can't handle right now, I understand.

Please see my website for a comprehensive list of content warnings for each book.

Take care of yourself.

Love,
Kirsten

Table of Contents

When I Found You

Can't Fight This Feeling

She Gives Love a Bad Name

Owner of a Lonely Heart

Just What I Needed

PLAYLIST

"Why Can't I Have You" - The Cars
"Affair of the Heart" - Rick Springfield
"Talking in Your Sleep" - The Romantics
"Magic" - The Cars
"Owner of a Lonely Heart" - Yes
"She's a Beauty" - The Tubes
"I Guess That's Why They Call It the Blues" - Elton John
"Can't Fight This Feeling" - REO Speedwagon
"More Than a Feeling" - Boston
"You Might Think" – The Cars
"Tell Her About It" – Billy Joel

CHAPTER 1

Katherine

New Year's Eve, 2020

This year sucked. Every single brutal moment. I'm glad it's over, but a new year doesn't mean a fresh start. So, I took a walk to clear my head and ended up in the one place I could breathe. The place I associate with Dad, and now Mom. The loneliness intensifies as I stare out over the expanse of Lower Manhattan, an ominous twinkling maw of dark disappointment.

I embrace the howl of the wind whipping my hair. My eyes water and my cheeks and nose burn from the icy chill. I turn my back against it, snagging a perfect view of Freedom Tower gleaming in the distance.

I had to bribe the guard to give me ten minutes on the observation deck. My father worked in this building years ago. I can't see the Empire State Building without thinking of him. Or Mom. It seems only fitting to spend my final moments where I feel closest to them.

The past few months only added fuel to the raging dumpster fire that will forever be known as the year from hell. After the beginning of the year where a pandemic tipped the economic scales right into the toilet, I found myself unemployed as well as grieving. Not only did the six-year relationship with a man I thought I loved come to an abrupt end, but it happened only days after I lost Mom.

When this year started, I had hope, now I want nothing more than to join my parents in Brooklyn cemetery. Life is a joke, and I am no longer amused.

The city lay in eerie silence below. It should be raucous and vivacious celebrating the end of the shittiest year on record. Instead, everyone hides inside their homes terrified of what the new year will bring.

A cold gust of air from the Hudson River and some scattered snow flakes wrap around me. I'm reminded of a film tucked somewhere in the back of my mind where two lovers meet on the top of the Empire State

Building. But I'm not here to meet a lover. No, I'm here to end the miserable existence I call life.

This year took the very last fuck out of my savings account of fucks to give. I've got nothing left. Cancer took Mom in November. That was the final straw, honestly. While Mom was here, I had a purpose, a reason to keep going. Now, there's nothing. I can't even see a silver lining in the distance, it's all hazy and distorted like a mist hovering over the edge of a cliff. I might as well embrace the inevitable.

It's over.

I glance over the edge of the railing of the towering skyscraper. Since the lockdowns, the building management began construction on the observation deck, which removed the typical barriers protecting pedestrians from dealing with items being tossed from a hundred floors up. But now there's nothing between me and the ledge. The lights of Freedom Tower flicker in the distance. A beacon of hope and perseverance, but I remember, and it does nothing to quell the hopelessness constricting my heart.

I lean over the rail. A gust of wind pushes against my back giving me the nudge I need. Reflexively, I grip the rail tighter. If I die, it'll be on my terms, damn it. I won't let fate take this from me too.

The once great, thriving city that never sleeps slumbers beneath my feet. I close my eyes and pray. I ask for forgiveness, for some semblance of clarity. Something. Anything.

My phone rings and one hand slips from the railing. I flounder for a moment, and my heart lodges in my throat. I grip the railing with one hand, my back to the world below until the ringing stops. Carefully, I remove my phone from my pocket.

Unknown caller.

Figures. I swipe up to unlock my phone. A gust of wind blows across the deck. I stumble back, but the phone slips from my grip and falls. I watch in slow motion as my phone tumbles through the air and drops toward to the street below.

It's a sign. It has to be. I take a deep breath. Maybe this isn't the solution. Maybe I should give the new year a chance. How could things possibly get any worse?

"Hey, lady. What the hell are you doing?" A beam of light shines right in my eye.

My heart pounds in my throat. I jump and my hand slips, making me twist around in a blur. The whole world sinks into slow motion, just like my phone, as I fall back into the open space surrounding the Empire

State Building. A scream tears from my throat as I grab for the railing, but it's too late. It's over. I'm falling.

I watch the beam of light grow smaller and smaller until it's a pinprick in the distance. The lights of the Empire State Building create a halo overhead as I fall. This is better, falling backward. That way I don't see what's coming.

My mind accepts the inevitable. I'm on my way, Mom. Dad, I'll see you soon. I stare into the heavens as I drift through the cold air, but surprisingly, I'm no longer cold. What a way to celebrate New Year's Eve. Is it midnight yet? Does it matter?

Not anymore. I close my eyes and embrace the inevitable.

The impact I expected never comes. I wait for a moment, and it stretches into several moments. Did I survive the fall? No, this can't be right.

I crack open one eye.

The sun rises over the bay casting the city in beautiful shades of red and orange. Huh? Maybe I imagined falling. I grip the railing and whip my head around in disbelief.

The observation deck is empty except for me. I check my pockets. Nope, my phone is definitely gone. I inhale deeply wondering if I somehow passed out last night and woke up from the nightmare which seemed so damn real.

The skyline spreads before me like a panoramic photograph. It's gorgeous. Wait.

I blink twice before it hits me like a dump truck on the Washington Bridge.

"No, it can't be." I mutter before rubbing my eyes and looking again. But the scenery doesn't change.

It's the skyline I've known my whole life, but there's something wrong. Instead of Freedom Tower, there are two identical towers stretching into the sky on the southern tip of Manhattan Island. The Twin Towers. The ones that fell on September 11th, 2001.

"No. They're not there." I turn and face the building. After several deep breaths, I spin around and take in the view once more.

They're still there. The World Trade Center Towers stand tall against the sunrise.

I back up until I hit the wall. No, what's going on? This can't be right.

A garbage can in the corner catches my eye. There's a newspaper tucked behind it. I rush over and pull it out.

Spreading it on the ground, I scan the headlines and search for the date. December 31, 1984. I read it over and over hoping it's a joke, a prank. Someone's mad at me for trying to kill myself, so they've decided to pull a fast one on me, show me how lucky I am or something stupid.

I stand up and spin around. No one. Nothing. No cameras, no phones recording my reaction. Not a goddamn thing. What the fuck?

I snatch up the paper and tuck it under my arm. There has to be a reasonable explanation for this. There has to be. I chew on my lip and run through the possibilities in my mind.

Damn. I've got nothing. The paper crumples under my arm. Okay, I need a minute.

One more peek to confirm I'm not insane. Nope. The towers are still there. I take three deep breaths focusing all my energy on filling my lungs with air. The cold stone beneath my fingertips grounds me. After several minutes, a calm settles over me.

I open my eyes and find the sun rising in the distance. The towers cast shadows over the city below. If I'm actually in the year 1985, then I haven't been born yet. My birthday isn't until June. Shit. Mom is pregnant with me right now.

What the hell is happening? I take another deep breath and focus on the facts I have. Where did we live when I was born? Dad. Holy shit. Dad.

Excitement bubbles up from the pit of my stomach. Dad's alive. Tears fill my eyes. I can see Dad again. I cry out in relief.

Wait. Remember. What did Mom tell me?

Dad died when I was three years old. February 17, 1989. That's more than enough time to find him. Where did she say he worked?

It hits me like a slap to the face. The Empire State Building. It's why I came here in the first place. To find a connection to Dad. To have him talk me out of this insanity. In some strange way I wanted him to reach out and stop me, to give me some hope for the future. Is it possible he had a hand in this?

I shake my head. No. This is insane. All of it. I didn't try to kill myself. I didn't end up traveling through time. This isn't 1985. I'm dead. This isn't real.

"Ma'am?" a voice echoes across the small observation deck.

I jump and spin around to face the voice intruding on my existential moment with the universe. "Yes, sorry."

"Ma'am, what are you doing up here? The deck doesn't open for another two hours."

"Oh." I laugh and wave a hand. "It's a long story. I'll go." As I head for the elevator, the man follows behind me.

"Are you okay, ma'am?" he asks as the doors close sealing us inside the elevator car.

"Yes, of course." I clear my throat. "Why do you ask?"

"If you don't mind my being blunt, ma'am, you don't look well." He pressed the button for the ground floor.

A memory flashes in my mind. The number fifty-four. I grasp it with both hands. "Would you mind pressing floor fifty-four? I forgot something."

He eyes me suspiciously. I force a smile, and he shrugs before pressing the button I requested. When it stops, he turns to face me.

"I'll be on the ground floor. Let me know if you need help with anything."

The doors slide open. Nervous excitement churns in my gut. "Thank you. I will."

I step into the hallway and turn to the left, unsure of which direction I should go but knowing I need to put some distance between me and the man who found me on the rooftop.

The elevator doors close and the numbers start declining on the illuminated panel over the elevator. I breathe easier.

It's early. No one is in any of the offices yet. Right? I locate the information board and scan the list of offices on this floor.

Lawyers. Bankers. There it is. Lincoln Architecture Firm. Beneath it, I read the list of employees barely registering the names until one douses me with ice water. *Jackpot.*

I rest my hand on the name. Mr. Victor Cohen. *Dad.* I close my eyes and breathe deep.

Is this really happening? Shit. It's New Year's Day. If it wasn't a holiday, he would be arriving for work shortly. I glance around the deserted floor and spy their main office door. I try it, but it's locked. Damn.

I could wait here until he shows up. No. That could be days. I haven't showered, and there's nothing to eat. My stomach rumbles at the thought.

Then a stray thought built from years of watching science fiction paralyzes me. What if I screw up some space time continuum or create a paradox by seeing him? But nothing's proven. It's all theoretical. I mean, everything will be fine, right?

Besides, I think a paradox only happens when you encounter

yourself, and I haven't even been born yet since my birthday isn't until June. I clap my hand over my mouth and stifle a chuckle. Holy hell, this is freaky. If this is New Year's Day 1985, then Mom is in her mid-twenties and Dad's just hit thirty. I'm older than my parents now.

But they're alive. A small voice whispers. Hope blossoms in my chest. I can see them again, then reality hits me with a baseball bat. They don't know me, and they'll think I'm crazy if I tell them who I am.

It doesn't matter. It's Dad. Nothing can stop me from seeing him. Not a goddamn thing.

I need a plan.

My foot crunches on a piece of paper as I step away from the door. I retrieve it, noting the name at the top of the page. *Mr. Arthur Maxwell.*

A noise behind the office door startles me, but before I can react, the door swings open. A shooting pain thunders through my head and over my shoulders. The world goes dark.

CHAPTER 2

Arthur

The door meeting resistance should have worried me, but it didn't. This wasn't the first time some idiot put a chair or trash bin in front of the office entrance. For an architecture firm, the floor layout was as unfortunate as the door placement since it aligned perfectly with the elevator doors creating all types of traffic issues during the workday. I shove the door open with my shoulder, and it slams into something.

I peer around the edge of the door and frown. There's no one there. Then I glance down at the floor and my blood turns to ice. Shit. A dark-haired woman wearing winter boots and an oversized wool coat lay sprawled at my feet. Is she breathing?

Tossing aside my briefcase, I kneel beside her and feel for a pulse. Okay, she's alive at least. I roll her onto her back with little resistance. Her pale skin reflects a hint of color, and she's breathing steadily, as though trapped in a deep sleep. Her thick eyelashes lay heavy against her cheeks.

She looks familiar. Maybe one of the maids working overtime on the holiday? I brush my hand across her forehead, removing the dark waves when I notice the smear of blood across her hairline.

"Fuck." I gently rock her. "Ma'am. Can you hear me? Ma'am? Goddamn it, wake up." My prodding does nothing, and there's no way to hide the panic rising in my voice.

I can't call the cops or an ambulance. The last thing I need right now is an investigation into why this woman is lying on the floor outside my office with a headwound. I know enough lawyers to know involving the cops is a one-way ticket to trouble. With the upcoming proposal meeting with the Hudson Group for a new hotel in Manhattan around the corner, I can't take any chances of having an incident, no matter how accidental, ruin such a prime opportunity.

I sound like a heartless bastard. With a groan I place my briefcase inside the office and lock the door. The woman doesn't even whimper when I pull her into my arms and shift her body against me. I stumble a bit under the weight but quickly find a comfortable position. I'm too old for this shit.

I press the down button next to the elevator. When the car arrives, I step in and select the ground floor. Her head rests against my shoulder lolling from the elevator's wobbly descent. My driver should still be waiting outside. I only meant to come into the office for a moment and verify some paperwork. Then she happened. I glance down at the woman in my arms and squash the protective instinct rising from the pit of my subconscious.

No. You're not her knight in shining armor. You knocked her out. Now you're kidnapping her. What kind of man are you, Arthur? If I could reach inside my own mind and rip out the part of my brain now accosting me, I would do it without hesitation. Instead, I ignore it and focus on the numbers as they count down.

When we reach the ground floor, the guard's eyes widen when I step from the elevator carrying the unconscious woman.

"Mr. Maxwell." He rushes forward. "What happened, sir?"

"Oh, one of my new temp secretaries. She fell asleep in the lounge late last night, and I can't seem to wake her." I shrug but it's lost under her weight pressed against my chest.

The guard doesn't seem too convinced with my lie, but he doesn't need to believe me. One of the regular guards appears around the corner. Mike. He's worked at the building since I started here fifteen years ago.

"Oh, I see you found her." Mike gestures to the woman in my arms. "She was up on the observation deck this morning. Asked me to stop on your floor. She one of your employees?"

I nod. "Yes, started last week. A temp."

"She looked a little lost up there on the deck this morning." He stuffs his hands in his pockets. "Might want to keep an eye on her."

"Yeah. Found her passed out on the couch in the lounge. I guess the party was too much for her." I tsk. "Well, gents. I need to get her home."

"No problem, Mr. Maxwell. Happy New Year." Mike tips his head and motions for the other guard to open the door.

Once I step out into the cold morning air, I exhale with relief. The black Cadillac pulls up to the curb ahead. When my driver, Cyril, steps around the car, his brow arches in surprise. He says nothing and opens the rear door.

It takes a bit of fancy maneuvering, but I manage to get her comfortably situated in the back seat and slide in next to her. She's still unconscious. I sigh. What a way to start the new year.

Cyril slides into the driver's seat and glances at me in the rearview. "Where to, sir?"

"Home." I catch the glimmer of curiosity and open criticism in his eyes.

"Yes, sir." He pulls away from the curb and out into the early traffic.

I pinch the bridge of my nose and take a deep breath. What the hell am I going to do with this mess? I peek at the woman beside me. A pronounced smear of blood mars her forehead. I'm a horrible person. I should have called for help or at least let her rest in the office until she woke up. But no. I didn't need this kind of gossip spreading through the office, let alone the building.

Within fifteen minutes, I'm inside the penthouse elevator with the mysterious woman limp in my arms. It takes some time to slide the key in the lock, but once we're inside the apartment, a weight lifts from my shoulders. I carry her to my bed and lay her on the down coverlet.

She moans and shifts but doesn't wake. I unbutton her coat and slip it from her shoulders. The oversized monstrosity hinders me from assessing whether or not I did more damage than a knock on the head. I set it aside, noting the familiar designer style much like the new coat Victor bought last month, but the material is worn and well-loved. I shove the thought aside. A puzzle to ponder later.

After a quick inspection, I note no other injuries with a sigh of relief. I gather towels, a wet cloth, and the first aid kit I keep for emergencies.

Her lashes flutter when I brush the cloth over her hairline. The blood washes easily enough from her dark hair, but the raised bump above her hairline bleeds afresh when I dab it. A cut, not too deep, but enough to cause a deceptive amount of visual trauma. I must have caught her with the edge of the door.

Guilt washes over me. Maybe I should have taken her to the hospital. At least then I could be assured of her care, even if the circumstances of her injury seem suspicious. I take a breath and head into the kitchen to get something cold to compress over the wound.

I grab the phone and dial the number I know by heart.

"*Dr. Thompson.*"

"Hey, it's Arthur."

"*Hey. You're up early. Didn't you have a party at the office last night?*"

I rake my hand through my hair wishing I had cut it last week. "Yeah, but we went home shortly after midnight. Are you on call today?"

"*No.*" Rob pauses. "*Do you need something or are you calling to wish me a*

Happy New Year?"

"Can you come over? I need your help with something."

"*Did you murder someone and you need me to help hide the body?*" Rob chuckles. "*That shit will cost you. We're not kids anymore, you know. I have ethics I'm bound to.*"

"Exactly, which is why I need you to get your ass over here." I groan. "Bring your bag of miracles."

"*What happened?*" The tone of Rob's voice shifts, and I can tell he's worried.

"I'll explain when you get here." I hang up the phone before he has a chance to respond. He'll keep me on the line all day if I let him. Hopefully it's enough of a teaser to convince him to come over.

When I return to the unconscious woman in my bed, I place the bag of frozen peas in a towel and place it on the lump. Then I pull a blanket up over her. A soft moan makes me pause. She twitches her nose and exhales.

My gaze drifts over her features. Delicate brows, full lips, and a nose curved slightly off center. I wonder what color her eyes are. Probably a bewitching shade of brown or vibrant blue. The thought swiftly fixes itself in my mind and I'm thrown off.

I don't know anything about this woman. I've already dug myself into a nest of lies and perjured myself for her. I push aside any idle curiosity I have for her and focus instead on at least establishing an identity.

Carefully, I peel back the blanket to check her pockets. Wait, no pockets. What kind of garments are these? Some form of exercise leggings I expect, only made from thick material to provide warmth. The oversized cream sweater hides her figure. I search her innocently, ignoring her soft curves. *No pockets and no identification.* I frown. The overcoat.

I pick it up from the chair and search every pocket. A handful of crumpled papers, a key, and a stick of gum wrapped tight in silver paper. Great. Nothing.

The doorbell startles me. I dash across the apartment and open the door.

Rob steps inside carrying a small leather case. "What the hell is going on?"

I lock the door and lead him into my bedroom, gesturing to the woman lying in my bed as though it were a grand revelation and would explain itself.

"What the fuck did you do?" Rob rushes to her side and checks her pulse. He's quick and thorough. I watch him follow the same methodical procedures he learned when he was in med school.

"I went to the office this morning to get some paperwork I forgot. When I went to leave, I hit her with the door." I lift my hands in supplication when Rob turns and shakes his head. "By accident. It was a fucking accident, okay?"

He returns his attention to the woman. "How long has she been unconscious?"

I shrug. "I don't know. An hour maybe?"

"An hour?" Rob grits his teeth. "You should've called me right away."

"Why?" Fear grips me and I know I'm going to hell for not calling the ambulance. "Is it bad?"

Rob peels back the makeshift ice pack and inspects the wound on her head. He tuts and replaces the cold pack. "No. But I don't like the fact she hasn't regained consciousness."

I stand steadfast in my decision as he takes her pulse and checks the dilation of her eyes.

"What's her name?" He reaches into his bag.

"I don't know. I've never seen her in the building before."

"Does she have any identification? A driver's license?" He fishes around searching for something in the bottom of the bag.

"No." I cross my arms, bracing against the judgement emanating off Rob in waves. If we weren't friends for the last twenty-odd years, I would tell him exactly where to take his sorry ass. Truth is, I need his help, and he knows it.

He opens a small case and withdraws an ammonia capsule. I catch a brief hint of it when he cracks it open and waves it under her nose.

She jolts against the assault of chemicals. Her eyes fly open, not blue. Not brown. A mixture of the two. *Interesting.* Wild, she lurches upright and grips her head with a tentative hand, hissing as her fingertips brush the abrasion.

"Take it easy. You're safe." Rob sits on the edge of the bed and smiles. I want to slap him already. His bedside manner always earns him bonus points at the hospital. I stay back and observe from the side.

"Where am I?" She blinks, trying to remember but obviously struggling. "Who are you?"

"I'm Rob. This is Arthur. You're in his apartment. You are injured. Do you remember what happened?" Rob's soothing voice seems to work its magic as she relaxes her shoulders.

She licks her lips and scrunches her nose in thought. "I was at the Empire State Building..." She mutters almost to herself. Her eyes widen. "Am I dead?"

Rob chuckles. "No, most certainly not dead."

Her gaze drifts to the window overlooking the southern tip of Manhattan. I chose this apartment for the skyline view of the most iconic skyscrapers in the world. It cost me a fortune, but it was worth every penny.

When her gaze fixes on me, her enchanting eyes are wide with terror. I want to reach out and comfort her, but I stand my ground, watching and waiting.

Rob takes her hand. "What's your name, sweetheart?"

"Katherine." She turns to face him. "But everyone calls me Kate."

"Okay, Kate. You rest here for a minute. I'll get something to replenish your fluids. Stay in bed, okay?" Rob stands and motions for me to join him.

With one last look at the lost soul in my bed, I follow Rob into the living room and brace myself for the lecture of the century. At least she's okay. *Kate.* What the hell have I gotten myself into now?

CHAPTER 3

Katherine

A rancid smell rips me from the tormented dreams. The moment I open my eyes pain shoots through my head. Holy shit. Am I dead? In a slow-motion delayed reaction, I realize I'm no longer at the Empire State Building. I'm in a bed in a fancy apartment, and I'm not alone.

The man hovering beside the bed has dark blonde hair, cropped close in a military-esque style, but professional with a length that makes him approachable. His soft hazel eyes scan my face and he smiles. He sits on the edge of the bed.

"Take it easy. You're safe."

"Where am I?" I struggle with the words. My tongue feels thick and my head aches so much I can barely think. "Who are you?"

"I'm Rob. This is Arthur." He gestures to the man behind him standing at the foot of the bed.

I'm struck stupid at the sight of Arthur. He's tall with dark brown hair, nearly black. His steel gray eyes pin me with unyielding curiosity. There's nothing soft about his expression or his features. He looks carved from marble, like he belongs in a museum alongside David, not here painted in warm hues and vibrant colors.

"You're in his apartment." Rob continues, his voice soothing and calm, "You were injured. Do you remember what happened?"

It takes me a minute to remember. "I was at the Empire State Building..." Oh, shit. Maybe I did jump. "Am I dead?"

Rob chuckles. "No, most certainly not dead."

I relax only a fraction until I glance out the window. The southern tip of Manhattan lays on the horizon with the Empire State Building standing tall against the blue sky, then I see the World Trade Center buildings. The Twin Towers. Holy shit, it wasn't a dream. I really did travel through time.

The memories flash through my mind. My phone dropping off the top of the building. When I slipped. The guard finding me. The elevator. The realization. Dad and Mom. They're alive. His office. The paper. Shit, the door.

I meet Arthur's gaze and his jaw ticks almost imperceptibly. Oh, lord. Am I in trouble? What the hell happened?

It barely registers when Rob takes my hand. "What's your name, sweetheart?"

"Katherine." I meet his warm, friendly gaze. They don't need my full name, right? I left my ID in my purse, and who knows where the hell it is now. "But everyone calls me Kate."

"Okay, Kate. You rest here for a minute. I'll get something to replenish your fluids. Stay in bed, okay?" Rob rises to his feet and motions for Arthur to follow him.

I'm relieved, because being in the same room with that man brought a wave of awareness I wasn't quite ready to examine yet. When the door closes, I slowly rise to my feet and cross the room to crack it open hoping they don't notice. I peek into the room ignoring the thundering headache pounding through my skull. Both men stand in the kitchen, their backs to the bedroom where they left me.

"What the hell did you do, Arthur?" Rob keeps his voice low and rips open the refrigerator.

What did he do? I rub the extremely tender lump on my head and wince when my hand brushes the cut and comes away damp with blood. I remember standing outside the office and leaning down to pick up a paper, then shooting pain and darkness.

"It was a fucking accident, Rob." He rakes his hand through his hair making it stand on end. "What should I have done? Huh? Called the cops. Rushed her to the hospital in an ambulance. Made a scene."

His restless discomfort makes me pause. It was an accident. For all I knew, I was alone on the fifty-fourth floor. My body sways and I brace myself against the doorway determined to hear what they're discussing about me.

"You should have called me. I could have met you at the office." The handsome doctor sets the orange juice container down on the counter with little grace.

"I know. Okay? I fucked up. Is that what you want me to admit? I panicked and made a stupid ass decision. There's nothing I can do about it now."

Rob pours some orange juice into a glass and replaces the cap on the jug. "Do you recognize her? From the building?"

Arthur shakes his head. "No. I mean she seems familiar, but hell, there are so many offices in the building and so much foot traffic. She could be any one of a hundred faces I pass every day."

Familiar, huh? I nearly laugh at the absurdity of the whole situation. There's no way in hell anyone in this time would recognize me. Mom always told me I looked like Dad, but I never quite saw the resemblance in the photographs she showed me over the years.

"You're going to keep an eye on her, right?" Rob asks with a pointed glance at his companion, whose grim expression casts a dark thundercloud over his head.

"Yeah," Arthur snaps. "I'm not a heartless bastard."

The duo moves back toward the bedroom and I jump away from the door hurrying back to the bed in time to collapse against the soft bedding as the door opens. My head pounds. I press my palm to my forehead and hiss in a breath.

Rob enters the room first bearing a glass of orange juice. He sets it on the nightstand and helps me sit up.

"Take it easy." His voice is soothing and calm. "I don't need you passing out. Here." He offers the orange juice and turns back to dig through the bag he brought. "Take these too."

I take the two pills from his palm and pop them in my mouth, washing them down with a few sips of juice. The sweet tart of the liquid tingles on my tongue. I drink the rest down quickly and sigh before handing him the glass.

My gaze drifts from the deep calm pools of Rob's hazel eyes to the tumultuous maelstrom raging in Arthur's, who stands at the foot of the bed with his arms folded across his chest. I can't tell if he's watching us with avid attention or barely restrained irritation.

I turn my gaze to the window overlooking the city. The sunset reflects off the buildings creating an illuminated maze weaving through the streets below with skyscrapers jutting up from the concrete jungle.

"Kate." Rob's soft but assertive voice pulls me from the view. When I face him, he smiles. "Is there anyone we can call? Family? Friends? Your husband, maybe?"

I shake my head. Hopelessness threatens to choke me. "Not married." I show my bare fingers. Scrambling for excuses I lunge for the most cliché of them all and it's enough to make me cringe. "But honestly, my head is a blur. I can't remember."

"Amnesia isn't uncommon after a head injury." Rob nods solemnly. "A few days of rest should help." He turns to his friend. "Can she stay for a few days, see if her memory comes back?" At Arthur's nod, he turns his attention back to me. "I'll make some inquiries at the hospital to see if anyone's been searching for you."

Unable to trust my ability to lie, I smile. "Thank you."

"I'll check on you tomorrow." He slowly rises to his feet and closes his bag. "Stay in bed. Rest. No sudden movements and no alcohol. Doctor's orders." His lopsided grin is so endearing it makes me forget I'm in the wrong decade if only for a moment.

"Yes, sir." I return his easy banter but my smile disappears the moment I see Arthur's heated stare. And by heated, I mean furious, not hell bent on seduction. The image seared in my mind at that brief thought leaves me breathless.

"Arthur, a word." Rob leaves the room with Arthur following in his wake.

I can't very well chase after them to eavesdrop a second time without getting caught. My head weighs a ton and even with the medication, the pain stabs through my skull. I touch the cut once more and groan. What I want is a shower, some warm pajamas, and to curl up and sleep. Hopefully I'll wake up and I won't be trapped in 1985 with a grumpy businessman and his doctor friend as my only allies.

Reality weighs down on me. Do I want to return to the present? I mean after the bang-up year I had, I'd much rather be stranded in the middle ages than 2020. But it was more. I lost so much this past year, I considered ending it all.

Now I'm stuck in the past. Right where my beginning started, and I can't help but wonder if this is fate playing some cruel joke on me.

I slowly rise to my feet and walk to the floor length window and lose myself in the rising darkness beyond. As the last remnants of sunlight fade beyond the horizon, I press my face to the cold glass.

How the hell am I going to make this work? There must be some laws of physics and time I must be violating by being here. I can't imagine trying to live in a transported time wondering if I'm meddling with the fabric of the universe.

Take it one day at a time, I hear my mother whisper through my memories. One thing is certain, I will see my parents again, and that alone is worth the risk of a paradox and the wrath of the man in the other room who is now my only ally in this world.

With no money, no job, no apartment, I am at his mercy. A shiver of excitement grips me.

Be careful, my mind cautions. I catch a glimpse of my reflection in the glass and behind me, through the door, I see Arthur appear.

"I see you're going to be a handful." His disappointment echoes clearly in his heady baritone voice.

When I spin around, I sway at the quick motion and lean against the glass.

In a flash, he's by my side, his hands firmly planted around my waist. "Lie down before you fall down."

His words are harsh, but his gentle touch says something completely different, leaving an ache deep in my chest when he helps me onto the bed and backs away. "Stay there. I need to make a phone call."

I expect him to pull out a cell phone, but instead, he leaves the room. I squeeze my eyes closed. *Cell phones aren't a thing yet, idiot.*

Yeah, being stuck in 1985 is going to be more difficult than I thought if I expected to be able to maintain any semblance of normalcy.

CHAPTER 4

Arthur

It takes every ounce of effort not to shove Rob out the door and slam it in his face. Instead, I stewed while he lectured and guilted me into taking responsibility for this lost little lamb. Hah. Lamb, my ass. After he left, I found her staring out over the city when she should have been in bed resting. If I hadn't seen her unconscious firsthand, I would have thought it all an act. The question is, why go to all that trouble? What is her angle?

Rob may be blind to her wiles, but one look at those wide, mesmerizing eyes and I knew. This woman is trouble. Maybe it's my own bias. I don't exactly have a great track record with women, but none have given me a reason to trust them. Vultures and vixens, all of them. Well, except one. And unfortunately, she is the only one I can call for help right now.

I rake my hand across my face in irritation and retreat into the living room. Once I make this call, I'll never hear the end of it. But I don't have any other course of action. I lift the phone receiver to my shoulder and dial a number as familiar as my own. After a few lengthy rings, the line connects.

"Hello, this is Marcy Maxwell."

"Hi, Marcy."

"Arthur." Her business tone shifts to one of amusement. "Happy New Year."

I grunt and ignore the stabbing irritation in my skull. "You busy?"

"Just reorganizing my closets with Donna and Liana." She snaps the gum she's chewing. "Why?"

Taking a deep breath, I push forward. "I need a favor."

"Holy shit. Did hell freeze over? Who are you and what have you done with my brother?"

"Laugh it up." I growl knowing I'll never live this down.

She sobers quickly. "What can I do for you? Get you a new wardrobe? A blind date? Maybe find you a sense of humor?"

"I need you to make up a bag. Toiletries, makeup, and clothes." I brace myself for the deluge of questions I'm about to face and march into the gaping maw of hell. "For a woman."

"Get the hell out of here." She gasps. "Did you snag yourself a babe?"

"I'm not even going to dignify that with an answer." I sigh. "Can you do this for me?"

"Under two conditions." She snaps her gum again.

"Name them." I stare at my reflection in the window wondering if I haven't signed a contract with the devil.

"Nonna's blanket." She tuts when I groan. "And the recipe for her chicken noodle soup." Marcy knows exactly what she wants, which is why she's the most sought-after stylist in the city.

"Fine." I sit on the arm of the couch and carefully twist the cord so I don't knock the whole thing to the ground. "How fast can you be here?"

"As soon as you give me her measurements, I can be there in thirty."

My head spins. Measurements? What the hell? "I don't know her measurements, Marcy."

"Ask her, idiot." She tuts again in exasperation.

"Hold on." I set the phone down and head toward the bedroom. Inside, I find my uninvited guest staring at the ceiling chewing on her lip.

"Everything okay?" she asks when I open the door.

"Of course." I bristle. No, it goddamn isn't okay. You've upended my plans and you're lying in my bed. I bite my tongue and ignore the frustration curdling in the back of my throat. "What are your measurements?"

Her eyes widen and she sits up enough to meet my gaze fully. "Why do you need those?"

"You can't wear the same clothes for days on end and I doubt you'll fit in mine."

"I wear a large top and a size fourteen jeans." She brushes her hair away from her eyes.

"Shoes?" I add taking mental note and trying not to imagine those curves I now know she's hiding beneath her baggy sweater.

"Eights."

I nod and leave the room, closing the door behind me. Shit. This can't be good. It's bad enough I don't know anything about this woman and here she is tormenting me without even trying.

I snatch the phone off the table. "Large top, size fourteen jeans, and size eight shoe. That work?"

"I can make it work for now." She sounds almost disappointed in my clipped response. "I'll be over in thirty minutes. Ciao."

After I hang up the phone, I stare blankly at the new television and state of the art stereo system sitting like huge bricks stacked against the wall. I don't know why I bought them. I never watch television or listen to music. The architecture firm takes up all of my time. My gaze drifts to the bedroom. At least it did.

If I had known what was waiting for me on the other side of the door at the office this morning, I wouldn't have gone in. A fleeting memory of Kate's soft body pressed against me makes me pause. I remember the sweet, teasing scent of a tropical island drifting up from her hair and pulling me closer. Guilt crashes over me again when I remember the sight of her crumpled on the floor, blood marring her pale forehead.

I shoot to my feet and pace the floor. Rob, being astute and noble as ever, has a valid point. I was responsible for her injury, therefore I am responsible for her recovery. Until we get some answers as to where she came from and who she is, I guess I'll have to cope with the inconvenience.

This time I knock on the bedroom door.

"Come in." Her voice filters through the wood.

When I push open the door, I expect to find her exactly where I left her moments before. Instead, she's sitting on the edge of the bed staring out the window. I clear my throat and stalk to the far wall where the en suite bathroom is located. I flip on the light and turn to face her.

"Here's the bathroom." I stuff my hands into my pockets and lean against the door.

She's still staring out the window as if entranced by the city lights flickering outside. "Thank you."

Silence fills the void between us. "I'll be in the other room if you require anything else." Without waiting for a response, I leave the bedroom, making sure to close the door behind me.

I unfasten the buttons on my wrists and roll my sleeves up. In the kitchen, I gather some vegetables from the refrigerator. Breakfast was a cup of coffee and a bagel from the shop on the corner. In all the chaos, I completely forgot about lunch. A reminder my stomach punctuates with a loud grumble.

Chopping peppers and onions gives me something to do with my hands. I'm careful not to let my mind wander too deeply into the mess I find myself mired. I pop a slice of pepper in my mouth as I set a pan on the stovetop. My recipe isn't quite as good as Nonna's, but it works when I don't have the time for a full ragu simmer. As I fill the pot with water for the pasta, the door buzzes. Quickly, I toss the onions in the first pot and let the hot oil work it's magic.

When I open the door, I'm stunned to find not only my sister, but her two associates carrying bags in her wake.

"Arthur." Marcy regards me with a smile and a once over. "You look like a train wreck."

"Hello, Marcy." I nod to her associates. "Liana. Donna. Come in." They pass without hesitation when I step aside.

"Smells good." My sister sniffs the air. "Nonna's ragu?"

"No one has that kind of free time." I disappear into the kitchen and stir the onions ensuring they caramelize evenly.

Marcy leans against the counter next to the stove. "So, dish. Who's the chick?"

"Your slang has gotten worse." I scowl. "Working with all those rock stars and celebrities is starting to rot your brain."

"You're a grumpy old man. Don't take your issues out on me." She sneaks a pepper from the cutting board and snaps it between her teeth. "So, where is she?"

"In the bedroom." I regret the words the moment they leave my mouth.

Marcy's brows shoot straight up. "You sly dog. That was fast!"

"It's not what you think." I groan and backpedal knowing she won't let this rest now or ever if I don't tell her the truth. In the fewest possible words, I explain what happened at the office and how I brought the woman here. I assure her Rob came and offered his professional advice.

"Are you kidding me? Professional advice, my ass." She rolls her eyes and snorts.

"You and Rob have your little rivalry or whatever it is, but he's my friend and a doctor. As much as his advice wasn't what I wanted to hear..." I shrug and let the implication slide into oblivion.

"You feel guilty for whacking her over the head and knocking her out." Marcy chuckles. "Good. You should." She snatches another pepper as I pour wine into the onions to deglaze them.

I glare my sister wishing I had another female in my life who I could have called, but unfortunately, this is the curse of being a man married to his work. "I don't need you to heap more guilt onto my shoulders as well, Marcy." I jab my wooden spoon in her direction. "Just take the clothes and stuff into the bedroom."

"I bet you didn't even tell her I was coming or who I am." She winks and disappears before I can stop her.

Shit. I didn't tell her. I hang my head and chase after my sister. "Liana, keep an eye on the sauce, would you?" I motion to my sister's assistant who gives me a strange look.

Marcy spins around at my command and glowers. "Don't tell her what to do. She works for me, not you."

"Shit." I step between my sister and the bedroom door. "No, okay, you win. I didn't tell her you were coming or who you were. Just...give me a minute."

I open the door and find the room empty. The sound of running water echoes behind the closed bathroom door. My eyes drift closed. If she's lying on the shower floor unconscious, I'll never forgive myself.

"Go stir your ragu, genius. I got this." Marcy steps toward the bathroom door and knocks.

Liana and Donna carry the bags into the bedroom as I head back to the kitchen. Well, the new year is off to a promising start. I've accosted, kidnapped, and possibly killed a stranger. Fantastic.

Even better, my best friend and my sister are witnesses to my failure. Fucking perfect. What else could possibly go wrong?

In the kitchen, my wine has evaporated leaving burned onions sticking to the bottom of the pot. I rinse it out and start over. Maybe I should order food from Lorenzo's and drown my misery in a bottle of chianti.

The scream from the bedroom makes my heart stop.

CHAPTER 5

Katherine

The shower in this place can fit three people, at least. I lean against the tan tiles and let the water run through my hair, sluicing over the sore lump my generous host gave me earlier. It wasn't his fault, honestly, if it happened the way he says it did. Damn it. I wanted to ask him about it when he came back, but the scowl on his face drove all thoughts of conversation from my mind.

While my head ached, the pain seems to have dimmed enough to tolerate being on my feet. I pray I don't pass out while I'm in the shower. The thought of not showering crossed my mind, but one look in the mirror confirmed the truth. I'm a hot mess. Dried blood caked against my scalp, blotchy skin, and dark circles highlight my eyes. Before I could stop myself, I was naked and in the shower.

I use some of the soap and lather a washcloth. The subtle hint of lemon zest reminds me of the soap Nanna used to have at her house. My hair will be a beast to untangle without the proper shampoo and conditioner. I use whatever's in the shower knowing I'll smell like him. But the thought isn't a complete turn off.

The thought of my unwilling host even smiling is almost comical. He looked every inch the disapproving dad. Hah. Dad. Daddy. He certainly is daddy as fuck which seems super creepy considering the fact I haven't even been born yet.

I chuckle and slip on the tile. My heart lurches and I brace myself against the glass door until my body is in complete control once more. Shit. I need to pay attention or I'll die naked in a stranger's shower. What a thought.

Carefully, I finish rinsing my hair and toss it over my shoulder.

"Don't use his shampoo. Damn. We'll never get those curls sorted."

I spin around and slip again, this time falling on my bare ass. There's a hazy figure of a woman on the other side of the glass.

"Christ, I didn't mean to scare you. I knew that bastard didn't tell you." She mutters the last sentence under her breath, but I can hear her clearly.

I cross my arms over my naked breasts and cross my legs for all the good it does at hiding my childbearing hips.

"Oh honey, don't be modest. I've seen more naked women than Hugh Heffner." She slides open the door and I catch a glimpse of crimped hair and a neon headband as she sets some bottles on the rack inside the shower. "Try these. There's a leave in conditioner that's amazing." The door slides shut, but she doesn't leave.

"Uh..." I slowly climb to my feet and read the bottles provided. "Who are you?"

"Oh, sorry, sugar. I'm Marcy." She snaps her gum.

"Why are you here?" The moment the shampoo touches my hair it thanks me by allowing my fingers to comb through the stubborn curls.

"Cause I'm the best." She giggles to herself. "And I'm the only one Arthur calls when he's in freak out mode." She huffs. "Well, the only woman."

I rinse the soap out of my hair and listen with confusion. "I don't understand."

Marcy sighs. "I'll let you finish up. We'll talk once you're out of the shower." She moves toward the door. "Don't take too long."

While I'm thankful for the salon quality supplies, I still don't know who she is or why the hell Arthur called her. I finish my shower and wrap my head with a towel before bundling up with a second one. My head aches with the weight of the fabric and my ass hurts. I'll definitely have a bruise there tomorrow. Damn. My ego and my ass. Awesome.

In the bedroom, I stop at the sight of three women, two lounging on the edge of the bed chatting and the third drawing the blinds across the windows. They all turn toward me.

"Awesome," Marcy says, rising to her feet. She's tall and willowy with dark hair and sparkling eyes. Her polka dot neon green shirt drapes over her shoulders and nips at her waist beneath a wide black belt.

It's like a bad dream where I'm trapped naked in an eighties music video with a bunch of strangers. I pull the towel tighter around my chest.

"Donna. Grab the kit. We'll give her some beauty essentials." Marcy snaps her fingers like she forgot something. Finally, she grins. "Liana, let's try a few of the pieces you picked. Not feeling the glam vibe, but I think she's got the bod for the rock look."

"What are you doing?" I protest when Marcy hooks her arm through mine, dislodging my towel.

"Don't worry about it. We're professionals." This time I see the lime green shadow and flecks of gold glitter at the corners of her eyes.

"Professional what?"

"Fashion mavens." She cocks her head and inspects me, walking around me twice before nodding. "Trust me."

"You still haven't told me who you are." I squeal when she pulls the towels off my head. A mass of heavy wet curls falls across my face hiding my shameful blush.

"Marcy. I told you." Two pieces of silk and lace are pressed into my hands. "Try these."

I tug on the lace demi bra and high wasted panties. Lord, these are a blast from the past.

Someone nudges my side. "Sit down, hon. Let me take care of those curls for you." Donna, I think she said her name was, pushes me toward the chair where she begins detangling my curls. I point out the tender spot on my scalp which she carefully avoids.

"Arthur didn't specify how long you'll be staying or what you'll need, so I brought a variety. They should fit, but if they don't, call me and I'll change them out. They're all last season's wardrobe." Marcy flips through the pile of clothing growing on the bed.

The colors and styles are most definitely last century's wardrobe, that's for sure. I bite my tongue as she shows me each outfit combination. Oh, my God. I remember dress up for the eighties day at school, but I don't remember these patterns and fabrics. What is wrong with this decade?

An hour later, I'm exhausted. She's wrapped me in some kind of pink leggings and a billowy silk shirt. I wiggle, unfamiliar but not uncomfortable, with the new duds. Her word, not mine. I scramble through my mind for any memories of movies from the eighties in which I can pull references and slang. All I can think of is *Back to the Future* and *Top Gun*. Not helpful.

"Well, I think we've done our best, ladies." Marcy gestures to the other two women who wave as they step out of the room. "I'll let you get some rest." She smiles and this time it feels more genuine.

"Thank you." I glance at myself in the mirror one last time.

"Of course. It's the least I can do." She rests her hand on my shoulder. "If my brother gives you any crap, just give it right back to him."

My gaze meets hers in the reflection. "Arthur is your brother?"

"Well, yeah, duh." She laughs. "You didn't think we were together, did you?"

I study the carpet and a wave of shame washes over me. "Yeah. I did. Sorry."

"No reason to be sorry. I thought he told you." She snaps her gum again. "Guess he owes me double." Her hug startles me for a moment, but it feels like heaven and I sink into it. "Just give me a ring if you need me to kick his ass."

"I will." A sense of loss envelops me as she steps back.

"Come on, let's show him how I work my magic." Marcy pulls me into the living room by the hand. "Hey, Arthur."

On cue, Arthur steps out of the far room. My heart stops at the sight of him. His shirtsleeves are pushed up exposing strong forearms. The vee of skin at his throat draws my attention upward to his angled jaw and full lips. Oh God, he's hotter. How is that possible?

His sharp gaze narrows as it skims over my body. "It works."

I want to grab the vase off the mantel and hurl it at him. Really, so much work for this pathetic reaction. I mean, honestly, it wasn't to impress him in the first place, but my ego is already battered.

"You're welcome." She gives my hand a squeeze. "Get some rest. Ciao!"

Without further fanfare, the three women leave the penthouse surrendering me to the company of the sexy, grumpy Daddy. I shake my head. No. Not going there. Never going there.

"Are you hungry?" he asks, stuffing his hands into his pockets.

The question pulls me from my twisted thoughts. "Yes. I'm starving."

His lips twitch, but he remains stoic. "Come into the kitchen."

The penthouse has a spacious openness making it feel grand and leaving little privacy when in the main common areas. The living room and kitchen sit side by side, although the kitchen is elevated a fraction making it the main functionality of the room. There's a small dining area off to the right along with several closed doors. The opposite side is where his bedroom sits along with a glass door leading to what looks like a balcony with greenery. How did I miss that? Curiosity pulls at me, but the tantalizing scents emanating from the kitchen draw me back to the moment and my hunger.

He hands me a plate and piles pasta mixed with sauce on it. "There's cheese here." He gestures to the counter beside the stove.

I slide past him, my hip grazing his thigh. The touch is innocent enough, but a weighted undercurrent pulls me toward him. I force myself away. After sprinkling on a healthy dose of parmesan, I cross through the kitchen to the dining room and sit near the window to get the best view while I eat.

Once Arthur joins me, I dig in. The sauce coats the noodles perfectly. My headache eases with each bite. I must have been hungrier than I realized.

Arthur's staring at me. I can't tell if he's more horrified by my manners or my appetite. He arches a brow.

"Sorry. It's just..." I lick my lips and smile. "It's really good."

He takes a bite.

I focus on eating slower. "Did you make this?"

He nods. "My Nonna's recipe."

"Nonna?" I ask wiping a stray bit of sauce from my cheek.

"Italian for grandma. She emigrated when she was young."

"Wow." I stuff more pasta in my mouth so I don't trip over my words and say something that makes the universe implode. Silence descends like a heavy fog.

I finish my last bite and push the plate away. Satisfied and grateful. But the silence is killing me. The man across the table doesn't seem interested in talking any more than I do, but I am curious. Maybe my curiosity is what contributed the events which led me to the top of the Empire State Building in the first place. It doesn't matter. I don't have any friends here and we're stuck together, so I might as well make the best of it.

"So, Arthur, what do you do?"

"I'm an architect." He swirls the wine in his glass, and I stare at my own water with regret.

Then it clicks. "Wait, you work at Lincoln Architecture Firm?"

"I started it." Arthur sips his wine taking full measure of me as he does so.

My face heats and I remember the paper I found lying on the ground outside the office. "Arthur Maxwell," I mutter under my breath and hide my face in my hands. "Of course."

"Your amnesia must be clearing up. I never told you my surname." His eyes glint with challenge.

"When I was outside your office, I found a paper on the ground. I bent down to pick it up and saw that name...your name on it. Right before you knocked me out with the door and kidnapped me." I fold my arms across my chest and hold his gaze.

"It was an accident." He leans forward and braces his bare forearms on the table. The light catches the hint of gray starting at his temples and my body goes into hyper alert.

Shit, am I supposed to be scared or horny right now? I'm confused. I shove both away with force and clear my throat. "Accident or not. It happened. Nothing we can do about it now."

"I find it difficult to believe you can remember your name and the fact you have no family or friends to call, but nothing else."

I swallow convulsively. "Well, I don't, and that's all I know." It's not a lie per se, but it's definitely not the truth. I pray he doesn't press me further.

Arthur looks more skeptical than before.

"I'll be out of your hair in a few days. I'll find a job and pay you back for the inconvenience," I lie. How the hell am I going to legally work? I don't exist. "If you want, I can cook, I'll clean, whatever I need to do. I don't want to be an inconvenience."

He harumphs. "Too late."

It stings, but I brush it off and take the opening I've recognized as the perfect opportunity. "Do you need help at the office? I can answer phones or run errands."

He scoffs and takes another drink. "No. The last thing I need is you at the office as well as my apartment."

I stand and collect the dishes. "Fine. I offered."

Without waiting for a reply, I carry the dirty plates to the sink to clean them. I can tell when my company isn't appreciated. The familiar feeling bites even more now because I'm completely out of my element.

As I wash, Arthur sets his glass next to the sink. His presence and the spicy cologne I'm beginning to associate with him distract me. He turns and leans against the counter, crossing his arms over his broad chest.

"Today has been strange for both of us." He exhales sharply. "Stay. Recover. We'll figure something out."

"I can't stay here and do nothing. There must be some way I can pay you." I meet his gaze and realize my mistake instantly. He's close. Too close. My heart races faster.

"Your eyes." He blinks twice before finishing his thought. "They're two different colors."

"Yeah," I murmur. Heterochromia runs in the family, but I can't tell him because I'm supposed to have amnesia. Shit.

His lips curl into a smile and my fucking heart stops beating. No man should look so delicious when he smiles. Arthur's smile could tempt a woman to sin and then lure her to the end of the universe. As quickly as it appeared, it vanishes.

Oh, sweet baby Yoda. I can't fantasize about my dad's boss. I refuse to flirt with him, no matter how sexy and brooding he is. What the hell am I going to do?

CHAPTER 6

Arthur

What the hell has gotten into me? I take a step back and shake this unnerving attraction away before it can dig its talons into me.

This woman. Damn it. I'm no closer to knowing who she really is or where she came from, but I can't deny the tension building between us. Watching her savor the dinner I made from scratch has me pinned between pride and lust. I can't reveal how much she affects me. Mostly because I don't understand how that's even possible.

How the hell did I get to this point? As she washes the dishes, I war with the conflict tearing apart my conscience. I don't need this complication, not now, not ever. The women in my life, my mother, grandmother, hell, even my sister, would never let me live a day longer if they discovered I turned this vulnerable woman out into the street without money or protection.

The vixen doesn't even need protection. The fire in her eyes when I challenged her at dinner revealed a passion hidden deep within. She would put up a fight, and the thought intensifies this desire I never expected.

I shift my weight trying to hide the effect she has on my libido. I may be an asshole, but I'm not blind. She's fucking gorgeous. My sister definitely knows her craft. She took what was already present and highlighted it with ease. The billowy silk shirt amplifies those curves I knew lay beneath her oversized sweater. I felt every one of them pressed against me earlier when I carried her.

"I'm going to take a shower," I mutter before pushing past her. I'm halfway across the room when I hear her call out.

"Thank you for dinner."

My heart softens a fraction, but I just wave in acknowledgement and keep walking. Once I'm safely locked in the bathroom, I lean against the door and take a few deep breaths. The sweet, floral scent of the soap she used lingers in the room. I pinch my eyes closed.

She's marking everything, leaving reminders of herself across my apartment. After years of living alone, blissfully untethered by marriage or even a steady relationship, having someone living in such close quarters is more challenging than I remember. It's only temporary. By mid-month, she'll be out of my life permanently. Why does the thought of her leaving piss me off?

I tear open my shirt with more force than necessary and glare at my own reflection. A long, cold shower should help me refocus. I have a firm to run and projects to finish. This year I intend to land the contract which will set both my firm and myself up indefinitely. Early retirement is sounding pretty good. Maybe a new venture will come along and carry me into my golden years.

It sounds ridiculous. I'm barely forty. I have my whole life ahead of me.

The cool spray of the shower rinses away thoughts of Kate and the events of the day. After a long soak, I step from the shower and dry off, wrapping the towel around my hips. I crack the door open expecting to find Kate, but the room is empty.

I pull a pair of sleep pants from the dresser and slip them on. Normally, that's all I wear, but I don a sweatshirt. The fabric rasps against my skin, but I shrug off the annoyance.

In the living room, Kate is bundled beneath a blanket on the couch where she's made a bed of sorts from blankets I had in the closet. *Make yourself at home why don't you.* I bite back the words when I notice her eyes are closed.

The thought of her rifling through my apartment should have irritated me more than it did. I cock my head and study her. The crochet afghan lay against her chin. All I can see is her face surrounded by a halo of dark curls. Innocent? Most assuredly not. This woman has burrowed beneath my skin, and the knowledge doesn't sit well with me.

"Take the bed." I tug on the blanket around her feet. "I'll sleep out here."

Her eyes fly open and fix on me with open suspicion. "No. I'm fine here."

"After my actions today, it's the least I can do. Take the bed. You need to recover."

"I can recover on the couch as well as the bed." She clutches the blanket tighter.

I grab a handful of the blanket and pull it off her.

"No!" She squeals when it slips from her hands and reveals her whole body. Her hands immediately grapple to cover her bare skin. The silk and lace camisole and shorts leave nothing to the imagination.

Sweet merciful God, what is she wearing? And why the hell would my sister give her sexy lingerie to sleep in rather than functional pajamas? I resist the urge to call my sister and instead toss the blanket back over Kate's shivering form.

"What the hell is Marcy thinking?" I shake my head. "You'll freeze in that getup."

Without waiting for her response, I stalk back into my bedroom and pull out the smallest set of pajamas I have. I typically buy sets but only end up wearing the bottoms. They're an unflattering plaid with red and blue stripes, but they're warmer than what she's wearing.

I return to the living room and toss the clothes on her lap. Her eyes widen when she unfolds the fabric. The motion draws attention to the silken camisole as it slips over her shoulder revealing the tempting curve of her breast.

"I don't need you freezing to death. Rob will kill me."

"Thanks." She stands up and the blanket falls away for a brief second as she struggles to wrap it around herself. The silk clings to the plush curves of her body.

With the effort of a saint, I turn and retreat into the kitchen to get a glass of water.

The sound of my bedroom door closing fills me with relief. I lean against the cabinet and set my water aside. My cock twitches as my mind replays the moment the blanket drops. I groan and adjust myself regretting I didn't take the opportunity to relieve this sexual need when I was in the shower. As if it would have helped, I scoff.

After I finish the water, I flop down onto the couch where she made her little bed. The fabric is still warm and the tantalizing scent of her soap teases my nose. I close my eyes and visions of silk and lace sliding from Kate's body fill my mind. I grit my teeth. Great, now I'm painfully hard.

"You tricked me."

I open my eyes and Kate's standing over me, her hands on her hips, my pajamas hanging from her luscious curves, her full lips upturned in a scowl.

"I didn't trick you." I shift a pillow across my lap to hide my uncomfortable situation. "Those pajamas are much more comfortable, aren't they?"

Kate nods. "Yes, but I can't take your bed."

"You will." I fix her with my most intimidating and unwavering stare. "Go. I'll sleep here."

She huffs, her cheeks flaring with color, and her eyes flashing with challenge. "Fine. I'll sleep on the floor."

When she moves to kneel, I launch to my feet and snatch her by the arm. "Why must you be so stubborn?"

She glares up at me and tries to wrench herself from my grip. "You're the one who's being stubborn!"

Damn it. I snatch her by the waist and lift her over my shoulder.

"Put me down!" She squirms and writhes trying to free herself. My arm bands her legs down to keep her from kicking.

After two steps she's shouting profanities that would make a sailor blush. Without thinking, I bring my palm down hard on her ass. The satisfying crack echoes through the room. She stills completely.

"Now, settle down before I drop you." I stalk the rest of the way into the bedroom and toss her onto the bed.

Her indignant grunt ignites a surge of pride. She's a fighter, and I'm enjoying it much more than I should be.

"That's not how you treat someone with a head injury." She crawls to a sitting position on the bed and glares.

"You'll live." I jab my finger toward the bed. "Now, go to sleep."

Her gaze drifts over me pausing halfway down my body. She gasps and her gorgeous eyes widen as they meet mine.

Shit. There's no hiding it now. I prop my hands on my hips. "Is there a problem?"

She shakes her head so hard her curls obscure the blush creeping into her cheeks.

"I didn't think so."

As much as I want to join her in the bed and take full advantage of my situation, I turn and leave the room, slamming the door behind me.

I turn off the lights and settle on the couch, pulling the warmest blanket over me. Taking a few deep breaths, I attempt to cool the heat raging through me. My body reacts of its own will, and I smooth my hand over my cock. The movement only aggravates the need pummeling my system.

No. I refuse to succumb to this base sexual need. I don't know her. She doesn't know me. We are not friends. We're certainly not lovers. And hopefully in a week, we'll never cross paths again.

But as I lay in the dark staring at the ceiling, I hear my conscience whisper through the stillness. *Is this what you really want? Or do you want to see where the other path leads?*

Irritated, I roll onto my side. The other path can only lead to trouble. Curvy, soft, intoxicating trouble. Only a mad man would follow it.

CHAPTER 7

Katherine

After a horrible night unable to sleep thanks to the unnecessary sexual attraction blossoming between Arthur and me, I must have hit a wall, or a door with my luck, because the next thing I know it's nine a.m. The makeshift bed on the couch lay empty and a note sits next to the still warm pot of coffee in the machine.

At work. My number is 555-8940. Use only in an emergency. Do not leave the apartment. Make yourself at home.

I toss the paper aside. Damn it. I had every intention of badgering him into letting me come with him to the office. I want to see my dad.

The note stares up at me. I read it again. It's no declaration of undying love, but deep beneath the brusque sentences, there's a glimpse of concern for my wellbeing. Maybe he's trying. I don't know.

Last night confused the hell out of me. One minute I can almost feel the sparks flying between us and the next he's built a brick wall ten feet high. The expression on his face when he saw the pajamas his sister brought. Oh, holy night. He looked ready to jump me then and there. But a cool displeasure smothered whatever heat ignited in that brief moment.

The way he tossed me over his shoulder and threw me on the bed. Hot. The way he dismissed me and left me completely confused. Well, dick move on his part.

I grab a cup of coffee and something to nibble before planting my butt in front of the TV. After messing with the ancient entertainment system, I finally get the damn thing turned on. I need something to distract me from the fact I'm attracted to my father's boss.

Three hours of non-stop soap operas is enough to rot anyone's brain. I rotate through the channels three times until I realize there's nothing good on television during the day. Not only was this true in my time but also in the past it seems.

I groan at the manufactured drama on the television. I don't even know which one this is. *Days of our Lives. Young and the Restless.* Hell, it could be *Dallas* for all I know. It's so over the top. I groan. How the hell did Nanna watch this garbage?

I click through it again and find MTV. Like actual MTV playing music videos. I instantly recognize the song. REO Speedwagon playing "Can't Fight This Feeling." I stare at the television entranced by the video. I've heard the song a million times, but I don't think I've ever seen the video. The lyrics return without hesitation. Oh man, the power of an eighties rock ballad.

I crank up the volume and sing along as I wander into the kitchen to find a snack. Inside the cabinet I find a bag of Doritos and a box of Famous Amos chocolate chip cookies. Score! There's only juice and water in the refrigerator. The cup of coffee and toast I ate this morning has long since worn off.

After tucking my snacks under one arm, I carry the juice and a glass into the living room. The bed I made the night before is still there. Blanket thrown over the back of the couch haphazardly. I pick it up and wrap it around me before settling down onto the couch.

The spicy scent of Arthur creates a cocoon around me. I nestle deeper into the fabric. Why does he have to smell so damn good?

Ten minutes of music videos and I'm nodding off. Just as I snuggle against the pillow and give in to the exhaustion, the phone rings.

I bolt upright and search the room. Where the hell is the phone?

It rings again and I see it sitting on a glass table beside the couch.

"Hello?" I nearly knock the whole contraption to the ground. Damn corded phones! Don't they have cordless yet? He's rich enough.

"*I must have the wrong number. I was looking for Arthur,*" a woman's voice purrs through the receiver.

"No, this is the right number." I cradle the phone in both hands. "He's at work right now. Can I take a message?"

Silence fills the line.

"Hello? Are you still there?"

"*I see Arthur hasn't wasted any time finding some hussy to warm his bed,*" the woman hisses.

Stunned, I choke on my reply before getting it out. "Excuse me?"

"*You heard me, tramp. Moving in on another woman's territory, huh?*"

I blink twice completely blanking on how to reply. "You misunderstand..."

"*No. You misunderstand. Arthur is mine. So, you'd best get your shit and get out,*" she growls into the other line.

"Lady, I don't know who you are or what the hell you're smoking, but you have issues." I slam the phone down so hard it makes me flinch. Damn, that was satisfying. Ending a call on an iPhone doesn't have quite the same effect.

The soap opera drama has somehow transferred from the television and into my life. Great. I flop down onto the couch and burrow beneath the blanket once more.

With the music playing in the background, I find myself drifting off. Exhaustion plus the warmth of the blanket and his scent lull me into a contented state. I fall into dreamland and find my dad waiting for me.

He's wearing a dark pinstripe suit with a crimson tie standing in the oversized window overlooking the city. A blinding smile transforms his dour expression when he sees me. I run toward him with my arms open. He scoops me up and spins me around.

I'm a little girl again. Clinging to him, I'm lost in the moment. He sets me down and holds my gaze. His eyes brim with love and pride. One blue while the other is nearly engulfed in amber. The eyes I see reflected in the mirror every day.

"I love you, Dad." My voice cracks. "I miss you."

"Me too, Peanut." His joyful smile takes on a sad hue before he steps away. "Don't cry. We'll see each other again soon." His outline fades against the sunset over the city until all I see is the imposing presence of the Empire State Building.

"Kate," a familiar, imposing voice rumbles behind me.

I spin around and see Arthur leaning against the wall. The sunset plays across his features casting half of his face into shadow. He's wearing the same suit as Dad, but it fits him differently. Broader, more powerful. Intimidating. Sexy as hell. He uncrosses his arms and stalks toward me.

My back hits the glass. He pins me against it. His scent, his heat, his presence...they disorient me. My heart races, and I fear it will tear free from my chest.

Arthur's gaze drifts over me, a slow wandering perusal, before locking with mine. A crooked smile pulls at his lips. "You're mine now, Katherine." His hands grip my shoulders as he leans closer, his mouth a breath from mine.

"Kate."

Somewhere in the haze I hear my name. Before I feel the press of Arthur's kiss, I'm tumbling through the darkness.

"Kate."

I wrench my eyes open to find Arthur staring down at me. His hands grip my shoulders. He sighs with relief.

"Thank God." He releases me and rakes his hand through his hair. "I wasn't sure you were going to wake up." He stands and pulls his tie loose. "Must have been some dream."

Consciousness slaps me in the face like a cold winter gust of wind. I sit up and shake my head.

"What do you mean?" I clear my throat.

Arthur tugs the tie from his suit and unbuttons the top of his shirt baring a hint of skin at his throat. "You didn't want to wake up. Must have been a good dream."

My face heats. "Yeah." I turn my gaze away, unable to quell the thirst building at the sight of him practically doing a striptease compounded with the haunting memory of the dream kiss. Damn it.

"I'm gonna change." He walks toward the bedroom, giving me a full view of his ass clad in fitted dress pants.

Sweet mother of Captain America, that ass.

"Would you please set the table? I brought dinner. Hope you like Chinese food." He gestures toward the kitchen with one hand before disappearing into the bedroom.

I press my hands to my face. Yup. Flaming hot. I'm sure it's a hideous shade of maroon. Great. Fanfuckingtastic. Is it possible to die from embarrassment? I don't know if I can even have a conversation with him now. Not after a sinful, sexy dream starring him. These thoughts need to stop. He's too old for me.

But is he really? The question pops unbidden to my mind flashing in big bold neon font. I need to be honest with myself. I'm stuck in 1985 indefinitely. Unless whatever powers that brought me here suddenly decide my time is up and they beam me right back to 2020.

I shake my head. No. There's nothing there for me. Not now.

I sound insane. Why would I be better off in the past?

A million reasons, the voice in my head whispers. I shush it with a wave of my hand and climb from the comfy nest on the couch. Darkness has already fallen over the city. I blink a few times and glance at the clock. Six p.m. Holy shit! I slept the day away.

In the kitchen I gather plates and silverware. On the dining room table there's an assortment of containers. I glance at the names on the top as I set the dishes on the table.

"I wasn't sure what you liked. So, I got a few of the basics," Arthur says from behind me.

Steeling myself, I turn and smile. "It looks great. Thanks."

"I was going to call, but one of my meetings ran late." He grabs a bottle of wine from the refrigerator and two glasses. "You want some?"

"Yes, please." I sit down and open the containers. "Unless you think I shouldn't. Rob did say I shouldn't drink."

"It's been twenty-four hours. I think you're good." He grins. "One glass won't kill you."

A grin. Be still my damn heart. Who knew one simple action could make someone twenty times more attractive? I don't know if I can resist him if he keeps revealing these little hidden treasures. I nod because I can't trust the words to not come out of my mouth sounding like *please take me to bed and ravish me now.*

As I put food on our plates and he pours the wine, a silent awkwardness falls between us.

"*Buon appetito.*" He gestures, raising his glass.

I tap mine to his and sip the refreshing white wine. It has a delightful fruity taste, but I'm sure it's not nearly as heady as Arthur's mouth. I'm riveted by it as he sips his wine.

"Something wrong?" he asks, setting the glass aside.

"No." I take a bite of lo mien and chew thoughtfully trying to desperately avoid fantasizing about my dad's boss. "Oh, you got a phone call today."

"Is that so?" He takes a bite of chicken.

"Yes. A woman called."

Arthur set his fork aside. "Shit." He leans his elbows on the table and exhales sharply. "I hope she wasn't rude."

"Well, she called me a hussy and a tramp. But I've been called worse." I shrug.

"I'm sorry."

"It's not your fault." I take another bite. "Your girlfriend?"

He scoffs. "Not really. We dated a few times. Social functions around town. But nothing serious."

I laugh. "Well, she never got the memo."

"What do you mean?"

"That woman thinks whatever you two have is the real deal." I break it to him as honestly as I can. "I guarantee she was expecting you to put a ring on it."

Arthur shakes his head and laughs. "A ring on what?"

I wag my left hand and point to my ring finger. "On this."

His eyes narrow. "I guess I'll have to clarify our agreement then it seems."

"Is everything a business arrangement with you?" I ask, genuinely curious as to the innerworkings of his mind.

"Yes." He replies without hesitation and takes another bite of food.

The wheels in my mind spin. "Then how about we make an arrangement?"

Arthur nearly chokes on his fried rice. "What?"

"An arrangement. Between you and me."

Skepticism seems so natural on his expression. "What are you proposing?"

"I need a job and a place to stay."

He grins and leans forward. "What's in it for me?"

"I keep the bitch off your back." I shrug. "Plus, I'm a whiz at Microsoft Office."

"I'm not sure what the hell you're talking about." He leans back and studies me carefully. "But it seems I could use a bit of help at the office. My secretary quit this morning and the temp agency is shorthanded."

"No problem. I can handle it."

A wicked grin crosses Arthur's lips and I'm transported to the dream instantly. My heart pounds and my appetite for dinner is replaced by something much more carnal.

"Oh, I'm sure you can, Kate."

I walked into that one, and I don't regret it. But I'm about to see my dad again. This now overshadows the longings I'd much rather not inspect too carefully.

CHAPTER 8

Arthur

Those springs are lethal. I don't know if I can spend one more night on the torture device also known as my sofa. It's barely six thirty, and I'm already up with a cup of coffee staring out the window. The blue haze of dawn breaking into a cacophony of orange and pinks lays over the horizon.

I debate leaving her at the apartment again, even though I agreed to her insane plan. Truth is, I'm not against having her in the office. I could use the help. The real concern is how the hell I'm going to function with her being a physical distraction in my space all day.

There is no logical reason for this attraction. I mean, of course, she's gorgeous as well as quick witted. I even enjoy the way she challenges me rather than accepting her fate meekly. But none of this explains the chemistry building between us. It's been forty-eight hours since we met, for Christ's sake.

The alarm rings in the bedroom. I pour a second cup of coffee and take it in hoping it will entice her to get up.

The bed's empty. I turn off the alarm and knock on the bathroom door.

"I'll be done in a minute," she calls out.

"Take your time," I shout back. "I brought you..." The door opens and my eyes drift over the woman standing before me. Kate's wearing a black pencil skirt and a flowy green blouse with a wide belt tucked around the narrowest part of her hourglass figure. Her dark curls are tamed in a bun and loose tendrils frame her face. I don't know what kind of witchcraft my sister utilized, but holy shit, the transformation is night and day.

"Coffee." She sighs with contentment and takes the mug from my hand. "Thanks." The look on her face as she sips the brew is pure bliss.

I'm half-jealous of a coffee mug the way her lips press against the porcelain. Would they taste sweet with a hint of the earthy caffeinated beverage? Ignoring the persistent fantasy, I clear my throat.

"We leave at seven thirty." Without waiting for her response, I push past her and shut the bathroom door creating a solid barrier between us.

Instead of allowing myself to think about Kate and this growing fascination, I run through the mental checklist for my day. I have two meetings with clients and one with the head of the development office. It will only be me today since Victor is out of the office for the remainder of the week. We can schedule a meeting for Monday morning to discuss plans for the month and assess the quarterly goals for the year.

Twenty minutes later, I'm showered, shaved, and dressed. As I fasten the watch around my wrist, my reflection in the mirror convinces me I'm prepared to face whatever the day may bring. When I open the door and find Kate sitting on the loveseat flipping through the paper, my confidence trips and falls face first into rush hour traffic.

"Do you have a coat that doesn't look like it came from a thrift bin?" I cross the room and open the closet near the front door.

"Yes, your sister gave me one." She stands and retrieves the oversized monstrosity I found her in.

"Why are you wearing this one then?" I frown. "It looks ancient." I pull it toward me and check the tag. "It's a man's." An unfamiliar pang of jealousy nags at the back of my mind.

"It's much warmer." She smiles and pulls the worn wool jacket around her shoulders. "Plus, it was my dad's."

"He's probably freezing."

A forlorn expression steals her smile and she drops her gaze. "Yeah." She shakes her head. "Anyway, shall we go? I don't want to be late on my first day."

The moment passes as quickly as it arrived. "I'm sure your new employer will understand."

I open the door, and she steps into the corridor, pausing to wait for me. Once we arrive at the ground floor, she grips my arm but quickly releases me.

"Sorry. I guess I'm more nervous than I thought."

"About what?" I hold the door for her and we step out into the street. The bustle of the city surrounds us and as usual it invigorates me, breathing life into my routine.

She doesn't respond. I turn to find her watching the people walking past the front of the building. Her wide eyes dart back and forth, her lips parted in awe.

"Something wrong?" I come alongside her and nudge her toward the car where Cyril is waiting.

"No." Kate shakes her head almost a bit too quickly but smiles when she sees my driver.

"I'm glad to see you've recovered, ma'am." Cyril tips his hat to her before shifting his attention to me. "Good morning, Mr. Maxwell."

"Kate, this is my driver Cyril."

"Nice to meet you." She shakes his hand.

Cyril reacts slowly, dumbfounded at her reaction. "Likewise." He grins. "If you need anything, don't hesitate to ask."

"When I asked you to swing by Grant and pick up my suit at the cleaners, you told me you're a driver, not a manservant." I shove my hands in my pockets and stare pointedly at my driver.

Cyril shrugs. "You're not a beautiful woman recovering from an injury, are you?"

Kate chuckles before climbing into the backseat of the car.

Pride and indignance rear their heads in unison at his snappy retort. "Careful, Cyril, or you'll be hard pressed to find another gig in the city once I fire you." I climb into the car behind her.

The driver scoffs. "Whatever you say, sir." The door closes, firmly punctuating his statement.

"I like him." Kate smiles.

I study her bright expression. This is the first time I've seen her smile. My heart stirs at the way her eyes crinkle at the corners and her grin reveals a small dimple in her right cheek.

"Well, don't. He's impertinent." I straighten my tie and face forward as the car turns into traffic.

Kate leans closer, her breath brushing against my ear. "You won't really fire him, will you?"

The teasing floral scent of her soap sinks into my brain, and the caress of her breath creates a riot of desperation shooting through me like fireworks over the bay. My fist clenches to keep from reaching for her.

I shrug a shoulder noncommittally, not trusting myself to face her or even respond.

She leans back against the seat and stares out the window. The ride to the office continues in silence. It takes me that long to reign my unruly thoughts into some semblance of cohesion.

Once we arrive at the office, the world around me clicks into synchronization. A calm settles over me, even with Kate, a factor of the unknown, by my side.

Gladys looks up from the typewriter when I open the door. Her smile faulters for a moment at the sight of Kate.

"Good morning, Mr. Maxwell." She abandons the typewriter and rises to her feet.

"Gladys, this is Kate. She'll be working as my temporary assistant for a few weeks until we find a permanent replacement." I keep the conversation simple and unfettered with details. "Would you please show her around and give her an idea of how we do things around here?"

"Of course, Mr. Maxwell," Gladys replies with a sincere smile. "Welcome, Kate."

"I'll be in my office preparing for my nine-thirty. Please hold all my calls." With a parting glance at Kate, I turn and barricade myself inside my office. I don't know what I was thinking bringing her to work with me. How the hell am I going to concentrate knowing she's running loose in my business where I found her snooping on New Year's Day?

I pinch the bridge of my nose. Doesn't matter. There's a reasonable explanation. When her memory returns, I'll ask her. Until then, there's nothing I can do except keep a close eye on her.

I hang up my jacket on the coat rack and pause. She mentioned her old, oversized coat belonged to her father. Is this a sign of her memory returning?

Bolstered by hope, I sit behind my desk and prepare for the upcoming meeting. As much as I want her to recover and move on, I can't ignore the pinch of regret at the thought of her leaving. Shaking my head, I focus on the papers before me and not on the woman who's fallen directly into my path and aroused these unnecessary desires.

CHAPTER 9

Katherine

Being productive gives me life. Seriously. Ever since I lost my job in November, compounded by Mom's death shortly after, and then jackass breaking up with me right before Christmas, I've been adrift. Today, I feel like my life has purpose again, and that alone gives me hope.

I glance at Arthur's closed office door. He's been in and out of the conference room all day with various clients. While he's given direction and made requests, our interactions have been minimal. I can't say I'm not disappointed, because I am. I like having his sole attention.

Two stacks of papers sit twelve inches deep on my desk. My most pressing task today is to organize and file them. This I can handle. No problem.

Gladys smiles from across the room. She's sweet and friendly. Her humor reminds me of my mother. After Arthur left me in her capable hands, we became friends quickly. We're about the same age—a technicality, I know. She's worked at the firm since Arthur started it fifteen years ago, so she knows the ins and outs and what's expected of the staff.

Once I got the grand tour of the office, she explained the details of what my job entails and where to find supplies, files, and so forth. The office is so well organized, it makes my job easy. She directed me to take the desk outside Arthur's office and answer any incoming calls in between filing the paperwork piled on the desk.

The day passes quickly. More quickly than sitting in Arthur's apartment watching soap operas all day, that's for sure. In an era where Netflix and Google and the internet are distant dreams, having a job is certainly a welcoming diversion. I can't believe how different it feels not having those things at my fingertips. Even walking around without my phone makes me feel like I'm naked. I think I miss digital music most of all. Waiting for a familiar and loved song to play on the radio is painful. How did people survive monotony? The answer is obvious now. Work.

Gladys sashays across the room in her mauve dress with the wide padded shoulders and poufy blonde hair. Ugh, the fashion during this decade certainly leaves a lot to be desired.

"That's enough for today, hon." She smiles and grabs her purse and jacket from the closet. "How was your first day?"

"Good." I lean back and stretch. "Thank you for all your help."

"Any time. If you have any questions, don't hesitate to ask." She pulls the coat on and fluffs her hair over the collar.

"Aren't there three architects with the firm?" I ask, hedging around the one question I've been dying to ask all day. "I already know Mr. Maxwell and I met Mr. Brooks."

"Oh yeah, Mr. Cohen. He's out this week. Took his wife on a special trip." Her eyes glaze over at the thought. "Lucky woman. Mr. Cohen is a great guy. You'll like him."

"I'm sure I will." My heart constricts when she mentions Dad. I miss him so much I could burst. I'd been so hopeful at the thought of meeting him today.

"He'll be back in the office on Monday." She slips her purse over her shoulder. "You heading home now?"

"Not yet. Mr. Maxwell wanted me to stay until after he finishes this last meeting."

"Okay." She winks. "Don't let him take advantage of you. Maybe we can grab a drink after work one day next week."

"Sounds good to me. Thanks again, Gladys."

"Any time, honey." She waves before heading for the elevator.

I stand up and arch my back stretching to the right and then the left. I'll definitely need some yoga stretches added to my daily routine if I keep this up.

"You finished with the filing already?"

My heart stops at the sound of Arthur's voice behind me. I whip around and find him leaning against the doorframe of his office with his brow arched and arms folded across his chest.

I glance at the bare desktop. "Yup. Just finished." Pride fills me.

"I see you and Gladys work well together." He pushes away from the wall and retrieves his coat from the closet, followed by mine. "You didn't find the work too boring?" He holds my coat open inviting me to put it on.

"Not at all. Organization is a hobby of mine." I slip into the warm, familiar embrace of dad's wool coat. "I enjoy a challenge."

"Of course, you do," he mutters, stepping away. "Shall we?"

I exit the suite first, and he locks the door behind us. In the elevator,

I study his profile. The strong line of his jaw, those full kissable lips, the hint of a five o'clock shadow along his jaw. He's handsome. Classical silver screen handsome like Cary Grant or Mel Ferrer.

He glances at me out of the corner of his eye as the elevator slowly descends. "Are you hungry?"

"Starving," I confess dramatically. "I can make something when we get home. It's only fair."

"I have a better idea." A smile tugs at the corner of his mouth. "Would you like to get coffee first?"

"Starbucks?" My voice overflows with excitement. I've been craving a caramel macchiato since yesterday morning.

His brow furrows. "What's Starbucks?"

Shit. Oh, no. I broke the cardinal rule of time travel. No spoilers. "Nothing. Never mind."

"Is your memory coming back?" he asks as the doors slowly open on the ground floor. "You mentioned your coat belonging to your father this morning and now Starbucks. I can only assume these are familiar things to you."

"Snippets and flashes. I'm not sure how they all fit together yet," I lie.

"Well, I'll take that as a good sign." He opens the door for me, and we step out into the city shrouded in darkness and noise.

Cyril is waiting for us. He smiles when I rush toward the car. "Hello, Miss Kate. How was work?"

"Lovely, Cyril, thank you. I trust you had an uneventful day?"

"Always." He focuses on Arthur and sobers instantly. "Where to, boss?"

"Take us to the Red Maple, Jeeves."

Cyril glares at Arthur. The two men face off and I forget how to breathe. Are they going to fight?

"Yes, sir." Cyril opens the car door and helps me in.

Once the car weaves into traffic, Arthur relaxes beside me. I want to ask him why we're going there, but I sit quietly beside him and stare out the window. Everything looks so different and yet it's almost like nothing changed. The colorful characters who occupy the streets of New York are a bit more vibrant thanks to the preference for neon shades. But the hustle and bustle roars through the streets the same as it always has and always will.

The car rolls to a stop in front of a chrome and glass diner with a flashing red and white neon sign hanging over the door. The Red Maple.

I remember Mom telling me about it, but I'd never been there. She once said they made the best pies in all five boroughs.

Arthur steps from the car and offers his hand. I take it feeling more like a spoiled princess than a temporary employee and uninvited houseguest. The warmth of his touch sends shivers of electricity coursing through my arm and directly into my chest. As soon as my feet are steady on the sidewalk, he releases me. Did he feel it too?

He escorts me inside where we take a booth in the corner next to a window giving us a view of the pedestrian traffic outside. Arthur sits with his back to the wall, his observant gaze flickering across the other patrons in the diner.

"How do you feel about pie?"

"I love pie." I settle back against the booth.

"What kind are you in the mood for?" He gestures to the glass case where a variety of choices await.

"Surprise me." Damn, this is reckless. I'm supposed to have amnesia and keeping track of my lies is becoming exponentially harder.

As I debate telling him the truth, a pretty waitress rocking Madonna's early signature look combined with her uniform sidles up to the table and lays two menus down.

"What can I getcha to drink?" She pops her gum and glances between us.

"Two coffees." Arthur slides the menus back toward her. "And two orders of apple pie a la mode."

The waitress scribbles down the order and retreats behind the counter.

Arthur leans back casually draping his arm across the seat. "How was your first day?"

"Great." I shift under the intensity of his gaze. "The work was pretty straight forward once I figured out the filing system."

"No problems otherwise?" He nods to the waitress who appears next to the table bearing two coffee mugs, creamer, and a steaming pot of coffee. After she fills both mugs, she leaves.

"No problems at all." I pull the mug closer and focus on adding some cream and sugar even though I normally only take a dash of milk.

"Do you have any questions?" He lifts his mug and sips the unadorned black coffee.

I stir my concoction and cringe when I taste how sweet it is. Shit. "About the job itself, no. I can't think of anything."

"My colleague, Mr. Cohen, will return to the office on Monday.

You'll have a chance to meet him then."

My heart leaps at the thought and I smile at the prospect of seeing my father again. "I'm excited to meet him." I sip the coffee and choke it down. "Have you worked with your partners long?"

"Brooks and I have been together from the beginning. Cohen's only been with us for the past few years, but his work shows great skill and an eye for detail."

Hearing his high praise of my father's work makes me swell with pride. Dad had a talent for design. It surpassed most of the other architects of his time. Getting a position with this firm at the age of thirty proved to be the single greatest accomplishment of his short life.

The waitress appears again bearing our pie heaped with ice cream. "Enjoy."

I pick up my fork and take a bite. The buttery crust and sweet tang of apple filling melts in my mouth along with the decadent vanilla ice cream. The combination wrenches a moan from my throat.

Arthur pauses mid-bite and stares at me with an arched brow. "That good?"

"Better than sex," I murmur before stuffing another forkful into my mouth.

He chokes, and I meet his gaze across the table. In their stormy depths I see his hunger, and it has nothing to do with apple pie and coffee.

CHAPTER 10

Arthur

"Better than sex."

The pie barely touches my tongue when her words strike me like a lightning bolt. I half-choke down the bite of now flavorless pie before meeting her innocent gaze. Maybe innocent isn't the right word, but I honestly don't know any other word to describe it. Those mesmerizing eyes widen with realization but no regret.

A volcanic heat rushes through my veins and a memory of her wearing skimpy lingerie flashes through my mind. Her tongue darts out to wet her lips before she presses them firmly together. It's becoming harder to deny this blossoming chemistry. Reckless, I dive headfirst into the flames.

"Perhaps you haven't found the right partner." I lift another piece of pie and grin at her dazed expression before consuming it.

Kate clears her throat and turns her reddening face away from me, focusing instead on the street outside. Her reflection in the glass betrays her reaction to my words. Her eyes drift closed for a brief moment. Her breath quickens. Her lips move silently, but I catch the way her teeth brush her lower lip when she mutters an unspoken curse.

I eat, patiently, calmly, waiting for her to regain some composure. Within moments she faces me again and picks up her fork. Kate and I resume our meal, ignoring the tension.

My words must have struck a chord, because her cheeks remain stained with a lovely blush until the last of the pie disappears from our plates. She sips the cold coffee and avoids making eye contact.

After I pay, we exit the diner and find Cyril waiting for us at the end of the block. The ride back to the apartment is painfully silent. I wonder if she's mulling over the possibilities of my response to her assessment of the pie. I am. I haven't stopped.

But questions remain. And until I have answers to those questions, I cannot indulge in what I truly want. No. Not yet. It is obvious Kate is keeping secrets, and I will uncover them through any means necessary.

Once we arrive at the apartment, Kate disappears in the bedroom, locking the door behind her. I pull off my jacket and jerk my tie free. Coming home to an empty apartment never bothered me before, but this week it became apparent something vital was absent for the past twenty years.

I turn on the TV desperate for some kind of distraction. MTV pops up on the screen in full annoying color. I'm more of a fan of the sixty's hits than this new shit. Most of it is loud and abrasive. I don't understand the fascination with heavy metal and hair bands. Even the pop racket grates on my nerves. But right now, I'm thankful for whatever distraction it provides.

A new video plays. I read the name of the band at the bottom. The Cars. The beat is catchy. It's not Elvis, but it works.

"Oh man, I love this song!" Kate steps from the bedroom wearing my plaid pajamas.

Suddenly, I wish I hadn't given her my clothes to wear. Her bare skin hidden beneath the thin layers of cotton fabric. I want to peel it off and explore every inch of her.

She sings along with the song completely oblivious to the wicked ideas crossing my mind. When she curls up on the couch beside me, my whole body tenses. I want to reach for her, drag her across my lap and taste her. I close my eyes and try to focus on anything besides this white-hot lust pulsing through me. So much for my plan to draw out her secrets.

Unless I use seduction. My cock pulses at the fleeting idea. No. I won't play that game. I can't. It wouldn't be fair to either of us.

"I haven't heard this song in so long." Kate leans back against the cushions and frowns. "It was one of my favorites as a kid. Dad loved The Cars."

Her confession makes me pause. "A kid?" I face her. "How old are you?"

A look of panic crosses her face. "A lady never reveals her age." She laughs. "I mean it makes me feel like a kid. My Dad loved all kinds of music. He got into their early stuff."

Kate shifts uncomfortably beside me. I'm not sure I believe her or not, but honestly, I may have misunderstood her. Since my cock's insistent demands distracted me.

"You like this crap?" I gesture toward the TV where a Michael Jackson video is blaring across the screen.

"Of course." She nods and remains focused on the TV. "Don't

you?"

"No. I prefer Elvis, Bob Dylan, and Johnny Cash. Stuff I grew up with." I undo the top two buttons of my shirt.

She spins and scrunches up her face at me. "Bob Dylan? Seriously? I mean, his lyrics are iconic, but his voice...no, no way." Her gaze drops to where my hand at my throat.

"Doesn't mean I enjoy it any less." I shrug and work on my cufflinks.

"So, you don't enjoy any modern music?" Her voice cracks at the end as her curiosity keeps her attention fixed on my hands.

"Not really." I shrug. "My sister loves it. She works with all these people. I don't see the appeal."

"Wait? Marcy works with musicians?" Her jaw drops, revealing a beautiful row of pearly white teeth and a tongue I'd love to see put to good use.

"Musicians. Actors. Celebrities of all sorts. She's the most sought-after stylist in town." I steer my dirty thoughts back into neutral territory. "She didn't tell you?"

"No. I mean, she's stylish and knows her stuff," Kate sputters. "But she didn't give me any details or drop names."

Drop names? What the hell does that even mean? I push the question aside. "Yeah. After her divorce a few years ago, she got this great opportunity through one of the networks downtown and her business went through the roof."

Kate beams, and her smile hits me like a punch to the gut. "That's amazing! It sounds like she's living the dream."

Living the dream. I marvel at the way she speaks. Her choice of words sometimes doesn't make sense without context. "Yeah, well, it used to be a nightmare."

Her smile faulters. "Her ex?"

"Yeah. The guy is an asshole. Rob and I tried to warn her, but she married him right out of high school." I dislike even thinking about it, but I keep talking unable to stop myself. "He controlled everything she did. Who she saw. Where she went. Hell, he even tried keeping her from visiting and calling her family."

"One of those guys." Kate nods solemnly. "I understand."

"When she finally caught him in bed with his co-worker's wife, she filed for a divorce." I ignore the emotions recounting this story brings to the surface. "I gave her a loan to get her on her feet. She refused to take a handout from anyone."

"Yeah, I would've been the same way." Kate props herself against the couch facing me. "You're a good brother, helping her when she needed it the most."

"She deserves the best, but she worked hard for what she has now." I chuckle at my sister's stubborn streak. "And she paid me back the full loan with interest. I'm proud of her."

Kate rests her hand on my shoulder. "Family is important. I don't have any siblings."

"Oh?" I ask, noting the shift in conversation. I press her further to see if her amnesia has finally lifted. "Were you close with your parents?"

She chews on her lip as she stares at the television. "Yeah. Dad died...a while back. Mom passed a few months ago. I miss them."

Interesting. I can't help but wonder if her memory recovered or if she even had amnesia to begin with. With the conversation so personal, I decide against calling her bluff and instead focus on drawing more out of her.

"Did you grow up in the city?" I ask, searching her profile.

Kate shifts her attention back to me and I note the panic etched deep in her mismatched eyes. "I think so." She laughs uncomfortably. "I don't remember exactly. The details are still kind of fuzzy."

"I understand. Rob did say the memories may be slow to return." I slowly rise to my feet. "I'm going to change."

"Oh, yeah. Of course."

"There's some leftover Chinese in the refrigerator if you're still hungry. The pie wasn't dinner. It's not nearly satisfying enough." I add the last part on a whim, teasing her. Another wave of blush stains her cheeks and she glances away.

"You're never going to let me forget I said that, are you?"

"Said what?" I shove my hands in my pockets. "Your assertion about pie being better than sex." Taking two steps backwards, I move closer to the bedroom. "Nope, probably not."

Inside the bedroom, I change into my pajama pants and an NYU sweatshirt. When I come back into the living room, Kate's in the kitchen heating up plates in the microwave. I hate the contraption and barely use it. She's bouncing around with the music on the TV.

Maybe I should call Rob and update him on her recovery. I slip into my drafting room and close the door. Of the two phonelines in the apartment, I rarely use this one, but this isn't a conversation I want to have in front of Kate.

After the fifth ring and no answer, I hang up and try the hospital number. The nurse transfers me to his line. Three rings and it connects.

"*Dr. Thompson.*"

"Rob, it's Arthur."

"*Hey, I meant to call yesterday, but the ER was chaos. How is your victim, I mean guest?*" Rob chuckles.

"Funny." I lean against the drafting table and lower my voice. "She's up and moving around. She went to work for me today."

"*You knock her out, take her home, and now she's your personal slave?*" Rob deadpans. "*No wonder you're a hit with the ladies.*" He clears his throat. "*Has she had any episodes of fainting, nausea, vomiting, or seizures?*"

"No."

"*Is she eating? Drinking fluids? Resting?*"

"Yes."

"*Has her memory returned?*" Rob asks methodically, running through a mental checklist.

"That's what I wanted to ask you. What should I expect? Will it all come back at once?" I don't mention her strange claims or the tidbits she's revealed about her family and her past.

"*It depends. I've seen some patients where it comes back all at once. Sometimes it never comes back. And then there are others who seem to remember bits and pieces, but forget larger chunks of their memory.*" Rob exhales sharply. "*Has she mentioned anything about her past?*"

"A few details, but nothing giving me any idea who she is or where she came from." I tap my fingers on the desk.

"*Damn. Well, don't push her too hard. Do you need me to stop by?*" Rob shuffles some papers on his end of the line.

"No. I'll give you a call if anything changes."

"*Sounds good.*"

"Have you found anyone looking for her at the local hospitals?" I ask, half-hoping he doesn't.

"*No. Do you want me to put in a call to Richards down at the station, see if he can find anything to help us locate her family?*"

"If you think it would help, yeah, but I don't have a lot of information to give him." Involving the police isn't ideal, but it's the last avenue to chase any possibilities.

"*I'll give him a call after my shift. I need to run, some of us have lives to save.*"

"Thanks, Doc." My sarcasm earns me a brusque goodbye.

I rest my hand on the door and take a deep breath. Honestly, I shouldn't be this invested in someone I just met, but I can't help it. There's definitely something between us. I feel it. A gentle pull every time she walks into the room.

But there are too many unanswered questions, too many variables I have no control over. There is a reason I stay single and only casually date. I don't want complicated. I have no place for a wife or even a steady relationship.

Kate is most definitely a complication. She's worse than that. She's a distraction. I have a firm to run. The last thing I need or want is a curvaceous hellcat tearing up my well-maintained life.

My fist taps against the wall repeatedly. It's like I have no control over my hormones when she's in the room. Even thinking about her pulls me deeper into fantasies I haven't allowed myself to indulge in—ever.

Yet, she rose to the challenge at the office today. Even though my schedule was full, I watched her carefully. She learns quickly and follows instructions to the letter. A strange sense of pride wells up deep in my chest. *Mine.*

No. I shake my head at the strange possessive thought. She's not mine. The irrational thought makes me recoil in horror. What would make me think such a thing?

The way she moaned while eating her pie. The way she so innocently claimed it was better than sex. The way my clothing caresses the sweet curves of her body. Her in my apartment. Naked in my shower. In my bed.

I pace the length of the room and rest my forehead against the cool glass of the window.

"Stop," I whisper to the voice in my mind telling me how easy it would be to seduce her, to lay claim to her.

You want her. You can't deny it.

I growl and my breath fogs the glass. No. Maybe I should ask Marcy if she can stay with her until she recovers. I can't ask Rob. That would be like feeding a lamb to a lion. It has to be Marcy. But I can't ask my sister to go out of her way because I'm uncomfortable. She has her own life and thriving business.

The memory of Kate lying unconscious on the floor outside my office haunts me. I did this to her. I hurt her. I can set this right. But I cannot concede to my baser desires.

Until Kate recovers, she is my responsibility, nothing more.

When I return to the living room, Kate is curled on her side, her head on my pillow, fast asleep.

My heart aches at the sight. I shove the tender emotions aside and pick her up. She nestles her face against my neck.

Fuck.

I carry her into the bedroom and lay her down on the bed. She sighs when I pull the blankets around her. Her sweet smile and bewitching eyes may be hidden from me, but they're burned into my memory.

Kate needs to get her memory back and fast, because if she doesn't, I don't know what I'm going to do. Part of me wants to crawl into bed beside her and hold her close. I can't shake the feeling this is exactly where she belongs, and that thought terrifies me more than anything.

CHAPTER 11

Katherine

After a long morning, I take my short lunch to retreat to the observation deck. The brisk air refreshes me and I feel closer to Dad than I have in years. It's Friday, which means in three days I'll finally get to see my father. Monday morning. I can hardly contain my excitement. I've waited this long, two more days should be no problem.

Less than a week into my new position and I've already fallen into a comfortable rhythm. Gladys helps me work through any issues and Arthur, while continuously busy, checks in periodically. There's definitely something to be said for the pace of the office setting without all the technology cluttering it up, but then again, I'd kill for a decent PC with a word processor over a typewriter.

The clear blue skies stretch for miles. Even though the sun shines brightly overhead, the air is crisp and cold. I pull my coat closer around me. Tourists bustle around the platform, but after living in the city for so long, I'm used to their presence. I lean against the railing where I stood only a few days ago contemplating the darkness around me. Today, there's a blossom of hope I never could have imagined.

I admire the city scape in the distance, but my attention always returns to the World Trade Center buildings. The constant visual reminder of my displacement in time leaves me uneasy. So many events take place during my lifetime, I never took the time to think about them before. Could I even influence major events and save lives? No, probably not.

Every book, movie, TV show featuring time travel I've ever seen shows the consequences of messing with past events. Then why am I here? If not to change the world, then to change my own destiny? Frustration overwhelms me.

I wish there were a handbook or an instruction manual to help me navigate time travel. I don't want to be the reason for nuclear war in the twenty-first century by accidentally stepping on a dragonfly. Ugh, the idea definitely leaves me queasy.

A glance at my watch tells me I should get back to work. Gladys wrote out a list of projects for me to tackle today. I'm glad for the challenge. I need something to occupy my thoughts. Between my excitement at seeing Dad next week and this complicated tension building with Arthur, my brain is overwhelmed.

The thought of Arthur makes my body heat. I push away from the railing and retreat into the elevator. Once I'm back inside the building, I unbutton my coat and refocus. This job may be temporary, but I'll do my damnedest to make sure it's done to the best of my ability.

I weave around a handful of people when I reach the fifty-fourth floor.

"Hi, Gladys. Did I miss anything?" I greet my co-worker as soon as I walk in the door.

Gladys jumps to her feet. "Oh, thank goodness you're back. Arthur wants you in his office the moment you return."

Fear grips me. What happened? What did I do? Did he somehow uncover the truth? I pull off my coat and hang it up.

"Did he say why?" I smooth my hands over my skirt.

She shakes her head. "No, but he's in there with Mr. Cohen right now. I'll let him know you're available."

Mr. Cohen. *Dad.* My heart stops. I'm not prepared. I'm not ready. Shit. Just breathe. I quickly adjust my blouse and pat my hair. Oh, God. I can't do this.

"Kate has returned, Mr. Maxwell." Gladys props the phone against her shoulder listening to his response. "Yes, sir. I will." She hangs up the phone and nods to me. "Go ahead in. They're waiting for you."

"Gladys, I..." My throat constricts.

"Don't worry. They won't bite. Go on, don't keep them waiting." She shoos me toward Arthur's office door.

I take several deep breaths before opening the door. Arthur glances up from behind his desk. He stands as I walk in and close the door behind me.

"You asked to see me, sir?" I keep my attention focused on him, but I can feel Dad's presence in the room. Those piercing eyes ground me. I take a breath and steady my racing heart.

"Yes, Kate. I want you to meet Victor Cohen, my associate." He turns away, and I follow his gaze. "Victor, this is my new assistant, Kate."

"Good to have you on board, Kate." Dad extends his hand and offers a sincere smile.

There's a stabbing pain in my chest from my heart exploding. I choke back a sob at the sight of him. His familiar mop of hair slicked back with precision, kind eyes, and commanding presence. He looks exactly like he does in the photograph I keep of him on my dresser. I want to scream and cry and throw myself into his arms, tell him how much I missed him. The desire to do it nearly overwhelms my sense. But I refrain.

Instead, I reach out and take his extended hand. "An honor, Mr. Cohen. I'm excited to work with you."

The heat of his hand engulfs mine. After thirty-two years of being deprived of his presence, his touch, I'm engulfed by a torrent of emotion by the simple contact. Pain, relief, joy, sadness, and every possible emotion in-between seems to catch me up in a hurricane. I may die, but it would be worth it for this one moment of reconnection. I shake his hand firmly and ignore my heart screaming inside my chest.

"Likewise." He releases me and steps back. His smile is kind and warm.

I clear my throat and smile turning back to Arthur. His expression is guarded and stern. I drop my gaze, unable to stand the intensity of the moment.

"Kate, would you please pull the file for the Mulligan Building as well as the Firehouse and Webber projects?" Arthur's deep voice reverberates off my soul.

I swallow the lump in my throat and meet his gaze. "Of course." With a parting smile at Dad, I turn and leave the room.

Once I'm outside Arthur's office, I head directly for the filing cabinet and retrieve the files he requested. Staking them in a pile, I place them on Gladys's desk.

"Here are the files Mr. Maxwell requested." I gesture toward the door. "I need to use the ladies' room."

Gladys nods without glancing up from her typing. "Go ahead, dear."

The walls compress inwards. My head spins. I step out into the hallway and rush toward the restrooms located at the end of the corridor. Inside, it's empty. I collapse inside a stall and hang my head over the toilet as the nausea rolls over me. But nothing comes up and for once I'm glad I skipped lunch.

I slam the toilet seat down and collapse against the wall. Tears fall freely as the rush of emotions slam into me like a freight train.

How the hell can I do this? How can I work alongside Dad and not tell him the truth of my identity? How can I continue this charade with

Arthur after all he's done for me? My heart splits with indecision. Even if I tell the truth, no one will believe me.

Arthur is a practical man. He won't believe I'm from the future. He'll think I'm insane and send me off to some asylum somewhere for psychiatric evaluation. Fear grips me. I'll never see Dad again. I'll be trapped here forever.

Too late. I'm already trapped here, in a time I don't belong. How is this even possible? I'm no closer to understanding how I got here than I am to understanding if there's even a way to get back to my time? I thump my head against the wall. Not that I want to go back to the future. The thought alone makes my skin crawl. I shiver. No. I'll make it work here, but I don't exist and this presents a problem.

At some point, I'm going to have to ask for help. The question is, who can I possibly trust with the truth of my situation? Another wave of nausea rolls over me and I wrap my arms around my waist.

What am I going to do? Maybe I should reach out to Marcy or even Rob, the doctor friend of Arthur's. Deep in my mind, I know doing either would cause a rift between me and Arthur. If anything, I've learned Arthur is a fiercely loyal man, and while he may not understand my situation, he deserves the truth at some point.

I choke back a sob because I know the moment I tell him, whatever we have will be over. And the thought of losing him terrifies me more than the possibility of never seeing my parents again.

Chapter 12

Arthur

I send everyone home early. Since it's Friday, no one questions my dismissal. It's been a while since I granted such a boon. Gladys beams at me when she exits the office reminding me to tell Kate when she returns from the restroom.

That won't be a problem because Kate is the very reason I'm sending everyone home early. After her unusual reaction to meeting Victor, the pieces are starting to fall into place. Finding Kate outside the office. Her questions about my associates, Victor in particular. But seeing her flustered response to his presence solidifies my suspicions.

What I hadn't anticipated was the surge of possessive jealousy to commandeer my common sense and rational thought. Jealousy because I want her to react to my presence. Possessive because Victor already has a beautiful wife. The undercurrent hums through me, and I pace my office unsure of how to even approach the conversation with Kate.

The outer office door closes. Kate's shadow falls across the frosted glass of my door.

After a deep breath to steel my expression, I open the door. The words die in my throat when I see Kate bent at the waist searching the bottom drawer of the filing cabinet. Her skirt rides high on the back of her thighs and all I can imagine is slipping my hand along those curves and baring her backside as she bends over my desk.

The filing cabinet slams shut.

I shake my head and clear my throat.

Kate snaps to attention, spinning around and pressing her hand against her chest. "You scared me."

"I apologize."

"Where did everyone go?" Kate asks glancing around the office.

"I gave them the rest of the day off." It's monumentally harder to gather my thoughts now since I've allowed my imagination to run free with that naughty fantasy. "Can I have a word with you in my office?"

Kate draws her lower lip between her teeth drawing my focus to her mouth. "Of course," she stammers before setting aside the files in her hand.

She looks nervous. Damn it. I didn't mean to make her uncomfortable, but she needs to understand. I need to understand.

Inside my office, Kate stands demurely with her fingers interlaced. "Did I do something wrong, sir?"

"Arthur." I lean against the desk in an attempt to make this conversation informal but still show the importance of its content. "When we're alone, call me Arthur."

She nods.

"Kate. I'm going to ask you a question, and I want you to be honest with me."

Her wide eyes flash with fear. "Okay."

"After I introduced you to my colleague, you seemed upset by the encounter." I tap my fingers on the edge of the desk. "What happened?"

Kate drops her gaze to the carpet. "It's nothing. I...well, he seemed familiar. The meeting must have triggered something in my memory." Her head shakes back and forth as she speaks.

"He reminds you of someone from your past?" My body tenses at the thought.

"That must be it." She shrugs her shoulders. "Although I still don't remember any details."

Disappointment settles over me, but I remain skeptical as to her designs on Victor. She doesn't seem like the type of woman who would set her cap on a married man. And yet I find myself addressing it with no qualms about my perspective.

"Victor came to tell me the good news." I straighten to my full height and shove my hands in my pockets. "He and his wife are expecting their first child. She's due in June."

"His wife. Pregnant." Kate sways but steadies herself on the back of the chair beside her. The color in her cheeks fades.

"Yes. They found out last week." I step closer.

"Last week." Kate pinches her eyes closed and nods slowly.

"Are you well?" I reach out and rest my hand on her shoulder. "You look like you're going to faint."

"I'm fine."

"Are you sure?" I pull her toward the chair. "Sit down. Do you need something to drink?"

"Yes, I'm sure." She waves her hand. "Don't worry about me."

"Kate." My voice is soft but firm. "Do you have any intentions of pursuing Victor?"

"Pursuing?" She stills and her bewitching gaze meets mine. "You think I'm attracted to Victor?"

I replay the memory her physical reaction to meeting Victor and her response to the news of his wife. "Yes. I do."

"What?" Her lips part in surprise. She covers her mouth and laughter fills the room.

"Why are you laughing?" I refrain from grasping her by the shoulders and demanding she explain herself. My hands clench into fists by my side.

"Because," she replies between peals of laughter. "You think I...Victor." Kate buries her face in her hands and her body shakes with mirth.

"When you're finished." I stare completely bewildered at why my comment would elicit such a response. "Please, take your time."

The sarcasm sobers her. "I'm sorry. It's, well, that's the most ridiculous thing I've ever heard."

I will never understand this woman. "I'm glad you find it amusing. Victor isn't only my colleague; he's my friend. I do not approve of flirtations, however innocent, with a married man."

"So, I can flirt with an unmarried man?" Kate's response comes with a smile.

Jealousy flares hot in my veins. "You cannot flirt with anyone in my office. Period."

Rose blooms in her cheeks as she closes the gap between us. I stand my ground when she wraps her hand around my tie. Desire pulses around us, hot and desperate. She licks her tempting lips.

"Even you?" She tugs on the tie.

I grip her shoulders, keeping her from pulling me toward her. "I don't think this is a good idea."

"I agree. It could be an absolute disaster." She cocks her head. "I didn't ask for any of this, but here I am. We're in this together now. Why not make the best of it?"

"Kate." My reserve slips with the word. She's right. Heaven help me, she's absolutely right. I'm only a man. A man with needs and a willing woman in his arms. How long can I fight this magnetic pull? Reason begins to slip as she rises up on her toes.

"Arthur." She jerks on my tie, and I concede, closing the distance with a muttered curse.

Her mouth collides with mine, soft and pliant. I wrap my arms around her and deepen the kiss. She tastes like mint and lemon. Her curves press against my body teasing me with the innumerable possibilities. My hands wander along her spine until one cradles the back of her head and the other settles on her lower back. I want nothing more than to push her back on my desk and explore all of her.

Kate moans and flicks her tongue against mine. She runs her fingers through my hair, tugging and caressing. Soft breathy moans punctuate each kiss. My cock rubs against the zipper of my dress pants. She grinds her hips against me.

I break the kiss and hold her at an arm's length. "Kate. Wait."

Each breath is torture. I want to bury myself inside her. I want to taste her, commit her to memory, possess her completely. But I can't.

"We can't do this." I force myself to put up the barrier knowing my restraint is hanging by a few thin threads.

The passion in her eyes fades at my words. She straightens and steps away, her pained expression sends regret surging through me. I hate myself for ripping this moment from both of us, but it needs to be done.

"I'm sorry." I drop my hands to my sides. "Until your memory returns, I don't want to take advantage of you." Her stricken face makes his conscience twist.

"My memory might be gone, but I'm still able to decide what I want...and who." Kate pushes past me and pauses in the doorway. "Don't worry. I won't flirt with *anyone* in the office."

"Kate." I reach for her, but she's already gone.

Son of a bitch. I kick the trashcan and knock it over. What the hell did I just do? Raking my hand through my hair, I pace the office.

For years, I've been satisfied with my life. I never wanted a family, a wife or kids. Traditional expectations meant nothing to me. At least they didn't until I found myself at the end of my sanity over a curvy brunette with no memory of who she is or where she comes from.

I should drag her back into my office and show her exactly what she does to me, but I can't. I won't. And the damnedest part of it is...I can't think of a single, logical reason why I shouldn't.

CHAPTER 13

Katherine

One week since the disastrous kiss, and I'm still not over it. Arthur locked himself in his studio the moment we got back to his apartment. He only came out to eat and use the bathroom, barely sparing me more than two words every time he emerged from his dungeon over the weekend.

I stole an empty notebook from the drawer in the closet and spent my copious amounts of free time writing while the television played in the background. I had no other way to document my thoughts since there was no one I could trust with the truth.

Over two days, I poured my heart and soul into the notebook, documenting everything from the events of the past year to my conflicting emotions for Arthur. Part of me hoped I could somehow make sense of what was happening, but my words sound like the rantings of a lunatic. I sincerely doubt there would ever be anyone who would understand and not want to ship me off to a shrink.

Come Monday morning, we were back on speaking terms. I wanted to talk to him about what happened in his office last Friday, but the stern expression and steely determination in his eyes warned me of another week of silent treatment should I pursue the subject.

Then I saw Dad. We formed a fast friendship right away, and he asked for my opinion several times over the next few days. I did what I could to help. It felt so good to spend time with him.

I tried not to stare or seek him out. After what Arthur insinuated last week, I did my best to contain my emotions around my father. Last thing I wanted was a misunderstanding, awkward as that would be. I wasn't here to make trouble. A second chance dropped into my lap, and I am determined to enjoy all of it.

"Kate, I need you to take a letter for me," Arthur calls from his open office.

Wrapped in nerves and anticipation, I grab my notepad and join him. When I walk into his office, I remember how his lips tasted, how hard he was for me. How he pushed me away. Taking the seat across from his, I'm keenly aware of his presence. I poise the pen over the paper.

"Ready." I refuse to look up. If I meet his gaze right now, I may combust.

At his silence, I glance up to see if he heard me. His stare pins me to the leather chair, and I shift uncomfortably under his scrutiny. Then, as if nothing were amiss, he launches into dictating the letter.

I write quickly, but he slows enough for me to keep up. I wish I could type it in Word directly. My typing skills are faster than my makeshift shorthand. Another downside to the eighties, I guess.

When he finishes, I stand, ready to retreat back to my desk. The resignation in his voice stops me.

"Kate, you don't have to run away from me."

"I'm not running." I fold my arms across my chest shielding my heart with the legal pad. "I have work to do, as do you."

He scoffs but shakes it off. "Have you finished organizing the projects for the promotional packet I requested?"

"I'll have it for you by the end of the day." I tap my fingers on the pad. "Anything else I can do for you?"

The tick in his jaw is prominent even from ten feet away. He wants me to remain professional, and I will. Even if my whole body screams for his attention. I want his mouth on me again. I want more than I should and knowing I affect him as much as he affects me has my willpower burning to ash.

"No, that will be all." He clears his throat. "Type this letter up for me to sign and then mail it before the end of the day."

I nod, swallowing my disappointment, and retreat to my desk. As I begin to type the letter, Gladys waves from across the room. I stop clicking on the keys and return the gesture.

Within moments, she's by my side. I pause midway through the letter.

"Did you hear the news?" Gladys squeals with excitement.

"What news?" I ask. Her energy seeps into me dispelling the lull left in the wake of my interaction with Arthur.

"Mr. Cohen's wife is going to have a baby!" She dances around in a tiny circle. "Oh, I'm so excited for them."

"That's wonderful." I choke out the words with a fake smile while my mind spins. *Pregnant with me. My mom, pregnant with me.* The whole situation is trippy as fuck.

"I found out while you were in the office with Mr. Maxwell. She told me the good news herself!" Gladys snatches a butterscotch candy from the bowl on my desk and unwraps it.

"Wait." The room spins like a carnival ride, and I grip the chair to keep me steady. "She's here. Now?"

Gladys pops the candy in her mouth and nods. "She's in her husband's office now. Brought him an afternoon snack. Isn't she sweet? Those two are adorable together." She sighs dramatically. "I hope I can find a love like theirs one day."

My heart twists in my chest, pounding so loud I hear the repetitive beat pulsing in my skull. I stare at the door to Dad's office. Two shadows move beyond the tinted glass. My parents. Behind that door. Together. I press my hand over my heart and breathe deep.

"You okay? You're a little flushed?" Gladys eyes me with concern.

"Fine. Just heartburn. Lunch was too spicy I think." I brush it off with little effort.

"I have some Alka Seltzer in my purse, if you need it."

"I'll be fine. Thanks though, I appreciate it." I smile. "I should finish this. Needs to go out today."

Gladys nods. "Don't work too hard. No reason to let him work you into the ground."

Once she retreats, I focus on the letter. But my mind drifts back to the office where I know my parents are talking. On the last line, I type out Arthur's name and leave room for a signature before reading through the letter for any errors. As I pull it from the machine, Dad's office door opens.

"Don't forget to stop by the bank on the way home." Mom's voice drifts through the room and I'm transported through the past thirty odd years of my life.

"Oh, you're here. Good." Dad comes up to the desk with his arm around Mom's waist. "Kate, I'd like you to meet my wife, Nora." He radiates love as he gazes at Mom. "Honey, this is our new secretary, Kate."

Mom holds her hand out. "Lovely to meet you, Kate."

I want to burst into tears. But even more, I want to launch myself across this desk and hug her. God, I miss her so much. I swallow the emotions clawing at my chest screaming for release. My gaze drifts between my parents and I muffle a sob behind a gentle cough before taking her hand.

"Nice to meet you as well."

Mom looks the same as I remember even though she's younger than I've ever seen her, except for photographs. Her dark hair holds no trace of gray and no worry lines mar her fair skin. She's positively glowing. Even beneath the flowing fabric of her gown, I note the soft curve of her stomach.

"Kate. Is that short for Katherine?" Mom muses tapping her finger on her chin.

"Yes, it is." The words spring from my lips without hesitation.

"It's so elegant." She laughs. "I'll add it to the list of possible girl names. What do you think, Victor?"

"I like it." He grins. "Very classy."

"You're having a baby?" I play it off wanting a bit more time with both of them, together.

"Yes. Our first."

"Congratulations." I force a smile remembering the stories Mom told me about how lucky they were to have me. I was her little miracle. "That's wonderful news."

Her hand rests protectively over her stomach. "We're extremely fortunate. Our little miracle."

My heart aches at the words I heard so often over the years. Tears form at the corner of my eyes and I blink furiously in a vain attempt to stop them.

"Arthur, there you are." Mom turns away, thankfully missing my emotional display.

I dash the tears away with my sleeve and swallow hard while their attention shifts to Arthur.

"Nora. You look radiant." Arthur hugs Mom and places a kiss on her cheek. "Did you get the flowers I sent?"

She slaps his shoulder playfully. "You charmer. I don't know why you sent me such an ostentatious bouquet."

"You didn't like it?" He frowns.

"She loved it," Victor adds. "Don't let her modesty fool you."

"How did you know my favorite flowers were peonies?" Mom teases him. "Did you ask Victor for help picking them out?"

"Actually, I chose them at Kate's suggestion." He steps closer and rests his hand on the back of my chair. "She's very detail oriented."

The compliment melts over me and I stare at Arthur in shock.

"You have wonderful taste, Kate." She grins. "I think we're going to be good friends."

Oh, Mom. "I think so too."

No matter how much I want this moment to last, how much I want my parents wrapped in a protective shield to be happy and together forever, reality lingers in the back of my mind hovering like a storm building a dangerous momentum.

"Well, I should get home." Mom waves. "I enjoyed meeting you, Kate. We'll talk again soon."

"I'd love that," I reply as Dad leads her to the exit.

"Is the letter ready yet?" Arthur's voice startles me.

I hold the paper up, bitter at his ability to ruin the moment. "Yes."

He takes the letter and leans down until his breath brushes my ear. "Is my portfolio ready?"

My fingernails dig into my palms. If I turn my head, I could easily press my lips to his. I could take what I want. But I don't. He's toying with me now. Testing me. I refuse to play his game.

"Is the day over?" I snap under my breath.

"I want it on my desk by five." His voice burrows beneath my skin infusing me with heat.

"Yes, sir." I couldn't stop the sarcastic bite to my words.

"Don't test my patience, Kate," he growls.

I close my eyes and the heat of him disappears. When I spin around, his door closes with a forceful thud.

Whatever battle began last week, Arthur seems determined to win at all costs. Is he trying to break me? Trying to get me to admit something?

I have no idea what his problem is, but if he persists, I'll have no choice but to call his bluff.

Victor saunters back into the office and knocks on my desk. He's beaming with optimism, bouncing on the balls of his feet. "Smile, Kate. It's a good day to be alive."

His grin infects me with hope. "Yes, it is."

Once he disappears in his office, I slump in my chair. I should be happy for my parents, but I know what's coming. All I can do is pray I haven't caused a fracture in the space-time continuum or a paradox or some insane butterfly effect.

Pushing the existential crisis aside, I focus instead on finishing the portfolio for Arthur. The insufferable ass won't let me hear the end of it if I don't meet my deadline. I will not let him win.

Not this round.

CHAPTER 14

Arthur

The moment I close the door to my apartment, the infuriating woman cloisters herself away in my bedroom. The only words she spared during the ride home after work were directed at Cyril. She treated me like I wasn't even there. Each passing moment grew heavier with the weight of our silence.

Part of me wanted to grab her by the shoulders and kiss some sense into her. I swore to show some restraint. One of us needs to act with some sense.

She claimed she had no romantic interest in Victor, but I saw the way they interacted at the office. All week they worked together, laughing and talking. I wanted to say something, but their actions never broached the boundaries of propriety. No one would even suspect Kate and Victor of crossing that line. And yet, like an insatiable itch, it festered in my mind.

When I saw her talking with Victor and Nora, my curiosity commandeered any rational thought. Even though she thought no one noticed, I saw the shift. The sadness beneath the smiles. There was something there, and Kate was determined to hide it from the world. From me.

Over the last week, I did my best to give her a wide berth. The kiss seared me like a brand. Every time I close my eyes, I can feel her in my arms, taste her on my tongue. She wants me, just as I want her. But it doesn't feel right. With her still recovering her memories, I would only be taking advantage of her vulnerability. At least that's what I tell myself.

What if she's already taken? She said she wasn't married, but that doesn't mean she's not in a relationship with someone. The thought haunts me. I can't admit it aloud, and I'm terrified to ask for fear it may trigger a memory.

But we can't avoid each other indefinitely. There needs to be a compromise if we're stuck together.

I cross the room and knock on the door. "Kate. We need to talk."

She opens the door and I'm distracted by the skin tight leggings and a loose sweatshirt draped precariously low on one side baring the creamy expanse of her shoulder. Kate eyes me as she pushes past, heading directly for the kitchen.

"Goddamn it. Kate, you can't ignore me forever." I follow trying not to catch a glimpse of her ass when she bends over to grab a bottle of wine from the refrigerator.

"I'm pretty sure I can." She spins around and grabs the corkscrew off the counter beside me before heading for the living room.

With a muttered curse, I find her curled on the couch drinking directly from the bottle.

"How classy." I cross my arms and shake my head. "Would you like a glass?"

Bold as gilded lettering, Kate meets my gaze and swigs from the bottle.

"Very mature." I'm two seconds from snatching her off the couch and bending her over my lap.

She ignores me and turns on the television with the remote. Music fills the room. Her attention fixes on the screen behind me.

"At some point, you're going to have to talk to me." I stand directly between her and the television.

Kate licks her lips and her glare sends a shiver of need straight to my cock. Pliant Kate may be attractive, but feisty Kate is sure to bring a whole new dimension to the bedroom.

I shake the inappropriate thoughts from my mind. "Must you behave like a child?"

"How would you like me to behave, Arthur?" The emphasis she places on my name sets my teeth on edge.

As I open my mouth to respond, the phone rings. I snatch it from the receiver. "What?" I snap.

"Easy there, Arthur. I need you to buzz me in." Marcy has the damnedest timing, but honestly, I'm thankful for the reprieve. Maybe Kate will open up to my sister if she won't talk to me.

"Fine." I hang up and hit the button on the panel near the door.

Kate's drowning in chardonnay in front of the television, so she doesn't even notice when Marcy arrives.

I pull her aside out of view of Kate the moment she walks in the door. "What the—"

"I need you to do me a favor."

"Oh, another favor? Does this earn me Mom's crystal vase?" Her eyes glitter.

"You're a heartless vulture, you know?" I sigh. "Fine."

"What do you want me to do?" she asks, popping her gum.

"I want you to hang out with Kate tonight. See if you can get her to open up."

"Hang out with Kate?" Marcy laughs. "I was planning on doing that anyway. Would've done it for free."

"I hate you."

"You love me." She grins. "Wait, has her memory come back?"

I run my hand through my hair. "Honestly, I have no fucking idea. She won't talk to me, and I'm about to strangle her."

Marcy's smile widens. "What happened? You two fuck?"

"No. We didn't fuck." I tip my head back and stare at the ceiling. "We kissed last week."

"No way." Marcy shoves me. "About time you showed some interest in someone who isn't a goddamn brainless mannequin."

"What do you know? You spent all of what, an hour with her last week?"

"And you're an expert on the female mind?" Marcy laughs. "Well, whatever happened. I'm glad. You needed your orderly existence disrupted."

"I don't think she's being honest with me. Some of her memories seem to be coming back, but I can't shake this feeling there's more she's not telling me." I glance around the corner. Kate's riveted by whatever's on the screen.

"I doubt she's plotting anything nefarious." My sister pats me on the shoulder in a sad effort to placate me. "But I'll sacrifice my Friday night to sit on the couch, drink wine, and gossip, if it will ease your conscience."

When she phrases it like that, it sounds ridiculous, but I'm already committed to this plan. "Fine."

"Good. Why don't you go out? Call Rob. Hit the bar." She cocks her head at my hesitant expression. "I can't work my magic with you here, Arthur. Go."

"Okay." I square my shoulders and head back into the living room. "I'm going out."

Marcy pops around the corner, and Kate's scowl transforms into a brilliant smile.

"Marcy! What are you doing here?"

"I thought I'd come over and we could spend some quality time together." Marcy turns and shoos me with her hand. "Go. Out with you. Girls' night."

I roll my eyes when she collapses on the couch next to Kate and grabs the bottle. If anyone can help me now, it's Marcy. She may seem flighty and eclectic, but I trust her with my life.

Their laughter fills the room. They don't even notice when I walk past them. Once I'm in the hallway, I push aside any hesitancy at leaving Marcy alone with Kate and press the button for the elevator.

Rob lives on the twenty-third floor of the same building, which can be both a curse and a blessing. I hesitate before aggressively pressing the doorbell outside his apartment.

I'm shocked when the door swings open, and Rob fills the doorway wearing a robe over his t-shirt and sweatpants. "Arthur? What the hell are you doing here?"

I push past him and head right for his stash of booze. "Marcy came over to keep Kate company." I pop the lid off the scotch and pour it in a glass.

"Let me guess, you weren't invited to their little pajama party?" he says leaning against the bar beside me.

"Nope." I down the shot without a second thought.

"Well, I'm glad you came." Rob saunters over to the dining room table and picks up a thin manila folder. "Richards came by the hospital today and gave me this."

I take the folder and flip it open. Inside is one sheet of paper. I read it and toss the paper back in the folder. "What the fuck does this mean?"

"Your mystery woman." He pours himself a scotch and lifts it in salute. "She doesn't exist."

I scoff. "What the fuck do you mean she doesn't exist? She's sitting in my apartment right now."

"I don't know what to tell you." He shrugs. "I gave a description and all the information you provided. Richards says there's nothing. No missing person's file fitting her description. Nothing."

I toss the file aside. "Bullshit. She's as real as you and me."

"I know." He pours two more shots. "It doesn't make any sense, does it?"

"Someone has to know who she is?"

"Cheers." Rob lifts his glass in salute.

Raising my glass, I drift off into my own mind. If there's no record of her and no missing person's report, then who the hell is she? How the hell did she end up in my lap? I toss the alcohol down my throat and grimace at the burn.

"What are you going to do?" Rob asks eyeing me with interest.

"What do you mean?" The alcohol doesn't sit well. I tap my chest with my fist.

"She can't stay with you indefinitely." Rob leans against the bar.

"Well, she's working for me for the moment." I shrug. "I guess we'll have to find a place for her somewhere besides my apartment."

"Yeah, sure." Rob laughs. "You can't fool me."

"Fool you about what?"

Rob stares at me like I've sprouted a horn in the center of my forehead. "In twenty-some years of friendship, I've never seen you this worked up over a woman."

I pour another shot. "I'm not worked up over anything."

"Yes, you are." Rob moves the bottle out of reach. "Listen. You can't kick her out. She has nowhere to go."

I down the liquor and immediately regret it. "I missed the part where that's my problem." Before he can remind me how I assaulted her, however accidental it was, I continue. "She may not have recovered all her memory, but she's perfectly capable of fending for herself. I gave her a job, which provides a lifetime worth of torture on a daily basis. I don't need her fucking up my personal life too."

"What personal life?" he scoffs. "All I'm saying is, it sounds like you two need to fuck and get it out of your system."

"Yes. Sex will obviously solve all my problems. Perhaps her memory will magically return afterwards." I tap the glass on the bar. "Then I can get her off my hands."

"I'm used to you being an asshole, but this is overboard even for you." He snatches the glass from my fingertips and walks around the bar. "What gives?"

I hang my head. "I wish I knew. This woman has me all twisted up. The moment I think we're on solid ground everything gives out beneath me and can't tell which end is up."

He offers a glass of water. I sip it wondering if I can even voice my concern out loud and not sound like a raging lunatic.

"I can smell the smoke from the gears spinning in your head." He sips his water. "Just say it."

"I don't think she has amnesia." I stare into the glass. "She's not being honest with me."

"What makes you say that?" Rob straightens and sets the drink aside.

"The way she talks. The way she interacts with people. With me." I shake my head. "I don't know how to explain it, but it's like she has this carefully constructed persona and every now and then she'll say or do something that doesn't make sense. I don't know."

"Have you asked her about it?"

"No."

"You should."

"Why? What good is asking about it?" I rub my forehead. "She'll only deny it."

Rob throws his hands up. "All I know is it wouldn't hurt for you two to talk about it, you know, like adults."

I cock my head and pin him with a disappointed glare. "Yes, because behaving like honest adults has worked so well for you and Marcy."

"Don't bring us into your shitshow." He gestures between us. "I'll talk to Marcy when I'm good and ready."

"Better hurry, the window of opportunity narrows with every date she goes on." I click my tongue. "Gotta catch her before she realizes she's better off alone."

"I'm not discussing this with you." Rob rinses his hands and pats them dry. "Let's go. We're going to crash the pajama party so I don't have to deal with your miserable ass all night."

I can't believe this man has been my best friend for as long as he has. I should have killed him long ago. I hate when he's right.

My stomach lurches at the prospect of confronting Kate, but the nausea doubles when I think about Marcy and Rob together. That's a visual I didn't need.

CHAPTER 15

Katherine

Halfway through the second bottle of wine, Arthur fades into the back of my mind. Marcy and I watch MTV while she tells me spills all the delicious gossip about working backstage with all the celebrities.

It's so difficult not to say anything. I catch myself a few times nearly spilling spoilers for the next thirty-five years. Having this kind of foreknowledge is a curse.

As she tells her stories, I listen intently asking questions and finding ways of relating to the conversation.

"Oh, there are some tasty stories about that man, let me tell you." She launches into an encounter she had with one of the most prominent men in New York. I bite my tongue because...spoilers.

We finish the bottle of wine, and Marcy volunteers to get a new one from the kitchen. She pops the cork and pouts. "Arthur should really invest in a better wine selection."

"I don't know. This stuff isn't bad." I sip the red wine. It's drier than I would normally drink, but overall, it's good.

Marcy scoffs. "My brother has great taste in everything except wine and women."

Her words strike my own insecurities. "Why do you say that?"

"His prior string of girlfriends were complete idiots. Pretty faces with empty heads." She sticks her tongue out in disgust. "I mean, I get it. He's focused on his career. His buildings are his children, so he's not interested in tying himself down to a real family."

Disappointment tugs at my conscience, which I shove away.

"It's sad, really. To see him so successful and yet at the end of the day, he has no one to share it with." She swirls the wine in the glass and shrugs.

"He has you." I counter. "And Rob."

Marcy tilts her head and fixes her blue shadowed gaze on me. "It's not the same as having a loving wife, maybe some kids." She sighs. "I shouldn't talk. After my shitty marriage ended in flames, you would think

I'd be against the whole institution."

"I understand the feeling." The alcohol loosens my inhibitions, but with Marcy, I find it so much easier to forget the reality of my situation. "My ex broke up with me three weeks before Christmas."

"Wow. What an asshole." Marcy shakes her head.

"Yeah. I mean, it had been over for a while, but I had so much invested in him and kept hoping it would get better." The memories assault me, and I bat them away angrily. "It never did."

"Yeah. Sounds like my ex." She raises her glass in a toast. "To new beginnings. Fuck those boys who couldn't handle how awesome we are."

"I'll drink to that." I drink deeply. "This year is already shaping up to be better than the last, although that doesn't mean much. Last year was hell." I tick the reasons off on my fingers. "I lost my job, my mom died, and asshole left me high and dry." A harsh laugh escapes. "I should be thankful for the last one though."

"Oh honey." Marcy rests her hand on my knee. "I'm so sorry about your mom."

"She'd been sick for a while." My voice cracks. "We knew she didn't have much time left. But damn it all if life had to kick me at my weakest moment."

"That's the worst. Come here. You need a hug." Marcy embraces me.

I relax against her, the scent of Aquanet tickles my nose and tugs at my memories. I can almost picture mom holding me close, telling me it'll work out in the end. The brutal pain of the last year slowly ebbs into acceptance. It feels good to vent and get it off my chest. I didn't realize how much I missed having someone to talk to and trust.

When we break apart, she fills our glasses. "So, I have to know. What is going on with you and Arthur? He seemed a little pissy earlier."

I wave my hand. "Honestly, I don't know. One minute he's distant, the next he's thoughtful and kind."

"Sounds like Arthur." Marcy heaves a dramatic sigh. "He wouldn't recognize a good thing if it slapped him in the face." She grins. "I guess I'll take it as a good sign he hasn't kicked you out of his apartment yet."

"What do you mean?"

"He never lets anyone stay here. Even when I separated from my ex, he didn't offer to let me stay with him." She chuckles. "Not like I would have. He's impossible to live with, and I'm much too free-spirited to share a space with a control freak."

Her admission hits me square in the chest and steals my breath.

"He's only doing it because he feels guilty for knocking me out."

"Yes, that's probably true. Or it was in the beginning." She props her elbow on the back of the couch and leans her head on her hand. "I almost offered to let you stay with me, but seeing him all twisted up and tripping over himself over having to take care of someone other than himself, well, it's good for him to step outside his own perfect box once in a while."

A snort-laugh escapes before I can stop it. I clap my hand over my mouth.

"I'm an evil genius, I know." She winks. "I half-hoped he'd be in love with you by now."

"We met last week!" I gape at her. "You didn't know anything about me."

"Honey, it's my job to be able to read a client's personality and find their perfect fit. This extends to matchmaking." She laughs at the stunned expression on my face. "Chemistry, baby. That's all it is. When you try on a dress and its instant love, the same thing applies to people."

I snap my jaw closed. "I'm not sure whether to be horrified or impressed by your confidence." She's right about the chemistry between us, but Arthur overcoming whatever hurdle he's erected between us has proved to be damned irritating.

"He's being stubborn, isn't he?" Marcy groans.

"Yes." I finish the wine and set the glass aside. "After we kissed, it's like he's actively trying to keep me as far from him as he can."

"You kissed?" Marcy damn near spills her wine. "When the hell did this happen?"

Heat rises in my cheeks. "A week ago."

"Hah! Chemistry." She punches the air with her bangled fist. "Told you."

"It only made things worse." I hang my head. "The only time he's ever around me is when I'm talking with someone else."

"Is this with anyone else or only other men?"

"Anyone, really." I think about the past week. "If I didn't know any better, I would think he's possessive, but honestly, he probably doesn't trust me."

"He doesn't trust anyone." Marcy taps her manicured fingernails against her lips. "But this is more than that for sure."

Before I can even ponder her words, Rob and Arthur appear in the doorway. Rob hangs back, his gaze appraising as it skims over me and lingers on Marcy.

"Sorry to interrupt the party, ladies." Rob and Arthur share a look.

Arthur's stiff posture and the gentle clench and release of his fists by his side betray the tension radiating from him. He seems uncomfortable, and that's putting it mildly.

"No problem." Marcy jumps to her feet. "Want something to drink, Rob? Come to the kitchen."

I know what she's doing and she's not even trying to hide it. Rob joins her in the kitchen. Even though it's open to the rest of the apartment, there's a shift in energy with Arthur and I remaining in the living room.

"You should find your own place." Arthur's statement cuts straight through the tension stealing all the warmth from the room.

What little confidence I gained from my conversation with Marcy pops like a bubble. My chest constricts under the intensity of his gaze. He remains firm.

A scuffle of commotion in the kitchen behind me brings me to my senses. "Yeah, you're right."

When I stand up, I grip the sofa to keep from falling. Three bottles of wine hit me at once.

In a flash, Arthur's across the room and catches my elbow. I jerk out of his grasp. "No. You don't get to play hero, Arthur. You want me to leave. I'll go."

"I didn't mean right this second." His voice grates against my mind creating friction and heat. "You're drunk. I'll help you find a place tomorrow."

"No." I stumble back out of his reach. The tenuous connection we have pulls tight, a fraying thread barely holding. "You've done enough."

Arthur roughly runs his hand over his face and through his hair. "Damn it, Kate."

The biting edge of his words cuts the final tether. An alcohol induced haze filters through my reason. My heart plunges to the pit of my stomach and bile burns the back of my throat.

I race past him stumbling around the furniture. He reaches out and grabs my wrist.

"Kate. I want you to be honest with me."

My stomach churns and I shake my head. "No. You don't."

I wrench myself out of his grip and dart into the bedroom. By the time I reach the bathroom, it's too late. I double over the toilet heaving as my body purges the copious amounts of wine I drank.

Tears sting my eyes as my stomach heaves. My body shakes. Stupid.

So stupid. My hand grips the toilet.

"Easy now," a man's gentle voice echoes behind me. It's not Arthur, it's Rob. He gathers my hair in his hand and rubs a cool cloth against the back of my neck. "Better get it all out."

Mortified, I pinch my eyes closed wishing I were still in my present. No matter what the decade, I am still a hopeless disaster.

"Leave." I try to shoo him away.

"Nice try, Kate." Rob's soft chuckle echoes off the tile. "I'm a doctor. A little vomit doesn't scare me."

My stomach heaves again. I want the ground to open up and swallow me, put me out of my misery.

Arthur wants me to be honest with him, but I know the truth will do nothing but drive a deeper wedge between us. Maybe that's better than lying. No one would believe me anyway.

CHAPTER 16

Arthur

The bathroom door slams from inside the bedroom making me grit my teeth. What the fuck did I do? Kate looked ready to shatter into a thousand delicate pieces. I knew the moment I opened my mouth, something bad would happen.

"You're an asshole!" Marcy charges from the kitchen after breaking free from Rob's hold.

I brace myself for impact. She's got a mean right hook and isn't afraid to use it. But instead of lunging at me, she heads for the bedroom to help Kate.

Rob catches up to her and they exchange a few muffled, heated words. Marcy nods and crosses her arms, spinning around to face me, while Rob ventures into the bedroom after Kate.

I swallow the jealousy raging deep inside me. I can't go after her, not after what I said. What I did. Marcy's right, I am an asshole.

"What the hell was that about?" Marcy lays into me. She's a good six inches shorter and half my weight, but I hate being on the receiving end of my sister's wrath.

"What?" I shrug as though it doesn't bother me, but it does. It tears me apart. "She can't stay here any longer. I did my part. I even gave her a job. End of story."

"You're a goddamn saint." She glowers. "Do you want a fucking award for being a decent human being?"

"No. I just want my life back."

"Yeah. It's such a charming existence living in your penthouse all alone." She spits venom. "I was right, you wouldn't know a good thing if it fell out of the sky and danced in your lap."

"What the hell is that supposed to mean?" I snap.

"Kate." Marcy says her name like it's the answer to the ultimate question of the universe.

"I've known her for less than two weeks." I gesture toward the bedroom where she and Rob are locked in the bathroom. "She doesn't even know who she is."

"Has it ever occurred to you she knows who she is but decided not to tell you because it's none of your goddamn business?" Marcy stalks closer and jabs a finger in my chest.

Her words stun me for a moment, but I focus on the first part of the question rather than the later. "Yes. I had a feeling she lied to me from the very beginning about having amnesia."

"And yet you didn't ask her directly?"

"I tried." I exhale growing exhausted. "When I ask, she hedges around it."

"What if it's painful for her to think about her past? Did you ever think about that?" Marcy's eyes flash with anger and unshed tears. "Did you ever think maybe she was like me? Trying to break free from a horrible, inescapable situation? Not everyone has someone to come to their rescue, to give them a chance to start over."

Goddamn it. My mood takes a nosedive into misery. "No. I didn't even think of that."

"Of course not. Who would? You live up here in your gilded penthouse with everything you could ever want and no one to challenge you." She wipes the tears with the sleeve of her shirt leaving tearstains on the neon fabric.

"Marcy." I reach for her, but she steps back and shakes her head rapidly.

"No. I'm not the one you should apologize to. I'm not the one you strung along and then kicked to the curb."

Indignance rises up to defend me. "I didn't string her along. We kissed once. It was a mistake, and I told her I had no intention of pursuing anything further between us."

"You think it matters?" Marcy laughs. "The tension between you two is so thick I could cut it with shears. You can deny it all you want to, big brother, but the sparks flying between you two don't lie."

"I don't need a relationship." Even the words sound weak when I speak them aloud. "I don't want one. I'm happy with my life."

"Not everything is about you, Arthur."

"I helped her out, gave her a place to stay. Hell, I'll even help her find a place and get a permanent job."

"And then what? You'll both go your separate ways and live happily ever after."

"Something like that."

"Where did you find her?" Marcy's voice softens a fraction. "New

Year's Day."

"What's that have to do with this?" I'm confused by the shift in the conversation.

"The guard said he saw her on the observation deck, didn't he?" Marcy continues. "Before you conked her on the head with the door outside your office."

My eyes drift closed. "No. That can't be right."

"A lot of desperate people have taken the jump." Marcy shrugs. "From what she told me, last year was a hell of a struggle. Desperation makes us do crazy things."

"But she didn't jump. I found her outside my office." I reason. "Why come to the fifty-fourth floor?"

"Maybe you should ask her."

"She won't tell me." I swallow my pride for a moment.

"You're asking her to be honest with you, when you can't even be honest with yourself." My sister rests her hand on my arm and squeezes. "You feel something for her and it scares the ever-loving shit out of you."

The sincerity of her words sends a bolt of realization straight through my heart. I shake my head, unable to think or even speak.

"I love you, Arthur. You came to my defense when no one else would." Her soft tone makes my heart ache. "I want you to be happy, and you can't be happy until you face the truth. One day you're going to wake up alone and realize you let *the one* get away."

Unable or unwilling to face the reality of her words, I turn away. Halfway to the door, Marcy's voice stops me.

"Don't be an idiot!"

Without hesitation, I stalk toward the door, grab my coat from the rack, and head out into the night. I need to think, so I retreat to the one place where I know I can clear my head. The observation deck of the Empire State Building.

Out in the cold, January night, I bundle myself deeper in my wool coat. It seems even in trying to escape facing Kate, I run directly into her arms by putting myself in her exact position.

Marcy may have a point, but I'd rather die than admit it to her.

CHAPTER 17

Katherine

After a hot shower and a warm cup of peppermint tea, I feel almost human. Exhausted, both physically and emotionally, yes, but Rob and Marcy make sure I have everything I need. With the alcohol purged from my system, all I want is sleep.

Once I'm tucked in a warm pair of oversized pajamas and snuggled beneath the soft warm sheets, it hits me. Arthur wants me to leave. I try to protest and climb from the bed, but Marcy gently pushes me back. I'm too weak to fight.

"Rest," Marcy instructs in her most maternal voice.

"Arthur said..." I lick my lips as the words trail off.

"Don't you worry about him." Marcy glances at Rob whose brow furrows in concentration. "Just sleep."

"But he said." I protest weakly falling into the welcoming arms of sleep.

"It's okay. We spoke to him. It's important you rest now. Do you need anything?" Rob sits on the edge of the bed and feels my forehead.

His touch comforts me. "No. I'm good. Thank you."

"You're welcome." Rob stands and nudges Marcy. They step off to the side, their voices low.

I close my eyes and welcome the respite. Drifting in and out of consciousness, I can still hear Rob and Marcy whispering.

"I'll stay." Marcy's voice raises a fraction. "You have to work in the morning. Go. I'll call if I need anything."

"Okay. I'll check in tomorrow," Rob's reply carries across my fading consciousness.

I mumble goodbye and fall into the darkness, tuning out the world at last.

When I struggle to open my eyes breaking free from a dream I can't quite remember, there's sunlight streaming through the gaps in the curtains. I stretch and slowly roll to the edge of the bed. Exhaustion slowly fades as I stand and head for the bathroom.

One glance in the mirror makes me cringe. My frizzy hair resembles an unraveling loofa. I tame it with a brush, tying it back before brushing my teeth. Considering how fucked up I was last night, I'm stunned to find I'm even able to function this morning.

Hangovers in my thirties are ten times worse than they were when I was in my twenties. Fortunately, the wine didn't linger, so there was no evidence of my blunder complete with headache and misery.

However, the memory of the night before lingers and pierces me with regret. I hide my face, embarrassed to even meet my own gaze in the mirror. How can I even show my face after that? Maybe I can gather some things and slip out the door before anyone realizes it.

Rob and Marcy were more than kind. They were amazing. I wince at the knowledge they were even present to witness the events of the night before. But in the end, I am grateful they were there in the aftermath of hurricanes Arthur and Kate.

I vaguely remember a conversation between Marcy and Rob before I drifted off. Did she stay last night? But where was Arthur?

Steeling myself for whatever I might find, I take a breath and leave the safety of the bedroom.

Marcy glances up from her seat on the couch and sets her coffee mug aside. "You're awake."

"Yeah." I shuffle closer.

"Want some coffee?" She's already on her feet and halfway to the kitchen when she asks.

"Sure." I follow and lean against the counter watching her pour the steaming brew into a plain white mug.

"Hungry? I can whip you up some eggs or pop some toast in for you if eggs are too heavy." Her concern warms my heart.

"Toast first." I smile. "Thanks, Marcy."

"Of course, what are friends for?" She puts some bread in the toaster and gets some butter and jam out of the fridge. "Go sit at the table. I'll bring it over."

I take the chair closest to the huge window. The sun streams over the city, nearly cresting in the sky. I glance at the clock. Just after eleven am.

Marcy bustles in and sets a plate with buttered toast with a side of jam in front of me right beside my coffee. She drops into the chair next to mine and smiles.

"Feeling better today?"

"Yeah." I take a bite of the perfectly browned toast. "I'm sorry about last night."

She waves it off. "Don't even worry about it. We all have those moments, hon. I'm glad I was here to help."

The question burns my mind and I'm terrified to ask her even though I know it's inevitable. "Where's Arthur?"

"I don't know." She shrugs with a sigh. "He went out and never came back."

Fear grips me. "Aren't you worried about him?"

Marcy chuckles. "Worried? About my brother? No. I mean, I am, but not because I'm afraid something bad happened to him because he didn't come home yet. This wouldn't be the first time he wandered off to clear his head."

I sip the coffee and it warms me instantly.

"When we were kids, Arthur would wander off after an argument. Some days he wouldn't return home until after midnight." She laughed at the memory. "Mom would get so mad, but it didn't stop him."

"Where did he go?"

"No one knows. To this day, he still won't tell me where he goes to think." Marcy shakes her head. "He calls it his spot. I bet that's where he went last night. It's where he always goes, especially to get away from me."

"You're lucky." I sniff and stare out the window. "I wish I had a bond like you two have. I don't have any siblings. My dad died when I was three, and mom never remarried."

"Do you remember him?" Marcy asks, cradling her coffee mug in her hands. "Your dad."

My gaze fixes firmly on the Empire State Building. "Not really. I have a few memories, but nothing bonded us, you know?" A sad smile crosses my lips. "Mom filled in the blanks. She told me all about him." I stop myself from saying anything more knowing it will only complicate things.

"Kate." Marcy reaches across the table to take my hand. "You're not alone. I'm here for you." Her warm smile brings tears to my eyes.

"Thanks, Marcy." I wipe the tears away with my free hand. "I appreciate your support."

"Don't worry about finding a place right away either." She squeezes my hand. "If you need a place to crash, you're welcome at my place until we can find you something, okay?"

Relief washes over me. "Thank you."

"Of course." She releases me and sits back. "And we can start looking for a new job on Monday morning."

"A new job." I nod at the realization and my heart sinks. *Dad.* I won't get to see him every day. I panic.

"I mean, if you want to work for my brother, that's completely up to you."

"No. I mean, yes. You're right. I should branch out and start looking anyway. The job at the firm was only meant to be temporary anyway." I fake a smile even though my heart weeps at the thought of abandoning all contact with both my father and Arthur.

"Awesome! There might be a couple of places we can check. Oh, maybe down at the station." Marcy's already listing out possibilities, and I'm stuck, mired in my own disappointments. So much for this being an opportunity to spend time with my parents.

Marcy jumps to her feet and carries my empty plate into the kitchen. "Monday morning, for sure," she calls from the kitchen.

"What's on Monday morning?" Arthur's deep voice echoes across the room.

I gasp and spin around. He's standing beside the television wearing the same suit he wore to the office the day before. His tie is missing and a shadow darkens his jaw.

"Oh, you're alive. Good." Marcy props her hand on a hip. "I was about to call the cops and fill out a missing person's report."

"Don't you have somewhere to be?" he growls the question.

"No, actually, I don't." She glances at me. "Do you want me to help get your stuff together now?"

Arthur looks like he's been dragged down an alley and pummeled, but even worse than that, the moment she mentions gathering my stuff, Arthur's countenance darkens.

"Kate. Can we talk?" He ignores his sister's indignant huff and steps closer. His intense gaze focused solely on me. "I fucked up. I'm sorry."

My throat constricts at his apology.

"Call me if you need anything, okay, hon?" Marcy grabs her coat and escapes the apartment as though the whole building were on fire and about to explode.

Arthur's shoulders slump the moment his sister leaves. "Last night." He gestures helplessly. "I was an asshole."

"Yes, you were." I stand but don't move any closer. My hands rest on the chair maintaining a barrier between us.

"When this year started, I had plans. Big plans." He rubs his hand over his jaw. "None of these plans involved a relationship."

I bite my tongue and hold his gaze steadily. If he wants to dig himself into a deeper hole, I'll gladly let him. It'll make it easier for me to walk away.

"But that was before." He exhales, and lightning flashes in his stormy eyes. "When I found you, I never expected to feel anything this strong. It's terrifying, honestly." He scoffs. "We barely know each other, and yet I find myself wanting to not only protect you but possess you."

"Possess me?"

He licks his lower lip and nods. "All of you. Your body, your mind, all of you. I want to keep you all for myself."

"That's a bit misogynistic, Arthur." My heart races at the thought of being possessed by this man. As much as I want to deny his words affect me, I can't. Even my physical response to him leaves me confused and aroused.

"I'm not asking you to do anything against your will." He steps aside. "If you want to leave, I won't stop you. If that's what you want."

"Suddenly you care what I want?" Heat bubbles inside my chest, and I can't tell whether it's fury or passion.

"Marcy set me straight." He rests his hand on the table. "I understand why you felt you had to keep up the amnesia premise."

The amnesia...oh, God. The wine. I will never again. I pinch my eyes closed and my lapse in judgement rushes back in vivid shades of mortification. The alcohol loosened my inhibitions all right. It completely blew my cover. Shit. It was only a matter of time before the truth came out, no matter how convoluted this version is.

"I had a feeling you weren't being honest with me." Arthur watches me, his expression since. "But I misunderstood your intentions. I apologize."

I clear my throat unsure if I should rip off the bandage now and reveal the truth. But the longer the moment stretches, the more I lose my nerve.

"I apologize as well. I shouldn't have lied." The half-truth slips from my tongue in a rush. "It was selfish of me to take advantage of your kindness."

Arthur scoffs. "Kindness?" He shakes his head and laughs. "If we're being honest here, then I should confess I also had selfish reasons for my actions."

He's five feet away, but I can feel the heat pulsing between us.

"When I hit you with the door, an accident, I swear, I panicked." He swipes his hand over his face and groans. "I lied to the guards and carried you home because I was too fucking scared to call the cops and admit I injured you."

"I know." My words are soft. "I'm glad you didn't call the cops, honestly."

"It was stupid. You could have been permanently injured or died."

"You called Rob. That's almost as good as a trip to the ER in my opinion." I chuckle. "He's a very attentive physician."

Arthur growls and his eyes darken. Possessive and jealous, he stalks closer.

I back up until the cold glass stops me. Arthur crowds me, placing his hands against the glass, caging me between his heat and the frosted pane. His eyes shift from mine, down to my mouth, and back as he studies me intently.

"That kiss haunts me, Kate." He licks his lips. "All week. I couldn't think of anything else except how much I wanted another taste."

My pulse echoes in my ears rushing like a waterfall. "Me too."

I rise up on my tip toes and end both our misery.

CHAPTER 18

Arthur

The memory of her kiss is nothing to the reality. I grip her waist, lifting her closer and angling my head. I want to devour her completely. Not a sample, not a taste. She's heady and a fizzy type of magic infuses the moment. I'm drunk on her with one kiss.

I should be terrified, but I'm not. I want more.

She arches her body against me, and I seize the invitation without hesitation. My hands slide beneath the cotton fabric. A moan breaks from deep in my throat when my fingers brush her bare skin.

There have been women over the years, but none of them seem to entice me, burrowing beneath my conscience, like Kate. I worship her curves molding them with my palms, kneading and pulling. I curse the oversized pajamas she stole from my closet.

They're my favorites. Seeing her wearing them when I walked into the apartment nearly threw my composure out the window. I've dreamed of ripping those cotton pajamas from her body every night since she arrived. It's about time I make my fantasy a reality.

Her palm slides down my chest and over my stomach. I suck in a breath when it comes to rest on my cock. Even through the fabric, the heat of her touch stokes the fire hotter.

As much as I want to strip her down and take her up against the glass in view of the whole city, I refrain. We have all the time in the world to christen each surface of my apartment. Right now, I need her sprawled beneath me while I memorize her glorious, bare skin with my mouth.

Without warning, I scoop her into my arms. She squeals and clings to me.

"What are you doing?" She laughs as I carry her into the bedroom.

"I intended to take you up against those windows at some point." I whisper against her temple. "But right now, I have other plans for you."

I set her down on the bed and step back enough to give me room to strip. I toss my coat off to the side. Kate lays back against the pillows and watches me. Her parted lips and glassy eyes betray her hunger.

Instead of rushing to strip, I slowly unbutton my shirt while holding her lust filled gaze. She runs her fingertip down the vee of her top and mimics my motions. Every button I release, she matches. The creamy expanse of skin she reveals leaves me speechless. Her soft, ample curves push against the fabric, and her deep breaths reveal more. She arches her brow when I pull the shirt off my shoulders and toss it aside.

Kate shakes her head. The blue fabric barely covers her areolas. I need to see her breasts in their full glory, but she gestures to my waist.

"Pants next." Her husky voice makes my cock painfully hard.

I unfasten my belt and slide the button free. As I push the pants down over my hips, Kate again surprises me. Her hand slides beneath the waistband of her bottoms. The moment her fingertips reach her cleft, her eyes drift closed and her breath hitches.

"Tease." I kick my pants and underwear aside before climbing into the bed.

She opens her eyes and moans softly. Her cheeks are flushed. I watch the fabric gently moving in rhythmic motions.

I grasp the fabric and pull it down her legs. She lifts her ass enough to allow them to slide free.

"Fuck, Kate." My gaze fixes on her delicate hand with two fingers pressed against her clit.

I press soft kisses along the inside of her thighs as I nudge them open, revealing her pussy slick with her arousal. I remove her hand and replace her fingers with my tongue.

Kate's moan echoes off the bedroom walls. Encouraged by the sound, I flick my tongue deeper between her folds, boldly tasting her. She's sweet and addicting. I suck her clit into my mouth and she arches off the bed.

God, she's responsive. I grip her hips with my hands, and she buries her fingers in my hair. Every tug only emboldens me. I spread her wider and give myself better access. She's mine, all mine, and I intend to savor each drop her when she comes against my mouth.

My name sounds sinful intertwined with her whimpered moans. Her breath quickens and I hear it catch as I push her higher and higher. When I slip two fingers into her, she bucks against my mouth. I find a generous rhythm between my mouth and my hand.

The telltale flutter against my fingertips warns me she's close. I redouble my efforts wanting her to surrender to me with her climax.

"Fuck. Oh, fuck." She mutters over and over when she comes. Her body clenches around my fingers. I smile as she slowly comes down from her blissful high. But I don't relent completely until she's trembling, her hands flexing against my scalp trying to push me away.

I pull back enough to study her face and wipe my mouth with the back of my hand. Better than a five-star meal, hands down.

A lopsided blissful smile pulls at her mouth. "That was amazing."

"You think that was amazing?" I scoff, climbing up over her until our noses touch. "That was just the appetizer."

She kisses me, and I melt against her. This time I take her full breast in my hand and roll her nipple between my fingertips. She gasps into the kiss and presses her body closer.

I trail kisses down over her jaw and capture a ripe nipple in my mouth sucking it until it pebbles against my tongue. Kate's urgent moans only intensify my need to pace myself. I want her so desperate for me she'll come even harder.

Kate scratches her fingernails over my head, her moans reverberate through my body. I dedicate attention to both breasts until she's writhing against me.

"Please, Arthur. Please." She licks her lips and gasps when I flick my tongue over her nipple.

"What do you need, sweetheart?" I lean back.

She arches her hips against my thigh. "I need you."

"Say the words," I whisper against her mouth before kissing her gently.

"Fuck me."

I chuckle at the crass demand. "Wouldn't you rather I make love to you?"

"Make love to me, fuck me, I don't care. All I want is you inside me...now." She wraps her legs around mine.

"Let me get protection." I murmur, leaning over to the nightstand drawer.

"Shit." She mutters under her breath and sighs. Her smile fades a fraction until I slide the condom down over my cock.

"Is this what you wanted?" I pull her close and slide the tip over her sensitive cleft.

Her gasp ends on a moan. "Yes." She clings tightly to me, her fingernails biting into my shoulders, when I push inside.

Kate tosses her head back. I sink deeper until I'm seated fully inside her. Fuck, she fits like a favorite pair of gloves. Her body grips me tight.

"How does that feel?" I nip the tender spot on her throat right below her ear. She shivers and holds tight.

"So good." She bites her lower lip and meets my gaze.

I kiss her and move, starting slowly and gently increasing momentum. She's tight and warm. It's been so long since I've been with anyone, I'm worried I may come too quickly.

Kate meets my thrusts with her own. I let her take control of the pace. She urges me faster. I close my eyes trying to keep from ending this before it's even had a chance to start.

She gently presses her hand to my heart. "Lie down."

"Something wrong?" I move to pull out, but she stops me.

With a little effort, she rolls me onto my back without unsheathing me from her warmth. Staring up at her, I'm struck dumb. She's fucking stunning as she shucks the top and shakes her hair back.

Her bewitching gaze locks on mine and she grinds her hips down taking me deeper than before.

"Holy shit." I rest my hands on her hips and inhale deep. "You're gonna make me lose control if you do that, sweetheart."

"Mmmm, I like the thought of you losing control." She leans forward, her hair creating a curtain of dark waves around her flushed face. "I won't break. I like it rough."

The thought alone gives my cock a burst of strength. "Show me, baby." I lick my dry lips. "Take what you want."

She pouts. I wrap my hand around her delicate throat and kiss her mouth firmly. "I'll give you what you need later."

Her eyes glitter with lust and her hips buck against mine. She thrusts at her own pace, slowly increasing the tempo, using me until she's panting.

"That's it, sweetheart. Come for me." The words trigger something inside her.

Kate's mouth opens on a breathless scream, and I hold my fingertips against her pulse. She rubs her clit against me enough to trigger her climax. I drop my hands to her hips and thrust up, pounding into her until my own release rushes up and capsizes us both in a listless ocean of sexual satisfaction.

Weak from the intensity of her orgasm, she collapses against my chest. I wrap my arms around her and hold her close. Slowly, our overheated bodies cool and our breathing slows. I run my fingers along her spine, stroking her like a contented kitten curled in my lap.

I've never had sex rock me to my core. Even with the most enthusiastic lovers, sex was passable at best. Normally I'd find any excuse to leave, but now I'm desperate for any reason to stay, to keep her like this forever. But, holy hell, this is unlike anything I've ever experienced.

My heartbeat mimics hers. How is it possible to be so synchronized with someone at such a basic level and yet be practical strangers? One thing is certain, I want to know everything about her. What she likes. Her favorite things. What makes her smile.

Fate may have blindsided me when she appeared in my life. I was a fool to fight it, but now I have no intention of letting her go.

I slowly roll her onto the bed and kiss her forehead before pulling the blanket over her.

She sighs sleepily and smiles. "Where are you going?"

"To clean up." I kiss her head again. "Rest now. I have plans for you."

"Promises, promises." Kate snuggles deeper into the blankets.

Halfway to the bathroom, I glance over my shoulder at the woman in my bed.

Kate looks so vulnerable and sated. A warmth infuses me and wraps its tendrils around my heart. I didn't expect to find someone who would make me feel this much contentment.

In the bathroom, I toss the condom into the trash and turn on the shower. The heat renews my energy. Under the spray, I wash away the uncertainty and regrets. This is a new day, a new opportunity. I wash the sweat from my skin, but the memories remain. When I close my eyes to rinse off the soap, a sweet floral scent surrounds me.

The press of her body against mine has my cock jumping in response.

"I thought you were resting?"

"While you're in here all naked and wet?" She slides her slick body against mine and wraps her hand around my cock.

"Damn it, Kate." Her hand gives enough pressure to make me see stars. I brace my weight against the wall and the water sluices over us both. I swear again when she strokes twice and drops to her knees.

My Kate. Mine. It doesn't matter where she came from or what troubles lay in her past, together we can face anything.

When her mouth closes around my cock, I lose all coherent thought and surrender to this wonderfully wicked woman.

CHAPTER 19

Katherine

Hot water runs over me as I take him in my mouth. I'm not a fan of oral. Maybe it's because I never had a partner I trusted to give me what I needed or trusted my own abilities to reciprocate.

Arthur makes me feel like a goddess. He worships my body. My insecurities faded the moment he kissed me, and then disappeared when I saw the look of hunger on his face in the bedroom. Emboldened, I teased him, pushing him to the bounds of his restraint. I fucking loved every moment.

He let me take control. This is the first time I was able to tell a partner what I needed. While Arthur knows what he wants and how he wants it, he gave me the reins and let me take control. When he disappeared into the bathroom and I heard the shower running, it drew me like a siren's call.

I wanted him, even after he made me come. Twice. I've never even been able to bring myself relief like he did. He knew exactly what my body needed.

My tongue strokes the length of his cock and it pulses against my lips. I know exactly what he needs, and I'm more than happy to give it to him. His balls rest in my right hand while the left encircles his shaft teasing the head of his cock.

"Kate." He groans and his legs tremble. "Deeper, sweetheart." He gasps when I slide him in as far as I can. "Good girl."

His praise emboldens me. I quicken my pace alternating pressure with my hand and my mouth. His hips rock back and forth almost until he's fucking my mouth gently. I intensify my efforts and am rewarded with a whimper.

Water runs over my face. I close my eyes and focus only on pleasing him. After his magnificent tongue brought me a toe-curling orgasm, I want to give him a gift of my own.

"Damn, sweetheart, I'm going to come. If you..."

I quicken my pace determined to swallow every last drop. He tries to pull away, but I grip him tighter.

Arthur's groan echoes off the tiles mingling with the steam from the shower. His cum coats my tongue. I swallow quickly, gently working the length of him to wring his body into submission. He trembles beneath my touch.

Pride suffuses me. I rise to my feet and he pulls me under the spray holding me against him, his face buried against my throat. He rocks me gently until he regains his senses.

"That was amazing." He kisses me deeply. "You're amazing."

There's no shame, no disappointment, no judgement between us. Nothing but pure satisfaction.

He shakes free from his thoughts and smiles. "I'll let you rinse off."

"Okay."

When he steps from the shower, uncertainty consumes me. I like having him near me, but I know there are still things unspoken between us we need to address if we're going to make this relationship work. Like the truth of where I come from.

He wraps a towel around himself and leaves me alone in the bathroom. I take the moment of peace to wash quickly and put some conditioner in my hair to keep it from looking like a poufy disaster. Once I reach a semblance of cleanliness, I dry off and wrap the towel around my body and another around my hair.

Arthur isn't in the bedroom. I hear noise in the living room, so I peek out the door. He's in the kitchen sorting through the cabinets.

"Looking for something?" I walk in the room blotting my hair dry.

"Food." The towel hangs low on his hips. One tug and I could have it around his feet.

"There's some leftovers from the other night in the fridge." I walk past him, trailing my fingertips over his lower back. I bend at the waist when I reach into the fridge to pull out the containers.

"We could order take out." His voice echoes behind me.

I freeze when his hand slides beneath my towel and glides over my sex. My legs part of their own volition.

"But that would mean I have to get dressed." I glance at him over my shoulder.

"This is true." His grin transforms his face with a mischievous charm. "I much prefer you naked."

"You can't be ready for me again?" I arch my brow and moan when he slides one finger into me.

"Are you complaining?" he asks with a smirk. "Damn it, you're so wet. Maybe I should have another taste. A little dessert before dinner."

I straighten quickly knowing my legs won't hold me if he continues to tease me. His hand falls to his side.

"Let's eat first." I set to arranging some leftovers on plates and putting them in the microwave.

Arthur wraps his arms around my waist and pulls me firmly against him. The towel slips and he captures my breasts in his hands. His merciless lips tease along my throat.

I brace myself. He's relentless and commanding. I love every minute, every touch.

The microwave timer goes off.

"Arthur."

"Hmmm." He moans against my throat.

"Your food is ready." I try to pull it from the microwave, but he's distracting me. I nearly drop it.

"After food. After!" Trying to pry myself from his grasp is nearly impossible. But I'm able to shake him off long enough to put the plate in his hand. "Go. Eat."

"Yes, ma'am." His teasing smile flashes, and I swear my body went *sploosh*. If he keeps this up, I'm going to run out of dry underwear quickly.

Once my food is heated through, I join him at the table.

We eat quickly and in silence. I hadn't realized how hungry I was. After last night, I wasn't sure if I would be hungry at all today, let alone be in the mood for sex.

Arthur's gaze drifts from the skyline to me. The sun is starting to descend over the city. The Empire State Building casts a long shadow over the buildings near it.

I collect both of our empty plates and put them in the sink. When I come back, Arthur's sitting in front of the oversized window.

"Come here." He pulls me down into his lap.

Joy overwhelms me. His arms lock around my waist and I nestle my head against his shoulder. Together we stare out over the Manhattan.

"I love this view of the city." He lets his hand run across my thigh, slipping beneath the cotton towel as he travels the path up to my hip.

"It's perfect." My gaze lingers on the Empire State Building, then on the twin towers beyond it. I turn and study Arthur's profile, ignoring the tug of guilt deep in the pit of my soul.

"Millions of people down there." He teases the seam where my thighs meet and parts them with a gentle nudge. "All blissfully ignorant of everything around them."

A moan catches in my throat at the gentle pressure of his fingertip on my clit. I'm embarrassingly wet from his teasing earlier. He coats his fingers in it before making slow circles over the sensitive bud.

I cling tighter to him. "Arthur." His name is a plea, an offering, an admonishment all wrapped together in delicious heat.

He continues to tease me, taking his sweet time, bringing me close and then easing the pressure. Within moments he has me panting, trembling against him, I can't stop myself from begging.

"Please, Arthur. Please. I need to come."

In an instant, he drops his hand and lifts me to my feet. I stumble forward and catch myself against the window. My towel falls away. I'm completely bare in front of the whole city of New York, if they cared to look up. The thought sends a bolt of need straight to my pussy.

Arthur's heat presses into me. His towel is gone. I know because his cock brushes against my ass when I lean into him. He pins my wrists against the glass and nudges my stance wider with his foot.

"Keep your hands on the glass, Kate," he whispers against my ear. "No matter what. I want you to keep your hands right there. Do you understand?"

I exhale and fog the glass with my breath. "Yes."

"Good girl." He slides his hands down my arms, over my torso, until they rest on my hips. He pulls my ass against him.

I'm shaking. The cold glass does little to chill the flame burning through me. I tilt my hips giving him access to the place I want him most.

His hand smooths over my hip before disappearing. I open my mouth to protest in disappointment, but the loud crack followed by the sting of his hand connecting with my ass brings me up short.

"What the hell?" I glare at him and my hand slips from the position against the window.

He brings his hand down on the opposite cheek and I quickly reposition it. Pain and pleasure radiate through me.

"I told you not to move." He wraps his hand around my throat and strokes with a hint of pressure.

"Why did you spank me?" My outrage dims at the caress. It's difficult to remain outraged when it's what I crave.

"Did you lie to me?" He takes the lobe of my ear between his teeth and tugs.

"No." I whimper.

"You told me you like it rough." He presses his cock against the cleft of my ass.

I thrust my hips back against him. "Yes, please."

With his hand on my throat, he positions his cock at my entrance and slides in with little effort. I'm soaking wet, practically weeping for him to fill me.

"You feel so good, Kate." He nips at my earlobe again and his grip on my throat tightens a fraction.

There's no way to stifle the moans as he thrusts into me. He has me pinned where he wants me, taking me without mercy, without hesitation. I focus on maintaining my position against the glass and see his reflection. The focused concentration and firm set of his lips as he drives deeper into me. Fuck, yes. This is what I've been missing.

As if reading my body, Arthur shifts his grip on my throat to my breasts, rolling each nipple in turn sending shockwaves of pleasure ricocheting through my limbs. I'm helpless, and yet I know he's there ready to catch me should my legs fail. He caught me at my weakest moment, even though it went against his judgement. He caught me. My knight. Arthur.

A spiral of pressure unfurls in the pit of my stomach. I'm going to come; all I need is a gentle push over the edge.

"Please, I'm...please." My words are broken, but Arthur knows.

"That's it, baby, come for me." He reaches between my folds and applies the perfect amount of pressure to send me cascading over the waterfall. I tumble headfirst into my orgasm, my fingers trying to dig into the unforgiving glass.

He thrusts a few more times before pulling out. I feel the hot spray of his release against my back, and I smile at his consideration. Although the thought of him coming inside me makes my pussy clench with another spasm.

"Don't move." He disappears, and I take the moment of reprieve to catch my breath.

Arthur returns and wipes me clean with a damp rag. "Did I hurt you?"

I turn and wrap my weakened arms around him. He holds me steady and kisses me. I'll never get enough of this man. He holds me and we linger, mouths searching, our actions speaking louder than words ever could.

The kiss breaks and we're both breathless. He rests his head against mine.

"Thank you." Satisfaction seeps into my bones.

He grins. "You're welcome."

Together we stand naked in the window staring out over the city. The prominent buildings stand tall against the failing light and reality slowly consumes me. The towers. The Empire State Building. Mom. Dad.

I press my eyes closed and a tear slips free even in the midst of the most amazing sexual encounter of my life, I'm caught up in a life not my own. And for the first time, I'm terrified of losing what I found here. Of losing Arthur.

"Are you crying?" He tips my chin to glance at my face.

I swipe my tears away and sniff.

"What's wrong?" His tone is gentle, and I know I have to tell him the truth even though it's unfathomable.

Mustering all the courage I have, I take a breath and face him. "There's something you should know."

He leans forward to kiss me, and I stop him, my hand against his chest. Concern fills his steel blue gaze.

"My name is Katherine Cohen." I brace myself and push through. "And I'm from the future."

Whatever expression I expected, Arthur exceeds it with spectacular flourish. Disbelief makes him laugh, but when I don't join in, he sobers instantly.

I know whatever we shared has fractured, and I wish I could take it back the moment he releases me and puts space between us. The last year of my life might have been horrible, but it's nothing compared to the pain of the man I love staring at me the way he is now.

CHAPTER 20

Arthur

Part of me thinks this is a joke, but her expression is fragile and earnest. I shake my head and step back, running my hand through my hair. She reaches for me, but I need answers first. Her touch will only cloud me with confusion.

I need to think, damn it, but it's difficult when her scent still clings to me and the evidence of our lovemaking surrounds us. I snatch the towel off the floor and wrap it around my waist.

Kate does the same, wrapping the fabric tightly around her torso. I'm almost saddened at the loss but right now I need to focus. Both of us being naked doesn't help at all.

Her eyes fill with tears and she bites her lower lip. She's searching for something to say, I can almost see the gears spinning in her mind.

She can't be serious, can she? Cohen? As in Victor Cohen, my colleague? None of this makes any sense. After spending my whole life in this city, I've heard some crazy stories, but this one definitely takes the grand prize. I can't help but feel like she's toying with me, but she's upset and I can tell it's sincere. I groan and try to face this information with an analytical mind.

"Katherine Cohen." When I speak her name, she snaps to attention. "That's your full birth name."

She nods and a sad smile parts her lips. "Mom didn't want me to have a middle name."

"And your date of birth?" I monitor her reaction to each question carefully.

"June 24, 1985." She cringes.

"I see." But I really don't. If she's telling me the truth, then she hasn't even been born yet. "And you're from the city?"

"Yes. We lived in Manhattan until..." She pauses and drops her gaze. "When I turned four, we moved to Staten Island to live with my grandma."

"Why?" I press.

Tears fall fresh pooling in the corners of her eyes and spilling down her cheeks. "Dad died."

An icy tendril of dread touched the base of my neck. "Kate, who is your father?"

She hiccups and her voice cracks. "Victor Cohen."

The events of the past two weeks fall into place, and I stumble back until my knees buckle and I collapse against the couch arm. "Is this why you were outside my office on New Year's Day? You were looking for him?"

She hides her tearstained red face behind her hands. "Yes."

I shake my head in disbelief. The questions she asked about him, every conversation they shared. Her smiles. Her laughter. She wasn't in love with him in the way I assumed. Not even close. But none of this explains how the hell any of this is possible.

"This can't be possible." The gruff edge to my voice makes her jump. "How the hell did you end up here?"

"I don't know." She uses the edge of the towel to wipe her face and sniffs trying to contain her emotions. "One minute I'm standing on the observation deck, and the next I'm seeing the sun rise with the twin towers."

Her words are pure nonsense. "What do you mean?"

Kate stomps her feet and groans. "I can't tell you what it means even if I wanted to. That's like the first rule of time travel. No spoilers! I don't want to be the reason we declare war with Canada and dinosaurs rule the future."

More gibberish pours from her mouth. "Wait? What the hell are you talking about now?"

She sighs heavily and collapses in one of the dining room chairs. The towel rides up her thigh. I refocus my attention on her face wishing I had told her to put some damn clothes on before we dove into the specifics.

"Haven't you seen *Back to the Future*...shit, never mind." She pinches the bridge of her nose. "I can't tell you what's going to happen in the future because it could alter future events causing a rip in the space-time continuum. Or a paradox. Or an alternate timeline. I mean, there are a lot of theories as to what would really happen, but I am *not* interested in finding out which one got it right."

I fold my arms across my chest. "Well, it may be a bit late for that considering you've told me you're from the future and your dad dies when you're four." I push aside the anguish attached to this knowing I'll have to address this piece of information later, but she's right, we can't take the chance of altering the future for personal gain.

"Shit." She bites her thumbnail. "But if we don't interfere in any events, then nothing will change, right?"

I laugh. "Kate. The door must have hit you harder than I thought." The possibilities are too fantastical for me to believe a word out of her mouth.

"You don't believe me?" The color drains from her face.

"You want me to believe you're the daughter of my colleague who's come from the future." I do the math in my head. "From what year?" I lean forward.

"2020."

"Ah," I reply as though it's obvious. "You don't know how you got here or why."

"No idea."

I nod and slowly rise to my feet. "Maybe I should call Rob and have him see if they can get you in for a scan down at the hospital?"

Kate jumps to her feet and charges toward me. "There's nothing wrong with my head!"

Those delectable lips and delicious curves I enjoyed only an hour ago distract me from the truth. The girl is delusional. She has to be. None of this makes any sense.

"Sweetheart," I place my hands on her shoulders ignoring my body's response to the smooth texture of her skin and the heat simmering between us. "There's nothing to worry about. I'll call Rob, and we'll get this figured out."

"You think I'm crazy." She wrenches herself away. "I'm not crazy."

"I never said you were crazy." I reach for her but she's already sprinting toward the bedroom.

I'm on her heels, but she slams the door in my face. "Kate. Kate!"

Silence reaches me. "Shit."

I cross the room and pick up the phone. Rob doesn't answer at his place, so I call the hospital. When the nurse tells me he's with a patient, I leave my name and ask for her to have him call me right away.

The bedroom door opens, and Kate emerges wearing the same clothes I found her in on New Year's Day. She crosses to the door and gets her oversized wool coat.

"Where are you going?" I stand between her and the door blocking her exit. "I can't let you leave. You need help."

A glare, one I can only describe as murderous, pins me in place. She hisses in a breath. "You have no right to keep me captive here. I'm perfectly sound in body and mind. Now move, before I move you."

A good six inches shorter than me, Kate poses no threat. I scoff and hold my ground.

"It's not safe for you out there. I've called Rob. He'll help, just stay here, Kate. We'll figure this all out." My pleas fall on stubborn ears.

"There's nothing for me to figure out." She jabs her finger in my chest. "You, on the other hand." Her shoulders shrug with the implication of her words. Determination flashes in her mismatched eyes.

I lift my hands in supplication. "Explain it to me then, Kate."

She shakes her head and the determination in her gaze fades into sadness. "I tried, Arthur. I bared my soul with the truth."

"The truth?" I scoff, but sober the moment she scowls. "I'm a practical man, but I'm sorry, your truth goes against all reason."

"Goodbye, Arthur." She tries to push past me and grab the door handle, but I block her. "Move."

"No. You're not going anywhere." I wrap my hand around her wrist and tug her away from the door, but she bristles at the touch.

"Let me go." The low growl of her voice sets off warning bells in my head.

"Not until we get to the bottom of this." My grip tightens, and I pull her against me.

Without hesitation, she jabs her elbow into my side with her weight, stomps on my foot, slams the back of her fist into my nose, and drives her elbow into my groin.

Pain radiates through me. I double over in agony and stumble forward, blood dripping from my nose onto the carpet.

By the time I regain some of my senses, I realize Kate's gone. Gingerly, I hobble into the bedroom, glaring at the phone on the other side of the apartment. I should call the guard on the ground floor, but what would that accomplish? If she's willing to injure me to this degree for her freedom, then I have to let her go.

Warmth coats my face. Shit. I'm bleeding everywhere. I stumble into the bathroom and run the water, washing my face in the sink and blotting the mess smeared across me with white towels. Fuck, my bathroom is a murder scene.

The ache in my side and foot dissipates long before the throbbing where her elbow connected with my balls. It takes much longer to stem the waterfall of blood coming from my nose. It's already turning purple. Great. I gently press the side of my nose, and there's a screaming pain.

Yup, it's broken.

Looks like I'll be paying Rob a visit at the ER. As I pull on some old clothes, I worry about Kate. Obviously, she's lost, but what if she's telling the truth?

This is crazy. Time travel isn't real. There's no way in hell. It's science fiction, not reality.

But the more I think about it, I can't shake the feeling there's a piece of this puzzle missing. Maybe I should give her time and space. Kate may not be dangerous to anyone but herself at this point. Except my well-ordered life.

First, I need to deal with the broken nose she left me along with a broken heart.

CHAPTER 21

Katherine

Guilt and anger twist in the pit of my stomach gnawing away at my insides leaving a dark void of regret. Maybe I shouldn't have told him. It's a lot of information, and even though it conflicts with his perception of reality, it doesn't negate the truth.

I don't belong here. And by extension, I don't belong with him.

Assaulting him when he blocked the door may have been a stretch, but I knew he would never let me go of his own volition. Not since he truly thinks I'm a mental case. No, I had to get out of there before he locked me up in the psych ward. Mimicking Gracie Lou Freebush and her dramatic display of self-defense, I gave myself the window I needed. Oh God, I probably broke his nose. He'll definitely be sporting a pair of black eyes and some bruises in the morning.

If Arthur thought I was crazy before, he certainly will now.

When I reach the ground floor, I half expect the doorman to stop me or have security throw up barricades hindering my escape. But I walk out the doors without any issue. The attendant even holds the door open and wishes me a good evening.

The cold evening air stings my cheeks. I walk along the street tugging the wool collar higher to block the wind from my face.

My act of instinctive defiance ensures several things. I have no job, no home, and no belongings. I did manage to grab the cash he gave me for my first payday. But a hundred bucks isn't going to get me far.

I find the first subway station and stare at the signs. I should try to find a shelter for the night, at least then I won't be sleeping under the bridge down by the river. But instead, I take the line to the Upper West Side.

The address is a fixed point in my memory. I don't remember the details, but Mom told me stories about their first place on 73rd.

After a quick ride, I emerge from underground and integrate myself into the bustling Saturday night pedestrian traffic. Normally I enjoyed the anonymity of walking the city without anyone noticing my presence, but tonight it leaves me anxious and lonely.

My feet take me down the sidewalks and around the corners past shops and restaurants. I admire the hustle of the city. Some of these things will still be here years from now. Some won't, and that's the part twisting a hole in my sanity.

Obviously, there's no way for me to get back to 2020. I don't have much keeping me there, but here in 1985, I'm an outsider with too much knowledge. It would be simple to use it to my advantage and manipulate the future ensuring my success.

I'm no expert on quantum mechanics and the physics of space and time, but I know doing so would be playing with fire. Fear seizes me. What if I've already ruined something by telling Arthur? Does it matter? He doesn't believe me anyway.

I thought he did. Then I saw the cognitive dissidence jerk him right back into denial. Tears appear again, and I blink them away. No. No more tears. I can't change him. I can't make him understand. I can't control anything but my own actions and how I respond.

In one of the last conversations I had with Mom, she imparted these words of wisdom. She admitted it took her years to realize their truth, but when she applied it to her life, it made things more manageable.

I'd lost my job. My apartment. Justin and I were on the rocks, and with her in hospice, I knew it was only a matter of time before I lost her too. I didn't want useless platitudes and deep insights on life. I wanted something I could grasp with both hands and hold tight. I was losing control and it scared the fucking shit out of me.

Her words echo in my mind giving me strength with each step.

When I reach number twenty-three, I stop and stare up at the narrow brick townhouse squeezed between neighboring buildings. Light illuminates the first-floor window. They're home.

Mom and Dad. Alive. Happy. Excited for their future family, with me. My grin falters. No, not *me*. I pause on the bottom step.

What the hell am I doing here? I should leave before they see me. They don't need my drama. It was stupid of me to think I could scavenge whatever time I could with them stuck in this nightmare time slip.

"Kate?"

A dictionary of curse words zings through my brain at lightning speed. I regain my composure and spin around. Dad's standing on the sidewalk with a bag of groceries in one arm. His warm smile and kind eyes instantly soothe the ache in my heart.

"Hi, Da...Victor." I wave and sway catching myself against the railing.

"Whoa, easy there. These steps can get slippery sometimes."

"Yeah. I'm good."

"Did Arthur send you?" He chuckles. "I swear sometimes he can't turn off work. The man needs a hobby or a wife."

My throat constricts at the mention of his name. "No."

Dad's smile falters. "Is something wrong? Did something happen?"

I shake my head, but there's no stopping the tears. My lip trembles and I fight hard to keep myself from falling apart on my parent's front steps.

"Kate?" Mom's voice echoes behind me.

I tumble over the precipice and burst into tears.

"Oh, honey." Mom rushes down the steps, careful not to slip, and wraps her arms around me. "Victor, what happened?"

"I don't know. One minute we're talking, and the next—"

"Come on, honey. Let's go inside. You need a cup of tea and something to eat." She tucks my hair behind my ears. "Then you can tell me what's wrong."

I can't fight her kindness or her tender touch. I missed it so much. All I can do is nod and follow her up the stairs.

Inside, she tugs off my coat and deposits me on the couch. "You sit here, and I'll be right back. I have a kettle already on the stove."

"Thank you, M...Nora."

"Of course." Mom carries my coat into the hallway. I can hear their voices carry down the hall, but I can't make out the words.

My gaze drifts over the room. The avocado green and goldenrod patterned sofas seem to be holdovers from the seventies, but the rest of the room is tame enough. The pictures on the wall opposite the front window catch my attention.

I cross the room and inspect them. Mom and Dad at their wedding. Grandma and Grandpa on their front porch. A few other familiar family members are scattered across the wall, but I keep coming back to their wedding photo.

"We got married in Las Vegas." Mom comes up beside me with two mugs in her hands. "I told him I wanted a house, not a wedding. So we compromised."

I take the mug she offers and blow across the top. "You look so happy."

"It wasn't traditional, but it was fun." She laughs. "I even allowed Elvis to officiate the ceremony."

"I remember." The gaffe slips from my tongue and I sputter in an attempt to correct myself. "Arthur mentioned it."

Her brow rises. "I'm surprised Arthur pays attention to anything aside from his business." She waves her hand. "He's a wonderful man and a good friend of ours, but the man does nothing but work."

"I noticed."

Mom gestures to the couch, and I sit down beside her. We both take a sip of tea and it warms me instantly.

"Feeling better?" she asks.

"Yes, thank you." I clear my throat and shift uncomfortably. "I apologize for breaking down like that. It's been—" I heave a shaky exhale. "—A rough couple of months."

"Do you want to talk about it?" Her understanding smile nearly breaks my heart. She's so damn young, but I see her older self beneath the surface. It takes all my restraint to keep the tears from bursting over the dam again.

"I shouldn't." I shake my head. "It's complicated, and I don't want to drag you into my drama."

"Honey, don't you worry about dragging me anywhere. You seem like you need a friend, and I'm glad you had the sense to come here." She pats my hand. "Now, what did he do?"

I laugh. I can't help it. Mom always was too observant for her own good.

"Are you talking about Arthur?" Dad comes in and sits in the armchair a few feet away.

My face warms. I don't want to talk about what happened with Arthur in front of my parents, but they don't know how awkward this whole situation is. How could they? I take a fortifying sip of tea and cradle it in my hands.

"Honey, we already know there's something between you two." Mom nudges me. "Victor told me about it on Monday night. Why do you think I came to the office this week?" She winks. "I had to meet the woman who caught Arthur's attention."

I nearly choke. "But...we weren't even talking then."

Dad snorts. "Yeah, Arthur was in a right foul mood all week." He laughs. "I even caught him working on the wrong proposal."

"See?" Mom lifts her mug in salute. "You've got him all kinds of distracted. Besides, I saw the chemistry between you two. Positively nuclear."

This conversation has taken a strange turn, but I forge ahead thankful to even have the two most important people in my life in the same room with me.

With a deep breath, I launch into a brief, non-descriptive account of my relationship with Arthur touching lightly on the events of the last twenty-four hours leading up to this moment.

Their reactions range from horrified to angry to appeased and then circle right back again. Only I don't reveal exactly what caused the fight, but the mere mention of an argument has Dad on his feet.

"Why is he so stubborn?" He stalks toward the door. "I'm going to march over there and give him a piece of my mind."

"Sit down, Victor," Mom admonishes him. "You're not going anywhere. This is between Kate and Arthur." She turns back to me. "I'm sure he'll come to his senses at some point during the night."

Thoughts of Arthur and his sore...ego and busted nose make me cringe. "I doubt it."

Mom tilts her head in concern. "Do you need a place to stay?"

"No. Thank you. I couldn't impose."

"It's not imposition. We have a spare room for guests, and it'd be nice to get a chance to get to know you better."

My soul warms at her words. "I'd love that."

"Good, it's settled. I'll get the spare room ready after dinner." Mom gestures to the kitchen. "I need to check on the roast."

After Mom leaves, I catch Dad staring at me when I reach for my tea. "Something wrong?"

He shakes his head. "No. It's just...I have this odd feeling about you. Who are your parents?"

I nearly spit out the tea and sputter before swallowing it. "Uh. Why do you say that?"

Dad leans close. "Your eyes. Two different colors, like mine." He chuckles. "It's not a common trait. We could be related. How crazy would that be?"

"Crazy." I reply uncertain of what I should say.

"Don't worry about Arthur." He winks. "He'll come around."

"I hope you're right." I finish my tea and stand. "Where's the kitchen? I'll take my cup in."

"Don't worry about it. You're our guest." Dad takes my cup and gathers up the others. "Relax."

Once he leaves, I stand and pace the floor. This feels so surreal, staying with my parents like this. I wander down the hall and peer into the rooms taking an inventory of the home's layout.

The phone rings and I nearly jump out of my skin.

"Hello." Dad's voice echoes from the kitchen.

I lean against the wall and listen.

"Yes, she's here." He pauses. "No. She's staying here." Another pause. "Okay. I'll let her know. Bye."

"Who was it?" Mom asks him.

"Arthur's sister, Marcy. She was looking for Kate."

Fear grips me. He knows I'm here. I can't stay. Not now. Without waiting for Mom and Dad to come find me, I bolt down the hallway, grab my coat, and venture back out into the cold.

I don't know where I'll end up, but I let my feet carry me wherever my heart leads.

CHAPTER 22

Arthur

The cold, sterile hospital environment does nothing to settle my anxiety. Where the hell did she go? I made sure to call Marcy before I left my place, in case Kate tried to contact her. Did she even have my sister's number? Or her address?

I press the towel covered bag of peas against my nose. They're turning to mush in the bag, but they're still cold and soothing. While it treats my physical discomfort, it does nothing to soothe the gaping hole in my conscience.

The more I think about Kate's confession, the more I realize how horribly I reacted. I should have been more understanding. She's obviously in some kind of delusional state caused by her injury. Now she's out roaming the city with nowhere to go.

A gentle knock on the door stirs me from my thoughts. Rob enters the room with a clipboard in his hand. He glances up and freezes instantly.

"What the hell happened to you?" He closes the door and sets the board aside.

"I ran into a door." My pride hurts enough, I can't bring myself to tell Rob the truth.

He pulls on a pair of clean gloves and nudges the cold bag from my face. His eyes narrow as he inspects the damage. I wince as he presses and prods my face, asking stupid questions about whether this hurts and then jamming his thumb into the aching protrusion that used to be my nose.

I hiss and mumble one-word responses littered with a few choice swear words to emphasize my enthusiasm.

"It's broken. I'll have to reset it."

"Do whatever you need to do." I brace myself

He braces his hands on my face and screaming pain ricochets through me as he applies pressure. There's a distinct crack as it realigns.

"Son of a bitch!" My whole body trembles at the rush of pain and immediate release of pressure. The ache remains, but it doesn't throb like it did before.

Rob backs away and prepares some bandages. "So, you going to tell me who hit you?"

I scoff. Rob's too observant. This makes him an amazing physician, but it also makes him an annoying friend. I've never been able to hide anything from him.

"Kate." I dab the towel to my nose to catch any remaining blood.

"Kate did this to you?" Rob's laughter fills the small room. When he sees my serious expression, he sobers. "Wait, you're serious?"

"Have you ever known me to joke about anything like this in my life?"

"Good point." Rob grabs a few pills from a bottle and pours me a small cup of water. "Take these. They'll help with swelling and pain."

I pop them in my mouth and wash them down.

Rob leans against the counter and crosses his arms. "What the hell happened?"

Deflated, I shake my head. "I don't know. One minute we're all over each other and then the next she's spinning some crazy story."

"Hold up," Rob interjects. "You two had sex?"

I nod. "Yeah, I came home this morning and well, we worked things out."

"I'm glad you came to your senses." He eyes me with skepticism. "After your behavior last night, you're lucky I didn't break your nose first."

"I admit. I was an asshole." I replace the ice pack on the right side of my nose. "I came home this morning and apologized. Then things got a little heated."

"You two fucked like rabbits." Rob nods. "I get the point, please feel free to skip to the part where she kicks your ass."

"After the most amazing sex I've ever had..." I pause for emphasis and to annoy Rob, stopping only to admire the look of disgust on his face. "She tells me the truth."

"She never lost her memory?" Rob asks with a slow grin.

"Well, that, yes, but also when she's from." I wait for it to hit him.

Rob's brow furrows. "You mean where she's from?"

I shake my head with slow precision. "When."

He blinks in confusion. "What?"

I lean close regardless of the fact we're the only two people in the room and keep my voice low. "She thinks she's from the year 2020."

Rob's jaw drops. "Maybe the whack on the head did more damage than I thought? We should definitely get her in for an evaluation."

"That's what I said to her." I gesture wildly. "She stormed into the bedroom. I tried calling you, but you were with a patient. Then when she came out, she was determined to leave. I tried to stop her." Helplessly, I point at my swollen nose. "She gave me a broken nose and bruised...ego before storming out." I clear my throat.

"Where did she go?"

"I don't know." I hiss when I shift the icepack to the other side. "I called Marcy before I left and told her to keep an eye out for her. I told her to call everyone at the office and have let me know if she contacts them."

"Good idea. She's got nowhere to go, so she may reach out for help."

"I hope so." The thought of Kate out in the city alone with no direction and no support stirs guilt and regret in my gut. "I should have...I don't know, done something different. I mean what the hell am I supposed to say to someone when they tell me they're from the future?"

"Your reaction is normal." Rob grabs his notepad and scribbles a number down. "Did she seem lucid when she told you?"

"Yes." I sigh. "I mean, the way she said it, I could tell she believed every word."

"Hmmm." Rob ponders this for a moment. "The day you found her, did she have anything on her that would give you any indication as to where she was from or confirm she's telling you the truth?"

I scoff. "You're not actually saying you believe her, do you?"

Rob shrugs. "There are a lot of possibilities. I'm saying maybe we should investigate a little bit more before writing it off. When we find her, we can run a scan and make sure she's physically okay." His gaze sharpens. "I've met a lot of patients with serious mental issues over the years. Kate doesn't exhibit any symptoms which cause me to think she's unstable or crazy, so to speak."

"You're right." My rational mind wars with my instincts. "I just...I need her, Rob. I feel like shit."

"I know." He pats me on the shoulder. "Go home and look through her stuff. See if you can find anything."

"She left wearing the clothes I found her in." I try to remember the morning when she was unconscious and I checked her pockets for identification. There was nothing but some garbage. "I doubt I'll find anything to help us."

"Then we need to find her." Rob hands me the paper. "This is the detective's number; in case we need to enlist some help finding her."

I slip the paper in my pocket and nod. "Thanks."

"Okay, let me clean up your nose so you can get out there and find her."

Twenty minutes later, I step out into the brisk January night. Gentle flakes of snow fall from the sky dusting my face and clothes. From here I can see the lights in the Empire State Building reflected in the falling snow. I wish Kate were here to see it. It's peaceful and beautiful. I can almost see her dancing in circles trying to catch the icy flakes on her tongue.

Shit. I need to find her. She's tainted everything, leaving impressions of herself across the city. I fucked up. I pray it's not too late.

I locate the car where Cyril is waiting and climb inside. Neither of us speak, but once we reach my building, I give him instructions to watch for her.

There's no one home when I come in the door. I half hoped she would return, or that I would find Marcy with her sitting on the couch laughing at the whole situation. But the apartment is dark and vacant of all joy.

In my room, I sort through all the clothes and makeup my sister brought. There's nothing there revealing anything of relevance. Her scent lingers in the room. My gaze fixes on the bed where I buried myself inside her and made her come with my tongue.

I shake the memories away and search the drawers beside the bed, hoping I'll find something. After a thorough search, I realize there's nothing, and if there is, she's taken it with her.

I collapse on the edge of the bed and stare out over the city. Snow cakes to the glass leaving a frosted imprint wherever there's moisture. The lights glitter beyond the pane and I'm mesmerized by the sight.

She's out there. Somewhere. I whisper a prayer for safety. Nonna used to say it at night before she went to sleep. Her way of asking for protection for those she loved. I'm not a religious person, but I can't ignore the peace it gives when I murmur the words.

My head swims, and I lie down. Her scent clings to the pillow. I slide my hand beneath it and inhale deeply careful not to bump my nose. My fingertips brush against something.

I pull a small notebook from beneath the pillow. It looks like one of mine, but when I open it, it's Kate's handwriting I see.

As I read, my jaw drops. The words are a direct portal into her thoughts. Over the past week, she's filled the pages with details and information I can't even fathom. The more I read, the more I realize how wrong I was.

Kate's not crazy. She knows things no one can possibly know. I flip through the pages, devouring the words and their implications. Then I see the papers I found in her pocket the morning we met. They're pressed flat between the pages. A ticket stub and a receipt. Nothing of consequence, until I read the dates. December 29, 2020.

Then I remember her coat. Victor's coat. No wonder it looked so familiar. It's the same coat, but hers is worn and ragged from years of use. *Holy shit.*

When the detective said there was no record of Kate, I didn't understand. But now I do.

The phone rings in the other room. Taking the notebook with me, I run to try to catch the call.

"Hello?" I pray it's Kate.

"Hey. I found her. She was at Victor's place." Marcy's voice cuts through the line.

"Was?" My heart sinks.

"Yeah. She bolted without a word." My sister's voice cracks. "But we'll find her."

Disappointment and anger, mostly at myself, coagulate into a mass pulling me into darkness. "Shit." I throw the notebook down and it splays open on the floor. A simple, rudimentary sketch of a building lay between the creased pages. Then it hits me.

"I know where she is. I'll call you later." Without waiting for Marcy's response, I hang up the phone and snatch the book off the floor. As I dart out the door, I tuck it into my pocket and race down to the lobby.

Cyril is the best driver in the city, but I feel I could have made better time on foot. We're stuck in a traffic jam two blocks away, so I climb from the car.

"Go get her, boss." He shouts before the door slams.

I take off down the street shoving through anyone crazy enough to be out in this cold snowy night. When I reach the building, I wave to the night guards and punch the number for the observation deck.

Excitement builds inside me. She has to be here. It's the only possible place she could be. The elevator reaches the main deck, and I step out, anticipation thrumming through my veins.

I round the corner and see her standing against the railing. The snow falling around her creates a beautiful ethereal halo of light against the dark sky.

Careful not to startle her, I step forward and call her name. "Kate."

She turns, and the last remaining hesitation falls away. I may not understand why she's here or how, but it doesn't matter. I love her and nothing can change that.

CHAPTER 23

Katherine

I sense his presence. The snow creates a globe of silence encasing the observation deck. When he speaks my name, it's almost as if he's standing beside me whispering in my ear.

Apprehension coils around my heart protecting it. Coming here was selfish on my part. This is my spot. Dad's spot. But now I know for certain, this is Arthur's spot too. His love for this building is obvious. Perhaps that's why I followed my heart when it led me here because I knew he would find me.

I turn and gasp at the sight of the bandage across his nose highlighted by the darkening bruises. He shortens the gap between us, and I reach out to gently brush the skin of his cheek below the bandage.

"I'm sorry, Arthur." My apology is sincere, but the guilt lingers. "I didn't mean to hurt you."

"It will heal." His sad smile makes my heart ache. "Rob took care of it. Says it'll be as good as it was before it was broken."

"Oh, God." I hang my head. "I broke it? I'm so sorry. I reacted on instinct."

"Kate, it's okay." He tips my chin up. "I was worried about you."

I tense at his touch unsure if this is a trap or if he's sincere. "Because I'm crazy?"

He drops his hands and tucks them in his pockets but maintains our close proximity. "I didn't say you were crazy."

"You didn't have to say it." I exhale and a plume of steam engulfs us. "Don't you think I know how insane my story sounds? Why do you think I lied? I had to. No one would believe me." Tears sting my eyes. "I don't belong here."

"Do you want to go back?"

The question stops me, and I search his face for any signs of duplicity. I find only sincerity in the depths of his gaze. "No. Everyone I love is gone. They're all here." I laugh at how stupid it sounds. "But I'm not part of this world. I haven't even been born yet. I'm a random piece of a second-hand puzzle that got tossed in the wrong box. I want to belong, but I don't know how it would even be feasible."

"There must be a reason this happened."

"When you figure it out, let me know." I scoff and narrow my gaze. "Are you saying you believe me?"

"The world is full of endless possibilities." He shrugs one shoulder. "Who am I to question the will of the universe when it drops a beautiful and talented woman right on my doorstep?"

"You make me sound like I'm special." I tease him, but his words ignite an ember of hope deep in my soul.

"You are special, Kate." He brushes a snow crusted curl away from my face. "In two weeks, you've upended my life in the best way, and I was stupid to fight it. You challenge me and make me want to be better. I can't imagine going forward without you by my side."

His touch warms me and the ember sparks into a flame.

"I apologize for my reaction earlier, and if you'd rather stay with your parents..." He pauses as though still coming to terms with the concept of Victor and Nora being my parents, but pushes forward. "Then it's fine with me. I'll even help you find your own place, if you want to take things slow."

"Thank you." I cup his hand against my cheek.

"I love you, Kate."

His confession steals my breath.

"I love you, and I don't care if you came from another planet, let alone another millennium, I want you by my side from this moment forward." Snow nearly covers his hair making him look like a sexy silver fox. His eyes shine with hope and desire.

I can't imagine any place I'd rather be than right here, right now.

"When I found you, I had no idea what to expect. Last week, the thought terrified me, but as long as I have you, I'm ready for whatever challenge lies ahead."

"Even if I refuse to give any spoilers for the future?" I grin.

"Keep all your spoilers, Kate." He hugs me tight. "All I want is you."

"I love you, Arthur." I grasp his coat in both hands and pull him closer. He kisses me, and I melt against him.

The kiss turns passionate and I brush the tip of his nose with mine. He hisses in a breath.

"Oh, I'm sorry." I wince. "Maybe we should take it easy until you recover."

"Wherever you learned that self-defense trick, it's definitely effective."

I grin and think of the first time I tried it on my ex after I watched *Miss Congeniality*. Poor bastard ended up with two black eyes, and we didn't have sex for a month afterward. It should have been a warning sign. I shove the memory to the trash bin in my head.

My past doesn't matter, because now I have a clean slate. It's a do-over in a way, and my heart feels lighter than it has in years.

"Shall we go home?" Arthur offers his arm.

I loop mine through and lean against him. "Yes. As much as I'm enjoying this *Sleepless in Seattle* moment, my toes are frozen."

Arthur shakes his head. "I have no idea what that means."

We head for the elevator, and I tug on his arm. "Spoilers without context. You'll figure it out one day." I chuckle. "This is going to be more fun than I thought."

"I'm glad you're amused, sweetheart."

Inside the elevator we dust each other off leaving a layer of snow on the carpet. Mike, the guard, waves when we exit the building, unconcerned with our presence in his building.

Cyril grins when he sees us. "I'm glad you're safe, ma'am."

"Kate." I return his infectious grin. "Call me Kate."

He nods and opens the door. Once we're in the car, Arthur pulls me against him and kisses my cheek.

"Will you stay with me?" he whispers hot against my ear.

I suppress a shiver of need and nod. "I'll stay."

"Are you going to tell your parents?" His voice is low.

"No. I don't think that's a good idea." I sigh at the thought. "It's better this way."

"I agree." He brushes my hair away from my face and smiles. "But you can spend as much time with them as you want."

"That sounds like the perfect plan." I'm blindsided by a thought and it makes me hesitate. "But what about me? I mean, not this me, baby me?"

He ponders this for a moment. "I don't know. I guess we'll address that once you're born."

"Do you think the universe will implode if I meet my infant self?" My mind spins with insane possibilities.

"I doubt it." He interlaces his fingers with mine. "Don't worry. We'll figure this out together."

"I know." I rest my head against his shoulder and close my eyes.

After a few breaths, my body relaxes and peace settles over the chaos in my mind. "How did you know where to find me?"

"Educated guess." He shifts and pulls something from his pocket. "I saw your sketch in here."

Straightening, I take the notebook from his hand and hold it against my chest. "You read it?"

"I did."

"Arthur! Spoilers." Panic starts to rise once more.

"I highly doubt the universe will implode if I know a few details about the future." He chuckles. "If I wasn't financially secure, I would say there are a few prime opportunities one could take advantage of."

"You can't. It wouldn't be right." I clutch the notebook tighter.

"Don't worry, sweetheart. I'm perfectly capable of managing my wealth without the aid of insider information." He winks. "As for some of the other events you discuss, well, I doubt anyone would believe us even if we tried to warn them of impending destruction."

"You're probably right." I tap the notebook and ease my grip a fraction. "Is this why you came after me? I mean, after reading it, you must have realized I wasn't crazy or you would have called the cops."

"I came after you because I love you and I wanted to ensure your safety." He kisses my forehead. "But yes, the *spoilers* in your little journal helped solidify my belief in your story."

"I should burn this damn thing."

"If that's what you wish."

The rest of the drive is silent. A gentle contentment settles around us once we arrive home.

Home. It's so strange to think of it as my home.

I glance up at the massive building and then at the man standing tall beside me. He takes my hand and squeezes infusing me with confidence. The snow falls around us gently enfolding us in snapshot of picture-perfect winter magic.

I may not understand how I became stranded in 1985, but I understand the reason I'm meant to stay. Arthur, my dad's boss, and the man I love beyond reason. Beyond time itself.

CHAPTER 24

Arthur

New Year's Eve, 2020

Spoilers. Such a simple, inconspicuous word, and yet for the last thirty-five years, it has been our secret code for knowing the unknowable.

"Did you fall asleep already?" Kate calls from the doorway.

"How can anyone sleep with you nagging them to death?" I snap back in a loving tone.

"For that comment, I'm drinking both these hot cocoas." She ambles into the room with a tray bearing cookies and two steaming mugs.

Her hair, as well as mine, turned white years ago. She may have a strange little shuffle when she walks and her face is careworn with the passage of time, but she's still the same beautiful woman I married in 1985.

"Are we watching *Doctor Who* reruns?" I ask as she sets the tray down on the table.

"I was hoping we could watch *An Affair to Remember.*" She smiles. "It's a classic."

"It's better than *Sleepless in Seattle.*" I snort and reach for a cookie.

She slaps my hand. "Not better. Different. I prefer Grant to Hanks."

"You like older men," I tease her and plant a kiss on her cheek before snatching the cookie with awkward grace.

Kate sticks her tongue out and pulls her phone from her apron. "Nearly midnight, maybe we should wait for twelve and then turn in."

"You want a little New Year nookie." I add a wink, and she blushes. I love that after all these years, I can still make her blush.

"Oh, Arthur, you never change." She turns up the volume on the television and flips until a movie catches her attention.

I study her profile. She's my best friend, the love of my life, and the woman I didn't know I needed to keep me in line. How did I get so lucky?

My gaze drifts to the row of photographs lining the wall and taking up all the space on the bookshelves. Photos of us through the years, with her parents, with her holding herself as a baby, which still makes me chuckle. But the best photographs are of our kids and grandkids. My heart swells with pride at the life we created together and how amazing the journey has been.

Kate never did tell her parents. She spent as much time with them as she could up until the day her dad passed. I held her as she wept the day before and then every night for a month after. We mourned his death together. I lost my friend the day she lost her father. She never regretted stealing those final moments with him, even though he didn't know her role in his life.

When Nora and little Kate moved away, we kept in touch, but time and distance, like everything else, pushes people in different directions. We often spoke about checking on Nora and little Kate, but we knew their lives were on a set path and wanted to give them their memories together. So, we focused on our own blossoming family and left the future in the past.

Kate pulls the phone out again and glances at the time. She heaves a sigh and sips her cocoa.

"Shall we retire?" I rest my hand on her thigh.

She stares at me over her silver rimmed glasses and shakes her head. "You're still a randy old goat."

"Your magic still works on me, love." I grin, but it softens when I see the concern in her eyes. "Don't worry about her. It'll work out."

"I know." Unlocking her phone, Kate pulls up the directory. Before I can stop her, she's hit the call button.

"Kate." I reach for the phone, but she jerks it away. My voice softens. "Let it go, sweetheart."

The phone rings a few more times. Kate's eyes fill with tears.

"You already know how this story ends." I take her hand and kiss her fingertips.

She sobs and ends the call, tossing the phone aside. I gather her into my arms and hold her against me.

"I love you, Kate."

"I love you too, Arthur."

"Thanks for the memories." I kiss her tenderly. "And the spoilers."

"Let's text the kids and go to bed."

I slide my hand over her hip and squeeze her backside. "Good idea. I've got plans for you, sweetheart."

Outside in the streets, the city erupts into celebration as the new year arrives right on time.

PLAYLIST

"Bad Medicine" - Bon Jovi
"Can't Fight This Feeling" - REO Speedwagon
"Cold as Ice" - Foreigner
"That's All" - Genesis
"Livin' on a Prayer" - Bon Jovi
"Keep on Loving You" - REO Speedwagon
"I Hate Myself for Loving You" - Joan Jett & the Heartbreakers
"Dr. Feelgood" - Motley Crue
"I Won't Back Down" - Tom Petty
"You Might Think" - The Cars
"Lights" - Journey

CHAPTER 1

Marcy

Manhattan, NYC 1985

I hate weddings.

That's the first thought I had when my brother told me he was getting married. I love Arthur and Kate, but the thought of helping to plan a wedding and being an active participant in the whole event leaves my skin crawling.

I tried it once, the whole marriage thing. It's bogus. I'd rather use my toothbrush to clean the bathrooms in Grand Central than tie the knot again.

But this isn't about what I want. This is about my brother finding the love of his life across time itself. I don't know how much of Kate's story I believe. I mean, it's pretty hard to swallow the yarn she told me.

From the future? Yeah, sure. Whatever.

But she makes my brother happy, and she's pretty awesome. So I'm not going to rain on their parade.

I slide a tip into the caterer's hand. "Thanks."

"Enjoy your party." He nods and leaves with his crew in tow.

"Did you finish those favors yet?" I ask my assistant, Liana, while I inspect the cake.

"Yeah. When did Arthur say Kate would be back?"

"Rob should be bringing her any minute." I glance at the clock. Five to five.

Arthur suggested I throw a small bachelorette party for Kate instead of a bridal shower. I had no idea what it was until he explained. I guess it's a big deal in the future. I don't know. But it gives me an excuse to kick back and relax. Work has been crazy lately, and I'm in desperate need of some downtime.

Besides, Kate doesn't have a lot of friends. And that resonates deep. I remember a time when I had no one but Arthur looking out for me. Well, Rob was there too, in a way offering support, especially that night…

I shake my head at the direction of my thoughts. I will not think about that night or my brother's best friend. Not now. Not ever.

We put the finishing touches on the decorations. The moment the door opens, Liana pops the champagne.

Kate jumps and laughs, her eyes wide as she enters Arthur's penthouse. "Marcy." She puts her hands on her hips. "Did your brother put you up to this?"

I wrap my arm around her waist and lead her into the living room I converted into our party oasis. "He may have mentioned it in passing."

"Thank you." Kate takes a champagne flute from Liana.

"You've given us a reason to celebrate." I wink and take the offered glass from Donna. "I never thought I'd see Arthur delirious in love."

"To love then." Kate lifts her glass. The small group of women around us cheer in agreement and drink.

I can't toast to that. I won't. Love ruined me. My hand trembles as I bring the glass to my lips.

A shadow flickers by the door.

Rob stands in the entryway, leaning against the doorframe, his blue eyes narrowed on me. His dark blond hair is short enough to keep it out of his eyes but long enough to run fingers through it. From a distance, he's the perfect image of a medical professional. But I've seen him up close and personal.

That man is a hazard to my health.

While Kate is distracted by the small buffet and animated conversation, I cross the room, bracing for an oncoming storm with Rob.

"Thanks for bringing Kate." I gesture to the door. "You can go now."

A lopsided smile transforms his face from serious to amused, and he presses his hand to his heart. "That eager to kick me out? I'm hurt."

"You're so dramatic. Don't you have somewhere to be?"

"Arthur hasn't even left work." He straightens, and I'm reminded of the staggering height difference between us. He looks down at me. "Why do you hate me, Marcy?"

"I don't hate you." A lump lodges in my throat and I swallow it. "I just don't have time for playboys."

Rob scoffs. "I'm not a playboy."

"Whatever. Now shoo. This party doesn't include you." I press my hand against his chest, urging him back toward the door. He's like a brick wall beneath my hand. I ignore the way his body flexes beneath my touch.

"Fine. We'll be at the bar, then crash at my place." He collides with the wall by the door and rests his hand on the knob. "Enjoy your evening."

The moment the door closes behind him, relief and regret simultaneously slam into me. Why does he make me feel this way—twisted up and confused to the point I can't think clearly? I know there's sexual tension between us, but exploring it is not an option. Period.

I return to the party. The half dozen ladies I've gathered to celebrate Kate's status as bride-to-be are ready for food and booze. By the time we cut the cake, the tension between Rob and me has lessened to a nagging pinprick in the back of my mind.

Kate curls up on the couch beside me, balancing her plate in one hand and stabbing bits of cake with a fork. "Thanks for the party, Marcy. You didn't have to do this."

I wave my hand. "Don't worry about it. I like the idea of this much more than a stuffy, boring bridal shower."

"The only thing missing is some strippers." Kate laughs and stuffs a bite of cake in her mouth.

"Strippers?" I gawk at her before chuckling. "Why didn't I think of that?" My voice drops low so only she can hear me. "Is that a big thing in the future?"

She nods adamantly.

"The future sounds like a wild trip."

Kate's mood sobers, her eyes glistening with tears. "It's...different."

My heart goes out to her. I have no frame of reference for the emotions she must be feeling—torn from her life and thrown into the past. It must be terrifying and heartbreaking. She doesn't offer any details, but she doesn't have to. Arthur's told me enough to know she felt like an outsider in her own time.

I wrap my arm around her and pull her against me. She leans her head on my shoulder. We've all felt that way at some point, and even though she can't talk about it, I want her to know I'm here if she needs me.

"So what's going on with you and Rob?"

Well, that shatters the heartwarming moment. Kate sits up, her gaze curious when it fixes on me.

"Nothing. Why?" I sip my drink and focus on a streamer hanging on the far wall.

"Come on. I may have been here less than six months, but I'm not blind. You two have some kind of *thing* going on."

"We most certainly do not have a *thing*," I growl. "He's my brother's best friend. That's it."

"Really?" She looks unconvinced.

"Look, it's simple. The only thing we have in common is Arthur. That's it. There is nothing between us."

"Would you want something?"

"With Rob?" I scoff. "Not in a million years."

"Why?" Kate's question is like a blade through my heart. "He's a nice guy. I think you two would make a great couple."

"I just don't look at him that way."

"Why not? He looks at you like he wants to—"

"It's complicated," I snap.

Hurt fills her eyes at my harsh response.

I sigh and take her hand. "Let's not talk about this non-existent thing between Rob and me."

"I just want to see you as happy as Arthur and me." She squeezes my hand. "You deserve to be happy, Marcy."

She knows the truth of my messy past; she's just too kind to bring it up. I'm sure Arthur has filled her in on the details of my failed marriage and my subsequent struggle. How I refused to take his money and clawed my way up from the ground to reach this point. Arthur walked beside me the whole way, but I wouldn't let him help me.

It was something I had to do myself. To prove I am strong enough to overcome what that bastard did to me.

"Thanks, sugar." I kiss her cheek. "Let's focus on you for now. In a week, you'll be married and off on your honeymoon."

"It's so exciting." Joy fills her eyes at the reminder.

"Have you picked a destination yet?"

"Italy. He's promised to show me Rome, Venice, Florence, and Milan. A whirlwind tour of the country over two weeks."

Jealousy rears its head. Not over the trip to Italy. I could buy a ticket and spend a year roaming the country with the funds I have tucked away. No, it's not the destination causing me pain; it's that she'll have Arthur by her side for the adventure. They'll share the experience, and it'll be a memory they carry into their golden years together. I can't help but envy that.

"Nona would be so proud." I beam at her, swallowing the sting of my own disappointment. "Be sure to take plenty of pictures."

"I wish I had my iPhone. This film stuff is so old-school." Kate claps her hand over her mouth. "Forget I said that."

"Oh, honey, if I don't recognize something you say, I block it out." I wink. "At some point, I'll figure it all out, but I don't need to know the future. The present is enough of a challenge."

"That's true." Kate leans back against the couch. "If there's no stripper, then what do you have planned for us?"

"Well, I have two options. Games or gossip," I tell the group as the guests gather around us. "What'll it be?"

"You work with the hottest celebrities on a daily basis," Kate's coworker, Gladys, says with a glint in her eyes. "Let's gossip."

"What about both?" Kate asks, sitting up. "Marcy can name a celebrity, and we'll ask her yes-or-no questions. If it's yes, she drinks. If it's no, we drink."

"Sounds like a dangerous game but I'm in." Liana settles a chair nearby and fills her wine glass.

While the other women scramble to fill their glasses, I prepare myself mentally for this game. Normally, I wouldn't encourage gossip about my clients. But these ladies know me well enough to keep it within the bounds of my established rules. I may work in an industry that allows me to rub shoulders with the elite of New York City, but I'm certainly not a snitch or a sellout.

"Here is the only rule." My gaze skims over the five guests and the bride-to-be. "I reserve the right to not answer a question if it crosses the line of client confidentiality, but I'll entertain all questions before making that decision. Deal?"

"Deal," they chime in unison.

"All right, Kate. You pick the first celebrity."

"Jon Bon Jovi." Her eyes sparkle. "Is his hair as soft as it looks?"

With a wicked grin, I salute her and take a drink. The ladies cheer my confirmation.

The evening continues with laughter and scandalous revelations about our favorite celebrities. Since I found success as a stylist to the stars, my view of celebrity culture has changed. I see them as people first, not commodities. Not all of them are pleasant, but for every asshole, there are ten who treat me with respect and courtesy.

I've spent a lot of time building my reputation as the top stylist in the city. It doesn't put me in the spotlight like being an actor would, but it's my passion and I'm proud of my accomplishments.

By the end of the night, I'm pleasantly exhausted. I'm not as young as my mind thinks I am, and these late nights take their toll. I'm closing in on forty. That alone terrifies me. The last thing I want is to wake up at seventy with regrets. Maybe I should start figuring out what I want to do outside of my established empire.

In one week, my brother will be married to a wonderful woman, and I'll be on my own again.

That's not true. My family will expand with Kate's presence. I just can't help but feel the gaping hole in my chest expanding.

Why should I need a man? I've done just fine without one. The last thing I need is another asshole barging into my life, ruining my hard work, and stealing my thunder before beating me unconscious.

To hell with marriage and men.

After Arthur and Kate's wedding next week, I'll wash my hands of the whole institution.

CHAPTER 2

Rob

There isn't a woman alive who gets under my skin like Marcy Maxwell.

The warm spring air intensifies the heat simmering in my veins. As I make my way across town, my mind wars with my body.

How can one woman be both the bane of my existence and the object of all my fantasies?

I grab the subway heading toward Hell's Kitchen. It's a lovely day, and I should take the opportunity to walk through Central Park. It would burn off this thrumming need threatening to tear me apart. But I promised I'd meet Arthur at six.

It's already twenty after five. Shit.

After fighting the work rush, I manage to find a spot on the subway. The crush of people does nothing to quell the heat. It's going to be a hot summer if this is any indicator. Heat inevitably leads to more work for me.

Arthur has told me countless times to give up the grind of the emergency room and start my own practice. But I can't. There's something about triage medicine—the rush of adrenaline in saving someone's life—that brings my purpose on this rock into focus.

Granted, Arthur uses me as his own personal physician 90 percent of the time. Like the whole fiasco with him knocking Kate unconscious and refusing to take her to the hospital. In that specific case, I understood. Her situation was unique. I wouldn't have wanted to explain it to the boss. Sometimes, bureaucracy gets in the way. I won't turn down help for someone who needs it, regardless of whether they're in my ER or on the street.

The subway reaches my stop, and I make my way out of the station, desperate for some fresh air. Sunny blue skies stretch overhead, but I'm focused on weaving through the crowded sidewalks.

Today's the first day I've had off in two weeks. I took Kate to finalize a few last-minute wedding arrangements at Arthur's request, and

Marcy wanted to surprise her with a bachelorette party, whatever the hell that is. I thought women were supposed to have bridal showers? Not that it matters. Any excuse to see Marcy is worth it.

By the time I reach the Black Penny, it's after six. There's a decent gathering already. The dockhands often stop to grab a drink before heading home.

Claude appears when I slide onto a bench at the bar. He's already pouring gin over ice with his one hand. "The usual, Rob?"

"Yeah." I admire his ability to navigate the bar with one arm. Well, one hand really. We've been coming to the Black Penny for years. Claude took it over from his grandfather after he came back from Vietnam. Amputation of the left proximal radial and ulna can take a toll on anyone. But he's adapted. He never talks about it or his time in Vietnam. We never ask, although it does pique my medical curiosity.

He places my gin and tonic on a napkin and slides it toward me. I place a twenty on the bar. "I'm paying tonight, got it? Don't let Arthur tell you otherwise."

"No problem." Claude's gaze flickers to a spot over my shoulder as his hand closes around the bill.

"Don't let me do what?" Arthur materializes behind me.

I jump and press a hand to my heart. "Fuck, Arthur, why do you have to sneak up on me like that?"

"I didn't sneak up on you. You're distracted." He takes the stool next to mine. "Scotch, neat."

Claude's already placed the drink in front of him. "Just flag me down when you need a refill." He crosses to the opposite end of the bar.

"Kate surprised at her party?" Arthur lifts the drink and inhales deeply before indulging.

"Yeah." I chuckle at the memory of Kate's expression, but it's immediately replaced by a vision of Marcy's fury. "Your sister did good."

"Glad to hear it." He sets the glass down.

"Your sister hates me." The words spill from my mouth. I'd blame the gin, but I've barely ingested any.

"She doesn't hate you." Arthur glances at me, his eyes dark. "She doesn't like men in general. Can you blame her?"

"No. But after twenty years, you'd think she'd warm up to me." I scoff. "It'd be nice not to have my head bitten off every time I try to talk to her. I'm not like her asshole ex."

"I know." He claps his hand on my shoulder. "Don't take it personally."

"I don't." Yes, I do. Every fucking time. It's exhausting.

"Good."

Several tense moments pass, and I wash thoughts of Marcy down with my gin. Claude returns with a bowl of pretzels. I grab one and nibble on it. I should order something to eat, but my stomach is twisted in knots.

"Are you ready for the wedding?" I watch Arthur's profile.

"Ready as I'll ever be. I never imagined I would get married." He shakes his head and laughs. "Especially not to a girl from the future."

"Yeah, I still have a hard time figuring out the logistics of that." I chuckle. "But she's good for you. I'm glad you found someone who'll deal with your grumpy ass."

Arthur straightens. "I'm not grumpy."

"Whatever you say."

"I'm not."

Claude reappears, and I seize the opportunity. "Claude, is Arthur grumpy?"

The bartender's expression remains neutral as his gaze drifts between us. "Don't drag me into this. I'm here to serve drinks, not mediate your petty bullshit."

I frown. "You're no fun."

Claude shrugs and retreats to the far end of the bar.

"He knows us too well." Arthur smirks before finishing the last of his scotch. "I booked the flight to Rome. We leave the day after the wedding."

"I'm jealous, man. I've always wanted to see Italy."

"So go. Nothing's stopping you."

"That's not the point. You have someone to share it with."

Arthur sighs and pivots to face me. "So find someone and go."

"You say that like it's the easiest thing in the world."

"If you'd stop mooning over my sister, you'd find someone."

I choke on my gin. "I'm not mooning over Marcy."

"Yes, you are. You have been for years. It's fucking exhausting—you two go back and forth like two stray cats. Admit it, she's not interested. You should move on."

But I don't want to. The words echo in my mind. I finish the gin and slide the glass away. "Point taken."

"Oh, speaking of my sister, she'll be staying at the penthouse while we're away. Kate insisted on getting a cat, and Marcy offered to keep an eye on her." He pauses, tapping the glass on the bar. "I told her to call you if she has any issues."

"Thanks. That'll help me move on." I groan and rest my head on the table.

"You're welcome."

Claude appears and refills our glasses. The conversation shifts to more neutral topics, mostly work and snatches of gossip about our mutual friends. I enjoy spending time with Arthur when he's not breaking my balls. But I can hand it right back to him.

Right now, though, I don't. He's getting married, and we're celebrating. I'm happy for him and Kate. They deserve each other. I couldn't have envisioned a better match.

The longer we sit at the bar, the more we drink. Claude cuts us off at ten o'clock and starts pushing water in our direction. By the time midnight rolls around, we're drunk and carefree, but not completely wasted.

Claude kicks us out shortly after midnight.

A black town car appears, and Cyril steps from the driver's seat. He opens the back door, and with a disapproving shake of his head over our state of intoxication, he nudges us into the car.

Thirty minutes later, we arrive at our building. Arthur lives in the penthouse, and I'm in one of the smaller apartments several floors below. It's convenient, living near my best friend. But it's also a curse.

As we enter the building, we pass a gaggle of women. Arthur returns to Cyril for a hushed conversation as I stand with the door open, like a gentleman.

Then I see her. Marcy. The only woman in this world who I crave. Her eyes flash bright beneath the streetlight overhead, and her lips purse when she sees me. The rest of the women pass by, leaving me to face her alone.

"I trust you had a lovely evening?"

Marcy faces me. "It was illuminating."

"What does one do at a bachelorette party?" I muse, my voice swaying from the effects of the gin.

"Drink. Gossip. Play games. Watch men strip and throw money at them."

"What?" My eyes widen. Surely I misheard her.

"Looks like indulging in half-naked men before you're married is all the rage in the future."

"But why?"

"I guess girls just want to have fun." She brushes past me.

"Marcy…" My voice trails off when she stops and turns.

She props her hand on her hip, and the neon glow of her top catches the streetlight, making her shine.

"What, Rob?" She snaps her gum.

"Nothing." I shake my head. "Sleep well."

With a scoff, she walks away. Arthur helps her into the car along with the other women. Cyril casts a pleading look my way before rounding the car and getting in the driver's seat.

"You're having him drive them home?" I ask Arthur when he joins me.

"Of course. I pay him well enough. He'll be fine."

I follow Arthur to the elevator and press the button for my floor. He presses his. Silence descends in the car as it rises.

"Thanks for tonight," Arthur says as the elevator comes to a stop on my floor.

"Of course." I exit and turn, saluting him. "Go home to your wife."

A smile tugs at his lips. "With pleasure."

The doors slide closed.

When I open my apartment, the soft glow of the lamp next to the sofa lights the room. It's small but tidy. I don't spend all of my money on a lavish place. I rarely sleep here. It fits my needs.

With a groan, I head for the shower. I let the warm spray soothe me as I lean against the wall. Thoughts of Marcy flood my brain. Why does she plague me? I'd give anything to purge her from my soul, to find someone who actually likes me…wants me.

My cock hardens at the memory of her pink lips and her glow under the streetlight. I take it in my hand and stroke until I'm consumed by nothing but her, by the pleasure lying just out of reach. Panting breaths echo off the tiles. When I come, I imagine her face. Her body. Marcy.

Fuck. I'm a goddamn lost cause.

After drying off and brushing my teeth, I collapse in bed, then stare at the ceiling. I have to work at eight a.m., but sleep eludes me. I'm wrapped up in her. I can't keep fighting this pull.

But how can I convince someone of something when they're dead set against it?

I roll to my side, and the sheet slides low on my hips. Shit, how am I hard again?

Somehow, I have to convince her of the truth. I love her, and I've loved her for years. But how the fuck do I show her?

Convincing her of anything is like walking on broken glass. But I'll gladly do it if it gives me the chance to make her mine.

CHAPTER 3

Marcy

Come Monday morning, it's business as usual. Stale cigarette smoke and expensive perfume cling to the air when I walk into the studio. I wave to the crew as I weave through the equipment. My staff will arrive any minute with the garment racks and accessories.

The manager points me to the area they've set aside for costumes and styling. The makeup artists and hairstylists have already arrived and greet me with air-kisses. We've worked together on projects in the past. At this point in my career, I know most of the major players in the industry with roots in the city.

"How was your weekend?" I ask when my reliable employees arrive with the covered garment racks.

"Totally rad," Trixie gushes. She's a whiz when it comes to hair. "Hit a party on the Upper East Side. What about you?"

"Oh, yeah. Me too. It was an intimate get-together though. Very exclusive."

Liana catches my eye and hides a grin behind her hand. We're very selective about the information we share within the industry. Too much propensity for gossip. I like to keep my personal details under wraps, so I cultivate a persona that fits the bill. My girls know this and support it 100 percent.

"Bitchin'." Kit, the makeup artist, slides from her seat by the window and stubs out her cigarette. "Did they tell you who we're styling today?"

"A couple of new artists for an MTV slot and an actor from that show everyone's raving about."

"Vic Simmons." Trixie swoons dramatically. "He's so choice."

I snap my gum and shrug. "Never heard of him."

"Seriously?" Liana gawks at me. "You've watched that detective show he was in—"

She snaps her mouth shut at my stern look. I peel the cover off the rack and skim through the clothing selection I packed yesterday.

"Oh, that's him? Huh." I play it off while Liana positions the other racks along the wall.

"That role as the brooding detective set him up. He's hot stuff now." Kit pops her gum and fixes her hair in the mirror. She readjusts her crop top, ensuring her breasts are at their most visible. "I heard he's single. Dumped that actress he was with last month."

"Really?" Trixie perks up. "Dibs."

"You can't call dibs," Kit snaps. "All's fair in love and war, honey."

Trixie sticks out her tongue and then applies a generous gloss to her already pouty lips.

These two are ten years younger than me, and they act it. They have no idea what a steady relationship is, judging from the banter I regularly hear. Not that I hold it against them. Truth is I'm jealous. I wish I had spent my twenties having fun and hitting on every guy who crossed my path. Unfortunately, most of that decade of my life was spent hidden in a small apartment afraid I'd end up in the ER because I'd made him mad. Again.

I shake the thoughts away. No. He doesn't warrant a moment of my time. The past is gone, and I'm not going to give another man that kind of power over me. Ever.

"Isn't he in his forties?" Liana asks. "I didn't know you guys liked older men."

"It's Vic. He's hot for an old guy." Trixie tugs her pink-and-gray ripped tee shirt to the side, exposing her shoulder.

I bite my tongue. They're only after the sex and the status. They don't care about the nitty-gritty details of a relationship.

Oh, to be young and carefree again.

A knock at the door interrupts us. The stage manager pops his head inside. "Ready when you are."

"Bring them in." I nod and take charge. Trixie and Kit ready their stations while Liana and Donna organize the rest of the clothing.

Three gorgeous women enter the room. They all look vaguely familiar. But then again, everyone does in this industry. I've worked with them before, but they don't acknowledge the prior connection. They see so many stylists throughout the course of their careers. I don't take it personally when they're so distracted they forget they've met me. In this industry, we're just the magicians behind the scenes. And even though we don't get the recognition we deserve on camera, the studio knows exactly who they want working for them. After a quick greeting, we launch into action. Time to make some magic.

We rotate stations—one with hair, one with makeup, while we dress the third. It's fluid and effortless.

I live for this job. It's my only love. Style. Fashion. But most of all, I love the control. Being my own boss. No one questions my taste…not anymore. I've worked for heads of state and Hollywood's elite. Nothing surprises me at this stage of the game, and best of all, they trust my judgment when it comes to wardrobe.

When I've finished the second artist's look, the manager appears in the doorway. "Marcy, Mr. Simmons is ready for you."

Kit and Trixie glance up simultaneously to meet my gaze in the mirror.

"I'll be there in a moment." Once he disappears, I gather the garments I set aside for him and motion for Liana to join me. "Donna, finish up here." I glance at Trixie and Kit. "I'll send him over when I'm done."

Their expressions fluctuate between jealousy and disbelief. I almost make a sexual innuendo, but I refrain. I don't need gossip to spread that I've set my sights on a client. I certainly don't mix business with pleasure. No matter how tempting it might be.

Liana grabs the garments in my hand and follows as we step from the dressing room. The manager leads us to a room down the hall and leaves us.

I knock on the door. "Mr. Simmons?"

"Come in." A deep voice echoes within.

When I enter, my whole body ceases to function. Mr. Simmons is standing in only a robe, his dark hair tousled, his blue eyes sparkling, and his lips curved in a tempting grin. Shit. He's even more handsome in person than on TV.

Somehow, I manage to regain control of my brain and my limbs. "Good morning. I'm Marcy, this is Liana. I'm your stylist for the day."

"Lovely." His gaze rakes over me, and I can't stop the heat from rising in my face.

I turn and take the garments from Liana's arm. Keeping my back to him, I hang them on a hook behind the door. With a deep breath, I face him once more. My gaze lingers on his broad shoulders as I take in his form, estimating measurements.

"We'll go with the navy blue. It'll bring out his eyes, and the fit should be perfect." I gesture for Liana to prepare the suit. "Now, Mr. Simm—"

"Vic." His deep voice rumbles through me. "Call me Vic."

"If you insist." I clear my throat. "Vic, do you have an undershirt?"

He tugs the hem of the robe aside to reveal only bare skin beneath the fabric. "Never wear one."

"I see." My heart pounds in my chest and I struggle to ignore the allure of this man. "Well, in that case, we'll go with a darker shirt. I think the black will work, don't you, Liana?"

"Yes." She frowns as she skims through the bag. "It must be on the rack. I'll go get it."

"Perfect. Thank you."

Liana steps out of the room, leaving the door cracked, and the earlier tension transforms into a physical presence.

Vic patiently stands at a reasonable distance, yet I feel claustrophobic. It's not a bad feeling, but it's one I've purposely avoided for years.

"Here…" I pull the pants from the hanger and cross to where he's standing. "Put these on. I'm pretty sure they'll fit like a glove."

Vic's gaze doesn't waver as he pulls the robe off his shoulders. There's only a tempting expanse of skin dusted with hair and an intoxicating scent of his aftershave. He drapes the robe over the chair and takes the pants from me. My gaze dips to his waist. I stifle a moan at the sight of his muscular thighs and the briefs gripping his hipbones, barely containing his obvious arousal.

I avert my gaze as he draws the pants up and fixes them around his waist.

"They fit perfectly." He grins. "You've got a good eye."

"What can I say? I'm good at my job." I snap my gum.

"You certainly are."

I don't miss the glint of hunger in his eyes. Why did I send Liana for that shirt? I know better than to break my own rule—never remain alone with a client, male or female. It leaves too much room for unwanted drama. I've seen too much shit that could have been avoided if there were witnesses.

And yet here I am. Alone with a client who obviously sees something he likes.

As if summoned by my thoughts, Liana opens the door. "Found it."

"Thank you." I gesture to Vic. "If you'll give him that, I'll get the tie and jacket."

Taking a moment to regain my composure, I pull the jacket and tie off the hanger. When I turn, my mouth waters at the sight of Vic shrouded in dark colors, molded to his body like a second skin. It should be illegal for him to look that good.

I pass the jacket to Liana and hold up the tie. "Can you handle this part?"

He scoffs and grabs the silk tie from my hand. The fabric slides between my fingers, making me shiver.

My mind wanders as he loops it around his neck, beneath his collar. He works quickly, tying it in a perfect Windsor knot. All without glancing in the mirror or breaking eye contact.

"How does it look?"

"Fantastic," Liana says with awe. "You're a magician."

Vic laughs. "No. I had a lot of practice tying them on set. I didn't have gorgeous stylists to help me then."

Liana's face turns pink. She hands me the jacket. I hold it open. He turns and places his arms in the sleeves. It slides over his shoulders and settles into place, perfectly framing his body. I suppress a shiver caused by the heat building between us and step away.

"Magic." He meets my gaze. "Thank you, Marcy."

"Any time." I drop my hands to my sides. "I'll have hair and makeup come to your room in a moment."

Liana gathers the remaining items and opens the door. I'm half in the hallway when his voice stops me.

"See you around."

I meet his gaze, and my pulse flutters at the sincerity on his face. With a smile, I close the door behind me, cutting him from my view.

Liana nudges me with her elbow. "Was he flirting with you?"

"Yeah." I shrug like it doesn't matter, but inside, my body's humming. I've had clients flirt with me before. Senators, actors, musicians, talk show hosts—you name it, they've hit on me.

But it's never affected me the way Vic's flirting has. He's all charm, the way Dan used to be. It's a red flag, and I know better than to get involved with a client. That's a one-way ticket to disaster.

"Why didn't you flirt back?" she asks, keeping her voice low.

"Because I don't fool around with celebrities. And I certainly don't date clients." I pin her with a knowing look. "You've worked for me long enough to know this. I don't mix business with pleasure."

"I know." She pouts. "But he looked like he wanted to throw you over his shoulder and find the nearest bedroom."

I chuckle. "You don't need a bedroom…just a door with a lock."

"That's true."

I open the door to the main dressing room. Kit and Trixie spin around expectantly, then frown when it's only me. "Mr. Simmons is waiting for you both in his dressing room."

"Finally." Trixie grabs her gear and heads for the door. Kit follows close behind.

I shake my head and focus on the young woman Donna is dressing in a long shimmery dress.

As we finalize her look, my mind wanders to Vic.

It's not like I haven't been interested in any men. I am. But I'm not interested in anything more than a one-night stand. That doesn't work well in this industry. And the one man I'd even consider breaking my longstanding rule for…well, he's not even an option. Vic isn't Rob. No one is.

My brother's best friend is completely off-limits. Rob deserves a woman who will give him everything he's always wanted. And I can't give him that.

I'm broken and jaded. No one wants the *real* me.

CHAPTER 4

Rob

It must be a full moon. The ER is crammed to full capacity. It's even busier than usual for a Friday afternoon. I've only been on the clock for four hours, and I'm already exhausted. The bustle of commotion around me leaves me in an adrenaline-induced haze.

On days like today, I'm actually thankful for the activity—keeps my mind off the rehearsal dinner tonight and my best friend's wedding tomorrow.

But it doesn't block the ever-present thoughts of Marcy. Shit.

Summer, one of the nurses on duty, rushes up to me with a chart in her hand. "Dr. Thompson, I need your assistance in exam two."

"What do we have?" I take the chart and flip through it.

"Female. Mid-twenties. Came in complaining of stabbing pain in her abdomen." She rushes on before I can ask any standard questions. "She has bruising."

I glance up from the chart. "On the abdomen?"

"Yes, but that's not where it concerns me." Summer lowers her voice. "She has a black eye and swelling on her left cheek and along the jaw."

"You asked her what happened?"

"Yes. She says she tripped over the mop bucket in the kitchen and hit the counter when she fell." Summer doesn't seem convinced by this story, and neither am I.

"Does she have anyone with her?"

"Her husband." Summer shifts her weight from one foot to the other. "He refuses to step outside so we can speak to her alone."

"Shit." I rake my fingers through my hair. "Okay. I'll take a look."

The unknown variables play in my mind as I head for the exam room, Summer following. She takes her place by my side in the curtained area. The woman on the gurney glances up. The left side of her face is swollen and purple, exactly how Summer described. She's clutching her side, just over the liver. Fuck.

The man beside her hovers, his arms folded across his chest. He doesn't look the part, but you don't have to look like a bully to beat the shit out of someone. Flashbacks to the night Marcy left her ex flood back in a rush. The bruises, the cuts, the blood. I shove the memories away and focus on the patient in front of me.

"Hello, I'm Dr. Thompson." I offer a friendly smile. The man grunts when I sit on the chair beside the bed. I ignore him and focus solely on the patient. "What's your name?"

"Grace."

"What's going on, Grace?"

"I fell. In the kitchen." The woman's voice is strong, but her hands tremble. "My side hurts. Feels like something's broken."

"Do you mind if I take a look?" I hand the chart to Summer and gesture to Grace's side.

Her gaze shifts from me to the man beside her. He nods. Fury shoots through me, but I maintain calm. I don't want to escalate this situation. Confrontation in an emergency room isn't uncommon, but it's highly disruptive. I try to avoid it if I can.

She moves her hands and I gently palpate the area. She winces at the pressure and fists her hands in the sheets. Her face pales, and she bites her lip to suppress cries of pain. Poor kid. I inspect the area thoroughly before leaning back to give her space once more.

"There's definitely something going on here. But before I make a definitive diagnosis, I'd like to get a CAT scan of the area to get a better idea of the possible damage."

"A CAT scan?" The man huffs. "Is that necessary?"

"I need to be sure there's nothing broken and her liver isn't damaged or hemorrhaging. It could just be inflammation, but I need to be sure before settling on a course of action to treat it." I turn my attention back to Grace, who looks terrified. "Do I have your permission to get a CAT scan?"

She glances at *him* again. I clench my hands into fists and take a deep breath. I want to kick his ass out of the room, but if I do, he'll surely throw a fit and lash out. No, I have to play this with finesse.

Reluctantly, the asshole nods.

Grace breathes a sigh of relief. "Yes, please, it hurts terribly."

"Don't worry, Grace. We'll give you something for the pain and have you right as rain in no time." My reassuring smile seems to ease her discomfort.

I turn to her husband. "Sir, if you'll step into the waiting room, I'm going to need you to take care of some paperwork while your wife is in having the scan done."

"She can't go alone. I have to be with her." His agitation is growing. "She needs me."

"Sir, it will only be a few moments. As soon as she's done, we'll bring you right back here," I assure him. But I wish I were lying. I have no legal recourse to keep them separated. My hands are tied for the moment.

"Fine." He steps aside as two nurses come in to wheel the gurney from the room. Summer guides the agitated husband to the front desk while I follow the patient down the hall toward radiology.

The moment we pass through the doors. Grace bursts into tears. She grips her side.

"It's okay, Grace. We'll get you fixed up in a jiffy."

She shakes her head, and the tears continue.

"Grace, I'm going to ask you some questions. I'd like you to answer them as honestly as possible."

Her wide green eyes are full of tears. She hiccups, then gives me a tiny nod.

"Good girl." I keep my voice low. "Do you feel safe at home?"

A fresh round of tears bursts forth. "I can't…I can't answer that."

"Sweetheart, if you're not safe and need an advocate, now is your chance. I'll do everything in my power to help you."

"I can't talk about it." She whimpers between sobs. "He'll…I can't." She hides her face with her hands. The force of crying makes her moan with pain.

"Shh, it'll be okay, Grace. I understand." Regret stabs me. Too many times I've been in this position, and there's not a damn thing I can do. I can't help her if she doesn't want my help. If I step in without her consent, she'll catch hell when they're alone again. It's a twisted situation, and I'm not mentally prepared for the onslaught of past emotions rising to the surface. I shove them aside and focus on my patient.

We reach radiology. I ask to the nurse wheeling the gurney to retrieve some medication from the pharmacy. The CAT scan tech appears by my side. I give him instructions and request a female tech to come on board with this particular patient. I want her to feel safe. Having that extra layer of protection isn't because I don't trust the tech. It's because she's vulnerable, and damn it, she deserves a moment of peace.

The two technicians take her into the room.

I lean against the counter at the nurse's station and take a breath.

All I can do now is pray the CAT scan comes back clear. It could be broken ribs, a lacerated liver, hemorrhage, or a dozen other issues. I can't be sure of anything until I get a look at what's going on inside her. But I sure as hell know what's going on outside.

That fucker raised his hand to her. He put those bruises there. I can tell by the way she looked to him for answers to every question. She waited for his approval before agreeing to anything.

This is a classic case of domestic abuse.

And there's not a goddamn thing I can do about it. The pencil in my hand snaps in two.

I wait until the CAT scan is done and escort Grace back to the ER. There are a half dozen patients waiting for me, but I can't leave her. Not until I'm sure it's not life-threatening.

When we reach the exam room, he's waiting for us. Grace blanches at the sight of him and drops her gaze to her hands. I instruct the nurse to give her the pain meds. I ask a series of questions about her medical and family history. By the time I finish, the tech arrives with the CAT scan report. I review the results with a critical eye.

Nothing. Relief fills me. Her liver is enflamed, but there's nothing concerning on the scan. I explain this to her, and with a sigh, she relaxes against the pillow.

I give her instructions to follow and a scrip for medication to bring down the inflammation. "Now remember, if the pain persists or increases, I want you to come right back here. Okay?"

"Yes, Doctor."

My gaze drifts to her husband, whose eagle eyes are narrowed on me. I meet his glare with one of my own, one that clearly states I know exactly what he did to his wife and I will not tolerate it happening again. Telepathy doesn't work, but I think he gets the point.

The asshole shifts his weight uncomfortably. "Can we go?"

"Yes." I glance at Grace. "Take care of yourself."

"Thank you, Doctor." Her tentative smile pierces my conscience. Before I make a fool of myself, I exit the exam room.

The rest of my shift passes in a blur of activity. I don't have a chance to dwell on what happened with Grace or the horror it dredged up from my past. I couldn't protect Marcy, and I can't protect Grace. I did the best I could under the circumstances and curse my restraints.

When I finally leave the ER, I'm fucking exhausted. I want to go home and crash. But I can't.

I glance at my watch. I have just enough time to get home, shower, and run out the door again. The rehearsal dinner starts at seven. I don't want to be late. Arthur will kill me.

But I'm in no mood to be sociable. The weight of the day rests heavily on me, like a vice constricting my chest. I can't push it away. The cloud hangs over my head and threatens to unleash hell.

Goddamn it.

Seeing Marcy tonight isn't going to improve my mood.

It should. She's the one bright spot in my life, and I would give anything to spend time with her, even if she hates me. But after the incident in the ER, I'm reminded of just how close I came to losing her. Even though she was never mine to begin with.

I love Marcy. I loved her before she married that asshole. When she showed up on Arthur's doorstep with a suitcase, bleeding and broken, I patched her up. But she wouldn't let me close. I couldn't blame her. Who the fuck would want another relationship after that?

But it didn't curb my feelings for her. It intensified them.

Her resolve and determination after her divorce fed her success. She made something beautiful from the wreckage of her life. I commend her.

When I get home, I manage to throw myself together in a presentable manner and head for the restaurant. It'll be fine. I'll be fine. I'll just bury my disappointment and pain and deal with them later. Tonight is about Arthur and Kate.

The closer I get to the restaurant, the more I want to turn around and go home. I'm in a fucking mood, and I'm afraid everyone is going to see it.

Especially Marcy. And the last thing I want to do is upset her.

CHAPTER 5

Marcy

I don't like this—Rob and I having dinner with Kate and Arthur. It feels too much like a double date.

We're seated at a round table in one of the most prestigious restaurants in the city. The lights are low, and the instrumental music is atmospheric with a whimsical touch of romance. Sitting here watching my brother make calf eyes at the woman of his dreams is making me uncomfortable.

No, actually that part isn't bothering me nearly as much as the undeniably masculine presence to my left. Rob's somber mood radiates off him in waves as he picks at the chicken on his plate. He hasn't spoken more than six words all night. It's not like him.

Kate's outlining the itinerary for their trip to Italy. Since Rob isn't invested in the conversation, I jump in and ask questions. I'm happy for her and Arthur, but I won't lie, I'm a bit jealous of the lovely honeymoon they have planned.

"You've been to Rome, haven't you, Rob?" Kate asks, turning her attention to the brooding beast beside me.

"Once." He sets his fork aside and takes a drink of his wine. "For an international conference."

"Did you get to see any of the historic sites while you were there?" Kate's eyes flash with interest.

"Not really. I think we drove past the Colosseum, but I didn't get to look around."

"That's a shame." Kate pouts. "Arthur's promised to point out all the architectural wonders during our trip." She covers his hand with hers.

I take a drink of my wine to stop a sarcastic comment. *Be happy for them. It's not their fault you're a jaded old woman.*

"You're still able to stay at the apartment and watch the cat, right?" Arthur focuses on me.

"I…uh…well, I don't know if I'll be able to." I shift uncomfortably in my chair. "My schedule changed and I need to be at the studio early.

My apartment is closer to work, so it'll save me some time if I stay at my place. Sorry."

"What about you, Rob?" Kate turns to him. "Would you be willing to stay at the penthouse while we're gone?"

"I probably won't be there much. I'm on call next week." Rob fidgets with the stem of the glass.

"Oh, that's fine. I just want to be sure Tabby's taken care of."

"I mean, I can check on the cat in the evenings, if you want," I add, sensing conflict brewing.

"No, don't go out of your way." Kate beams at Rob. "Tabby's pretty shy anyway. Just feed her twice a day, and you'll have a friend for life."

"I can handle that." Rob's relenting nod doesn't foster confidence.

I search his profile, noting the firm set of his jaw and the crow's-feet at the corners of his eyes. I recognize his body language. He's holding back. Putting on a front. It's as familiar to me as my own reflection. A pinch of sympathy manages to infiltrate to my walled-off heart.

"Are you sure?" Kate asks.

"Positive." A tight smile curves his lips.

"Thank you. You're a lifesaver." Kate shifts the conversation to the wedding, but I'm still fixed on Rob's profile.

He finishes the wine in his glass and sets it aside. His gaze shifts to me, and I see exhaustion in the depths of his kind eyes.

I lean closer. "Rough day at the office?"

"You could say that." He drops his gaze to the half-empty plate on the table.

"Too many nurses to choose from?" I tease. It bothers me when he's in such a somber mood. I miss his smile and poke a little to stir the pot. "Did one of them shoot you down?"

"Damn it, Marcy." He shakes his head and pierces me with a stern look. "Just sitting in your ivory tower judging everyone beneath you doesn't give you the right to make assumptions about my life. Or my job."

"I—"

"You're what? Sorry?" He scoffs. "Save it, all right? I'm not in the mood for your bullshit tonight."

My jaw drops when Rob shoves away from the table and stalks across the room. After he disappears through the archway into the bar, I turn to Kate and Arthur. Their stunned expressions mirror mine.

"What did you say to him?" Arthur narrows his eyes at me.

"Nothing. I…I made a joke…" My voice drifts off when my brother shakes his head.

"After all these years, you just can't ease up, can you?"

Shame settles in the pit of my gut. I drop my hands to my lap. "I didn't mean anything by it."

"You never do." Arthur stands and kisses Kate's forehead. "I'll be right back." He trails after his best friend without another word.

Damn it. I bite my lip and stifle the tears threatening to ruin my mascara.

Kate slides into Rob's seat and rests her hand on mine. "It's okay, hon. I'm sure he's just had a rough day at work. He didn't mean to take it out on you."

"Yeah, he did." I sniff. "I shouldn't have teased him like that. I thought it would make him laugh."

"Has he ever done that before?"

"Never."

"Hmm." Kate pats my hand. "How long have you known Rob?"

"Years." The memories flood my brain. I can still remember the first time I saw him. Young and determined. Handsome as hell. "He was premed at Georgetown, where he met my brother. Arthur brought him home for Christmas. I was seventeen."

I fell in love with him at seventeen, but he wouldn't give me the time of day.

Kate's eyes brighten. "You had a crush on him, didn't you?"

"Maybe a little one." I push aside my rising emotions. "But it vanished quickly. He wasn't interested in anything but studying medicine and chasing older women."

"What happened between you two?"

"Nothing." I straighten up and finish my wine. "He went on to med school, and I got married."

"When did you see Rob again?"

"The night I left my husband." The encounter is vivid in my mind. "Rob and Arthur helped me."

My body ached as I had dragged myself to my brother's doorstep. Arthur's horrified expression when he saw the extent of my injuries is forever seared in my brain. I begged him not to call the cops. But he insisted. I refused to go to the emergency room. So he called Rob.

The cops took my statement while Rob tended to the cuts on my arms and the bruises on my face. He never said a word. I could see how desperately he wanted to ask what happened, but he kept his mouth pressed in a thin line. Cold fury burned in his eyes. Both Rob and Arthur wanted to kill the bastard for what he had done to me. Their argument remains fixed in the darkest part of my psyche.

I push it aside and smile at Kate.

"It's okay, Marcy." Kate hugs me.

It's only then I realize I'm crying. I snatch the napkin and dab my eyes, cursing when the white linen comes away smeared with mascara. "Damn expensive shit should be waterproof."

Kate pulls away. Her tender gaze searches my face. "I'm sorry you had to go through such hell."

"Thanks, hon." I force a smile. "I'm stronger now because of it."

She knows the details of that night. Arthur told her. But even after ten years, I can't talk about it. I don't want to talk about it.

"You always give Rob a hard time." Kate treads carefully with her words. "Do you really hate him?"

Her question lingers, turning over again and again as I inspect it with curiosity. *Do I hate him?* No. But I don't want to examine the other emotions left behind. "No."

"Then why are you so mean to him?"

"Because he irritates me." I exhale sharply.

"Why?"

"I don't know." I twist the napkin in my hands. "He just gets under my skin. I don't like it."

Kate nods, understanding. "Maybe it's about time you two find some common ground. I don't know. Maybe you could be friends."

I scoff. "Rob and I aren't friends. Never will be."

"Why?"

"We have nothing in common."

"How do you know? Have you had a conversation with him that didn't end in one of you getting stitches?" She chuckles.

"No, and I'm not interested in being friends with Rob." It's true. Friendship is the last thing on my mind when it comes to Rob. I want more than that…

Nope, I'm locking that door right now. Not even entertaining those thoughts. I'm done with relationships.

"Then why are you upset that he snapped at you?"

Well, fuck. Isn't that the ultimate question? I toss the napkin on the table. "Because he's never done it before, and I'm worried he might go postal."

Kate's shrewd gaze fixes on me, and I pointedly ignore it.

"Are you going to be okay at the wedding tomorrow?" she asks.

"Yeah." I flag down the waiter and order another glass of wine. "Why wouldn't I be?"

"I know weddings aren't your thing." She beams. "But I'm thrilled to have you as my maid of honor."

"Well, don't expect any sappy speeches from me."

"I won't. I'm just glad you'll be there to celebrate with us."

I click my tongue. "You're lucky I love you and my brother enough to suffer through this."

Kate nudges my shoulder with hers. "I'm beyond lucky."

"Enough with the sentimental stuff—can we order dessert?"

"Yes, please." She bites her lip, hesitating. "Shouldn't we wait for Arthur and Rob?"

"They're on their own. I need some chocolate cake. Stat."

Kate laughs and waves to the waiter. She places the order for our dessert while I nurse my wine.

I should apologize to Rob. He's right; I don't know anything about his life or his job. For years, I've kept such a distance between us, it's hard not to be defensive.

What worries me most is this lingering concern for him. I don't want to think about Rob. I sure as hell don't want to worry about him. But I do.

Fuck. Years of erecting this perfectly structured wall around my heart, and now I'm trying to climb over it for a better view.

Rob and I aren't friends. I doubt we ever will be. If I ever open the door to that possibility, it will only be a matter of time before I find myself falling head over heels for him. Again.

I try to convince myself I never loved Rob. It was just a stupid, silly teenage crush. There was never anything between us, and there never will be.

I'm not interested in anything longer than a one-night stand, and Rob's not that kind of guy. He's a respectable doctor and a compassionate man. We have nothing in common and no future.

The waiter places a decadent piece of chocolate cake on the table in front of me. My mouth waters. It's a temptation, just like Rob. One taste will never be enough.

Ignoring the turmoil churning inside me, I indulge in the cake, knowing *it* won't come back to bite me in the ass.

CHAPTER 6

Rob

Regret hangs over me like a specter as I make my way through the restaurant.

I shouldn't have snapped at Marcy like that. But my restraint was already cracked, and having her beside me put unbearable tension on the weak points. There's no reason for me to take my shitty mood out on my friends. Shit, I'm an asshole.

After the day I've had, seeing her happy and healthy beside me should have infused me with gratitude. Instead, it unleashed a torrent of emotions I hadn't anticipated. Memories of Marcy covered in blood, sobbing in Arthur's arms, her struggle to find herself again after that asshole tore her apart. The rage resurfaced with a vengeance, and I wasn't prepared for the fallout.

Then she looks at me with those intoxicating eyes, and I'm lost. I want nothing more than to kiss her senseless and drag her back to my place. I want to make sure she's loved thoroughly for the rest of her fucking life. She deserves it.

But it doesn't matter. I could be the last man on the planet and Marcy would reject me.

Still doesn't give me the right to bite her head off for teasing. Fury curls like a ball in my chest, pressing on my sternum.

There's an empty spot at the bar. I take it and flag down the bartender. I've already had two glasses of wine. I know better than to compound my misery by dousing it with more alcohol.

"What can I get you?" the bartender asks.

"Tonic water."

He arches his brow in surprise but pours me the drink. My gaze is lost in the small bubbles floating to the top of the glass.

"What the hell was that?" Arthur's admonition echoes behind me.

I turn to face him. He's an angry brick wall.

"It's been a shit day." I offer the lame excuse. Arthur doesn't buy it. We've known each other for too long. He can see right through me.

"Bullshit. I've seen you stressed to the breaking point. You've never taken it out on Marcy. Ever." Arthur keeps his voice low, but it's stern.

Words fail me. I stare into my glass.

"Whatever happened, she didn't deserve that."

"Don't you think I know that?" I growl, causing the man beside us to glance over suspiciously.

Damn it. I stand and move toward the shadowed hallway. Arthur follows. The moment we're alone, he crosses his arms.

"Then what the hell made you snap like that?"

I cradle the drink in one hand. My grip tightens as the earlier confrontation in the ER replays through my mind. "There was a patient today." A dull ache forms at the base of my skull. "A woman. We suspected domestic abuse. But…"

"But she didn't want help." Arthur finishes the thought for me.

I clench my jaw and nod. "The girl was terrified. She was the same age as Marcy when…"

"Rob." Arthur's posture softens, and he rests his hand on my shoulder. "You did the best you could."

"Did I?" My voice cracks. "She wouldn't even answer the questions herself. The bastard stood there, cocky and smug, while I took care of her injuries. The ones *he* caused."

"Do you have any proof he did it?"

"No." I hang my head and collapse against the wall. "And when I got her alone for the CAT scan, she still wouldn't talk."

"I can't imagine working in an environment where you're put in that position." Arthur leans against the wall beside me. "You offered. There's nothing more you could have done."

"I know. It's just…"

"Marcy."

"Yeah." I rub my hand over my face. The image is burned into my brain. Every time a battered woman comes into my hospital, I see Marcy, broken and bleeding.

"The stress is too much, Rob. Maybe you should take a break. Step away from the intensity of working in the emergency room."

"I can't. It's my calling."

"Well, it's killing you. If you keep burning yourself out like this, you're gonna have a heart attack before you reach fifty."

I scoff, but he's right; the burden is overwhelming. "It's all I have, Arthur. It's my life."

"I didn't say give up medicine, but maybe you should consider alternate employment possibilities." He pauses as though pondering those options. "You could easily start your own practice. Keep office hours. Take a vacation once in a while."

Alone? No thanks. While his suggestion makes sense, it would leave me miserable. If I take away my work, the only thing I have is the gnawing ache for a woman who doesn't want me. I'm fucking pathetic.

"Are you going to be okay for the wedding tomorrow morning?" Arthur's question breaks through my mental fog.

"Yeah. I'll be there."

"You'd better not make my sister cry at my fucking wedding. I don't care how long we've been friends. I'll kill you with my bare hands."

My body tenses at the undercurrent of his tone. He means it. "I promise I'll be in a better mindset. I just need some rest."

"Good." He straightens and offers his hand. I take it. "Now, let's go back and get some dessert."

"Fine." I follow him back to the table. My mood hasn't changed, but I force a smile when we return to find the ladies enjoying chocolate cake without us.

Arthur resumes his seat, and Kate abandons the spot I had occupied before my outburst.

"Everything okay?" Kate asks, sitting beside Arthur.

"We're good," Arthur responds, glancing at me.

Marcy takes a bite of cake, her gaze fixed on the half-eaten slice before her. Her shoulders are tense.

Apologize, you idiot, my mind screams. But nothing comes out. Fuck. My mood takes another nose dive.

I manage to squeak out an apology and excuse myself from the table. My mumbled apology and excuse seem to mollify Kate. But Arthur continues to eat his cake in silence, watching me.

"Goodnight, Marcy."

She waves her hand, unable to meet my gaze. Shit.

I fucked this up. Damn it. How do I rebuild the tenuous bridge between us?

The duration of my commute home, I ponder all the ways in which I can fix the fragile relationship between Marcy and me. It may be too late. She's already made it perfectly clear how she feels about me. Maybe it's time I take a hint and give her the space she asks for.

When I reach my apartment, I strip on the way to the bathroom. I've already showered once, but I need it again. I feel dirty. But a shower won't cure this. Nothing will.

Leaning against the cool tile, I let the warm water slide over me. I imagine it's the featherlight touch of Marcy's lips and fingertips. The fantasy takes root and I'm transported.

My cock hardens at the mental image of Marcy naked and wet as she explores me. I refrain from seeking release, no matter how much I need it.

No. I shake my head and turn off the shower. I can't keep doing this. Dreaming of Marcy and all the delicious things I want to do with her—it's torment. It has been for years.

I've dated other women. I've tried to find someone who fits my world, who understands me. But they're not Marcy.

Her comment about the nurses cut deeper than she realized. I've had nurses throw themselves at me. Hell, I've had other doctors flirt with me while on duty. But I'm a professional. I take my job seriously.

I don't mix work and pleasure.

The fact that she would even think I'm that kind of man hurts like hell. She knows me better than that, even if she won't admit it.

It took every ounce of strength I possess not to tell her the truth. She's the only woman I want, the reason I breathe. I would do anything for her if she would only ask. Instead, I let my overwhelmed emotions get the better of me, and I hurt the woman I love.

I'm no better than that asshole who abused her.

Burdened by this knowledge, I climb into bed and pull the sheet up. The darkness surrounds me, and I succumb to it. Marcy's waiting for me in my dreams, but they quickly turn to nightmares when she abandons me completely.

CHAPTER 7

Marcy

"How do I look?" Kate spins around, her ankle-length skirt lifting like a flag on a summer breeze. The gown is a bold choice—A-line with a sweetheart neck, without the popular puffed organza sleeves and over-sequined fabric. When she asked me to help her design it, I thought she was crazy. Turns out I was the crazy one. It's lovely and classic and suits her to perfection, accentuating her generous curves.

"You look gorgeous." A lump forms in my throat as I adjust the pearls nestled against her throat. "Arthur's going to flip when he sees you."

"Well, this is your handiwork." Her face turns pink. "Thank you for everything."

"Of course. We're sisters now." I kiss her cheek, then busy myself with packing the makeup kit to keep from making a sentimental fool of myself.

Sunlight streams in the windows of the Empire State Building, illuminating Kate like an angel sent from heaven. My heart twists at the sight of her in her wedding gown with a crown of flowers in her curled hair. She looks lovely.

I'm happy for them. Truly.

Even though the circumstances of Kate's appearance in our lives seem a little farfetched, I can't help but be grateful for the twist of fate. This should be a joyous day. My brother is getting married to the love of his life. And I'm left with this gaping hole in my chest, the burden of painful memories haunting me from the past.

Marriage should be a partnership. A uniting of two souls who were made for each other. At least, that's the fairy tale. But marriage left me shattered and floundering. The institution lost all its meaning after my hellish experience.

Gladys, Arthur's secretary, appears in the doorway. "They're ready for you on the observation deck."

"Thanks, Gladys." Kate turns to face me, her eyes sparkling and her wide smile infectious. "Shall we go?"

I step to the side and sweep a dramatic bow. "After you."

Kate grabs the bouquet of lilies and roses sitting on Arthur's desk and swans out of the office. I follow, making sure the doors are locked behind me. When we reach the elevators, Kate takes my hand.

"Nervous?" I press the button for the observation deck.

"Yeah." Her hand trembles, and I squeeze it tight.

"Those nerves will disappear the moment you see Arthur. I promise." My comforting words ease her trembling.

They decided to have the ceremony in the same place where it all began on New Year's Day—the Empire State Building. Some would say it's romantic, like an homage to that old film, *An Affair to Remember*. I'm just thrilled they're opting for a non-traditional wedding. I'm pretty sure I'd burst into flames if I set foot in a church.

When the elevator dings, I release her hand. The doors open, and Arthur's business partner, Victor, stands waiting for us. He offers his arm to Kate.

"May I?"

Tears well up in her eyes. "I would be honored, Victor. Thank you."

Kate slides her arm through his, and they step out into the bright May sunlight.

I slip around them and make my way toward the small area they transformed into a lovely, romantic oasis. A dozen chairs lay on either side of the makeshift red-carpet aisle. At the end of the aisle, near the railing, stands my brother in a dapper black tuxedo. Beside him stands the pastor, and off to the side is Rob, wearing a matching tuxedo and a bright blue bow tie.

My heart flutters at the sight of him standing there. Damn it, why is he so handsome?

Soft strains of music fill the air. The string quartet is an elegant touch. I make my way up the aisle and take my position to the left of the priest.

When I turn to watch Kate's procession, I'm struck speechless. Her radiant smile only compounds the effervescent joy pouring off her in waves. She grips Victor's arm tightly as she walks down the aisle to Arthur, her eyes shining bright. When they reach the small dais, she hugs Victor and kisses his cheek. Tears roll down her face.

Arthur takes her hand as she steps forward to take her place beside him. She turns and hands me the bouquet.

I step closer, take the flowers, and place a handkerchief in her hand.

My gaze skims over the crowd as Kate turns to Arthur. There's only a handful of guests. Victor and his extremely pregnant wife, who looks like she's about to burst. Gladys, Cyril, and a few other friends of the family. The music fades before coming to an end.

"Dearly beloved..." The pastor begins the ceremony, and I clutch the flowers tightly in my hands.

These words. They're painful. They dredge up memories I would rather leave buried at the bottom of the Hudson River. I close my eyes, wishing I had something to focus on. Something to distract me from the twisting, gnawing ache that rips my head and heart apart.

When I open my eyes, my gaze fixes like a laser on Rob. I inhale sharply.

He's not watching the ceremony or the guests. His attention is focused on me.

Only me.

The pastor recites the vows, but it's background noise. Every fiber of my being is on fire. Rob never wavers. It's like *we* are standing on the dais before the pastor and the congregation. I brace myself for panic to overwhelm me, but it never comes. Instead, a peace settles around me. We're transported, the two of us, to a stolen moment in time amid family and friends.

Kate and Arthur repeat the vows. As they speak the words and exchange the rings, Rob flexes his jaw, pressing his lips together in a thin line. It's almost as though he wants to speak but stops himself. Strange.

"I now pronounce you husband and wife," the pastor announces. "You may kiss the bride."

Arthur sweeps Kate into a passionate embrace. The crowd erupts in cheers and applause. Rob and I remain steadfast, our gazes locked.

Kate spins around and hugs me tight, breaking the spell. "Now we're truly sisters!"

She takes her bouquet and links her arm through Arthur's. They make their way back down the aisle, greeting their guests and smiling while the quartet plays an uplifting tune.

Rob closes the gap between us and offers his arm. "May I escort you to the reception?"

My throat closes. "I...need to take care of something first." Brushing past him, I head for the elevator.

My heart pounds as I press the button for the ground floor. I lied. The only thing I need is to put some distance between Rob and me.

My hand rests against my chest; I will my heart to stop racing. What the hell just happened? One minute I'm at my brother's wedding, and the next, I'm tangled in some staring contest with Rob.

No. It was more than that. The intensity of his gaze remains firmly fixed in my mind. There was no mask. No hiding the hunger I saw in the depths of his eyes. He didn't flinch. Didn't blink. That single-minded determination, open and bare for all the world to see. Has it always been there?

The car reaches the ground floor, and I hail a cab. During the ride to the restaurant, my mind spins.

After the way he reacted at dinner last night, I thought Rob had finally had enough of my sarcasm and biting wit. I didn't expect a resolution—or even an apology. But when he abandoned us so quickly, I had the distinct impression he wanted to be as far from me as possible.

The way he looked at me during the ceremony, though, told me there is something else going on. I swallow and lean my head back against the seat. Do I even want to know what it is?

Uncertainty curls inside me, and I wonder if I could possibly get away with skipping the reception altogether.

No. Arthur and Kate would be disappointed. Besides, they're leaving right after the reception. Their bags are packed and their flight leaves tonight.

The car pulls up to the restaurant. I manage to keep my composure as I go into the building and find the small ballroom reserved for their reception. The decorations are minimalistic but lovely. I admire the pink-tipped orange roses and white calla lilies nestled in dark green ferns in the crystal vases on each table. A banner hangs across the bride and groom's table. *Congratulations, Mr. and Mrs. Maxwell.*

My heart takes another hit. I might have to see a doctor after this. *Rob?* No. I pinch my eyes closed. I most certainly do not need to see *that* doctor.

I make my way to the ladies' powder room, where I collapse on a velvet-cushioned lounge chair. What the hell am I doing here? This is supposed to be their special day, and I'm having a full-on heart attack.

The time alone gives me a chance to collect my thoughts.

I can do this. It's only for a few hours, then I can go home and get back to business as usual. No problem. I just have to avoid Rob until then. Easy.

Gladys, Victor and his wife, and a few other guests have arrived by the time I return to the ballroom. Kate and Arthur enter, and I'm struck by how perfect they are for each other.

I find a seat at a table near a huge potted plant, far from the commotion. With such an intimate affair, it's difficult to blend into the crowd. Kate waves when she spots me. I wave back.

Where's the bar? I scan the room and frown when Rob appears at the entrance. As if drawn by a freakishly large magnet, his gaze homes in, directly on me. Fuck.

I shift uncomfortably, wishing I could dissolve into the carpet.

The familiar strains of REO Speedwagon filter over the speakers. Shit. It's my favorite song. Kate and Arthur are on the dance floor, swaying in time to the ballad.

Rob crosses the floor, his gaze riveted on me like I'm the only person in the room. He offers his hand. "Dance with me? Please."

"Fine." The word slips from my traitorous mouth.

Then it's too late. Rob takes my hand and leads me toward the dance floor.

My body thrums with need at his touch. When he rests his palm on my waist, I bite my lip. His warm hand engulfs mine as our movements fall in time with the music. I've never danced with Rob before. I imagined it once, long ago, when I was a naive teenager.

But I'm not a teenager or naive anymore.

He pulls me closer, and I stifle a moan before it betrays me.

"Marcy." His warm breath brushes my cheek.

I try to focus on anything but him, knowing if I meet his eyes, I won't be able to hide the desire burning inside me. "What?"

"I owe you an apology for my behavior last night."

I become viscerally aware of his proximity when my pulse spikes and my chest constricts.

He sighs. "I had a stressful day and I shouldn't have taken it out on you. I'm sorry."

Rob apologized. Hell must have frozen over.

What on Earth do I say to that?

CHAPTER 8

Rob

"I understand." Her grip tightens on my shoulder, and I'm desperate to hold on with both hands to draw her flush against me. "Your job is stressful. I shouldn't have made such a stupid joke."

"Sarcastic comments are your trademark, Marcy." I soak up her warmth. "I'd be worried if you hadn't responded that way."

A small smile settles on her lips. "Still, I'm sorry."

"Already forgiven." My hand slides to the base of her spine, and I pull her closer.

Marcy softens and rests her head against my shoulder.

I'm trying my damnedest to keep the inferno under control, but having her in my arms is pushing me to the limit. I've dreamed of this moment for as long as I've known her—holding her close, keeping her safe. Marcy might be an independent woman, but she's not a machine. She's flesh and blood…and all heart when she deems someone worthy.

I want to be worthy. More than anything.

The song ends and another ballad begins. We continue dancing, spinning around on the dance floor. If she takes a half step closer, she'll know exactly how much I want her. My cock is rock hard. I'm glad I kept my jacket on. If I remove it now, the whole assembly will see the effect she has on me.

Part of me wants to tease her, to bait her into the sharp banter she embraces so easily. But I don't want to break this tender moment.

No. I finally have Marcy where I want her. Peaceful in my arms.

There's a soft tap on my shoulder. "Excuse me, Dr. Thompson?"

The magic moment is shattered. Marcy comes to a stop, and we both turn to the intruding party. It's one of the restaurant staff, looking quite repentant for interrupting our dance.

"Yes, that's me."

"There's a call for you, sir."

Marcy drops her hold on me, and the loss of her touch strikes me with the force of a lightning bolt. "Go ahead. I'll be here when you get back."

Those words lodge in my brain, and it short-circuits. Have we finally taken a step forward? I nod at Marcy and follow the man off the dance floor to the front of the restaurant. He gestures to the phone behind the partition.

"Dr. Thompson speaking."

"It's Summer." Her harried voice carries through the phoneline. Something's wrong.

"What's going on?"

"Sorry to interrupt, but I need you here. Stat." She takes a deep breath. "Grace is back."

"What happened?" My body tenses, and adrenaline dumps into my system.

"I don't know, but it's bad. How fast can you get here?"

"Ten minutes." I glance around the room, searching for someone from our party. Shit. I don't have time to waste. I'll apologize later. They'll understand. "I'll need clean scrubs."

"I'll have them waiting in the locker room. Hurry."

I hang up the phone and dart from the restaurant. Fortunately, I'm able to snag a cab and get to the hospital in five minutes. I murmur a prayer of thanks that Arthur and Kate chose a restaurant in our neighborhood.

By the time I walk into the ER, Summer's waiting at the entrance. She fills me in as we walk to the locker rooms.

"She came in an hour ago by ambulance. Unconscious." Summer keeps her voice low as I strip out of my suit. She hangs it up while I pull on scrubs. "I think there may be internal bleeding." She lists what they've already done and the meds they've administered.

I pull the top on and follow her out of the room. "Where's her husband?"

"Down at the police station." Summer stops speaking, but I can tell there's more to the story. She doesn't want to tell me everything.

I can't blame her. Fury is pulsing through me, red hot. I'm about to rip this building apart.

"Summer. Tell me."

She groans but finally relents. "Cops showed up for a suspected domestic altercation. Found Grace unconscious and called the ambulance."

"Is he under arrest?" My hands flex into fists. He's lucky he's not here because I'd fucking kill him myself.

"No, but they're investigating what happened."

"As they should. It's better he's not here." I head down the hall. "Where is she?"

"Exam room four."

I stop outside the door. Keeping my voice low and my emotions contained, I ask, "Is there anyone here to advocate for her?"

"No. She's alone."

"Fuck." I take a deep breath to calm myself. I need a level head before I go in. "Okay."

I'm her advocate. The unspoken words take up space in my brain, expanding until they consume me with determination. I push aside the curtain and step into the room.

My heart plummets.

Grace lays quietly on the gurney. The wires and tubes attached to her look like something out of a science fiction film. I should be used to it, but no one should be complacent about seeing a young woman in such a way. An individual who should be full of life and vitality has been transformed into a bruised and battered victim of her circumstances.

Like Marcy had been.

Shit. I shove the thoughts aside and allow myself to fall into a familiar rhythm. I'm a doctor damn it. I can help her. I can save her.

I flip through a mental checklist as I examine her. Oxygen, fluids, medication, all good. Heartrate, elevated and irregular. The bruises on her face are now two distinct shades. Yellow—from the aging ones—and deep purple and red. Those are fresh. Fuck.

My examination leads me down a dark path. The suspected injury from yesterday seems to have worsened. There's hemorrhaging beneath the skin of her abdomen and chest.

Summer watches from the other side of the bed with a worried expression. "What do you want to do?"

"I want a full CAT scan. The swelling on her face looks like it may be a fracture. I also want bloodwork done. What's her type?"

"A-positive."

"Okay, let's make sure we have some on hand."

"Got it." Summer darts from the room. I can hear her barking orders on the other side of the curtain.

I rest my hand on Grace's. "Don't worry. We'll take care of you. You're safe now."

A crew appears and wheels her down the hall to get the tests I requested. I follow behind, going through all the possibilities in my mind.

I was on call today, but they didn't actually need me. There's no logical reason for me to be here.

Except that Grace needs me. She needs someone who cares. Someone to fight for her, damn it.

As they do the CAT scan, I watch the monitors. Shit. Liver and spleen look like they're damaged. There's a lot of subdermal hemorrhaging, and it's filling her abdominal cavity. I grab the phone.

"Yeah, Dr. Thompson here. Page the trauma surgeon and have an OR prepped for surgery, stat."

"Yes, sir." The nurse on the other end of the line doesn't question me when I give her the details.

I hang up the phone.

The tech sitting behind the console glances at me. "Should I finish the scan?"

"Yes. Finish it."

I analyze the results before stepping into action. Mandibular fracture. Hairline fracture of the cervical spine. Subdermal hemorrhaging. Fuck. Did he hit her with a baseball bat?

Grace is in critical condition. It's a blessing she's unconscious. The pain would be excruciating. I help the trio of nurses wheel her back to the ER while we wait for the surgical team to prepare. We have to get the bleeding under control before we can address the other issues.

Summer joins me when we return to the ER. "What do we have?"

I fill her in. My composure slips when I see Grace on the table. So fragile. So alone. I've worked in the ER for years, seen similar cases a million times, but nothing prepares me for the slap in the face I feel when I see the damage this poor, sweet girl has endured. I could have stopped it.

No. I can't think that way. I need to focus. With a deep breath, I clear my head. Summer comes beside me, a silent but steadfast support.

I'm mentally drained, but I can't give up on Grace. I won't. She deserves better.

Grace's vitals drop. Her oxygen plummets and she seizes. Her battered body relinquishes the fight.

"Code blue!" I shout before Summer and I spring into action, screaming orders, directing the chaos that descends on the claustrophobic room.

When her heart stops, I choke back a sob. No, damn it. Don't die on me.

Summer grabs the crash cart and we attempt to resuscitate her, but nothing helps.

The horrific flatline tone echoes through the room.

She's gone.

Exhausted, we step away from the table as a nurse calls the time of death. A horrifying numbness settles around me.

I cradle her cheek in my hand. "I'm sorry, Grace."

Summer nudges me with her elbow. I take a deep breath and leave her.

She's at peace now. He can't hurt her anymore. She's safe.

"Hey, you did the best you could." Summer claps me on the shoulder after we clean up.

"Yeah." She's right. I did. But knowing that doesn't stop me from dropping into my own pit of self-deprecation. I could have done more. I could have stopped him the first time she came into my ER, broken and scared. I toss my scrubs into the bin and head for the shower.

No matter how hard I scrub, I can't wash away the shame of my failure. Tears mingle with the water running over my face.

What if it had been Marcy on that gurney?

I can't dwell on that. Grace isn't Marcy. Marcy escaped that fate. But it doesn't stop me from wondering what would have happened had Arthur and I not been there to help her cut ties with her ex.

Somehow, I manage to scrape myself together. Summer tells me she'll put the file on my desk for Monday morning. Everything blurs together as I make my way home.

What started as a joyful day, full of hope and new beginnings, evolved into an epic disaster. I feel like I'm on a flaming rollercoaster and it's just gone off the rails, hurtling toward certain doom. Maybe a good night's sleep will help…but I doubt it.

It's nearly ten when I get home. I change and grab a beer from the fridge before collapsing on the couch in the darkness.

Kate and Arthur are on their way to Italy. Marcy…fuck. She probably thinks I'm an asshole for ditching her at the reception. I would give anything to start the day over and not blow it.

The image of Marcy in her hot pink, sequined gown, standing beside Kate on the top of the Empire State Building is burned into my mind. I couldn't stop staring at her. I wanted her more in that moment than I've wanted anything in my whole life.

I wanted her to speak those vows to me.

But I'll settle for another dance. Another chance to prove I'm serious about her.

I only hope I haven't fucked it up beyond repair.

CHAPTER 9

Marcy

Rob never came back.

The wedding was two days ago, and Arthur and Kate are safe in Rome, enjoying their honeymoon, while I'm lying in bed on a Monday morning replaying Rob's apology in my mind. I wrench myself out of bed and head for the shower.

Something changed between Rob and me on that dance floor. His apology. The way he held me as we moved to the music. It's like the Earth shifted, the sun now rising in the west and setting in the east. My whole world feels off-center, but not in a bad way.

I waited for him to come back to the reception, even ordered him a drink. But after two hours, I drank it and plastered a fake smile on my lips. I was there to celebrate Arthur and Kate's wedding, not to moon over Rob. I thought I had put that childish crush far behind me, but whatever spark ignited between us on the roof of the Empire State Building followed us to the reception.

Warmth floods me at the memory. I can't imagine what would have happened had we not been interrupted. Would I have confessed my longstanding infatuation with him? Given into the heat building with every sway to the music?

He promised he'd come back, but he never did. I can't help but wonder if it's my fault.

I shouldn't be thinking about him. Whatever feelings I have for him—whether they're lust or something more—should sit firmly on the shelf. I don't want to complicate our tenuous friendship…if I can even call it that.

The spray of hot water washes the need away, but the thoughts remain in the back of my mind. I need to work. It will keep me distracted…I mean focused on what's important.

Last night, I got a call from Donna. Studio 35 has requested us to take care of their guests this week since their previously booked stylist had a family emergency. It's a last-minute addition, and I'll have to split my stylists between two locations. But I can't say no to Studio 35. They host celebrity news interviews as well as MTV. I'd be insane to turn them down. I've worked with them in the past, and they're top-notch. We'll just have to make a few adjustments to fit it all in.

Somehow, I manage to get myself looking halfway decent, and I head to the station. The commute is minimal since both locations are close to my apartment. I make it in the door at five to eight.

"Hold the elevator!"

A massive hand grabs the doors before they snap closed. I breathe a sigh of relief when they open.

"Thanks." I nearly trip when I reach the elevator.

Vic Simmons is holding the door. A smile curves his mouth when I step into the carriage. "Fancy meeting you here."

"Likewise."

The door closes, and I realize we're the only two people in the elevator. I fix my gaze on the mirrored surface before me.

"What floor?" he asks.

"Twelve."

He drops his hand, and I see the button is already illuminated. My gaze shifts to his. "You're going to twelve too?"

"Yup. I have an interview for an upcoming action film." He shoves his hands into his pockets.

The man's shoulders are so broad, I feel like he takes up half the elevator. But it could just be his presence.

"Oh, congrats on the new film." I straighten the bag strap on my shoulder.

"Thank you." He glances at me in reflection. "You look lovely today."

My face heats, and I nearly choke on my gum. What are words? I can't seem to string two of them together. He complimented me…I'm wearing a white leather skirt and a hot pink top. I grabbed them in a rush, and I look like a fucking mess with big hair and sparkly eye shadow. Granted, I'm supposed to look that way. It's all the rage right now, but it doesn't scream sex appeal to me.

Judging by the way Vic is drinking me in, I'd say it *does* scream that to him. And I'm not completely wigged out by it either.

"You're quite good at your job." Vic flashes a disarming smile. "Do you enjoy it?"

"Totally." I snap my gum and try to play it cool. I'm a thirty-five-year-old woman spazzing out over a hot actor giving me a compliment.

What the hell is wrong with me? "I mean, I've always been into fashion. Why not make it a career, right?"

"Absolutely. You should do what you love what makes you happy."

"Well, it didn't start that way. It was more about paying the bills." I glance at the numbers above the door to distract me from his charming presence.

"I can understand that." He chuckles, and the sound ripples through me. "I wasn't always the successful leading man you see before you."

"Get out of town. I never would have guessed."

"It's true." He sighs dramatically. "But I've been fortunate to turn my passion into my livelihood. Something we have in common."

The elevator reaches the twelfth floor, and the doors slide open. A vague connection doesn't mean anything, does it?

"I guess I'll see you later." I step from the carriage.

"I look forward to it." Vic gives a jaunty little salute and heads down the hall.

A cluster of people surround him, and I'm left staring after him in confusion.

Was Vic flirting with me? Or am I just a hotbed of lust-fueled coals left simmering after my dance with Rob? I shake off the lingering tension and weave my way through the studio to the dressing rooms.

Liana glances up when I walk in the door. "Finally! I'm freaking out here." She bustles around me with five hangers dangling from her fingertips. "I wasn't sure which ones we would—"

"Honey." I take the clothes and put them on the rack. "Take a breath. We got this. Okay?"

"I know. I just hate when we spread ourselves this thin." She bites her lip. "Do you know who we're styling today?"

"I haven't seen the list yet, but Vic Simmons is here." I waggle my brows.

Liana's eyes widen, and I swear there are hearts dancing in her pupils. "He's a dreamboat."

"He is easy on the eyes, I won't deny that." I skim through the selections and make mental notes on what we have on hand. "Plus he's charming. I ran into him in the elevator."

"You were alone with him?" Liana grabs my arm. "Tell me everything."

"Not much to tell, honestly." I warm from the inside out. "Although, I think he was flirting with me."

"Whoa." Liana gapes, her crimped hair falling across her eyes. "Did he ask you out?"

"No." I wave my hand and laugh. "Like I would ever date a client. You know me better than that."

"Yeah, I know all about your rules, but this is *Vic Simmons* we're talking about here."

"You act like that's supposed to mean something to me, Liana?"

A knock at the door interrupts us. It's the stage manager with the list of clients. I take it and tell him to send the first client in when they arrive.

Liana snatches the list from my hand. "So back to Vic. You gonna give him a shot or what?"

"For the hundredth time, I don't date clients. Period."

"Maybe you should break your rule this one time?" Liana winks. "Come on...just one little date."

"He hasn't even asked me out. Don't you think you're getting ahead of yourself here?"

"He'll ask." Liana nods in certainty. "I saw the way he looked at you last week."

"Oh stop, Liana. Seriously, I'm too old for these games." I rifle through the garment rack and pull a few dresses for the first client.

Another knock at the door saves me from Liana's incessant nagging. "Come in," I call without turning.

Liana nudges me in the ribs.

"What?" I spin around to find Vic standing in the doorway. "Oh, it's you." I replace the gowns and pull a casual menswear ensemble from the rack, taking into account his dark hair and bright blue eyes as I select the colors.

"I'm gonna go grab that box I left in the hallway," Liana mutters as she slips out the door, clearly breaking the rule she knows I live by.

For the second time today, I'm left alone with Vic Simmons. Typically, I'd be worried about being alone with my client, but after the ride in the elevator, I'm oddly at ease with his presence. That should be a flaming red flag all by itself.

"Here. These should fit. I'll just wait outside for you to change."

"I hope I don't make you uncomfortable..." He seems to search for my name like I never gave it to him, but he knows exactly what it is.

I humor him regardless. "Marcy." I clear my throat. "And no, you don't. I just wanted to give you some privacy."

"How thoughtful."

My heart flips at his sheepish smile. The hell is wrong with me?

I step outside and lean against the door. There's no sign of Liana in the hallway. Traitor. She bailed on purpose, trying to play matchmaker. I should fire her ass. But I won't. She's practically family.

After a few minutes, I knock on the door. Vic opens it.

I gasp at the sight of him in a blue polo with a flipped collar. The tailored tan slacks perfectly hug his thighs.

"You're sure about this?" He gestures to the shirt.

"For sure." I smooth the collar, and my fingertips brush his neck. With a gasp, I drop my hands. "You look gnarly."

"Is that a good thing?" he asks with a laugh.

"Totally." My gaze skims the length of him, one last appraisal of my styling before I send him out on camera.

"Marcy." His voice cuts through the silence.

"Yeah?" I snap my gum and meet his gaze.

"Would you have dinner with me next week?"

"I don't know, Vic." My heart does two somersaults, then lands like a rock in my stomach. "I don't date clients." Even as I say it, my traitorous heart pushes back against my conscience, demanding I pursue whatever this is.

He pulls a card from his wallet and hands it to me. "My number, in case you change your mind."

"Thanks." I take the card and slip it into my bra. His gaze follows the movement. "But I told you, I don't date clients."

"Well, it doesn't have to be a date. Just two people having dinner, getting to know each other."

That grin devastates me with its undeniable charm. Warning bells should be going off in my head, but I'm too smitten to care.

I tap my chin. "I'll think about it."

The stage manager pops his head in the door. "Vic, you're on in five."

"Got it. Thanks." He shoves his hands in his pockets after the manager leaves. "I'm in town for two more weeks. Just call if you change your mind."

Something's wrong with me because I can't find a single response in my brain. It's not until Vic leaves the room that I can breathe again. What the hell just happened?

I can't seriously be considering going out with Vic? That would break every promise I've made to myself. No relationships. No dating. Nothing serious.

Definitely no dating clients.

Am I honestly giving this serious thought?

What about Rob? What about what happened Saturday on the dance floor?

No. I'm not letting Rob influence any decisions I make pertaining to my sex life. He doesn't get a say.

When Liana returns, I play it off. She doesn't need to know about Vic's invitation. No one does because it's none of their damn business.

Shit. Why does this have to be so damn difficult?

CHAPTER 10

Rob

I miss my bed. Don't get me wrong, Arthur's penthouse has a better view of the city and more space, but it's not the same as my shoebox apartment and lumpy mattress.

Being here reminds me of Marcy. I haven't seen or spoken to her since the wedding reception. Since our dance. Between my regular shifts and overtime, I can't seem to get a break this week. This is the first free moment I've had, and I'm taking it to relax and read a book.

I set aside the Chinese takeout menu and sink back into the couch cushions. Dinner's on the way, and I've disconnected the phone. Tabby jumps onto the empty space beside me. Her inquisitive green eyes search my face.

"Hello, sweetheart." I scratch her head, and she arches into my touch, rubbing her face against my hand. Her purring resonates through my fingertips. She mews in response and climbs onto my lap.

"Can't let you languish here alone, can we?" I stroke her fur, and she curls against my chest. "Affectionate thing, aren't you?"

Her sweet little mew melts my heart. I'm not typically an animal person, but Tabby's been wonderful company these past few days. It's nice knowing someone's waiting for me to come home, craving my attention.

Am I talking about a cat or something else?

Even though Marcy keeps me at arm's length and seizes every opportunity to sink her claws into me, I know it's because she's scared she'll lose that precarious balance she's fought so hard to gain. Her protective instincts run deep.

I turn on the television while we wait for the food. Tabby purrs contentedly against me while I flip through the channels searching for something worth watching. I pause on the local news. I don't really care what it is; I really just want some background noise.

A knock at the door pulls me from my search.

"That was fast," I murmur to Tabby and set her aside. They knock again just as I reach the landing. "I'm coming."

When I open the door, my heart flips twice. "Marcy." I lean against the doorway and drink her in.

"Rob." The neon top and sparkly gray pants don't detract from her natural glow. She looks like a rock star and every fantasy I've ever had. Even her eyes shimmer in the hall light. "Can I come in?"

"Yeah, sure." I open the door and step aside. "You just get off work?"

"Yup." She brushes past me, and the scent of her perfume and Aqua Net lingers in her wake. A bag dangles from her hand. "I forgot to drop off my wedding gift. Figured I would do it now while I have a chance."

"Busy week?" I ask, closing the door before Tabby can escape into the hall.

"Totally." Marcy snaps her gum and ventures into the living room. "I'm gonna put this on the counter so they'll see it when they get back."

"Be my guest." Tabby weaves through my legs. I scoop her into my arms and scratch behind her ears. I might be grasping at straws, but Marcy showing up like this seems like a sign. I should take a chance, right?

"You got plans for dinner?"

"No, why?" Marcy sets the bag on the counter and turns. "Are you cooking?"

"Not tonight. I just put in an order for takeout." Tabby's purring amplifies my heartbeat in my ears. "I ordered double if you're hungry."

A slow grin curves on the sinful lips I've imagined wrapped around my cock. "Are you asking me to stay for dinner?"

"I am. But if you'd rather not spend time in my presence, I understand."

Marcy crosses the gap between us to pet Tabby, who's contentedly cradled in my arms, purring up a storm. "I'll stay, but only if you tell me why you didn't come back to the reception on Saturday."

Pain flashes through me at the reminder, but she deserves an explanation for my disappearance. "Deal."

Grinning, she takes Tabby from my arms and nuzzles her face in the cat's fur. I've never been jealous of an animal in my life, but here I am, glaring at Tabby. Marcy settles on the couch with the affectionate kitten.

I'm about to speak when a knock at the door cuts me off. This time it's the delivery boy. I take the food, give him a little more than the cost of the meal, and bid him farewell. Burdened with two bags of takeout, I return to the living room and set them on the coffee table.

Marcy puts Tabby on the couch and scoots closer. "What'd you order? The usual?"

I arch my brow at her. "How would you know what I like?"

"Rob, seriously." She scoffs and pulls out the container of lo mein. "You've been friends with my brother since I was in high school. I know a lot more about you than you think I do."

"I doubt that." I snort and sit down beside her.

She hands me the broccoli and beef. I snatch chopsticks off the table with a huff.

"Try me." She opens her chopsticks and takes a bite of the noodles.

"Fine." I push aside the broccoli, searching for the beef. "What's my mom's first name?"

"Martha." She slurps down another bite. "Come on, give me a hard one."

"Okay. My favorite sport?"

"Baseball." She shakes her head. "You played in high school and college. Your favorite team is the Yankees."

I narrow my gaze. Confidence oozes out of her. She's practically gloating. "All right. I didn't always want to be a doctor. What did I want to be before I went to college?" There's no way she can possibly know this. I've never told another soul. Not even Arthur.

Marcy stops chewing and levels her gaze with mine. She holds it while she thinks. I can see the flecks of gold in her eyes. It's taking all my restraint to not hook my hand around her neck, pull her close, and kiss the smirk right off her lips.

"A spy."

Astonishment floods me. How the fuck…

I jab the chopsticks in her direction. "How the hell did you know that?"

"I can read your mind." She gasps dramatically before chuckling and taking another bite of her noodles.

"No, seriously. I never told anyone that."

"Like I said before, I know you better than you think I do." She winks, and my passive desire increases to a simmering boil.

I stuff a piece of broccoli in my mouth. If I hadn't been head over heels for this woman already, I certainly would be smitten now. We lapse into silence as we eat. I grab two beers from the fridge and pop the tops.

She takes one and sighs in contentment. "Thanks for dinner. It hit the spot."

"Thanks for keeping me company." I salute her before taking a drink.

"So what happened Saturday night? Why'd you bail?"

"Hospital called." I hesitate, wondering how much I should actually tell her. There were too many similarities between Grace and Marcy. I swallow the lump in my throat. "There was an emergency with one of my patients."

"Oh no." Her teasing demeanor fades at my revelation. "I should've known it was important. You'd never bail on my brother like that if it weren't." She spins the bottle in her hands. "Was everything okay?"

I shake my head, unable to find the words, and hide my face behind the beer bottle. "She died."

"Oh, Rob. I'm so sorry." Marcy's hand rests on my knee. "I'm sure you did everything you could."

If I had a nickel for every time I heard that phrase, I'd be richer than Arthur. I sniff and tip my head back. "Yeah, well…it wasn't enough."

Marcy bites her lip and takes my hand. The touch infuses me with comfort and hope. I squeeze it and smile.

"Thanks for trying to cheer me up, Marcy." I sigh. "It's part of the job. It fucking sucks, but I'll get over it. I can't save them all."

Marcy rests her head on my shoulder and threads her fingers in mine. "You'll try though. If I know you, you'll do your damnedest to save every last person who comes to you for help."

"You know it." I chuckle at how well she does know me.

"It's gotta be better than being an international spy." Her words are soft, but I hear them clearly enough.

"I don't know. Travel the world, dine in fancy restaurants, stay in the world's classiest hotels, make love to the most beautiful women in the universe. It's a toss-up."

She shoves her weight against me. "You watch too many Bond films."

That's when it clicks. "Ahh, now it makes sense."

"What?" She draws back and looks at me, confused.

"How you knew I wanted to be a spy."

"What?" Her cheeks turn pink. "I've seen your collection of Ian Fleming novels, and I know you've seen every James Bond film."

"You're observant, I'll give you that."

"Well…" She pulls away, and I feel a sharp loss at the absence of her touch. "It's my job to be observant."

"Mine too." We're both observant, but not enough to get past this tension that has kept us at odds for years. If she could only see how much I want her, how much I love her.

Just tell her. Do it.

Marcy stands and stretches. "Well, I should get home. Long day tomorrow."

"It's Saturday." I walk her to the door.

"Yeah, but stylists don't run normal schedules like the rest of the world."

"You mean like doctors?" I chuckle. "I work tomorrow too."

"Day shift?"

"Yup."

Her smile warms me. "Well, don't work too hard."

"You too, Marcy." I open the door for her. "Be safe."

"I'm always safe, Rob." She waves as she walks down the hall. "Later!"

I close the door and Tabby appears at my feet. Scooping her into my arms, I return to the living room and clean up the remains of our meal.

If someone had told me Marcy and I would be sitting around like old friends, laughing and joking, I would have called them crazy.

But I like it. It gives me hope there could be something more between us.

I just wish I had the courage to tell her how I feel.

CHAPTER 11

Marcy

What the hell am I doing?

I twirl the card for the Plaza Hotel between my fingers. There's a room number scrawled on the back. Fuck. I can't seriously be considering this. Can I?

After the impromptu dinner with Rob last night, nothing has eased the ache—not cold showers, not self-stimulation. I should have been honest with him, but I couldn't do it. Whatever tenuous friendship we've formed over the past few weeks is hanging precariously by a thread. I don't want to ruin it by throwing myself at him.

No. I need to distract myself. Maybe have a little fun. Work has been stressful, and between the wedding and Rob's strange behavior, I deserve a break from the usual.

By break, I didn't mean to disregard my *no dating clients* rule. But Vic seemed sincere enough when he issued the invitation earlier this week. It's just dinner. Right?

I pick up the phone and punch in the digits for the hotel. When the front desk clerk answers, I request Vic's room.

"Hello?"

"It's Marcy, the stylist." I lick my lips, and my heart pounds like a drum in a cave.

"You changed your mind?"

"Maybe." I twist the cord around my fingers. "You want to grab dinner?"

"I could eat. The restaurant in the hotel is fantastic. Meet you there at seven?"

"Perfect." I hang up the phone and nearly drift off into space.

This is the craziest thing I've done in a while. It's been too long since I've had any kind of action. The last guy wasn't even worth the effort. Such a disappointment. The guy I want is the one I can't have. There's no Rob tonight. It's just Vic and me. Whatever happens, happens. I'm not going to stress about it.

After an hour of primping and prepping, I manage to nail that effortless, not-trying-too-hard glam I see so many women wasting hours to perfect. Looking good is my brand. I need to stay on top of it. I pop in a stick of Doublemint gum and slip on my glasses.

I manage to flag down a cab and take it to the Plaza. Inside, the concierge points me toward the hotel restaurant. Shit, this place is high-class. I tug at my skirt, knowing I must look like I'm in the wrong place. Screw it. I straighten up as I enter the restaurant.

Vic stands when he sees me. "You look lovely."

"Thank you." I warm at the compliment and take the seat across from him.

"Would you like something to drink?" Vic waves to the waiter.

"Red wine, please." I address the waiter before turning back to Vic.

He's wearing a blue-and-red pinstripe button-down dress shirt and black trousers. It's simple, but the color amplifies his eyes. He's handsome. Definitely movie-star quality handsome. And charming to a fault.

Guilt creeps in. Why should I feel guilty? He asked me to join him for dinner, and damn it, I'm going to soak up the attention.

I scan the menu and steal a glance at him over the top. "So how's the promo tour for the new movie going?"

"Great. We have a few more interviews here next week before flying to LA for the red-carpet event." Vic's gaze lingers on me as he reaches for his glass of water. "Perhaps I could entice you to be my date for opening night."

It takes me two whole seconds before the implication of his words sinks into my addled brain. "We haven't even gotten through dinner and you're inviting me to LA for a massive, highly televised event?"

"I have a good feeling about you." He winks.

The waiter returns with my wine and takes our orders.

Once he leaves, Vic leans closer. "So tell me about yourself. How did you become such a gifted stylist?"

Typically, I don't mind talking about my business, but this feels personal, intrusive, like he's asking about my private life rather than my professional skillset. I can't form a realistic response so I take a sip of my wine, giving myself time to figure out what I can offer without revealing too much.

"Well, my grandmother taught me to sew when I was a teenager." I spin a yarn a mile long, hoping he'll eat it up. There are nuggets of truth woven through the story, but nothing that could be traced to my broken past. I might be outlandish in my clothes and personality, but I prefer to keep my past buried and locked away from prying eyes. I'm not one for wearing my shame in public for sympathy or ridicule.

The more I speak, the more he listens. It's like he's absorbing all of the information, and I can't help but wonder if he's interested or just placating me. Finally, I shift the conversation to him.

"Enough about me, tell me about you." I smile and sip my wine. "Did you always want to be an actor?"

"No. I kinda fell into it." He rakes his fingers through his hair and chuckles. "I was working construction on a film set when the lead actor was injured trying to do a stunt. I stepped in for the stunt work. After that gig, the director called me to audition for a role in his new film." Vic shrugs. "I fell in love with it."

"That's wonderful. It's a relief when you love your job. I mean, I couldn't imagine doing a job I hate." I shiver at the thought of being stuck in a thankless job I didn't enjoy, and I'm reminded how fortunate I am for all I have.

Dinner arrives, and we eat while enjoying conversation scattered throughout the meal. Being in his company is the reprieve I need. His presence garners looks from neighboring tables, but he's kind and gracious to those who recognize him. Vic Simmons is an enigma, and I find myself wanting to know more about him.

But that's not how this works. I only accepted his invitation because I knew there could be nothing between us. Just distraction and maybe some hot sex.

After dessert, a decadent crème brulee, Vic signs the check and meets my gaze. "Shall we?" He stands and offers his hand.

I take it and let him escort me from the restaurant. I feel like a celebrity myself as we weave through the tables to the exit.

In the corridor, he leans down. "Would you like to come up to my room?" He whispers the question against my ear.

"That depends on what you have planned?" I tease, brushing against his body with my own.

"I have every intention of seeing those lips put to good use." His blue eyes blaze with heat and unspoken promises.

But there's something beneath it. Something dark and unnerving. A warning to walk away.

"Mmm. Tempting, but maybe another night." I pull my hand free.

In a flash, the blue in his eyes turns to a raging, stormy gray. He snatches me by the wrist and pulls me into an alcove leading to the bathrooms. I try to wrench my hand from his grip, but he's too strong. My heels twist uselessly on the carpet as I try to catch my balance, stumbling behind him.

"Vic!"

He smothers my shout with his mouth as he pins me against the wall. We're alone in the dark hallway. I push against his chest, but he doesn't budge. His hot, unwelcome kiss leaves me stunned, and I squeal in protest when he shoves his tongue between my lips. He steals my breath, plunders my mouth.

The roast chicken I had for dinner churns in my stomach. No matter how hard I shove against his body, he doesn't move. He's a brick wall of solid muscle and determination.

Help! I'm screaming in my head, but no one can hear me. I have to get him off me before I choke on the panic.

In desperation, I bite his tongue. He rears back and glares at me. There's a flash of movement and a burst of pain as his hand connects with the side of my face. Warmth blooms across my face.

I gasp and clutch my cheek. It's wet. He strikes a second time, sending me reeling. Then he grasps my shoulders and slams me against the wall.

My skin burns and my brain shorts out.

It's not Vic, it's Dan. He's standing over me with a wooden rolling pin. I barely scream when he swings it at me. My body aches from the countless strikes. I sob and pull inside myself, covering my head with my hands, hiding my face. *Stop!* I scream, but he doesn't listen. He keeps going until he's content with the damage.

Just like that, Dan is gone and Vic is back.

"You'd best not decline such a gracious invitation." He grits his teeth.

No, I can't let him win. I won't let him best me like Dan did. I'm stronger now. Stronger than I was. I can fight back.

With all the determination I possess, I tip my head back and meet his gaze. I spit in his face.

"You'll pay for that, bitch." He draws his arm back to strike me again. A shadow appears at the end of the hallway.

Thank God! Before I can shout for help, Vic drops his hand over my mouth.

"Ah-ah. Before you scream for help, consider your business. Your passion." His breath against my skin makes me gag. "It would be a shame for you to lose such a prestigious connection." He sneers. "No one will believe you anyway."

Vic drops his hand and walks away, leaving me alone in the hall. I manage to stumble into the bathroom and lock the door. My heart's racing and my legs feel like they're about to give out. But I can't stay here. I need to get home. I need…

Fuck.

One glance in the mirror tells me exactly what I need: a doctor.

There's blood smearing my face. I manage to clean it the best I can and find the cut. With a paper towel pressed to my cheek, I manage to keep a low profile during my escape from the hotel.

The cabbie doesn't spare me a second look when I climb into his car. I pay him extra not to ask questions and get me home quickly.

Inside the safety of my apartment, my composure shatters. I crumple to the floor in a broken heap. Dragging myself across the floor, I slowly progress to the phone by the couch.

I dial the number I know by heart. The line is picked up.

"Hello?"

The quiet sobs transform into heart-wrenching gulps of air as the panic and pain coalesce inside me.

"Marcy?" Rob's voice echoes in my ear, and relief fills me.

"Help me." I hiccup. "Please."

"Fuck. Where are you?"

"Home. Hurry." I disconnect the phone and curl up in a ball as the emotions consume me.

I knew better. I fucking knew better than to trust him.

And now I'm right back where I started all those years ago.

CHAPTER 12

Rob

The heart-wrenching sobs echo through the line.

Help me. Please.

The moment I hear those words, I reach for my shoes. All the air disappears from my lungs as my world is ripped out from under me.

Hurry.

"Fuck." I race down to my apartment and grab my medical bag. Within five minutes, I'm in a cab, racing downtown.

The drive is torment, but I shove aside my impatience. I can't get to her faster by foot or subway. By the time I reach her place, it's nearly midnight. Panic infuses me.

What the hell happened? Why was she in tears? The last time I heard her in such a state was the night she left her ex. The night I stitched her wounds and bit back my fury.

I felt a shift last night during our friendly dinner. The soft transition from tolerating someone's presence to friendship. I shouldn't hope for much, but knowing she called me for help instead of one of her other friends leaves me certain there's something more.

Then again, she called her brother's number. I just happened to be there to answer the phone. Maybe she was reacting out of desperation, out of survival, calling the one person she could trust. Her brother.

But he's not here. I am. I answered the phone. I heard her sobs, her plea for help.

The uncertainty mixes with the adrenaline coursing through my system. I need to see her. I need to be sure she's okay. Fear pulses through me, hot and suffocating. I urge the driver to speed up, tell him it's an emergency.

Because it is.

When the taxi driver pulls up outside her building, I toss some bills at him and dart from the cab. A quick glance down the alley reveals her bedroom light glowing like a beacon. The curtain sways in the faint breeze, and I catch a glimpse of her shadow beyond the fire escape that crisscrosses the side of the building.

She must have stepped outside for a smoke.

I slip past a couple exiting the building and head inside. When I reach her door, I'm breathless, and my pounding heart echoes in my chest like a jackhammer.

"Marcy." I pound my fist on the door. "It's Rob. Open the door, baby."

My hand flexes impatiently at the distinct sound of the deadbolt and chain. When the door opens, it's like someone's taken a sucker punch straight to my solar plexus. Rage, red hot and all-consuming, floods me.

"What the hell happened, Marcy?" I rush inside and close the door behind me, then lock it. My gaze never strays from her.

Her eyes are red and swollen from crying. But it's not the tears that have me fuming. It's the darkening bruise framing her face and the gash high on her cheek, leaving a trail of blood against her pale skin. She presses a bloodstained rag to it and the tears flow anew.

Without thought, I pull her into my arms. Her shoulders tremble as I hold her close. She sobs against my chest, and I let her.

A million thoughts slam into me at once. Was she attacked on the street? Did someone mug her? I hold my tongue. I'll have to wait for answers. Right now, she just needs to be held. To know she's safe.

"It's all right, baby." I rub my hands gently across her back in a soothing rhythm. "You're safe now. It's over." I repeat it, over and over, until she quiets in my embrace and the trembling dissipates to soft hiccups.

When she finally pulls away, she groans at the sight of her blood on my shirt. "Sorry." Marcy sniffs.

"I work in the ER. Bloodstains might be a bitch to get out of my lab coat, but they don't scare me." I offer a smile and guide her to the couch. "Sit down. Let me take a look."

Marcy sits beside me, her gaze fixed on the floor. I put my bag on the coffee table before turning toward her.

"Chin up. Let me see."

She drops the bloody rag into her lap. I gently cup her chin in my hand and rotate her face in the light. Contusion on both sides with bruising. A laceration in the soft tissue across her zygomatic arch. It's not deep, but it's still bleeding. Damn it.

I reach into the kit and withdraw antiseptic and some cotton swabs. I'll clean it, then put some ice on the swelling. Hopefully, it'll stop the bleeding as well.

"It'll sting." I dab antiseptic on the wound, and she flinches, hissing in a breath. "Sorry."

I take the rag from her hand and place her fingers on the cotton ball against the wound. "Hold this. I'll get some ice."

In the freezer, I find a frozen bag of peas. That'll work. My mind races as the onslaught of emotions propels me to action. Even though I want to push for details, I don't. I grab a clean hand towel from the closet and wrap the peas before replacing the cotton with the cold pack. Years of training kick in, and I walk through the motions to ensure she's cared for properly.

"This should calm things down," I assure her, but she still won't meet my gaze. She's withdrawn due to the trauma.

I sigh. "Marcy. Look at me."

Those bewitching eyes, full of pain and shame, finally meet mine. Her lower lip trembles.

"What happened?" My breath catches in my throat at the way she cringes at the question.

"Don't. I can't, he'll…" She bites her lip and shakes her head. "Don't ask."

"He?" The barely suppressed rage boils to the surface. "Who did this to you, Marcy?" I grit my teeth, trying like hell not to snap in half from the pressure building inside me.

She shakes her head harder. "I can't."

The normally tough-as-nails woman I've loved for years sits before me like she had that horrible night. Fragile and bruised, fearful and angry. But this time, there's more. She's embarrassed about it. There's a layer of shame across the surface.

"Who are you protecting?" I ask, my voice stern.

"I'm not protecting anyone!" she snaps.

In that moment, I see the fire ignite in her eyes once more. There's the fighter I know and love.

"Fine." I lift my hands in surrender, but I remain steadfast beside her. "Do you have any other injuries? Ribs, arms, legs, abdomen? Any discomfort?"

"No." She shifts the peas away from her cheek, and the cold has staunched the bleeding to a drop or two.

"Why didn't you just go to the ER?" I open the pill canister and pour two ibuprofen into my palm.

"Because I didn't want anyone asking stupid questions." Her strength must be returning if the forcefulness of her responses is any indicator. She takes the pills and pops them without water. "It's not a big deal."

"Bullshit, Marcy. You called your brother's penthouse in tears, barely able to get the words out."

"I panicked. I needed…" Her voice falters. "I forgot he wasn't home."

"But I answered." I nod with painful understanding. "You weren't calling for me."

"I was."

Her soft response leaves me stunned.

"You helped me just as much as Arthur did that night. I'm glad you answered the phone. I didn't have your number."

My heart can't take the goddamned roller coaster much longer. I can't care for her unless she wants me to, but she won't tell me what happened. And I'm afraid if I pry, she'll push me away again.

"Marcy, I want to help you. But if you don't tell me what happened, my hands are tied."

"I made a mistake." Her jaw clenches. "I trusted someone I shouldn't have, and this is what I get." Her lip quivers again, but judging by the steely glint in her eyes, this time it's from fury, not fear. "I shouldn't have gone, but I did. There's nothing I can do about it now."

"You went out on a date?" Disbelief mingles with the anguish churning in my gut. Once the realization settles, the rage ignites like an inferno. "He fucking hit you."

"It was just dinner. But he wanted more than that." Her gaze settles on the far wall. "I told him no. He wasn't pleased with my response."

"Fuck, Marcy." I spit the words out not realizing how they'll affect her. She flinches. "Sorry." The emotions rise to a rolling boil. "Did anyone see him hit you?"

"No." Her hand is shaking where it presses the cold pack to her cheek. "But someone walked past, and I was able to get away from him before he could do worse."

"Tell me who he is, Marcy," I plead. "Tell me, and I'll make sure that bastard never walks again. Never touches another woman. Never knows another moment of pleasure in his miserable life."

A hint of a smile touches her lips. But it's sad and lost in painful memories. "I can't, Rob. Please. I know you want to help me…" Her words trail off, and she shrugs.

Resigned, I put my kit back in the bag and close it. "Well, make sure you rest. I'll check on you tomorrow."

I stand, and her hand grabs my wrist. "Please stay, Rob." Fear reflects in her eyes again. "I don't want to be alone tonight."

Damn it.

I exhale sharply, praying for strength. Of all the nights for her to invite me to stay…and not for the reason I want her to ask me to stay. I must have been a goddamned saint in a prior life.

"Okay. I'll stay." I place the bag on the table. "Come on, let's get you to bed."

She leads the way, and I place a butterfly bandage on the cut before I put a larger bandage over that. She doesn't need to wake up with a blood-soaked pillow if it bleeds during the night.

I pull the sheet over her. A gentle breeze drifts in from the cracked window. It's warm tonight, so I turn on the fan. The rhythmic noise lulls her.

"Goodnight, Marcy."

"Night, Rob." She closes her eyes. "Thank you."

I nod, but she's already dozing. I bend down and kiss her forehead. The scent of her sweet shampoo lingers in my nose as I retreat to the living room and crash on the couch. I punch the throw pillow and lay my head on it, staring at the dark ceiling.

Yeah, I'm a goddamned saint. But at least I'm doing what I've always wanted to do, what I should have been doing from the start.

Keeping her safe.

CHAPTER 13

Marcy

He's chasing me. The hallway stretches out before me, an endless tunnel leading into darkness. My screams evaporate in the void.

He snatches my hair and pulls me back to him. There's no escape.

I claw at his arms, his chest, his face, but nothing stops him. He sneers as he shoves me against the wall and rips my clothes.

When I fight him, he beats me into submission.

Exhausted, I'm naked and bleeding. He unbuckles his belt and reaches into his pants. I cringe, tightly closing my eyes.

No, no, no! This isn't happening. It's not real. The light streams across his face.

Rob?

I jerk awake. Sweat coats my skin. I'm wearing my pajamas, tucked into my own bed. Slowly my gaze focuses in the darkness. What a fucking dream. I wipe my brow and freeze when I see shadows shift in the far corner of the room. Even the blood in my veins stops flowing.

Someone's in the room with me.

"Rob?" I hazard the word, but it's not him.

A figure materializes in the darkness. The light from outside amplifies the shadow on the wall. The dream returns with a vengeance, gripping me by the throat and shaking me.

A scream wrenches free.

The shadowed figure bolts across my bedroom toward the open window. When they pass the door, it flies open, colliding with the intruder.

"Marcy." Rob flicks on the light switch. He's shirtless and has a frying pan in his hand. Eyes wild, he scans the room.

The dark figure groans in a heap on the floor. Rob reaches down and snatches them by the arm, dragging them to their feet.

Black leggings, black shirt, and black domino mask.

What the fuck? A burglar? The fear slowly dissolves at the reveal of the intruder. They attempt to pull away from Rob, but he tightens his grip.

"You're hurting me," the burglar cries out, pulling against his hold.

"A woman?" I gape at her and untangle myself from the sheet.

"Let me go." The woman sidesteps me when I reach for her mask.

"Knock it off." Rob gives her a firm shake.

I pull off the mask and the cap holding her hair in place. A mess of frizzy, dark red curls tumbles free, framing a pair of wide green eyes. She could be a model if the industry weren't hellbent on every woman being a size two. In the light, her generous curves fill out the black ensemble.

Any other day, I'd say she was a knockout, but not here, not now. She broke into my fucking apartment.

"Well, well, looks like we caught ourselves a cat burglar." Rob grins as he drags the woman into the living room.

I follow behind and retrieve a carving knife from the kitchen. Better safe than sorry.

Rob shoves the woman onto the couch and points the frying pan at her. "Don't move."

With his attention still focused on her, Rob picks up the phone. He struggles to dial the number. "Watch her, Marcy. If she tries to run, aim for her throat."

The woman's eyes widen. Her gaze shifts to me, and I recognize the fear hiding there, just beneath the surface. The adrenaline drains from my body, replaced immediately with fury.

"Why the hell did you break into my apartment?" I hiss at her. "I don't have anything worth stealing."

The cat burglar cocks her head and studies me, but she says nothing.

"Richards, it's Thompson. I need you to give me a hand with something." Rob glances at me, irritation on his brow. "Yes, I realize it's four in the morning." He sighs. "No, this can't wait."

Who in the world did he call? I keep my focus on the intruder, who seems as invested in Rob's conversation as I am.

"I'm at a friend's place, and we've had a break-in." Rob taps the pan against his thigh, and I'm drawn to the way his shoulder muscles flex beneath his skin. "No, I can't call the cops." He looks at the ceiling. "It's complicated. Look you're going to have to trust me. Get your ass over here." He rattles off the address and hangs up the phone.

"Who was that?" I ask when he turns toward us.

"Just a friend." He sits on the coffee table across from our uninvited guest. "A detective. He owes me a favor."

The intruder's mouth gapes. "You're not calling the cops?"

Rob snorts. "Trust me. When Richards gets ahold of you, you're going to wish I had called the cops."

"Is that the guy my brother knows down at the precinct? The one you—"

"Yeah, he's the cop I saved the night Arthur and I went club-hopping after graduation." Rob shakes his head. "He made detective a few years ago."

"I didn't realize you were still friends with him." I sit on the arm of the chair.

The woman shifts uncomfortably when she sees a glint of the blade in my hand, and her gaze shifts to Rob. Once the detective shows up and takes her off our hands, she'll be a distant memory. I'm not even paying attention to her anymore.

No, it's Rob's half-naked form driving me to distraction. And it seems the woman in black is having the same problem. Hunger fills her bright eyes. I want to claw them out of her head.

"Yeah, we get together at the bar for drinks once a month. I've worked with him on cases before too." Rob's response pulls me from my fantasies.

"So what do we do with her until he arrives?" I glare at the intruder who's drinking in every inch of Rob's bare skin.

"Just sit tight. He said he'd be here in twenty."

"Could you at least cover yourself? She looks like she's about to eat you alive." I grab his shirt from the chair behind me and toss it at him.

Rob chuckles and pulls on the shirt.

The cat burglar pouts. "Spoilsport."

"You shouldn't even be talking. Felon. You broke into *my* apartment, remember?" I jab the knife toward her.

Gently, Rob pries the blade from my hand and sets it beside him. "I don't feel like filing a police report tonight just because you were jealous."

I barely register his comment before the intruder protests.

"What? You mean you were bluffing about the knife to the throat?" She huffs.

"*I* was." Rob jabs his thumb at me. "But I don't think she would have hesitated to slit your throat. You're not exactly an innocent bystander here." He sobers and leans closer. "What the hell were you thinking?"

She shrugs and tosses him a saucy wink. "I was thinking I'd get lucky."

Red fills my vision. I'm about to rip this girl to pieces. Her cute nose, those sensual curves, her intoxicating eyes. She knows exactly what she's doing. Trying to throw herself on Rob's mercy.

Over my dead fucking body.

"Sorry, sweetheart. You're not my type." Rob leans back and shakes his head. "Besides, breaking and entering isn't exactly a romantic way to meet someone."

"Your loss, honey."

I can't take any more of this bitch. I'm going to do something drastic if I don't get some air. I shoot to my feet and stomp to the bathroom. Inside, I splash some water on the unbandaged side of my face and dab it with a towel. My whole face pulses with a bone-deep ache.

The bruises are starting to appear beneath the skin. It'll take heavy concealer to hide this shit from my clients, but I'll manage. Big sunglasses and a wide-brimmed hat does wonders for curious onlookers too. Hell, if it works for celebs, it'll work for me.

After using the toilet, I stop in my bedroom and lean out the open window. Yup, the fire escape ladder has been lowered. Bitch must be a damned spider monkey. I retreat into the room and close the window, ensuring I lock it. It's too hot to sleep with the windows closed. Guess I'll have to figure out another way to keep cool this summer…or splurge on an AC unit.

A knock at the door pulls me from my thoughts. I dash into the living room and wave to Rob. "I got it."

Peering through the peephole, I see a tall, somber man with a day's worth of scruff on his jaw and a scowl deep in his brow. I unlock the door and open it.

"Ma'am." He nods in respect, but I note his long perusal of my face. My hand covers the bandage protectively. "I'm looking for Dr. Thompson."

"He's in here. Please, come in." I step aside and allow him entry.

"Thanks for coming." Rob rises to his feet and extends his hand.

"This better be worth dragging my ass out of bed, Thompson." He glowers at Rob. "What the hell is going on?"

Rob gestures to me, encouraging me to tell him what happened.

"Well, I woke up and found this burglar in my bedroom looking through my things." I point to the woman seated on the couch.

My nerves are exposed, frayed, sparking like live wires of electricity. It feels like one more thing heaped on top of everything else. I'm about to scream into the sun.

"Did she do this?" He massages his own cheek with a fingertip, referring to my injury.

"No. Different incident." I fold my arms across my chest.

"Okay." His gaze narrows before shifting to the intruder. "And why didn't you just call the department?"

"I don't want a whole bunch of questions and paperwork right now," Rob says, his voice low. "I'm sure you can talk some sense into our…guest here."

A grin splits the detective's lips. He's handsome in that rough and tumble, brash, hard-boiled detective way. Dark hair, dark eyes, an even darker soul. This man has seen some shit. I shiver at the thought, even though my skin is overheated from the stale air in the room.

"I'll take care of her." The detective reaches down and grabs her arm, pulling her from the couch.

"Wait, don't let him take me! Call the cops. But don't let him take me. Please." Panic fills her eyes. "Please," she begs as he drags her toward the door.

"It's too late, kid. You're my problem now."

He pauses at the door and murmurs something in her ear. She stills immediately, her mouth pressed in a thin line.

"Thanks, Richards." Rob waves. "See you next week."

"Yeah, yeah." He nods to me. "Good night, ma'am."

"Night."

I lock the door behind them. Relief fills me at their absence.

Rob returns the frying pan and knife to the kitchen. "Good thing you told me to stay." He grins. "You might have killed someone tonight."

Irritation floods me. How can he tease me at a time like this? My emotions are all over the damn place. After the incident with Vic and now this burglar, I don't think I'll be able to sleep for a month. At least.

"Fuck you, Rob." I stomp past him, determined just to be out of his insufferable presence.

"Whoa." He grabs me by the hand. "Stop. Hold on."

I can't face him. Tension pulses between us. His hand burns like a brand against my skin. My body tenses when he steps closer. I pinch my eyes closed and take several deep breaths.

If I do this, if I face him now, my restraint will snap.

"Look at me, Marcy." I can feel his fingertips against my chin.

No. No. No. Don't do it. Fight against it. Don't say or do something you'll regret.

"Please, baby."
His plea breaks me.

CHAPTER 14

Rob

I fucked it up again. Damn it.

I meant it as a joke, something to lighten the mood. But instead of easing the tension, it inflamed her temper. There were a hundred things I could have said to offer comfort and support, but I stuck my foot in my mouth instead.

Her pulse pounds beneath my fingertips pressed against her wrist. My other hand lingers on her jaw, and I plead for her to look at me. A smart man would let her go, let her be angry at him. But I can't bear the thought that I caused her even a moment's pain.

Marcy spins around, pulling away from my touch. Her eyes blaze with internal fire.

"You're right. I almost killed someone tonight. Is there anything else you'd like to point out?" She folds her arms across her chest, emphasizing her breasts hidden by the thin tank top.

"Marcy, I didn't…"

"Didn't what? Think before you spoke? No shit." She huffs and throws her hands up. "Thank you for coming to my rescue tonight. Now get the fuck out."

One step forward and two steps back. My hope deflates at her dismissal, but I've gained this ground, and I refuse to give it up so easily. "I'm not leaving until you tell me what the fuck just happened?"

"What happened?" She scoffs. "That bitch happened. Breaking into my house is one thing but throwing herself all over you to try to get out of any punishment is a whole new low."

I blink twice. She's actually jealous. The realization strikes me like a physical blow and leaves me reeling.

But this is progress. I've never seen her truly jealous before. The flush of pink on her skin, the flaring nostrils, the firm set of her lips. She's livid, and now I know why.

"Wait a minute, are you telling me you're more upset because a woman flirted with me than you are that she broke into your apartment and scared the hell out of you?"

"No." She stiffens at the accusation, but it's too late. I see the truth through the cracks of her facade.

"I've known you for too long, Marcy, and I can read you like a book." A smile tugs at my lips, but I force myself to suppress it. I'll have the truth from her if it kills me.

"No, you can't."

"I can." I step closer, and she backs away from me, eyes wide. "What? Are you afraid I might take her up on her unspoken offer?"

"No."

"Wrap my hand in those curls and pin her against the wall. Take my fill of those lips and her dangerous curves." Satisfaction pours through me at her indignant gasp.

"I don't care what you do or with whom." She jabs her finger in my chest right before she hits the wall. "But I'll be damned if I let you screw some hussy in my living room."

My hands rest on the wall, framing her shoulders, holding her in place. Her quick breaths amplify the rise and fall of her chest. My gaze dips to the creamy skin exposed by the gaping tank top.

Enough games. I'm tired of denying the truth. I want Marcy, but she needs to know exactly how I feel first.

"So that's how it goes, huh? You're allowed to criticize my choices, but I can't ask you about your date."

She shivers when my words strike true.

"I'm only good enough when you go out with some asshole and he gets rough. Then you call me to patch you up."

"No." She shakes her head, and her scent surrounds me. It drives me wild.

"Is that all I am to you? A bleeding heart with a medical degree who's got a soft spot for his best friend's sister?"

Her mouth drops open. "I have never taken advantage of your kindness or your friendship with my brother."

"Not knowingly, perhaps." I lick my lips and hold her gaze steadily. "But you have to know, after all these years, I don't care solely because you're Arthur's little sister."

"What?" Her slow blink confirms the realization sinking into her brain. "I don't understand."

"I've wanted you since the first day we met." My heartbeat thunders in my chest in an arrhythmia. I might be dying, but I don't care. I've waited years to say this.

"But…" She shakes her head. "Why tell me now?"

"There's never been a good moment. Until now." I exhale a breath lodged in my chest. "I want you, Marcy. I've always wanted you."

Those luminous eyes hold mine for what feels like eternity. Marcy grabs my tee shirt and pulls me down to her level.

Her mouth is on mine in an instant, hot and sweet. She kisses me hard and fast.

Suddenly, I'm pulled into a vortex of pleasure, and I surrender completely.

I moan as the final piece of my restraint falls away. My hands drop to her shoulders and pull her close. My mouth opens beneath hers.

I'm lost in the kiss. In her. She tastes like pure bliss. I'm as close to heaven as I'll ever get.

Her arms encircle my neck, and I lift her off the ground, pinning her to the wall. Those slender legs wrap around me, and she grinds her hips against mine. I hiss at the pressure of her heat rocking against my aching cock.

Fuck. I need to be inside her.

I stumble back and carry her to the couch. When I sit, she comes with me, straddling my thighs.

I've fantasized about this for so long, it feels like a dream. Like she'll vanish in a plume of smoke.

I softly cup her injured cheek in my hand, and she draws back. Her eyes are glazed with passion and desperation.

"Are you sure you want this?"

"Rob, I swear to God, if you don't fuck me now, I'll spontaneously combust." She pulls her tank top over her head and tosses it to the floor.

I suck in a breath, and my hand slides up over her side. I take one breast in my hand. It overflows, and I squeeze, drawing a guttural moan from deep in her throat. She grinds her hips against me.

"Condom?" she whispers in my ear while her hands unfasten my belt.

"I don't…have any." Regret fills me. I know better than to take the chance, but I'm desperate. Reason breaks through. "I'm sorry. I'll…"

"When was the last time?" She nips my earlobe and tugs my pants down my hips.

"Years. Fuck. It's been years."

Marcy slides off my lap, pulling my pants to my ankles. She kneels and removes them completely. Her thumbs hook in the waistband of her shorts, and as she stands, she draws them down.

The sight of the curls between her thighs leaves me ravenous. I snatch her by the waist and pull her back into my lap.

She collides with me, and my cock brushes against her slick center.

"You?" The question is more of a gasp than a word.

I'm two seconds from taking her hard and fast. But I won't…not if she doesn't want me to. My restraint is hanging by a fraying thread.

"Too fucking long." She whimpers when I rock my hips against hers. "Rob, I need you. Now."

"But…"

"On the pill." Marcy grasps my jaw in her hand and kisses me hard. "Make me come."

My body responds immediately to her command. I lift her hips and position her over my cock. She sinks down, and I watch with fascination as she takes me.

Her eyes flutter closed, her nails dig into my shoulders. The heat of her surrounds me, clenching tight around my cock.

Once she's taken all of me, I take three deep breaths to keep myself from coming on the spot. My hands grip her hips to keep her from moving, and I rest my head on her chest.

Her fingers thread in my hair, and her laugh rumbles through me. I tease her nipple with my teeth, coaxing a moan from her wicked mouth.

Marcy bucks against me, and my cock swells even more.

"I won't last if you keep that up."

"We have all night," she croons in my ear as she gently rocks back and forth.

"Fuck it." Gripping her waist, I thrust deep.

She gasps and holds tight as we fall into a rhythm. I'm drowning in sensations of her, trying to hold out until she takes her own pleasure.

"That's it, baby." I urge her on as her soft moans fill the space between us. "Take what you need."

This unleashes something within her. Gone is the hesitancy. The restraint. She holds tight as she grinds her hips, searching for friction and pressure. I slide my thumb over her clit and circle it in time with her panting gasps. Her head falls back in surrender.

I've never seen anything more beautiful in my life. A goddess taking her pleasure, eyes closed, mouth parted. Her whimpers tell me she's close to orgasm. When she finally breaks, it's my name on her lips that tips me over the edge.

I come hard, filling her. Her pussy clenches around me with the aftershocks of her climax, milking every ounce of pleasure from my body.

Fuck. Me.

When she collapses against me, we cling to each other, covered in sweat. It's not how I imagined it. It's so much better.

I stroke my hand over her spine and she moans, arching deeper against me. "Shower?"

"Hmm?"

"Shower. To cool off."

"That sounds amazing." Marcy kisses me. Slow and drugging. My cock twitches inside her. She laughs. "Ready again so soon?"

"What can I say? I'm making up for lost time."

We manage to disentangle ourselves and stumble into her small bathroom. I let her shower, and then step in behind her.

There's not nearly enough room to do what I want to do to her, so instead, I slide my fingers deep into her cunt.

Her lovely moans echo off the tile when she comes, soaking my fingers. I lick them clean, making her eyes widen. She's sweet. I can't wait to taste her again.

And again. And again.

Marcy is mine, and I'll be damned if I'm going to let her go now that I've finally claimed her.

CHAPTER 15

Marcy

What is happening to me?

Every fantasy I ever had about Rob never came close to the reality. I don't know what finally snapped, but his confession should have left me reeling. Instead, relief flooded me.

I've wanted him for so long, actually having him is surreal. And when he let me take control on the couch? Fuck, that was the hottest thing he could have done. I don't think I've come that hard…ever.

"Bed, now," he whispers against my skin, gently nudging me out of the shower.

"You love giving orders, don't you?" I towel dry my torso and step aside, giving him room.

He cocks his head. "Sweetheart, I've wanted you in my bed for a long time. Now that I finally have you there, I intend to explore every inch of you with my mouth."

Gooseflesh pebbles my skin at the sinful promise. "My bed, you mean."

"Semantics." He gives my ass a playful swat. The sting warms me.

Rob is more adventurous than I ever imagined. Granted, I may have tried to downplay the possibility of him being a thoughtful lover to quell the need burning inside me.

The sun is rising, but I'm wide awake and desperate for Rob to make good on his promise. I toss the towel over the chair and sprawl on the bed like a starfish basking in the early morning light.

He watches from the doorway, towel slung low on his hips, damp hair hanging across his forehead. He pushes it back and stalks closer.

I never knew all those muscles were hidden beneath his polos and scrubs. I want to trace my tongue over every ridge and leave my mark on that pristine skin.

Holding his gaze, I draw my leg up and let the warm air brush against my pussy. He pauses at the foot of the bed as if waiting for an invitation.

I draw my finger along my swollen lips. His eyes darken two shades while they follow my gentle strokes.

A growl rips from his throat as he climbs on the bed, settling between my thighs. He shoves my hand away and nudges my legs wider, exposing me. My breath catches when he blows across my aching clit. Then his mouth covers me, and I'm caught up in the storm once more.

While his tongue teases my folds, I run my fingers through his hair, gripping tight. He suckles my clit in his mouth. The sensation overwhelms me. I buck my hips, and he deepens his exploration, devouring my pussy with the same hunger he showed in his kiss. His moan sends shockwaves through my body.

Panting and gasping, I cling to him, unable to relieve the tension building inside me.

Rob lifts his gaze to meet mine. He's taking his time making good on his promise to explore every inch of me with his mouth.

When he finally slides two fingers in, rubbing with the perfect amount of pressure, I combust, my head falling back against the blankets.

"Fuck." My grip tightens as the orgasm hits. Sparks of pleasure radiate through me like fireworks against a black sky.

But Rob doesn't relent. He doubles his efforts and drinks me dry.

When I release him, he leans back and grins, his lips glistening with my arousal. He wipes his mouth with the back of his hand. That shouldn't be as hot as it is.

"I'm not done with you, sweetheart." He pulls my weightless body up and kisses me. "Put your hands on the wall."

I manage to shift my pleasure-wrought body to the head of the bed and place my palms against the headboard. Anticipation sparks like a live wire through my limbs.

Rob trails his hand along the inside of my thigh, nudging my legs wider. "Arch your back." I do as he instructs, and he groans in appreciation. "Good girl."

"Rob." His name falls from my lips when he trails his fingers over my pussy. "Please."

"Is this what you want, baby?" He slowly enters me from behind, and I'm drowning in him. With one arm around my waist, he encircles my throat with the other. "Keep your hands right there. Don't move."

The pressure of his arms is featherlight, but with his cock buried deep inside me, I'm grounded. My head spins. I've never been this vulnerable during sex, not since…

I pinch my eyes closed and tense at the unwelcome memory.

"Marcy," he whispers against my ear. "Breathe."

I exhale the breath I'd been holding, and Rob withdraws. He drives deep when I gasp. His teeth graze my shoulder, making me shiver as he pounds into me. Over and over, he takes control and pushes me higher. His hand presses on my lower abdomen, fingers skimming my sex.

The build is slower, more intimate, but Rob has me. Holds me close. His whispered endearments soothe me, his dirty words stoke the flame burning inside me.

I've never felt this before. This bond forged by pleasure and trust. I bask in it.

Rob pulls me away from the wall and lays me on the bed facing him. My pussy aches at the loss of his cock, but before I can protest, he's filling me again, deeper still.

His mouth covers mine, and I wrap my arms around him. The kiss consumes me.

My legs encircle his waist, and I ride the waves of pleasure, bucking my hips in tandem with his thrusts. I want all of him, every last drop of his being, bound to me.

Throughout years of longing, I feared I would never experience the passion I knew Rob possessed. I fought against it. Convinced myself he could never feel the same.

Lies. All of it. Why did I waste so much time?

Another orgasm crests, and Rob murmurs my name when he follows with his own release. He rolls to his side and pulls me against him.

After a few quiet moments, Rob presses a kiss to my forehead. "Are you okay?"

"Never better." I nestle closer and drape myself across him. This I could get used to…the quiet moment of repose between bursts of pleasure. With Rob. Only with him.

He trails his finger across my bare arm. "You hungry?"

"Starving."

"I'll make you something." Rob kisses me softly on the lips and climbs out of bed.

I stretch across the mattress and watch him leave. Who has an ass like that? So squeezable.

Rob grabs his towel and turns, catching me red-handed. "Stop looking at me like I'm a piece of meat."

"What's good for the goose is good for the gander."

He huffs. "I've never looked at you like that."

"You just did. Right before you ate my pussy like a man starved."

"I did." He chuckles. "Fine. Stare all you want. I guess it's yours now anyway."

"Oh? So does that mean I can smack your ass in front of my brother?" I laugh at the look of horror on his face.

"Within reason, Marcy. Geezus, we're not animals in heat."

I crawl on all fours toward the end of the bed. "Speak for yourself."

"No." Rob holds his hand up, warding me off. "I'm making breakfast. Save that insatiable lust for later."

I pout, but the growling in my stomach agrees with Rob. "Fine."

Once Rob heads into the kitchen, I clean up in the bathroom and pull on a silk robe.

There's something so sexy about a man in an apron. Rob's donned my blue apron and has bacon sizzling in a skillet. He adds a little cream to the eggs before whisking.

"Smells delicious." I rest my cheek against his shoulder.

He kisses my forehead. "Grab a plate for the bacon."

I hold the plate as he places the bacon on it and drains some of the grease. When he pours the eggs into the skillet, I can't help but admire his fluid movements and his gracefulness in the kitchen.

Curiosity overwhelms me. "Do you like to cook?"

"I don't mind it." He smiles and it softens his features. "Don't really have a choice. I have to eat."

"Bachelor life can be rough."

He nods. "It's more fun to have someone to cook for."

I lean against the counter beside him. "Why didn't you ever marry?"

Rob's gaze fixes on me, honesty reflected in his handsome face. "Thought that would be obvious now."

My face warms when the realization hits me. "Marriage isn't all it's cracked up to be."

"With the wrong person, I agree. But with the right person…" He shrugs his shoulders, leaving the implication hanging in the air.

"Rob…"

"It's okay, Marcy. I understand." He pushes the egg around in the pan as it cooks. "You mind setting the table? Coffee should be ready."

Regret settles in the pit of my stomach. This wasn't how I wanted our morning to go. I have so many things I want to say, questions I want to ask, but suddenly, my brain doesn't want to cooperate. I set the table in silence and pour some coffee.

Rob puts the eggs on our plates and returns the skillet to the stovetop. I fidget with my fork until he joins me. Sitting at my small dining table like this seems even more intimate than the multiple rounds of sex we just enjoyed.

Breakfast in silence. I'm used to it when I'm alone, but with Rob's larger-than-life presence across from me, I can't focus on anything but him.

"Arthur and Kate will be home in a few days. I'm sure you're excited to see them." Rob sips his coffee.

"I am." I push the eggs around on my plate and take a halfhearted bite. "What do we tell them?"

"About us?" Rob arches his brow.

"Yeah."

"What do you want to tell them?"

"I don't know." I finish the last bite on my plate and shove it away.

"We don't have to tell them anything if you don't want to. Not until you're ready." Rob reaches across the table and takes my hand. "But I guarantee your brother will figure it out. He's not an idiot. He has eyes."

"Can we just enjoy the day together? Please? I don't want to worry about my brother or Kate or anything else." I drop my gaze to the table.

We should talk about us. What are *we* now? I can't bring myself to broach the topic knowing it'll make this all too real. If it's real, then it can end, and I can't handle that right now.

"Whatever you need, sweetheart."

Rob gives my hand one last squeeze before collecting the dishes and carrying them to the kitchen. We work as a team to clean up, and he wraps his arms around me when I finish the last dish.

His lips reignite that heat when he presses them to my neck. The hard press of his cock against my ass makes me wiggle my hips. He growls in response and tightens his grip on my waist.

"Come with me. I want to taste you again."

"No." I spin in his arms. "It's my turn to taste you."

Rob's eyes drift closed, and he murmurs a silent *thank you* to the heavens. I jab him in the ribs and laugh when he winces.

Caught up in the moment, he sweeps me into his arms and carries me into the bedroom. I spend the rest of the day exploring him as thoroughly as he explores me.

There's never been a more perfect day. Eat, sleep, fuck. With Rob, it's heaven. I never want it to end.

But when Monday morning comes, my alarm wakes me and the bed is empty. Was it just a dream?

There's a note on his pillow.

Marcy,

I left for work early. Didn't want to wake you. Had to go home and change. Working doubles all week. I'll call you when I have a free minute.

Love, Rob

I tuck the note into a book on my nightstand and manage to drag myself out of bed. My whole body burns with residual bliss at this recent adventure into sexual activity. I don't know how many times we had sex, but I'm not complaining. My body, however, is having second thoughts.

In the shower, my muscles relax under the spray. The note plays in my mind. I wish he would have woken me, but I understand. We both have jobs and lives. And they've intersected. What do we do now? Where do we go from here?

Part of me hopes I didn't fuck everything up by sleeping with Rob. I don't regret it—not even a little bit—but what the hell happens next?

What do I want?

This hasn't changed my mind on marriage. And Rob still deserves to have that option, should he desire a wife and a family. I'm just not sure it's something I might want in the future. Although, the thought of living with Rob has its appeal. We've been in each other's lives for so long, there's nothing about him I don't already know.

Then why the hell am I scared to death to tell him? To say the words?

What if he wants something totally different? I don't want to lose whatever this is.

But I know we'll have to talk it out at some point.

We'll both be busy all week. Maybe it'll give us both time to think things through. I just hope he doesn't start having second thoughts.

I just hope *I* don't start having second thoughts.

CHAPTER 16

Rob

I haven't spoken to Marcy in two days. Not because I don't want to, but the ER has been chaos since Monday. Even Tabby has felt the brunt of my absence. Good thing Arthur and Kate returned from their honeymoon yesterday.

I spent the night at the hospital, curled up on a cot in one of the back rooms. We had two physicians call in this week, so I'm picking up the slack. I expected double shifts, but I didn't expect to move into the hospital permanently.

Thank God for Summer and the other nurses in the unit. They're more capable than some of the doctors on staff and give me a chance to breathe between cases. The stress of being on the floor has now overcome the adrenaline rush I used to get in my thirties. This shit is starting to take its toll on me. And now that Marcy and I are finally on the same page, a quiet life of office visits is starting to sound appealing. I've wasted too much time already; I'll be damned if I waste any more.

In my small office, I leaf through the files on my desk. These cases need notes. I glance at the phone. Maybe I should call her. It's two in the afternoon, and I'm pretty sure she's at work. I have the evening off, so I'll call her tonight when I'm home. Maybe we can grab some dinner.

Refocusing my wandering thoughts, I open the first file. The phone rings.

"Dr. Thompson." I lean it against my shoulder and finish a note in the patient's file.

"Rob, it's Arthur. Am I interrupting?"

I toss the pen aside. "No. What do you need?"

"Kate wants to know if you're free for dinner. She's making lasagna with a recipe she got in Italy. A thank you for watching Tabby."

My stomach growls at the thought of a home-cooked meal. I've eaten cafeteria food for the past few days, and my body will revolt if I imbibe one more gelatin bowl or chocolate pudding. As much as I don't want to intrude, this reprieve is exactly what I need. I can't help but wonder if Marcy will be there too.

"Yeah, my shift ends at six." I glance at the clock. Only four more hours.

"Perfect. Dinner will be ready at seven. See you then."

"Thanks." I hang up the phone and return to the stack of files.

As if the universe could sense my anticipation, it throws everything at me at once. Three traumas from a car accident, a sprained ankle, two screaming toddlers, and a very irritable octogenarian who has no interest in cooperating with the nurses round out my afternoon in the ER.

Exhausted, I manage to leave the hospital at six thirty. It takes me thirty minutes in traffic to get home, ten to shower, and five to pull on some clean clothes. God, I hope they're clean. When did I last do laundry? I really need to spend some time getting my place in order. The days swarm together, but all I can think about is Marcy.

It's quarter after seven when I knock on Arthur's door. Kate answers it.

"We were getting worried." She steps aside and lets me in.

"Yeah, sorry. Work was chaotic today." I hand her a bouquet of flowers I had picked up from a corner vendor on the way home. "How was Italy?"

Kate's cheeks pinken, and her eyes glaze over in that nostalgic way people get when remembering a happy memory. "It was heavenly."

Tabby weaves through my legs and mews. I pick her up and scratch her ears. "I'm glad you had a great time."

The scent of tomatoes, rosemary, and meat fills the air. My stomach growls. Kate takes Tabby from my arms when Arthur appears.

"About time, I'm starving." He claps his hand on my shoulder. "Let's eat."

While we eat, Kate tells me all about their adventures in Italy. The lasagna is perfection, like a tiny slice of paradise. Kate and Arthur's united culinary skills are unmatched by any other couple I know. When she brings out the tiramisu, I'm practically swooning. This woman knows the way to a man's heart.

"Do you know what tiramisu means in Italian?" Kate's eyes glow with amusement as I take the first bite.

A moan rips from my lips at the decadent bliss on my fork. I shake my head and savor another bite.

"*It makes me happy.*" She chuckles. "That's what the waiter told me. How fitting is that?"

Arthur laughs at her giddy response.

"Makes total sense to me," I say between bites. "I guess *orgasm in a bowl* was taken?"

Kate snorts with laughter. Arthur shakes his head, but I see the smile on his lips.

"Any problems while we were gone?" Arthur changes the subject when Kate takes the plates into the kitchen.

Saturday night with Marcy covered in blood and bruises flashes through my mind. Damn, I guess there's no avoiding it. He'll figure it out the moment he sees her. Better I tell him now and give him time to assimilate the news before he sees Marcy.

"There was an incident." I hold my friend's gaze. "With Marcy."

The muscle in Arthur's jaw ticks. His eyes darken, and his hands clench into fists. "What about Marcy?"

"She went out on a date Saturday. He roughed her up good." I hold up a hand when Arthur looks ready to explode. "She called me when she got home, and I took care of it. A couple of bruises and a nasty cut on the cheek. She was shaken up. So I stayed with her."

Arthur's deceptively calm response leaves me unnerved. "Who did it?"

"She refused to tell me." I'm honest with him, but it's killing me not telling him the whole truth of what happened that night. Between her and me. "Even though she wouldn't come to the ER, I wrote up a report at the hospital in case she decides to file charges."

"But she won't tell you who it was?"

I shake my head. "I didn't push either. She's scared. It brought all that past trauma rushing to the surface. So I stayed at her place on Saturday. It's a good thing I did too, because a cat burglar broke in early Sunday morning and scared the hell out of her."

"What?" Arthur rubs his hand over his face.

"Some young woman with more stealth than sense. I took care of it." I correct myself. "Well, I called Richards and *he* took care of her."

"Richards?" He furrows his brow. "Why didn't you call the cops?"

"Because I didn't need a whole bunch of questions about what happened to Marcy on top of everything else. She didn't need that circus either." I shake my head. "You remember what happened the last time."

"Yeah." Arthur relaxes a bit, his hands flexing against the table's surface. "But she's all right?"

"Marcy? Yeah, she's good. Tougher than she looks." I sip my wine.

"I'll check on her tomorrow." My friend slumps back in his chair looking exhausted. "Fuck. Why didn't she tell me when I called her last night?"

"She probably didn't want you to worry. You can get a little overbearing when you're all worked up." I smile. "It's not a bad thing, but sometimes she wants to fight her own battles, big brother. You can't do it for her."

"I know…but shit, I hate feeling so damned helpless."

"Amen to that." I salute him with the glass.

"Thanks for coming to her rescue."

"It's the least I could do."

My stomach twists in knots. I should tell him that we hooked up. But I don't think he needs to hear how many times I railed his little sister after confessing my longstanding affection for her the same night as two traumatic events.

"I should go. It's been a long day."

Kate appears with a frown. "Leaving so soon?"

"Yeah, it's been a long week."

She laughs. "It's only Wednesday."

"It's Friday in my mind thanks to these eighteen-hour shifts." I kiss her on the cheek. "Thanks for dinner. It hit the spot."

Arthur shakes my hand. "Thanks again for everything. The Black Penny on Friday night?"

"Sounds great." I head for the door, petting Tabby on my way out.

The emptiness of my apartment leaves a lot to be desired, but I'm too tired to care. With a full belly, the exhaustion sinks in fast. I manage to change into sleep pants before collapsing into bed. My head hits the pillow, and I'm sinking into dreamland fast.

Shit. I forgot to call Marcy. Fuck.

Sleep evades me, and I stare at the ceiling, wondering if she's going to kill me for neglecting her all week. It's not that I wanted to. Far from it.

I want her all the time. Her company. Her conversation. Her pussy clenched around my cock. Her taste on my tongue. I want all of her. But I haven't figured out how to convince her to take the next logical step.

Now that I've had her, I want everything. Nothing will fill this ache in my chest. I should know; I've tried to fill it before. Marcy's the only one I want.

I love her, and I don't want to live without her. But how the hell do I make her see sense?

I'm not like them.

Shit. Time's ticking, and I'm not getting any younger. I'd rather negotiate with a strung-out addict than Marcy. She's dead set on remaining single. But I've tasted what we could have together. So has she. Maybe it's time I upped the ante.

CHAPTER 17

Marcy

I miss him. When I woke alone on Monday morning and my heart ached at his absence, I told myself it wasn't a big deal. The feeling would wear off. But it hasn't. It's gotten worse.

I tried to call him, but no answer. He must be working overtime at the hospital. It's nothing personal. Right? We each have our own lives and careers. I have plenty to keep me busy this week. I refocus my attention away from the multiple orgasms Rob gave me during our time together over the weekend.

Monday and Tuesday were spent reorganizing inventory for the upcoming summer spectacular event hosted by MTV. Today, I spent all day going over the books with my accountant and the upcoming month's schedule. By the time I make it home, it's after nine.

My apartment feels empty without Rob. He filled that space without effort, making it feel more like a home than it has since I moved in. I toss my purse on the couch just as the doorbell rings.

"Who the fuck…" I trudge to the door and peek out the peephole. Of course. I open the door for my brother. "When did you get back?"

"Yesterday, right before I called you to tell you I was home."

Oh yeah, I forgot that.

He stands like a concrete pilar in my doorway. "Are you going to invite me in?"

"With that scowl on your face, no." I sigh at the pathetic twitch of his lips and step aside, sweeping my arm wide in invitation. "Please, come in."

He scans the apartment while I close and lock the door. "Is anyone here?"

"No. I just got home from work." I push past him and open the refrigerator. "Want a drink?"

"I'm fine."

"Suit yourself." I grab the open bottle of chardonnay and pour a glass. "So what brings you over so late?"

"What the hell happened?" Arthur reaches out and touches my cheek.

"Nothing." I shove his hand away. He's always too protective, too observant, but I don't feel like rehashing it right now.

"Bullshit, Marcy." He puts his hands in his pockets, and his eyes narrow. "Rob came over for dinner."

"Fuck." I down my wine in one swallow.

"Anything you want to tell me?" His patience burrows a hole in my conscience.

"No."

"I'm your brother. You can't hide this shit from me." His tone softens. "Rob told me someone roughed you up."

"Rob's got a big mouth."

"He came to your rescue, and he's my friend. Why would you think he'd keep this from me?" Arthur cocks his head, studying me with his all too observant eyes. At my silence, he continues. "He told me he was here during the break-in too."

"Oh great." I twist the glass in my hand.

"Marcy, if you don't feel safe here, you're welcome to stay with me and Kate." He clears his throat when overwhelming emotion seeps into the words. "You're family, and I want you safe."

"Thanks, but I'll pass." I fidget in my seat. "It's too close to…"

Rob. I can't bring myself to say it. It sounds stupid. I don't want to sound weak and helpless. And I certainly don't want Rob to think I'm desperate. Even if I do miss him, I can't be that close. No matter how much I want him in my life and my bed.

"Too close to what?" Arthur presses.

"Nothing. Never mind."

"No, it's not nothing." He sits on the couch beside me and takes my hand. "Whatever's going on, you don't have to face it alone. Kate and I love you too much to see you struggle in silence. Rob's worried about you too."

"Of course he is." I meet my brother's gaze.

"I don't know why you hate him so much. He's practically part of the family."

The words strike my heart with a force that leaves me breathless. *He's more than that,* I want to scream. He's everything I've ever wanted, ever dreamed of.

But I'm too damaged, too broken. There aren't fairy-tale endings and rainbows waiting for me. I'm a magnet for assholes who treat me like shit.

Rob's different. He's too pure, too righteous. He deserves a woman who isn't shattered and terrified of commitment.

"I know," I whisper as tears well up in my eyes.

"Look, he didn't tell me all the details. He just wanted to check on you, make sure you're okay."

"Why didn't he do it himself then?"

"He's been working all week. Double shifts." He pats my hand. "I'm sure he'll check on you this weekend, once he has a break."

"Sure." I nod, ignoring the twisting guilt in the pit of my stomach.

Does Arthur know something happened between us? I mean, he's not blind, but I'm not volunteering any information. Not tonight. My body twitches and I stand, unable to sit under his scrutiny.

"You don't look convinced." His gaze follows me. "Did something else happen?"

"No." I bite the edge of my fingernail. "Isn't it bad enough I got beat up and robbed in the same night?"

"I wasn't talking about that." He cocks his head and furrows his brow. "Rob…did you two have a fight or something?"

Images of Rob with his head buried between my thighs flash to the forefront of my mind. My body tingles at the reminder of his warm mouth and talented fingers. I shake my head, trying to purge the wicked, tempting thoughts from my brain.

"No. Nothing like that." My tone is too adamant, and I take a deep breath.

"Something happened between you two. I've been friends with Rob long enough to know when he's not being completely honest." He rises slowly to his feet. "And you…well, I know when you're keeping things from me."

"Nothing happened between Rob and me." I hold his gaze determined to make him believe me. Willing him to believe my blatant lie. "He came over, patched me up, saved me from the cat burglar, and that's it. End of story."

"Okay. Fine. It just seems like you're both a bit on edge now." He lifts his hands in supplication.

"After everything that happened, you expect me not to be?" I scoff.

"That's not what I meant, and you know it."

"Then what are you trying to say?"

"Look, I know you and Rob aren't exactly friends. I'm not even sure when the animosity started between you two." He rakes his fingers through his hair. "But Rob's not your enemy."

"I know that."

"Then stop treating him like he is." Arthur exhales sharply. "He's trying to be nice, the least you could do is to not act like you want to claw his eyes out every time he walks into the room."

"He walked away completely unscathed this weekend."

"Did he?" He arches a brow, frown firmly in place.

Guilt burrows deep into my bones. *Did he really?* I shake my head to clear the invasive thought.

"Listen, I'm not going to pry into your personal life. You've done a hell of a job getting yourself back on track after Dan. I'm proud of you and all you've accomplished." He sighs. "I just don't want to see you throw it all away over another asshole."

Even if he's not an asshole and your best friend? I swallow the retort, knowing I won't like the conversation that follows.

Rob isn't asking me to throw away my career or my dreams. It was one night. I have no idea where it's going to go from here. That's the part that scares the hell out of me.

"Thanks," I mumble, my head spinning with the hundred possible directions this conversation could go if I pursue it. Instead, I wrap my arms around my brother's waist and lay my cheek against his chest.

He squeezes me against him and kisses my forehead. "I love you, Marcy. I just want you to be happy."

"I love you too."

Arthur releases me. "I'll let you get some sleep. Call me if you need anything."

"Will do. Tell Kate I said 'hi.'" I walk him to the door and lock it behind him before collapsing against it and closing my eyes.

Why didn't I just tell him the truth? Because it's Arthur, and he's known Rob for years. I don't want to start some ridiculous feud between them because we hooked up. My brother is protective of me, but he respects my decisions.

After a soothing shower to cool off, I pull on my pajamas and curl up in bed.

I washed the sheets, but the pillow still smells like him. The memories, like whisps of smoke, curl around me, pulling me into a play-by-play review of every sexual act we indulged in.

Rob has always been my dream, my fantasy. Crushing on him as a teen was hard because I knew he would never see me as more than Arthur's little sister. Then after Dan...well, I was broken and scared. I didn't want or need a man to rescue me. But Rob stood beside me, as steadfast as any brother. Never asking for anything, never pushing me.

How I convinced myself he hated me, I'll never understand. Rob's always been there. My knight in bloody scrubs. I pushed him away because this feeling, it terrifies me.

I love Rob, and I always have.

But what the hell am I supposed to do now that we've crossed that line?

Maybe it's time we sit down and have an adult conversation. I need to know what he expects from me.

But first, I need to figure out what I want from him. Am I really willing to break my own vow? Being Rob's wife doesn't sound bad now that I've had time to think about it. I mean, time to seriously consider it.

Sleep evades me while my brain struggles to make sense of my change in plans. I hug Rob's pillow to my chest and inhale deeply, wishing he were here with me now.

CHAPTER 18

Rob

"Sir, you can't just barge in here like that." Summer's voice carries through the waiting room.

"I must speak with him now."

Wait…I know that voice. Following the sound of commotion, I open the door to the waiting room and see my best friend arguing with one of the nurses.

"It's all right, Summer. I'll handle it." I chuckle when she shakes her head and turns away in a huff.

Arthur faces me. "Finally. I tried to catch you before you left this morning."

"My shift started at four a.m." I hold the door for him. "Come on. My office is back here."

The handful of patients waiting to be seen follow us with curious stares. I don't have much time, but Arthur looks agitated and I don't need an incident in the waiting room. There are far too many of those every day or so as it is.

Summer glances at us as we pass her. "The patient in five is ready for you."

"I'll be there in a moment." I push open my office door and motion for my friend to enter. "Thank you, Summer." With a wink in her direction, I close the door.

"Now, what's so important—"

My words die when Arthur turns around, grabs the lapel of my lab coat, and shoves me against the wall.

"What happened between you and Marcy this weekend?"

"I told you what happened." I grab his fist and slowly peel it from my coat.

"Bullshit." He releases me with a growl and takes a step back. "Something changed between you two. Did you sleep with my sister?"

Shit. This is not how I wanted him to find out, nor is it the best place to discuss it.

"Did Marcy tell you?" My hand runs along my jaw.

"No. She didn't. And neither did you." Arthur's eyes darken. "I figured it out on my own since you're both too chicken shit to admit it like grown adults."

"When did you figure it out?"

"Last night. When I went over to my sister's place. I wanted to check on her after what you said at dinner." He sinks into the chair against the wall. "I offered her a place to stay until she felt safe to be on her own, but she turned me down."

"Sounds like Marcy." I sit in the chair opposite him.

"She's so damned stubborn." He shakes his head. "I just wanted to make sure she was safe."

"Is she?"

"I guess. Hell, I don't know anymore. When I asked her what happened, she gave me the same story you did."

"What tipped our hand?"

"She didn't curse your name when I asked if you two got into a fight." He scoffs. "You two are always at odds with each other. Normally, she gets a sour look on her face when your name comes up, but this time…she smiled."

Relief fills me. "You say that like it's a bad thing."

"It's not. It's just different."

"Change can be a good thing, Arthur."

He nods. "You're right. But this year has been *all* change. It's a bit overwhelming…in a good way." His gaze holds mine. "I just want to be sure Marcy's taken care of. She's strong, but she's also fragile. I don't want her to go through that hell again."

"You really think I'd let that happen?" I rest my hand on Arthur's shoulder. "I've loved Marcy for years. Years, damn it. I will never let anyone hurt her again. Not while she's with me. Not while there's life in my body."

"I know, Rob. That's the only reason I didn't come through the door swinging." He smiles.

"At least you're not pissed off about it."

"Oh, I was. Kate calmed me down before she let me leave the house this morning."

"What did Kate have to say about it?"

"She told me you two were made for each other. She's seen the sparks fly between you firsthand." He chuckles. "I didn't want to admit it, but she's right. Even when you two were fighting, there were fireworks. I just refused to admit to myself that my best friend and my sister could be happy together."

Hearing those words set my heart free. For years, I worried about what Arthur would say or do if I confessed my affection for his sister, but now I feel as though a weight has been lifted. I'm free to pursue the woman I want without concern about losing my best friend.

"I promise, I will protect her with every fiber of my being." The vow seals over my heart. "I will love her until I draw my dying breath."

"So you want to marry her?"

"Absolutely. If she'll have me."

"That's good. I'm glad to hear it." He strokes his jaw. "Have you told her this?"

"No." Shame floods me. "I was planning on telling her over dinner this weekend, once my last shift ends."

"Better sooner than later." Arthur stands and offers his hand. I shake it. "Good luck."

"Thanks. I know she's not interested in getting married again, but I can hope. Right?"

Arthur laughs, and the booming sound echoes in my small office. "You've known her long enough to know that's going to be a long and bloody battle, my friend. But if anyone can make Marcy see the value in marriage, it's you."

"I love her. I'll wait as long as it takes, do whatever it takes."

He pulls me into a brief hug and shakes his head. "If you need backup, let me know. Kate and I are rooting for you."

"Thanks."

With a final goodbye, Arthur heads down the hall toward the exit. As I watch him walk away, my heart aches. I really need to talk to Marcy. Now more than ever. She has to know how much I love her.

But I've never said the words before. Ever. No woman has ever earned them. Marcy has. She has all my love. I would die for her.

"Dr. Thompson," Summer's voice cuts through my thoughts. "Five is still waiting for you."

"Yes, of course, my apologies." I take the chart she offers and skim through the notes.

It takes every ounce of effort to push thoughts of Marcy to the back of my mind while I work. Summer catches me daydreaming a few times and directs my attention back to the task at hand. I don't know what I'd do without the stellar nursing staff.

After ten years working here, I'm loath to leave them. We've become such a great team and have earned the recognition of the city three years in a row as the best emergency center in Manhattan. I don't know how I would function without them.

But weeks like this one wear on me. I'm exhausted, and now that I have Marcy, there's hope for something more than just emergencies and adrenaline-fueled shifts.

If I can get Marcy to say yes, maybe, just maybe, I can start my own practice and take some time to enjoy life with the woman I love. At least, it's worth considering now.

By four o'clock, I'm dragging. I've pulled eighteen-hour shifts, but ten is still exhausting. Especially after a week of back-to-back double shifts. One hour left, then I can go home and get some rest.

"Oh, my! I didn't even know he was dating anyone." Summer's voice drifts up from the nurse's station. She snaps to attention along with three other nurses when I round the corner.

"Who's dating again?" I ask, wondering if they're gossiping about me and just got caught red-handed.

"Oh, it's, uh…just this actor," Anne, the receptionist, says with a dreamy smile. "He's Hollywood's most eligible bachelor, but I guess he's off the market now." Her smile fades with a sigh.

"We don't have anything better to do than gossip about celebrities?" I chuckle.

"Yes, sir." The nurses return to work, but Summer lingers.

"Did you think we were talking about you?" She jabs me in the side with her elbow.

"Maybe. I don't know. You all seem to like talking about my personal life."

"Oh, you have one of those now?"

I scoff with mock indignance. "I'll have you know, I just found a wonderful woman who doesn't take advantage of my sensitive nature."

"Are you sure you're not just making her up?"

"She's real." I grin. "And she's amazing."

"Hmm, that's why you were glowing when you came in on Monday, huh? Finally got some action, Doc?" Summer laughs as we make our way down the hall to the last room where a patient waits for evaluation.

"I can't help it if you're jealous." I quickly sober when we reach the room.

The young woman looks up from the magazine she's reading. "Sorry." She tosses it onto the chair beside her.

My attention follows the colorful paper, but the moment it settles on the plastic seat, I freeze.

No, that can't be right. I snatch up the magazine and inspect the cover.

Vic Simmons Spied at Romantic Dinner with Mystery Woman is splayed across the front, over a photograph of a couple at an intimate meal.

"Oh shit." My brain replays Marcy's words over and over. Her insistence on not revealing the name of the man who hurt her. "Excuse me for a moment."

Summer covers my lapse as I toss the magazine on the bed and dart from the room.

This can't be happening. No. No. No. I reach the front desk and ask Anne for the magazine she was reading. She hands it to me with a curious look.

Different magazine, similar photograph. Only in this one, I recognize the sweep of her hair, the curve of her jaw, those lips I've tasted. Marcy on a romantic date with Hollywood hotshot, Vic Simmons. Son of a bitch.

He's the bastard who hurt her.

CHAPTER 19

Marcy

Today's the day. After work, I'm going straight over to Rob's and we're talking this out. It's been horrible trying to focus this week without knowing what's in his head. We need to figure this out. Period.

On the subway to work, I get a few more stares than usual. It must be the fishnet stockings and leather skirt. Maybe the neon top is too much? Doesn't matter. I want Madonna energy today, and I'm damn proud of my effort. Shrugging it off as typical New York, I continue with the commute by diving into the fashion magazine Liana gave me yesterday.

The moment I walk in the door, all hell breaks loose. Liana and Donna rush toward me. Their voices overlap as they ramble, and I can't make sense of the words.

"Whoa, slow down. What happened?"

"You haven't seen?" Donna turns to Liana. "She doesn't know."

"Shit." Liana darts down the hall and returns with a magazine. "You're front-page news."

"What?" I nearly choke on my gum after I take the magazine from her hands. *Vic Simmons Spied at Romantic Dinner with Mystery Woman.* Fear grabs me by the throat and squeezes. There on the cover is a photograph of Vic and me at the restaurant on Saturday night. Fuck. Fuck. Fuck. I pinch my eyes closed, praying it's a joke.

"That's you, right?" Liana points to the woman sitting across from Vic. "I'd recognize you anywhere."

"You went out with Vic Simmons and didn't tell us?" Donna gapes at me.

"Well, yeah, but it was just dinner. Nothing happened. I'm not dating Vic Simmons." My hand covers the cut on my cheek. "It was nothing."

"Hold on." Liana pulls my hand away and sucks in a breath. "Did he do that?"

"What? No. I fell, hit the corner of a table."

"Uh-huh. That's interesting. Because Monday you told me a cat scratched you, and the bruise was from an errant swinging door." Donna crosses her arms. Her eyes darken like a storm over the bay. "Spill it, sister."

"It's fine. Forget it." I shove Liana's hand away. Panic pulses thick around me, and I need space to breathe. Pushing past them, I head for my office. More tabloids litter my desk. I shove them all into the trash and sit down.

Taking out the checklist for the following week's jobs, I read the words, but nothing sticks. My mind swarms with building anxiety. What if Rob sees this? What if he finds out who I was with on Saturday? He'll know. Fuck.

I bite my lip and try to focus on the list. Tears prick my eyes.

"Honey." Liana's concerned face appears in my doorway. "You don't have to hide it from us. We saw the bruises on Monday."

"And the cut," Donna adds, coming in beside Liana. "Why didn't you tell us the truth?"

I sniff and hide the tears. "What truth? It's nothing. Really."

"Did Vic Simmons do this?" Donna sits on the edge of my desk.

My lip trembles as the memories slam into me with the force of a speeding train colliding with a brick building. Vic's harsh words. His hot breath. The unwelcome pressure of his mouth on mine. His firm grip. The pain shooting through my head when his hand collided with it. The sting of his ring slicing my cheek with the backhand.

I squeeze my eyes closed willing the memories to vanish. But they're replaced by darker, hazier visions of Dan throwing me to the ground. Punching me. Hitting me until I black out in a bloody heap.

"Shh, honey, it's okay," Donna whispers in my ear as she rocks me in her arms.

I'm sobbing. Decimated by memories of the two men who used me and then abused me. Every ounce of strength I've built falls away, and I find myself weak and vulnerable once more. This time, the whole world is watching.

They will recognize me. The photograph is clear as day. There is no way I can tell anyone the truth of that night. No way in hell. They will never believe me over Hollywood's most eligible bachelor.

"Tell us what happened." Liana retrieves the tissues from a small table and offers one. I blow my nose and blink up at them.

As I recount the evening's events, they listen with rapt attention. Both of them flinch when I get to the confrontation in the hallway.

Anger replaces their shock when I finish the story.

"Marcy," Donna murmurs. "You can't let him get away with this."

Liana offers another tissue, and I take it with gratitude. I wipe away the tears while shaking my head. "No one will believe me."

"Did you go to the ER?" Liana asks, sitting in the chair across from me.

"No." I hang my head. "I went straight home."

"Did you speak to anyone after that?" Donna presses. "Anyone who can testify to what happened."

Rob's face rises in my mind. His sweet, caring smile. His strong jaw and gentle eyes. "Yeah. I, uh, called a friend. He's a doctor. He came over and took care of my injuries."

"Yes. Good. So he can testify on your behalf." Liana beams.

I shake my head. "No, he can't."

"Why not?" Donna asks.

"Because I refused to tell him who did it." A fresh round of tears springs to my eyes. "If I told him, he'd rush off and try to defend my honor."

"And that's a bad thing?"

"Yeah. They'll arrest him for assault. There's no proof. No one saw Vic and me in the hallway. No one saw him hit me." My hands tremble as I take another tissue. "There's nothing to back my story."

"This was at the Plaza?" Liana taps a finger on her jaw.

"Yeah, why?"

"My cousin Milo works at the front desk there. I could make some calls and see if there's any chatter?"

Hope blooms, then quickly shrivels to dust. "What will it matter? No one will go against Vic Simmons. He'll deny the whole thing."

Donna hugs me tight. "It's okay. We'll figure this out."

"It's hopeless. And now Rob'll discover the truth, and he'll—"

"Rob?" Liana cocks her head.

"The doctor who helped me. He's my brother's best friend and my…" I can't even bring myself to say the words. *Friend. Lover. My heart and soul.*

A knowing look passes between Liana and Donna.

"You love him, don't you?" Donna rubs my back. I know she's not talking about Vic. Her words strike straight to the center of the problem.

"Yeah. I do."

Both of them burst into radiant smiles.

"Finally." Liana sighs. "We've been hoping you'd find a good man."

"But what will I do? He'll find out sooner or later, and then it'll be a shitstorm." I bury my face in my hands.

"Well, first things first. We need to make some calls and find out if someone saw you two in the hallway at the hotel on Saturday night." Liana stands and reaches for the door. "While I do that, Donna will call her lawyer friend and have him come over right away. We need to get these vultures under control before they make a bigger mess."

"What should I do?" I ask, uncertain any of this was going to make a difference. Vic is so influential and popular. How can I go up against that kind of power?

"Go splash some water on your face. Fix your makeup and be ready." Donna grins. "We're going to war."

"You realize this could amount to nothing, right?" I slowly stand, the weight of it all pressing on my shoulders. "This is Vic Simmons you're talking about."

"Listen. My ex was charming and sweet to everyone, but when it was just us, he was an asshole with a bad temper." Liana's eyes sharpen at the recollection. "I wasn't the first woman he beat, and I'm sure I'm not the last. If Vic hit you, there've been others. We just need to find them."

Donna nods. "Maybe if you speak up, it'll be enough to inspire other women to do it too."

"We can't let him get away with this so he can hurt the next girl." Liana holds my gaze and nods with confidence. "It only takes one with courage to bring the others forward. Are you willing to do that?"

Her words infuse me with determination. "Yes. Let's do this."

"Good." Liana disappears down the hall.

When I head for the door, Donna stops me. "We'll make sure this bastard pays for what he did."

"Thanks." I swallow the emotion lodged in my throat. The moment I reach the bathroom down the hall, I collapse against the sink. My chest tightens, my breathing shallow and panicked.

Facing myself in the mirror, I focus on deep breaths until the wave passes. My makeup is smeared, and I look like a wilting Salvador Dali painting. I grab a washcloth and soap and scrub my face.

The purpling bruises and small gash healing on my cheek are highlighted by the lack of product. Rather than reapply my makeup, I smear on some lotion and wear the injuries with pride. When the lawyer shows up, I want him to see what Vic did to me without the mask of makeup protecting my wounded ego.

I should call Rob, tell him before he sees it on the news. It's not something I want to tell him over the phone, but he's at work. I have until he gets off at five to get this shitstorm under control and catch him at home.

I'd rather him hear it from me than the tabloids, but it may be too late.

CHAPTER 20

Rob

Fucking finally. At five o'clock, I gather my stuff and bolt out of the ER.

It took every ounce of strength I possess not to storm out of the hospital and make a beeline for Marcy's office the moment I saw that magazine. Summer tried to ask me about it, but I didn't have the time or patience to explain it. Not when I needed to get across town and see her.

I hail a cab and give the driver her address. The entire trip is spent in torment, wondering what in the hell I am going to say, what she will do when I confront her.

She wouldn't tell me who hurt her, wouldn't go to the ER. But the truth is she couldn't. Vic Simmons is a Hollywood superstar. He has leagues of lawyers and agents who would throw themselves into the flames to protect their client. Especially a moneymaker like Vic. Even if Marcy came forward and filed an incident report with the police, they would sweep it under the rug. No one would be the wiser.

It's a damned disaster. I have half a mind to hunt the bastard down and make him pay for what he did to her. But where would that land me? Prison, that's where. And pretty boy would get off scot-free.

Fury bubbles up inside me. By the time I reach her apartment, it's a full-on inferno. I pay the cabbie and step back from the curb. A flash of neon catches my eye.

Marcy. She's walking toward the door to her building, her arms wrapped around her torso. It's mid-May and nearly ninety degrees, but she looks like she's shivering in the cold.

"Marcy!" I call out with a wave.

She comes to a stop, her gaze snaps up at the sound of her name. Then she spots me through the crowd of pedestrians filling the sidewalk. As I make my way closer to her, her eyes widen. At this distance I can't tell if it's out of fear or relief, but it doesn't matter.

"Rob, what are you doing here?"

I pull her against me. Her arms wrap around my waist, and her tense body relaxes. "I came to check on you."

When I draw back, I tip her chin up and search those mesmerizing eyes. Gone is the heavy eye shadow and dark liner. Without makeup, the bruises stand out against her pale skin. The cut is healing nicely, but it's still an angry red blemish against her porcelain skin.

Fury rises hot and heavy inside me at the sight. "I can't believe that bastard hit you."

"Not here," Marcy hisses. "Come on, let's go inside."

Without waiting for my agreement, she drags me by the hand to her apartment. Silence fills the elevator on the way to her floor.

Once we're safely tucked inside her apartment, I round on her. "You could have told me it was Simmons, Marcy. I would have believed you."

Marcy scoffs and skirts around me, heading for the kitchen. "It doesn't matter. It's over, I can't take it back. And if I could, I would give him a pair of swollen nuts to go with his oversized ego."

"That's not the point. You should have told me. I could have—"

"Could have what? Called the cops? Filed a report? Made me go to the ER?" She shelves her hand on her hips. "I know you, Rob. You would have stormed over to his hotel and punched him in the face."

"I have more restraint than that." I huff. "Give me some credit."

"It's not worth getting the cops involved." She shuffles her feet uncomfortably and grabs orange juice from the refrigerator. "Dan beat me to within an inch of my life."

"Not worth…" I cross the space between us and grip her arms. "Look at me, Marcy." She lifts her gaze, and I see the uncertainty swimming deep within her. "You're worth it. I don't care who he is, but he shouldn't be given a pass because of his celebrity status."

"He won't." Her jaw ticks. "I've already hired a lawyer and started the process."

I blink at her twice. "What?"

"Liana and Donna convinced me to file charges."

When I release her, she pours a glass of orange juice. Her voice wavers. "I spoke to the lawyer. He's going to start the process."

"That's great." Relief fills me, but the joy doesn't quite reach her smile. "Wait, what's the problem?"

"There aren't any witnesses to the actual assault." She sips the juice. "We were in a dark hallway. If there's no witness, there's no case. It'll be my word against his, and his agency will pay to keep me quiet. It'll all get swept under the rug."

"I can serve as a witness to your state after the incident. If I file a report in the hospital system, we can use it in the case."

"I appreciate that, but it won't help." She sighs. "Unless we can find someone who saw what happened in that hotel hallway, it's a lost cause." Her expression falters.

I gather her in my arms, and she rests her head back against my chest. "I'm sorry."

"I haven't given up hope completely." Her voice rumbles through me, and the sweet scent of her shampoo teases my sense of reason. I shove aside the temptation to drag her into the bedroom and make her forget about everything except for the pure explosive pleasure I give her.

"What do you mean?"

She arches back against me, and my hands tighten around her waist. "Liana's cousin works at the Plaza. She called and told him what happened on Saturday. He wasn't working, but he knows who was. He's making some inquiries among the staff to see if anyone happened to see Vic and me in the hallway."

Hope unfurls in my chest. If they're able to find a witness, it changes everything. I kiss her on the back of the head.

"Come on." I nudge her toward the bedroom.

"Where are we going?" She nearly drops the glass, setting it aside in haste.

"Pack a bag. You're staying with me until we figure this shit out."

"Why?" She spins around and glowers at me. "I'm not fucking helpless, Rob. I don't need a babysitter."

"Listen—until this shit blows over, I don't think you should be alone."

Her exasperated look brooks no argument.

I relent. "Fine. If you don't want to stay with me, at least stay with your brother and Kate."

Her nose scrunches at the suggestion. "I don't want to be in the apartment alone with those two honeymooners."

"Then stay with one of your other friends."

"But I want to stay here."

"It's only a matter of time before they figure out who you are and where you live." I rest my hands on her shoulders. "Before you know it, you're going to have paparazzi camped around your home and your office. Trust me. You're in the spotlight, whether you like it or not. The best thing you can do right now is lay low."

"You're right." She frowns, and I want to smooth the lines between her brows with my thumb. "I hate that you're right."

I can't help but smile at the win. "Okay, go pack a bag."

Marcy pauses in the doorway to her bedroom, resting her hand on the frame. "Were you serious?"

"About what?"

"Letting me stay with you?" She draws her lower lip between her teeth, and I suppress a growl of protectiveness.

"Of course." I take two steps and pull her into my arms. "For as long as you want."

My lips nearly spill the word *forever* but it's a delicate time. I don't want to push her. We'll talk about *us* later once we're at my place.

Twenty-five minutes later, I'm wheeling her suitcase to the curb and hailing a cab. Marcy climbs in beside me and gives the cabbie my address. I pull her against me to kiss her temple. She leans her head against me, and we ride in silence.

I like this. Having her nestled by my side, certain of her safety.

"We should tell Arthur." Her voice drifts up on a murmur.

"You should." I hold her tight. "He'll find out sooner or later. It's best if he hears it from you."

"I'm sorry." She sniffs. "I should have told you."

"It's okay. I'm just glad you're safe."

"How did you find out?" She leans back and searches my face.

"Some of the nurses were talking about it, and I saw the photo on a magazine cover."

She winces. "I should have told you."

"It doesn't matter now, baby." I press a soft kiss to her lips. "Let's make sure your brother doesn't find out the same way. I don't think he'll take it as well as I did."

"You took it well?" She scoffs.

"Hell no. I was about to tear the ER apart." Her smile warms my soul. "If I ever see him, I'll rip him to shreds."

"Don't." Marcy shakes her head, eyes wide. "Don't make it more complicated than it already is."

Something about her tone soothes the furious beast inside me. I nod and pull her into my arms once more. I love this woman. It feels so good to finally hold her.

And I'm never letting go. Until death do we part.

CHAPTER 21

Marcy

Arthur is going to lose his shit.

Rob squeezes my hand and knocks on the door of my brother's penthouse. "It'll be fine," he whispers in my ear when the lock rattles against the door.

Inhaling a deep breath as it opens, I brace myself for the oncoming storm. Kate's kind smile greets us.

"I was just about to call you!" Kate steps aside, inviting us in. Her voice drops low. "I saw the headlines. What's going on?"

"Is Arthur home?" Rob glances around the empty apartment.

"He just got here." She nods toward the bedroom. "He's changing."

Nervous energy skitters along my spine. Rob's grip tightens on my hand. His hazel eyes meet mine, reminding me that I'm not alone. He's right beside me.

"I'll let him know you're here. Help yourself to a drink." Kate takes two steps before Rob's question stops her.

"Does he know?"

Kate shakes her head. "I'm glad you're here. He'll take it better if it comes from you, Marcy."

I nod, unable to trust my voice. Rob leaves me in the living room, retreating to the side bar to pour two whiskeys. When he returns, he places one in my hand with a confident smile.

"This'll take the edge off."

"Thanks." I down it, letting the drink warm me through.

Déjà vu. A piss-poor decision has led me to my brother's doorstep once again. I want to melt into the carpet. *But it's different this time.* Yeah, it is. This time I was smart enough to know when to walk away. This time I have Rob beside me, giving me courage to do what I need to do.

His solid presence infuses me with courage. How was I so stupid for so long? Thinking he disliked me. Thinking him indifferent to my presence.

The signs had been there all along, and I was too fucking blind to see them. Rob didn't save me; he supported me. He cared when he could have walked away.

"Marcy." Arthur joins us. "Rob. To what do I owe the pleasure?" His gaze fixes on my face.

"I made a mistake." I swallow the lump in my throat. "Kate, do you have the magazine?"

"Yeah." She edges around Arthur and retrieves it from the kitchen. When she hands it to me, I clutch it to my chest, like a shield blocking my heart.

"What happened?" Arthur's scowl deepens.

"I wanted to tell you, show you, before you read about it in the tabloids." With a deep breath, I press on. "One of my clients invited me to dinner last Saturday. I said yes, and we were photographed together."

Rob takes the magazine from my hand and gives it to Arthur. The furrow between his brows deepens even further, and the kind face of my older brother skews into horror and disbelief.

"Is this the man who hurt you?" His gravelly voice is menacing.

If I had been worried about Rob's reaction, I was terrified of my brother's. Both men were overly protective of me, but since my divorce, Arthur has made it his life's mission to keep me from experiencing that pain again.

"Yes." I hold his gaze steady as I elaborate on the events of that night and the startling revelation of our relationship in the tabloids.

"I see." He clenches the magazine in his fist. "Have you filed charges?"

"My lawyer is working on it." The pressure of Rob's hand on mine encourages me. "But unless there's a witness, it's hopeless. His status will give him indemnity. Between his agents and the press, any whisper of wrongdoing will be swept under the rug, and there's nothing I can do about it."

"No one saw you together?" Arthur crosses his arms.

"Oh, people saw us together. Hell, the whole city now knows we were together that night." Bile bites the back of my throat at the thought. "But there was no one around when he hit me. He made sure of it."

"You think he's done this before?" Rob asks with surprise.

"Judging from his reaction, yeah, I think he has a nasty habit of beating women who don't fall at his feet and do what he wants."

"Do you have any proof that this isn't the first time he's done it?" Kate interjects.

I shake my head. "I don't have proof of anything. All I know is that a man of his stature, his status, isn't used to being called out for his shitty behavior. He's all charm until you say no."

"Someone must have seen something." Arthur's agitated movements do nothing to calm my nerves.

"They're making inquiries now with the hotel staff," I add, as though it will soothe him.

Before Arthur can respond, Rob stands up. "Why don't we go down to the Black Penny, see if Richards is around? He might be able to help."

A long look passes between Rob and my brother. Finally, Arthur relents. "Fine." He kisses Kate. "You two stay here. We'll be back in a few hours."

"Wait. You can't seriously expect me to stay locked away while we get this figured out?" I stalk toward them and grab my brother's arm. "I'm coming with you."

He turns to face me. "Listen, your face is plastered all over every tabloid and gossip rag in the city. It's only a matter of time before they figure out your name and where you live." Arthur pulls me into a warm hug. "Let us take care of this part. We'll do some digging, ask some questions. Then, when we have the ammunition, we'll let you take him down."

Arthur lets me go and disappointment fills me.

"I can't let you fight this battle for me." Defiance replaces disappointment. "I won't."

"We're not fighting your battle, Marcy." My brother sighs. "We're supporting you. Let us do this. It's going to be hard enough to face down Vic Simmons in court."

"I relish the opportunity." The thought should scare me, but instead it leaves me vibrating with certainty that this is the right course of action.

"Good. Save your strength. You'll need it for the long haul." Arthur presses a kiss to my forehead. "You've fought alone for years. Let us help you with this."

Deep in my heart, I soften at his touch and his words. "Fine."

Rob tilts my chin up. "Don't worry. We'll find something on him. He won't get away with this." He strokes his thumb across my jaw. "Promise."

The press of his warm lips to mine leaves me clutching his shirt. I don't want to let him go. I love him too much.

"Be careful," I murmur against his mouth.

"Always." With a smile, he and Arthur head out into the spring evening in search of something I'm not sure they'll be able to find. It's a wild-goose chase. Vic Simmons has the media by the balls. No one will cross him.

"Fuck." I slump onto the couch and clutch the pillow to my chest.

"You love him, don't you?" Kate appears beside me with a bottle of wine and two glasses.

"That obvious, huh?" I rest my cheek on the pillow.

"Yeah."

She pours a glass for me. I take it with a muttered thanks.

"I'm glad you two finally got together. I might not have been around long, but these last few months of you two hurling jabs at each other is enough to set the curtains on fire."

"I can't believe I was that blind."

"We all have those moments." Kate chuckles. "But it doesn't matter now. You're both on the same page."

"Are we?" I cradle the glass in my hands. "I mean, this is all so new. We haven't discussed anything yet. All we've done is fuck. Which, don't get me wrong, is nice. Better than nice. It's fantastic. But I don't know what he wants for the future. For us."

"You'll have to ask him." Kate salutes me. "Before you jump him again."

My face heats. "We've both been alone for so long. What if it doesn't work?"

"I guess you won't know until you try." She rests her hand on my knee. "I wouldn't worry about it though. Rob's a cinnamon roll. He'll do anything for you."

"Cinnamon roll?" I skew my nose up at her strange reference. "What do pastries have to do with anything?"

"Shit." Kate laughs, nearly spilling her wine. "Sorry. I keep forgetting. A cinnamon roll is someone who is sweet and kind but faces more hardship and suffering than they deserve."

"That sounds exactly like Rob." I smother a laugh behind my hand.

"I wouldn't worry about Rob. He loves you, and whatever comes next, he'll be right there beside you the whole time."

Emotion chokes me, and all I can do is nod.

"Why don't you help me in the kitchen? I was about to whip up some pork stir-fry with noodles." Kate stands and offers her hand.

My stomach growls at the mention of food. "That sounds amazing."

"Good. I've got everything ready." Kate ventures into the kitchen, but I pause halfway across the room and cast a longing look over my shoulder at the door.

At this point, I don't care about Vic Simmons. I care about Rob. Sweet, caring, wonderful Rob. He's chasing my demons, and I feel like there's nothing I can do to help him.

When he comes back, we'll talk. I don't want to be without him. Not for another moment. Life's too short to waste one more minute apart.

CHAPTER 22

Rob

"What the fuck are you thinking?" I round on my best friend.

Arthur glares at me as he settles back in the cab. The cabbie pulls away from the curb, heading toward the Plaza Hotel.

"I'm getting answers." He levels me with his gaze.

"We agreed to talk to Richards before heading to the hotel." Uncertainty twists in my gut. "We can't go in there half-cocked."

"Look." Arthur heaves a sigh. "We need to get answers before this spirals out of control."

"Exactly. And that's why we were going to consult Richards before starting an inquisition." I run my hand across my jaw, agitated at the recklessness of his plan. "Maybe we should call Richards and have him meet us there."

"No." He shakes his head. "Once we get there, we'll split up. You take the restaurant. I'll talk to management." His eyes glisten in the decaying sunlight. "Someone *had* to have seen something, damn it."

"Marcy said one of her stylists has a cousin who works at the front desk. Maybe if you drop her name, they'll be more willing to help."

"Which stylist?"

"Liana."

Arthur nods. "Yes, I remember her."

The silence stretches for a few blocks. The knot in my stomach expands the closer we get to the hotel. This could end badly if we don't play it right.

"So what's our story?" I ask as the city descends into darkness around us.

"The truth, but we keep it vague." He meets my gaze, unflinching in his determination. "My sister was here with a date on Saturday. They got into an argument in the hallway outside the restaurant. Did anyone see anything?"

"But what's our reason for asking?"

"Why do we need one?"

I shrug. "We don't, but they're not going to be as willing to talk if we don't have a legitimate reason."

"Then we tell them the truth. He got physical, and she's pressing charges." He cocks his head. "But I wouldn't volunteer that information up front. Let's see how far we can get on charm alone."

The cab pulls up in front of the hotel, and my hands are shaking when I step onto the sidewalk. Arthur pays the cabbie, and together we head into the towering hotel. It's been an intricate fixture in the skyline for years. But tonight isn't for admiring the architecture; it's for getting answers.

There are a few patrons milling around in the lobby. I follow Arthur to the front desk, where he asks for the manager. What did Marcy say Liana's cousin's name was? Miles? Mike? I catch a glimpse of the name tag of the man behind the counter. *Milo.*

"Are you Liana's cousin?" I ask, keeping my voice low.

"Yes." His eyes widen, and his voice drops to a whisper. "Are you here about what happened to Marcy?"

Arthur and I share a look. He nods at the man behind the counter. "Did anyone see anything?"

He nervously licks his lips and glances around, ensuring he can't be overheard. "I didn't. But I asked some of the staff who were working in the restaurant that night. A few of them said they heard arguing in the hallway when they were coming back from their break."

"Can we speak with them?" Hope blooms in my chest, but I tamp it down. Just because they heard arguing doesn't mean they saw anything.

Milo nods and calls over another employee to take his place behind the counter. "Follow me." He leads us to the elevator and up to the restaurant on the fifteenth floor. We pause in the hallway outside the restaurant, near the restrooms. "Wait here."

Arthur and I wait, impatient but quiet, our nerves lit like live wires. Neither of us speaks, but when Milo reappears, I let Arthur take the lead. Milo quickly appraises the waiter of the reason for his presence.

The waiter's eyes shift to us with skepticism. "You sure they're not reporters?" he asks Milo.

"They're not. They're friends of my cousin." Milo turns to us. "Ask him. I'll be at the front desk if you need anything else." He bolts to the elevator, leaving us with the tall waiter.

In this lighting, it's difficult to gauge his age, but I'd say he's not much older than Arthur and me. I offer my hand, and he shakes it. "Sorry to bother you, but we have a few questions about Saturday night."

"So you're cops?" He stiffens.

"No." Arthur steps in. "But my sister was here on Saturday night. About this tall, dark hair, hazel eyes…"

"The girl with Vic Simmons?" He rubs his jaw. "Yeah, I remember those two. Making eyes at each other all night."

My hands clench into fists, but I manage to maintain my composure. "That's her. Did you see them outside the restaurant?"

"I did. They were right there." He points to a dark nook in the bend of the hallway. "I was coming back from a smoke break when I heard arguing. Sounded like someone struggling. I crept close to get a better look, and I saw them making out."

I flinch at his words.

Arthur commandeers the questioning. "Did you see anything else?"

"Yeah, I saw the bastard take a swing at her. He got in two hits before I could react to what I was seeing." He shook his head. "By the time I stepped into view, he'd pulled away. I ducked out of sight again before he could unleash on me. When I came back a moment later, she was gone."

"Why didn't you come forward with this information?" I push, knowing I'm already running with a short fuse.

"To who? There were no cops, no inquiry." He scoffs. "Who's gonna believe me anyway? I didn't know who the girl was, and I wasn't about to lose my job and credibility by going up against Vic Simmons."

My hope deflates at his words. "So you're not willing to testify to what you saw that night?"

"I never said that." He narrows his eyes. "But there better be a solid case before I take the stand against him."

"You'd testify on her behalf?" Arthur asks, holding the man's gaze.

"If I know the bastard will get what he deserves, then yes, I'll testify."

"Why stick your neck out for a woman you don't know?" The question leaves my lips before I can bite it back. I can't just leave well enough alone. I need to know why he'd do something so selfless.

"My dad…he, uh…" The waiter sniffs and drops his gaze. "He beat my mom. No one spoke up for her, and she died."

The confession hangs in the air between the three of us. I can hear the unspoken shame and trauma this man endured. Even more, I sense the undercurrent of regret and guilt gnawing at his heart for not taking action against his father to save his mother.

"I'm sorry." My apology sounds weak, but it's sincere.

"Yeah…well, that was years ago." He clears his throat. "I figure I can do something this time around."

"We appreciate it." Arthur shakes his hand.

After we take his information, he retreats into the restaurant while Arthur and I head to the ground floor. Neither of us speaks until we're in the cab. I give directions for the driver to take us to the Black Penny.

If we get this information to Richards, he can vet the waiter. We can't do this halfway. It has to be airtight.

Vic Simmons will pay for what he did to Marcy.

After a few shots and a long conversation with Richards, we have our next step. He'll run a background check on both the waiter and Simmons. We can take the information to Marcy's lawyer and let him start the process.

I manage to keep it together until I reach my apartment. Inside, Marcy's curled up in my bed, sleeping. Kate must have given her the spare key. I'm fit to burst with all the information I have, but I don't have the heart to wake her.

Once I strip down, I slide beneath the covers beside her. She curls against me, and I'm reminded of just how lucky I am to have her in my life.

She deserves peace, and I'm determined to see this through to the end.

CHAPTER 23

Marcy

I snuggle in when his arm drapes across my waist, pulling me close. A contented sigh escapes me.

Rob's lips trail over my shoulder, and I squirm trying to get even closer. "I didn't mean to wake you."

"It's fine." I moan when he nips at my skin. "This is the best way to be woken up."

Artificial light filters through the windows, casting a hazy glow across the dark room. I turn in his arms until we're face to face. His careworn expression leaves my heart pounding. For years, I've dreamed of this, of sharing myself with him. This man has seen me at my worst, and yet he still wants me.

I bite my lip. "How did it go with Richards?" I trail my finger along his jaw.

"Good." Rob drops his gaze. "Listen, I don't want you to get upset, but you deserve to know."

"Upset? Why would I get upset?" I draw back slightly.

"Arthur and I went to the Plaza." He holds up a hand when I open my mouth to protest. "We spoke to someone willing to testify on your behalf. He saw everything."

My fury at their presumptuous action disintegrates into shock. "Wait…what?"

"There was a waiter who saw the whole encounter in the hallway. He's willing to testify against Vic Simmons."

"You're joking?"

"I would never joke about something like this." He takes a deep breath and cups my cheek in his palm. "Richards is going to run background checks on him and Simmons, get us some more information before you meet with your lawyer."

"I'm supposed to meet with him tomorrow afternoon."

"Do you want me to go with you?"

He's in earnest. I can see the unresolved agitation in the way he tenses his body as if he's bracing for rejection. "Let me think about it."

"Okay. There's no rush." He deflates at my response but nods in understanding. "I'm here for you, Marcy. Whatever you need, just say the word."

"I appreciate it." My heart aches at the thought of Rob and Arthur fighting my battle for me, even though they have both assured me they're only helping me. "But this whole mess is my fault. I shouldn't have gone out with him. I should have trusted my gut."

"You can't blame yourself for his actions." He hooks his finger beneath my chin and brings my gaze up. "You did nothing wrong. He's an abusive, entitled asshole."

"I know." Tears sting my eyes. "But you of all people should understand…I don't want to be rescued. I don't want charity. Facing him down is the only way I'll get any closure. I refuse to be scared of my own shadow just because he's a goddamn bully."

"I'm not trying to fight this battle for you, Marcy." His touch leaves me trembling with need. "I'm here for support. You've got yourself through worse scrapes than this, and you've thrived because of it. I couldn't be prouder of you than I am right now. Facing this takes courage. There are a lot of people who break under this pressure."

"Trust me, I've been tempted to just walk away and let him win this round." Heaviness settles around my heart at the thought of Vic hurting another woman when I could have stopped the cycle. "I can't bear the thought of someone else being on the receiving end of his unwanted attention. What if he goes too far and does major damage?"

"You're right. He could easily hurt someone or kill them." Rob closes his eyes and exhales sharply. "I've seen it happen more times than I care to remember. Abuse should never be tolerated."

"No one should be subjugated to that." A shiver racks me, regardless of the spring heat.

Rob draws me closer and kisses my forehead. "I'm proud of you for standing up."

"Rob?" I cling to him, wrapping my leg around his thigh. "Why are you doing this for me?"

"I love you. I've always loved you." His breath ghosts over my cheek.

Fireworks ignite in my chest at those three little words. I close my eyes.

"I want to cherish you. Protect you. Love you. It's all I've ever wanted to do."

"But why?" I ask, inhaling the scent of him and committing it to memory. "I'm broken and difficult."

"We're all broken, sweetheart." He rests his hand on my hip, drawing small circles with his thumb. "But that doesn't mean you're not worthy of my love."

His words leave me breathless and confused, but I hear truth ringing in their depths. I try to disentangle myself from his embrace, but he grips me tighter.

"Don't push me away." His murmured plea makes me stop. "I'm not asking you to get married and start a family. I'm not even asking you to move in with me. I would never ask you to sacrifice anything for us to work. I'm willing to take it slow if that's what you need."

The tears finally spill free. He swipes them away with the pad of his thumb. For years I kept him at arm's length because I was terrified of letting myself feel anything for him. Because I valued him too much to have him disappear from my life if he didn't feel the same way.

"I love you, Rob." A whimper breaks out when the words leave my mouth.

With crushing tenderness, he presses his lips to mine. Every ounce of tension leaves me at the loving expression. He deepens the kiss, exploring with reverence. He pulls me close, pressing our bodies together, tangling our legs and tongues. I want to get lost in him and never resurface.

Rob, with all his faults, is the only man who has ever seen the true me.

The friction building between us reaches the point of desperation. My hips grind against his thigh. Naked and needy, I climb on top of him, straddling his thighs. He's hard and ready, his cock brushing my slick pussy.

He grips my hips tight as I guide him to where I want him. One thrust and I gasp when he's buried deep inside me. Emotions pulse through me in waves, I rest my head against his chest and take several deep breaths, trying to ground myself.

His hand comes around the back of my neck, tender, soothing against my skin. I meet his gaze. He's grinning. My heart does a little flip.

I buck my hips against his, and a groan of pleasure tears from his throat.

"Do it again, baby." He sucks in a breath when I repeat the action. "Take what you need."

"Oh, I intend to."

Bracing my hands on the bed beside his head, I find my rhythm. His eyes drift closed as I ride his cock, grinding my hips against his to fan the flames higher.

Our mixed moans echo in the dark room. The speed of my panting gasps increases as my orgasm builds. I need more of him, and my release hovers just out of reach.

As if sensing my frustration, Rob switches our positions and drives deeper, pushing me into the mattress. I wrap my legs around him and meet his thrusts with my own.

This is what I want. What I need.

I dig my nails into his skin, holding tight. He kisses me hard, doubling his efforts.

A cry rips from my throat as I reach the pinnacle and tumble over the other side. Pleasure rocks through me with the force of a tidal wave, leaving me trembling and sensitive.

Rob takes his own release. His warmth fills me, leaving me sticky and sated. I've never been more content.

"You okay?" He lifts his weight off me and searches my face.

"I'm fabulous." I arch up and kiss his lips softly.

"Wait here." Rob climbs off the bed and disappears into the bathroom.

"I couldn't move if I tried." I languish in the bed, unable to move my limbs after such an earthshattering climax.

He chuckles from the other room. When he returns, he cleans me with a warm rag and rejoins me. Tucking me against him, he sighs in contentment.

"Why don't we stay home tomorrow?" I muse, half asleep and sex-drunk. "We can stay in bed all day and fuck each other senseless."

"That sounds like a great idea." He groans. "But I have to work."

"What time?"

"Three."

"We have all morning then." I snuggle closer.

"We have our whole lives." He quickly adds, "If that's what you want. No pressure."

My response lodges in my throat.

It is what I want, but I've been alone for so long, I can't jump into something so quickly. Can I?

With Rob by my side, I can do anything. The soft, steady breaths against my shoulder tell me I don't have to answer him tonight. He's fast asleep.

I stare at the wall, wondering what happens next. Is this too good to last?

CHAPTER 24

Rob

We spend half the day in bed, wrapped in each other and sheltered from the realities of the world outside. It's heaven, and I never want to leave.

Until I get a call from Arthur at noon. Richards has the reports on Vic Simmons and our witness from the restaurant. He wants to meet and discuss them at the Black Penny.

My call into work leaves my superiors shorthanded, but after all the hours I pulled this week, they can find someone to fill in for me this time. If things go well, I won't be working there much longer anyway. Now that I have Marcy, I have bigger plans that don't include working doubles in the ER.

I press a kiss to Marcy's forehead, and she pulls me in for one last drugging kiss before I leave. She's not thrilled about being left behind, but Kate offered to go with her to the meeting with the lawyer. We'll meet up with them there.

Downstairs, Arthur's waiting for me by a shiny black town car. Cyril gives me a wave from the driver's side. Must be nice to have one's own personal driver in this city. No subway. No taxis. No walking. Just…onward, Cyril.

I slide into the back beside Arthur. "What's the game plan?"

"Richards has the information. We'll meet him first, then head over to Marcy's lawyer."

"What time?"

"Five." He glances at his watch. "I've already given the lawyer an update with the new information. He agrees she should lay low for a while, but she needs to file a formal complaint today to get the charges started. With this, we'll have enough ammunition to get this guy more than a slap on the wrist."

"He deserves a *lot* more than that," I grumble, leaning back against the seat. "I don't think this is the first time he's done it."

"You're probably right." Arthur watches the city pass outside the window.

For the rest of the drive, we're silent. My mind churns over the information, again and again. Personally, I'd like nothing more than to make this asshole disappear forever, but that goes against every ethos I have. This needs to be methodical and focused. I don't want him or the paparazzi coming after Marcy. I just want it over.

When we reach the Black Penny, Claude waves us toward the back where Richards is waiting for us. I slide into the booth across from him, and Arthur takes the space beside me.

"I did some digging, and it took some sweet-talking to get the tyrant in records to release this shit." Richards's eyes flicker with amusement. "Looks like your boy here has a long history of taking things that don't belong to him. Three rape charges, two assaults, and one breaking and entering."

"Holy shit." I run my hand across my jaw as I skim through the reports. My instincts on this asshole were spot-on. "Has he ever been convicted?"

"No." Richards leans back. "Every single case got settled out of court and conveniently swept under the rug."

"Fucking figures." Arthur sneers.

"Do you think these are the only incidents?" I ask Richards.

He shakes his head. "These are only the ones where he got caught. In my experience, there are always more. He's got a taste for it. Gives him a rush. Chances are, there are a lot more, but because of his status, they disappear fast...*if* they come forward at all."

"Is it worth pursuing this?" Arthur asks the question burning in the back of my mind.

"It'll be complicated and drawn out. Because he's a celebrity, it will get national coverage and could get messy. They'll likely try to settle out of court." Richards shrugs.

"But he'll do it again." Anger bubbles within me.

"Yup." Richards takes a drink. "Another thing. If Marcy testifies against him, they'll dig up her past and throw it in her face. You think she's ready for that?"

Arthur and I exchange a long, knowing look. This could get ugly. Really ugly. We've spent years trying to protect Marcy, but this will rip open the scars to bleed anew. Is she willing to put herself through that?

"She can handle it," Arthur replies. "But it'll be hard."

Richards nods. "Okay. I'll make a few calls, see what I can dig up." He takes the folders and tucks them out of sight. "I'll have these delivered to the lawyer when she files the official charges."

"Thanks." I shake his hand, and we part ways.

Cyril has the car waiting for us outside the bar. Arthur gives him an address, and we climb in.

It's a quick ride, barely enough time to compose myself to face the fight I know is coming. It'll be hard to convince anyone to take this fucker on in court. I can only hope her lawyer isn't a chickenshit who'd rather take a plea deal than make the bastard see the inside of a courtroom. If I have to scour the city for someone willing to take this case, then so be it. Marcy deserves a chance at justice. Every one of those women does.

Walking into the building, Arthur falls into step beside me. We take the elevator up, tense silence pulsing around us. I step out onto the twelfth floor and freeze.

Two men are standing outside the office, shaking hands with a third man. The taller one turns, and recognition slams into me with the force of a well-placed punch to the gut.

Vic Simmons. The same smug face I've seen on the cover of countless magazines and movie posters.

He hurt Marcy. *Bastard.*

His gaze fixes on me.

The sound of a door opening behind me makes me turn. Marcy steps into the hall, her eyes bloodshot, her chin raised high. Our eyes meet for a brief moment, but the second she sees Vic beyond us in the hallway, she pivots on her heel and retreats to the exit. Kate follows her, casting an apologetic, concerned glance at Arthur over her shoulder.

He fucking *hurt* her again. I don't even care what he said or did, I saw the look of pain on her face. My control snaps.

"What the fuck did you do to her?"

His eyes widen as I approach, and he lifts his hands in defense. The moment I'm within reach, I strike. Hauling back, I let my fist fly. A perfect jab catches him square in the face. The crunch of his nose breaking mixes with the crack of my knuckles fracturing from the impact. Blood pours from his nose, but he hauls back, throwing a hook, and catches the side of my face.

He lunges for me, and it's World War III. I feel like Rocky but without experience or confidence. The only thing I know is I want this asshole to bleed for what he did. We get a few more hits in before they drag us apart.

Arthur puts himself between Vic and me and hands me a

handkerchief. His stern expression fixes on me like I'm a kid caught fighting at school.

"What the hell is your problem?" Vic shouts while two men in suits hold him back.

"That's for what you did to Marcy, asshole." I flip him the bird. "I'll see you in court."

He smirks. Blood stains his teeth. "I doubt that."

I lunge forward again, but Arthur catches me by the arm. "Save it," he growls against my ear. "This isn't the time or the place. Come on." He drags me into the office, out of the hallway.

As Simmons passes, I catch the twisted grin on his lips. He thinks he's won, thinks he's on top of this. But he doesn't know how determined I can be. Fucking with Marcy has earned him a one-way ticket to prison.

"What the hell were you thinking?" Arthur shakes me. "He could come at you with assault charges now."

"He won't." I dab the blood from my face, wincing at the sting and the pulsing throb in my right hand.

"You don't know that." Arthur keeps his voice low as the lawyer approaches.

"Putting himself in the spotlight will only draw more attention to his imperfections." I snort. "Guys like him are self-centered with egos the size of Mount Rushmore. I'd like to see him fucking press charges, then I'll drag his name through the mud."

Arthur shakes his head when the lawyer appears. "Let me do the talking."

"Fine."

I manage to keep calm during the meeting. As I judged from the look on Marcy's face, Vic's team has already intervened and tried to sweep this "misunderstanding" under the rug. The lawyer doesn't seem optimistic about the case should it come to court, unless there are other women who come forward with similar stories. If that were to become the case, then he would be more open to pursuing it.

We have our work cut out for us, but honestly, the only thing I care about right now is getting home to Marcy. The pain and fury etched on her beautiful face haunt me. I won't rest until she's safe in my arms again.

She's the only thing that matters to me, and I'll be damned if I let anyone else hurt her. I'll rip the city apart if it ensures her protection.

I love her. And nothing will ever keep us apart.

CHAPTER 25

Marcy

"What the hell happened to you?" I rush across the room when Rob walks in the door. The right side of his face is swollen, and a dark purple shiner is forming around his eye. He winces when I cup his cheek to inspect the damage.

"Had a run-in with Vic Simmons at the lawyer's."

Bile bites the back of my throat at the mention of that name. "Did you hit him first?"

"Yes." He grins.

"That was stupid. Now he'll come after you."

"I'd like to see him try." He kisses my forehead. "I'm sorry he hurt you, baby."

My heart pounds at the sweet gesture. "Sit down here." I motion to the couch, then grab a bag of frozen veggies from the freezer and wrap them in a tea towel. "Here, put this on it."

He presses the bag gingerly to the side of his face, focusing on me with his good eye. "Thanks."

"I hope he walked away with one to match." I gesture to his face.

"Better." Rob grins like he won the lottery. "I broke the bastard's nose."

A gasp rips from my throat even as pride fills me. "You didn't?"

"I did." His grin fades to a self-satisfied smirk. "Caught him off guard too." Rob flexes his right hand. "I think I fractured my metacarpals though."

"Your what?"

"The bones in my hand." He chuckles. "I think they're broken."

I shake my head. "You're a mess."

"Yeah, but I'm your mess now." He pulls me close and presses a soft kiss to my lips.

My heart warms at the action. "You're lucky I love you."

"Luckiest man alive." He flinches at the uncomfortable position.

Pulling back, I settle beside him and study his handsome face. "So what happened after I left? The lawyer didn't seem too convinced we could win. Then Vic's team showed up and offered a deal to keep it all quiet."

"They're trying to reach an agreement so we don't take it to court."

"Did the lawyer say we should take a deal?"

Rob exhales sharply, the sound of exhaustion echoing through the room. "At first, that's exactly what he thought we should do. Then I offered some deeper insight into the charming Vic Simmons's history."

I nudge him with my elbow. "The suspense is killing me. Out with it."

"Richards did some digging and found some unflattering records on Simmons. Old charges that were dismissed out of court. Probably paid off to keep their mouths shut."

"How does that help me?" I pout at the disappointing revelation. "If he's gotten away with this before, there's no way in hell we'll get him this time."

"Not necessarily." Rob lowers the ice pack and holds my gaze. "It establishes he has a history of this type of behavior. If we can find other women he's assaulted, we might be able to throw a wider net. Plus, we have a witness who's willing to testify on your behalf. That counts for something."

"How are we going to find other victims? He travels extensively, and no one is going to want to air that kind of dirty laundry." I bite the edge of my nail in a lame attempt to quell my rising anxiety.

"Richards is calling in a few favors. I'm sure he left a trail. Trust me"—Rob's face softens—"he won't get away with this, baby. I promise."

"I do trust you." I take his hand and kiss the reddened knuckles before placing the ice-cold bag on them. "But I can't just sit here and do nothing."

"Maybe it's time we took your story public."

The suggestion leaves me off-kilter.

"If you step forward, maybe it'll encourage others to do the same."

Fear lodges in my throat, choking me. Unwelcome memories flood me, and I pinch my eyes closed.

You're safe. You're safe. Breathe.

"Breathe, Marcy. Just breathe."

When I open my eyes, Rob's kind eyes are filled with compassion. "There you go. In. Out. In. Out. Breathe, baby."

Slowly the panic subsides, and I'm able to focus again. "I don't know if I can."

"I won't force you. This is your decision." He licks his lips. "But if you take your story public, I guarantee others will come forward."

"Who would run a story like that? Simmons's powerful and popular and influential. No media outlet in their right mind would run the story."

"They might if they were granted first rights to any information pertaining to the case and exclusive interviews."

"You want me to parade myself in front of the press?"

Rob's eyes darken two shades. "No. I don't. I want to protect you as much as I can from these vultures." He sighs. "But the truth is, if this goes to court, they're going to start digging regardless, and it would be better for us to stay out in front of it."

"Fuck." My head droops.

Rob hooks his finger under my chin and lifts my gaze. "I have faith in you. Whatever happens, we'll do this together."

Tears prick my eyes. "What if it's all for nothing and he gets away with it?"

"Could you live with the regret if you don't follow through?"

I shake my head vehemently. "No, especially if he hurts someone else and I could have stopped him." A sob sticks in my throat. "I can't let that happen. Not while there's a breath in my body."

"I didn't think so." He wraps his arm around me and pulls me against his solid chest. "You have support. Me. Arthur and Kate. Donna and Liana. We're all right here with you, all the way."

Even though I'm not at peace with the decision, confidence infiltrates every fiber of my being. "Thank you."

He kisses my forehead. "For what, baby?"

I lean back to meet his gaze. "For loving me even though I'm a beautiful disaster."

"You're beautiful without a doubt, and this is quite a disaster. But that doesn't mean you're broken in any way." He brushes a lock of hair away from my face. "I love you regardless."

Our lips meet in a sweet kiss. My hunger for him soon overwhelms my sense. I climb into his lap and cradle his face in my hands, deepening the kiss. My touch is gentle, aware of the bruising.

Rob grasps my hip with his left hand, gently pressing my thigh with his injured right one. He hisses against my lips.

I pull away, but he hooks his arm around my waist and holds me still.

"I don't want to hurt you."

"I'll be fine," he murmurs against my cheek. "I need you just like this."

When I search his eyes for a flicker of pain, I'm lost. This sweet, compassionate, wonderful man…how have I lived this long without him? And how can I ensure I never have to be parted from him for a moment longer? "I love you, Rob."

"I love you too." He nuzzles against my neck. "We'll get through this together."

"Then what?" I gasp when he kisses the sensitive spot below my ear.

"Guess we'll figure that out when we get there."

"Will you marry me?"

The moment the words leave my lips, the weight of them dissipates into the air.

"Wait. What did you say?" Rob grips my shoulders and holds my gaze. "Say it again."

"Marry me, Rob."

"Are you feeling okay?" He presses the back of his hand to my forehead. "Are you feverish? Delusional?"

I laugh and shake my head. "No. I'm serious."

"Oh, thank God, I thought I was imagining things for a moment." His smile turns effervescent. "Is that what you want?"

"Absolutely."

"You're sure?"

"Positive."

He sighs in relief. "Good, because I'm getting too old for this waiting-around bullshit."

I roll my eyes. "Don't be so dramatic."

"I wasn't being dramatic. I was just waiting for the woman of my dreams to realize I've wanted her for years."

My hand rests on his heart. "Why didn't you say something sooner?"

"Trying to convince her of anything is like walking on broken glass."

"Totally dramatic." I chuckle. "So what's your answer?"

"Yes." He kisses me softly. "I will marry you, Marcy."

Elation consumes me. Together we fall in a mass of tangled limbs and murmured groans, dinner forgotten. After the first two orgasms, I stop counting and enjoy the bliss of finally securing the love of my life. Neither of us can fight this feeling anymore, and for once, I surrender willingly.

We have a long road ahead of us, but together we can conquer anything life throws our way.

CHAPTER 26

Rob

A Year Later…

"In the case of Vic Simmons, we the jury find the defendant guilty on all counts."

A round of applause shakes the courthouse. Marcy visibly relaxes when the verdict is read. I wrap my arms around her.

"It's over, baby. We got him."

"Finally." She buries her face against my chest.

On the other side of the room, Kate and Arthur beam with pride.

Six months of interviews and testimony gave us all the ammunition we needed against the bastard. When Marcy's story hit the stands, a flurry of calls came in. With Richards's connections, we were able to put together a case against Simmons. He tried to settle, but the allegations kept piling up until he couldn't hide any longer. It went to court.

And we won the suit against him.

Later that night, we gather at Arthur's penthouse to celebrate.

"You should be proud, Marcy." Arthur offers his congratulations. "He'll finally get what he deserves."

"Even better than that, he'll think twice before trying that shit with another woman now that he's been branded an abuser." Kate hugs Marcy. "I can't believe the number of women who came forward with their stories."

"Your bravery gave them courage." Arthur pours another glass of tea from the pitcher on the table. "I'm extremely proud of you for standing up and speaking out against him, even though it put you in an awkward position."

"Airing your own dirty laundry for all the world to see isn't easy, but you did it." Kate takes Marcy's hand.

"It wasn't easy, but I'm glad I did it." Her gaze turns to me. "I couldn't have done what I did without you by my side." She leans back against me.

I wrap my arm around her waist. "I told you. We're with you until the end, baby."

"What'll happen now?" she asks.

"Jail time. Restitution." I shrug. "We have to wait until sentencing."

"They don't castrate them?" Marcy jokes, half-serious.

"I wish," Kate murmurs.

"So it's still a problem in the future, huh?" Arthur rests his arm on his wife's shoulder.

"Yes. I wish I could say it gets better, but it doesn't."

I hold Marcy tighter.

"So what's next for you two?" Kate changes the subject.

"We have an appointment next week in upstate New York to look at a house." Marcy's excitement is infectious. "Rob's taking a job there as the local doc."

"That's wonderful. You both deserve a break after the last year." Kate claps her hands together.

Marcy wiggles against me. It was difficult for both of us, putting ourselves in front of the cameras and exposing her difficult history. We fought hard trying to protect ourselves, but in the end, she took a hiatus from her job when the story broke and the press went wild. Liana and Donna took over the business, leaving Marcy to indulge in her other passions—namely me.

It didn't stop her from helping other women find their voices and their freedom. Claude thanks her every day for helping Gwen last winter. I'll miss seeing them together at the Black Penny every week.

When she found the perfect location to open a cute boutique upstate, that sealed the deal. I put in my notice at the hospital last month. It's time for a change. As much as we both love the city, we're ready for a new adventure. Together.

"The boutique will be just up the road from Rob's office." She glances at me with an infectious grin before returning her attention to her brother and Kate. "You'll come visit, right?"

"You won't be able to keep us away." Kate leans against Arthur. "We'll be looking for a new place soon. There's no room here for a baby."

"Baby?" Marcy jumps up, wrenching herself from my arms. "You're pregnant?"

Kate nods. "I just found out."

"Congratulations." I offer felicitations to my best friend and his time-traveling bride. "I'm so happy for the both of you."

Marcy and Kate hug, falling into chatter about their plans and possible names. I stand and stretch my legs, walking to the window overlooking the city. Arthur comes alongside me.

"You're going to be a father. How does that make you feel?" I clap my hand on his shoulder.

"Terrified." He grins, and there's a sparkle of joy in his eyes. "But I wouldn't have it any other way."

"I'm so excited for both of you." I chuckle. "As improbable as it is, you knocking Kate out with a door is the best thing that has ever happened to you."

"Yeah. There are days I wonder if she's really here…if she's real."

"She's real, and after watching *Back to the Future* last year, I can't say I'd completely discount time travel as real."

Arthur snorts. "She didn't come here in a DeLorean."

"No, but there's a lot of shit we can't explain in the universe."

"Maybe I'll just chalk it up to fate."

I laugh. "Fate, huh? Listen to you. Never thought I'd hear you say something like that, Mr. Practicality."

"I'm too old to fight it."

"Yeah, me too." I look out over the city as the sun sets in the west, setting the buildings alight with bursts of orange and red.

"So where are you planning on moving?"

"Not sure yet. We have a few months to figure it out. But I'm sure we'll stay in the city."

"Any word from your driver, Cyril?"

"Not since Christmas." Arthur leans against the window. "I've put all his stuff in storage at the garage."

"What are you going to do with it?"

"What he would have wanted. If he shows up, it's his. If not, well…"

The implication of the words settles between us, weighed down with regret.

"He'll show up. You'll see."

"I hope so." Arthur shakes his head and straightens. "How about we go out for dinner? My treat. Today is a day for celebrations."

Kate's head snaps up. "Can we go to the diner? I've been craving apple pie and vanilla ice cream."

We all laugh, and the sound soothes like a healing balm.

"We'll stop for dessert, I promise." He retrieves her purse from the table.

"Shall we?" I offer Marcy my arm, and she takes it, fitting her hand in the crook of my elbow like it was always meant to be there.

This moment was a long time coming, but it was well worth the trials along the way. Contentment settles over me.

I finally have the woman of my dreams, and she has my heart. Forever.

I can't fight this feeling anymore, and I wouldn't have it any other way.

PLAYLIST

"What's Love Got to Do with It" - Tina Turner
"Pour Some Sugar On Me" - Def Leppard
"You Give Love a Bad Name" - Bon Jovi
"Runaway" - Bon Jovi
"Every Rose Has Its Thorn" - Poison
"Rock You Like a Hurricane" - Scorpions
"Poison" - Alice Cooper
"Rainbow in the Dark" - Dio
"Hold On Loosely" - 38 Special
"Love is a Battlefield" - Pat Benatar
"Heartbeat City" - The Cars

CHAPTER 1

Grant

Manhattan, NYC 1985

I'm too old for this bullshit.

Rob and Arthur are lucky we've been friends for as long as we have. When Rob called to say he had an issue and needed my help, it took all my effort not to tell him to drop dead.

But my conscience wouldn't let me roll over and go back to sleep. So now I'm standing in Arthur's sister's apartment with an irate cat burglar fighting me.

Why didn't he call the cops? Rob's explanation is simple. The woman broke in, and he didn't want the hassle of paperwork. I can't say I blame him. I'm just irritated to have been torn from the comfort of my bed at this god-awful hour of the morning. Seems like he forgot I don't handle petty breaking and entering bullshit. I'm strictly homicide.

"I'll take care of her." I hook my hand around the thief's arm and drag her to her feet.

She tenses under my grip. Her narrow eyes take me in, like she's looking for a soft spot on my throat to sink her teeth into.

I meet her gaze, unflinching, hoping she catches my unspoken warning—if she doesn't behave, she's gonna wish they had called the cops. My grip tightens as I pull her toward the door.

The reality of her situation finally reaches her stubborn brain. "Wait, don't let him take me! Call the cops. But don't let him take me. Please." Panic fills her wide green eyes.

Doesn't matter how young or pretty she is, she crossed the wrong person today. I'm in no mood to negotiate.

"Please."

Her pleas do nothing to my cold, dead heart. She fucked up and she knows it.

"It's too late, kid. You're my problem now."

She fights my hold, clawing at my hand on her arm. I pull her against me with a firm tug.

"Keep it up," I whisper in her ear. "And I'll make sure you're locked up so tight, you'll never see sunshine again."

The hellcat stills immediately, pressing her lips together in irritation.

"Thanks, Richards." Rob waves. "See you next week."

"Yeah, yeah." I turn to Arthur's sister. "Good night, ma'am."

The moment we step into the hallway, the door locks behind us. Exhaustion creeps over me. What the hell am I going to do with this stray cat who seems hell-bent on causing trouble?

She stumbles behind me as we make our way down the hall. Silence then fills the elevator as we descend to the ground floor. When we step into the May air, she tries to break away from my grip. I glance at her, amused by her futile attempt to escape.

"Please, let me go." She bats her thick dark lashes. "I promise I'll behave."

I scoff. "Sure, kid, and I'm Superman." The soft flicker of neon light filters through the street. "Come on."

She mumbles, and I pull her alongside me down the street. When a diner comes into view, my stomach growls. A late-night diner is a perfect place for me to question this little street rat to see if she'll be of any use.

Inside, the middle-aged waitress glances up from her station. "Morning," she calls out. "Sit anywhere."

I nod in thanks and take a booth at the back of the diner. The thief slides in first, and I sit next to her to block her escape.

"What can I get ya?" The waitress appears with two menus.

"Two coffees." I glance at the breakfast selection and choose two basic dishes without consulting my unwilling companion. "Thanks."

I give the menus back, and she disappears into the kitchen.

There's no one else in the diner at this early morning hour, and I'm thankful for that. We must look like an odd pair to the waitress, but she doesn't stick her nose in it. I'm sure she's seen her fair share of crazy shit in this city. She returns with the coffee before retreating again.

I push one of the cups toward the burglar. "You got a name, kid?"

She snorts. "Why do you care?"

"Look, I'm not above dragging your ass down to the station and booking you for breaking and entering and attempted theft. But by all means, keep testing my patience."

Her shoulders slump. She reaches for sugar and cream, dumping a ton of each into her steaming mug. I sip my black coffee, watching her closely.

She samples the drink that was once coffee and sighs. "Quinn."

"She speaks." I try not to focus too intently on her, but being this close makes me uncomfortable. I keep waiting for her to lunge at me with a fork or to toss the coffee in my lap before racing to the exit.

But she doesn't move. Instead, she pushes her riotous curls away from her face and exhales sharply. Her gaze lifts from the coffee mug and settles on me.

I've never been swayed by a pair of pretty eyes and a flirty smile, but damn it if this little minx isn't the definition of pure temptation. She's all curves beneath a skin-tight black top and leggings. The light catches the red woven deep into her auburn curls. This close I can nearly count the freckles across the bridge of her nose.

"Irish." The word tumbles from my lips, and I cringe.

"What?" She gapes at me.

"Your name. It's Irish." I lean back and cover the slip with a shrug of indifference.

"Yeah. So?" She cocks her head and narrows her eyes. "The red hair, green eyes, and freckles didn't give it away?"

"Calm down, smart-ass." I sip my coffee and redirect my attention when the waitress appears with our breakfast.

Quinn licks her lips at the plate coming to rest in front of her.

"Dig in." I grab my fork and take a bite, ignoring the way my heart aches.

We eat in silence. She's done before I even make a dent in my eggs. I arch a brow as she mops her plate with a slice of toast and licks her fingers.

Her gaze meets mine. "What?"

Her tongue curls around her index finger, and a thousand wicked thoughts fly through my mind. I slam a lid on them before they can take root.

"You were hungry." I pull my attention from her face and resume my meal.

"Yeah. I don't exactly have money to indulge in a fine meal at such a quality establishment." Heavy sarcasm laces her words.

"Is that why you're breaking into people's apartments and robbing them blind?"

"Look, I fucked up, okay? You gonna take me in? Or keep rubbing it in my face?"

I finish my last few bites and wash them down with coffee. She crosses her arms and glowers expectantly in my direction. When I lean back, I give her my full attention. Those luminous eyes blink at me, full of irritation and hate.

"Do you want me to take you in?" I wipe my mouth and toss the napkin aside. "I mean, it's up to you, kid."

"First of all, stop calling me 'kid.' I'm twenty-six." Her scowl deepens as she folds her arms across her ample chest, drawing my attention there for a split second. "And secondly, I don't appreciate you fucking with me—either you're gonna take me in or you're gonna let me go. Pick one."

"Why are you in such a hurry?" I smirk. "Got better places to be?"

"Yeah, I do."

"You got someone waiting for you?"

Her cheeks flame, turning a delicate shade of rose pink. "No."

"Someone to fence the loot you were supposed to snatch tonight."

"Fuck you." Indignant, she shoves me. It's a feeble attempt, and I can tell I've struck a nerve.

"If I were interested in that, I would've taken it behind the diner."

"Asshole." Her eyes spark with fury. "Like I'd let you touch me."

"Come off it, kid. You were ready to throw yourself at me at the slightest chance I would let you go."

"Damn you," she mutters under her breath.

"I might not be old enough to be your father, but I'm not interested in taking advantage of women or desperate thieves." I pin her with a no-nonsense stare.

"I'm not getting off with a warning, am I?"

"No." I shake my head, and a slow smile spreads across my lips. "But I'm willing to offer an arrangement that might benefit both of us."

She arches her delicate brow. "I'm listening."

"There's been a string of murders lately. They look like break-ins gone wrong, but I think there's something more." I cock my head and study her expression as she takes in the information.

"What's that got to do with me? I don't know anything about that shit."

"Yeah, but you've got connections." My hand flexes against my thigh.

"I won't be a rat. I've seen what they do to people who snitch to the cops."

"I don't want low-level scum. I'm homicide. I don't give two shits about petty theft." What I do is different. It consumes me, and I'm running out of patience.

"I've been chasing this fucker all over Manhattan, and I got nothing."

"What do you expect me to do?" She eyes me with distrust.

"Keep an eye open for anything suspicious. If you hear something—anything—contact me at the Twenty-Fourth Precinct." I pull out my wallet and drop a few bills on the table. "If I'm not at work, come to the Black Penny in Hell's Kitchen. The bartender's a friend."

Her eyes widen when I hand her a twenty. She tucks it into her bra, giving me a glimpse of pale bare skin beneath her black top. "The Black Penny. Hell's Kitchen."

"Right." I stand, and she follows suit.

When I step out into the night, she comes beside me. "Why are you doing this?"

"Because stopping this bastard is more important than locking you up." I glance down at her. The twilight fog swirls around us, and a curl slides across her cheek. I clench my fists after I nearly reach out to brush it away. *She's not your responsibility. She's nothing. Leave her alone. Walk away.*

"Thanks for breakfast." Quinn offers a half smile, but I can see the skepticism in her eyes. Like she's waiting for the rug to be pulled out from under her.

"Stay out of trouble, would you?" I pull a pack of cigarettes out of my pocket. "If you get caught, I won't be able to bail your ass out."

Quinn rolls her eyes and tosses her hair over her shoulder. "I got sloppy tonight. Won't happen again."

I light the cigarette and take a drag. "I'd tell you to give it up, but I know you won't listen."

"You asked me to be your snitch." She puts her hand on her hip. "I can't give it up *and* be your informant."

"Point taken. Just keep your head down, kid."

Quinn glowers at me, then snatches the cigarette from my hand. She tosses it to the ground and grinds it beneath her boot. "Thanks, dad."

I shake my head. This woman will be the death of me. I can feel it. "Get out of here before I change my mind." I shove my hands in my pockets and start down the sidewalk.

"Wait," she calls.

I stop and turn, meeting her green gaze.

"What's your name?"

"Detective Richards."

"They don't issue a first name or what?" She inclines her head with a teasing grin.

"You gotta earn the right to use that name." I wink. "See ya around, kid."

The sound of her swearing follows me down the street. I doubt anything will come of this fiasco, but I need all the help I can get. There's a serial killer loose in Manhattan, and I'm scraping the bottom of the barrel to catch the bastard.

CHAPTER 2

Quinn

The detective's words haunt me every day. Even as I pull on the little black dress, I can almost hear the disappointed grinding of his teeth and feel the heat of his gaze burning into my skull.

I have tried to go straight over the last three months, but with jobs thin on the ground, money is too tight to live comfortably in the city. My gaze shifts around the cozy, little, East Harlem apartment I share with two other girls. This isn't cutting it. I barely scrape together the money I need for rent and utilities each month. I was lucky to find the ad searching for a roommate. Beth and Nancy are nothing like me. They have legitimate jobs and goals.

Me? I'm floundering.

Ever since the night I got caught breaking into the wrong house, it's like I've suddenly grown a conscience. I blame Detective Richards—a thorn in my side and an ever-persistent pain in my ass. I haven't spoken to him since he bought breakfast and offered a deal. His simple request burns me. *Stay out of trouble.* How the hell am I supposed to stay out of trouble and be his informant? I can't do both.

Not that it matters. There are whispers on the street, but no one knows anything about the string of break-in–murders. Thieves don't really share information. But there's enough chatter to put us all on edge.

Eddie Fink, the guy who fences all my goods, isn't taking chances. He told me he's keeping low. Everyone is. Though not because they don't want to cross whoever this guy is. They're worried the cops will somehow pin the murders on them if they get caught.

Can't say the thought hasn't crossed my mind, but I have an ace in my pocket. Richards knows I'm not the murderer. That doesn't guarantee he'll come to my aid. I just know I won't be pinned with a bullshit murder charge. But I could still be a target.

I forgo any makeup and tie my hair back, pinning it in place before fixing a white cap on my head. I'm not used to the new color of my hair. Too dark. Makes my face even paler, if that's possible. But without red hair, I blend in better. I'm less noticeable. When I show up, no one spares me a sideways glance.

This maid gig is sweet. Tempting too. Nancy managed to secure me a part-time position in a swanky uptown mansion. Rich bankers. No one who would recognize me. After the first week, the possibilities presented themselves. Jewelry boxes open in the bedroom. Crystal and silver ornaments littered throughout the house. Cash stashed in random drawers in random rooms.

Who the hell leaves all that valuable shit just lying around the house?

Temptation pulls at me from every direction. For the last month and a half, I've kept my head down and done my job. No one blinks when I walk into a room; servants in this place are a dime a dozen. There's a permanent chef and kitchen staff as well as six full-time maids, two butlers, and a high-dollar security team keeping tabs on the outside entrances.

If I didn't know any better, I'd say the banker who owns this house is into some shady shit. Mafia or something. That's what kept my hands off the enticing morsels the first month. But the longer I'm here, the more alluring those little gems have become. Certainly, they wouldn't miss a trinket here or there, right?

I tie the apron around my waist and sigh, glimpsing the dour maid reflected in the mirror. It's not the most flattering outfit, but it could be worse. I could be stripping or picking up johns on the East Side.

A shiver wracks me. I'd rather starve than sell my body to perverts. I've met too many girls over the years who lose their minds and their lives dipping into that line of work. I'd rather leave the city than sell my soul.

"Off to work?" Nancy asks as I step into the living room.

"Yeah." I sit beside her on the couch and put on my shoes.

"Be careful." She bites her lip.

"I'm always careful." I soothe her with a smile. She's sweet and innocent. If they knew my past and half the shit I've done, both my roommates would kick me out.

"I know. Maybe you could ask for the day shift? It might be safer."

"I like working nights. Gives me time to myself." I rest my hand on hers. "Don't worry. I'll be fine."

Nancy sighs, then nods her blonde head. Her blue eyes are full of worry, but she doesn't persist.

"I'll be home late." I grab my purse and head for the door. "See you later."

"Bye."

I'm halfway down the stairs when I start contemplating the logistics of my situation. I haven't officially met the rich bastard I work for, or his family, but I've seen pictures scattered throughout the house. They're ridiculously loaded with too much time on their hands. It's almost the perfect opportunity.

The old man's on his sixth trophy wife, it looks like. He's got kids with each of them, all ages from adult to infant. I think the oldest is older than me, some hotshot broker on Wall Street. He stopped by a few times. Once he stumbled in on me cleaning the library. Snobby shit took ogled me for half a second before turning his nose up before kicking me out of the room.

Asshole.

If I were going to steal anything, I'd take it from that prick. Being raised with a silver spoon in his mouth was terrible for his manners. Fortunately, he hasn't been back.

For now, the pay is decent, and I can keep my nighttime hours. As long as I restrain myself, I'm in the clear. Shiny things are my downfall.

As I make my way down into the station, a shadow appears behind one of the pillars. Nancy's warning rings in my head. I sidestep, ready to run if needed. The city at night isn't a friendly place. I've seen too much shit in this town to take anything for granted.

On the subway, I settle into an empty seat in a half-full car. I don't even glance up when someone brushes past and slides into the seat beside me. First rule of survival in Manhattan, mind your own business. Sticking your neck into something that doesn't concern you is a surefire way to get yourself killed.

"You've been hiding from us, Quinn."

The rough tone pulls me from my thoughts, and my whole body stiffens at the familiar sound of Jack's voice.

"What the hell do you want?" I keep my own voice low.

"The boss sent me with a reminder. You're past due on your payment."

His hand rests in his jacket pocket. Doesn't take a genius to figure out what he's got in there. Jack's always packing heat. That's what mobsters do.

"I told you before, I'll have it by the end of the month."

He tuts. "Interest has gone up, sweetheart. Boss wants double by next week."

"Double?" I gape at him.

His dark hair falls across his vacant brown eyes. I don't doubt the truth of his words. He's a bulldog for one of the biggest crime lords in the city. I'd be stupid as fuck to cross either of them.

He shrugs. "Costs have gone up."

"That's not fair." Fear flutters through me, but I retain the strength in my voice. "We had a deal."

"Deals change." His sadistic smile makes my stomach churn. "If you want to take it up with the boss, I'll escort you over there now."

"No." My heart stops at the thought of facing him before I have the funds. "Fuck. I'll have it to you by next week. But after that, I'm done. We're done."

"Good girl." Jack pats my knee.

It takes all my effort not to puke at his touch. The silver medallion around his neck catches the overhead light when he stands. I barely maintain my composure until the subway comes to a stop. He exits, leaving me in a state of fury and disbelief.

I know better than to make a deal with a devil. Even one I thought I knew.

There's nothing I can do about it now. It would be better if I disappeared, vanished into thin air. But I can't. Not yet. Not until I take care of my debts. Mom's safe, but not me. I'm fucked.

How the hell did I let myself get into this mess?

When I finally arrive, the mansion on Riverside is quiet. Milly tells me the family is out, on a yacht in the Caribbean or something ridiculous. Relief fills me. I don't have to deal with the family. With that many ex-wives, drama is never in short supply.

Milly hands me the cleaning carrier, and together we climb the opulent staircase to the second floor. We work in relative silence, but inside my mind, I'm screaming.

This job gives me enough money to get through day-to-day life, but it won't take care of the debt hanging over my head. Jack's stark reminder of my predicament leaves me nauseated and miserable.

I can't let them pull me under. Not when I've fought so hard to stay afloat.

Fuck them for putting me in this position.

Milly takes the master suite, and I work on the bathroom. Glittering sapphires and diamonds lay in an open jewelry box on the bureau. My gaze lingers as I pass by. The sparkle calls to me, promising security and closure. *Freedom.*

I close my eyes and press forward. *No.* I'm not going to do this. Not tonight. There has to be another way.

There isn't another way, and you know it, my mind whispers as I spray the vanity in the bathroom. *No one is coming to your rescue. If you don't seize this opportunity, it's done.* I double over at the thought of Jack's disgusting grin as he hovers above me, taking his payment in flesh and blood.

"You okay?" Milly asks from the doorway.

"Yeah, fine. Just the fumes." I wave my hand to disperse the invisible gases.

"Crack the window. It helps." She smiles and returns to her duties.

I open the window, and a cool breeze ghosts over my skin. The sounds of the city filter in on the night air, and I know I'm fucked either way.

One last heist, then I'm done.

I swear on my mother's grave.

CHAPTER 3

Grant

Upper East Side…two victims…white male, age fifty-two…white female, age forty-seven…multiple abrasions and contusions…evidence of a struggle…both found with throat slit…forced entry and robbery confirmed…no evidence of sexual assault to either victim…no witnesses.

"Shit." I close the file and toss it aside. It's been eight months since the first case hit my desk, and I'm no closer to connecting the handful of unsolved murders plaguing the city.

I run my hand through my hair and groan at the ache in my shoulders before opening the second file to scan the contents.

Harlem…one victim…black male, age forty…gunshot to the chest…forced entry and robbery confirmed…no evidence of sexual assault, no witnesses.

It's similar across the remaining three files. There's no pattern in the relationship between the victims or the location of the thefts. Totally random. The only connection shared across five cases is that what started as a burglary ended with murder. Not a single cop in the city believes these cases are related.

Except me.

I rub my thumb into my temple and reach for the top drawer of my desk where I stash pain pills. Pouring two into my palm, I grimace at the possibility that I'm chasing a figment of my imagination. After swallowing the pills, I wash them down with the cold coffee in my mug. The bitter taste lingers in my mouth, and I shudder.

"How's it going, Richards?" Mickey collapses in his chair on the other side of our two back-to-back desks. He glances at the files spread out before me. "You still looking for connections?"

I nod.

We've been partners for a few years, but I've known him since we went through the academy together. He works hard and holds up his end. I'm thankful for that, but he doesn't believe me. Not about this.

"You sure there's something here?" He arches a ginger brow when I shrug. "Half those cases aren't even ours to worry about."

"Yeah, I know…but I got this feeling." My fingers drum on the desk, mirroring my agitation. "They're connected, Mickey. I know it."

"You need to find yourself a woman." He scoffs. "All work and no play makes you a pain in the ass. Maybe if you got laid, you'd relax."

My mood darkens at his statement. "I tried that, remember? It made shit worse."

"I didn't tell you to run off and get married to the first blonde who winked in your direction."

I glower at him and say nothing. My ex was a mistake. A big-breasted, unfaithful, expensive mistake. Thoughts of her do nothing to improve my sour mood.

"Look, I'm just saying maybe you need to take a break. Find something outside of work to distract you." He leans forward on his elbows, concern glinting in his eyes. "This job will chew you up and spit you out if you let it."

"I just can't help but think this is another Son of Sam situation." I shake my head. "There's a connection here. I just need to find it. Or find someone who saw something."

"You sure you're not just looking for something to keep your mind busy?" Mickey leans back in his chair.

I am. But he doesn't need to know that.

Truth is, something about these cases bothers me. I just can't put my finger on it. I had hoped my thief-turned-informant would have something for me, but I haven't heard from her. She vanished into the wind. Which means one of two things—either she wised up and got out of the game or she hasn't gotten caught again.

An unsavory third option leaves a sour taste in my mouth. I shake my head.

"You going to the pub tonight?" Mickey stands and pulls on his coat. "I'll buy you a drink."

"No, thanks. I need to get some shit done before I head home."

"Suit yourself." He waves. "I'll see ya around."

I wave him off with a nod and a halfhearted smile. Mickey's a good guy, but I really didn't feel like being around other cops tonight. The pub around the corner is always full of cops—retired, active…it's the precinct hangout. Not exactly the best place to go when I'm already a pariah among my peers. They don't say anything to my face, but I know what they say about me behind my back. What they call me. Rabid Richards, a dog with a bone. Relentless and single-minded.

Truth be told, I'd rather drown my sorrows at home alone with a bottle of whiskey. I tuck the files into my leather satchel and switch off the lamp on my desk. Here's hoping for a quiet weekend so I can get some research done.

I'm one of the last to leave for the day. The minimal night crew waves as I step into the fading sunset. It's nearly eight. My stomach growls, demanding sustenance.

Maybe I'll stop downstairs when I get home to grab something to eat before I dive back into these files.

By the time I reach the Black Penny, it's bursting with local patrons. Much more discreet than the pub cops frequent. A few regulars slap my back as I walk through the crowd. I greet them with a smile, wondering if I should have just gone up and wrangled some food from my sparse cabinets.

Claude notices me from behind the bar. I find an empty stool toward the back of the Irish pub, and he sets a double on a coaster, eyeing me with warmth.

"Rough week?" He leans close as two of the waitresses push past him to help the Sam, the weekend bartender.

"Yeah, you could say that." I sip the whiskey, thankful my brother has a stash of my favorite brand behind the bar. "Looks like you've got your hands full." I gesture to the bustling commotion around us.

"Weekends are good business." Claude rests one hand on the edge of the bar and pivots the missing one away from me. "But we can manage well enough."

I ignore the ever-present guilt about my brother's missing hand. Should have been me in the jungle, not him. Never him. Claude's too good-hearted to be a soldier. Me? I'm a jaded asshole. That draft number should have been mine. But somehow, I slipped through without being called to duty. Claude wasn't so lucky. I'm just glad he made it home alive.

"Pap would be proud of you, keeping up the pub like this." I salute my brother.

He smiles at the mention of our maternal grandfather. An Irish immigrant, who came to America at the turn of the century, trying to find a better place to raise his family. He built this place, poured everything the family had into it. Then, when Claude returned wounded with an honorable discharge, Pap gave him the bar to instill purpose and direction. Which it did. Damn it if Claude isn't the best bartender on the East Coast.

"And what would he say about you?" The corner of my brother's mouth twitches. "You're gonna work yourself into an early grave."

"Do I really look that bad?"

"Like death warmed over." Claude refills my glass, the bottle clinking against the glass rim. "It's a great look for a homicide detective though."

"Smart-ass." I take another drink. "What's the special tonight?"

"Bacon cheeseburger and fries." Claude smirks. "Same as always."

"You need to liven up your menu." I sigh. "Fine. I'll take it."

Claude stops one of the waitresses and gives her the order. She nods before heading to the kitchen.

"Looks like you'll need to hire more help." I glance around the bar as it grows louder.

"Good help is hard to find, Grant." He arches a brow at me.

So many of my own features are reflected in his face. Everyone assumes we're twins, but we're not. I'm two years older. We share some strong traits from our father—dark hair hiding ears that stick out a bit, strong, angular profiles, and pale skin splattered with what mom liked to call our beauty marks. She always said we were handsome, but it wasn't until we grew out of our awkward teen years that we even remotely believed it.

"Isn't that the truth." I finish the whiskey and set it aside.

He takes the glass and ambles off to wash it. An old veteran sidles up to the bar and flags him down. I chuckle. They certainly have their own little club, don't they?

"Hey there, handsome." A husky voice echoes behind me.

I spin around, and my brow furrows at the interruption. A leggy blonde, her hair poofed and crimped, cocks her hip and rests her hand on it. Her eyes drift over me from head to toe, and I can almost feel those glittering nails scratching a chalkboard when she speaks.

"You looking for a good time?" She winks.

My gaze roams from her overstyled hair to the fishnet-covered toes peeking out of her platform heels. A neon top hangs precariously off one pale shoulder. She snaps her gum and smiles, hoping I'll take her bait.

I reach into my pocket and pull out my badge. "Why don't you try the pub down the street?"

Her eyes fly wide at the sight of my shield. With a huff, she spins around, nearly tripping over herself in her haste to get out.

I chuckle as the door slams behind her. Even if she weren't a hooker looking for her next client, I'm not interested in picking anyone up.

Especially at my brother's bar. I'm not *that* masochistic.

Claude shoots me a look from the opposite side of the room. I lift my shoulder in response. He shakes his head and returns to his conversation with the vet.

It's sad. The only people I can trust are my brother, Claude, and my friends, Rob and Arthur. One's been with me nearly my whole life and the other two are like family. It's not often you have friendships like that. Especially in my line of work.

Is it lonely? Yes, more so than I care to admit. But I wouldn't trade it for anything.

The waitress sets my burger down.

"Thanks."

"You're welcome, honey. Anything else I can get ya?"

"No, I'm good."

With an embellished pout, she turns and heads back into the kitchen.

Claude better keep an eye on his employees. Something tells me they can get into a lot of trouble with very little effort.

I tuck in and savor the crisp bite of bacon and greasy cheeseburger. I need something to fortify me through the night. Whoever's out there killing people isn't going to take a night off just because I'm exhausted.

I need to find that loose thread and pull it before this whole case unravels around me.

CHAPTER 4

Quinn

Another uneventful night cleaning a rich asshole's home. It's getting harder to come to work every day and *not* steal something. There have been at least a dozen opportunities.

But I've behaved, just barely reining myself in before I pocket his wife's gaudy gems or his gold cufflinks.

They'd immediately know it was me. Especially if I disappeared into the night with a pocketful of loot. Fuck.

It's so much easier when there's nothing to tie me to a location. That's how I did it before I tried to walk the straight and narrow. I never hit the same neighborhood twice. I always moved boroughs afterward. I cased the place for a week or two to learn who had the most predictable schedule and to find the quickest access. Middle or upper class.

Never kids. That was my limit. The last thing I needed was kids in the mix when I was trying to sneak in and out. Kids didn't need that kind of trauma. Not that it's anything like the shit I had to deal with, but still. Kids deserve to be kids. So I never hit a place where there was a chance I'd be caught or seen by a child. They deserve the opportunities I didn't have growing up.

The door opens behind me, and I cringe at the sight of my employer's oldest son entering the foyer. I duck into the nearest room, blending into the darkness. His presence makes me uncomfortable. I've caught him leering on the small handful of occasions we've been in the same room. He's never said anything to me, but I refuse to give him a chance. I avoid him at all costs.

My brow furrows in confusion. Milly told me the family went out for the evening. The house is empty except for the nanny and baby in the nursery on the fourth floor. What is he doing here? I can only pray he hasn't come to harass the staff.

He climbs the stairs, taking two at a time, glancing around the open space. Then he enters the old man's study. Is he looking for something?

Curiosity gets the best of me. I take the servant stairs to the second floor and creep down the hall. The door is cracked open. The thud of books hitting the floor echoes through the narrow space. I spy his agitated flurry of movement as he tosses books from the massive bookcase behind the mahogany desk.

A flicker of light from the desk lamp casts deep shadows across his face when he turns to raid the contents of the desk. I hold my breath and slowly back away from the door as he crosses the room. He bursts into the hallway, intent and focused as he makes his way up to the third floor. I cling to the shadows, watching his progress. Where is he going now?

It's obvious he's on the hunt for something in particular. Something he thinks must be hidden.

Shit. I can't be involved in this.

Without hesitation, I make my way downstairs to the parlor to finish cleaning. Milly is in the living room. If he comes downstairs to cause trouble, I can call for help.

Busying myself, I ignore the burning curiosity and fear nestled at the base of my neck, making the fine hairs stand on end. This is none of my business. If he came to start shit, then the old man can deal with it. I'll steer clear of that family drama. There's no reason for me to stick my nose into it, not with my record.

Ten minutes later, the front door slams, the sound echoing off the marble floors in the foyer. Relief fills me. I don't have to deal with whatever that was. I manage to finish the parlor and gather my cleaning supplies.

If I hurry, I can finish the hallway on the third floor before calling it quits for the night. Milly waves as she heads to the kitchen. I slip into the servant stairwell. The house feels like a museum in the still quiet of the night. Without the old man and his trophy wife home, sound resonates like a tomb.

Outside the master bedroom, I set down the cleaning kit and take out a rag to dust the hallway surfaces. The decorative lighting casts a dull sheen on the walls and floor. I can't really tell if I'm getting the surfaces clean, but it doesn't matter. No one checks anyway.

The soft murmur of voices fills the air. I glance down the hallway. Perhaps the old man and his wife have returned home. I move to gather my things when I realize the sound is coming from behind the master bedroom door.

I lean closer, and the voices elevate. From here, I can't tell who it is. It sounds like two men arguing, but I can't be sure. I jump back when the handle of the door shifts. I press myself into the shadows against the wall, wishing I had stayed home tonight.

"Go to hell." The old man's voice echoes through the open door. I didn't even hear him come home. If he steps through and glances to the right, he'll see me. Maybe I should leave.

"Get out of my house!"

My heart stops. I press my hand to my chest. The flutter beneath my palm reminds me this is real. I look toward the servant stairs at the end of the hallway and contemplate how fast I can get there without being seen or heard.

Then comes the sickening crunch of flesh striking flesh, the unmistakable thud of a body hitting the floor. I pinch my eyes closed, willing myself a thousand miles away as a scuffle ensues. The flurry of activity in the master bedroom escalates. A gurgling groan drifts through the open door, and I hear the slide of heavy fabric on the hardwood floors.

I should run. Turn and leave.

But I can't just leave the old man to his fate. Can I?

With as much care as I can muster, I slide closer to the doorway and peer around the decorative molding framing the doorway. A dark figure dominates the open space of the master bedroom, face hidden from view. In a motionless heap at his feet, lies the old man. Dark liquid spills across the hardwood floor, pooling around his body, glinting in the lamplight. The broad masked figure stares down at the old man for a long moment, then he shifts his position. I catch the flash of a knife in his hand as he wipes blood from the blade.

A gasp rips from my throat as a wave of nausea overtakes me.

The intruder jerks around, and even though I can't make out details in the dim light, I know he sees me.

Shit.

I turn and run like the cops are chasing me. I stumble over the cleaning kit but manage to right myself before the intruder clears the doorway.

His stride matches mine.

I need to put something between us. As I round the corner, I overturn a table, forcing him to slow. He swipes the blade at me, catching the back of my right arm.

The stinging bite of the cut pulses through me, and warmth runs down my arm dripping onto the floor.

I grasp the wound with my other hand and race down the stairs. My breath comes in heavy pants as panic consumes me.

How the hell do I get away from him? Where do I go?

I dart down the hallway toward the main entrance. He's nearly reached me when I fumble for the door. This time, the blade catches my left shoulder. I slam into the wall and grab the iron coatrack with both hands, jerking it down between us. It catches the back of the murderer's head and he swears beneath the black ski mask.

Seizing my opportunity, I wrench open the door and run out into the night. Just up the street, there's a dark passageway between the houses. I race toward it, unsure of the assailant's whereabouts.

I don't care. At this point, I just want to get away. Fast.

When I reach the opening, I slide between the brick and the iron grates, stepping into a hidden garden behind the buildings. I weave through the overgrown vegetation, half hoping the owner will see me and call the cops. Anything to deter the man chasing me. I find a quiet corner where another gate lets me out on the next street.

I silently retreat through the darkness of the city, letting the shadows conceal me from the evil lurking in the distance. My heart races with every step, and I jump at every sound.

Glancing over my shoulder, I take comfort in the fact there's no one behind me. He'd be crazy to chase me through the streets of the city.

I manage about ten blocks before the adrenaline wears off and the blood loss hits me. Feeling weak, I lean against the nearest building, still keeping to the shadows. Blood seeps between my fingertips as I try to staunch it. Fuck.

I can't go to the hospital. Too many questions. The cops will find me. They'll think I did this. With my record, they'll lock me away and throw the key into the Hudson. I'll be screwed.

That's what I get for trying to go legit. Damn it.

The Black Penny. The words float into my mind between spasms of pain. Detective Richards told me to go there if I needed him. The bartender would contact him.

I don't have a choice. No hospital. I can't go home to embroil my innocent roommates in my fucking mess. No. He's my only hope. If I can convince him of the truth, then he can keep the cops off my ass.

The Irish pub is on the edge of Hell's Kitchen. It's not far. If I can make it, the detective will help me.

It's either that or bleed out on the streets.

Shit.

I drag myself to the pub. I can't go in the front door like this, so I sneak down the side of the building and bang on an unmarked door. My hand slides down the metal, my legs giving out. Exhaustion threatens to drag me under as adrenaline wears off.

The door opens and casts a halo of light on me, rendering me blind for a moment. My eyes adjust, and I'm staring at a tall man. He looks a lot like the detective, but I know it's not him when I see his missing hand. His scowl softens when he sees my state and the blood on my hands.

"Detective…Richards." My voice is weak. I lick my lips.

"Damn it." The man reaches down and pulls me inside. "Wait here."

He dashes up the stairs, and when he reaches the next floor, he shouts, "Grant!"

The sound of pounding and raised voices echoes through my head as I succumb to the darkness.

CHAPTER 5

Grant

"Grant!"

I hear shouts through my front door followed by the repeated pounding of a fist against the wood. I manage to pull myself from the chair where I'd been sorting through cold case files.

My brother's never this demanding. What the hell?

"What?" I rip the door open.

"Downstairs, now." Without waiting for a response, he darts back down the stairs.

"What the fuck?" I follow but freeze on the landing when I see a woman in a heap at the base of the staircase. "Who is it?"

"Don't know." Claude kneels to check her pulse. "She's still alive but unconscious. I don't know where all this blood is coming from. Let's get her to your apartment."

"My apartment?" I hesitate before crouching next to the unconscious woman with dark brown hair, wearing a maid's uniform. "Why?"

"Because"—he glares up at me—"she mentioned your name before she passed out."

I kneel beside her and brush the hair away from her face. *Shit.* The cat burglar I gave a second chance to. Her clothes are soaked in blood, and her breathing is shallow.

"What the hell happened to you, kid?" I murmur before gently lifting her.

She's not petite by any standard, but she fits perfectly against me in my arms. Careful of her state, I carry her up the stairs into my apartment. I lay her on the bed, not caring about bloodstains. That's the least of my worries.

Claude lingers at my elbow.

I turn to give him directions. "Call Rob. Tell him to get his ass over here now."

With a nod, my brother retreats to the living room. His voice carries through the open doorway.

I turn my attention to the bundle of trouble bleeding all over my bed. My fingers brush her sweat-slick forehead, pushing away the stray locks curling across her face. Her pale skin glows against the dark blankets.

"Rob's on his way." Claude returns with an armful of towels. "Here. I'll get some hot water and a rag. Get her out of those clothes so we can find her injuries." He hands me the pocketknife on his hip.

Those military instincts never disappear. Even though I'm a cop, Claude's always been more level-headed and methodical in a crisis. It's like all my training goes out the window when I'm faced with a medical emergency. Thank God for my brother.

I manage to cut the dress off. She doesn't react as I carefully roll her to the side and pull the material from beneath her. That's when I spot the gash on her left shoulder blade. I press a damp rag against the wound, hoping the pressure of her body will staunch the bleeding until Rob arrives. On the other side, I wince at a deep cut marring her upper right arm.

"Maybe we should take her to the hospital?" Claude asks when he appears with a bowl of hot water.

"No hospital," she mutters, her green eyes fluttering open. They lock on mine.

"What the hell happened to you, kid?" I ask, wrapping another damp cloth around her arm.

She winces, and her eyes roll into the back of her head as she falls unconscious again. Fuck.

I look at my brother. His eyebrows draw close in a deep furrow.

"Go. Send Rob up when he gets here. I can handle this."

Claude presses his lips together like he wants to argue but nods.

The moment the door closes, I turn my attention to the woman in my bed. After more than two months of radio silence, why did she show up here? What kind of trouble did she stumble into? Why did she come to me of all people? I shake my head. She's nothing but bad luck. A cat burglar who ended up in the wrong place at the wrong time. I'd put money on it.

She looks young, but there's nothing innocent about her. If I'm going to learn anything about what happened to her tonight, I need to patch her up.

It takes me about twenty minutes to clean her. I draw the blankets up to protect her modesty. She's wearing only a bra and panties, and I don't want to put any other clothes on her until Rob addresses the wounds on her arm and back. She's got some scrapes and bruises too, but those should heal without intervention.

"Grant?" Rob calls from the front door.

"In the bedroom."

Rob steps into the room, and his gaze drops to the bed. "What the hell happened?"

"I don't know. She showed up at the back door and passed out." I stand and shove my hands in my pockets. "She's got a deep cut on her right tricep and another on her left shoulder blade."

He pushes me aside and sits on the bed. His hands methodically inspect the wounds. "Hand me my kit."

I snatch the bag from the foot of the bed and give it to him.

He shuffles through it until he finds what he's looking for. "They're deep. I'll have to stitch them." He threads a needle. "Can you hold her while I work?"

Uncertainty floods me, but I take the spot where Rob was sitting and gather her unconscious form into my arms, resting her head against my shoulder. After readjusting the light, Rob sets to work. He's quiet and precise, making the stitches small and effective so they don't scar.

I stare at the wall above my bed, acutely aware of her skin against my thin T-shirt. I ignore the clean floral scent of her hair. My fingertips are light against her back as I hold her in place. Her breath ghosts against my neck in soft puffs. A thousand questions burrow into my mind, but I won't have any answers until she wakes. Right now, she's safe; that's all that matters.

Once Rob finishes bandaging her shoulder, he shifts and scowls. "You're going to have to hold her like this."

He shows me how to position her in my lap to give him access to her arm. I do as he says, ignoring the brush of her body against mine and the brash reminder that it's been a while since I've been intimate with anyone.

No. Not going there. I shove aside the rush of desire. Even if I were interested in pursuing something, it wouldn't be with a kid fifteen years my junior who has a snarky mouth and sticky fingers.

Rob finishes the last stitches on her arm and wipes his hands on the towel before cleaning around the wound and affixing a clean bandage. "So." He looks at me over her sleeping form. "Gonna tell me who she is?"

I clear my throat. "Remember that break-in at Marcy's a few months ago when you asked me to take care of the thief?"

"Yeah." He furrows his brow and his gaze drops to the woman he just patched up. "No way! This is the cat burglar you took care of that night?" He chuckles at my nod. "What happened? She seduce you and win her freedom?"

"No." I put her down after Rob removes the bloody towels, then I draw the blanket over her sleeping form. "I gave her a choice—either prison or become my informant."

"Which did she pick?" Rob asks from the restroom where he's cleaning his tools in the sink.

"I don't know. I haven't heard from her in months. Not until she showed up a bloody mess on my doorstep an hour ago." I sigh and glance at her. "But it looks like she got herself into some trouble, that's for sure."

"What are you going to do with her?"

I run my hand through my hair. "Who the fuck knows. I can't kick her out looking like that."

"You're such a softhearted grizzly bear." Rob grins. "Always a sucker for big eyes and long sad stories."

A scoff rips from my throat. He's not wrong, but in this case, he's not right. This kid might have information I need. She's useful in gaining evidence for my investigations, nothing more. The moment she's on her feet, I'll kick her out. No skin off my back.

"You got your hands full, that's for sure." Rob stuffs his tools back in the kit.

"Yeah, I know."

"Keep the wounds dry. No showers or anything that could get them wet. Change the bandages every day and give me a call if anything comes up."

"Thanks, Rob. I owe you one." I walk him to the door.

"Yeah, I'm racking up those favors this year. First Arthur, now you." He claps his hand on my shoulder. "Get some rest. I'll call you later this week to check in."

"Thanks again."

"No problem." Rob heads down the stairs and out into the night.

I close the door and slide the deadbolt into place. When I return to the bedroom, she's still out cold. I rake my hand over my face.

What the hell did I do to deserve this? A beautiful problem dropped right in my lap. Her delicate lashes lay against her pale cheek. In sleep, she almost looks like an angel. But I know the inferno beneath that innocent exterior. She's a firecracker, and I'm not interested in getting burned.

With a sigh, I retreat to the bathroom to take a shower, rinsing her blood down the drain. Once I put on fresh clothes and get some rest, things will calm down.

I just hope I did the right thing by making her problem mine.

CHAPTER 6

Quinn

He found me. How did he find me?

The tantalizing scent of coffee pulls me from my dark, twisting dreams. The madness of nightmares slowly lifts as I open my eyes. Sunshine streams in through the window, illuminating the unfamiliar space.

I wince and groan as pain shoots down my arm and across my shoulder. Memories rush over me in a flood. The mansion. The murder. Running. Pain. The Black Penny. A familiar face. Detective Richards.

I can't be sure any of it is real. I know for certain I'm not dead. When I sit up, the blanket slips to my waist.

Shit. Where are my clothes? I'm wearing my bra and underwear, but my uniform is gone. I wince at the pull of my skin and the ache in my arm and shoulder. My hand drifts over a spot on the back of my arm. *Bandages.*

My gaze drifts to the floor where the torn remnants of my uniform lay in a dirty heap. *The knife.* Whoever attacked me left a mark. A hazy memory resurfaces, and I bite back a wave of nausea. Desperate for something to cover myself, I slowly rise, careful of my aching arms, and spot a man's robe hanging from the back of the door. As I tie it around me, the warm, spicy scent of aftershave drifts up from the fabric. It's comforting in a way.

I take inventory of the room. Two dressers littered with clothes and papers. A messy full-size bed. Drab, dark blue curtains framing a single window. On the other side of the room is a doorway. I glimpse yellowing tile and a sink pedestal in the shadows. It's messy and simple. Certainly no woman's touch that I can see.

My hand rests on the doorknob. Even though the door is cracked, I can't hear anything. This must lead to the living room. Is that where I'll find him? The lingering scent of coffee and bacon teases my hunger to life.

I take a deep breath and open the door. The apartment is smaller than I anticipated. A combined kitchen and living room with a table and two chairs against the far wall.

A tall, broad figure hunches over the stove. With every step I take, domestic sounds fill the space around me. The clatter of dishes. The sizzle of bacon. The occasional scrape of a spatula against metal.

When I reach the place where the frayed edge of the carpet meets the worn linoleum, I pause. My attention remains fixed on the gentle sway of his body as he moves, the flex of his shoulders beneath his plaid shirt. A breath catches in my throat when I catch a glimpse of his strong profile.

The detective is even more handsome than I remember. I push aside this strange attraction and clasp my hands together. "Good morning."

"Morning." He points to the coffeepot on the counter. "Help yourself."

"You knew I was awake?" I cross the floor, and my bare feet stick to the linoleum.

He nods. "I cracked the door, hoped the bacon would do the trick."

I pour a cup and fill his half-empty mug sitting on the counter. "Actually, it was the coffee."

The corner of his mouth pulls back in a smirk. "You're up and moving around. That's all that matters."

As I watch him work, he focuses on the eggs, cracking them one at a time into the bacon grease. I sip my coffee, grimacing at the bitterness. It nearly burns my tongue.

"Got any cream and sugar?" I set down the mug and open the refrigerator.

He snorts. "You'll be lucky if that milk is still good."

I glance at the date on the carton and open it. A quick sniff confirms his suspicion. The milk is bad. I toss it in the trash.

"Sorry, kid, I wasn't expecting company."

With a shrug, I retrieve the coffee. "I wasn't expecting to drop in on short notice either."

He turns and studies me. His brow rises as he takes in my frame wrapped in his robe, but he doesn't say a word. He snatches up a plate and places two eggs on it beside some bacon before thrusting it in my direction. "Sit. Eat."

I take the plate and my coffee to the small table. There are papers and files all over it. With a sigh, I set the plate on the chair and carefully stack all the papers before moving them to the solid wood coffee table in front of a floral sofa. A holdover from the early seventies, judging by the harvest gold pattern and wood trim.

When I return, he's set my plate on the table beside my coffee.

"I'm not used to having guests."

"I couldn't tell." My gaze drifts over the apartment, taking in the dust bunnies along the wall and a thin layer of dust on the television.

I settle on the chair and pick up my fork. The first bite is delicious. I quickly devour the eggs between bites of crispy bacon.

The detective watches me as he eats, allowing silence to consume us. I can tell by the look in his eyes, he's got questions. Who wouldn't after finding someone bleeding out on their stoop?

I use a piece of toast to clean the plate. A sigh of contentment echoes between us.

He pushes aside his own empty plate and cradles the mug in his hand. "Now that you're fed, care to tell me what the hell happened last night?"

Part of me wants to tell him the truth. Just spill it and hope like hell he believes me. But whatever I tell him is going to open me up to more questions and more digging. I don't want anyone fishing around in my past. He could easily look up my rap sheet at the station, but that's nothing compared to the skeletons still hiding in my closet. The people I've worked with, the shit I've seen...and done.

No. I can't tell him. Not yet. Not until I'm sure I can completely trust him.

I shake my head and sip my coffee. My attention drifts to a smudged window to my right. Outside, I see the brick of the neighboring building and hear the distant sound of traffic flowing through the city.

He heaves a heavy, melodramatic sigh. "Listen, kid, I want to help you, but if you don't trust me, my hands are tied."

"Thanks," I manage despite the loud pulse of my heartbeat in my ears.

"For what?"

"Taking me in. Patching me up. For not dumping me at the nearest ER and making me their problem." I offer a halfhearted smile.

"Listen, kid. I'll help any way I can, but I'm gonna need you to give me something if you want more." He clutches the mug tighter. "That deal we made? You got any leads for me?"

"No." I shift uncomfortably in my seat. "I've been keeping my nose clean. I haven't stolen anything since the night you caught me."

His brow shoots up in surprise. "Trying to go straight, huh?"

"Something like that." I pick at the edge of my nail, unable to meet his gaze. "Found a job. It doesn't pay much, but it's something." I slump and mutter under my breath, "At least, it was."

He narrows his eyes, and I anticipate his next question, but I'm saved when the telephone rings.

In three strides, he's across the kitchen, pulling the phone from the receiver. "Richards."

I stand and gather the plates, carrying them to the sink. While I do my task, my attention remains fixed on the man standing three feet away.

"When?" His voice rumbles through the stillness of the apartment. "Only one victim?" Another pause. "I see."

My heart pounds in my chest. I try to calm down. I tell myself it has nothing to do with what happened last night. He's a detective. They could be talking about anything.

He grabs a pen and notebook from the corner of the counter. Leaning the notebook against the wall, he scribbles a few notes before turning to face me.

Our eyes lock. The intensity of his gaze burns a hole of guilt through me. I should tell him, but I can't bring myself to do it.

His amber eyes narrow, like he knows I'm withholding vital information.

"Got it. Yeah. I'll be there in thirty." He hangs up the phone. "I need to go. There's been a murder."

I don't flinch at the word. I knew it before he formed the syllables on his lips. "I should go anyway."

"No. You're not leaving this apartment until you come clean."

"I don't have anything to tell you." Fury builds in the pit of my stomach. I clench my hands into fists against the robe.

"Bullshit, kid. Whatever happened to you last night scared you enough to drop you on my doorstep looking like death warmed over." He shakes his head. "You must have been desperate to come to me for help."

He's not wrong, but I won't give him the satisfaction of hearing me say it. I pinch my lips together in pure defiance.

"I'll have my brother keep an eye on you while I'm gone."

"You're just going to lock me up like a prisoner?" I prop my hands on my hips. "That's illegal."

"Sue me, kid." He reaches into the small closet and retrieves his jacket. "I've got bigger things to worry about right now. We'll discuss this when I get back."

I throw my hands up in the air. "This is totally bogus."

"Stay in this apartment. I'm serious." He points his finger at me. "And don't try to sweet-talk Claude. He may look like a nice guy you can manipulate, but he's smarter than he lets on. He'll see through you in a heartbeat."

I glower at him as he opens the door.

"Claude!" he yells down the hall.

"What?" comes the answering shout.

"Come here."

I stare in disbelief as another man approaches the detective. They're the same height, the same coloring and build. I blink twice. Are they twins? No. They have marked differences. But one difference stands out more than the rest—Claude has only one hand.

"Keep an eye on her for a couple of hours. I have a case."

The brother turns toward me. His overlong hair brushes his collar. Eyes similar to Grant's bore into mine. "I can handle her. Go."

Disbelief and anger bubble inside me. "I don't need to be *handled*."

The detective ignores me. "Thanks. I owe you one." He turns to face me. "Behave, Quinn."

"Yes, dad." I scrunch my nose at him.

Without another word, he disappears, leaving me with his brother who comes inside and closes the door. My gaze falls on his missing hand, and a memory niggles at the back of my mind.

"You found me last night."

He nods.

"I'm Quinn." I hold out my hand.

"Claude." He shakes it and smiles.

No, they're definitely not twins. But most certainly brothers. His presence exudes warmth and safety. I like him already.

If I'm stuck as a prisoner, at least I won't be completely miserable.

CHAPTER 7

Grant

"What the hell happened here?"

"Looks like a murder." Mickey tips back his hat and scratches his forehead.

The click and flash of the photographer's documentation pulls my attention to the victim lying facedown on the hardwood floor.

"What do we got?"

Mickey opens his notebook. "Lionel Madison. Sixty-three. CEO and founder of Victory Mutuals."

I listen as I circle the body, careful not to disturb any evidence.

"Family was out for the evening. Most of the staff had the night off."

"So no one was here?"

"According to the housekeeper, there were two maids last night. Neither of them came forward with any information."

Blood spatter covers most of the floor near the door. Some of it smudged by undiscernible shoe prints. Arterial spray, judging by the laceration on the victim's neck. We'll get more information after the coroner does their report, but something doesn't sit right. I step through the door and assess the hallway.

To the right, a basket of cleaning supplies lays overturned beside a table holding an expensive-looking vase. I walk down the carpeted hall, cursing the crimson fabric beneath my feet. I can't see bloody footprints.

Returning to the master bedroom, I study the scene from the doorway. The position of the body tells me he was facing the door when he was killed. Nothing blocked the path of the blood, so the killer must have been behind him.

"Did you find a weapon?" I rub my hand along my jaw. I already know the answer to the question, but I have to ask.

"No weapon." Mickey clicks his pen and tucks it in his pocket with the notebook. "But get a load of this."

He steps around the body and leads me from the room. I follow him down the stairs to the narrow entry at the front of the house. Earlier, I came in the back door since the reporters and photographers were out front, hungry for whatever morsel of gruesome detail they could get.

Blood coats the white tile. Drops lead to the entrance where there's a smear on the door and blood coats the handle. A metal coatrack lays sideways across the path. I step around it and kneel to investigate. "The killer's?"

Mickey shrugs. "Who knows? Could be. But my guess is someone stumbled upon the killer and made a run for it."

I retrace the trail of blood and find sporadic droplets hidden in the carpet. They lead directly to the third floor, stopping at the top of the stairs.

"You might be on to something." I turn to face my partner. "I want the names of anyone who was in this house last night."

"On it." Mickey grabs the nearest uniformed officer. Once he gives the instructions, he turns back to me. His brow furrows at the look on my face. "What are you thinking?"

"As soon as they're finished in the master bedroom and the victim is taken to the coroner, I want the family to inventory the house. See if anything is missing."

Mickey groans. "You can't think this has any connection to that stack of cold cases you've been working on?"

"I won't rule it out."

"You're obsessed, Richards."

"Maybe. But I'm not discounting anything."

The officer returns with a piece of paper. I snatch it and skim the names on the list. *Milly Parker, Jane Murphy, Alice Jones.* Two maids working on the main floors and a nanny on the fourth floor.

"Get them here."

"Sir, the nanny is downstairs in the parlor along with one of the maids."

"We'll start there."

Mickey and I make our way to the parlor. Inside, the ashen countenances of two women transform from apprehensive to relieved at our entry.

"Morning. This is Detective McArthur and I'm Detective Richards. I'd like to ask you a few questions."

They both nod. I ask them some basic questions to establish their positions in the household and their routines. A few personal questions give me a better feel for their reliability.

"Did either of you see or hear anything last night?"

"I was fast asleep with the baby." The nanny, Alice, twists the handkerchief in her hand. Tears fill her eyes.

I turn to Milly and offer a smile. "Did you hear anything?"

She shakes her head, her eyes darting back and forth, unable to meet my gaze.

"What about the other maid, Jane Murphy? Did she see anything?"

Sobs spill from her. "I don't know. She disappeared. I tried to call her this morning, but her roommate told me she hasn't come home." Finally, she meets my eyes. "Something bad happened to her. I know it."

I pass Milly a clean handkerchief from my pocket and tell her we'll post a bulletin to ensure her friend's safety. My gut twists. That nagging feeling from before returns with a vengeance.

"Can you describe her for me?"

Milly nods. "Five-five. Green eyes. Curly, dark brown hair."

My jaw clenches. "Slender? Curvy?"

"Curvy." She nods emphatically.

Son of a bitch. It's Quinn. I'll bet my last paycheck the missing maid is the bedraggled kitten I bandaged up last night. Oh, she's gonna catch hell when I get home.

I thank the women for their time and ensure them we'll get to the bottom of this murder.

Once we're back in the hallway, Mickey nudges me. "What's up? You're wearing that look again."

"What look?" I growl.

"Your *don't fuck with me* look."

"Listen, there's something I gotta look into. Finish up here, then check with the missing maid's roommates. Call me if you find anything."

"Richards, what the hell is going on?" he calls after me, but I'm already at the door.

"Later," I tell him and slip outside.

The commute back to my apartment does nothing to calm the rage simmering inside me. When I get home, I'm a volcano ready to erupt.

Then I see Claude on the couch with Quinn.

Her easy smile directed toward my brother vanishes when she catches sight of me. Claude spins around and rises slowly.

"Glad you're home. I have to open the bar in twenty minutes." He waves to Quinn, who flashes a warm smile in his direction.

"Thanks for keeping me company, Claude."

"Any time, Quinn." Claude leaves without another word. Smart man. He knows my moods, just like I know his. And he knows I have something on my mind that doesn't include him.

"So what? You and my brother are friends now?"

"Well, you did leave him here to babysit me." She scowls.

I rub my hand across my face and unclench my jaw. *This woman.* My hands fist at my sides. "Do you want to tell me what the fuck is going on?"

"What do you mean?" Those luminous eyes go wide, but I know it's not innocence.

"There was a murder last night."

"What does that have to do with me?" She carries her glass to the sink, effectively turning her back on me and the conversation.

I grab her wrist and spin her to face me. "Don't bullshit me, Quinn. Tell me how you got those stab wounds."

She doesn't fight me, but she doesn't go limp either. Quinn holds her ground. I'm not sure whether she's gutsy or stupid. I can't bring myself to give a shit. I need to know the truth. Now.

Her eyes glass over as if lost in thought. She pinches them closed and exhales a deep breath before opening them again. "This murder? Was it on Riverside Drive?"

I nod.

"Fuck." She bites her lower lip. "Okay, look. I wasn't involved in this shit. I don't know who it was, or what the hell was going on—"

"Did you see the murderer?"

Quinn swallows hard. "I saw him kill the old man."

"Shit." I drop her hand and cover my mouth.

"I was minding my own business. Cleaning. Like I'm supposed to. And I heard voices in the master bedroom. No one was home. At least, that's what I thought." She wraps her arms around her torso and shivers. "He saw me and I ran."

"How the hell did you get away?"

A harsh laugh escapes her throat. "I almost didn't. He had me, twice. But I managed to give him the slip. I know these streets better than most."

"Did you get a good look at the killer?"

"I was too busy running for my life." She crosses her arms. "And he was wearing a black ski mask."

Fury turns my vision red. The thought of finding Quinn dead on the red-carpeted steps in that mansion or in a street leaves my stomach churning. "You could've died!"

"No shit, Sherlock. You think I don't know that?"

"Listen, kid, I don't know what kind of bad luck charm you've got hanging around your neck, but if you don't get your shit together, you're going to end up another file at the bottom of my stack. You need to wise the fuck up." I'm breathing like I've just run up a flight of stairs with a wicked hangover after a long night.

"Fuck you." She spits the words at me like a viper bite and stomps to the bedroom. "Asshole." The door slams, punctuating the word.

I collapse against the counter, bracing my hands on the edge, and hang my head. What the fuck is wrong with me? This kid isn't my problem. She means nothing to me.

Then why the hell is my chest tight and my head spinning? Shit. I need to get a grip on whatever this is.

Quinn might not be my responsibility, but she's certainly my solution. She's a murder witness. The only clue I have to solve this damned case. I can't afford to lose her now.

Chapter 8

Quinn

That son of a bitch.

How dare he lecture me on safety.

He knows nothing about the hell I've been through. Nothing about my past or the things I've done to survive.

I pace the length of the bedroom and kick a T-shirt lying on the floor. It skitters across the faded carpet, stopping on the ruins of my bloody, ripped uniform.

I could have died. I *should* have died.

The events of the night before come back in a rush. Adrenaline pulses through me. Snippets of memory flash in my brain like lightning across the night sky. The struggle. The chase. The sound of the old man's rattling final breath.

I shiver and wrap my arms around my waist, then curl into a ball on the bed and close my eyes.

I've been in more scrapes than I can count, and I've always gotten out of them. But this time I nearly ended up a statistic.

No shit, I almost died. I thought I was dead there for a minute.

It was pure dumb luck I got out of that place alive.

I roll onto my back to stare at the ceiling. My shoulder aches at the motion, pulsing beneath the bandage. Two deep breaths ease the pain, but it's a constant reminder of my brush with death.

On the other side of the door, he's in a mood. The sounds of slamming cabinets and the distinct clinking of glass against glass fill the void. The detective is a grumpy asshole.

And yet he took you in and patched you up. The whispering voice in the back of my mind is smug. *Ungrateful shit.*

I scowl at the door, wishing it would burst into flames.

He did help me, but that doesn't mean I have to let him treat me like garbage. We mean nothing to each other. Nothing.

Maybe I shouldn't have told him about last night's mess. I should have taken the opportunity to go while he was out and left it at that.

When he came back looking like someone ran over his favorite puppy, I couldn't lie to him.

Fuck.

Even his brother makes me feel guilty for wanting to leave. I could have slipped out the door a few times, but those sad, pensive eyes just followed me around the apartment. Claude's not the typical New York barkeep with a big mouth and bad attitude. He's quiet and sweet. I noted the American flag pin on his lapel, less obvious than the missing hand. He's a Vietnam veteran. I'd put money on it.

He kept me company while his brother was off being a detective. I'll admit I craved the company. I don't want to be alone. Not after last night. Claude cuts an imposing figure, but his kind smile is reassuring.

Then Detective Grump Ass came back and ruined everything.

He makes me want to tear my hair out. But now he knows I saw the murderer, and he'll never let me go. Honestly, as much as I want to bash him over the head with a frying pan, I feel safe here.

Plus, I don't have anywhere to go. There's no one I can trust.

What are the odds he'd be the detective in charge of this damned case?

I'm no help, and I've told him as much. I didn't see anything that could uncover the identity of the murderer.

Wounded, with nowhere to go and nothing to offer, I'm useless. No matter what, I have to talk to him. We need to come to an agreement. Something.

I drag myself up to sit on the edge of the bed. My hand rubs the bandage on my arm. I don't mean to be a selfish little brat, but after years of taking care of myself, trust comes hard.

Can I trust him?

Do I have a choice?

With a sigh, I stand and slowly walk into the living room. The moment I open the door, I see him slouched in a shabby recliner, staring out the window. A glass dangles from his fingertips. Amber liquid catches the light from outside.

He glances up when I cross the floor, his gaze narrowing as he sips the drink.

I sit on the couch, and the silence stretches between us, pulling tight like a rubber band. Then it snaps.

"Done with your temper tantrum?" He eyes me over the rim of the glass.

"Are you done being a dick?"

A corner of his mouth pulls back in a lopsided smirk.

"Look, I don't know how much help I'm gonna be. Maybe I should leave?" I rub my hands on my bare thighs. Claude found some women's clothes stashed in a box in the office downstairs. I didn't ask him how they got there or why he had them. Some questions are best left unanswered.

Detective Richards's gaze skims over the ripped neon-yellow T-shirt and acid-washed jean shorts. His countenance darkens, and a frown replaces the smirk. He exhales sharply and leans forward, resting his forearms on his knees.

"Even if you can't point out the murderer in a lineup, I can't let you go." He shakes his head. "Not until we nail this bastard."

"How long is that going to take?"

"I don't know." He sets the glass aside. "Depends on if we get any leads."

"So you're just going to lock me in your apartment indefinitely?" I fold my arms across my chest and slump. "How generous."

"Would you rather go back to your life and let the murderer find you? Finish what he started?"

Gooseflesh prickles along my arms. "What do you mean?"

"He knows what you look like, sweetheart."

His attention fixes on me, and I shift uncomfortably.

"He could be anyone in this city. Your neighbor. The guy who takes the seat next to you on the subway. A random person you pass on the street during rush hour."

"Shit." I bite the edge of my nail.

"Even if you didn't see well enough to make a positive ID, I can't take the chance."

Can't take the chance? What the hell does that mean? Before I can respond, he cuts through the fog of my thoughts.

"I won't force you to stay here, but I can't let you go without protection."

"Protection?"

"Yeah. I can get you into a safe house with a rotation of guards assigned to you."

The thought of someone following me around, watching my every move, leaves me unsettled. I shake my head and curl my lip in disgust. "No."

"Then you stay here with me."

Gritting my teeth, I consider the alternative. I go back to business as usual and risk running into the murderer. Worse, I could lead him to my roommates and put them in danger.

No. I can't do that. I'll have to take my chances here with the detective if I want to outrun this bastard.

"Fine. But I have a few stipulations."

"I'm listening." He plucks his glass from the table and downs the remaining liquid.

"I'll need clothes and toiletries."

"Easy enough."

"We'll need groceries." I glance around the room, noting the dust gathering in corners. "And cleaning supplies."

"I'll make it happen." He cocks his head. "Anything else?"

"Yeah." I pin him with a firm look. "I get the bedroom."

He scoffs. "You expect me to spend nights on the sofa?"

"You'd make your guest sleep on the sofa?" I feign horror and press my hand to my chest.

"Nice try, kid. I'm not falling for that shit."

"So I'm supposed to sleep on the sofa?"

"Honestly, I don't care where you sleep." He jabs his thumb at the door to his bedroom. "But that's *my* bed, and I'm not giving it up."

I fold my arms across my chest and grumble under my breath.

Slowly, he stands. "We done?"

"Why?"

"Because I've got work to do." He carries his glass to the sink.

"You're going out again?"

"Yeah."

"When will you be back?" I follow him to the door.

He glances at his watch. "Later."

"You're no help."

"I'll send Claude up with some cleaning supplies." He pauses halfway to the door and turns. "If you need anything else, make a list. I'll take care of it when I get back."

"And what am I supposed to eat?"

"There are some TV dinners in the freezer. Heat one up."

"Such a gracious host."

"Don't leave the apartment."

"Yes, dad."

He sighs. "Grant."

"What?" I lean closer, pretending I couldn't hear him.

"My name is Grant."

"Sounds like a hard-ass's name."

He shakes his head and leaves the apartment. I lock the door behind him. Leaning against it, I close my eyes and take several steadying breaths.

"You can do this. It's temporary. Just…breathe."

A gentle calm settles over me. As long as I'm here, I'm safe. No one knows about my connection with the detective…with Grant. No one knows where I am. It's like the earth opened up and swallowed me whole. If anyone can protect me, it's him.

Ten minutes later, I'm armed with supplies courtesy of Claude. I thank him before he leaves, and with a renewed sense of determination, I head to the bedroom and begin cleaning.

I can make this work. Right?

Without regret, I toss my bloodstained uniform into an empty garbage bag and tie it off. That's one reminder I don't need lingering around the apartment.

Is it sad the one spark of joy I found today was discovering the clean set of sheets in the small linen closest? I remove the bloodstained ones from the bed and pile them in the corner.

If Grant thinks he's getting the bed tonight, he's crazy. That bed is mine.

What if he climbs into bed with you? a teasing voice echoes in my head.

My gaze lingers on the full-size bed. Need pulses through me at the thought of Grant lying beside me on the clean sheets.

Maybe this is a bad idea. But what choice do I have?

CHAPTER 9

Grant

The haunting presence of my uninvited guest-turned-murder-witness lingers like a weight on my shoulders as I step into the summer evening. After a quick word with Claude, I retreat from the one place I thought was my haven. The sun is finally drifting below the towering buildings, but the heat remains in the pavement, radiating up in waves as I amble down the street.

I can't let this kid out of my sight. Whether she saw details or not, she's a witness to a murder. I'll have to jog her memory to see if any subconscious facts tumble free from that smart mouth.

She's trouble with a capital T. If I were smart, I'd put her in a safe house and have a guard posted at her door round the clock. But I'm desperate, and that overrules my common sense right now. We need to catch this fucker before he strikes again.

I have no proof it's the same person who killed those other people. All I have is a gut feeling and a hunch. But I can't prove anything. Quinn's the closest I've come to finding answers.

As I walk to the nearest bodega, I run through the information she gave me. She saw the killer, and he nearly took her down. She's lucky. But this curious little kitten doesn't have many lives left. If the killer figures out where she is, she's done for. He'll take her out just to cover his own ass.

When I step into the air-conditioned bodega, I grab a basket and start tossing in basics. Eggs, milk, bread, lunchmeat for sandwiches, cheese, a variety of junk food, chips, pasta, a jar of marinara sauce, and some frozen meals. Chicken's on sale, so I grab some thighs as well as a pound of ground beef. Cooking isn't exactly my forte, but the kid deserves to eat better than a convict or a broke cop.

After I pay, I give the shop runner a five to deliver the stuff to my apartment. I'd take it myself, but honestly, I'm not ready to face her again. It's tense between us...and not just because I'm a cop and she's a hellcat with a kleptomaniac streak.

By the time I step back outside, darkness has stretched its arms around the city. I wander a few blocks, taking the long way home. I need to clear my head.

Quinn.

She's a pistol with a hair trigger. In the short amount of time she's been in my life, she has tainted everything. Her presence ruins the peace of my space, of my life. As pathetic as it was, it was mine. I didn't have to worry about anyone or anything except the job.

Now she's put her fingerprints all over my world, and I can't say I'm upset about it. More like disconcerted. I'm not used to it. Not since the ex packed her shit and took off.

I like my dingy little apartment. It's home, and it's close to my brother. But now even that space isn't relaxing. Fuck.

On a whim, I stop at a payphone and ask the operator to connect me to the precinct. Something's nagging at me, and I can't quite put my finger on it.

The call connects. "Twenty-Fourth Precinct, this is Officer Jenkins. How may I help you?"

"Jenkins, this is Detective Richards. Can you check to see if there's anything from the coroner on the Riverside Drive case?"

"Yeah, give me a minute."

Leaning against the booth, I scan the pedestrians as they pass. My brain catalogs details as they go about their lives. A woman with a poodle rushes toward the subway station entrance. A mother with two kids in tow rounds the corner. Two men in suits also hurry to the subway. Another guy ascends the stairs and casts a cautious glance around before darting into a nearby street. A glint of light flashes in the distance.

"Richards, you there?"

I'm pulled from my people-watching. "Yeah, whaddya got?"

"Nothing yet. I'll call you at home when his report comes through."

"Thanks. I appreciate it." Disappointment chokes me as I hang up the phone. It's only been a few hours, but I anticipated a little more expedition since the victim was high profile.

The city buzzes around me as I wander the streets. When I finally make it home, I ignore the pull to go up to the apartment and instead venture into the Black Penny.

Claude glances up from behind the bar. Chatter surrounds me as I weave through the crowd and take a seat on a stool toward the back of the room. My attention skims over the patrons, noting regulars and a few new faces. I don't linger long. I'm not looking to make friends; I just want to drown my irritation in a barrel of whiskey.

"How's your guest holding up?" Claude asks as he slides a glass onto the bar's worn surface.

"She's a fucking delight," I growl. The liquor burns the sarcasm from my throat.

Claude chuckles and leans forward, resting against the edge of the counter. "That girl's got you in a twist."

"Tell me something I don't know." I throw back the rest of the whiskey, then tap the glass on the wood.

"She's nice once she warms up to you." Claude pours a refill.

My lips press into a thin line, and I regard my brother carefully before I respond. Claude's always been a decent judge of character. It's what makes him a great bartender. He listens. Watches. And nine times out of ten, he can spot a rotten apple from across the room. The fact that he's taken a shine to the cat burglar who is sucking the life out of my sanity has my eye twitching and my teeth grinding.

"I take it she hasn't warmed up to you yet."

"How perceptive. Maybe you should become a detective."

Claude shakes his head. "You could try being nice to her. She's been through hell."

I rake my fingers through my hair. "You think I haven't tried being nice?" I lower my voice when the guy two seats down glances over at me. "I saved her ass twice, offered everything in my power, including my personal fucking space, to keep her safe while I finish this investigation."

"You probably scare the shit out of her, Grant."

A scoff rips from my throat midsip, and I nearly choke. "I *scare* her? She told you this?"

"She didn't need to tell me anything. I can see the way she tenses when you walk in the room."

Stunned, I stare at him like he just sprouted another head or a brand-new hand. "I've been *nothing* but nice to her since she showed up half-dead on my doorstep."

"A little sympathy would go a long way."

"I don't do sympathy." A frown pulls at my mouth. "I'm not her fucking shrink."

"Maybe you should try to get to know her instead of barking at her."

"I don't bark at her." My fist tightens around the glass, and I take a deep breath.

"She's scared and alone. Right now, you're the only person who can offer her any comfort."

"I didn't ask to be her fucking babysitter."

"She's an adult. She doesn't need a babysitter. She needs a friend. Someone to talk to."

I take another drink. "If you're so worried about her, why don't I let her move in with you so you can coddle her?"

Claude's brows draw together. "Don't be a dick. She's your responsibility right now. If you don't take it seriously, she's gonna disappear, and then your case will be fucked."

I slap a bill on the table and finish my drink. "Thanks for nothing."

"Anytime."

My empty stomach protests the two glasses of whiskey as I climb the stairs to my apartment. I grip the railing tight with every step. When I reach my landing, I rest my hand against the door and take a deep breath. I should have eaten something. Fuck, it's too late now. I'm not going back down to the bar to face Claude again. Not tonight.

I unlock the door, and the scent of roast chicken nearly knocks me back. The savory aroma lures me deeper into the room. When the door shuts behind me, I snap out of my trance.

"You're back." Quinn appears in the bedroom doorway, her hand on her hip. "There's a plate in the oven if you're hungry."

My gaze skims over her. She must have changed at some point; she's wearing some of my clothes. I need to find her something more suitable. Seeing her wrapped in one of my button-down shirts has my mouth watering.

It must be the smell of the food.

I clear my throat. "Did you eat?"

She nods and takes a seat on the couch.

"Good." I grab the plate from the oven and sit down at the table. Chicken thighs with mixed veggies and a baked potato. I moan at the first bite.

Quinn's head whips in my direction. Her eyes narrow as her jaw slackens, making those plush lips part on a soft gasp.

"It's delicious." I jab my fork at the plate.

"Thanks."

I take a few more bites while I work up the courage to invite her to join me. "There's a bottle of red wine in the cabinet below the sink if you want to join me."

She slowly rises from the sofa and crosses to the kitchen. I bite my lip when she bends over to retrieve the bottle. This woman is endless curves in all the right places. My cock jumps at the thought of exploring every inch of her luscious body.

Quinn joins me with two glasses and the bottle. "Where's the opener?"

"Drawer by the fridge."

Once she retrieves it, she makes quick work of the cork and pours two glasses. I wash down the last bite of my chicken as she takes the seat across from me. Her hands cradle the glass, and she eyes me cautiously before drinking. Silence surrounds us as I polish off the veggies. Her gaze shifts between me and the window to her right.

"Did you get any leads?"

I push the empty plate aside. "Not yet."

Her shoulders slump.

"Don't worry, kid. We'll find him."

She closes her eyes and nods.

"Were there any calls?"

"Phone rang twice. I didn't answer it. I didn't know if you wanted anyone to know I was here."

"Smart thinking." I smirk. "They'll call back if it's important."

"Your brother dropped off cleaning supplies and some toiletries." A soft smile curves her lips. "He's very thoughtful."

I bristle at her kind words toward Claude. She's right, he is thoughtful. Apparently, more thoughtful than me.

I really am a dick. "I'm glad."

"I'm gonna take a shower." Quinn sets her wine aside and stands.

"Good idea." I kick myself for being a shitty human. Claude's words drift back to me, but I fear it might be too late for me to play nice. What she sees is what she gets with me.

Quinn disappears into the bedroom and shuts the door. It's only then I remember Rob's instructions about showers and bandages. Fuck. She'll figure it out quick enough.

I shove my chair back and take my dirty dishes to the sink. As I wash them, I try to ignore the burning image teasing my half-drunk brain.

Quinn. Naked. Wet.

And there's only one bed.

Fuck.

I'm never going to survive this.

CHAPTER 10

Quinn

This is a bad idea. Staying here. Being close to Grant. Letting him see me like this. Letting him help me.

Maybe I'd be better off on my own. A nameless face in the crowd milling about the city. I can take care of myself out there. I've done it before. I can do it again.

When mom brought home that deadbeat and dropped the bombshell she was married, I thought my world had imploded. I could handle Jim and his obsession with Jack Daniels, but his son pushed me over the edge. Billy ruined everything and gave me my first taste of lonely freedom.

Tarnished memories of my childhood rear their ugly heads, and I jerk the bathroom door closed behind me. I cleaned the bathroom earlier today—it took a lot of elbow grease to get the fixtures to shine and the grime off the tiles. But the thought of taking a long, hot shower gives me the boost I need after the last two days.

Thankfully, the button-down shirt doesn't give me any trouble when I strip it off, but the moment I step into the shower, the bandages soak up the water. Fuck.

The stitches pull my skin tight. Warmth seeps through the cotton and soothes the itch beneath.

It does nothing to ease the ache from earlier with Grant. His gruff but well-meaning concern left me bewildered and desperate for even a scrap of attention.

Aware of my injuries pulsing in protest, I wash my hair and scrub my skin with the floral soap Claude brought up. When I step out of the shower, I almost feel human again.

I wrap my hair in a towel and twist another around my torso. Shifting the fabric, I catch a glimpse of red staining the white towel beneath my arm. When I lift it, a warm trickle of blood traces over my skin, dripping to the floor.

"Fuck." I grab a dark wash cloth and press it to the wound.

I can't replace the bandages myself. My gaze drifts to the door. I hate asking for help, especially after everything he's done for me. But I need him. I can't do this alone.

After cleaning up my mess, I exit the bathroom and peer through the cracked-open door leading to the living room.

Grant's leaning against the window frame, staring out into the night. He turns when the door creaks open. His jaw clenches, and those dark eyes narrow. Everything softens when he sees my hand covering the wound on my arm.

"What the hell did you do, kid?" In two strides, he crosses to the kitchen and pulls out a first aid kit.

"I need the bandages replaced."

My mouth snaps closed. He knows exactly what happened.

"Sit down." He gestures to the couch and opens the kit on the coffee table.

The towel rides up my thighs when I sit. I can't fix it, but I whisper a prayer for the extra-long fabric to hold tight where I tucked it.

"Turn that way." He points to the far wall. "I should have warned you about the bandages."

The couch depresses, pulling me toward him, when he sits beside me. His hand covers mine over the cloth, and a bolt of awareness shoots through me. I shift uncomfortably and tug the towel tighter to ensure it doesn't unravel like my sanity seems hell-bent on doing.

"Too late now." I bite my lip to keep from saying anything to antagonize him more.

He angles my arm back, and my hand grazes the inside of his thigh. I ball my hand into a fist as he peels off the soaking bandage.

Every press of his fingertips against my skin leaves fire in its wake. I press my eyes closed and breathe deeply, ignoring the building need in the pit of my stomach.

It's been too long since I've let anyone touch me, since I've basked in the bliss of a simple brush of skin against skin. I bite my lip to suppress the moan nestled in my throat.

He's so gentle, so tender for such a gruff, jaded man.

Grant places a fresh bandage over the wound and tapes it in place. "Doesn't look like you tore the stitches, but it'll be tender. Try not to overextend your arm."

Words completely fail me. I nod dumbly as he grasps my shoulders and angles me so he can focus on the bandage on my shoulder. A whimper escapes at the soft caress when he tenderly removes the old bandage.

"Sorry," he mutters.

"For what?" My voice cracks, and I curse my touch-starved body.

"Hurting you."

"You didn't hurt me."

I glance over my shoulder. His brows are drawn together in concentration, his lips parted, and soft breaths caress my neck. He meets my gaze, understanding reflecting in his brown eyes. He refocuses on cleaning the area before applying a fresh bandage.

"Someone did." His fingers trace old scars on the opposite shoulder and down my spine. "Looks like you've gotten into some scraps."

"A few." My body hums at his innocent touch. I want him to trace every inch of me with his fingers, with his tongue. Anything to keep this desire burning inside me. With it to warm me, the vacant cold has no hold to pull me into the darkness.

I don't want to be alone. Not anymore.

"The murderer really did a number on you, kid." His fingers tease along my collarbone, where the skin is turning purple. "You're lucky you got away."

"Luck had nothing to do with it."

I shift beneath his scrutiny. I might as well be completely naked. Grant sees me more clearly than most, and the thought doesn't scare me like it should.

"I was just faster."

"That's luck, kid."

I spin around to face him. "Why do you do that?"

"What?"

"Call me kid." I study his expression, guarded as it is, and glean nothing. "I'm not a kid."

Grant's gaze dips to the towel clinging to the curve of my breasts and clears his throat. "I noticed."

I lean closer and arch my neck toward him. He doesn't retreat.

"See this?" I trace my finger over a scar behind my ear. "Got that from a job when I was sixteen. My stepbrother forgot to warn me about a broken window. Just missed the artery, the doc said." My finger lingers on my pulse for a few heartbeats, as if to remind me I'm alive and this is real.

"That who roped you into becoming a thief? Your stepbrother?" Grant cocks his head. His eyes glint in the dim lamplight, shifting from amber to something darker, something richer.

He cut straight to the heart of it. I nod, unable to fix the lie on my tongue. I don't want to talk about me or my family. I need him to see me. Not a kid. Not the petty thief, the troublemaker, or the murder witness. I want Grant to see *me*.

"How old were you?" His voice is soft, with a smoky hoarseness that lends to his appeal.

"Twelve." I shrug a shoulder like it's no big deal. "I played distraction while the older boys picked pockets on the subway."

"Where were your parents?"

"Dad died when I was two. Mom remarried when I was eleven." My gaze drops to the fraying carpet. "She got sick shortly after."

"Fuck. I'm sorry, Quinn."

I angrily wipe away tears forming at the corners of my eyes. "We didn't have money for medicine. I had to do something."

My stepbrother saw my desperation to help mom as a weakness, and he exploited it. For years. It kept her alive for a while, at least until Jim disappeared. Then her health took a dive. But by that point, I was in too deep. It was all I knew.

"Once you're in, it's hard to get out." Grant gives voice to my unspoken thoughts.

"Yeah, something like that." The towel on my head slips, and my curls tumble free. "Damn it." I push the hair away from my eyes and shake my head back.

Grant takes a damp curl in his hand and twists it around his finger. "The red is coming through again."

"Maybe I should pick up some dye."

"The red looks good." He slides his finger free of the curl coiled around it.

"Makes me easier to recognize."

"That's true." He regards my hair thoughtfully for a moment before shaking his head. "You should get some rest."

My protest dissipates when he rises from the couch and gathers up the first aid kit. Frustration and shame wash over me.

I grip the towel tightly to keep it from slipping and stand. Grant's halfway across the room when I turn around. "Thanks for your help."

"Any time, kid." He shelves the kit, keeping his back to me.

"Good night."

"Night."

A tangle of emotions pierces me as I retreat to the bedroom. Inside, I claw at the towel constricting me and climb into the bed. It's too hot to wear pajamas.

My body's on fire. I writhe beneath the thin sheet, desperate for the tender caress of a hardened detective. It only intensifies the desperation singing through my veins.

Come to me. Please. Touch me.

The distant sound of the door closing tells me what I already know. Grant's gone. He's not coming. I pushed him away with that glimpse into my past. With a look at the real Quinn. And he pulled away, putting space between us.

I expected it. Knew it was coming. And yet…I held out hope he might want something more from us.

He doesn't want me. He's just doing his job. Just keeping me safe until he solves the case.

I'm nothing to him.

And I always will be.

CHAPTER 11

Grant

The sofa springs are lethal. My back aches as I arch it and roll my shoulders. I've been surfing sofa city for the past three days, and it's fucking killing me.

I can still feel the softness of her skin beneath my fingers as I applied fresh bandages. The soft floral scent of her damp hair has haunted me every night, following me into my dreams, beating me over the head with a longing I haven't felt since I was a randy teenager.

I've gotta snap out of this.

The conversations around me dull to a low hum as I focus on the witness statements in my hand. Everyone in the precinct moves with purpose, yet I'm caught somewhere between obsession and torment.

For the love of God, I can't shake the kid from my thoughts. She's safe in my apartment. Claude's keeping a close eye on her while I'm gone. And I can't focus on anything but her and this damned case.

Problem is, I've read the statements three times, seen the autopsy report, walked the crime scene multiple times. Nothing about this makes any sense. The old man was as well-loved in society as he was wealthy, and he donated frequently to local charities. According to his family, he had no enemies. Is it possible he was just a random target?

"Well, that was a waste of time." Mickey tosses a notebook on the desk across from me.

I set aside the paper in my hand, breaking off my train of thought. "Nothing?"

"Not a damn thing." He shakes his head and loosens his tie. "The family's clean. Their alibis all check out."

"All of them?"

"The wife was with friends at the theater. The older kids were visiting family."

"What about ex-wives?" I run my hand along my jaw as I check the mental list of family members and suspects.

"All clean and accounted for. I double-checked."

"What about the oldest son?" A hazy image of the young man I interviewed yesterday pops into my mind. He seems pretty torn up about his father's death, but since he stands to inherit a sizable chunk of his father's estate, I don't trust a damn word he says or those crocodile tears.

"Clear. The doorman puts him at Clubhouse 54 at ten fifteen. Staff saw him in the club until well after two a.m. Time of death is estimated at five after ten. There's no way he made it across town that fast." Mickey leans back in his chair. "As much as I want to pin it on the slimy little bastard, he's clean."

"Fuck." I take a deep breath and run through the list again. "And you've already double-checked the staff?"

Mickey nods and throws his hands up. "The staff, the family, his business partners. It's like whoever killed him is a goddamn ghost. Are you sure he didn't just off himself?"

"The coroner said that's unlikely. Knife went too deep, and there are no hesitation marks." I know the truth thanks to Quinn's testimony, but I keep it to myself for the moment. "Besides, no weapon was found."

The captain is willing to entertain the possibility that this old man had the strength to slit his own throat down to the bone but not that a stranger could possibly have targeted him, breaking into the house to add another kill to his list.

"Too bad we don't have any witnesses." Mickey pulls a small flask from his pocket and takes a sip. "Did you ever track down the other maid?"

Conflict claws inside my chest. I didn't tell anyone about Quinn's run-in with the murderer or that the only murder witness is currently sleeping in my bed. Shit. There's not a possible scenario in which I can explain this without looking suspicious as hell.

"Not yet, but I have a contact who might know where to find her." I tap my pen on the desk. "Did you talk to her roommates?"

"Yeah, nothing there. Said they'd call if they heard from her."

"I'll do some digging on my way home after work."

"Need me to come with you?"

"Nah, I got this. Get home to your wife at a decent hour, before she comes after me."

Mickey chuckles. "She's still pissed about last weekend. We had tickets to see *CATS*, and I had to bail."

"I know. I'll never hear the end of it if I make it a regular occurrence."

"Eh, she knew it was part of the deal when she married a cop." He tidies up his desk and closes the drawer. "You need any backup, call me at home, okay?"

"Thanks, Mickey. Give Sue my best."

"Will do." He stands and pulls on his jacket. "I'll see you tomorrow."

With a nod, I turn back to the mess of papers on my desk and organize them into folders. I hate lying to my partner, but I can't reveal I've been keeping our only witness in my apartment since she showed up on my doorstep a bloody mess.

Quinn. She's a piece of work, that's for sure.

The first night I met her, she was a ball of fire and vinegar ready to tear my head off for looking at her. But when she showed up covered in blood with my name on her lips…

Fuck. I've never been so fucking scared.

Seeing the red gashes against her pale skin sent me into a mindless rage. They're healing, thank God. But the reminder only reignites my fury.

For how damned wounded she is, I would think she'd recoil at the thought of someone touching her. Her internal scars run as deep as the old marks marring her silky skin. I tried to ignore them, but they're branded on her.

Who could do such a thing to another person? Her story broke me. No one should have to struggle and suffer as she has. We all have ugly pieces of our history, but they shouldn't start when you're still a kid.

If I ever get my hands on her stepbrother, I'll fucking kill him. How could he take someone with so much potential and break her down into a petty crook? She might be a thief, but she's an innocent. I can see it in her eyes. This isn't the life she wants.

I wanted to ask her, to draw the truth from her full, tantalizing lips, but when she leaned into my touch and moaned, I lost all sense. I'm a gentleman, but damn it if I didn't imagine tracing my fingers beneath the hem of that towel and peeling it away from her damp skin.

Even though I want her, I shut that shit down. She's still under my protection, and I'll be damned if I'm going to take advantage of her like some goddamned predator. She deserves better.

Once I put the files away, I grab my suit jacket and head for the door. It's warm outside, even in the shade. August weather is suffocating, like a wet rag over my face. I need to take a shower. Which I can't do at my place.

Wandering through the nearest side street, I head for home.

Claude's been letting me use his shower and borrow his clothes since I'm obviously not man enough to reclaim my own fucking space.

Truth is, since that night, I can't take chances being close to Quinn. Her scent, her simple presence is enough to twist me into knots. If I linger, I might do something stupid…like kiss her, claim her.

Can't do that. She's a murder witness. The only lead I have. I can't risk chasing her off or fucking this up.

I've been coming home after she goes to bed, crashing on that damned sofa, and leaving before she wakes. I grabbed a couple of things from my closet yesterday and just about lost my mind at the sight of her in my bed, her curls draped across my pillows, her bare skin peeking out from beneath the sheet. I could have lived the rest of my life not knowing that she sleeps naked, but instead, I'm cursed to carry that painful knowledge to my killer sofa night after night while I refrain from taking myself in hand to ease the ache in my balls.

Claude hasn't said anything about our little arrangement, but I know he's watching. And harshly judging me. I can't blame him. I'd do the same if I were in his position, but he's smart enough to keep his head down and his mouth shut.

When I reach the Black Penny, I slip inside the door. At barely six, there's already a crowd. Years ago, this was a popular hangout for local dockworkers and the blue-collar crowd. Now it's brimming with sharp suits and gold Rolexes. My gaze roams over this new class of patrons as I make my way to the back of the bar.

Claude appears from the back room and nudges past a waitress as I slide onto a barstool near the hallway leading to the restrooms.

"Hey." He acknowledges my presence with a nod. "The usual?"

"Make it a double."

The corner of his mouth twitches as he pours my favorite whiskey over ice. He slides it across the bar.

"How is she?" I let the liquor work its magic, burning a hole in my gut.

"Bored."

"There's a television and food. What else does she need?" I keep my voice low.

"She's not a fucking cat, Grant." He scowls at me. "You plan on leaving her to fend for herself again tomorrow?"

Guilt twists my stomach into cords of regret. The whiskey bites the back of my throat. Shit.

I look away, my attention focused on a cluster of men sitting in the nearby booth. I have no idea who these people are or why they're in a dive bar in Hell's Kitchen when they could be at some swanky club uptown.

"Fine. I'll give her something to do."

It takes two full seconds for my brother's statement to sink through my thick skull. I whip around to face him. "Like what?"

Jealousy rears its head like a starving serpent when a million inappropriate thoughts fly through my brain. Claude flirting with Quinn. Them sitting together, talking over coffee. Him helping her cook in his small kitchen. Her resting her hand on his shoulder and smiling at him like he hangs the moon.

Fuck that. She's mine.

A knowing grin curves my brother's typically stoic lips. He leans against the bar. "If you don't take care of her, someone else will." He arches a brow in challenge and slowly rises, then quickly swishes his rag across the counter, drapes it over his shoulder, and retreats.

"Son of a bitch," I mutter under my breath. I've never been jealous of my brother, at least not as an adult. But right now, I want to take him into the street and beat his ass for insinuating I can't take care of her.

He's right though. If I don't step up, someone will—him or the murderer or some other asshole down the road. Good or bad, there will always be someone waiting to take my place.

No, I can't let that happen. She deserves better than the miserable cards she's been dealt.

I cringe at the pain in my chest and ignore the burning desire to march up those stairs to sweep her into my arms. I want to kiss the hurt away, tell her she'll be safe with me forever.

But that's not how the world works. My horrific past relationships prove this.

I can protect her from the murderer, but I can't protect her from the pain of her childhood. I can't protect her from my shit either. Nothing I do will heal her or give her the fulfillment she deserves.

Claude gives me a long look when I slap a ten on the bar and slip down the hallway. When I reach the landing outside my apartment, my hands are shaking. I don't know what to say to her. She deserves company, conversation with another adult. But I'm shit at that.

For her, I'll try.

I unlock the door and push it open. The television flickers in the corner of my eye. There's food on the table. One place setting, just for me. Her dirty dishes are in the sink.

I creep closer to the sofa and find her passed out, her arm draped over her head. She's wearing the clothes Claude found for her, the T-shirt riding up her side to bare her curves. Fuck.

I should let her sleep here and take the bed, but I can't bear the thought of the sofa springs hurting her. With a groan and the restraint of a saint, I lift her and carry her into my bedroom. She nestles against me, burying her face against my neck.

Her scent surrounds me, and I'm lost.

By the time I reach the bed, I'm rock hard. I put her down and draw the sheet over her. She burrows her face into my pillow and hugs it close. A sleepy moan drifts up, arousing me even more.

With a sigh, I grab some pajamas from the closet and head for Claude's apartment. I need a shower then food.

But I'll never be able to sate my hunger in this state.

At Claude's place, I turn the shower on cold and step under the spray. It doesn't touch the heat coursing through me. Only after I take my cock in my hand and alleviate the pressure inside me am I finally able to wrangle some control of my brain.

I eat the dinner she prepared and clean the dishes. By the time I lay down on the sofa, it's after eleven. I leave the television on and try to sleep, the background noise distracting me from the thoughts racing through my head.

This time, when I take my cock in my hand, it's a steady hum of need pulsing through me. I stroke, slow and firm, imagining it's Quinn. The thought of her touching me does the trick, and I'm spilling over my hand, leaving a puddle on my bare stomach.

Shit. I'm a fucking mess.

The quicker I solve this case, the better off we'll both be.

CHAPTER 12

Quinn

I heard him last night.

When he came into the living room and lifted me from the sofa, I pretended to be asleep. His touch burned through my sleepy haze. It took every ounce of restraint not to bury my face against his neck and arch into his warmth.

His scent lingered long after he placed me in his bed and pulled the sheet over me. Temptation pulled me into madness. I should've dragged him into the bed with me and taken what he clearly wanted.

The moment the front door closed, I ran to the bathroom and splashed water on my face to cool down.

But when he returned, I heard him. His low moan drew me to the door. From this angle, I could see him on the sofa. A peek through the crack made my heart stop—Grant with his hand wrapped around his cock, his head thrown back in tormented ecstasy.

A gasp lodged in my throat. My mouth watering, I watched, frozen like a statue as he stroked himself. My arousal grew with every soft moan. Grant came, his satisfied groan echoing in the small space.

How I wanted to go to him. To tease him. To make him come again…this time at my persuasive touch.

Without acting on my impulses, I returned to bed and buried myself beneath the sheets. My heart beat loud in my ears.

Even though I was frustrated with him, I couldn't throw myself at him in a desperate attempt to ease the ache between my thighs. Instead, I slid my fingers along my slick folds and urged myself to a quick but unsatisfying completion while imagining Grant's impressive cock pushing into me.

When I woke, the apartment was empty. Of course, it was.

For the past four days, he's left me to fend for myself. I cleaned the whole apartment out of pure boredom, music blasting from MTV the first two days. Yesterday, I lost myself in endless hours of daytime drama on television.

He always comes home just after I've eaten and fallen asleep. He must have some kind of sixth sense. I tried waiting up last night but fell asleep on the couch. He did wake me when he came home, but if I had confronted him then, I would've made an ass of myself climbing him like a needy little kitten.

Part of me wants to resent him for abandoning me to the confines of his apartment and my own devices. Even though I know I'm safe, I hate feeling trapped and isolated. No one knows where I am. Or if I'm even alive.

A shiver wracks me. Must be the guilt sliding along my spine at the thought of my roommates freaking out when they realize I'm not coming home. Have they reported me missing yet? I wish I could send them a message to let them know I'm okay, not to worry. But there's little chance Grant will let me talk to anyone.

There's no way the killer identified me. Right? He can't possibly know who I am. The police haven't named me as a person of interest…have they?

I turn on the morning news. The old man's murder is the lead story on every network. There's a ton of speculation but nothing substantial. No leads. Curiously, there's not a single mention of a witness.

Is Grant keeping me a secret?

Chewing on my nail, I watch for a few minutes before changing to another station. After an hour, I'm certain of it. Grant hasn't revealed he has a witness to the murder of Lionel Madison.

That means the murderer and Grant are the only two people who know I was there.

The realization strikes like a lightning bolt. I really am safe here, even if he leaves me alone all day to fend for myself.

A knock at the door makes me jump three feet off the couch. Clutching my hand to my heart, I peel myself from the sofa and cautiously approach the door.

"It's Claude." He pauses, and I hear him shift. "I'd unlock the door with my key, but my hands are full."

After my heart resumes its normal rhythm, I unlock the deadbolt and open the door.

"Morning." Claude shifts the box in his arm and smiles before crossing the threshold.

"Good morning." I close the door behind him.

"What's that?" I reach for the box, but he pulls it away and heads for the kitchen.

He sets it on the counter before facing me. His grin is infectious and instantly brightens my mood. "Groceries. I need to make sure you're not dying from neglect."

I lean against the kitchen counter. "How chivalrous of you."

Claude shrugs and reaches into the box. "I also brought you some books."

"Please tell me it's Stephen King's newest one."

"It's not *Skeleton Crew*, but good to know I brought something you like." He hands me copies of *The Dark Tower* and *The Talisman*. I snatch them from his grip and hug them to my chest.

"You're a fucking godsend." Cradling the books, I stroke the spines with reverence. "I haven't read these yet."

"They're pretty good." Claude shoves his hand in his pocket. "I love Stephen King."

"Me too." I set the books aside with a loving glance at the covers before turning to the groceries in the box. "Which one is your favorite?"

"Of all of his works?" Claude ponders for a moment, his nose scrunching as he thinks. "It's a tie between *The Shining* and *The Dark Tower*."

Claude keeps me company as I put away the groceries, and we discuss the merits of King's literary works. I've always had a thing for the macabre, and his work hits the fine line marrying the supernatural to horror. I'm excited to dive into the books Claude brought and see where the master of horror will take me next.

"Can I get you something to drink?"

"A Coke would be great." He takes a seat on the sofa while I snatch two cold sodas from the fridge.

He cracks it open and lifts it in salute.

I mirror the action and take a drink. Curiosity pulls at me when I sit beside him. "Where's your brother?"

"Work, I assume. Heard him stomp down the stairs early this morning."

I chuckle at the thought of Grant making extra noise to emphasize his mood. "Is he always such a grump?"

"Yeah." Claude sips his Coke. "But you can't blame him. His job takes a toll on him. Plus, he hasn't been the same since his wife left twelve years ago."

"He's married?" I choke on the bubbles and my surprise.

"Divorced. Didn't last long. She gave him an impossible choice—her or the job." Claude shrugs.

"You didn't like her, I take it?"

"Not at all, but I didn't marry her." Claude studies me with narrowed eyes. "What's your story?"

"I don't have a story."

When I shift under his scrutiny, he smiles.

"We all have stories, Quinn."

"Tell me yours first."

"What do you want to know?"

"Well…" Instinctively, my gaze drops to his missing hand, and before I can correct myself, he sighs. "I wasn't going to ask about your hand."

"Everyone does."

"I'm not everyone." I lean my head against the sofa. "What I want to know is…" I bite my lip. "Are you single?"

Claude's brows shoot up to his hairline, and he bursts with laughter. "Not what I was expecting."

"That's me in a nutshell." I gesture to the length of me. "Not what you'd expect."

"How true." His eyes sparkle, and he rolls the can in his hand. "Yeah, I'm single."

Surprise pierces me. "Why?"

"I'm not exactly top shelf." His self-deprecating chuckle saddens me.

"Any girl would be lucky to have a guy like you, Claude."

"Well, they're not lined up around the block."

"They should be. You're sweet and thoughtful." I nudge him with my knee. "I know there's a handsome guy under that Lynyrd Skynyrd T-shirt and mop of unruly dark hair. Plus, you've got great taste in music and books."

Claude laughs aloud. "You certainly know how to boost a guy's ego."

"Hey, I just call 'em like I see 'em."

"What about you?" He leans forward, eyes keen with interest.

I shake my head. "There's no one to worry about me." A deep breath purges dark thoughts from my mind.

"I find that hard to believe."

"It's true." I hold his gaze. "I've been alone a long time."

He hums thoughtfully. "I know the feeling."

A wild thought strikes me. "Claude, would you do me a favor?"

"What do you need?"

"My roommates. I don't want them to think I'm dead in the street, but I can't reach out to them myself. Would you give them a call to let them know I'm safe?"

Worry creases his brow. "I don't know, Quinn. Maybe you should have Grant tell them."

"No, they'll worry more if a cop calls." I chew on my lower lip when the idea strikes. "You can tell them I gave you a message to deliver. I'm working on finding a better job, and I'll be home soon."

Skepticism is painted all over Claude's face. "I'll think about it. But I think you should have Grant reach out to them instead."

I muster a pout. "He's so busy. I don't want to burden him with one more thing."

Claude sighs. "I'll see what I can do."

"Thank you!" I launch myself into his arms and hug him tight.

The scent of his cologne teases my senses. The same scent as Grant last night, but on Claude, it smells lighter, almost sweet.

He gives me a gentle pat on the back and I pull away.

"Anything else you need?"

"Yes." I eye the basket inside the bedroom. "Where's the laundry?"

"Come on, I'll show you."

I grab the basket and follow him down the stairs. He shows me to the laundry room and leaves me to it, reminding me to return upstairs as soon as I'm done. The last thing either of us needs is a lecture from Grant.

Between loads of laundry, I sit on the sofa and read. Somewhere in between, I pop a small beef roast into the oven. By the time the last load is done, I can hear noise from the bar filtering through the doors. My curiosity pulls me closer. Just a peek before I go upstairs and start dinner.

After I slip through the doors, the scent of pub food and malt liquor hits me. My stomach growls even though I have food cooking upstairs. I peer around the corner and see the movement of bustling patrons enjoying a night at the neighborhood pub.

Claude moves behind the bar with purpose and grace. His gaze skims over the crowd before landing on me. He shakes his head.

A firm hand clasps my uninjured shoulder. Panic grabs me by the throat.

He found me. Somehow the murderer found me. Fuck.

CHAPTER 13

Grant

Fuck. Another day wasted chasing dead ends.

I toss the folder onto my desk and rake my hand across my face. A four-day beard scratches my palms, reminding me I haven't shaved since that night. I haven't had the heart to face her.

The moment I do, I'm bound to do something stupid or say something to set us off in a dangerous direction. I can't afford to do either.

Every waking hour is spent chasing down every lead for Lionel Madison's murder. Any possible cold case that could be tied to this has been combed through at least three times. There's just nothing overtly tying the cases together.

Each one was a break-in turned deadly, but there's not a single piece of evidence linking any of them. I might as well eat crow because my fellow cops will never let me live this down. I've made it abundantly clear I think they're all connected.

Shit, can one thing go right for once?

"Richards. My office." The captain stops beside my desk with a pointed look. "Now."

Every eye in the room turns to us, hyperfocused on me. Shit, this can't be good.

"Yes, sir." I push away from the desk and follow him across the hall to his spacious office with a bright sunny window blocked with fading blinds.

He sits behind his oversized desk and leans back, studying me. "Have a seat, Richards."

The tone reminds me of a frustrated parent about to lecture an errant child. I push the thought from my mind and sit down.

"Any leads on the Madison case?" He pulls out a cigarette and lights it.

I lick my lips, the lack of nicotine pulling at my nerves. I haven't had any in two days, and it's starting to wear on me. I shift in my seat, tearing my gaze from the cigarette between his fingers. "Not yet, sir. We're working on it."

His bushy brows furrow. "It's been a week."

"Exactly, sir. We're still digging through the evidence, and there are no witnesses to tie the murders to…"

"Jesus, Richards, are you still thinking this case is part of that string of home invasion murders?" He shakes his head. "Those cases are unrelated. You're grasping at straws trying to tie them together."

"Sir, I know it sounds crazy, but I'm telling you, they're connected."

"How?"

My vision clouds with frustration, and I blink, breaking eye contact. "I don't know yet."

"You don't know because there isn't anything connecting these cases." He takes a drag of his cigarette, and my irritation burns bright like its tip. "Those were home invasions gone wrong, Richards. Plain and simple. Let them go."

"But—"

"No buts. I've got the commissioner breathing down my neck on the Madison murder, and I need answers. Stop trying to find evidence that doesn't exist and get your shit together!"

My hands clench into fists. "So, it's political?"

"What?"

"You're only interested in solving the high-profile cases when someone high on the food chain wants answers?" Fury pulses through me.

"Don't push your fucking luck, Richards." He jabs a finger at me, the cigarette bobbing wildly between his meaty fingers. "I'll take you off this case if you can't handle it."

"I can handle it, sir. But—"

"No fucking excuses, detective. I expect an update on my desk by Monday, is that understood?" He grits his teeth and narrows his eyes, looking remarkably like an overstuffed badger. "Find evidence. A witness, a lead, something, or you're off this case. Is that clear?"

"Yes." The word tastes like bitter regret. I want to tell him exactly where to stick his order, but he'll just pull me off the case, handing it off to someone more interested in kissing ass than solving it. I swallow my pride and leave his office before I say something I'll regret.

Instead of burying myself in paperwork, I pack a few of the files into my messenger bag and leave the precinct. It's still early. I can't go home. Not yet. I can't face Quinn.

Reality slaps me in the face. I can't avoid her forever. She's the only witness I have.

Even though I've gone over her account of that night in my head a million times, I need to hear it again from her lips. There's something I missed. Something important.

If I want to solve this case, I need Quinn.

Problem is…I *want* her too. That's a messy fucking complication.

Goddamn it.

With a deep breath, I weave my way through the city. By the time I reach the Black Penny, I'm sweating. And not because of the August heat.

Quinn has me twisted into knots. I don't know how to untangle myself from this case and this stupid infatuation long enough to clearly see the details.

Maybe fucking her would purge whatever this is?

Nah. That's a bad fucking idea. Shit gets complicated when sex is involved. We're both in a bind. Until this case is solved, I can't indulge the whims of my overstimulated libido and demanding cock.

With a sigh, I shake the dirty thoughts from my brain and push open the door. I can hear the washer down the hall through the open door near the bar entrance. Bracing myself, I head upstairs.

The door's unlocked. What the fuck?

"Quinn?" I call, but there's no answer. "Quinn, where are you?"

I drop my bag on the sofa and check the bathroom, the bedroom…fuck, I check Claude's apartment and the rooftop.

No Quinn.

Sheer panic grips me in a chokehold.

Where the hell is she? Did they find her?

Claude. I dart down the steps and race along the hallway. Careful not to burst through the door looking like a madman, I quietly swing it open and my blood turns molten.

Quinn's peeking into the bar from the shadows. Where she's leaning, her halo of curls lights the wall on fire. She's wearing an oversized T-shirt pulled into a knot at the curve of her waist. A pair of cutoff shorts fray just above the indentation where her ass meets her thighs. I knew Claude brought her clothes a few days ago, but I'm going to kill him for giving her these tempting scraps of fabric.

Just beyond the wall, I catch sight of my brother. He holds my gaze and shakes his head. Like he didn't know she was out of the apartment. I'll deal with him later.

I readjust my lately ever-present erection and suppress the anger boiling inside me at her blatant disregard for rules I put in place to fucking keep her safe.

My hand grasps her uninjured shoulder.

She whips around, eyes wide, and strikes. Catching me off guard, her fist collides with the side of my face.

Fuck, that hurt.

"Grant."

Hearing my name on her lips with such soft surprise only makes me harder and infuriates me more. Ignoring the pulsing ache in my cheek, I snatch her by the wrist, then drag her through the door and up the stairs.

"Grant! Let me go!" She pulls against my hold, but I'm too far gone to care.

Once we're inside my apartment, I slam the door shut and round on her. "What the fuck were you thinking? Someone could have seen you!"

"No one saw me." Her green eyes are the size of fucking dinner plates. She bites her lower lip, letting it slide between her teeth as she releases it in slow motion. "I was doing laundry and—"

"You left the apartment, Quinn. Anyone could have seen you. That's when people start asking questions." I run my hand through my hair. "That's how the rumor mill starts."

I step closer and she backs up until she hits the door. Her panting breaths draw my attention to the white shirt pulled tight across her chest.

"So what?"

"All it takes is the right person to hear the whispers, and they'll piece it together." Her mouth parts on a gasp when I crowd closer. "The city might give you anonymity, but it can steal it away just as quickly."

A frown settles on those plush lips. "I was just trying to help."

"You can help by doing what I tell you to do."

With more force than I anticipate, she shoves her hands against my chest, pushing me away. "You don't get to tell me what to do. I'm not a prisoner. I'm here of my own free will." Fire sparks to life in her eyes. "I didn't go anywhere, no one saw me, and I haven't spoken to anyone except Claude."

I can't help but bask in pride at her tenacity. Heaven help the murderer if he catches up to her. Unarmed, she's a firecracker; she'd be a goddamned force of nature with a weapon in her hand. Maybe I should leave a gun with her.

"You're not a prisoner, but I can't protect you if you're out wandering around. You need to stay inside where it's safe."

She cocks her head to the side, and a look of pure animosity pins me in place. "You mean stay here with nothing to do but clean your pigsty apartment, wash your nasty sheets, and cook my own meals? You're right. You're not my jailer. You're an asshole who wants a maid and a personal chef."

I stare at her, dumbfounded. Quinn shakes her head, throws her hands up, and storms past, knocking into me as she thunders by. I snatch her by the wrist and pull her to a stop.

"Quinn, wait."

Her wrist locks beneath my touch, and I release her. She doesn't turn, but I can see the restraint pulling her body tight like a rubber band at its breaking point.

"I'm sorry…okay? It's just…" Defeat slams into me. "I've got no leads. Nothing. And I—"

"You didn't tell them about me, did you?" Her voice is low and steady.

"No."

"Why not?"

Exhaustion consumes what remains of my restraint. The truth pours free. "Because if I tell them I have a witness. This"—I gesture between us—"disappears. It's over. I can't protect you then. They'll put you in protective custody, and I don't fucking trust them to make sure you're safe."

"That's it?" She turns to face me. "That's the reason you're keeping me a secret?"

"I'm not keeping you a secret." I shake my head, but it feels fake. All of it. I shift uncomfortably under her scrutiny.

"I'm your dirty little secret." A wicked smile appears and her cheeks pinken. "Is that it? You like being in control and don't want anyone to know you've got me stashed in your apartment, tucked safe in your bed?"

The image of her curled beneath my sheets, her hair splayed across my pillow, lips parted on a soft sigh, lost in dreams consumes my vision. I blink to chase it away, but it's too late. It's there, and she can see exactly how much I want her. Shit.

"I'm taking you in tomorrow. You can give your official statement, and they'll take care of you from here on out." The lie falls from my lips in a rush.

Quinn reels as if I struck her, and she stumbles back a few steps.

While she composes herself, I can see it build like a storm gathering on the horizon over the open sea.

Whatever is simmering between us needs to stop. I can't take what I want from her, even if she willingly offers it. I have a job to do, and I can't do it if I'm emotionally and sexually invested with a key murder witness. I won't put the case in jeopardy. I won't put her in danger.

I'm already in over my head. There's nothing I can do to put these feelings back in the bottle. I'm drowning in them. And it fucking terrifies me.

Risking her life isn't an option. She was in the wrong place at the wrong time, and now she's stuck with me. I won't ruin what remains of her life.

But I can help her close the door and move on if I solve this case.

I can't do that with my dick buried in her and my mind lost in the possibilities of a future neither of us can ever have. We're too different. Like oil and water.

Judging by the tempest brewing before me, I'm in for one hell of a fight.

Good. I'd rather have her mad at me, makes this break clean and easy.

Hurricane Quinn unleashes her fury, and I brace for impact.

CHAPTER 14

Quinn

"I don't fucking think so." My patience has reached its limit, and I erupt like a long dormant volcano, unleashing upon anyone in my path. "I came to you for help. *You* promised I would be safe here until you solved the case. You left me here all week while you were out chasing leads."

Grant stands still as a statue, his only movement the tension pulsing along his jaw and the spark of fire flickering in his dark eyes. I step closer, invading his space, pushing him like he pushed me.

"I kept myself busy with whatever domestic bullshit I could find. I cooked. I cleaned your goddamn pigsty of an apartment. The least you can do is tell me why you suddenly want me as far away from you as possible."

My finger jabs his chest where his withered heart should be. Deep inside, my heart beats frantically, screaming for release from its bony prison. I want to understand why he finds my company so abhorrent. Why am I not welcome?

His hands clench into fists, then release. A heavy sigh fills the space between us before he glances heavenward and closes his eyes.

"Fine. I get it." I step back, pain lancing my pride. "I'll give my statement, but I'll take care of myself from here on out. I don't need cops to protect me. And I sure as fuck don't need you."

Choking back tears, I study his expression. Stoic and unreadable, it's like he's carved from stone. Fuck this. I'd rather take my chances on the street than deal with this bullshit for another moment.

Safe, my ass. Grant burrowed beneath my skin and infected my life with his presence. I'm already ruined. I'll be damned if I stay when it's blatantly obvious he doesn't want me.

Fuck him.

Halfway to the door, a firm arm catches me by the waist. Panic and relief flood me in equal measure, but my brain riots against his hold.

"Let me go."

I struggle to pry his hand from where his fingers dig into my side. Twisting and pulling, I try to wrench myself from his grip, but he snares me with his other hand. I'm trapped.

"Quinn. Stop."

"No. You don't want me here. I'm leaving." I flail my arms and rear back, away from his solid frame.

Grant catches my arms in his hands and backs me to the wall beside the door. His body crowds me, his knee pressing between my thighs, his hands pinning mine to the faded blue wallpaper. The scent of his soap and the heat of his body surround me, consume me. I bite back a whimper at the contact. His touch isn't rough, but it's firm. It's more comforting than it should be. But I can't concede. I won't. He wants me gone? I'll go.

When I push against his hold, he leans into me instead of tightening his grip. His heat pulls me in, lulling me into compliance. The rough pad of his thumb caresses the inside of my wrist, and I stifle a whimper.

"Breathe, Quinn." His gentle caress seeps into that long-deprived piece of my soul.

I close my eyes, trying to resist how good it feels, how it tames the beast raging inside me. My inhaled breath shutters, like I can't get it out past the ball of pain in my chest. When I release it, my tension goes with the exhale. I sink into his hold.

"Good girl."

My heart flutters at the praise, and I soak it up with his caress, like a flower kept in the dark for years suddenly exposed to the bright sunshine.

He flattens the back of my hands against the wall and traces his fingertips over the sensitive skin of my palms. "Take another deep breath."

I obey, desperate for more of the feeling expanding inside me. I can't name it, I can't explain it. It swells and fills the spaces inside me that have been barren for too long. A brazen part of my mind tells me to fight against this, to steel myself against this fleeting rush. But I melt against him. I want more than he's offering.

When I meet his gaze, I'm struck by the complexity of his expression. Dark eyes wide and vulnerable. Full lips parted. Skin flushed.

My tongue darts over my dry lips. "Grant, please..."

Let me go. It's what I want to say but not what it sounds like. That's not what my body demands. It wants everything he has to offer and more. It craves the chance to fill the voids, to embrace the moment.

I want him, all of him.

I close my hands around his fingertips, gently caressing them in my limited capacity. He relinquishes his hold on my wrists to slide his hands over my arms before tracing along my throat. His touch burns, leaving heat in its wake.

There's nothing stopping me from arching into his touch. My body curves into his, craving contact. I want his hands everywhere.

"Quinn." The reverent murmur of my name from his lips snaps what remains of my restraint.

I throw myself against him, my fingers tangling in his hair, and I drag him to me, closing the minuscule gap between us. My lips brush his.

It's the only encouragement he needs to crash through the invisible barrier separating us. With a moan, his lips part, and I'm lost in him.

Grant cradles my face in his hands, his fingertips brushing my earlobes. I pull myself closer, needing more contact. More of him.

He tastes like sin and salvation with a bite of wintergreen. I delve deeper, tasting him completely. The warm strength of his lips against mine leaves me breathless.

Then he's gone. He rests his head against mine for a long moment.

My racing heart pounds with uncertainty. Doesn't he want me? What's wrong?

I swallow the knot in my throat as he leans back, his eyes leveling with mine. He caresses my jaw and hooks his finger beneath my chin, forcing me to hold his gaze.

"Tell me you want this, Quinn." He licks his kiss-bruised lips. "This is your chance to walk away."

"Why would I want to walk away?"

"Because I can't make any promises."

"I don't want promises, Grant." My hand caresses the back of his neck. "I want you."

A growl escapes his throat as he closes the distance between us and unleashes his passion. The kiss evolves from curious to ravenous. His tongue is rough against mine, dueling and dancing.

I can't get close enough. Any remaining hesitation disintegrates as he lifts me into his arms, wrapping my legs around his waist.

I'm no delicate, dainty flower, but he carried me before and I loved every stolen moment. This time, I can openly appreciate the flex of his shoulders and the hard length of him against me. He crosses the short distance to the sofa and sits, taking me with him.

Straddling his thighs, I settle onto his lap. His hands rest on my hips.

I wiggle against him and tease my fingers across the collar of his blue dress shirt.

The light catches flecks of gold in his eyes when a lopsided smile steals across that sinful mouth.

"What's this?" I run my finger across his lower lip.

"What?"

"You're smiling." I grind my hips against his, eliciting a groan from the grumpy detective. "I didn't think you knew how to do that."

"Keep teasing me and you're going to learn *exactly* what I know how to do." His hand glides beneath my T-shirt, and I shiver as his warm touch skims my spine.

Grant's slow exploration leaves me panting. I take his scruffy face between my hands and kiss him. All my desperation and need pour into that kiss. His hands roam over my skin, leaving goosebumps in their wake. I pull my shirt over my head and unclasp my bra.

His chuckle brushes my neck before his lips seek out the sensitive space behind my ear. I wrap my arms around him and press myself closer.

"You drive me crazy." His whispered confession leaves me shaking.

"Why did you push me away?" I arch back when he trails soft, open-mouthed kisses along my collarbone and down between my breasts.

"To keep you safe."

He takes my breasts in his hands and rubs his scruffy cheek against my pale skin. The abrasive rasp against my nipples leaves me trembling. I thread my fingers through his hair.

"From what?"

I gasp when he takes a nipple in his mouth, gently tugging and rolling it over his tongue.

"Me." He glances up, and I drown in his dark gaze. "You shouldn't want an old, jaded detective, Quinn. I have nothing to offer you."

My hand wraps around his tie, and I slowly loosen it. "You're not old." I finger the fabric as it slides free. "You're experienced."

"That's not always a good thing." There's pain in his derisive laugh, and it lances through my heart.

"Do you still want me?" I ask, curiosity tugging my touch-starved soul.

"Fuck, kid. I've wanted you from the first moment I dragged your ass out of that apartment." He brushes his thumb along the curve of my breast, and I shiver.

"Then why fight it?" My hips rock against his, earning me a gentle slap on the ass.

"It's complicated."

"Not that complicated." I slowly unbutton his shirt. Knowing he's wanted me since the first night leaves me dizzy with desire. He's always been handsome, and his kindness that night earned him special admiration. I hadn't anticipated any serious attachment between us, not until the murderer forced my hand and pushed me into the path of this gruff detective.

"I can't give you what you want, kid."

"I'm not asking for anything." I tap my chin playfully. "Well, except the obvious."

The lopsided smile returns. "What would that be exactly?"

"You want me to say it?"

My face warms under his scrutiny. He's toying with me, and it sparks heat through my body.

"I want you to tell me what you want. Spare no details."

My pussy weeps at his demand.

"I want you to touch me. Everywhere. I want your mouth everywhere your fingers touch. I want you to fuck me."

"Good girl."

He shifts me beneath him onto the sofa and removes my shorts, tossing the garment away. He leans over me and spreads my thighs, hooking one knee over the back of the sofa.

His gaze skims my exposed pussy. "Beautiful."

My fingers glide over my sex, parting the folds for his perusal. I'm wet, embarrassingly so, and Grant slides down and tastes me. His tongue drags over my swollen clit, and I thread my fingers in his hair.

No man has ever touched me like this. What little sex I've indulged in has never included foreplay. It's always been *wham*, *bam*, and I'm done.

But this…this is what I've been missing. This raw connection. This uninhibited need. I've never wanted anyone the way I want Grant. The thought terrifies me.

I want this.

A moan rips from my throat when he slides two fingers inside me. His mouth and tongue tease me as he slowly fucks me with his fingers. My grip in his hair tightens as unrelenting sounds pour from my throat.

He devours me like a man starved. I offer him everything, even though I know I could very well lose my heart in the process.

Grant quickens his pace, and I'm caught in the pleasure. When he sucks my clit into his mouth and curls his fingers, I'm catapulted to another plane of existence.

The orgasm hits with the force of a hurricane. I'm pulled out to sea, blissfully dissolving into nothingness. My eyes close, heavy and sated like my body.

Even through the pleasure, I choke back a sob when the reality of our situation creeps back into my mind.

This can't last. Nothing this good ever does.

CHAPTER 15

Grant

Her scent wraps around me, and I'm harder than I ever thought possible. The taste of her arousal lingers on my tongue. It's been so damn long since I've eaten pussy.

But this is nothing like those uncomfortable past encounters.

No. Quinn is nothing like Veronica, nothing like any of the women I've been with before. She challenges me, pulls me out of my comfort zone, makes me crave more than I should dare to want.

This insatiable temptress is a dream come true, even if she is nothing but trouble with a capital T.

Quinn trembles beneath me, her body shaking with the force of her orgasm. She bites her lip, and her eyes flutter open, her gaze landing on me. I make a show of licking her cream off my fingers. Her eyes flash with desire, and a whimper escapes those tantalizing lips. It takes all my effort not to lean down to kiss her senseless, to let her taste herself on my tongue, to sweep her up in the moment and stake my claim.

"Please…" Her voice is breathless. She's drunk on her orgasm.

I plan on drowning us both in orgasms before the night is over.

"What do you need, hmm?"

"You."

"What about me?" I tease a fingertip along the crease of her thighs.

"I want you inside me."

The words heat my blood.

"I want you to fuck me, Grant." She takes my shirt in her fist and pulls me down. "Now."

Her mouth crashes on mine in a torrential kiss.

My words are lost on her tongue. Her breasts press against my chest, and I curse the fabric of my shirt for blocking the sweet slide of her skin against mine.

She tugs the shirt from my pants and fumbles with my belt while her lips work their magic on mine. Her hand grazes my cock as she moves, and need pulses through me, hot and sharp like a knife drawing blood.

Fuck, I want her with every ounce of my being. I can't seem to get enough of her heat, her scent, her touch.

After nearly a week of torment, I can't fight the pull any longer. She might not be what I expected, but she's exactly what I need.

A knock at the door echoes in the back of my mind like a distant explosion. I draw back, panting against her kiss-swollen lips, my cock aching for her, her body slick and hot arching against mine. I must be hearing things.

The knock shakes the door this time.

"Grant!" My brother's voice reverberates through the wood.

"Goddamn it to hell."

Quinn's eyes widen in horror as I steal a quick kiss and stand up. She scrambles to grab the crocheted afghan draped over the back of the sofa and wraps it around her body.

I manage to refasten my pants and belt as I walk toward the door. Unlocking it, I take a breath to calm my racing blood. In two seconds, I would've been buried deep inside her, and now this. My cock aches, and I've never wanted to tell my brother to fuck off more than at this moment.

I swing the door open. "What do you want, Claude?" I hiss through my teeth, keeping the door between my brother and the disheveled woman on the sofa.

His gaze skims over the haphazard state of my clothes. He has the decency to look embarrassed and clears his throat. "Sorry I interrupted. There's someone downstairs you should speak with. Now."

"Now?"

"Yes." He leans close. "It's about the murder. He says he'll only speak to you."

"Fucking hell." Quickly, I rebutton my shirt and put myself in some semblance of order. "Did they say anything else?"

"No. Only that they wanted to speak to you before they go to the cops." Claude shifts from one foot to the other. "He looks suspicious. Want me to call Mickey for backup?"

"No. I'll talk to him first. Just let me get my gun." I leave Claude at the door and return to the sofa where my .38 lays in its holster. Tugging it on, I meet Quinn's curious gaze.

"What is it?"

"There's someone downstairs I need to speak to." I kiss her softly. "Throw some clothes on. I'll be back in a bit."

"Is that it? You're done with me?"

I pin her with a hungry stare. "No, sweetheart, I'm not done with you. When I come back, I'm going to finish what I started."

Pink suffuses her cheeks, and her grin makes my heart pound. "Promise?"

"I promise." My fingers graze her cheek. "Why don't you check on dinner?"

Her eyes pop wide, and she shoots off the couch, wrapped in a blanket, making a beeline for the oven. I laugh at the sight.

"We're good!" she proclaims with a laugh as she retreats to the bedroom to change. "Hurry back."

"Yes, ma'am." I catch the flirty wink she sends my way and fasten my holster in place.

When I return to the doorway, Claude's leaning against the frame with a smirk on his lips. He backs away as I step out of the apartment.

"Don't say a word." I close the door behind me.

He shrugs. "I didn't say anything."

But the look on his face belies the thoughts in his mind. He knows exactly what was happening in my apartment; I have a feeling he approves. I'm not in the mood to talk about it right now.

"Where is this guy?" I lead him down the stairs.

"In my office. I told him to wait there."

"He didn't give a name or anything?"

"Nothing."

"Okay." I pause outside the closed office door. "Go back to the bar. I'll take care of this."

"Yell if you need anything." He drops his voice to a whisper. "I'll be back in five minutes to check on you."

I nod, knowing it's his way of having my back. Once he disappears into the bar, I open the door. The small space has few pieces of furniture—a desk, two chairs, a bookshelf, and a filing cabinet. A lamp glows in the corner.

I step deeper into the room and…no one's here.

Fuck. Where the hell did he go? Couldn't wait five minutes? I turn to leave, and the door slams shut. I barely see the flash of a neon-green-and-black running jacket with the hood pulled over the person's head before the door slams closed.

I dart forward, grasping the doorknob, then shaking it when it doesn't budge. Shit. I try to turn the lock, but it's jammed. Fuck.

What the hell? I beat my fists on the door and shout, but silence meets my fury.

There's a phone on the desk. I pick it up. There's no dial tone. A frayed bit of cord hangs from the receiver. Shit.

It's a trap.

I kick over a chair and curse my stupidity. I can't believe I walked into a fucking trap.

But why would they…

They need me gone so they can get to her.

Panic races through me, setting my teeth on edge. I grab the handle again and shout, but it doesn't budge.

Quinn.

CHAPTER 16

Quinn

Part of me wants to hate Claude for interrupting us, but he couldn't possibly have known what was going on between his brother and me. Hell, I wasn't even expecting it.

The stillness of the apartment fills me with apprehension. Grant will be back any moment. He promised to finish what we started.

But first, I need to get dinner out of the oven.

I put on a T-shirt and loose shorts. No reason to put fifteen layers back on if he's only coming back to strip them off again. The timer dings, and I check the roast, pulling it from the oven before it dries out.

With the roast done, I put some water on the stove to boil potatoes. Pretty standard fare, but a hearty meal nonetheless. I wanted something comforting, even though it's warm outside. The air conditioner in the window barely keeps the living room cool during the day.

The hum of the air conditioner lulls me into a rhythm. My mind drifts to the moment just before Claude knocked on the door.

Grant kisses like a man staking his claim. He tastes like stolen chocolate from a high-end store. Decadent and forbidden. His strength shouldn't have surprised me, but I was left stunned when he carried me to the couch and stripped me bare. That wicked mouth and those talented fingers brought me the best orgasm I've ever had.

Holy shit. I giggle and do a little dance in the middle of the floor. I didn't think he wanted me.

Reality steps in, looming like a shadow over my post-orgasm bliss. This can't last. Whatever *this* is between us. Once he solves the case, he'll go his way and I'll go mine. No grand gestures, no long-term promises.

Just a short-term indulgence.

Disappointment tugs at my heart. I don't necessarily *want* something more, but Grant's grumpy, unorganized presence is growing on me with every passing day. He's handsome, and I can't help but smile when I catch a glimpse of the charm hidden beneath his gruff exterior.

He may claim to be jaded, but he's an overstuffed teddy bear who just wants to be held and loved.

Whoa. Where did that come from? Love's a little strong.

I nibble on my lip. Damn it. Why does this shit have to be so damn complicated?

While the water comes to a boil, I dart to the bathroom to fix my hair. It's a tangled mess, and I'm sure it'll become even more of a mess when Grant returns.

Giddy delight consumes me. Heat curls in my chest, radiating down to where he thoroughly licked me until I came against his tongue. I can't wait to see him completely bare. To get my mouth around his length. To torment him until he fists his hands in my hair and begs for me to end his torment. Then I'll let him fuck me all night. I shiver with delight at the thought.

I tie my hair up and hear the door close. He's back. With a deep, fortifying breath, I saunter out of the bedroom and lean against the doorframe.

There's no one there. The apartment is empty. Maybe I'm hearing things. I check the water, which hasn't started boiling yet.

The air conditioner is off. Hmm, I must have tripped a breaker. I'm not sure where the box is, but I flip the window unit's switch on and off a few times just in case. Nothing.

I jump when a glass shatters on the floor behind me. I spin around, but the moment I do, a firm hand clamps over my mouth while another wraps around my waist.

Shit. It's not Grant.

The murderer! He found me.

My head pivots, trying to catch a glimpse of him, but I'm pinned in place.

How did he find me? Is he going to kill me? Fear grabs me by the throat and chokes me. I try to scream, but when I inhale, I instead gag on a sweet, astringent, chemical scent.

The potent aroma stings my nose and triggers vague, abandoned, memories of mom's hospital room. Of sterile hallways and empty gurneys and polite nurses offering their condolences. Memories I'd rather leave buried and forgotten.

I fight their hold, trying to wrench myself free from the memories, from the panic rising around me. I'm a ship sinking beneath the waves.

My head aches beneath the weight of the overpowering smell, and my eyes water causing my vision to waver. My arms push uselessly at my attacker's grip. With a jerk, my legs give out beneath me.

My scream dies, muffled against the rag pressed to my face. Desperation claws at my consciousness.

Grant, help me!

The words fade away, and I unwillingly surrender to the darkness.

CHAPTER 17

Grant

Four minutes of shouting and pounding on the door, and it still doesn't budge. I'm half tempted to shoot the lock, but that'll make more of a mess than I'm willing to deal with—even without the fact that the bullet could hit someone on the other side of the door. Fuck.

I kick the damn thing one last time, then rest my head against the impenetrable wood. Quinn's in trouble, and I walked into a fucking trap. What kind of shitty cop am I? Running in like some rookie with a lead before scouting my surroundings. Shit.

A sturdy knock vibrates beneath my hand.

"Damn lock's broken," I shout through the door. "Quinn's in danger. Go!"

"Top drawer in my desk," Claude shouts back. "I'll check on Quinn."

In the drawer, there's a small tool kit. I grab the screwdriver and attack the knob screws with a vengeance. By the time I get the screws out, my hands are slick with sweat and my heart's racing so fast, I worry I might go into cardiac arrest.

Please be there. Please be okay. The thoughts race through my brain and over my lips, a mantra of protection. A Hail Mary.

It was stupid of me to rush off without verifying the information.

But how could the murderer have discovered where she was? How could they possibly know? Why go to the trouble of getting me out of the apartment first? Nothing makes sense.

I manage to get the doorknob off and unfuck the lock. The door swings open, and I nearly collide with Claude when I round the corner. He catches me by the shoulder, his eyes wide, his mouth set in a grim line.

"She's gone, Grant."

"No." I push past him and race down the hall, tear around the corner, and climb the stairs two at a time. The .38 Special is steady in my hand as I approach the apartment. My chest nearly bursts from the exertion on top of the panic crushing it like a two-ton stone.

The door's wide open.

"It was like that?" I ask Claude, who comes up beside me.

He nods, and I notice the revolver in his grip—the Smith & Wesson Pap used to keep under the bar for rowdy patrons and light fingers.

We slip into the apartment and clear it. Strange. The air conditioning is off, but the stove burner is on, water boiling away. I turn it off. There's no sign of Quinn or the intruder.

What's even stranger is there's no sign of a struggle. Quinn would have put up a fight.

Confusion leaves me angry. This can't be the murderer because it doesn't fit their MO. In all the cases, none show any attempt to abduct a victim. They were killed on the spot and left for dead. If this were the killer from the Madison case, he would have removed her as a threat and left her lying in a pool of blood as a reminder. A shiver courses through me at the thought.

No, this is something else entirely. But I have no idea what it could be.

"Are you sure she didn't decide to leave?" Claude tucks the gun into the back of his waistband.

My mind conjures the moments before Claude interrupted us earlier. Her body wrapped around mine, her pussy tight around my fingers as I coaxed her to orgasm. The sweet, sinful promise of continuation on her lips as I walked out the door.

"There's no way in hell she just left." I shake my head and holster my weapon.

"You sure?"

"Positive." I shoot him a narrow glance to convey my affirmation. Claude doesn't need to know everything that goes on between Quinn and me. Not yet. But my brother's smart. I'm sure he's figured it out.

"This guy who wanted to speak with me?" I pace as I work the details through my mind. "What did he look like?"

"Thirties, brown eyes, brown hair. Nothing remarkable. No tats or scars that I noticed."

"Black-and-neon-green running jacket?"

"Yeah." Claude straightens. "Did you see him?"

"Bastard is the one who locked me in your office. Must have disabled the phone and the lock before I showed up. He shut the door behind me." Regret stings like bile at the back of my throat. "I should have known it was a trap."

"How could you have known?"

"With more than twenty years in the department, you'd think I'd know better than to let some punk blindside me." I run my hand over my jaw, ignoring how the oversight physically pains me. "Did you recognize him?"

"Never seen him before today. Just figured he was with one of the groups of uptown punks who keep coming in recently." Worry creases Claude's brow. "What do we do now?"

"I can put out a missing person's report, but she's only been gone a few minutes."

"Then put it out she's wanted in connection to a murder investigation."

"And run the risk of the murderer catching wind of it? Hell no." I run the options through my head, but none of them are remotely realistic. "I'll have to go after her."

"And how are you going to do that?"

"Start with the obvious and then go down the list."

"I'll come with you."

I shake my head. "You wait here for her…if she comes back."

"Don't sound so fucking optimistic." Claude skulks toward the door. "She'll be back."

Before I can round on my brother, he's gone. I grab my suit jacket and take one last look around the apartment. There's nothing in this room to tell me where she is. I need to look for her. Time's ticking, and I'm not about to waste it on an optimistic hunch she might come back on her own.

I put a call into the department to issue an APB for the fucker who locked me in the office. That will at least give me a direction. If she's alive, she's with him. And if she's not with him, he'll know exactly where to find her.

Once that's done, I'm out the door. The minute my feet hit the pavement, I pull the notepad out of my jacket pocket. Inside is the address to the apartment Quinn shared with two roommates. It's not a great lead, but it's all I have to work with.

It's fully dark by the time I reach the small apartment building in East Harlem. A lovely old woman on the front step confirms the two roommates are home. I slip in the door behind her and make my way up the dark staircase.

I reach up to straighten my tie, but my hands meet nothing. I must have forgotten to put it back on after Quinn removed it. Shaking the steamy reminder from my brain, I knock on the door.

My body tenses at the sound of footsteps, a muttered curse, and the satisfying click of the deadbolt and tinkle of the chain sliding across the latch.

A pretty blonde answers the door. "Can I help you?"

"Yes. I'm Detective Richards. I'm looking for Quinn Murphy. Does she live here?"

"Did he say he's looking for Quinn?" a voice echoes behind her.

The blonde pushes open the door, and another young woman approaches. Her black hair and complementary eye shadow give her a sullen look that appears out of place with her bright orange top and denim skirt.

"I am. Have you heard from her?"

"I'm Beth," she says with a smirk and gestures to the blonde. "This is Nancy. We haven't heard from Quinn since last week. She left for work but never came home."

"Is she in trouble?" Nancy's gaze drops to the floor before her soft blue eyes meet mine. "She was working at the mansion where that banker got murdered, but she never came home. I'm worried something happened to her."

"No, she's not in trouble." I bite down the frustration rising at the need to keep her two friends in the dark, but I don't want to overplay the importance of Quinn's role in the events of that night. "But I do need to speak with her."

"A detective came asking questions, and we told him the same thing we're telling you." Beth folds her arms across her chest. "The cops haven't found her yet?"

"Not yet, but we're following some leads." My teeth ache from forcing a polite smile. I pull a card from my pocket and hand it to them. "If you hear from Quinn, or know where she might be, please give me a call."

"We will." Nancy takes the card, but Beth snatches it from her hand.

"Her stepbrother's friends have been snooping around. Asking all kinds of questions." She tucks the card into her back pocket. "Been creepy as hell, them hanging out on the front stoop, waiting for her to come home. It's freaking out Mrs. Martinez, but the cops won't do anything."

Her stepbrother. She hadn't mentioned much about her family, except the stepbrother who got her into trouble as a teen.

I curse myself for not pursuing more information on the guy she mentioned in passing. "Do you have a name or an address where I can find him?"

"No idea." She shrugs. "Was there anyone sitting on the step when you came up?"

I shake my head. "Only an old woman I passed coming inside."

"That's Mrs. Martinez, our landlady. She's so sweet." Nancy beams, but I can see worry marring the skin beneath her eyes. She's lost sleep over this whole murder business. But I can't tell them Quinn's safe. Not yet.

"You lucked out. Those bastards are always hanging around at random hours trying to find Quinn."

Nancy drops her gaze once more. It leaves me uneasy. I turn my attention to her.

"Is there something else you want to tell me?"

Her eyes are full of tears. "A man called. He told us Quinn was safe and she would be home soon. He promised."

"When was this?"

"Yesterday."

What the hell? How does that play into what happened today? "Did you recognize the man's voice?"

"No, but the background was busy. Like he was calling from a bar or somewhere."

The pen I'm making notes with slides across the page and my head snaps up. "A bar, you say?"

"Could have been a pay phone, I guess. I can't be sure." She twists her fingers in the hem of her shirt. "But he promised she was safe, and he had a nice voice."

"A nice voice?" My gut twists at the implication of her words. Claude. I tuck the notebook away and nod to them both. "I think I have all I need, ladies. Thank you for your time. Call me if you remember anything else."

The door closes and locks behind me.

I'm halfway down the stairs when the fury ignites into full-blown rage. My brother went against my explicit instructions. I'm sure Quinn sweet-talked him into calling her roommates to let them know she was okay. Now I'm wondering what else they discussed in my absence and who else he contacted on her behalf.

It's not bad enough Quinn is fucking missing with no leads to go on, but now I can't even trust my own brother with a simple task.

I hope to hell she's alive because when I find her, I'm going to wring her pretty neck…along with my brother's.

CHAPTER 18

Quinn

The sting of cold air and the overpowering aroma of raw meat jerk me from blissful darkness.

I wake with a start. Panic chases away the haze of my drug-induced sleep. My mouth is dry. I try to lick my lips, but there's something in my mouth. A piece of fabric pins my tongue down. I choke for want of spit. A gag? What the hell?

When I reach up to remove it, my body refuses to respond. I twist my wrists in the ropes binding them behind me. My feet are tied to the heavy, metal chair beneath me. Fuck!

My head snaps up, taking in my surroundings, searching for something or someone to free me. Cool air drifts around me. A warehouse…no, a meat locker. I eye carcasses hanging against the far wall. It's a gigantic cooler for storing meat.

I shiver, and I can't blame it solely on the cold.

Did the murderer find me? Is he going to torture me for information and then kill me? It'd be easy to dispose of a body from a meat locker.

But he'll probably leave me for someone else to find. The rapid beat of my heart chases the breath from my lungs. I can't breathe.

Desperate for escape, I pull against the bonds, jerking my arms, kicking my feet. It's no use. The knots are tight. Cold air bites my lungs with every sharp inhale. It's hard to breathe with this scrap of cloth jammed in my mouth.

I close my eyes to focus on gaining control. Panic makes it worse. Breathe in. Breathe out.

A soft click echoes through the large room. My eyes snap open and search for the sound.

"She's awake." A voice drifts from the distance, and a warm breeze follows, ghosting over my back and bare arms.

There's another click and the warmth disappears.

A stream of muttered curses rips from my throat, but the words are muffled by the damn gag. I fight against the ropes. It's no use.

My body stills at the gentle brush of fingertips against my neck. I nearly puke at the thought of someone taking liberties with me in such a vulnerable position. They could have done anything they wanted when I was unconscious, but they didn't. I choke back the nausea and jerk away from the touch.

A soft chuckle surrounds me.

Before I can register the sound, they pull at the gag, and the sound of a blade slicing through fabric stops my heart. The gag falls away, and I cough, relief filling me at the loss of pressure against my tongue and jaw.

"What the fuck do you want?" I choke out the words, my voice hoarse and raspy.

"Is that any way to greet your brother?"

He steps into view, and rage fills me.

"*Step*brother." I hiss and lunge forward, pulling against the bonds, making him laugh. The sound sparks a thousand memories, none of them good or comforting. "Why the fuck did you kidnap me?"

"Oh, that. Well, I had to get your attention since you've been avoiding me." He hovers over me like a dictator interrogating an unruly subject. His blue eyes flash with amusement, but the twitch of his mouth belies his impatience. "Apparently, Jack's warning wasn't enough of a reminder."

He's right. I've been avoiding him for months. I should have known he would hunt me down if I didn't comply with his demands for repayment in a timely manner. I had forgotten about Jack's warning on the subway. His lackeys' constant reminders were annoying, but I should have known he'd respond in a dramatic manner if I kept maintaining my distance.

"I haven't been avoiding you." I hold his gaze, hoping he'll buy the lie. "I've run into some problems."

"Problems?"

He leans down and takes my chin in his hand. When I attempt to jerk away from his touch, he grasps it tightly, and I flinch at the painful grip.

"Shacking up with a cop is more than a problem, little sister."

"Stop fucking calling me that," I spit. My defiance dissipates at the smile slowly curving his lips. I should have known they'd be following me. But how did they know I was with Grant?

"Until you repay your debt, I'll call you whatever the fuck I want."

He releases my chin and steps back. "Why are you hiding under the pig's roof?"

Lies won't help me here. I'm at his mercy. Damn him. I don't know how he found me, but he did. And he knows about Grant. *Fuck*. It's a catch-22. I don't have any choices left.

"He's protecting me."

"From what?"

I take a deep breath and exhale slowly. "The place I was gonna hit…there was a complication."

"What kind of complication?" He cocks his head, and a dark curl falls across his forehead. He looks more rock star than mobster, but the effect is paralyzing nonetheless.

"There was a murder."

A sadistic grin splits his lips, revealing perfect white teeth. "Well, well. I didn't think you had it in you."

"I didn't kill anyone, jackass. I was working when the old man was killed." I choke on the next words, barely able to get them out. "I saw him die."

"You're a murder witness?" His left brow rises. "And the good detective is keeping a close eye on you?"

"He's keeping me safe. Yes."

"Is that so?" The wicked smile returns.

Whatever thoughts are churning in Billy's deviant mind don't bode well for me…or for Grant. I know him too well. He'll use whatever means at his disposal to get what he wants. With the criminal ties he has, nothing is off-limits. Murder included.

I tread carefully. The last thing I want to do is make him my enemy. Our agreement is already hanging by a tenuous thread. I'm fucked either way.

Perhaps I can negotiate my way out of this. Somehow.

"What do you want?" I lick my parched lips.

"I want what you owe me." His eyes narrow. "And I want it now."

"I don't have ten grand." Familiar panic creeps in, stealing my breath.

"Perhaps we can make an arrangement then." He shoves his hands in his pockets. "You keep up your little charade with the cop and feed me information."

"He doesn't tell me anything about the cases he's working on."

I can't betray Grant. If I lose his trust, it'll be gone forever. No, there has to be another way.

"Then you can seduce him and get him to trust you. He'll spill his guts if you let him fuck you."

Those words coming out of my stepbrother's mouth make me physically ill. My stomach roils, and if I had eaten anything tonight, it'd be all over his shoes. I might be a thief, but I'm not a snitch. Period. Grant went out of his way to protect me, to give me a chance at success. I can't just throw it in his face to clear my debt.

I shake my head. "I can't do that."

"Then how, exactly, do you propose to repay the debt hanging over your head?"

My mind spins a hundred miles per hour. I fully intended to go legit when I started working at the old man's mansion, but the temptation was always there, the opportunity almost too perfect. But even with the debt hanging over my head, Grant's words remained implanted in my mind. I could go straight. I didn't need to rely on petty theft to cover my debts.

And yet fate intervened, throwing me into yet another shitstorm. Now I have no recourse but to sacrifice whatever fragile bond exists between me and Grant. There are no good options. All of them land me on his shit list.

Maybe I should just turn myself in to the police. Or let my stepbrother take his pound of flesh. If I'm lucky, he'll kill me, putting a stop to this endless cycle of suffering.

"You have no other options, Quinn. Admit it." His voice cuts through the dark thoughts swarming inside my mind.

He checks his watch, and inspiration strikes.

"Wait." My voice echoes off the walls. Too desperate, but fuck it. "I can pay you."

He glances up. "Please enlighten me as to how you're going to pay your debt. In full."

"The detective. He can get me inside the house." Regret boils inside me as the words escape my traitorous mouth. "If I can get him to take me back to the scene, I can get my hands on enough to pay you back."

"Cash?" He strokes his jaw. "I have no patience for fencing stolen jewelry or trinkets. Cash only."

"Yes, cash." My conscience abandons me, leaving me to fend for myself. "Let me go, and I'll have it to you by the end of next week."

His expression pinches, as though he's skeptical. "Why should I trust you?"

"Because you know me." It takes all my effort not to flinch under his scrutiny. “I always pay my debts.”

The seconds stretch into hours.

Finally, he nods. “You have one week to bring me the money.” He traces a finger along my jaw. “If you fail, I’ll take what I’m owed from your body. You’ll belong to me.”

Fear wraps around my heart, constricting it. He’ll sell me off to the highest bidder. I’ll be well and truly fucked. He’ll do it too. There’s nothing he won’t do. Nothing is sacred. Not even our tenuous familial bond. I hate him.

He drops his hand and steps away. “One week, Quinn.”

I sag against the bonds as he retreats behind me. There’s a faint click followed by the murmur of voices.

A sack drops over my head, and the ropes around my hands and feet disappear.

“Any funny business, the boss said I can slit your throat.” A hoarse whisper accompanies the rough grip on my bicep.

I don’t fight him, even though I know he’s bluffing. My stepbrother needs the money, whether it’s cash or my body. He’d be pissed if either opportunity were wasted. I follow the goon’s lead.

The sounds of the shipping yard and traffic reach my ears. We’re still in Hell’s Kitchen, close to the water. They didn’t take me far. I don’t know how the hell they found me, but they did, and it means Grant is in danger now.

If I don’t give him what he wants, he’ll kill Grant and use me for his own financial gain. No matter how this plays out, it doesn’t end well. For anyone.

The goon throws me in a car and gives the driver an address. When we reach the destination, he pulls off the hood and I climb out of the car under my own power.

The neon glow of the bar’s sign lures me closer in the darkness. I turn but the car is gone. Standing in front of the Black Penny, I take a deep breath.

I thought there was something between me and Grant. I hoped there was. But this debt keeps drawing me back to the same old game. I can’t avoid it, but I can’t let them hurt Grant. The choice lies before me like a harrowing specter of death.

There’s no happy ending for someone like me. I should have known better than to try to go legit.

With a deep breath, I round the side of the building and pray the door is open. I can’t bear the thought of anyone seeing me like this. Not

Claude. Especially not Grant.

Fortunately, the door is unlocked, and I climb the stairs, trying to figure out how I'm going to play this.

CHAPTER 19

Grant

I've searched the whole damn city.

Well, realistically, not the whole city, but I've looked in every place I could think of to find Quinn. She vanished without a single clue of where she could have gone.

Thick darkness clings to the streets as I walk home. The bustle of the city surrounding me fades into the background as my mind spins uselessly.

I shouldn't have left her alone. I fucked up.

Over the years, I've gotten really good at kicking myself for doing stupid shit. But I've never held onto regret and let it beat me down the way this does.

I round a corner, and a strangled relief fills me at the sight of the neon sign over the bar entrance. Maybe I should check with Claude to see if he's heard anything. I won't hold my breath that she's come home.

Home?

I rake my fingers through my hair and reach into my pocket for a cigarette. Since when did I start thinking of Quinn making my shitty apartment her home. If she bailed on me, she's not coming back. Simple as that. She's gone for good.

Maybe I should've taken her into the station that night. Let them patch her up and put her in protective custody. Guilt twists my gut at the thought of her in their care. Damn it, why do I even care who watches her?

Because you like her, idiot. I curse the voice in my head. These constant reminders do nothing to fill the void.

Whatever happened between us, she's not going to stick around afterward. Once she's free and clear, she'll leave. And I don't blame her.

Who wants a washed-up homicide detective with a sticky, complicated past?

I light the cigarette and take a drag. The smoke soothes my nerves, but it doesn't solve my problem. I fucked up. It was my job to protect her, and I failed miserably. Some fucking cop I am.

I shove the self-loathing aside and open the door. The familiar setting offers some form of comfort, but knowing Quinn isn't upstairs waiting for me hurts like a punch to the kidney. I shake the thoughts free. There's nothing I can do to track her down until morning. Tonight, I fully intend to drown myself in a bottle of whiskey.

I weave through the crowd, ignoring the boisterous conversations and overdressed idiots. Claude appears behind the bar. The moment he catches sight of me, he nods toward the back room. Following his lead, I duck around a pair of women dancing to *The Power of Love* and slip past the bathrooms into the narrow hallway.

Claude's leaning against the doorframe when I reach his office. "Find her?"

Defeat reclaims my soul. "No."

"Did you find out anything?" His typical casual stance seems tense. I guess he's still shaken up about the whole incident, worried about Quinn. Then I remember the little detail her pretty blonde roommate shared with me before I left.

"Spoke to her roommates." I narrow my gaze and cross my arms. "They weren't too worried about Quinn since they got a call letting them know she was safe." I arch a brow. "Wouldn't happen to know anything about that, would you?"

Claude straightens. "Quinn asked me to let them know she was okay. I didn't tell them where she was or who she was with. She didn't want them to worry."

My irritation fades. "I know you meant well, but anyone could have been listening, watching."

"Goes for you too." He pins me with a harsh stare. "Everyone knows you're on this case. Maybe the killer had someone here, watching, waiting for *you* to lead them straight to Quinn."

Fuck. He has a point. Maybe keeping the sole witness to this case in my apartment wasn't the wisest decision. But damn it, they'd find her regardless. My conscience argues with me, this is the very reason we have a protocol in place for witnesses. I slam the door on those thoughts. They don't do me any good now.

"There's been a lot of new faces in the bar lately." Claude steps closer, keeping his voice low. "Most look like rich yuppies wanting to slum for a good time, but there's been a few who don't look too trustworthy. I've even seen a few of Donovan's crew hanging around."

"Donovan?" My teeth grind. "I told that bastard to keep his

criminal cronies away from this place. There are plenty of other places for him and his boys to conduct shady business."

"The mob doesn't listen to reason. You know that."

"Well, I'll have to give him a reminder."

"Good luck with that. I'll let you know if they cause any trouble."

"Okay. Anything else?"

Claude's stoic expression slips, and I recognize the concern in his dark eyes. "Find her. She's a good kid. She doesn't deserve any of this."

"I'll do my best." With a heavy sigh, I clap my hand on his shoulder.

Words are useless. We both miss her, but he's always had a softer touch than me. Has a way with those who are broken and need a friend. Quinn and my brother formed a friendship of sorts, and her disappearance has him on edge. He's not the only one.

The hinges on the door at the end of the hall creak. Claude and I take a few steps toward the sound, unsure of who it could be.

A tumble of auburn curls and curves appears in the doorway, gently easing the door closed behind her.

"Quinn?" Claude asks, his voice bursting with relief.

My heart seizes. "What the hell?"

She spins around, those wide green eyes rimmed red, highlighted with dark circles.

But damn it if she isn't the most gorgeous thing I've ever seen.

Claude and I rush toward her. Before either of us reaches her, she holds her hands up.

"It's okay. I'm fine. See?" She spins around. "Nothing to worry about."

Claude stops, allowing me to reach for her. I take her chin in my hand and inspect her face. Aside from exhaustion, she looks fine, no fresh cuts or bruises.

"Where the hell were you?" I drop my hands, unable to bear the temptation of her soft skin beneath my fingertips.

"I went out." She shrugs like that explains it.

"You went…out?" I deadpan. "You just decided to take a walk and not tell anyone where you went or when you'd be back?"

"Yeah." She blinks up at me with a defiance unmatched by anyone in the city. "It's still a free country."

Whatever remains of my patience completely evaporates. Ignoring my brother, I grab Quinn by the arm and drag her up the stairs to my apartment.

"Glad you're safe!" Claude's voice drifts up behind us.

By the time we reach my floor, my blood is pulsing hot in my veins. I jerk the door open and shove her inside. She whips around, glaring at me, a wildcat with claws drawn.

"What the hell was that about?" She wears her displeasure like a crown.

"You're not leaving this apartment again until you tell me where the hell you disappeared to."

She sniffs. "I told you. I went out."

"Stop fucking lying to me, Quinn." I close the gap between us, and she pulls back, holding her ground, searching me with uncertainty in her eyes. "Why would you walk out when you knew I would be right back to finish what we started?"

Heat burns through me at the memory of her sweet release on my tongue. I want her more now than I did before.

But I'm furious. I won't give that lust any attention until she comes clean with me. I'm sick of the lies and the subterfuge.

She either tells me the truth or it's over.

Lips parted, she stares at me. Each breath draws her shirt tight against her chest. I ignore the ache in my balls at the temptation before me. She knows exactly what I'm talking about. Her pupils grow wider, consuming the green of her irises. Her tongue darts out to lick her lips. I'm at my fucking breaking point but manage to hold on to a few threads of self-control.

"Tell me the truth or I take you in tomorrow morning." My hands clench into fists by my side. "I spent hours searching the city for you. I thought…" The words lodge in my throat, but I push past the emotion and choke them out. "I thought he came for you. I thought the murderer found you and carried you off to do God knows what to you."

"I'm fine, Grant. I promise." Her voice is soft, but she's still holding back, like she doesn't want me to know the truth about why she left.

"He could have seen you…taken you." I close the tiny gap between us, bringing the tips of our shoes together. "You can't be so careless."

The delicate scent of her drifts around me, pulling me back to the memories of earlier on the sofa. I want to dive back into that moment so much it hurts. But it's gone, like a leaf on the ebbing tide.

Her gaze finally drops. "I'm sorry. I didn't mean to scare you. There was something important I needed to take care of. No one saw me, I promise."

"You don't know that." I tip her chin up until I'm lost in her eyes once more. "This isn't a game, Quinn. He's out there, and if you give him the opportunity, he'll finish what he started."

"I know." A thin coat of tears appears. "I won't do it again."

"I need more than your word."

"I promise." She rises up on her tiptoes and presses a soft kiss to my lips.

The sweet gesture releases a beast inside of me. I take her in my arms and deepen the kiss, tasting what I thought I had lost forever. She melts against me. I take what she offers, the slow, teasing slide of her tongue against mine. This woman, infuriating as she is, unsteadies me. I'm drunk on her, unwilling to function without her intoxicating presence.

She gently eases away, breaking the kiss. "I'm sorry."

"It's okay." I reluctantly release her and withdraw.

Her hand catches mine. "Will you stay with me tonight?"

"If you want me to."

"I do." Her smile widens. With a teasing kiss, she turns and disappears into the bedroom.

I retrieve the bottle of whiskey from the cabinet. Barely enough for one shot. My cock can't continue to take this torment. Somehow, I manage to keep myself from barging into the bathroom and instead retreat to the bar downstairs to get another bottle from Claude's stash in the office.

On the floor, I find a small piece of metal lodged against the door jam. I pick it up. A St. Jude pendant on a thin chain. Strange. Neither Claude nor I carry St. Jude. I wait for Claude to finish behind the bar, then ask him about it. He's adamant he's never seen it before. I tuck it into my pocket and return upstairs with my bottle of whiskey and a persistent hard-on.

Inside, the apartment is silent. I peek into the bedroom and find Quinn passed out on the bed. Fuck.

I pour a double, take a long, hot bath, and crawl into bed behind her. My mattress feels strange after so many nights on the sofa, but it's even stranger to have her in bed with me. The moment I settle on the mattress, she rolls over and nestles against me, throwing her thigh over mine. The oversized shirt she's wearing rides high enough to give me a glimpse of her creamy ass.

I must be a goddamned saint because I drift off without acting on the impure thoughts in my mind. A thousand unanswered questions haunt my dreams.

CHAPTER 20

Quinn

My conscience is killing me.

Guilt weighs on my head, pulling me closer to confession. When Grant left last night, I seized my opportunity. After a hasty shower, I crawled into bed and pretended to be asleep.

The prickling unease of my actions made me restless. It took all my effort to ignore Grant's warm presence when he lay down next to me. I rolled toward him, aware of the magnetism of his body beside mine. Even though my conscience wouldn't let me rest, I found a little peace wrapped up in him.

Sunlight streams through the window, and I don't have the heart to move and wake him. His arm is draped over my torso, my hair pinned beneath his shoulder, our legs entwined. One slow rock of my hips would bring my aching pussy flush against his thigh. The pressure would be enough, but there's no way I could take my pleasure without him knowing.

It doesn't matter. We can't do this.

Billy made himself perfectly clear. If I don't get the money to pay him back, he'll kill Grant and sell me to the highest bidder. I've seen him do far worse for far less.

Somehow, I need to convince Grant to take me back to the mansion. The key to my freedom is there, just out of sight. I heard them arguing one night, the old man and his son. He retreated to his room and returned with a wad of cash. His son left with a bounce in his step. There's money stashed there. I know it.

Grant's soft breath caresses my cheek. I snuggle closer, and his grip tightens around me. The firm press of his cock is insistent against my hip. Tempting as it is, I can't make this more complicated. No matter what happens, Grant will be pissed when he discovers my plan.

The morning light casts a halo around his dark head. In sleep, his expression has softened, and he looks ten years younger. His hair curls over his forehead, hiding the scar above his right eye. He's in desperate need of a shave and a haircut. My heart squeezes at the thought of this man, with his jaded past and gruff bark, holding me like I'm the most precious thing in the world.

No. I have to do this. I can't let Billy hurt him.

With a deep breath and resolution for my plan, I shift against him, slowly peeling myself from his embrace. He clings tighter, his brow furrowing. I kiss his lips softly, and he groans, loosening his hold, only to readjust his grip on me.

His hands draw me closer, the gentle slide of his lips becoming more persistent. I grind my hips against him, allowing myself to indulge in a flicker of pleasure. My thigh rubs against his cock. Grant groans, breaking the kiss.

Those impossibly dark eyes open, fixing on me. "Morning."

"Hi." I wiggle against him, trying to pull away.

He pouts. "Where are you going?"

"Bathroom." Regret fills me when I withdraw from his hold completely.

"Hurry back." Grant stretches, and I'm mesmerized by the bare expanse of his chest. The sheet slips giving me a tantalizing glimpse of the hair disappearing into the waistband of his shorts.

I shake my head and disappear into the bathroom. Once I'm alone, I take care of the most urgent business before facing myself in the mirror. How the hell am I going to convince Grant to take me back? I can't lie to him outright, but if I can convince him to take me there, I can make my move. A splash of water on my face leaves me refreshed, but it doesn't bolster my confidence.

When I open the door, I'm not prepared for the sight that greets me. My body sways, catching against the doorframe.

Grant walks toward me, wearing nothing but a pair of cotton shorts. He's broad and muscular. Where the hell was he hiding those abs? The dusting of hair across his chest creates a vee that disappears beneath the fabric dipping low on his hips. I want to run my fingers over every inch of his chest.

He stops in front of me and grins. "You done gawking?"

I snap my mouth closed and meet his amused gaze. "I'm not gawking. I'm admiring."

"Isn't that the same thing?" He chuckles, and the sound goes through me leaving nothing but need in its wake.

"Not the same." I manage to choke out the words and step aside.

"Thanks." He kisses my forehead before stepping into the

bathroom.

Warmth infuses my cheeks, and I duck out of reach, heading for the living room. "I'll just go make breakfast."

"Thought you'd want to go back to bed," he says, popping his head back into view.

"Don't you have to work today, detective?"

He shrugs. I'm distracted by the motion of his broad shoulders. "Technically, yes."

"Technically?"

"I was planning on going over the files for this case. Don't need to be in the office for that." Grant retreats to the bathroom, leaving the door open.

A perfect opportunity presents itself, and I balk. With a gentle shake of my thoughts, I redirect my brain to my original plan. "About that." I bite my nail. "Do you think you could take me back to the scene of the murder?"

"Why?" he asks from inside the bathroom.

"I was thinking…maybe if I go back, I might remember something. A detail about the killer." I slump against the wall. "I can't keep living in fear of this creep. If it'll help me remember, then we should give it a try, right?"

Silence greets me, and I'm afraid I've overplayed my hand.

"Get dressed. We'll stop for breakfast on the way." The door closes between us.

Relief drowns out the guilt. I can't think about what will happen next. I have to focus on the moment, on stealing that money. I don't know how I'm going to get it past Grant, but I'll cross that bridge *if* I get that far.

With a renewed sense of purpose, I retrieve the clothes Claude gave me. The ripped denim jeans and Van Halen T-shirt aren't my style, but they fit. My body is still humming from Grant's touch, from the residual pleasure of his kiss. I crave more but stomp my desire down into a neat little box to be opened later…possibly never.

Grant reappears as I put on my shoes. I focus on lacing the high-tops as he dresses. My attention slips as he tugs the khakis over his hips. I've never thought of a man dressing as an attractive act, but damn it, Grant has my full attention as he pulls on his dress shirt. He turns as he buttons it.

"Are you sure you want to do this?" he asks, slipping on a pair of shoes.

"Positive." I tuck my hair behind my ears in an attempt to not bite my nails. "I need to do this. Help you solve the case so I can get back to my life."

He scoffs. "Is that really what you want? To go back to living like that?"

His tone stings, and I bristle at the implication of his words. "Like what?"

"You can't *want* to go back to scrimping and scrounging for money to pay your bills? Always being one step away from living on the street."

His observation hurts, but he's right. I ignore the bite of his assessment. "Are you saying I can't go legit?"

"I never said that." He runs his fingers through his hair. "Damn it, Quinn, you know what I mean."

"I do, but I'm capable of taking care of myself." I push past him but come up short when he grabs me by the waist.

"Take it easy, kid. I'm on your side." His voice filters through my hair. I stand strong against the allure of his touch, even though I want to surrender.

"Let's just solve this case and I'll be out of your hair." I twist to free myself from his hold, but he clings tighter.

"And what if I don't want you to go?"

My heart stops. "What did you say?"

He spins me in his arms and tips my chin up until our eyes meet. "Stay with me."

This time, the guilt pierces me straight to my soul. I pinch my eyes closed and sigh. "You don't mean that."

"Look at me, Quinn." He strokes his thumb across my cheek. When I open my eyes, I'm lost in his, a dark, endless sea full of promise and uncertainty. "I mean every word."

A jumbled mess of conflicting emotions chokes me. I blink back tears and swallow a lump in my throat. Grant holds me tight, keeping me upright, and for a moment, I nearly break, nearly spill the truth.

"I've done nothing but cause you problems." My voice cracks. "You don't want me."

"I do." He cups my face in his hands, and my knees wobble.

"You sure this isn't the case talking?" I chuckle, making light of the situation because I can't function any other way. What he offers is exactly what I want, but I can't say the words because I'm going to break his heart regardless.

"The case brought us together, but it's not why I'm asking you to stay."

"I need time to think." I gently push his hands away to put distance between us. "I've been alone so long. I can't…"

"I understand." He nods, his gaze dropping to the floor. "More than you know."

"Grant, I—"

"We should go." He steps away, heading to the door.

Just like that, the moment shatters. I should tell him. Explain. Something.

But I don't do anything except follow him out the door.

Outside in the sunlight, the pain dims, but it still throbs deep in my chest as we walk side by side. Grant needs to solve this case, and I need that money. Maybe we can both get what we want and no one will get hurt.

We stop for bagels and coffee at the corner market. I nibble on mine as we make our way to the station.

I should be happy. Everything is going to plan.

But why do I feel like I've just thrown away my best shot at happiness?

CHAPTER 21

Grant

I'm a fucking idiot.

Silence stretches thin between us as we sit on the subway. Quinn nibbles her bagel, and I drown my misery in black coffee.

What the hell was I thinking asking her to stay? Just yesterday, I couldn't promise anything more than my protection and a few orgasms. Now I'm offering her a place to live and a permanent spot in my life. What changed?

I nearly lost her, that's what. When she disappeared without a word, I knew I couldn't let her go. This scrappy little kitten has burrowed so far under my skin, I can't imagine life without her. It's true I can't promise her anything, but there's no way in hell I can walk away from her either. Not now.

My mission hasn't changed. Protect her. Catch the killer. Solve the case. Simple.

But it's been over a week, and I still have no leads. Taking her to the scene of the crime is risky, especially during the day when we could easily be spotted. The possibility of her reliving those traumatic events is a gamble. But it's one we need to take if I want answers.

All I can do is pray it unlocks something inside her mind. Something that gives us direction. Anything is better than nothing. I'm grasping at straws here, and I'll be damned if this murder gets lumped in with the rest of the cold cases sitting on my desk. If there's anything here, we'll unravel it. I'm certain.

By the time we reach Riverside Drive, my body is humming with anticipation. At least the place will be empty. The Madison family has gone to their home in the Hamptons while the police sort through the details of the case. Our department did a full investigation of the property and found no leads.

When we reach the back door, I unlock it with the key Mickey gave me. Quinn stares at it, her eyes glassy, her lips pressed into a thin line.

"You okay?" I ask, noting the pale flush on her cheeks.

"Yeah. I'm good."

"Sure you want to do this?" I stand between her and the door, offering a chance to back out. She doesn't need to do this if she isn't ready.

Those bewitching green eyes meet mine. "I'm positive. Let's do this."

I push open the door and lift the police tape for her to pass underneath.

Quinn runs her hand over the doorframe and pauses in the entryway. She presses her hand to her stomach and takes a deep, shuddering breath.

"Tell me if you need a break." I rest my hand on her arm.

"Got it." Her hand clenches into a fist, then releases.

"Walk me through what happened."

Step by step, she leads me through the events of that night. From where it began all the way to where he chased her out the front door and into the street.

Seeing her walk through the process leaves me shaken. Fury surges through me at the thought of how close she came to dying that night.

Then she leads me to the master suite.

"I stood here, like this." She assumes a position plastered against the wall outside the bedroom. "I could hear them…the old man shouting. Then I heard him fall to the ground. The scrape of his feet on the hardwood floor. His gasping breaths as he struggled to breathe." Quinn pinches her eyes closed and takes a few measured moments to compose herself.

"You looked into the room?"

"Yes. I saw him standing over the old man, wiping the blood off the knife." She gulps. "So much blood."

"How big was the blade?"

She holds her hands about a foot apart.

I write it down in my notebook and step inside the room. The blood has been cleaned off the floor, but there's still spatter on the baseboards and wallpaper. My gaze skims the room. Nothing out of place or disturbed. The family confirmed nothing was taken from the home.

There must be something I'm missing, a piece I haven't factored into the puzzle, but what is it? How does it fit?

"What are you doing here?" A young man appears in the doorway, his hand resting on the pistol on his hip.

"Whoa there, son. I'm Detective Richards, the lead investigator on the case. I just came back to double-check some things." I open my wallet to reveal my badge.

The man visibly relaxes. "I understand, sir. Would you mind coming with me for a moment? I have something for you downstairs."

"Sure." I turn to Quinn. "You gonna be all right by yourself for a moment?"

Quinn spins away from the window and nods. "I'll be fine."

I follow the young guard down the stairs and into the kitchen. It seems the family retreated to the country quickly and kept the security firm on duty to watch over the estate while the police finished their investigation. Not that I blame them—leaving the house empty could prove disastrous with so many expensive items.

When we reach the kitchen, I note the small area where the guard has taken up his post. "How many guards are on duty?"

"Two of us, sir." He retrieves a bag from the table and hands it to me. "I found this while walking outside the front of the building, behind one of the rose bushes near the neighbor's place."

Turning over the bag, I suck in a breath. It contains a knife the length Quinn described earlier. "How did you find this?"

"Glint of sunlight struck the blade while I was doing my rounds. It was half-buried in dirt."

The murder weapon. Luck smiles on me today.

"I'll take it down to the station and have it dusted for prints. What's your name?"

"Vincent Anderson."

"Good job, son."

He beams at the praise.

I tuck the blade back into the brown grocery bag on the counter. "Let me know if you find anything else."

"Absolutely, sir. Thank you."

I leave young Anderson to his post and return to the master suite. Careful not to make any noise, I pause outside the door, hoping to catch a glimpse of Quinn, staring out the window deep in thought. But she's not there.

There's a shuffling noise inside the bedroom. I rest my hand on the hilt of my .38 and step lightly, keeping my footfalls even. My heart stops when I see her in the wardrobe, bent over, drawer open, three thick wads of cash sticking out of her back pocket.

"What the fuck are you doing?"

She straightens instantly and spins to face me. "It's not what it looks like."

"You're *not* stealing from a dead man?" I close the gap between us and snatch her by the arm, pulling her away from the wardrobe.

"No." She doesn't fight me, but I can see the fear in her eyes.

"Because that's what it looks like."

"I can explain."

"Oh, you'll explain, all right." I holster my gun, grab the cash from her back pocket, and toss it back into the drawer before slamming it closed. "Let's go."

My blood pulses hot beneath my skin. How could I have been such a fool to trust her? I kick myself as I drag her behind me down the stairs and out the back door.

"Are you taking me to the station?" she asks, stumbling, trying to pull away from me.

I tighten my grip. She winces at the pressure. Our eyes lock, and judging by the expression on her face, she knows it's over. All of it.

"Grant?" My name is a plea on her sinful lips, and I flinch at the way it stings.

She says nothing while I flag down a cab and shove her inside. The ride is plagued by tense silence. Quinn twists her hands in her lap, refusing to meet my gaze.

The cab pulls up outside the Black Penny. Her demeanor shifts from uncertainty to hope.

But I'm not done with her yet. Hell, I haven't even started. I toss the cabbie the fare and climb from the car, pulling her with me.

We pass Claude in the hallway. He says nothing when I pin him with a firm glare.

Once we reach the safe confines of my apartment, I place the bag on the table beside the case files and lock the door.

Quinn stands in the center of the apartment awaiting her punishment.

"I'm only going to ask you once." I lean against the counter and cross my arms. "What the hell is going on? Is this a long con? Are you using me to gain access to the loot you couldn't steal the night your accomplice murdered Lionel Madison?"

"What?" She snaps to attention and fervently shakes her head. "No."

"Here's what I think." I pace the floor around her. "I think you decided to get a job that put you in the middle of all that money, and when you found the right moment, your accomplice came to help you steal the cash. But the old man came home and got himself killed. You didn't like that, so he turned on you."

Quinn's stunned expression doesn't shift. "No. That's not what happened. I told you already."

"You lied to me."

"Not about what happened that night."

"So, your suggestion to return to the scene of the crime just happened to put you within reach of a payday? Or was it a calculated plan, you showing up on my doorstep, an injured witness? Digging your claws into me until I relented and followed your suggestion to take you back?" My teeth grind at the possibility of her deception playing out in such a way.

"No, no. No!" She shouts, throwing her hands up. "I told you already. I was trying to go straight. I was in the wrong place at the wrong time. He would have killed me if he caught me. I came to you for help. I had nowhere else to go!" Her passion flares to life, and it's infuriating how sexy she is even when I'm pissed off.

I grab her by both arms. "Then tell me why I just caught you stealing?"

"Because I needed the fucking money."

"Why?"

Her gaze drops to the empty space between us.

"I have an outstanding debt."

"Who?"

"Does it matter?" She tries to pull away, but I hold her in place.

"If it makes you desperate enough to steal from a dead man right under my nose, then yes, it fucking matters." It takes all my effort to soften my tone. Even through the fury, I care about her. Damn it. "Tell me."

"My stepbrother." She pinches her eyes closed.

"Your stepbrother?" I shake my head trying to make sense of what she's saying. What the hell is he holding over her?

"Yeah. Yesterday he summoned me to let me know I had a week to repay the debt I owe him, or…" Her voice trails off.

"Or what?"

"He's going to make me pay it back another way." Her hopeless tone strikes me in the gut. "He's the reason I'm stuck like this."

"Who is your stepbrother?" I growl the words between gritted teeth.

She tugs free of my hold and backs away. "This isn't your fight,

Grant. Please. I can't let you get caught up in this mess."

"What do you mean he's the reason you're stuck like this?"

Quinn collapses on the couch and clutches a pillow to her chest.

"When mom got sick, I couldn't afford her care, not without his help. So I did what he told me to do. I broke free when I was twenty, but he still found ways to hold it over my head." Tears pool at the corner of her eyes, but she brushes them away. "He paid for her hospital bills in exchange for my services. After she died, I thought I was finally free and clear."

"So he sent for you to clear the last of your debt?"

"Yeah."

I cup her chin, forcing her to look at me. "Why didn't you tell me the truth yesterday?"

"Because it's not your responsibility. *I'm* not your responsibility. This is *my* debt." She tenses but doesn't pull away from my touch. "I don't want to put you in danger."

The roller coaster of emotions slows, and I shove aside what remains of my anger.

"You are my responsibility, Quinn." I pull the pillow from her embrace and gather her in my arms, pulling her across my lap. "I want to help you, but I can't do that if you're not honest with me."

She curls against my chest like a content kitten and grips my lapel. "He'll hurt you if I don't pay him. I don't want to lose you."

"You're not going to lose me, baby." I smooth the hair away from her face, and the words settle around my heart, easing the ache. "I promise."

"Did you mean what you said earlier?"

"What was that?"

"When you asked me to stay with you?"

"Of course."

A smile breaks through, brightening her whole face, and I'm caught up in the moment. I cover her lips with mine, chasing away the fear, replacing it with sweet, burning desire.

The torrent of need unleashes, and I'm swept away by the current. I deepen the kiss, determined to drive everything from her mind—her fear, her uncertainty, her pain. I'll keep her safe and show her just how much she's treasured. Loved.

Quinn is mine and I'll be damned if I let anyone take her from me.

CHAPTER 22

Quinn

Finally.

Grant takes control, and I'm more than willing to let him have it. Relief consumes me. I've craved his touch, his kiss. He should be furious with me, should drag me down to the station and have them lock me away.

But he doesn't. He cares too much.

My unexpected honesty stripped away the last resistance between us. He caught me red-handed yet continues to believe there's something beneath my criminal ways. Some good locked inside of me. I can't see it, but he can. That alone binds me to him on a deeper level.

I shift my weight until I'm straddling his thighs. His pants dig into my skin. There's too much fabric between us. My arms encircle his neck, and I lose myself in the moment, drowning in his darkness.

His mouth drifts along my jaw, leaving the burn of his scruff along the sensitive skin. I want to feel it all over my body, the sweet sting caressed by the soft brush of his lips. I crave the delicious pressure of his tongue against my clit.

"Grant, please," I murmur, threading my fingers through his thick hair.

A restrained growl escapes him, and before I can respond, he pushes me to my feet, stands, and lifts me in his arms. I cling to him as he carries me to his bedroom and sets me on my feet.

He wraps my hair in his hand and pulls back, exposing my neck, tipping my face up. His eyes are dark pits full of dangerous promises, and I teeter on the precipice of the void.

"What do you need, baby?"

His question simmers through me, sending a bolt of need straight to my core. I rub my thighs together to quell the ache, but it's useless. The only thing that will end my suffering is him.

Except he'll make me work for it.

"Everything."

"You're going to have to be more specific."

He grins, and there go my panties, ruined by my need for this insufferable man.

"Take off your clothes." I tug at the lapel of his jacket.

His slow striptease is almost cruel. He casually removes his jacket, tossing it on the dresser along the wall. My mouth waters as he unfastens his gun holster from around his torso and peels it off before carefully setting it and the loaded pistol on the dresser with his jacket.

When I reach for the hem of my shirt, he bats my hand away. "No."

"But I—"

"I'll undress you when I'm good and ready." That wicked smolder returns, and my heart flutters at the sensual promises hidden in such a simple expression.

I bite my lip, letting the pain dull the edge of the demanding sexual tension pulsing between us.

Grant holds my gaze as he frees each…little…button from its tiny noose. The flutter of fabric unfolds, baring his chest. I've seen him shirtless, nearly naked, and still, this is the sexiest thing I've ever seen in my life. This slow reveal is torment. I love it.

He unbuttons the cuffs and pulls his shirt off, adding it to the pile. By the time he toes off his shoes and unfastens his belt, I'm vibrating with need. My hands itch to touch him, to explore the bare expanse of skin before me. Never have I wanted someone as much as I want him. He's a buffet of decadent desserts, and I've been deprived of sweets for far too long.

I groan when he removes his last articles of clothing, revealing his thick thighs and impressive cock.

I can't stop my mind from wandering, from wondering how fast I could make him come with my mouth alone. He gives me no time to act on it. He steps closer and takes me by the waist.

"Is this what you wanted?"

"Yes." My voice is hoarse and breathy. I hate how desperate I sound, but I'm too far gone to really care.

Wrapping his hand in my T-shirt, he draws it over my head. My hair tangles in a heavy mess against my back when he pulls it free. His steady hands rest against my waist, and I shiver.

"What's wrong?" His gruff question slides over my bare skin.

"Too slow." I fumble with the button on my jeans.

He chuckles and brushes my hands aside. With more skill than I thought possible, he manages to tug the denim over my hips and remove it completely, along with my shoes and underwear.

"Still too slow…" My words fade when I look at the man kneeling before me.

"Quinn." The jaded detective holds my gaze and runs his hands along my thighs, up to my hips. "The only words I want to hear from you right now are *more* and *don't stop*."

The breath I'm holding catches on a whimper when he tips me onto the bed. I scramble back, but he's already climbing after me, eyes bright with intent.

He pins me to the bed and captures my lips. Kissing him is effortless and intoxicating, like sipping a fruity cocktail and forgetting how much liquor is in it.

I arch closer, needing him against me, inside me.

Of all the lovers I've had, none has made me feel this way. Like I'm treasured, loved, worshipped. Grant gives me a glimpse of his softer side, and I'm swept away by his attention. It's easy to soak up when I've never had anything like it before.

He explores my mouth, abandoning it to follow his questing fingers. They tease my breasts, smooth over my stomach. They part my thighs, giving him uninhibited access to the place where I ache for him.

The moment his tongue slides against my folds, putting gentle pressure on my clit, I moan. The sound echoes off the bedroom walls.

"More," I beg, uncaring of anything but him. Of us.

Grant licks my pussy until I'm squirming and panting. It's not until I thread my fingers in his hair and pull that he breaks free, lips gleaming in a proud smile.

"If you don't fuck me soon…" I leave the implications to his imagination.

His breath tickles my thigh when he laughs. Without hesitation, he pulls himself up and fits his cock to me. I groan with pure bliss as he slides in.

In a single thrust, he's bound to me. I wrap my legs around him and rock my hips.

It's corny and sentimental, but he fits perfectly. Thick and deep, his cock fills me in ways I never imagined. I could stay like this, wrapped in him, forever. Safe. Warm. Satisfied.

He matches my movements with his own, and I'm swept away by the storm. Pleasure fills me, wave after wave, until I'm lost in him.

"Don't stop," I murmur against his mouth.

Grant pins my wrists to the bed and drives deeper. Our frantic breath mingles as he pushes me harder, milking pleasure from both of us. He doubles his efforts like a man desperate to find absolution. I meet him, match his hunger with my own.

He rolls me onto my stomach, lifting my hips off the bed before filling me again. I'm so close, rocking back against his hips, impaling myself on his cock. He leans over me, his chest slick against my spine, and slides two fingers over my clit.

Pleasure shoots through me as he rubs gentle circles, coaxing my orgasm closer and closer.

"That's it, baby. Come for me." His words ignite the flame.

"Fuck." I choke out the word as my climax takes hold. It rips through me, and I collapse against the bed, boneless and weak as it pulses through me.

Grant grabs my hips and takes his own pleasure. His soft groan cuts through my sated haze. He smooths his hands over my ass and gently lowers me to the bed. My thighs are slick with our release, but he pulls me against him, holding me close.

After a few moments, he strokes my arm. "You okay?"

"Never better." I roll over and face him. "You?"

"I might have injured my hip."

"What?" I jerk back. "Which one?"

He laughs, and the sound infuriates me. He's teasing.

I shove him and pout. "Don't do that."

"Don't do what?"

"Joke about your age by faking injuries."

"I mean, my hip is pretty sore." He rubs it. "Maybe you should take it easy on me next time."

"Stop it. You're not old."

"You're right." He takes my hand and kisses my fingertips. "I don't feel *old* when I'm with you. I feel ancient."

"That's it." I scoot to the edge of the bed.

"Where are you going?" He reaches for me, but I slide from the bed.

"To shower."

"Good. I thought you were leaving." He flops down on the bed and tucks his arm beneath his head. "I was worried I'd have to chase you down again."

"Keep talking that way, and you'll never find me if I do leave."

"Okay, I'm sorry." Grant pats the bed beside him. "Don't go yet."

I climb back onto the bed, and he pulls me down on top of him.

"What are you doing?"

"Making love to you again." He kisses me, and I melt into his embrace.

"Already? We have all night. You're gonna wear yourself out."

He pulls back with a scowl. "Now who's taking jabs at my age."

"I'm not..." Exasperated, I bury my face against his chest. "You're infuriating, you know that?"

"I know. My mother always said I was a lost cause."

"You should wear a St. Jude medal."

"I would, but I'm not Catholic." He frowns. "Not anymore, at least."

"Doesn't matter. My stepbrother wears one, and he's not Catholic anymore either." I chuckle. "In fact, Eddie, my fence, might be the only Catholic I know who wears that medal. Like it does him any good."

"Eddie Fink?"

I nod. "He's not the sharpest tool in the shed, but he keeps his mouth shut."

Grant nods, deep in thought. He turns to me with a smile. "Why don't you go take a shower? I'll order us some food."

"Good, I'm starving." I kiss him once more, savoring the heat of him before abandoning the bed.

A long, hot shower soothes my sore body, but I'm already aching to join Grant for round two. After I dry off and pull on some underwear and one of his dress shirts, I sneak into the living room.

There's a large pizza sitting on the counter. I grab a slice and join Grant at the table. He's munching on the crust, reading through some documents.

"What's this?" I run my fingers over the pages splayed across the table.

"Some cases I've been working on." He pulls a file free. "Do you keep track of the places you've hit?"

Shame burns through me. I almost forgot he's a detective and I'm a petty thief. "Yeah, in my head. Don't need that shit coming back to haunt me."

"Do any of these addresses look familiar?" He pushes a piece of paper toward me.

The addresses on the list are scattered across the five boroughs, but I know them all. Dread fills me.

Grant meets my gaze and holds it. "You recognize them, don't you?"

"They're all places I've hit." I swallow the lump of dough in my throat. "Why?"

"These are locations of unsolved murders in the past two years."

"Holy shit." My half-eaten slice of pizza falls to the floor. "You don't think I had anything to do with this, do you? They were all alive when I stole from them. I swear."

"I don't think you had anything to do with these murders, Quinn." He sighs. "But I think you know who did."

"That's impossible. I have no idea who would do something like that."

My mind spins with possibilities. Nothing makes sense.

"I think you do, and you're going to help me solve these cases."

I still don't know how I can do that, but Grant pulls me into his lap and cups my cheek. His tender touch soothes the riot inside of me.

"I'm with you, Quinn, to the end. Do you trust me?"

Without hesitation, I nod.

"Good girl. Tomorrow, we'll go down to the station and get started." His words send a jolt of fear through me.

"What about my stepbrother? The money? He knows where I am, who I'm with."

"Let me worry about that, kid. I've got a plan."

The unease dissipates, but his words don't chase the fear from my mind. Grant kisses me until the thoughts vanish and then takes me to bed again.

I'm safe with him. He cares about me. I trust him.

So why does it feel like shit is about to hit the fan?

CHAPTER 23

Grant

After an adventurous night in bed and a few hours of sleep, I'm ready to take on the day. Waking with Quinn draped across me definitely improves my mood.

As we make our way to the station, I can sense her agitation boiling to the surface. She bites her nails, and I take her hand. The brown bag containing the murder weapon is clenched in my fist. I should have delivered it yesterday, but I was too distracted to leave Quinn alone in the apartment after everything that happened.

Her comment about the St. Jude medal led me down this rabbit hole, and I'm positive she knows the killer. All this time, I've been searching for a connection between these murders, and *she* has been the piece connecting them.

Before I can let her in on my plan, I need to clear it with the captain. With his stamp of approval, I can make this work. Otherwise, I'm setting myself up for failure.

Quinn pauses at the base of the stone steps leading into the station. "You sure about this? Taking me with you?"

"I'm not leaving you alone. Trust me." I squeeze her hand.

"Okay."

Having her by my side bolsters my confidence and my certainty. We climb the steps together.

The commotion inside the station doesn't bother me—I'm used to it—but Quinn is struck by the noise and movement. She moves closer to me, clinging to my arm. I walk through the lobby and take the stairs to the third floor.

Mickey stands when he sees me, his curious gaze shifting to Quinn. The rest of the room goes silent at the sight of the woman with me.

"Hey, Richards." Mickey steps closer, his voice low. "Who's the girl?"

"This is Quinn." I hold her hand tight, stroking my thumb over hers in comfort. She relaxes beside me. My attention refocuses on Mickey.

"Is the captain in?"

"Yeah, why?"

"I need to talk to him." I turn to Quinn and guide her to my chair and place the brown paper bag on my desk. "Sit here. I'll be right back."

"You're gonna leave me here?" she hisses under her breath.

"You'll be fine. Mickey will keep an eye on you." I glance at my partner, whose mouth is gaping. "It'll only take a minute."

"Fine." A defiant pout settles on her lips. Lips I remember crying out with pleasure as I…

Nope, not going to chase that thought right now. I have work to do. *We* have work to do.

I lean forward and kiss her forehead. Mickey chokes on his coffee. With a stern look promising retribution should he make a comment, I leave Quinn in his care. The rest of the detectives pivot in their chairs as I pass, blatant curiosity etched on their faces. I don't owe them an explanation.

At the end of the hallway, I pause outside the captain's office. With a deep breath, I knock, then wait for his summons.

"Richards," he says with surprise as I walk in. "Do you have an update on the case?"

"Yes, sir, I do."

He arches a bushy brow. "Well, are you going to brief me on it?"

"Not yet, sir." I stand firm. My gamble is risky, but I need him to trust me. "But I have a firm lead, and I'd like to make a request."

"Have you *solved* the case, Richards?" He slowly rises and rounds the desk, stuffing a half-burned cigar between his lips.

"I'm close." I lick my lips, knowing he's not going to like my next statement. "I believe I can solve not only the Riverside Drive murder but a handful of cold cases across the city."

Both of the captain's overgrown brows rise into his nonexistent hairline. "Bold declaration, Richards." He scoffs. "What makes you so certain?"

"I have a witness who has a connection to each location, sir." My gut tightens at the thought of naming Quinn, but there's no circumventing it. "I believe she's the key to finding the murderer."

"A witness." The captain rubs his jaw, his eyes narrowed. "I'm listening."

"Give me twenty-four hours, and I'll have the killer in custody."

The captain's guffaw echoes off the wood panels in his office. I straighten, standing my ground.

"You've got balls, Richards. I'll give you that." He stubs out the cigar and leans against the desk. "This witness of yours. Is she here?"

"Yes, sir. She's waiting with Mickey."

He regards me silently for a long moment. "All right, Richards. You have twenty-four hours to bring me a suspect."

My apprehension deflates, and I breathe with relief. "You won't be disappointed, sir."

"Whatever resources you need, take them. I want this case solved."

"Yes, sir. Thank you."

I shake his hand and take my leave. The moment I step into the hallway, my pace quickens. We have twenty-four hours to solve this, and I need to get my plan into action.

Quinn glances up from where she's sitting at my desk, setting aside her coffee mug when I appear. "Done already?"

"Yeah." I keep my responses measured to keep the gossip down. "Thanks, Mickey."

"No problem." He stuffs his hands in his pockets. "So, what's the story?"

"Walk with me." I pick up the brown bag and take Quinn by the hand.

"Where'd you find a woman to put up with your shit, Richards?" Jameson calls out with a laugh.

"At least I have a woman," I snap back. "Your cat doesn't count."

A ripple of laughter filters through the office as we retreat, leaving my fellow detectives in the dark. Once we're clear of the crowd, I direct Mickey and Quinn into an alcove near the window.

"What the hell is going on?" Mickey spins to face me.

"Remember that maid we couldn't find?"

"Yeah." His gaze drifts to Quinn, and his eyes widen. "You?"

Quinn nods.

"She saw the whole thing. Murderer came after her."

"How the hell did you find her?"

"She showed up bleeding on my doorstep."

Mickey scoffs. "Bullshit."

"She's been staying with me while I work the case."

"And you didn't think to tell your partner you found a witness to the biggest murder case of the decade?" Mickey scowls, and guilt jabs me at the reminder. "You sent me on a wild goose chase to interview her roommates."

"I couldn't tell anyone, not until I got more information."

"And?"

I hand him the brown paper bag. "Here's your murder weapon."

"What?" He snatches the bag and opens it. "Son of a bitch, Richards, where did you get this?"

"Went to the house on Riverside Drive yesterday. The security guard there found it buried under the rose bushes by the neighbor's place."

"Why didn't you call me right away?"

I glance at Quinn, whose face turns pink. She drops her gaze. When I face Mickey again, he nods knowingly.

"You're lucky I trust you." He closes the bag and clutches it in his fist. "What's the plan?"

"I'm working on it," I admit with a sigh. "Can you meet me at the Black Penny at six?"

"Yeah, why?"

"I'll explain later. Bring a dozen officers in plain clothes. Armed and ready for a fight."

Mickey's lip twitches. "We going to war?"

"Not if I can help it, but it's best to be prepared." Quinn grips my hand tighter, and I lace her fingers with mine. "We're ending this tonight, kid."

She gives me a shaky nod and a halfhearted smile.

"Tonight then." Mikey leaves, taking the evidence with him.

But the witness stays by my side.

"Do you have a plan?" she asks when we step outside.

"Kinda." I keep my voice low. "Can you contact your stepbrother? And Eddie? Anyone you've worked with who would have known your movements over the past year?"

"Yeah, why?"

"I want you to send them all an invitation to the Black Penny, tonight at nine."

"You want me to invite my stepbrother?" Her voice cracks.

"If he wants his money, yes."

"Grant…there's something you need to know."

"What?" I stop and pull her under the shade of a tree, out of the path of pedestrians.

"My stepbrother isn't just some street thug." She fidgets and takes a deep breath. "He's Billy Donovan."

The revelation pierces my confidence, and I grit my teeth. *Of course, he is.*

Billy Donovan, head of the most notorious Irish mob family in Hell's Kitchen. Shit, in the whole city. Goddamn it.

I should have known when she disappeared and came back shaken. This isn't some little family spat over money. He's fucking serious. Quinn owes him a debt, and he won't be satisfied until it's paid.

"That complicates things." I run my hand over my face. "Doesn't matter. Call him. This ends tonight, one way or another."

"He'll kill you, Grant."

"I'm more worried about you, kid."

"He won't kill me. I'm worth too much alive." Her sad smile stabs me in the heart.

I pull her into my arms. She smells like sunshine and flowers. Memories fill my mind, of us together, wrapped in each other, fucking until we're limp with exhaustion. No, this isn't over. Quinn is mine, and I want every moment with her. I'll protect her with everything I am.

"Come on, kid. We've got some calls to make." I kiss her softly, wiping away the sadness, replacing it with need.

The Black Penny is closed on Mondays. Tonight, Claude is going to make an exception for a special, invitation-only party.

Let's just hope this one doesn't end in fireworks…or death.

Whatever chaos ensues, I'm ready. Quinn deserves a second chance. I do too.

This isn't over, but I'm going to make damn sure her debt is paid in full, even if I have to take out every bastard who ever hurt her.

CHAPTER 24

Quinn

Whatever Grant is planning, he's not letting me in on all of it. That makes me nervous.

It's bad enough he wants me to extend an invitation to my stepbrother, but to summon everyone who knows what I've done and the places I've hit? That's practically begging for trouble.

I sit at the bar and stare at the phone in front of me. Grant is talking with his brother in the office. He's giving me time to make the calls, but I haven't yet worked up the courage.

Grant told me to use whatever tactic needed to get these assholes to show their ugly faces. Whatever his plan is, I don't think it'll work. Getting all of these men in one place is a recipe for disaster. I don't want any part of it. But if Grant thinks I'm letting him face Billy and his goons alone, then he's out of his mind.

Claude emerges from the back room and smiles. The tension in my body eases. He grabs a shot glass and pours a whiskey.

"Here, a little liquid courage will help." He places the drink on the bar next to the phone.

"Thanks, Claude." I down the shot and push the glass back to him.

He's right. The burn of the alcohol dims to a warm embrace and takes the edge off. It's not a solution to my problem, but it numbs the sharp edge of the blade I'm leaning against.

That sharp blade being Billy.

"Where's Grant?" I search the room, but it's just the two of us in the empty bar.

"Making some last-minute calls from the office." He cleans the shot glass and puts it away. "He'll be out in a few."

"Fine. Let's get this over with." I pick up the phone and dial the first number.

"Who's this?" Eddie doesn't even bother with a greeting.

"It's Quinn. You busy tonight?"

"I might be. What's the merch?"

"No merch, a business opportunity."

"What's the plan?"

"Come to the Black Penny in Hell's Kitchen. Nine o'clock. I'll fill you in on the plan when you get there." My voice holds steady. I missed my calling as an actress. This performance would put Meryl Streep to shame.

"What's the payout?" Eddie doesn't sound convinced.

"I can't talk numbers over the phone, but it's big, Eddie. Like *you don't want to miss this opportunity* big."

Silence descends on the line, and I'm afraid I'll hear a dial tone any second.

"I'll be there."

"Good." I hang up, and my body sags against the bar with relief.

"One down?" Claude asks.

"One down."

I pick up the phone again and dial Billy's number. My heart beats faster with every ring.

What if he's not there?

Three.

What if he tells me no?

Four.

Everything in me screams to hang up the phone.

Click.

"Deliveries." The stern voice on the other end of the line sounds irritated at my intrusion.

"It's Quinn. I need to talk to him." A tremor sneaks into my tone, and I chase it away. I can't show weakness. Not now.

"About what? He's busy."

The confidence from the whiskey falters, and I stumble, hitching in a breath. I shove aside whatever uncertainty remains and steel my voice. "Tell him if he wants his fucking money, he needs to talk to me. Now."

"Hold on." The line goes quiet, but I can dimly hear the distant shouts echoing through the room on the other end.

Drumming my fingers on the bar, I wait anxiously. A few tense seconds pass. Claude watches me from the corner of his eye, his face etched with concern. I offer a hesitant smile, which he returns.

I'm still not confident this plan of Grant's will work, but I have to hope he knows what the hell he's doing.

"Quinn." Billy's deep, silken voice drifts over me like an oil slick, leaving me feeling absolutely filthy. "I hope you have my money."

"I have what you requested." I grit my teeth to keep from telling him to go to hell.

"Where is it?"

"Come to the Black Penny at nine and you can have it."

He clicks his tongue in irritation. "You don't get to make demands, dear sister."

"I am not your sister." The vehement declaration comes out in a hiss. "If you want it, then you'll come get it at nine."

I hold my breath. This whole thing could go sideways if I say too much. Billy knows me too well. He taught me how to lie, how to steal. There's nothing about me he doesn't know. I'm an open fucking book, and he's read every line.

"Very well. I'll see you at nine." *Click.*

My breath whooshes out of my lungs when he disconnects the call.

"Good news?" Claude places another shot in front of me.

"Yup." I down it and grimace at the strong flavor. "I probably shouldn't drink any more. I need to be sober when they show up."

"You won't be here when they show up."

I stiffen at Grant's declaration and spin around to face him. "What do you mean I *won't be here*?"

"I'm not putting you in the middle of this, kid."

"Damn it, Grant. I *am* in the middle of this. I'm the reason for this whole fucked-up mess." I throw my hands in the air and slide off the bar stool.

Claude's lips press into a thin line. He says nothing as he wipes down the already clean bar. When I turn, Grant's at my elbow, looking one hundred percent like the gruff, no-bullshit cop from the night we met.

This time, though, I have an advantage. I know he cares about me.

"You were in the wrong place at the wrong time. I'm not putting you in harm's way tonight."

"No, but you'll put yourself and your brother in danger, right?" I prop my hands on my hips, wishing I were taller so I could face him eye to eye. As we stand, I feel like a kid who's being told it's not safe to go out after dark.

"I can't protect you properly if things go wrong." He growls when I crowd his space.

"I've told you before, Billy isn't going to hurt me. At least not physically." I jab him in the chest. "These are *my* people. They know me. If they come for anyone, it's going to be you and Claude."

"We can take care of ourselves." Grant's scowl deepens. "I've got backup waiting in the wings, and I have a plan."

"Let me guess." I tap my chin. "I'm not part of that plan."

"No. You're going to stay upstairs, out of sight, until I come get you."

"The hell I am!" I glower at him. "I told them I would be here. The moment they walk in and I'm not here, they're going to know something's up."

"Fuck." Grant glances up at his brother, who nods in agreement with me.

"She has a point," Claude says with a shrug.

I hazard a smirk at the small victory. "Just give me a pistol. I can take care of myself."

"Listen to me, Quinn." Grant grips my shoulders, forcing me to meet his gaze. "I won't let you make yourself a target tonight."

"I'm not asking to be a target. I want to help you." My hands clench into fists.

"You can help me by staying upstairs."

"No."

Grant swears under his breath and rakes his fingers through his hair, tugging on the ends.

"Tell me your plan," I say.

"My plan is to uncover a serial killer." His tone borders on exasperated.

"Serial killer?" The realization hits me, and I step back. "Are you telling me someone I invited here tonight *killed* all those people?" I swallow the lump in my throat.

"Yes, and I plan on unmasking them. Once they reveal themselves, Mickey and the rest of the undercover officers will arrest him."

"They tried to kill me."

"That's right." He nods with relief when I finally understand the severity of the situation. "And they're going to take the first opportunity to finish what they started."

"But I don't know who it is! It could be any of them." Panic grabs me by the heart and squeezes.

"Exactly. And they're counting on the fact that you trust them."

"Damn it." I shake my head. "It can't be Billy. He had the perfect opportunity to kill me and didn't."

"I don't think it's him. It may be one of his men." Grant takes my hand and holds it steady, tugging me closer. "When I went to your apartment the other day, your roommates said there were men hanging around outside. I think they've been waiting for you. Searching for a moment to finish it. I won't give them the chance."

"Surely, they wouldn't do it in front of everyone...would they?"

"I honestly don't know, but I'm not willing to take that chance. Are you?"

"No." I bite my lip. "But if I'm not here when they show up, they're going to leave."

Grant and Claude exchange a long look.

"She can stand behind the bar, take cover if shit goes sideways." Claude rubs his jaw. "Pap's gun is right here if she needs it."

"I don't like this. Not one bit." Grant sighs.

"I can take care of myself."

"I know, kid." His lopsided smile makes my heart pound. "Okay, let's run through this before Mickey comes with reinforcements."

CHAPTER 25

Grant

My stomach sours when I glance at my watch. Quarter to nine. The point of no return.

Everyone is in position. Mickey and the rest of the undercover officers are positioned around the building, covering every entrance and exit. There's another unit stationed down the street, waiting for our signal if things go south.

All I can do at this point is hope and pray my half-cooked plan goes smoothly.

I sit at the bar, waiting, watching the front door out of the corner of my eye. Claude stands behind the bar about three feet from Quinn, who's nervously tapping her fingers on the cooler by her hip.

When they walk in, she'll be the first person they see. That should give them enough courage to come inside, sit down, maybe have a drink on the house. But it's a tenuous peace offering, and they'll know it.

When I took on this case, I hadn't anticipated facing down Billy Donovan and his gang of thugs. They're as ruthless as the Italian mob families scattered throughout the city. I don't intend to make enemies tonight, but Donovan doesn't know that. He'll come at me, guns-a-blazing, if he senses I suspect him.

Which I don't. If he wanted to kill Quinn, he would've done so the day he snatched her from my apartment. No. He's a businessman—cutthroat to be sure, but if there's money to be made from something, he's not going to waste his resources. He'll milk them dry, then discard the husk.

No, whoever this sick, twisted bastard is, he likes to keep to the shadows. Judging from the six murders under his belt, he's got an appetite for it. He knows if he makes a show of his work, he'll get caught. Tonight, I get one shot at drawing him out, at unmasking him.

All I can do is play my cards and hope he falls for my bluff. Good thing I'm a shark when it comes to poker.

Quinn fidgets with a towel sitting atop the cooler. My grandfather's revolver is under that rag, within reach should she need it. I warned her if she pulls it, she'd better fucking use it. Never point a gun at someone unless you're ready to do what needs to be done. Or it will be used against you.

"You good?" I ask her, struggling to keep my foot from impatient tapping.

"I'm good." She flashes a quick smile, but I can see the flicker of fear in her eyes. It gives me confidence. A little fear keeps us from doing stupid shit.

My brother leans against the counter. "What about you?"

"I'm fine."

"You look like you're about to explode."

"Not helping, Claude." I glare at him and shift my position to face the entrance.

"Wasn't trying to help. Just making an observation."

"You're too calm right now."

Claude smirks and takes a drink of water. "I spent a year in Vietnam. This is a walk in the park."

The door opens, and a dark figure steps into the bar. He pauses in the shadow of the doorway to take measure of the three of us.

"What's this, then?" The figure points at me and Claude, his hand resting on the doorknob as though he's about to bolt.

"I'll explain, Eddie. Come in. Have a seat." Quinn gestures to the bar. "Want a drink?"

"Nah, I'm good." Eddie removes his hood and steps into the light. His curly hair is longer than when I last saw him. He shoots me a nervous glance before sliding into one of the empty seats farthest away from me. "What are you doing here, Richards?"

"All in due time, Eddie. It's not nine o'clock yet." It takes all my effort to keep my nerves from showing.

Over the past five years, I've had some run-ins with Eddie Fink. He's a low-level punk, dealing in stolen merchandise and a few inside tips if the price is right. I don't trust him…but then again, I don't know him. He lays low, keeps to the shadows, which makes him the perfect suspect. Quinn fences all her stolen merchandise through him, and he's the closest thing she has to a partner. If she trusted him with the location of her hits, my guess is there really is no honor among thieves.

The door opens behind him, and he jumps. I angle myself toward the new arrivals. Quinn tenses and rocks back on her heels. She wants to run, but she won't. Claude shifts a little, taking up position close behind her, like her own personal guard.

A handful of men enter the bar, all dressed in varying degrees of casual black, looking like they're the personal entourage of the president himself. They part like the Red Sea, and Billy Donovan steps inside. His shrewd gaze homes in on Quinn, and a sharp smile splits his lips. My fist clenches by my side.

I've never had the pleasure of meeting Donovan before, but the moment I see him, I pass judgment. He's a fucking dick. Handsome to a fault. Charming without effort. He's a goddamn walking nightmare if the stories I've heard about him are true.

I hate him on principle. He threatened Quinn, and I'll be damned if he has any sway over her ever again.

"Sister." Donovan crosses to the bar where Quinn is standing and takes a stool. He doesn't even acknowledge us. We're nothing to him. He's that fucking confident.

And that gives me an advantage. Cocky fucker.

"Billy." Quinn reaches for a decanter of top shelf whiskey and pours a shot. "On the house." She sets the drink in front of him.

"My thanks." He downs it and exhales with delight. "Excellent vintage."

His men fan out behind him, four on each side. I don't recognize any of them, but judging by the stance, they're bracing for a fight.

Eddie shifts uncomfortably in his seat.

Donovan doesn't even spare him a glance. "You don't have my money, do you, Quinn?"

She shakes her head.

"Then why am I here?"

The door swings open behind them, drawing attention away from Donovan's question.

Another goon enters the bar with bravado. "We're clear, boss."

"Thank you, Jack." Donovan doesn't spare him a glance. His gaze remains fixed on Quinn. It's not a brotherly look of affection. More like a lecher drinking his fill before indulging in his sin of choice.

I want to snap his fucking arms off and rip out his eyes. Instead, I stand and clear my throat.

His men reach for their sidearms in unison. I lift my hands, showing that they're empty and I'm not a threat.

Donovan finally looks at me. "Ah, detective. To what do I owe this honor?"

"I have a proposition. Tell your men to stand down." When he directs his men to lower their weapons, I drop my hands.

"Do you intend to pay off my sister's debt, detective?" He lounges in his chair, comfortable and unruffled by the shift in events.

"No, but I can offer a trade." I step clear of the bar, keeping all of them in view.

He scoffs. "What could you possibly offer me that's worth ten grand?"

"Information."

"I don't need your information, Detective Richards. As you can see, I have my own sources."

"True. You're a resourceful man." It's now or never. "But someone in this room is lying to you."

Donovan arches a brow. "You have my attention. Enlighten me."

"There's a murderer in this room."

He scoffs.

"They've been cutting in on your turf. Stalking Quinn. Murdering those she steals from."

"Has nothing to do with me." He shrugs.

"They came for Quinn," I continue carefully, taking measure of the men before me.

Donovan's eyes darken. "What makes you think it's someone in this room?"

"Because they're the only ones who knew where she would be and when to strike."

"What does this have to do with me?" Donovan throws up his hand.

"Their careless actions could be traced back to you. It'll look like *you* sanctioned these hits. Doesn't matter if you did or not, their shit will drag you to court and air your dirty laundry."

"You have no proof of any of this do you, detective?" He chuckles, and the sound is haunting.

"Actually, I do." I reach into my pocket and withdraw the St. Jude pendant inside a plastic bag. "This was found at the scene of the crime. The lab was able to get a full print off the back. We also located the murder weapon at the scene. It's being tested as we speak."

Donovan's face skews in irritation, his carefree expression replaced by a storm cloud. "What is that?"

"St. Jude, patron saint of lost causes." I tuck the evidence back into my pocket. "If you give me the murderer, I'll cut your connection to the case. We call the debt paid. Do we have a deal?"

His jaw works when he clenches his teeth. Bullseye. "Deal." He turns toward his men. "Show me."

Three of them pull medals from around their necks; the rest shake their heads, indicating they don't wear one. He turns to Eddie.

Eddie pulls a chain from his neck, a medal dangling from the thin chain.

"Fuck." Donovan turns the force of his rage on the man sitting beside him. "What the fuck were you thinking, Jack?"

Jack flinches, then jumps to his feet, drawing his pistol. He levels it at Quinn, and my heart stops.

"Nobody fucking move or the bitch dies. Got it?" He starts to back away, heading for the door.

I take a step toward him.

"Don't fucking tempt me, pig, or I'll put a bullet right between her eyes."

Quinn gasps, stepping closer to the bar, her thigh bumps the cooler blocking her advance. "Don't, Jack. Please."

"Shut the fuck up," he shouts, brandishing his gun. "I almost had you, bitch, but now I'll finish it."

A scream rips from her throat at the same moment Donovan's men rush him. But they're too slow. I bolt forward, ready to knock him to the ground.

He pivots and a shot rings through the bar.

The bullet tears through my flesh. Heat consumes me. I stumble, and a second shot hits my shoulder, knocking me sideways. I collapse, pain ripping through me as I hit the floor.

There's a scuffle and shouts, but they're muffled. Everything moves in slow motion.

I clutch my chest, gasping for breath. The bar fades to muted hues of color. My lungs burn. Warmth floods my hands.

In the distance, I hear shouts and commotion, but the ringing in my ears drowns it out.

Everything goes dark.

CHAPTER 26

Quinn

The world fades into slow motion as Grant hits the floor.

I climb across the bar, knocking over bottles in the process. Blood pools around his body. Shit. Panic pulses through me, stirring up the terror of losing him.

"Grant!" I drop to my knees and gather him in my arms. So much blood. It's everywhere. I turn to Claude who's on the phone.

He hangs up and tosses clean towels to me. "Compress the wound. Help is on the way."

I barely register a scuffle by the door as I press clean rags to the bullet wounds. "Don't you dare die on me," I growl, willing him to breathe, to survive.

The bar explodes with chaos when Mickey and the other officers burst through the door. They must have heard the shots. I let them take care of Billy and his men. Eddie meets my gaze and swears before dropping beside Grant to give me a hand.

"Please, don't die." Tears blur my vision as I brush his hair away from his face, leaving a streak of blood across his cheek. I want to punch him, to demand he can't die. "Please. I love you. You can't leave me." Sobs choke me, but I can't give in to the emotion. Not when there's still a chance. "Live, damn you."

The cops drag the quarreling mobsters from the building in handcuffs. Billy goes without a fight, catching my eye before disappearing from view. I can't worry about him. Not right now.

The scream of a siren outside tells me help has arrived. I whisper a prayer, hoping they're not too late. A team of medics comes in the door and pushes Eddie and me out of the way. Their quick assessment burns in my numb ears. The next thing I know, they have him loaded on a gurney and are rushing back out the door.

"Where are you taking him?" I chase the medics out to the street.

One of the EMTs puts up a hand when I try to climb into the ambulance. "Whoa there."

I repeat myself. "Where are you taking him?"

"Columbia."

The last glimpse I have of Grant is his ashen face with an oxygen mask and three medics hovering over him, keeping pressure on the wounds. Keeping him alive. The door slams shut, and the sirens wail, echoing through the streets as the ambulance speeds off.

Claude comes up beside me. "Come on. I'll take you to the hospital. I've already called Rob; he'll meet us there."

The adrenaline pumps through my veins. I barely remember making it to the emergency room or Claude's soft conversation with the nurses. They hand me some towels to clean the blood from my hands. My shirt is ravaged with red. It's ruined.

I'm ruined.

Without Grant, there's nothing.

And I didn't tell him how much I love him.

The tears fall freely, and I'm buried in my own grief.

Claude speaks with the nurses, the doctors, and another man I vaguely recognize from the night I met Grant.

It all feels like a drug-fueled trip. I can't focus on anything. My heart aches. I just want answers. Certainty.

A coffee cup appears before me, and I take it with numb fingers. "Thanks."

"Of course." Claude sits beside me on the waiting room bench.

I sip the coffee, letting the warmth soothe my hoarse throat.

"He's in surgery."

"Is he going to make it?" I stare into the Styrofoam cup, unable to meet his gaze.

"They don't know." He wraps his arm around my shoulder and pulls me against him. "He's strong, Quinn. All we can do is pray."

His words unleash a fresh torrent of tears. "I can't lose him, Claude. I love him."

"I know, sweetheart." He holds me steady, grounds me. "He knows it too."

Grief settles around us like a storm gathering intensity. The noise and chaos around us fade into the background, and I surrender to the pain. At some point, exhaustion pulls me under, and I fall asleep tucked against Claude.

A gentle nudge wakes me. "Quinn."

Somehow I manage to pry my eyes open. Claude's smiling down at me.

"What's going on?"

"He's stable. The surgery was a success."

I straighten and leap to my feet. "Can I see him?"

He shakes his head. "He's still asleep, and they're not letting any visitors in. We'll come back later."

Disappointment deflates me. "I need to see him."

"You will. Let's go home. You can clean up, and we'll come back in a few hours."

Reluctantly, I nod and follow him from the waiting room.

The apartment feels empty without Grant. Claude stays with me. He makes breakfast while I shower. I manage to eat something and take a nap while he retreats to his apartment to clean up.

Later that afternoon, we return to the hospital. Rob pulls some strings, getting us in to see Grant.

My heart leaps into my throat when I see him lying there, tubes and wires crisscrossing his body. The monitor beeps beside the bed, and I watch the lines moving on the screen with each beat of his heart. His face is pale, but there are small blotches of color. That's a good thing, right?

The nurse leaves Claude and me alone with Grant. He's still unconscious and on oxygen. I hate seeing him in such a state. It breaks me.

I gently take his hand in mine and lean down to kiss his forehead. "I'm here," I whisper against his warm skin. "I love you."

Claude pulls a chair beside the bed, and I sit, keeping vigil over the man who saved my life.

For two weeks, I don't leave his side. Claude brings me food. I make friends with the nurses on rotation, and they keep me updated on his progress and remove the oxygen mask.

But Grant remains asleep through it all. Daily, they remind me that it takes time for the body to heal from such trauma.

I'm reading the Stephen King novel Claude gave me when the beeps change tone. I glance up and find those intoxicating, dark eyes fixed on me. A tired smile accentuates his crow's feet.

"You're awake." I set the book aside and take his hand.

"Quinn." His voice is hoarse from disuse. He coughs, and I get him a cup of water.

"Take your time." I set the cup aside.

"What happened?" he asks, barely above a whisper.

"You got shot. Twice." I grip his hand tight. "I almost lost you."

"I'm still here." He gives me a lopsided smile. "What happened after I got shot?"

"Married to the job." I chuckle. "They arrested Jack. He confessed to all the murders, including Lionel Madison."

Relief smooths the lines on his face at the news. "What about Donovan?"

"They let him go."

"What about your debt?"

"Cleared." I smooth my thumb across his fingers. "It's over."

"Good." He closes his eyes.

The questions burning in my mind for the past two weeks linger on the tip of my tongue. He needs rest, but I need to know. "Grant?"

"Hmm?"

"How did you know?"

"About what?"

"Who the murderer was? How did you figure it out?"

"I didn't." He opens his eyes and grins.

"You didn't know who the murderer was?"

"No. I just knew it was someone who knew you and your habits, someone who followed you." He takes a deep breath. "Donovan kept tabs on you, had his goons tracking your movement. He even had them staking out your apartment."

I shiver with distaste at the thought of them reporting my every move to Billy. "Why?"

"Unhealthy fixation. He wanted you for himself. It was clear as day."

The lunch I ate an hour ago rolls uncomfortably in my stomach. I change the topic. "But the medal?"

"A bluff." He groans with pain when he tries to move. "When you mentioned it, I had a hunch."

"But you found the medal at the mansion."

He shakes his head slowly. "Claude's office the day Donovan took you from my apartment."

"How did you know there was a connection?"

"I didn't. Like I said, it was a hunch. I called their bluff."

"Oh, you brilliant, ridiculous man. I could punch you for putting yourself in such a dangerous situation on a hunch." Exasperated, I slump against the bed and lay my head on the blanket. His fingers thread through my hair.

"It's over. I survived. Case closed."

I lift my head and narrow my eyes at him. "You're lucky I love you."

"I am." His grin widens. "I love you too, kid."

My heart takes flight at those words, and I've never been so fucking happy. "Good, because I'm not leaving. I'm going to harass you for the rest of your life."

"Kid, loving you gives love a bad name, but I wouldn't have it any other way. You're mine, Quinn."

A nurse walks in and joy blooms through the wing. The flurry of activity disrupts our tender reunion, but there's plenty of time for us to talk later.

I'm just happy he's alive. He loves me. I love him. It's about fucking time both of us had something to look forward to.

Even if it means we both have to change careers, it'll be worth it.

Happy endings always are.

CHAPTER 27

Grant

One Year Later

My life would be shit without her. If someone had told me a year ago I would meet the love of my life after detaining her for breaking into my friend's sister's apartment, I would have laughed.

Quinn brought joy back into my life. She saved me.

I watch her toss breadcrumbs to the pigeons and smile. This is one of the routines I've come to love. On Saturday afternoons, we walk through Central Park. Rob recommended it as a good way to rebuild my lung strength after I took that hit last year. Frequent walks in a green space—those are hard to come by in a city of seven million people.

"Want to feed them?" She offers me a small paper bag full of crumbs.

"No. I'm not encouraging the flying rats." I nudge her with my elbow. "Let's walk."

She tosses the rest of the crumbs to the ground, and the birds descend like a flock of vultures circling a fresh kill. Her laughter echoes through the trees.

I'm still smitten with her. Her smile, the way she moves, her sass, her passion. She's everything I didn't realize I wanted and everything I need. I'm lucky to have her by my side, especially after everything went to hell last August.

This week marks a year since the Hitman Killer shot me. Fucking newspapers and their marketing ploys. No one called him that until they caught wind of the story and ran with it. Hopefully, this trend of giving sick, twisted psychos any attention dies out quickly. The victims and their families deserve peace. At least I was able to solve this one, but I still struggle to sleep at night.

"Let's get some ice cream." Her gaze lingers on the bright colors of a Mister Softee truck parked in the distance.

I scoff. "You really are a kid."

"You like ice cream just as much as I do, old man." She winks, and I feel lighter than I have in years.

"You're goddamn right I do." I steer her down a different path, away from the ice cream vendor.

"Then why…" She trails off and pouts. "You're no fun."

"I'm all kinds of fun."

"Sitting around watching daytime TV is not fun, Grant."

"It is when you struggle to breathe."

Her green eyes meet mine. "I'm sorry, I didn't mean to—"

"I'm fine, Quinn. It's been a rough year, but the docs say I'm through the worst of it."

"So glad that's over." She leans against me as we move toward the exit on 67th. "I don't know what I would have done without you."

"I ask myself the same question every day." I press a kiss to her head. "How the fuck did I get so damn lucky?"

"One of life's many mysteries."

We wander down the path and pause at the fountain so I can catch my breath. The department wants me to return to duty next month. I have to prove I'm fit enough to handle the stress, even though I'll be desk jockeying more than working active cases. Even so, it'll be good to be of use again.

I pull Quinn to a stop beside the water. She turns with an easy smile, her auburn curls vibrant in the sunlight. I take her hand in mine.

"Thank you for taking care of me. I know it wasn't easy, but having you beside me gave me a reason to live." I slip my hand into my pocket and pull out the ring that's been burning a hole since we left the apartment. "I can't imagine going forward without you."

She squirms and muffles her excited laughter when I open my palm and show her the ring. "Yes!"

"I haven't even asked you the question yet."

"Doesn't matter. Whatever the question is, the answer is yes."

She holds her hand out and lets me slide the ring on her finger. The opal glimmers in the afternoon sun.

She rises on her toes, wraps her arms around my neck, and kisses me. I melt into her embrace. This is where I want to be, lost in her, drowning in need, happy beyond measure. Every decision in my life has led to this moment, and I've never been more grateful to be a fucked-up, jaded divorcé. All of those miserable moments led me to Quinn.

When we finally break apart, she beams up at me.

"I could have been asking you to be my caretaker for life," I tease.

But she knows this is the kind of asshole I am. And she loves me anyway.

"Doesn't matter. As long as I'm with you, it's enough for me." She takes my arm and steers me back toward the ice cream truck. "Let's celebrate."

I pull her to a stop. "Claude and Gwen are meeting us at the restaurant. We'll be late."

"They know?"

"Of course. Did you really think I'd be able to keep it a secret?" I grin. "Besides, Claude told me he'd put another bullet in me if I didn't make an honest woman of you."

Her mouth drops open. "You sneaky bastard." A grin transforms her shock to pure bliss. "How did you know I'd say yes?"

"You stuck around."

"You sound surprised."

"I am." The path leads us to the busy street, and I pause to flag down a cab. "Divorced, work-obsessed, forty-something detectives aren't high on the eligible bachelor list."

"Those are all good reasons to keep you around." She chuckles when the cab pulls up and I open the door for her. "I think I found the only man in New York who can keep up with me."

My heart warms at her statement. I give the cabbie the address, and once the car merges back into traffic, Quinn leans against me. I wrap my arm around her, protecting her even though she doesn't need it.

We're good for each other, I think. This time I'm excited to see where marriage leads me.

"I love you, kid."

"I love you too, old man."

This looks like the beginning of a beautiful partnership.

PLAYLIST

"I Wanna Dance with Somebody" - Whitney Houston
"Holding Out for a Hero" - Bonnie Tyler
"Here I Go Again" - Whitesnake
"Tainted Love" - Soft Cell
"Owner of a Lonely Heart" - Yes
"Uptown Girl" - Billy Joel
"Need You Tonight" - INXS
"Heartbreaker" - Pat Benatar
"And We Danced" - The Hooters
"Magic" - The Cars
"Lights" - Journey

CHAPTER 1

Claude

Hell's Kitchen NYC, December 1985

I've had my fill of violence. I've had more than my fill of conflict and death, more than most people know. It's left a sour taste in my mouth. As a veteran of an unpopular war, I bear a daily reminder of the impact violence has had on my life, but I've learned to cope with it. Now I'm a pacifist, and I own a bar in Hell's Kitchen. That suits me right down to the ground. I tried joining the police force when I came home, but I didn't make the cut. I guess having lost my hand and the lower part of my arm put me at a disadvantage. Sacrifice always puts you at a disadvantage.

My brother is a homicide detective. A few months ago, he nearly died in the line of duty, which finally pushed me over the edge. I have no intention of putting myself in the midst of a horde of assholes with guns and itchy trigger fingers ever again. My life might not be perfect, but I've worked hard for it. I'm not about to throw it away playing the hero.

The door swings open on a gust of December wind, complete with copious amounts of snow. Such a storm is uncommon this early in the year, but it happens. The new arrival manages to close the door, then whips off the scarf around his head.

"Hey, Tom." I reach for the vodka. He's a regular who orders the same drink every night—a double shot of Russia's finest in a chilled glass.

"Claude." He sidles up to the bar, brushing off the remnants of the storm outside. "Looks like the weathermen were wrong…again."

I feel a lopsided smile on my lips as I set the glass in front of him. "You sure you don't want coffee? I can add some whiskey to spice it up."

Tom crinkles his nose at the mention of the drink. Even though many of my patrons come from hardy Irish stock, there are a few who don't have an ounce of Celtic heritage in their blood. Tom's family came from Russia, and he served in the Navy during the Korean War. After my honorable discharge from the Army, I took over my grandfather's pub, and when Tom stumbled in, our military bond made us fast friends despite a twenty-year age gap.

He taps the glass on the bar and lifts it in salute before downing the contents. Then he tells me about his day.

I soak it in.

This is my life. Service before self. Simple. Unfettered.

Lonely.

I have my faithful patrons and my family, but there's an uneasy distance between life and me. Since the war, I've played it safe, venturing only far enough to ensure the bar is taken care of and my brother stays out of trouble.

But he's not my responsibility anymore. He's got Quinn. She's good for him. They're a match made in chaos. That doesn't surprise me. Grant has always been a magnet for trouble, and Quinn personifies it.

I listen absently as Tom tells me about his adventure to the fish market across town. It's the same every week, but I don't mind indulging an old man his stories. It goes hand in hand with being a bartender. I watch, listen, and serve those who need a drink, an ear, or a smile.

A few more people arrive, coats and heads covered in white. Guess the storm must have picked up. They take a corner booth, and Sam scurries over to take their order.

He brings me the drink order before retreating to the small kitchen. We serve simple fare, burgers and fries, soups—hearty bar food to soak up the alcohol. No one comes here for the food.

The Black Penny is nothing fancy, but she's mine. My grandfather opened the bar before World War II. When dad didn't want to take over, Pap turned to me. I was a broken kid, fresh home from war. I didn't know the first thing about running a business, but he took me under his wing and showed me the ropes. Even without a left hand, I managed to pick it up quickly. Gave me hope I could make something of myself.

When Pap passed, he left me not only the bar but the building. I don't know where I'd be without him. His final request was twofold. Keep the bar in the family. Find a girl to make that happen.

It's been ten years, and I haven't been able to fulfill that promise. No one wants a warworn, one-armed bartender.

I can't say I blame them.

Tom waves me over for a refill. "Hell of a storm out there. Don't usually see these sorts until January."

"That's true." I pour him another round.

The door bursts open. A dark figure stumbles in, snow curling in a tornado around them as they struggle to close the door. Once they succeed, they collapse against it.

A brick drops into my stomach when the new arrival turns toward me.

Wide blue eyes the color of summer skies peer out from beneath long, thick, dark hair tangled with snowflakes. An oversized winter coat encases her whole body, gaping just enough so the sequined fabric beneath could catch the light. She moves like a skittish cat, shying away from light, from people. Then she sees me, and relief fills her delicate features. She rushes to the bar. Tearstained streaks of mascara stream down her cheeks. She leans her trembling hands on the counter, and her gaze darts around the room, searching for an oncoming threat.

"Can I help you, ma'am?" I lean close and keep my voice low in an attempt to soothe her. I'm afraid one quick movement or loud noise will shatter her fragile composure.

Flecks of white cling to her lashes. They flutter as she looks up at me, her eyes bloodshot and rimmed with tear-smudged mascara. "Do…do you have a restroom?" Her voice is low, and I hear a tremor beneath the words.

Her expensive-looking wool coat is open at her throat, exposing the delicate curve of her neck and a fancy gown beneath. My gaze lingers on the white glittering fabric…stained red. *Blood.*

"Yes, in the back." I point to the back of the bar. "Are you okay?" I keep my tone low and steady, but concern laces every word. "Are you bleeding?"

"I'm fine." She clutches the lapels of her coat, pulling the garment closed. "If someone comes looking for me, I'm not here, okay?"

I nod, but before I can press further, she darts to the back of the bar and disappears down the hallway.

I should check on her, make sure she's okay.

Tom pipes up from his nearby perch. "Poor kid looks like she's running from something."

"Yeah." I rub my hand across my jaw and look toward the back of the bar. Judging from her clothes and demeanor, she's not from around here. Probably an uptown girl caught in the wrong neighborhood. High-maintenance, with money burning a hole in her purse. A high-class broad looking for a good time. Not typical for this part of town. Strange.

As I wipe down the bar, the door flies open with another burst of cold air, swirling more snow into the room. Three men step through. The last one closes the door and stands against it, a guard blocking any possible escape. All three reek of power and corruption. Mafia.

The leader steps forward, his face half-covered with a bloodstained rag pressed to his nose. He pulls the cloth away and scans the bar with a sharp eye. The bridge of his nose is crooked, his fair skin bruised and smeared red. A trickle of blood runs down his lips. He wipes it away in irritation.

Perhaps it wasn't her blood after all.

Her plea echoes in my mind. *I'm not here.*

Tom and I exchange a look before he returns his attention to the empty glass before him.

"Can I get you gentlemen a drink?" I lean against the bar to hide the nervous energy pulsing at the base of my skull, warning me nothing good can come from this. From *them.*

The battered leader steps up to the bar. Bloodstained and proud, he looks like a warrior from a bygone era, vengeance in his blue eyes. He wears an expensive, well-tailored suit, but red mars the white dress shirt. He presses the bloody handkerchief back to his bruised nose.

"Did a woman just come in here?" His gaze fixes on me.

"Nope." I lift one shoulder, a halfhearted shrug, as I wipe down the counter.

The man's eyes narrow as if searching me for the truth. "You're sure?"

"Positive." I gesture to the nearly empty bar. "Can I get you a drink?"

A sneer curls the rich asshole's lip. He shoves away from the bar with a growl and motions to his men. "Look around."

Without delay, the two men split up and quickly search the bar. They disappear toward the bathroom.

My heart ices over. There's no way to warn her, to hide her. I maintain my calm and busy myself with small tasks behind the bar.

The bloody bastard swears, wiping more blood from his upper lip. His men reappear and shake their heads.

"She's not here."

"Fuck." Irritation radiates from the single word. "Let's go. The bitch can find her own way home. I'll deal with her then."

Without another word, the three men exit the bar, leaving a chill in their wake. I clench the rag in my fist and command my heart to stop racing.

"You think she went out the back?" Tom asks, his question quiet.

"I don't know." Tossing the towel aside, I head for the back of the bar.

When I pass Sam, I give him whispered instructions to watch for customers and yell if there's trouble.

With a look of confusion, he nods before joining Tom. He'll fill him in on the details.

Right now, I need answers, and the only way I'll get them is if I find the beautiful, bloodstained debutante hiding somewhere in my building.

CHAPTER 2

Gwen

He's going to kill me.

Standing in the small, two-stall bathroom, I stare at the wreck reflected in the mirror. My hair's a knotted mess, my makeup smeared beyond redemption. I groan when I pull open my wool coat to reveal the bloody bodice of the ivory Gucci gown I got for my birthday last year.

When I jammed my purse in his face, I was prepared for his rage but not for the blood. The struggle ruined my gown. How I managed to get out of the car and away from Nick, I'll never know. I suppose a few well-placed kicks must have given me the opening I needed. Thank God for the snowstorm. It covered me long enough to find this bar to hide.

I use a wet towel to clean my face, but the dress is unsalvageable.

Two gruff voices echo in the hallway beyond the door. I grab the towel and hide in a stall, locking it behind me. Carefully, I climb onto the toilet, cradling my gown so it won't show beneath the partitions.

Someone kicks open the door.

I clap my hand over my mouth to silence shaky breaths. Whoever it is, I shrink at their presence.

"She in there?" a deep, familiar voice asks.

"Nothing."

"Let's check the rest of the joint."

Footsteps recede, and the door closes softly behind them. I lean my head against the wall and breathe deeply. Focusing on a faint water stain on the ceiling panel, I count to one hundred. When I'm sure they're gone, I step down and sit on the toilet seat.

After a few more minutes, my racing heart slows to a steady rhythm. I dab the towel against my neck to wipe away the sweat and blood.

What the hell am I going to do now?

I can't go back to Nick. Not after that…not after he asked me to…

I pinch my eyes closed.

No. I won't do it.

There's no way I can crawl back to my parents either. Not after what happened. My father will force me to do whatever Nick wants. They want to keep him happy. He's my fiancé after all. Nothing, aside from death, can change that.

I hang my head and let the tears flow. This isn't what I want. I know what people see when I walk into the room. A spoiled rich girl with more beauty than brains. A shiny treasure to wear on special occasions.

Fuck that. Fuck them.

I'm more than that, and if I need to burn some bridges to secure my independence, then I will.

A soft knock at the door disturbs my solitude. I hold my breath.

"They're gone." The bartender's gentle tone drifts into the empty room. "Can I come in?"

I slowly stand and unlock the stall door. When I step out, I'm struck by the sight of the tall bartender, the bathroom door cracked enough for him to speak quietly to me. His long hair and neatly trimmed goatee hide a pair of kind brown eyes and a tender smile.

"Thank you." I smooth my hands over my coat. "I'm sorry to put you in such an awkward situation."

He meets my gaze. "You needed help."

I nod and turn away. "I don't want to cause any trouble. I should go."

The bartender refuses to let me pass. "Not tonight. Not in that storm." He pushes the door open and steps back. "Follow me."

We walk down the hallway until we reach a door labeled *Office*. The light flickers overhead. He reaches up to tap the fixture. The light resumes its full brilliance and holds firm.

I study his broad shoulders as he opens the door and switches on a lamp beside the desk.

"Come in." He rounds the desk and pulls open a few drawers, searching for something. When he stands, he holds out a stack of clothing with one hand. "You might want to change."

I take the garments with a grateful smile. "Thank you."

"Can't have you walking around looking like you just walked away from a murder scene." He smiles, and my heart softens at his thoughtfulness. "You can change in here. Just leave your clothes on the floor by the desk. Come out to the bar when you're ready."

Stepping aside, I allow him space to pass me. His scent surrounds me, pine and Old Spice with a darker note beneath it. Something only belonging to him, if I had to guess. It's comforting, like a glass of mulled wine on Christmas Eve.

He pauses in the doorway and glances at me.

"You sure you're okay? Not bleeding or injured?"

"I'm fine. I promise."

"Okay." He pulls the door closed behind him, leaving me alone in the office.

I wiggle out of the oversized coat and struggle to find the zipper on my dress. After a few minutes, I manage to unstick the zipper, and I peel the damp Gucci gown from my skin. Wadding it in a ball, I set it on the floor behind the desk. Gooseflesh pricks my skin, and I quickly pull on the oversized sweatshirt and sweatpants.

They hang loose in places, but it's a relief to not be wearing something tight and gaudy for once. I've caught plenty of grief from my mother for my ample curves. As if I had a choice. I wasn't blessed with a small waist or petite breasts. All of my garments are altered to fit, much to my mother's irritation.

Knowing I don't have anyone to impress or an image to project provides a keen sense of relief I haven't felt in a long time. I rake my fingers through my hair and twist it over my shoulder. I ensure my purse is still tucked safely inside my coat before draping it over the chair behind the desk. There's not much in it, just my pills, a compact, lipstick, and a few dollars. Still, I don't want to forget it. With a deep breath, I gather what strength remains and slip out of the office, leaving my coat and purse behind.

When I reach the bar, it's empty except for the bartender and a waiter wiping down the tables. The bartender's stern expression softens to a kind smile when he sees me, and he gestures to an empty chair at the bar.

"Would you like something to eat?" he asks as he works, placing the glasses on a shelf behind the register. He watches me in the mirror's reflection.

I shake my head.

"Drink?"

"After the night I've had…yeah, I could use a drink." I scan the bottles, searching for a selection. "I'll have—"

"Let me guess."

Stunned, I watch him retrieve a glass before turning for a bottle. With one hand, he scoops ice and pours it into the shaker. Every move is done with his right hand. That's when I realize my knight in shining armor is missing his left hand. I mean, I noticed something was different, but my addled brain didn't register what wasn't there.

He moves with grace, perfectly pouring the liquor, adding ingredients with ease. When he lifts the shaker in one massive palm, I'm convinced it's magic. He lifts the top, strains the concoction over ice, and adds a sprig of rosemary and a long thin strip of cucumber before topping it with a lime wedge.

"Try this." He sets the drink on a napkin and slides it toward me.

"What is it?" I raise the glass and inhale. The rosemary and lime mix with the herbal bite of the liquor. It smells divine.

"I call it a Tipsy Rose."

I snort. "Someone's been watching *The Golden Girls*."

"What's *The Golden Girls*?" He cocks his head.

I can tell his look of confusion is genuine.

"It's a television show." I wave my hand. "Never mind."

I take a sip, and the flavor surrounds me like a warm hug. It's a complex mix of sweet and floral with a bite of citrus. I feel like I've stepped into a fairy-tale forest, indulged in a heavenly drink created by elves. "Oh my God. That's amazing."

"I thought you'd like it." He grins, and I'm pretty sure he's pleased with himself.

"You're good." I take another drink, savoring the flavor. "How did you get so good at mixing drinks?"

"Practice."

"That explains a lot." I cradle the glass in my hands. "So do you have a name?"

"Claude." He brushes his hair away from his face. "Owner and proprietor of the Black Penny."

"Claude? That's a very French name for the owner of an Irish pub."

He shrugs. "My mother was obsessed with Monet."

His response stuns me. I'm not sure what to say without sounding overly inquisitive, but the desire to know more tugs at the back of my mind. I sip my drink to fill the lapse in conversation.

"And what about you?"

My face warms under the intensity of his gaze. "Gigi."

"Looks like my parents weren't the only ones obsessed with France." Claude chuckles.

"It's a nickname. My friends call me Gigi, but my name is Gwen." I curse the comfort of his presence for making me give my real name rather than an alias. It's too late. I can't take it back. I can only hope he doesn't read tabloids or watch the news. Once my family realizes I'm missing, there will be a citywide search. I'd rather blend into the woodwork and disappear than go back to my gilded prison.

"It's a lovely name." He smiles, and my heart softens again. "Are we friends now, Gwen?"

"You saved me, so I would say that makes us a bit more than friends." I lift my glass in salute. "To unexpected friendships."

Claude lifts a glass of water and meets my toast.

"It's bad luck to toast with water," I tease.

"I don't drink." He sets the glass aside.

"A bartender who doesn't indulge in alcohol? How odd." I chuckle. Am I tipsy already? Lord, what is in this drink?

"You'd be surprised." His cryptic answer lingers in the air. "The storm's getting bad. I'm going to close up. Make yourself comfortable." With a small salute, he goes through a small, swinging door.

I am surprised. I chew my lip and slowly finish my drink. This night has certainly taken a strange but welcome turn. My desperate escape from Nick led me to this place, and I couldn't be more thankful for the kindness of this one-armed bartender. He went above and beyond to make sure I was safe.

I don't think I've ever had anyone do anything for me purely out of the goodness of their heart. Normally, I'm surrounded by people who are willing to do things for me, but they always want something in return. Nothing is selfless when people know my name. My family. Everyone is a vulture, searching for the next score.

I've worked hard over the past ten years to put as much distance as possible between myself and those who would use me for their own gain. And yet, my father arranged my marriage to Nicholas DeLuca, the son of one of the most prominent mob bosses in New York City. I can't fight it. I'm bound by blood. At some point, they'll find me. They'll come for me. I'll go, kicking and screaming, biting and clawing. I will never give Nick the satisfaction of thinking he's tamed me. I'd rather throw myself off the Brooklyn Bridge.

If I could have my way, I'd disappear, vanish into the wind, start over. But how can I do that? I have no money, no prospects, no skills. I've never lived on my own or had a job. It's not that I can't take care of myself or do work. It's that they won't let me. What I want doesn't matter. I'm just a pawn in their endless game of chess. They'll sacrifice me without hesitation.

Claude appears from the hallway with a mop and a bucket. He crosses the room and turns off the sign before locking the door. He flicks a set of switches, dimming the lights until only the back of the bar remains illuminated

The waiter appears and takes the mop from Claude's hand.

"Do you have somewhere to go where you'll be safe?" Claude takes two tentative steps in my direction.

My mouth goes dry. With those broad shoulders and sharp features, he's like a towering oak tree reaching for the sky. Handsome in a strange, offhand way. His heavy brows and full lips contrast the bold angles of his face. A tiny, faded scar mars his cheek, surrounded by small, dark freckles. He's the night sky dotted with constellations and mystery. Those fathomless eyes search mine as he waits for a response.

"No. I don't. I'll figure something out." I smile, but it's forced and makes my throat burn.

"You can stay with me if you'd like. I have an apartment upstairs." He clears his throat. "I mean, for the night…until the storm lets up."

He seems flustered at the prospect, and I find it endearing. I don't like the idea of accepting charity, but I don't have much choice. Besides, I'd rather stay with this kind stranger than return to the lion's den and be devoured.

"Thank you, Claude. I appreciate the offer." I stand, bringing us toe to toe. "Are you sure I won't be intruding?"

"Positive." He rocks back on his heels, his throat working. "There's plenty of room."

There's something strangely sweet about this man. I study him carefully, weighing my options. I have no money, no prospects…and it's too late to find somewhere else to crash. Even then, they'll find me.

No, this is the best place. At least I'll be able to breathe freely for a few minutes without my family and Nick stalking my every move.

When my father finds out what I did, he'll force me to marry Nick. I wish he'd cut me off without regret. Somehow, that would be a more comforting solution, considering the alternative. Starting over without a penny to my name would be easier than enduring what Nick has planned for me.

Tonight, though, I have a reprieve. This is my chance to figure out what I want. How far I'm willing to go to break free from these vultures who would prey on me without thought.

"I'll stay." I smile at Claude, and the motion makes my cheeks ache. This time, it's sincere.

CHAPTER 3

Claude

Her smile leaves me devastated. There's something soft and vulnerable about her. The hesitant way she speaks counters the confidence in her words. Underneath that ruffled exterior, she's resilient and determined. She's a beacon of light in this dark, lonely bar. I'd be a fool to push her away in her hour of need. My mother raised me better than that.

"Come on, then." I pass her, heading for the stairs.

I don't need to turn to know she's following. Her presence radiates warmth and awareness.

Grant would call me a fool for inviting a perfect stranger into my home, but didn't he do the exact same thing just a few months ago? I mean, it was a little more complicated than that. The woman was a cat burglar turned murder witness who ended up on my doorstep, bloody and damn near unconscious. She dragged in a whole mess of trouble, but it was worth it. Quinn makes my brother happy. And surely, he wouldn't begrudge me the same hope.

Not that I expect anything from my time with this beautiful stranger. She's leaps and bounds out of my league, likely lives in an ivory tower. That bloody dress she was wearing was probably worth more than my whole year's income. And she didn't bat an eyelash at the ruined gown. I doubt she's had to struggle a day in her lavish life.

By the time we reach my apartment on the third floor, I'm exhausted by the argument in my head. It doesn't matter who she is or where she comes from. She needs help, and I can make sure she's safe and warm. It's the honorable thing to do.

Except…the way I want to unravel her secrets is far from honorable. I shake away the nagging desperation and focus on the door. It swings open, and I gesture for her to enter.

She swans into my world, wearing a pair of borrowed sweatpants and an oversized sweatshirt. Damn if she doesn't look like a queen surveying her kingdom, her curious gaze sweeping the room.

"It's so quaint." She brushes a hand over the afghan on the back of the sofa. "And clean."

"You sound surprised." I close the door and lock it behind us.

"I guess I am." Her cheeks flare a delicate shade of rose.

"Most people are." I gesture to the doors on my right. "Shower's through here and the bedroom's here. There's a door inside the bathroom to the bedroom. You'll find some toiletries you can use—shampoo, soap, new toothbrush under the sink."

"You sure you're not a Boy Scout?" She leans against the sofa, watching me.

"I was. Made Eagle at fifteen." I squirm under her scrutiny.

"I guess it left an impression."

Her smile warms me, like a strong shot of whiskey.

"It did." I grab two glasses and get water for each of us. "Can I ask you a question?"

"Depends on the question." She shifts.

So she is hiding from something.

"That guy who came looking for you, did you do that to his face?" I point to my own nose before handing her the glass.

"Yes. But he deserved it."

"I have no doubt he deserved it." I sip my water. "Who was he?"

"My fiancé."

The sharp word echoes through my skull, and an anchor drops in my stomach. "Your *fiancé*?"

"Well, kind of. Sort of." She struggles to find the words, but I'm lost in the fact that she's taken by someone who clearly doesn't deserve her.

What the hell am I thinking? I barely know this woman…and yet, I'm captivated by her. Hopeless.

"It's complicated." She sighs and shakes her head.

"I understand."

Judging by her stance, it's more complicated than she's willing to discuss right now. I drop it. If she wants to tell me, she'll do it when she's ready. After what she's been through, anyone would be terrified. But she's a fighter, if the bloodstains on her dress and her fiancé's broken nose are any indication. Strength flows through her veins.

"Can I ask you a question now?" She blinks at me.

"Anything."

"Are you hiring?"

I choke on my water. "What?"

"In the bar, do you need an extra hand?"

She closes her eyes and curses under her breath at the thoughtless use of the phrase. It doesn't bother me.

"I don't want your pity or charity. I'll work to earn my keep."

"Do you plan on sticking around?" I lean against the counter. "What about your fiancé?"

"Fuck him." Gwen clears her throat. "If you let me stay, I'll work hard. I promise."

My mood improves at her vehement response. Perhaps there's hope after all. "What experience do you have?"

"None."

"Then why should I hire you?"

She bristles and drops her gaze. After a few moments, those blue eyes meet mine, determination in their depths. "Because I need work, and I like it here."

I fold my arms across my chest. "How do you make a Manhattan?"

"Whiskey and vermouth."

A laugh escapes me. "It's more nuanced than that, sweetheart."

Her body tenses. "Then teach me. I'm a fast learner."

"Maybe tomorrow."

"So I'm hired?" A smile erupts across that sinfully plush mouth.

"I never said that." I push away from the counter and head for the bedroom. I pause in the doorway, then turn. "One more thing."

"Huh?"

Those blue eyes flash in my direction, and I'm momentarily blinded by need pulsing through me.

"What did you do with the dress?"

"Oh." Her cheeks flush again, and she straightens. "It's on the floor behind the desk in your office."

"I'll take care of it." I turn on the lights in the bathroom and bedroom before returning to the living room. "You can take a shower and rest."

"Thank you, Claude." She crosses the room, leaving the sweet scent of honeysuckle in her wake.

"Let me know if you need anything." I head out to give her some space.

Alone on the landing outside the apartment, I lean against the door. What the hell am I thinking? The temptation is too great. It's more than I expected.

This gorgeous—obviously wealthy—woman has secrets. I don't

hold it against her, but it puts me in an awkward position. What if her family comes looking for her? What if *he* comes back?

I'll cross that bridge when we get there. Tonight, I just have to make it work. It's only for one night. Tomorrow, I'll help her find a safe place and a job if that's what she wants.

But do I want her to stay with me? To work in my bar?

Yes, my mind insists without hesitation.

I make my way down the stairs and open the office door. Inside, I find the gown, wrapped in a tight ball, tucked behind my desk. I unravel it and savor her sweet scent clinging to the fabric. The stain is embedded deep in the beading, beyond salvation. Unless…

I pick up the phone and call Rob. He answers, even though it's after midnight.

"Hello?"

"Rob, it's Claude from the Black Penny."

"Is everything okay?" The concern is clear in his voice.

"Everything's fine." I study the intricate stitching on the gown and note the tag. "Had a patron come in tonight with blood on a fancy Gucci gown. Any idea how to get the stain out?"

Rob laughs. "What makes you think I know how to get blood out of a Gucci gown?"

"You work in a hospital. I just figured you'd know some tricks since you probably get blood on your clothes sometimes."

"Peroxide works, but…hold on." The chatter in the background turns into a full-blown argument.

"Hello?" A woman's voice comes through the line. "This is Marcy. Who's this?"

"Ma'am. This is Claude from the Black Penny. I apologize for waking you."

"You didn't wake me." She huffs. "I heard Rob mention Gucci and peroxide in the same breath. Do *not* listen to him."

"Would you happen to know what to use, then? It's her favorite gown, and I'd hate for it to be ruined."

A heavy sigh fills the void. "Send it over. I'll take care of it." She gives me her address.

I balance the phone against my shoulder as I write everything down. "I'll have it delivered tomorrow. Thank you, ma'am."

"You're welcome. Good night."

"Night." I hang up the phone and neatly fold the gown, tucking it into a trash bag. Tomorrow, I'll pay someone to deliver it.

Flicking off the light, I grab her purse and coat before locking the office and returning upstairs. Inside my apartment, the air has shifted. It's warmer, lighter…sweeter. I lean my ear against the bathroom door and hear the shower.

Quietly, I slip into the bedroom to retrieve the sweatpants and tee shirt I sleep in. The soft strains of her voice echo through the gap left by the slightly open bathroom door. It takes all my restraint not to peek in and drink my fill.

Chastising myself, I open the drawer to pull out a soft pair of pajamas. After laying them on the bed, I retreat to the living room. A quick change, and I'm as comfortable as I can be with a naked bombshell in the next room. In my bed.

I fluff a pillow and lay on the couch. I drape the afghan from the back of the couch over me, struggling to cover my feet.

In the next room, she moves and the noise makes me restless. I close my eyes, but all I can picture is her round face, her sea-blue eyes, her dangerous curves covered in sequins and blood.

For years, I've been comfortable with my life. With my status as a bachelor. Even with the promise to my grandfather hanging over my head, I was at peace with the cards I'd been dealt.

But now I can't help but dream of something…someone, who might be more trouble than she's worth. Damn my conscience.

CHAPTER 4

Gwen

His absence should relieve me, but it leaves me aching.

I'm in a stranger's apartment, in an uncomfortable and unfamiliar part of town. There's nothing about this situation that should give me comfort…and yet, I'm at ease.

Guilt pricks me for not being honest with him. I should have told Claude the truth. Who I am. Who the asshole downstairs was. I can't bring myself to reveal such details. Not yet. I feel horrible, especially when he so selflessly opened his home to me.

While he's gone, I trace my fingers along the back of the sofa. It's faded with fraying rips and tears, but it's clean. My gaze drifts around the small apartment. A bookcase lines the wall next to the bedroom. The sofa faces a television against the wall, between two windows. The galley kitchen opens to a small dining area with a table and two chairs. The furniture is worn and well-loved, holdovers from the seventies.

It's surprisingly tidy. Every surface dusted, the blanket on the sofa folded. I wander into the bedroom and find the same fastidious organization. A neatly made bed with sharp corners, two nightstands flanking it. One holds a cream-colored lamp and a stack of books, piled five deep. I scan the titles—all of them are Stephen King except one, a worn copy of Shakespeare's comedies.

I chuckle. My savior doesn't look like a horror or Shakespeare fan. He looks…well, he doesn't look like someone who likes to read. I guess that makes me a piss-poor judge of someone based on looks.

He's different from anyone I've ever known. My family. My fiancé. My so-called friends. It's refreshing to meet someone from outside my narrow social circle.

If my father knew, he'd rage, lock me in my room, restrict what little freedom I have. He's made demands on me for years, but this last act of betrayal has left me clawing to get away, desperate and with complete disregard for the consequences.

I can't go back to my father. To that family. Not when Nick is the person I'd really be going back to. I refuse to bind myself to a man who will exploit me for his own selfish gain. To a man who doesn't truly care about what happens to me. He'll use me until I no longer serve a purpose, then he'll discard me.

No. I can't go back. I *refuse.*

Groaning, I sit on the bed and take off my three-inch heels. The carpet soothes the aching soles of my feet when I retreat into the bathroom to turn on the shower.

There's a fresh, folded towel waiting on the counter. I appreciate the cleanliness and order, but I feel like I'm intruding on his personal space.

Quickly, I strip out of the borrowed clothes and push them off to the side before stepping into the spray of warm water. I manage to scrub whatever blood remains with a new bar of Irish Spring soap. My brow furrows at the coconut-scented shampoo and conditioner on the shelf. I use them, and the delicate scent indicates I must not be the only woman who uses Claude's shower.

Does he have a girlfriend? A wife? I chew my lip as I rinse the suds from my hair.

There's no sign of a woman in the apartment. Nothing noticeably feminine. It's simple. Concise. Orderly. And very masculine. Strange. Unless he prefers to wash his longish hair with something more effective than bar soap?

What other mysteries does Claude keep hidden? It seems there's more to him than meets the eye. My curiosity increases at the thought of unraveling complex layers beneath his stoic exterior.

The kindness of this one-armed bartender brought me here. Ensured my safety. And I shouldn't pry into his personal life. I'm a guest, however temporary, and should keep my nosy inquiries to myself.

Still, his immediate instinct to protect me leaves me in a soft, mushy place. He's handsome, though not in a traditional way, and radiates an appeal that goes beyond looks. His wavy dark hair, his soft brown eyes, his nose that should be too long but is somehow balanced in proportion to his face and height.

Part of me wonders how he would look in a tuxedo on my arm at a gala. I shake my head. He would be out of place at such an event. Here, behind the bar, wearing a dark plaid shirt, rock band tee shirt, and jeans—that's his element. I'm sure of it.

I finish showering and dry off before realizing I don't have anything to sleep in. Gathering the discarded garments from the floor, I return to the bedroom.

It hits me.

There's only one bed.

One. Bed.

The thought warms me. He never said anything about where *he* was going to sleep. He's not going to sleep on the sofa, is he? With his height and broad shoulders, that can't be comfortable.

I glance at the queen-size bed with its tidy blankets and cozy pillows. Longing strikes me. But I can't put him out in his own home.

I'll let him have the bed. I'll take the sofa.

That's when I spot the pile of clothes on the bed. I pick up the shirt and unfold it. No letters or words, just deep blue fabric. I hold it close, inhaling a subtle scent of detergent and something musky I assume belongs solely to Claude. When I slip the clothes on, they cradle me like a warm blanket, soothing my world-weary heart and restoring my faith in humanity.

After folding and placing the other clothes on the dresser, I open the door to the living room.

Claude's stretched out on the sofa, his feet hanging off the end and his eyes closed. Nothing about his position looks comfortable. How can he possibly sleep like that?

"Do you need something?" he asks, keeping his eyes closed.

"No, but…" I step closer and rest my hand on the back of the couch. "I can sleep on the couch…"

He peers up at me, those kind eyes fixing on my face, and it's almost as if he's taking measure of me. "I'm fine here. You take the bed."

"You don't look comfortable." I gesture to his feet dangling well past the end of the sofa. "This couch is far too small for you."

"It won't be the first time I've slept here, and I doubt it'll be the last." He shifts, folding his arms across his chest. "Take the bed. I'll be fine."

I twist the hem of my shirt between my fingers. "We could share the bed…"

He narrows his eyes, and I feel like I'm under a microscope as he studies me.

"I don't think that would be a good idea."

"I don't bite. I promise." A grin splits my lips, but it dissolves at the thought of his long limbs wrapped around me in the comfort of his bed. Warmth infuses me, flooding my cheeks.

"I don't think your fiancé would appreciate you sharing a bed with another man." He exhales sharply. "Just spending the night here is pushing it."

Disappointment fills me, and I bite back a retort. I want to tell him exactly how little I care what my *ex*-fiancé thinks of where I sleep. "Do you want me to leave?"

"No."

He answers so quickly, it gives me hope I'm not about to be kicked out into the storm.

"I don't want to be a bother. I'll leave."

When I turn away, Claude sighs and climbs to his feet. "Gwen."

His voice echoes behind me, and I turn around to face him. The moment our eyes meet, I feel that pull between us again.

"I'm sorry. I don't mean to be a burden."

"You're not a burden." He runs his fingers through his hair. "I just…I'm bad at this."

"Bad at what?"

"Playing the hero. Talking to beautiful women. Take your pick."

My heart beats faster. "You think I'm beautiful?"

He clears his throat and drops his gaze. The muscles in his neck work as he tries to formulate a response. When he looks up, his whiskey eyes sparkle in the dim light. "Please take the bed. I'm trying to be a gentleman."

"You don't have to try, Claude." I beam at him. "You're the only true gentleman I've ever met."

His lips thin into a line, and his cheeks flush pink. "Good night, Gwen."

I refrain from touching him, afraid he'll spontaneously combust at the contact. "Good night, Claude."

Without pressing the issue further, I slip around him and disappear into the bedroom, leaving the door cracked open. I turn off the light and crawl into his bed.

I nestle into the pillow, inhaling deeply. His scent surrounds me. The mild detergent and Irish Spring linger, but there's no denying the scent of *him* beneath it all. Spice and leather with the warmth of cinnamon.

No coconut. Interesting.

My eyes grow heavy as warmth surrounds my body, pulling me under until exhaustion finally closes my eyes. The sliver of light through the door draws me like a moth to a flame.

I wish he would have taken me up on my offer to share. I'm tired of being alone.

CHAPTER 5

Claude

I've slept better on a jungle hillside in a torrential downpour.

After cursing the aging sofa and my vivid imagination, I manage to steal a few hours of restless sleep. These couch springs should be classified as torture devices. I really need to get rid of it, buy something new. Something that won't stab me in my sleep.

But I can't completely blame the couch for my lack of rest. That fault lays firmly at the feet of the woman passed out blissfully in my bed at this moment. I thought the image of her naked in my shower would haunt me well into morning, but it was the invitation to join her in my bed that gave me a demanding hard-on and no peace.

I shouldn't be thinking about her like that. She's not mine, and judging by the expensive clothes and shitty fiancé, she never will be. Still, I wonder what she's hiding and why she's going to such lengths to run from her problems.

At daybreak, I concede defeat and get up. There will be no rest with her in my home. I can't purge thoughts of her long enough to fall asleep. Just knowing she's curled up, safe and warm in my bed, leaves my whole body aching for release.

I slip into the bedroom to grab some clothes. She's asleep, her back to me, blankets over her head. Careful not to make too much noise, I retrieve the clothes and tiptoe into the bathroom, closing the door softly behind me. Once I've showered and dressed, I return to the living room through the other door.

Frost cakes the windows and snow piles on the ledges, making it difficult to see the streets below. At least it's stopped snowing. Not that it matters. In a day or two, the snow will melt, leaving a mess of slush and mud coating the streets and sidewalks. This storm caught us all off-guard. It's not common to have this much snow in the first week of December. I'll have to replace the mat by the front door to catch the slop.

Exhaustion lingers, and I yawn as I set the coffee pot to brew. I grab a carton of eggs and some cheese from the refrigerator. There isn't a lot of variety in my pantry—I eat most of my meals in the bar—but there are always ingredients for cheese omelets here. They're a kind of comfort food for me.

I crack the eggs and whisk them in a bowl as the skillet warms, a tablespoon of butter melting in the center. I smile at the satisfying sizzle of eggs as I gently mix them while they cook. I turn the heat to low and let them sit. A sprinkle of cheese, and I pull them from the heat. Then I repeat the process, making an omelet for my guest without a second thought.

"Something smells delicious." Her voice, rough with sleep, pulls me from my silent motions.

"Good morning. Hope you're hungry."

"Starving." She takes the plate I've offered and retreats to the small table.

I finish cooking my own eggs and grab two forks from the drawer beside the sink. "Here." I hand her a fork and set my plate down. "Do you want some coffee?"

"Yes, please."

After I pour us both a cup of rich coffee, I turn. She's sitting with one knee folded beneath her. The worn material of my old shirt is stretched, exposing a creamy shoulder. She looks like a fairy princess relaxing beside a pool in a painting I can't quite place. Shaking the thought free, I hand her a mug.

She accepts it gratefully and inhales the aroma with a moan of delight.

I sit, painfully aware of the effect her presence has on my body. She's pure temptation. My clothes hug her curves in all the right places. Just knowing she's wearing them leaves me aching with a possessive need I've never felt before. I want to know what lies beneath the familiar fabric.

"Thank you." She takes a bite of the omelet and sighs. "This is delicious."

"Glad you like it." I poke at my eggs, my hunger replaced by something carnal. I manage to stuff a few bites in my mouth, and the motion nudges me to continue eating.

"You like to read?" she asks, gesturing to the bookshelf along the far wall.

"Yeah, when I get time."

"The bar keeps you busy?"

"It does, but I like it. Makes me feel productive."

She smiles, and my reservations melt.

"How long have you been a bartender?"

"Since 1973…so twelve years." I sip my coffee. "My grandfather owned the place. Taught me everything he knew before he let me take over."

"He must be very proud of you."

"He was." I clear my throat. "The building takes a lot of work, the bar even more. I feel like I'm constantly fixing something."

"I can imagine. They've got a lot of character though. The building. The bar."

"A lot of history here." Memories dance in the back of my mind. "Takes hard work to preserve them."

"And money," she says softly. When she meets my gaze again, she brightens. "What's your favorite Shakespeare play?"

I laugh, marveling at the way she bounces from one topic to another. "*Much Ado About Nothing*."

"Ahh, so you're a romantic."

Her teasing observation plucks my heartstrings.

"I've been called worse."

We continue to eat amid friendly conversation, and I like it. Her presence adds something unique and unfamiliar to my routine. The little bit of time I spent in Quinn's company a few months ago reminded me how much I miss the companionship of another soul. I've lived with roommates before, particularly during my time in the Army, but I've never shared my space—or my life—with a woman. I've always been terrified I'm going to say or do something stupid. With Gwen, that fear has vanished.

When she finishes her breakfast, she takes her plate to the sink and returns for mine. I sip my coffee in silence as she washes the dishes and sets them in the drying rack. Her question from the night before emerges in the front of my brain. "You really want to work at the bar?" I set the empty mug aside.

She spins around and nods. "Yes."

I rise from the table and grab my flannel shirt from a hook by the door. "Get dressed and come downstairs."

"I'll be right down." Gwen flashes me a smile and darts back into the bedroom.

My body protests every step as I descend the aging staircase. In all the years I've owned this place, I've never felt the need to make improvements or turn it into something it's not, and I've been remiss in updating the bar and the apartments above it. I've always just done basic maintenance to keep it functional, not stylish. Now that Quinn and Grant are always home on the second floor, I feel pressure to be a better landlord. I make a mental note to call Jack and have him start doing some work on the building. Pap left enough money to ensure that kind of stuff was taken care of. Old buildings deteriorate and need love. At least that's what I'm telling myself. My desire to improve the place has nothing to do with the curvy brunette who's wedged herself into my life.

She's not staying. I need to remember that.

The Black Penny is exactly how I left it the night before. I turn on the lights and flip the on switch for the jukebox in the corner. The bright colors illuminate the space. I'm home.

From behind the polished wooden surface of the bar, I pull out a variety of glasses. If Gwen is serious about working for me, she needs to prove she understands the basics. Any bar owner worth their salt should ensure the staff knows how to work behind the bar first. Everything else is easy.

"What time do you open?"

When I turn, Gwen is standing by the swinging doors, just over the edge of the tile.

"Five on a Sunday. Four every other day of the week. I used to be closed on Mondays, but people need a refuge."

She comes alongside me, eyeing the glasses. "What's this for?"

"Bartending 101."

"Is there a test?"

"This whole thing is a test." I lean against a shelf beside the register. "Pass it and you got the job. Fail it and…" I shrug my shoulder in a carefree way and leave the consequence unspoken.

"Okay." She takes a deep breath.

"What types of glasses are these?"

"This is a martini glass. This is for beer. That's for wine. Oh, that's a champagne glass." Her nose scrunches as she goes down the line. "Whiskey?" Defeat rings in her tone when she reaches a tall one. "I don't know."

"That's a highball glass." I point to the one that stumped her then move to the one she called a whiskey glass. "This is a rocks glass."

"Oh yeah." She bites her lip.

"Not bad." I shift closer and put all but two glasses away.

She stares at the martini and the rocks glasses left on the bar.

"Now for the true test. Make a Manhattan and a dirty gin martini with two olives."

She blinks at me like a stray cat caught in cab headlights. "What?"

"The couple who just came in wants a dirty gin martini with two olives and a Manhattan. I'm busy in the kitchen. You need to make the drinks without my help."

Tentatively, she searches the shelves for the gin. When she pulls a vodka bottle, I stop her and show her how the bar is laid out and where to find the proper ingredients. It's pretty simple with everything on display. I can tell she's nervous when the bottle nearly slips from her hand.

"Easy, darlin'." I grab the bottle before it crashes to the floor. "Why don't we take it a little slower?"

She nods in relief. "Yes, please."

I set the bottle aside and hand her a small metal container with all my drink recipes in it. I haven't used it in years, but every one of my employees starts with it and uses these recipes until they're comfortable on their own.

"Why don't you look here for the recipes, then try your hand at making the two I requested?" I turn to get my weekly checklist for liquor and food orders.

"Thank you for teaching me, Claude."

Her sweet words tug at my heart.

With a nod, I clear my throat. "I'll let you practice. Yell if you need anything."

Her plump lower lip disappears between her teeth, and she nods enthusiastically before turning back to the bar and opening the recipe catalog.

I run through my list, painfully aware of her warm presence behind me. I'm asking for trouble with this temporary solution, aren't I? This wayward kitten already has a home, and heartache is a foregone conclusion.

Being nice always leads to heartache.

CHAPTER 6

Gwen

The silence is too much. I feel like I'm drifting alone in the open sea, cut off from everyone and everything.

My gaze drifts around the empty bar and rests longingly on the jukebox. A little music would lighten my mood. I pat my empty pockets. No money. Damn.

Taking the little recipe box with me, I go to the other side of the bar and sit on a bench. The recipes are organized alphabetically, so I start with A and work my way through the catalog. The faint strains of a rock ballad play in my head while I read. I hum along as I skim the ingredients and instructions, and then set each card aside, keeping them in order.

I'm about halfway through the stack of recipes when Claude appears from the kitchen. He stalks across the room, drops some coins in the jukebox, and selects a song.

The strains I've been playing in my head come through the speakers. I bounce my foot with the beat and sing along. The music wraps around me, soothing me in ways I didn't realize I needed. The catchy beat fills the room, and suddenly, I don't feel alone anymore.

I shoot Claude a grateful smile when he returns. "Thanks, it was too quiet in here."

"It won't be once we open." He pauses in the doorway. "How's it going?"

"Good."

"Any questions so far?"

"No." I fan the cards in my hand, seeing how many I have left. "I hope you don't expect me to memorize all of these."

"I don't." He chuckles. "But it's good to be familiar with them."

"Yeah."

"You ready to try a few yet?"

"Almost." I hold up what remains of the deck.

"As soon as you're ready, you can show me what you've learned." He vanishes into the hallway, leaving me to my own devices.

I spend another ten minutes reading the recipes. Confidence fills me, even though there are terms I'm not quite sure of written in the instructions. What does it mean to *muddle*? What the hell is a *jigger*? What makes a dirty martini *dirty*? I mentally file these questions away. Once Claude comes back, I can ask him to clarify.

Pushing aside my apprehension, I return the recipes to the box and set it on the bar before venturing into the kitchen in search of Claude. He's taking inventory in the small walk-in freezer.

"I'm ready." My confidence takes a hit at his skeptical expression. I note the tension in his jaw as he finishes a note on his checklist.

He leads me back to the bar and sets the list aside. "Well then. Let's see you make something."

"What do you want?" I turn and smile.

His brow furrows for a moment, but it smooths instantly as he leans against the bar. "Let's start with the Manhattan."

I reach for the cards on the counter and pull out the one for the drink he requested. After a quick scan of the ingredients, I retrieve the whiskey, bitters, and sweet vermouth. When I reach for a rocks glass, he clicks his tongue.

I consider my options, then frown. "Is this a trick question?"

"Feels like it, doesn't it?" He takes out both a highball and a martini glass. "On the rocks," he says, pointing at the tall slender glass before moving to the martini glass. "No rocks."

"Rocks? That's a silly name for ice." I chuckle. "Let's make it on the rocks."

He watches silently as I take the mixing glass and search for a way to measure the liquor. His groan rips through me when I try to pour freehand.

"You're not ready for that yet, sweetheart." He grabs the liquor bottle and what looks like a small, uneven hourglass. Standing next to me, he pauses to make sure my full attention is on him. Where else would it be? His mere presence makes it hard to focus on anything *but* him.

"What's that?" I point to the hourglass thingy in his massive hand, ignoring the heat creeping along my neck at his close proximity.

"This is a jigger." He shows me the big end. "Two ounces." He flips it. "One ounce." Holding it between his fingers, he empties the haphazardly poured whiskey from the cup into the big end before deftly transferring it to the waiting empty glass. Then he measures the vermouth with the small end. He dashes a few drops from a small, awkwardly wrapped bottle into the mix. "Don't forget the ice." He pours a small scoop of ice into the glass and stirs it with a tall, red-tipped spoon.

"Make sure it's mixed properly, then add a cherry on top." He does so and slides the glass toward me. "Always wash your utensils after making a drink." Claude nods at the small sink by my hip.

"Can I try it?" At his nod, I sip the Manhattan. The burn of whiskey is dulled by sweet vermouth, and it has a bitter aftertaste. I scrunch up my nose and set it aside.

Claude chuckles. "Not your style, huh?"

"No. I liked the drink you made for me last night."

"Do you want to learn how to make it?" His smile widens as he reaches for the gin on the shelf behind him.

"Yes, please." My excitement bubbles up.

Step-by-step, Claude walks me through the process. I watch with fascination as he grinds rosemary leaves and cucumber with simple syrup at the bottom of a glass. He uses the word muddle, and a puzzle piece fits into place when I make the connection. Then he adds the liquor, gives it a shake, and strains it into a fancy glass.

"You make it look so simple." I pick up the glass and savor the refreshing cocktail. It may be only ten in the morning, but I deserve a treat.

"There's nothing to it." He shrugs and replaces the bottles. "Just practice."

His arm brushes mine as he reaches past me. Heat surrounds me, followed by the teasing whiff of his scent. A scent that's familiar and comforting. One that tormented me all night. It clings to my skin after sleeping in his bed, wearing his clothes. I lean into his path as he passes and inhale deeply. His back is turned, and I sigh in frustration when he steps away.

Claude gives me a quick introduction to the tools of his trade. He probably should have started here. I have no idea if he was testing me or challenging me, but it would have helped to know these things before I dove into making dirty martinis or fancy whiskey drinks.

When he finishes, he lapses into silence as he cleans the few dishes we used. I want to ask him more about himself, but he doesn't seem very talkative when he's not teaching me some tidbit or giving instruction.

The gin fizzles through me, sparking my bravery. I come up beside him and sway against him, nudging his thigh with my hip. "How come you don't drink?"

"Doesn't sit well with me." He dries a glass and sets it aside.

"Someone made you a bad drink?"

"Nope." He sighs. "Just gave it up when it hurt more than it helped."

"That makes sense." I study his profile as he works. "I'm sure you didn't always want to be a bartender."

"You'd be right."

"What did you want to be?" I sip my drink.

"A cop."

"Really?" I stare at him, surprised.

"Yeah, but after the war…" He raises his left arm with the absent hand. "I didn't quite meet the requirements."

I'm struck by the sadness in his tone.

"Is that how you lost your arm? The war?" I ask, my voice soft. Maybe I'm not supposed to ask such a question, but curiosity, emboldened by alcohol, increases my desperation to know.

"Yeah, but I didn't lose my whole arm." He pushes his hair back from his face. "I lost my hand and part of my forearm. Not that it matters. It was enough to ruin my job prospects."

Tears prick my eyes. All my life, I've been locked in my family's gilded apartments, toured the most elegant establishments, eaten the finest meals. I can't even make my own fucking drink, but this sweet, selfless man sacrificed so much in service to his country. I feel like a spoiled brat complaining about my problems. We're from separate worlds with completely different experiences. The gap between us is wide, but I'm determined to bridge it.

"Well, you're a damn good bartender." I rest my hand on his shoulder.

His eyes brighten and fix on me. "What did you want to be?"

"Free." The word slips out before I can stop it.

I shake my head and chuckle, trying to cover my mistake, but it's too late. The word is out there, floating on the air like dandelion fluff. He doesn't say anything, even though I can feel his curious gaze studying me.

"I mean, I always wanted to have my own place, maybe have a shop somewhere, selling jewelry or custom goods."

"Hmm." He turns back to his task.

I don't think he believes me. "I bet you get a lot of ladies in here."

Claude turns to me, confusion etched along his handsome face. "Why do you say that?"

"Come on…you're a handsome guy, with those soulful eyes and that charming smile."

His brow furrows as he ponders my words.

I warm under the tension, thinking I said something wrong.

When he finally speaks, his voice is rough. "Do you do that often?"

"Do what?"

"Flirt to redirect the conversation?"

I gasp at his question. "I…uh…no." I clear my throat. "I was just curious about why a good-looking guy like you is still single."

"As you can tell by the absence of a line of women around the block, no one wants a broken, one-armed bartender."

I do. A small, persistent part of my brain screams at the top of its lungs.

There's pain in his eyes. A pain I can relate to at a level most others can't even imagine.

"I understand."

My voice stops him, and he regards me like a hound with big eyes and floppy ears.

"It would be nice to be desired for what I am on the inside instead of for my looks or connections or what my family can give. I'm constantly rejected for my passions, my heart…hell, even my inexperience in the world outside my sheltered existence has left me with horrible self-confidence. I am an impostor among my peers."

I just want to be loved. The last sentence nearly strangles me. I shrug, thinking I went too far, revealed too much.

"I'm sorry, Gwen." Claude rakes his hand through his hair. "People can be assholes. Don't let it steal your sparkle though. You've still got some." His smile leaves me breathless.

"I doubt that," I mumble under my breath before pasting on a fake smile. I'm not sure I believe him. I've been reminded often how useless I really am. How stupid my dreams are. I'm half afraid I believe the lies.

"Keep studying. You'll figure it out," Claude says, turning away. "I'll be back in a few. If you need me, I'll be in the office." He retreats, taking his checklist with him.

Once again, I'm alone, left to wonder if I crossed a line by opening my big mouth. Shit. I thought we were getting to know each other. It's hard not to take it personally when you're desperate for some kind of connection.

I grab the cards and skim through them again, losing myself in the recipes, trying to focus on something other than the gentle pull of his presence and his kind words.

Don't let it steal your sparkle.

I'll try, Claude. I'll try.

CHAPTER 7

Claude

Even within the confines of my office, she haunts me. Working beside her could be dangerous. She's temptation incarnate, with a body made for sin and a smile that rivals a summer sunrise over the bay.

I collapse into my chair and toss the order sheets on the desk. What the hell am I doing? I'm tormenting myself. Honestly, I don't need the distraction of her in the bar every day. We haven't even discussed her living arrangements. Not that I'll be quick to throw her out in the street. She can stay with me as long as she needs to. As long as it takes to find a place of her own.

But having her in my life on a daily basis will only lead to heartache. I can see it coming a mile away.

With a groan, I lean back and close my eyes, stretching my aching back. Sleeping on the sofa didn't help, but I've slept in worse places under worse conditions. Crashing on the old worn couch my grandfather left behind won't be the death of me.

Gwen might be though.

Grabbing the phone, I dial the number for the courier my brother uses to deliver things across town. With a few quick instructions and payment arranged, I schedule the pickup for an hour from now. I'll pay for the quick turnaround, but I promised Marcy I'd have the gown in her hands today.

After I hang up, I stare at the bloodstained dress, wrapped discreetly in a small black garbage bag on the corner of my desk. I scribble a note with the name and address and tape it to the bag, ensuring it's firmly tied closed before pushing it aside.

The questions resurface in the back of my mind. Who is she? And what the hell happened between her and her fiancé last night?

It's really none of my business. I did my duty and stepped between them when she asked. Judging from the look of the guy who barged into my place demanding answers, I'd guess he didn't have her best interests at heart. And if she hit him, he deserved it. Best keep a little distance between them for the moment.

But the truth creeps in like ink spilled into crystal-clear water. He'll be back. And she'll have to face him.

Hell, maybe she'll want him back at that point. I don't know. I shouldn't care.

I *don't* care. It's her life. She can do what she wants.

Then why the hell am I sticking my neck out for her? Letting her stay with me? Hiring her to work at the bar? This is a guaranteed disaster waiting to happen.

The moment her fiancé shows up and shit goes south, I'll be caught in it. When she chooses him, whatever high I'm drifting on will be ripped out from under me and bring me crashing to earth.

I know the type. Entitled, indecisive. They sink their claws into people, use them, throw them away the moment something better comes along. I *can't* let her get under my skin. I have too much at stake—my business, my simple life. I won't let a beautiful stranger waltz in and rip it all away without a shred of remorse.

But is that truly who she is?

That's how people born with money are. I've met enough rich bastards to know they're only along for the ride while it's all ups. The moment things take a turn, they bail. They don't care who they ruin in the process.

A mental picture of Gwen in the blood-covered gown, shivering and desperate, pops into my mind. It's hard to believe she could be so cold and callous, but I actually know nothing about her. She refuses to share details. I get it. She'll tell me when she's ready, but damn if my curiosity isn't wearing a hole in my brain with the constant burning questions.

I want to respect her privacy. Maybe one day she'll trust me with her story, maybe not. But whatever trouble she's wrapped up in, she's tangled me in it too. She's clammed up and scared, which says enough. The girl is hiding something. I just wish she'd trust me.

The phone rings, jerking me from my thoughts. "Black Penny."

"Claude, what are you doing in the office on a Sunday?" My brother's voice booms through the line.

"Inventory, Grant, like I do every Sunday." I lean back in the chair.

"That's right. I forgot you're married to the bar." He pulls away from the phone, and I hear him mumbling to Quinn, his girlfriend. "You still coming for dinner tonight?"

Damn it. In all the commotion, I forgot about Sunday family dinner.

There's no way I can skip it or force Gwen to stay home alone. "Yeah, I think there's enough help to cover the bar tonight. We'll be there."

"We?" Grant picks out the one piece of information that doesn't quite fit. That's what detectives do best.

I curse the slip of my tongue, but it doesn't matter, he'd find out about her sooner or later. Better get it over with now. "Yeah, I have someone staying with me. Mind if she comes?"

"She?" His interest is piqued. "Who is *she*?"

"You'll meet her later. Now can I finish my inventory?"

"Sure."

"Oh, does Quinn have some clothes she can borrow?"

Grant chuckles. "Did she show up naked on your doorstep?"

My gaze lands on the bag containing her bloody gown. "Not exactly. I'll explain later."

"All right. I'll have Quinn bring some clothes down to the office."

"Just have her put them in front of my door. We need to change before we come over."

"I'm sure you do." Grant's tone brims with amusement.

I'll be bombarded with a thousand questions during dinner. I should probably warn Gwen before I drag her into the lion's den.

"See you then." I hang up without waiting for my brother's response.

The buzzer at the side door rings. I had it installed for deliveries and emergencies after the whole mess with Quinn a few months ago. Grabbing the bag, I head down the hall and open the door. A chilly gust bursts through the door and stings my skin, even through my warm flannel shirt.

"Afternoon, sir." The young man's breath curls in the cold air. The snow is melting into slush, but he's wearing boots and a warm winter coat. Beneath the wool cap, he flashes a smile.

"Hope you're staying warm." I hand him the parcel. He takes it in his mittened hand and tucks it beneath his arm. "Cold one today."

"That it is, sir." He nods.

"Address is on the package." I give him a generous tip. "Be quick about it, please."

"Of course, sir. Have a good one."

After he leaves, I close and lock the door. Hopefully, Marcy will be able to take care of the stains. Gwen looked amazing in that gown. I would hate to have it permanently tarnished due to her fiancé's incompetence as a decent human being.

When I return to the bar, Foreigner's "I Wanna Know What Love Is" plays over the speakers. I lean against the wall, remaining in the shadows, mesmerized by the sight before me.

Gwen is dancing in the middle of the bar, her arms moving with the beat, her hair swaying behind her like a dark veil. It takes me a moment to realize she's singing along. Her sweet voice fills the empty space.

My heart constricts. How could something so beautiful be so damned tempting? Or unattainable?

She's out of my league. Even in the old sweatshirt I loaned her, she looks like a goddess here to torment mortal men. Or maybe an elf.

I shake my head. I've been reading too much Tolkien. Maybe I should stick to Stephen King. At least there's no gilded temptation there.

Gwen spins around and stops when she sees me step into view. "Sorry. I just love this song. It makes me want to dance."

Her breathless laugh sends a bolt of need through me.

"We all have those moments." I clear my throat. "Would you be interested in joining me for dinner at my brother's?"

She blinks up at me with those luminous, intoxicating eyes. When she smiles, a small crease forms at the corners, charming and carefree. "You want me to come with you to dinner with your family?"

"Well, it's not my *whole* family. It's just my brother and his girlfriend. They live on the second fl—."

"I'd love to." Her smile fades, and she tugs at the hem of her sweatshirt. "But what will I wear?"

"Quinn has some clothes you can borrow."

"Quinn?"

"My brother's girlfriend." I motion for her to follow me. "Come on."

Gwen bounds over and rises on her tiptoes to kiss my cheek. "Thank you, Claude. You think of everything."

The warmth of her lips brands me. It takes all my effort to not drag her against me so I can discover just how soft and pliant her lips are under mine. My cock twitches as she disappears down the hallway.

I thought of everything, all right. That's why I'm mired in this mess, up to my old, lonely heart.

CHAPTER 8

Gwen

I tug at the sleeves of the borrowed sweater and struggle to relax. *It's only dinner with his family.*

But what if they ask questions I'm unprepared to answer? I don't want to get them involved. It's better if they don't know who I am.

Right? Indecision claws at me, and I bite my lip as thoughts race through my head.

Claude knocks on his brother's apartment door, then glances at me. "Are you okay?"

"Fine," I lie, flashing a halfhearted smile.

"They won't bite, I promise." He returns the smile.

Warmth radiates through me. How did I end up in the company of such a sweet man? All my life, I've lived in fear of the men around me. Their power. Their status. Their influence. Their lust. It's surreal to be with a man who isn't expecting anything from me…from us. I step closer, soaking up his heat, longing to be near him.

The door swings open, and I blink in surprise when Claude's brother steps into view. They're so similar, they could be twins. Claude's hair is longer and his demeanor more relaxed, but they have the same facial structure and dark features.

"Gwen, this is my brother Grant."

I shake myself from a stupor and take his hand. "Nice to meet you," I say, keeping my voice steady.

"Likewise." Grant opens the door wider and invites us inside.

I follow Claude into the apartment. Its layout is nearly identical to Claude's, but there's a distinct difference in décor and mood. Bright fabrics cover the sofa, a plush carpet brightens the dark space, and a bookcase filled with books lines the far wall.

"Dinner will be ready in a minute."

I spin around to see a gorgeous, curvy redhead wearing a green apron. She places a covered dish on a small table with four place settings. Her curls cascade in a mass over her shoulder. She turns with a smile, and I'm stunned by how lovely she is. And young. She can't be much older than twenty-four.

But looks can be deceiving…I should know. I hide the fact I'm twenty-five with a thick layer of makeup and the latest fashion trends. We're similar in body type, which makes sense considering her clothes fit me perfectly.

"That's Quinn." Claude comes alongside me. "My brother's girlfriend."

"Oh." I turn to see Grant limp toward her. He presses a kiss to her forehead and sits at the table. "What happened to him?" I whisper, curiosity tugging at the threads in my mind.

"He was shot a few months ago. Still recovering."

"Shot?" I gasp. "How?"

"It's a long story, but it's a risk a homicide detective takes."

"He's a cop?" Uncertainty tightens deep in my chest. This could complicate everything, especially if my family files a missing person's report.

"Yeah, but he's on leave while he recovers." Claude motions for me to join them at the table.

Slowly, the knot in my chest unravels. There's no threat here. It's just a family meal. Nothing sinister or underhanded.

Not like it would be under my father's roof.

Quinn pauses and offers her hand. "I'm so glad you're here." She beams. "It'll be refreshing to not hear them argue through the whole meal. You'll balance things out."

"Thank you for inviting me on such short notice." I take the seat opposite her. Tension zings down my spine at the intimacy of such an informal dinner. I can't remember the last time I had a casual meal with my family…or anyone else for that matter. Meals were always a production in my home. I hated them with a passion.

The brothers fall into a conversation about some court case blowing up the news. Quinn fills my plate. Pot roast, mashed potatoes, mixed vegetables. It all looks delicious. I take a few bites as the animated discussion between Claude and Grant continues.

Claude's attention drifts to me, even as his brother speaks. I smile, and the corner of his mouth quirks.

"So, Gwen, how did you meet Claude?" Quinn cuts through their conversation, obviously disinterested in it.

Claude chokes on a piece of roast beef and takes a drink of his water.

"Oh…well…" I search for the proper response.

"She came into the bar last night," Claude says. "Had some trouble and needed a place to stay."

Grant chews thoughtfully, his gaze searching me. I can't tell what's going on in his head, but Quinn interjects before I can think too much about it.

"You're such a sweetheart, Claude, coming to her aid like that." She rests her hand on his shoulder.

"He always was the sentimental kind," Grant grumbles under his breath. "Dad nearly had a fit when he brought home strays as a kid. But it never stopped him."

I bristle at his insinuation. Me? Is he comparing *me* to an abandoned pet? Warmth floods my cheeks. Thinking about the dynamics in my family, he's not far off.

"She's not a stray cat." Quinn shakes her finger at him. "And don't forget, you took me in when I needed help."

"Don't remind me." He flinches as she gently shoves his shoulder.

A smile breaks his stony expression, and my heart flips at the look they share.

They're in love. Absolutely head over heels. Smitten. Jealousy pierces my heart. What I wouldn't give to have someone look at me in such a tender way.

"How did you two meet?" I ask, curious about the romance playing out in front of me.

Quinn's face turns pink, and she clears her throat. "Well, that's a complicated story—"

"I caught her stealing shit that didn't belong to her." Grant stabs a piece of meat. "Two months later, she showed up on my doorstep with stab wounds, as a murder witness."

My fork clatters to the plate. "You…what?"

"Like I said, it's complicated." Quinn chuckles and lifts her glass in salute before taking a drink.

"How long are you staying with my brother?" Grant changes the topic.

I glance at Claude, who seems unbothered by the conversation's abrupt detour.

"She's welcome to stay as long as she needs to."

My heart swells. "Thank you."

Quinn shifts the conversation again, moving to lighter topics. I can't help but feel a twinge of jealousy at what she has with Grant. Their love is potent, obvious in every line shared, every glance, every smile. Even with their difference in age, I can see how much they care for each other, how they're in harmony with one another.

In all my life, I've never seen such unabashed adoration between two people. My parents didn't marry for love. It was a business transaction. Everything they did was for power and status. For show. And I am expected to play my part in an ongoing performance by marrying a man I loathe.

Throughout the meal, I'm haunted by thoughts of my past and the dread hanging over my head. I do my best to ignore the pressure from their weight, but seeing what I've been missing leaves an ache deep in my chest.

After dinner, I help Quinn clean the dishes. She's funny and full of energy. We laugh as we discuss the latest films and music. She has an affinity for Stephen King, like Claude, and enjoys movies, from classic films to modern action flicks. I like her already. In a different life, we could have been best friends.

I'll take these sweet kernels of friendship. These stolen moments of joy give me hope that there's something out there for me, beyond my family and their oppressive grip on my life.

Claude and Grant sip coffee at the table. I steal a glance at them and admire Claude's profile. Warmth surrounds me. I wonder whether his lips are as soft as they look. Do they taste like the apple pie we had for dessert?

Quinn nudges me with her hip. "Penny for your thoughts?" she asks, her voice low.

My face warms. "Oh, nothing."

"You can't fool me, honey." She grins. "I've seen that look before. Hell, I've worn it."

"I don't know what you're talking about." I dry the plate in my hands and set it in the cabinet.

"Mm-hmm." Quinn sighs. "Well, between you and me, Claude could use a distraction. He lives at the bar. It's his whole life."

"Isn't that a good thing? He has something he loves."

"Some*one* would be better." She sets aside the last plate and leans against the counter. "He's been alone for too long. It's nice to see him interested in something other than his work or his books."

My face heats at the implication of her words. She thinks there's something going on between Claude and me. I don't want to ruin her hope by correcting her, and I allow myself to imagine what it would be like to be with him.

"Are you ready to go?" Claude asks, breaking into my thoughts.

I jump and spin around. "Yes, I'm ready."

We exchange goodbyes, and Quinn hugs me tight. "Let me know if you need anything. I'll be here, taking care of the old man."

"I heard that." Grant grabs her by the waist and pulls her against him. "Nice to meet you, Gwen."

"Thanks again for dinner." I wave and follow Claude into the hallway.

When we reach his apartment, he lets me enter the room first, then closes the door behind us. My body thrums just being in his presence. Can he feel it too? I can't be the only one. I've felt more love in this place in the past two days than I've ever felt over the duration of my entire life.

"Did you enjoy yourself?"

Tears prick my eyes. "I did." I hastily wipe them away, hoping he doesn't see.

"Then why are you crying?" He steps closer and brushes his thumb across my cheek, catching a few stray tears.

I sway toward him at the tender gesture. "My family isn't nearly as welcoming as yours." I lift my chin to meet his gaze. "You're lucky to have them in your life." I sniff as the tears flow.

Claude embraces me, wrapping his one arm tight around my waist. His heat surrounds me, and I bury my face against the warm flannel of his shirt. He smells so good. Like spices and soap. The subtle aroma of *him* beneath it all unleashes a need inside me. I cling to his shirt until the sobs subside. When I finally feel grounded again, I lean back and wipe my face with my hand.

"Sorry about that." I laugh softly. "Thank you for everything."

When I press a kiss to his cheek, he goes still. I pull back, my lips hovering near his mouth. His eyes are closed, his lower lip trembling.

"Gwen." He opens his eyes, and deep in their dark centers, I can see hunger. Need.

Even though I want more than he may be willing to give—more than I have to offer—I refuse to ignore the tension simmering between us for a moment longer.

I take the chance and close the gap between us. My lips meet his, his goatee brushing my skin, and I kiss him softly. Reverently. With no expectation.

CHAPTER 9

Claude

Sweet merciful God. Am I dead?

I inhale sharply, taking the sweet scent of her deep into my lungs, my heart constricting. Her kiss catches me with an unsteady right hook. The press of her lips sends an electric pulse through me. My hand grips her waist. She leans into the touch, pressing her body to mine.

There's no part of her I wouldn't explore. Every delicious curve tucked against me drives my hunger deeper. She tastes like apples and cloves. A groan rips from my throat when she wraps her arms around my neck and buries her fingers in my hair.

Her gentle touch against my nape unleashes my restraint. I pull her toward me and slant my mouth over hers. She opens, and I'm lost in her glittering web.

When she walked into my bar, she shone with a brilliance I'd never seen before. Even in her blood-soaked gown, wearing tearstains like a badge of honor, she looked regal. A diamond shining in the darkness.

But now she fucking glows, brighter than the North Star.

She tugs my hair as I delve deeper, tasting her mouth, exploring her with equal parts curiosity and enthusiasm. Her gasping breaths mirror my own.

It's been years since I've kissed a woman, felt the heat of her surging through my blood. My body hums with desperate, clumsy emotions coursing through me. I want her. More than I should. She wants me, and I'm dumbfounded at the realization.

"Claude," she murmurs against my mouth, grinding her hips on my thigh. "I won't break if you touch me."

My fingers tighten on her waist. A slight shift of my hand and I could delve beneath the fabric of her shirt, feel the delicate skin I've been dying to explore.

She threads her fingers through my hair and pulls hard enough to force my head back.

Our eyes lock. The blue captures me, swirling in an endless sea. I want to surrender to the plea I see swimming in their depths. She wants me to make love to her.

But as much as I long to bury myself deep inside her, I won't. I can't.

"I'm sorry, Gwen." Her fingertips slide from my neck as I step away, releasing her from my hold. A chill surrounds me.

She comes closer, but I hold my hand up.

Her mouth gapes, and hurt replaces her hunger. "You don't want me?"

"No." I curse myself when she recoils as if I slapped her. "I mean, I want you, but we can't...*I* can't do this."

"Why?" She crosses her arms.

"We barely know each other." I rub my hand over my jaw and sigh. "Gwen, you're still engaged."

Fire flares deep within her, and I take an involuntary step backward.

"As far as I'm concerned, my *fiancé* can go to the devil. I agreed to that farce of an engagement, but he wasn't *my* choice." Her voice softens. "I don't get a choice."

"Gwen...I..." Confusion spins in my brain. What does she mean? I reach for her, but she bats my hand away.

"I don't need your pity." She sniffs and keeps her distance, her eyes brimming with pain and shame. "I don't want it."

Shit. I didn't mean to upset her or dredge up her past or her current situation. I was trying to be a gentleman. It would have been easy to give in to the temptation and take her right there against the wall. But she deserves better than that...better than me.

"I'm so—"

"Stop." She holds up a hand. "I don't want to talk about it. Let's drop it, okay?"

"I just don't want to take advantage of you, Gwen." My soft declaration echoes through the quiet room.

Tears slip from her eyes, and guilt pierces my gut. I reach for her again, but she pulls away and retreats to the bedroom, closing the door behind her.

Fuck.

I flex my hand and force myself not to follow her. I didn't pull away from her kiss because I wanted to. I pulled away because I needed to. My chest pulls tight at the thought of leaving her in such a state, but I won't intrude where I'm not wanted.

It's hard not to take it personally. I hurt her, that's true, but it's more like I ripped open an old wound that hasn't healed properly and then poured alcohol on it. But I didn't inflict the original injury.

Not that it matters. Scars like that run deep.

For a few tense moments, I hope she'll come back. Pray she'll talk to me. Trust me. But I can't even trust myself when it comes to her. I would let her unleash hell on me if it would help her heal.

Even though she only walked into my life twenty-four hours ago, I feel like I've known her for years. Our connection is that strong. It leaves me wavering, questioning everything. One thing is certain, though. I won't use her for my own selfish pleasure or bind her to me with careless actions and thoughtless words. That's a line I won't cross.

I stare at the closed door and groan. There's nothing I can do tonight. Regret bites the back of my throat.

I haven't been drunk since I got back from Vietnam, and even though the thought of alcohol does nothing for me, my subconscious offers up the suggestion.

Instead of dwelling on my thoughts, I venture down to the bar. Jan, Dave, and Sam have things under control. It's not busy, but there's a small group in the far corner as well as a few regulars seated at the bar.

I grab a Coke and retreat to my office, closing the door behind me with my foot. There's a mountain of paperwork on my desk. I collapse in the chair and take a drink.

Her taste lingers on my tongue. Nothing will wash it away. It's a memory I'll carry with me for years. I can't bring myself to regret it, but I won't allow myself to crave more.

Even as I try to convince myself it meant nothing, I palm myself through the fabric of my jeans. A quiet groan tears free at the pressure of my hand. I'm still hard, aching for her.

With a curse, I stand and lock the door. Resuming my seat, I take my cock out. It lays heavy in my hand. I close my eyes and grip it tight. It only takes a moment to imagine my large hand is her delicate one as I stroke myself.

Panting breaths fill the small space, and I relinquish myself to the fantasy. Gwen's bright eyes, her pouty lips, those dangerous curves. I want to bury my face between her thighs and not come up for air. I want her gasping my name, her fingers tangling in my hair as I lick her pussy. She'll moan, buck her hips against my mouth as I devour her. Right before she comes, I'll bury myself deep inside her.

My hand moves faster, stroking with a frantic purpose. The orgasm builds deep inside me. I squeeze my eyes closed and pump my fist, over and over. Visions of Gwen fill the darkness behind my lids. Her on her knees with her mouth wrapped around my length. Her beneath me as I bend her over the bar. Her straddling me in bed, hands braced on the wall as she rides my cock.

In my imagination, she tips her head back and cries out when she comes. It triggers my own release.

Warmth coats my hand as I come hard, my body shaking with the force of it. I can only imagine the reality would be more intense than my fantasy.

But it won't happen.

Somehow, despite my daze, I manage to clean myself with tissues and toss them into the trash. Mentally pushing aside the remains of my distraction, I pull the stack of papers close and open the top file.

I'll drown myself in paperwork if I have to, but there's no way I can go back upstairs. Not knowing she's in my bed. Knowing she wants me.

Whatever mess I've gotten myself into, I will find a way out of it. I always do.

I just hope I haven't fucked up beyond redemption.

CHAPTER 10

Gwen

Heart racing, I collapse against the door.

Stupid. I lean my head back and pinch my eyes closed. How could I be so stupid?

I practically threw myself at Claude. What did I expect?

He's unlike any man I've ever met. Quiet, reserved…restrained.

My lips tingle with the memory of his kiss. Beneath his calm exterior beats the heart of a passionate man. I'd bet my life on it.

And yet…he turned me down. Pushed me away.

Am I that horrid for wanting something new, something real?

The floor creaks on the other side of the wall, and I hold my breath. A door closes in the distance, and I sag against the wood, alone and unwanted.

I curse myself as I head for the bathroom. When I catch a glimpse of myself in the mirror, I wince. I can't even face my own reflection after that fiasco. Turning my back to the sink, I brush my teeth with the new toothbrush Claude set aside for me.

He's thoughtful and kind. I shouldn't have pushed myself on him. I've made everything uncomfortable and awkward.

And yet…he leaned into my touch. His hard body pressed against mine. The undeniable ridge of his erection brushed my stomach. He wants me. There's no denying it. But his rigid sense of honor won't allow him to take what I offer. To embrace the heat between us.

I strip down and put on the pajamas he lent me before flopping onto his bed. His scent surrounds me. Nestling into the blankets, I inhale deeply, committing his aroma to memory.

My body squirms at the reminder of his presence, his touch, his kiss. I huff and shift beneath the blankets. The soft glow of the bedside lamp flickers out when I press the switch.

Enshrouded in darkness, I stare at the ceiling. Nothing can purge Claude from my mind. He consumes my thoughts.

I slide my hand beneath the waistband of my shorts to find my pussy dripping for him. Those stolen moments of pleasure have left me in a state of need. I want him. All of him, not just the kind bartender who came to my rescue, the knight in shining armor. Even with his frustrating honor and chivalry, he has demons like any other man. Like me. There's more to Claude than he shows, and I want to peel his layers back, explore the darkness beneath.

My breath quickens as I imagine him stripping the clothes from my body, kissing his way down my bare skin. His head buried between my thighs. His soulful eyes locked with mine as he licks my pussy.

The fantasy pulls me deeper, and I circle my clit with two fingers. It's not enough.

I want to be filled by him. I want him to fuck all thought from my mind. To drive me to distraction before he makes me come, over and over, leaving me sated and suspended in bliss.

He'd tangle his hand in my hair while he drives deep from behind. Controlling me. Claiming me.

The men I've been with in the past, including Nick, cared nothing of my needs. For my pleasure. But I'm willing to bet Claude would make it his mission to satisfy me in ways I've only dreamed of. I imagine him pushing me to the edge and teasing me until I combust.

With every thought, the pleasure spirals higher until I'm positive I'll burst. The moment I picture him wrapping his hand around my throat, I come. Hard. Fast.

The orgasm radiates through me, and I milk it with gentle touches, arching my hips into my hand. As the effects wane, I roll to my side and sigh. It wasn't what I wanted, but it took the edge off. I still ache for him.

When I fall asleep, Claude greets me in my dreams. But even there, he plays the gentleman, and I drown in sexual frustration.

I wake to sunshine streaming through the window and the sound of movement in the next room. Peeling myself from the bed, I tiptoe to the door and peek into the living room.

"Good, you're awake." Quinn beams at me from the kitchen, her auburn curls woven into a braid over her shoulder. She pushes something in a skillet on the stove.

I open the door fully, and my gaze falls to the empty couch. "Where's Claude?"

"Down at the bar, most likely." She smiles and shakes her head. "I told you, he's married to that place."

"Are you making breakfast?" I cross the room and peer into the skillet.

"Yeah, figured you could use some girl time." Quinn points to a box on the floor behind the sofa. "I brought you some more clothes and other things you might need."

"Thanks." I fidget with the hem of the oversized shirt I'm wearing.

"Why don't you go get dressed and we can chat over breakfast?"

I carry the box into the bedroom. Inside is a variety of clothes, some makeup, hair products, deodorant, and a comfortable-looking pair of sneakers.

After I put on some clean underwear and a bra, I pull random articles from the box and match them the best I can. The stonewashed jeans and faded-black long-sleeved top are a definite step down from Gucci, but I'm not complaining. They're clean and comfortable. I'm grateful Quinn brought me something from her closet. While I enjoy Claude's oversized clothes, the lingering scent of him drives me crazy.

I wrangle my hair into a lopsided ponytail and brush on a little mascara. It's nothing fancy, but it does the trick.

When I return to the kitchen, Quinn is setting the second plate on the table.

She whistles low and winks. "You look smoking hot. Claude will love it."

My face heats at her praise. I'm used to compliments, but in my experience, they're nearly always insincere. Studying Quinn's face, I don't detect anything but honesty. I sit at the table across from her.

"How long have you known Claude?" I ask, pushing the eggs around on my plate.

"A few months," she says between bites. "We spend quite a bit of time together, now that I work in the bar four nights a week."

"You work at the bar?"

"Sure do." Quinn beams. "Grant isn't a fan of it, but he knows Claude won't tolerate anyone harassing his employees."

"Do you like it?"

"It's an honest living." She chews thoughtfully for a moment before setting aside her fork. "I was a thief when Grant met me. It's a long story."

I lean forward, curious. "I'd love to hear it."

"Of course, but not today. Claude told me he needs both of us downstairs by noon to get the bar ready."

"Ready for what?"

"Your first day." Quinn sips her coffee. "He asked me to keep an eye on you. Help you learn the ropes."

My face heats again. "I'm a fast learner. I promise."

"I don't doubt it." She narrows her eyes. "You look familiar. What did you say your last name was?"

"I didn't." I take a bite to hide my unease. I can't tell them my name. Not yet.

"Gwen." She reaches across the table to take my hand. "I promise, whatever happened to you, you're safe here."

"I know." With a sigh, I meet her gaze. "It's just…I like this. Being myself. Just Gwen. No expectations. No attachments."

"I understand." She squeezes my hand before releasing it. "Just know you can come to me any time if you want to talk."

A weight lifts from my chest. "Thanks."

We fall into general conversation about food and music. It seems we both have an affinity for Foreigner and Madonna. I reveal my burning love for Aerosmith, and she agrees wholeheartedly.

After we clean up, we head down to the bar. She knocks on the door to the office and pops her head in. "We're here," Quinn says to Claude, who glances up from his stack of papers.

"Good. Start with the prep work. I'll be out in a little while." His gaze shifts to me, and the butterflies that consumed me last night take flight again. "Morning."

I wave and smile, unable to speak, afraid I'll stick my foot in my mouth.

Quinn leads me into the bar and turns on the lights. She drops a few quarters into the jukebox and makes some selections. I sway with the bold strains of Journey, enthusiastic at her taste in music. Quinn and I are definitely kindred souls.

Thirty minutes later, we're laughing and singing to the music as we finish prepping. When the song finishes, Quinn nudges me with her hip.

"So feel free to tell me to get lost if I'm prying, but I've got to know." Her eyes sparkle. "What's going on with you and Claude?"

"Nothing." I grab a rag and wipe the counter.

"Come on." She leans closer. "I saw the way he looked at you during dinner last night. That *wasn't* nothing."

Heat creeps up my neck and into my cheeks. I shrug, unsure how to answer her. I turn to her and see Claude standing in the archway leading into the kitchen. Inside my chest, my heart flutters like a hummingbird.

His kind expression is impassive, but there's a tightness around his mouth that wasn't there the night we met.

"Are you done?"

Quinn spins around at his question. "Yes. We're ready to go."

"Are you sure this is what you want to do?" he asks, his gaze fixed on me.

"Positive."

He nods. "If there's any trouble, let me know. I'll take care of it."

"Why would there be trouble?" Quinn's confused gaze shifts from Claude to me.

"It's a long story." I offer a halfhearted smile.

"Looks like we're gonna have to make time to exchange long stories."

"Yeah." I rinse out the rag and drape it over the sink, ignoring the indecision twisting in my gut.

Maybe this isn't a good idea.

Claude's comment has left me floundering. It's possible Nick will return, searching for me. But I can't stay hidden away, living off charity. I can take care of myself; all I need is a chance to prove it.

When I turn around, Claude is gone. Quinn is leaning against the bar, watching me.

"What?"

"Nothing." She raises her hands and smirks. "But there's something going on between you two. I know it."

I busy myself with the tray of fruit to my right, hiding my red cheeks from her view. She's not wrong. There *is* something going on with Claude and me. But I want more than I should, more than he's willing to give. Right now, it's too complicated, and until I figure out what's going on in his mind, I don't want to confuse Quinn or Grant with complex explanations.

Whatever this is—even if we explored it—may not last. I shake my head. I'm not going to think about it. Not now. I want to enjoy this stint of freedom, for as long as I can, until I can figure out how to make it permanent. But that may require me to completely break ties with the city.

The last thing I want to do is lead Claude on and leave him with a broken heart when an opportunity arises. I doubt he'd be willing to come with me. It's not like he'd walk away from this place for a girl he just met. That's crazy.

But falling for a bartender in Hell's Kitchen after only two days seems insane too.

As we work, my mind keeps drifting to the soft-spoken bartender whose kiss left me breathless and wanting. Whatever happened between us, he's determined to ignore it. I just want to enjoy the moment. Can there be any compromise?

I will break down the wall he's built. One way or another.

CHAPTER 11

Claude

I'm beginning to regret my decision to let her stay with me.

A week has passed quickly, and I'm left with an ache in my spine from the ancient sofa springs. I *could* find somewhere else to sleep or find her a place to live, but the truth is, I like having her here, even if I've been avoiding her like the goddamn plague.

I can't trust myself to be a gentleman. Not after that kiss. The temptation is too great, and I'm not the kind of guy who takes advantage of a vulnerable woman. Not that she's completely vulnerable. She's dangerous. Ripe curves, sweet smile, kind heart. But she's also engaged. I don't take that shit lightly.

I've done everything in my power to avoid her this week. I give her space. Hell, I've been showering and retreating to my office before she wakes every morning. I've done more paperwork this week than in the last six months.

Why is this so damned complicated? And who is Gwen really?

After a brief conversation with Grant, I make a few phone calls to see if anyone is looking for someone matching her description. There are plenty of missing women in the area, but apparently, none of them look like Gwen. No one can tell me anything.

I have nothing to go on but the name she gave me…and her nickname, Gigi. Both of these could be pseudonyms. I kick myself for not asking more questions the night her fiancé barged into my bar demanding information. I don't regret not giving her up that night. On the contrary, I'm glad the asshole left empty-handed.

That doesn't make her mine. It just makes this whole situation fucking complicated. I should have never offered her a job or my bed.

Regardless, Gwen has shown she really is a quick learner. Even with no experience and no discernible skills, she works hard and takes no shit. In one week, she's not only learned how to do her job well, but she's become familiar with the regulars, who welcomed her as one of their own. I'm awestruck by the way she so seamlessly fits in. Who would have thought a debutante would be at home among blue-collar dockhands?

I push aside the last order request, then stand and stretch. A glance at the clock reminds me of my duties. Sam has to leave early tonight, and I promised to work the bar for him. The nights I stepped behind the bar this week put me in close proximity to Gwen, but the chaotic atmosphere kept us both busy. It took the restraint of a saint to not brush against her or whisper something to her in passing.

I wanted to. Lord knows I did.

Quinn took her to the corner thrift shop, and they came home, giggling, with six bags of clothes between them. She's blossomed from a wilting rose into a flower I don't recognize. Part of me wants to hide her, protect her. Someone with that much glow is bound to attract attention.

The bar is humming. Music blares from the jukebox, and nearly every table is full. A good night, so long as no trouble starts.

Quinn works the floor while Gwen mans the bar. I watch from the doorway for a moment as she pours pints and makes a dirty martini. She doesn't even reach for the cards to verify the recipe. Every pour is on point, and she makes it without error.

"Hey, Claude!" Frank, one of my regulars, shouts from his seat at the bar. A few of the patrons perk up at the sound of my name. I wave and step into the light.

Gwen turns, and her lips part in surprise before transforming into a smile when I cross the narrow space.

"I thought you were gonna leave me here all alone." She nudges me with her elbow.

"You were doing just fine all alone." I ignore the spark of playfulness in her eyes…and the ache it causes in my chest.

"There you are." A woman's voice rises over the noise of the crowded bar. "Claude! Over here."

I scan the room until I spy a quartet of familiar faces at the end of the bar and smile. Rob and Arthur have brought their significant others here for their monthly double date.

"This place is packed tonight. What's the special event?" Rob asks, sidling up the bar with Marcy. Behind them, Arthur and his wife Kate look for open seats.

"No event. People just like to come here to blow off steam." I lean forward, resting my elbow on the bar.

"Guess the best-kept secret in New York is no longer a secret," Rob says with a smirk.

"You'll always have a table here if you bring these lovely ladies." I wink at Marcy, who grins in response. "What can I get for you?"

"The usual." Marcy nudges Rob aside. "We'll be in the booth at the back."

"I'll have Quinn bring your drinks."

Kate and Arthur wave before disappearing to a back booth where a group has just left. I shake my head and smile, watching Rob and Marcy join them. I've known Rob and Arthur for over a decade. Years ago, they saved my brother's life…and his job. I owe them both, but they treat me like family. I guess we are family in a way.

In the last few months, I've seen sides of them I never thought I'd see. Relaxed, carefree, and absolutely smitten. Of all the men in New York, I never thought *those* two would find happiness in relationships. As both were confirmed bachelors, it left me speechless when I met Kate and Marcy. But love shakes things up.

"What do you need?"

I turn to find Gwen standing beside me. Her soft floral perfume encircles her like a halo, driving away the scent of cigarettes and booze. Those blue eyes hold mine, and for a moment, I forget what she asked.

Drinks. Right.

"Can you make an old-fashioned and a martini with lemon?"

"No problem, boss." Gwen pivots and retrieves the ingredients.

I manage to shake myself free of her spell and make Rob's gin and tonic. What the hell am I doing? I can't keep going like this, with this tension simmering between us. We need to talk, but it's not going to happen until after closing. And even then, I'm tempting fate, because being alone with Gwen is damned torment.

I place two drinks on a tray, and Gwen appears with the other two drinks. Quinn arrives with an empty tray and gives me another order. I slide the full tray to her and motion to Rob and Arthur's table, where Grant has joined them. Of course he has.

Quinn sweeps the tray into her arms and sashays toward the table.

As Gwen works beside me, I'm hyperaware of her presence. We move in sync, brushing past each other, working in tandem. It's almost a dance. The teasing sway of her body as she moves, as she glides from one side of the bar to the other. Her hair grazes my arm when she spins around to use the register.

Fuck me. I don't know how much more of this I can take.

"Claude!"

I turn to Marcy, who's leaning on the bar. The crowd is thinning. It's after eleven, and there are open seats everywhere.

"What do you need, Marcy?"

"I was able to salvage that dress." She grins. "Took some work, but I got it clean. I'll bring it over next week."

"What dress?" Gwen's arm brushes mine as she joins the conversation.

"The Gucci one," I say. "Marcy's a stylist, and she offered to try to clean it."

"It's yours?" Marcy's brows nearly disappear into her tufted bangs. "Honey, I don't know what happened, but you need to take care with a dress of that caliber."

"Thank you so much." Gwen presses her hand to her chest. "It was a gift. I thought it was ruined beyond salvation."

"Luckily, I'm a master at removing bloodstains."

I purse my lips, biting back the question burning in my mind: how does one acquire that mastery? But I really don't want the answer.

"I owe you." She extends her open hand, and Marcy takes it. "I'm Gwen."

"Marcy." Her eyes narrow in thought as they shake hands. "Have we met? I have this crazy feeling I've seen you before."

"Oh, maybe. I've lived in the city my whole life. It's possible we've passed on the street."

"No…" Marcy rubs her jaw. "I swear you look familiar."

"I just have one of those faces, I guess." Gwen blushes and hedges, busying herself with wiping a dry spot on the cooler near her hip.

"Holy shit." Marcy's eyes fly wide. "That's it. You're Gigi Monroe."

Gwen's cheeks turn bright red, and she shushes Marcy. "Not so loud."

"Shit. Sorry." Marcy drops her voice. "What the hell are you doing working here?"

"I'll try not to take offense at that." I cross my arms, confused by the exchange and Marcy's revelation.

"That's not what I meant." She shoots me a look. "I'm just wondering why the daughter of the richest man in New York City is working as a bartender in Hell's Kitchen when she should be schmoozing with the in-crowd."

"It's a long story." Gwen sighs.

"Are you ready to go?" Rob comes alongside Marcy and kisses her cheek.

"Yeah." She takes a napkin and asks for a pen. I hand it to her and watch her scribble something down before giving it to Gwen. "For if you ever need a stylist. I also make custom designs on the side."

"Thanks." Gwen tucks it into her pocket and turns away from me.

After they've gone, she keeps her distance. Now I know why she's hiding. Why she's trying to start over.

She's a Monroe.

The sole heir to the wealthiest family in New York City. The goddamn cream of the elite.

A family notoriously close to the mafia.

Son of a bitch.

I take a long look at the handful of patrons in the bar. The moment they leave, this game comes to an end. Gwen will come clean.

Or I'll call her father and tell him to come pick up his daughter before she can completely, irrevocably shatter my heart.

CHAPTER 12

Gwen

I saw the recognition light his eyes the moment Marcy's statement registered. Shit. There's no way I can play this off. He knows who I am, who my parents are.

Claude doesn't want me hanging around his bar. He doesn't want trouble. And that's all I am. Trouble in glitter and italics lit with neon light.

When he walks away without saying a word, I try not to take it personally. The unspoken tension between us has pulled tight over the past week. Even though he avoids me at every turn, it hums like an electrical current.

Instead of chasing after him, I busy myself behind the bar. There's still an hour until close. Quinn cleans the vacated tables while I focus on washing glasses.

Claude stands at the opposite end of the bar, talking with Tom, one of the regulars. It's difficult to ignore his presence. My attention gravitates to him as I work. His low voice drifts just under the music, making it impossible to hear what he's saying.

Quinn appears with a tray of dirty glasses. "There's only one table left and Tom. Should be able to clean up before closing tonight."

I nod and continue washing.

"Something wrong, hon?"

"I fucked up."

"How?"

There's no easy way to explain it, so I skip the details and go straight to the heart of my frustration. "Claude's upset with me."

Quinn scoffs. "Claude? No way. He's the most understanding man I know."

I shoot a glance in his direction. He remains firmly entrenched in his conversation with Tom. When I turn back to Quinn, her eyes are soft green pools of sympathy.

"Just talk to him. You'll feel better, I promise."

Before I can respond, Quinn turns and weaves through the tables. I stare at the far wall, my mind spinning with a hundred possible outcomes of a heart-to-heart with Claude, none of them ending well. I refocus on cleaning, and before I know it, the bar is empty.

Quinn locks the door at midnight. "Where's Claude?"

I scan the bar, but there's no sign of Claude or Grant. With a shrug, I place a few coins on the counter. "Put on some tunes while we work."

Quinn vacuums the floor while I mop behind the bar. We make quick work of the closing checklist, and for a brief moment, I forget my earlier concerns . To be honest, the music helps.

"I'll take the garbage out. Need anything else?" Quinn calls from the doorway.

"Nope, I can handle it from here. Go find your man." I wink.

She blows me a kiss and disappears into the kitchen.

Alone with my mop, I take my time, making sure to get under the shelves. A song by the Cars plays on the jukebox, and I sing along…of course I know the lyrics to "Magic." My body sways, and I'm caught up in the moment. The dim overhead lights reflect in the clean, wet floor.

My muscles ache nearly as much as my feet. I'm exhausted and sticky from some liquor I spilled on myself earlier, but there's nowhere I'd rather be. No upscale club or fancy dinner compares to the feeling of a job well done. Pride fills me, even as sadness tugs at the edges.

"It looks good." Claude's voice reverberates through me like a bell ringing in the darkness.

"Thanks." My face warms as I turn to face him.

He's leaning against the doorway, watching me, his brow furrowed.

"Something wrong?"

He presses his lips together and shakes his head.

I can't help but wonder if there's any way to cheer him up. Suddenly, I'm determined to make him smile, as if my life depended on it. "This is the second time you've caught me dancing." I set the broom aside. "Maybe you should join me."

"What?" His expression softens.

"Dance with me." I hold out my hand.

He straightens, but he doesn't move. "Gwen, I don't think that's a good idea."

"It's just a dance. I promise." I shimmy closer, moving my hips with each step. His breath hitches when I take his hand and pull him behind the bar. It's narrow, but I can dance anywhere.

He steps closer, and the music ends.

"I won't bite." I place his hand on my hip. Another song starts, "Cry to Me." It's bluesy and sexy.

I'm not sure I can keep my promise. I wrap my arms around his neck, and my body presses lightly against his as we sway.

His heavy sigh surrounds me, and I relax as his hand rests on my waist.

The memory of our kiss slams into me, but I bite my lip, stifling the urge to claim another one.

The music consumes me, and I grind against him. My hands wander over his shoulders, coming to rest on his chest.

He grabs my wrist and jerks me against him, pinning me against the bar.

"What do you want from me, Gwen?" Claude's deep voice is hoarse.

"The same thing you want." I trace my finger across his lips, trailing it over his broad chest. "I saw how much you wanted me when I was a scrappy, blood-covered wreck hiding in your bar."

"That's a bold assumption."

I shrug and lose myself in his whiskey-brown eyes, desperate to find some connection. Some revelation of truth. Of acceptance. "You want me, Claude. I can see it."

"You belong to someone else."

"No. I don't."

His eyes close for a breath, and when he opens them, I see hesitation amidst the pain. "You could have any man in the world. Why me?"

"You saw I needed help and stepped in." I lean into him, relaxing into his hold. I feel safe with him. Protected. Loved. "You didn't know anything about me. Not my name, not my family, nothing. You saw *me*."

Claude groans when I cup his cheek in my palm.

"You can't want this, Gwen. I'm no one."

"That may be true to the world." I bite my lip. "But not to me. You're *everything* to me."

"You don't know me."

"Then let me in."

"I can't." He hangs his head, and his voice cracks. "I'm broken and old. You don't want me."

"I do. You're kind." My fingers tip his chin up until our gazes lock. "And distinguished."

"I can't even hold you the way you should be held." He holds up his arms, making a show of his missing hand.

Without looking away, I rest my hand on the fabric covering where his hand should be. "You think that matters to me?"

"Doesn't it?"

"Not in the slightest." I slide my hand up his left arm, and he releases his hold on my other wrist. "I've seen you work. Nothing stops you from something when you set your mind to it. The only thing stopping us is *you*."

"Your fiancé, Gwen. What about him?"

I wince at the mention of Nick, but I shake off the nasty reminder and focus on the man in my arms. "I didn't choose him. I don't want him."

"It's not that easy."

"It is." I run my hand down the buttons of his shirt and over his belt buckle. My fingertips brush his cock, straining against the zipper of his pants. I grin at his sharp inhale. "The only man I want is standing right in front of me."

Claude dips his head and captures my lips in a bruising kiss. I cling to him, pulling him closer. The memories did no justice to the feel of him against me. Kissing me. His tongue delves into my mouth, and I moan at the onslaught of need. I'm a feather caught on the breeze, drifting higher and higher into the endless sky.

My hips rock against his thigh as his hand roams over my back, then caresses my ass. One massive palm grips me tight.

I want more.

His mouth trails across my jaw, my neck.

"Claude, please." I gasp against his shoulder as he runs his fingers along the crease where my thigh meets my ass. He grips my waist and spins me around, so my back is to his chest. I can see us in the mirror behind the bar. My tousled hair, flushed cheeks, kiss-swollen lips tell the same story as my lust-hazed eyes. I'm gone, lost in him.

"Hands on the counter." His brash command has my pussy weeping.

I place my hands on the sturdy counter beneath the shelves. His talented fingers unfasten my jeans and slide them down my hips. The cool air bites my thighs as he settles the denim at my ankles.

His fingers trail over the inside of my thighs as he slowly rises. In the mirror, I watch his dark head as he arches into me, blocking me with his body. His heat steadies me. When his palm cups my pussy through the thin fabric of my panties, I whimper.

"You don't have to be quiet for me, sweetheart." He pushes aside the fabric and glides his long fingers across my slick folds, parting them. "Is this what you want?"

"Yes. God, yes," I cry out when he slides a finger into me, stroking my sensitive walls. "Claude," I gasp as he adds another finger and slowly fucks me.

When I meet his gaze in the mirror, he smiles, and it's everything I ever dreamed of. His smile ignites something visceral inside of me. I rock against his hand, needing pressure against my clit. Claude quickens his pace, grinding the heel of his palm against my pelvis. Sweet tension spirals higher and higher. I tremble and shake as he moves deeper, pivoting his thumb to find my clit swollen.

"Come for me, sweetheart," he whispers in my ear, adding a little more pressure.

I buck my hips into his hand, and my climax slams into me. When I come, his name is on my lips followed by a string of curses.

I've never come that hard. Ever.

Claude kisses my shoulder, and I lift my head to meet his gaze. He spins me around, and my arms go around his waist. This time his kiss is tender.

"Shall we go upstairs?" I mutter against his mouth.

"Fuck, yes, that sofa will kill me if I spend one more night on it."

"You were always welcome to join me." I kiss him again, savoring the taste of him. "That bed is too big for one person."

"You'll be the death of me." He grins. "But what a fucking way to go."

I shimmy back into my jeans and follow Claude upstairs.

Finally. Fucking finally.

CHAPTER 13

Claude

What the fuck am I doing? I'm too far gone to care.

She follows me. I pause at the base of the stairs and allow her to go first. Her ass sways with each step, and I'm mesmerized by it. I can't wait to get those clothes off, to see all of her.

Her coming apart in my arms, moaning my name as her climax grips my fingers…it's the sexiest thing I've ever experienced.

I've been with women…before I lost my hand and part of my arm, before I sacrificed at the request of my country. When I came home, people looked at me differently. Treated me differently. They never thanked me for my service or my sacrifice. I didn't expect it.

But I never expected to feel like an outcast in my own neighborhood, among the people I grew up with either.

Years of working in the bar gave me purpose, a way to remind society I wasn't worthless, even with my injury. But when it came to women, I was still an outcast. Shunned for my quiet nature and lack of two functional hands.

Gwen opens the door to my apartment. She spins to face me when I close it. Her blue eyes sparkle in the low lamplight as she takes hold of my button-down shirt.

"I'm all sticky. From work," she says, grinning. She slowly slips the buttons free, her lashes fluttering against her cheeks as she makes quick work of my shirt. "I should shower."

"Don't let me stop you." I wrap my hand around the back of her neck, and she leans into the touch.

"Join me." Her hand trails up my stomach and rests on my heart.

Fuck, her touch has me hard as a granite boulder, as if I wasn't hard enough already.

"There's room for two."

"I doubt that." There's really not enough room for *me* in my shower, but she's insistent.

"We'll make room." She steps back, eyeing my chest and licking her lips. As she turns, heading for the bedroom, she peels the shirt from her torso and drops it to the floor.

I sway at the sight of her bare spine. Fuck. She wasn't wearing a bra this whole time. How did I not notice?

Then I remember how desperate I was to avoid her…to avoid this.

I was an idiot. She pauses in the doorway and glances at me, her body pivoting enough to show the generous curve of her breast and a soft, peaked nipple.

"Are you coming?"

"Not yet, but I'm close," I mutter under my breath even as my feet take action.

Gwen heads for the bathroom, shedding more clothing along the way.

I pull my shirt off, tossing it aside as I follow her. I fumble with my pants, unable to grip the button.

"Let me help." Gwen takes the button in her hands and unfastens it. As she slides the zipper down, her gaze dips to my waist. She hooks her thumbs into my jeans and pulls them down, taking my underwear with them. On her knees, she grasps my cock in her hands.

I brace my hand on the wall when she takes me in her mouth.

I nearly lose control at the sight of her full lips stretched around me. Her pink cheeks glow as she hums, the sound vibrating through my flesh.

"Fuck, Gwen." I gasp as she cups my balls and takes me deeper. As she pulls back, her tongue swirls around the head, and I nearly come. "Baby, if you keep going, I won't be able to stop."

She wipes her mouth with her thumb before rising to her feet. Every curve is bare, and I'm struck stupid at the sight of the woman before me. How the hell did I get so lucky? I can't even think about it. If I think too much, I might wake up and realize this is all a dream.

But it's not.

With a wink, Gwen disappears into the bathroom.

I kick off my shoes and pants before stumbling into the bathroom after her, my cock leading the way.

She bends over to turn on the shower, and the sight of her ass, with her soft folds bared to me, unleashes a beast. I hook my arm around her waist and pull her back against me. My cock rubs against her slick center, and she moans.

With the water running, the small space slowly fills with steam. My hand delves between her thighs to stroke her clit.

"Claude, please."

Her breathy plea tips me over the edge. I angle my hips and press the tip of my cock against her warm entrance. She reaches down to guide me in.

Holy shit.

She grips me tight as I drive deep into her. Her guttural moan echoes off the tiles.

It's been a while, but I never remember it feeling this fucking good. Like coming home, like being welcomed with open arms. I must have died and gone to heaven.

Being inside her leaves me breathless and panting. I hold tight as she bucks against me, taking me even deeper.

My balls ache. If she keeps this up, I'm going to come. I'll fill her until her pussy weeps with my cum.

The thought makes me feral. Possessive. I want to mark her, to ruin her with pleasure.

"Mine," I growl, withdrawing and thrusting into her, over and over.

"Yours," she agrees, whimpering, arching into the movements, taking me without hesitation.

Her fingers replace mine on her clit, and I band my arm around her chest, placing my hand on her throat. Her back bows, but she's pliant and willing in my arms.

The steam clouds my vision, but I don't need to see. I *feel* everything. Gwen melts into me. Her moans and panting breaths echo off the walls.

Gwen is mine. I am hers. Bound together like this, I've never been more grounded, more certain of anything in my entire life.

Her breaths quicken as she rubs her clit in tempo with my thrusts. I double my efforts, praying I hold out until she comes. I'm close. Too close. I'm amazed I've lasted this long. Her pussy grips me tighter.

"Come for me again, sweetheart," I murmur against her ear. "I want it."

She pushes her ass back, urging me on, wanting more. I oblige with a tilt of my hips.

Deeper. Harder. More.

I grit my teeth as her pussy tightens around my cock. Her orgasm ripples through her, and she cries out.

My body relinquishes control. I come hard, filling her.

Gwen collapses against me, and I hold her there. Our breaths mingling with the steam, our hearts racing in tandem.

I'm so fucking obsessed with this woman. I can't get enough. Even though I've just come, my cock is still hard inside her.

I press a kiss to her cheek and slide free. My cum leaks down her thigh and pride fills me. I should be ashamed because I wasn't careful. She could get pregnant, and whatever this is will become more complicated. But a secret part of me wants her to carry our child.

What the hell am I even thinking?

"I'm sorry." I drop my hand, letting it glide down her arm until it's by my side.

She turns and wraps her arms around my neck. "For what?"

"Not using protection."

"I'm on the pill." She rises up on her toes and kisses my lips.

I'm drunk on her touch.

"Still." My mind blanks when her hands glide down my arms, stopping to rest on my biceps.

"I liked it." A mischievous smirk plays on her mouth. "*Mine,*" she growls before kissing me again.

I blame the steam billowing around us for the heat in my face. "Take your shower."

Gwen takes my hand and guides me into the shower beside her. It's a tight fit, but I lean against the wall, and she steps into the spray. The sticky mess from work along with the remnants of our passionate sex swirl down the drain.

When she finishes washing herself, she takes the soapy washcloth and slides it over my chest. I'm more than capable of washing myself, but the way she moves the cloth across my skin leaves my heart aching, my mind blank, a blissful smile on my lips.

She cleans me with the same efficiency I've seen in the bar when she works. Dedicated, mindful, tender. She washes one arm, then the other, gentle when she reaches the stub where my forearm used to be.

"Do you miss it?" she asks, meeting my gaze before chuckling. "Of course you do. That's a stupid question. Sorry."

"Don't be sorry." I smile at her flustered expression. "It's been gone so long, I barely remember what it was like to have it."

"It hasn't stopped you."

"No."

"I'm glad." She lowers the rag and strokes my cock through the cloth.

I inhale sharply, sucking air through my teeth. Arousal spikes through me, and I need to be inside her again. Grasping her close, I switch our positions and rinse away the soap before turning off the shower.

"I'm not done." She pouts.

"Neither am I, sweetheart." I kiss her, arching my hips against her stomach.

She tangles her fingers in my wet hair and returns the kiss with unrestrained hunger. When we finally break apart, I wonder if we increased the steam in the room. Her blue eyes are dark, like midnight over the ocean.

She licks her lips. "Can I…"

She blushes, and I'm intrigued by her sudden shyness.

"Whatever you want, sweetheart."

Gwen squeals with joy and steps out of the shower, reaching for a towel. We both dry off, and I leave her in the bathroom while I move to the bed. She'll join me when she's ready.

Whatever she wants from me, I'm more than happy to give it to her.

She's mine as much as I'm hers. That thought alone makes me deliriously happy.

I'll savor every moment because God knows when it'll come to an end.

It always does.

CHAPTER 14

Gwen

My body is humming. I knew beneath that calm exterior beat the heart of a passionate lover.

I quickly dry my body and my hair, braiding it over my shoulder. I stare at the woman in the mirror. The familiar face greets me, but gone are the dark circles beneath my eyes, replaced by a glow I've never seen before.

A smile steals across my lips. For the first time in my life, I'm happy. Content.

As much as I want Claude, I know I'm playing with fire. Can this last? I don't know. But now that I've had a taste, I'm going to damn well try to make it work.

The butterflies in my stomach take flight at the thought of him waiting for me in the bed. After two orgasms, I'm hungry for more. I've never been with a man who put my pleasure first, who took his time, who savored every kiss, every moan of pleasure.

Hearing him stake his claim while offering himself in return is the sexiest thing I've ever experienced.

Mine. Yours.

Damn. I'm wet and ready for him again.

Draping the towel over a hook behind the door, I catch one last glimpse of myself. Kiss-bruised lips. Eyes dark with need. Skin flushed from heat.

When I open the door, I'm unprepared for the sight awaiting me. Claude's naked, sitting on the bed, back against the headboard. His long legs are crossed at the ankles, his eyes closed. My gaze drops to his cock, stiff against his thigh.

He looks like a goddamn warrior waiting for his victor's reward.

I bite my lip. *All mine.*

"You tired already?"

"No." His eyes snap open and fix on me. "Just resting before round two."

"So confident."

My hips sway as I approach the bed. His gaze dips down the length of my body like he's committing every inch to memory.

"I like that in a man."

He scoffs but doesn't say anything.

I trail my fingertips along his thigh, climbing higher until they brush the tip of his cock.

He sucks in a breath. "Don't tease me, Gwen."

His dark gaze matches the tone of his voice. He's holding back, straining with desperate need.

I climb onto the bed and straddle his thighs, rubbing myself along his length. "Who says I'm teasing?"

His hand rests on my hip as I guide him inside me.

He's deep, filling me in a way he didn't before, touching parts of me that have nothing to do with sex.

I rock my hips, ride him slowly.

"Damn it, Gwen," he gasps, meeting my movements with gentle motions of his own.

"You like that?" I murmur and grip his shoulders. He's solid beneath my touch. His muscles flex with bridled restraint.

He nods and stifles a groan. "Sweetheart, you're killing me."

His words encourage me to move faster, drive him deeper, take all of him, body and soul. *Mine.* The confession lingers in my mind, spiking my desire.

My knees ache, but I push myself more. My arousal spirals higher with every thrust. I meet his gaze, lose myself, focus solely on him, chase the pleasure dancing just out of reach.

"That's it, baby. Take what you need." The pad of his thumb presses my clit, making me buck my hips.

"Oh, fuck." Sparks dance in my vision as the sensations spike.

How does he know exactly what I need?

The pressure increases as he makes urgent circles, sending jolts of pleasure rocketing through my core.

His breath deepens, erratic between moans and muttered curses as my pussy clenches around him.

I'm deliriously close to coming, but my body refuses to relent.

"You gonna come for me, sweetheart?"

The question echoes around my brain. The switch flips when he gently pinches my clit and slides his fingers through my folds.

An orgasm rips through me, tearing a desperate moan from my

throat. I dig my fingernails into his skin and hold tight, afraid I might float away if I let go. He fucks me through my climax, and when I drift down from my high, I feel him come, filling me, making me a sticky, sated mess once more.

He leans his forehead against mine. "Good girl."

I've never preened under someone's praise before, but his words unleash a glowing warmth within me. I collapse against his chest, and he wraps his arm around me. His heartbeat resonates with mine, falling into a calming rhythm.

After a few moments, he kisses my forehead. "We should get some rest."

With a disappointed groan, I roll off him and curl up on the bed. Claude stands and disappears into the bathroom.

I nestle in the warm spot he vacated and sigh. Sex has never left me so blissfully exhausted.

Claude reappears with a warm rag and wipes me clean. His kindness leaves me in a gooey puddle. I can't help but want this man, with his consideration and his heart of gold.

When he climbs back into bed, he lays on his back and gathers me against his chest. My head rests in the crook of his shoulder, my hand on his beating heart.

We're like two puzzle pieces who fit perfectly together.

The cool air soothes my heated skin. Even though it's the first week of December, I'm overheated, tucked against him. He's an inferno, but I bask in his radiance. Within moments, I drift to sleep, content and safe in his arms.

When I stir from a dreamless sleep, it's well past dawn, and sunlight filters through the thin curtains. I'm curled around Claude, my thigh thrown over his, my hand on his chest, moving with the steady rhythm of his deep slumbering breaths.

I steal a glance at his face. He's so handsome. Some would disagree, with his crooked nose and the constellation of moles crisscrossing his pale face. But his inner strength bleeds through, even when he sleeps. A soft smile lingers on his lips, barely noticeable. I want to kiss him, steal that smile for my own.

But a wicked, playful thought strikes me.

Gently sliding from his embrace, I tug down the blanket and wrap one hand around his cock. He moans and shifts, but doesn't wake. His cock, however, swells. I stroke him slowly, savoring the heavy weight in my hand. He's soft as velvet and thick. Precum leaks from the tip, and I lick it away.

Bold curiosity takes control. I've never been a fan of blow jobs, but I want to see Claude lose control. Eager, I take him deep into my mouth, until he touches the back of my throat.

"Oh, God." Claude arches his hips off the bed, pushing into my mouth.

I look up and find him staring at me, his eyes glazed with sleep and lust. He runs his hand through my hair.

I wrap my hand tighter around his base and fuck him with my mouth. He thickens against my tongue, and I bask in the control I have over his pleasure. My pace quickens, and his hold on my hair tightens.

He gasps and pants, moaning when I hit a particularly sensitive spot.

I repeat the motion, driving him higher and higher.

He tries to draw me away, but I tighten my grip. I want *all* of him.

"Goddamn, Gwen," he cries out when he comes.

I swallow every drop.

He grins, and I'm smitten with his carefree, orgasmic glow. I did that. Pride fills me at my ability to disarm him with only my mouth and the promise of pleasure.

But there's more beneath it. A lingering sense of peace. Like this is where I'm meant to be. With him, in this moment.

I never want to leave.

Claude pats his chest, inviting me back into his embrace. When I'm settled beside him, he wraps his arm around my shoulder and kisses me.

"Thank you," he whispers against my lips.

"For what?"

"I've never been woken up with a blow job." He grins. "A guy could get used to it."

Gooey warmth fills me at his words. I settle against him, resting my head on his chest.

We lay in silence for what seems like forever. He traces patterns across the back of my hand with a finger. I hold him tight, losing myself in the beautiful simplicity of this moment. No expectations. No demands. Just two people consumed by desire and a need for connection.

"Why did you choose my bar?" Claude's question shakes me from my thoughts.

"It was snowing hard. I needed to hide from…him. The glow of your sign was a beacon."

"Can I ask why you ran away from your fiancé?"

I pinch my eyes closed, the desire to trust Claude warring with the pain of reliving the horror of that night. I take a deep breath and search for the right words.

"I understand if you don't want to tell me." His hand stops caressing mine.

"He asked me to help him with a job."

"A job?" Claude furrows his brow.

"Yeah." I blow out a shaky breath. "He asked me to seduce someone."

Claude scowls, his eyes darkening. "Your fiancé asked you to seduce someone else? Why?"

"Blackmail, extortion, who knows?" Panic grips me at the reminder of his betrayal. I knew he wasn't a good man, but this request broke me. I couldn't follow through with my father's demand to marry him when I would have to sell my soul in the process. "When I said no, he grabbed me, threatened to carve his name into my skin, to remind everyone who I belonged to." My voice trembles.

Claude sits up and gathers me to him. I cling to his torso, burying my face into his chest. He runs his hand up and down my arm, slowly pulling me from the memories back into the present.

"That's why you hurt him."

I nod. "When I hit him in the nose, it gave me a chance to get away. I ran through the snow until I reached your bar. It was a gamble, asking for help. But I had to try. I couldn't live life bound to a man who would brand me and demand I debase myself for his pleasure."

"Did you know he was like this?"

"Yes. He has a reputation for being cold and cruel. All the DeLucas are. He's the youngest son of the head of the family."

"Fuck." Claude tightens his hold on me.

"My father owes the mob a fortune." I bite my lip, terrified of the consequences if I voice everything I know. The details could get me killed…or worse. "He promised me to Nick DeLuca, a mutually beneficial arrangement."

Claude's breath hitches. "I'm so sorry, Gwen."

I snuggle closer, wanting to hide from the horrible reality of my past. For years, I felt like an outsider in my own family. A golden trinket, a pawn in my father's deals. A media darling to draw attention away from the family's questionable actions, from their dark, backroom negotiations. They foisted me into the spotlight, using me as a glittering, compliant distraction. And I let them. For years.

But no more.

When I'm with Claude, I realize what I've been missing all these years. Love and connection. Compassion and trust. Here, I'm safe and warm. Loved.

What we have might have come in with a snowstorm, but in the warmth of the sun, I know beyond anything, I can never go back to the life I once knew. Not when I know what true happiness feels like.

Being with Claude completes me in ways I never imagined possible. I may be a fool to throw away the glitz and glamour, but I'd sacrifice it all in a heartbeat if it means I can spend the rest of my life with Claude.

I can't say it aloud. It sounds insane. But I can show him. In every touch, every kiss, every glance. This may be the craziest thing I've ever done, but I don't care. I love him. I'd be even crazier to let him go.

I just hope he loves me too.

CHAPTER 15

Claude

The phone rings, shattering our tender moment of bliss. I was only a breath away from the confession of my life. Of course the phone interrupts.

With a kiss to her forehead, I roll off the bed and dart, naked, into the living room before the ringing stops.

"This had better be an emergency," I growl into the receiver, not caring who could possibly be on the other end.

"Am I interrupting something?" Grant's voice digs into my last remaining nerve and twists.

"Yes."

"Shit." Grant groans as the implication goes unspoken. "You're not gonna like this."

"What?"

"I called the station this morning to get an update from Mickey." He pauses, and it's almost like I'm waiting for a bullet to strike. "There was a missing person's report filed for Gwen last night. With a reward for any information to her whereabouts and safe return."

"Fuck." I keep my voice low, hoping it doesn't carry into the open bedroom door. A quick glance tells me she's in the bathroom. "What happens next?"

"That is entirely up to you, Claude."

Grant's words carry that older, wiser brother tone. I wince at the underlying truth within them.

"They won't stop until they find her." I sigh. "And if they find her with me, shit's gonna hit the fan."

"More than likely."

"I can't turn her in."

"Not saying you have to."

"You act like I have a choice." I watch the bedroom, keeping an eye out for Gwen's return from the bathroom.

"You do."

"Goddamn it." I bite back the frustration, and it turns to acid in my throat. "Give me a day to think about it."

"Okay, but do yourself a favor and tell her they're looking for her." Grant sounds sympathetic, which is unexpected. "If she knows, she can decide for herself."

"Got it." I shift my weight when Gwen appears beyond the doorway, her skin glowing in the morning sunshine. "Thanks."

Without waiting for my brother's response, I hang up the phone.

Gwen leans against the doorframe. My gaze wanders slowly down her generous curves. Pained regret stabs me, even as my cock twitches in appreciation.

I can't do it. I can't tell her. I can't ruin this perfect moment of domestic bliss.

I've craved it for so long, thinking it was beyond my reach. But it's right here, standing in front of me. Better than Kodachrome.

"Something wrong?"

I stiffen at her question, and she notices before I can shake it off. Her mouth pulls into a frown.

"No," I lie. "That was Grant. He always leaves me in a sour mood when he calls this early."

Her smile returns. My heart breaks over the little white lie. I have to tell her, but it can wait.

Right now, I want what we had last night. This morning. I want it to bleed into the rest of the day. A taste of what we could have in a perfect world. Something. Anything but the shitty cards we were both dealt.

I want to keep her for myself, but she needs to know her family is looking for her. And they deserve to know she's alive and well.

I have two choices. Turn her in, or tell her and encourage her to do it herself. Deep down, I know she won't do it. She's made her stance perfectly clear. She has no desire to return to that life or to the man her parents want her to marry. It's a catch-22, no matter how I figure it.

She steps into my embrace, wrapping her arms around my waist and resting her head against my chest. I want to keep her like this forever, but if I do and there's no closure with her family, it'll bite me in the ass.

"Are you hungry?" Her question breaks through my complicated thoughts.

"Starving." I kiss the top of her head. "Let me put on some pants, and I'll make breakfast."

"I'll help." Gwen bounds into the bedroom and puts on an old tee shirt. I admire the sight of her bare ass as she draws up a pair of dainty underwear, hiding it from view.

"Pancakes?" she asks, pausing in the doorway.

"And crispy bacon," I add with a smile.

"Crispy?" She scrunches her nose, and it takes every ounce of restraint not to pull her back into the room and bury myself between her thighs once more. "Not too crispy. If you burn it, it ruins the flavor."

I chuckle and shake my head. I'll never get enough of this woman. Ever. Even with her culinary misconceptions.

Her soft singing echoes through the apartment as she rummages in the refrigerator. I ignore her siren song and grab a pair of clean sweatpants from the dresser. Tugging on an old flannel shirt, I slowly button it with my one hand.

Gwen crosses the room to finish the job for me.

"I can do it myself."

"I know, but I wanted to help." Her eyes are like a crystalline ocean in a Caribbean vacation magazine. "Where's the mix?"

"Top shelf." I open the cabinet and pull down a box of Aunt Jemima's buttermilk pancake mix. When I hand it to her, she does a little dance. It seems a little over the top for pancakes.

She glances up and sees the expression on my face. "What? Our cook never made pancakes. Mom refused to serve them since she believed they were empty calories and made her fat." She pulls out a measuring cup and begins to scoop the mix into a bowl.

"So how do you know you like pancakes?" I steer the conversation away from her mother's controlling insecurity.

"Alfred, our chauffeur, used to sneak them to me when he drove me to school." Her eyes sparkle at the memory. "I was obsessed! Still am."

"I can tell." I turn on a burner and place a skillet on the stovetop. My unwavering moral compass demands I test the waters, and I carefully broach the subject burning a hole in my brain. "So you ran away because your mom refused to let you have pancakes?"

Her hand pauses midmix, and she spins to face me. For a moment, I wonder if I crossed a line, but when she sees my teasing smirk, she relaxes.

"No." She goes back to slowly stirring the batter, her eyes unfocused and dazed as she loses herself in thought.

I put a second pan on for the bacon and place some slices in it. She'll talk when she's ready. If I push, she'll clam up completely.

Her sigh twists the blade in my already bleeding conscience.

"My family is shit. They treat me worse than a servant. I'm nothing more than a pawn to them. There was no love in my childhood, only secrets and lies." Her words pour free, and even as she speaks them, I can feel their weight bearing down on her…and on me.

"They used me," she continues. "All the time. It's miserable. And their pristine image of wealth and success…it's a total sham. They're so wrapped up with the mob, it's only a matter of time until they're caught. They have to be. I mean, that's how it works, right?"

I study her closely. She's not really asking me, is she?

"We're always taught good guys win and bad guys go to jail." Gwen continues as she sets aside the batter and takes my hand. "That's how it works."

I pull her against me to hold her close. I can't tell her the truth, but I can't lie. "I wish it was, sweetheart. But this isn't a fairy tale. There's not always a happy ending."

She buries her face in my shirt. "I just want to stay here with you, forget they even exist."

That simple confession leaves me breathless with joy. "I would love that, Gwen."

"Really?" She draws back, eyes glistening with unshed tears.

"Really." I smooth her hair away from her face and kiss her forehead. "But they're not going to let you go easily."

"I know."

The sound of her breaking heart mirrors my own. If she only knew how much I want to ride in to save her, slay her dragons, give her the life she deserves. But it wouldn't solve the fundamental problem.

"The only way you'll have peace is if you break ties with them. Officially."

"If I go back"—her grip tightens—"they'll never let me go."

"You never know until you try."

Her eyes meet mine. The terror and uncertainty I find there ignites a fire of possessiveness I don't recognize.

Mine.

"I don't want to lose you," she says.

"You'll never lose me, sweetheart." I press a soft kiss to her lips. "I promise."

I know better than to make promises I can't keep, but desperation drives me beyond reason. All I want is to see her smile, to keep her safe.

How the hell am I supposed to go up against the richest man in

Manhattan *and* the mafia to protect this woman I love?

CHAPTER 16

Gwen

After a bliss-filled day with Claude, responsibility pulls us back to reality. By six o'clock, we're both behind the bar, slinging drinks to an eager, after-work crowd.

I could have bottled up my time with Claude and kept it in my pocket. A perfect memory to carry forever. But all good things must come to an end, even if temporarily.

Casting sly glances at him while I work leaves my face flushed and my heart fluttering. Deep inside the calm, relaxed bartender lies the soul of a romantic. His passion and dedication, once unleashed, know no bounds.

How can I *not* love him? I must be crazy for thinking this way.

I slide a beer across the bar to Tom and turn to find Claude smiling in my direction. I return it, wondering if he can read my thoughts.

If he could, he'd blush three shades of red before dragging me to the back office and bending me over the desk. I know it. The thought leaves my knees weak and my panties damp. I lick my lips and return to work. There'll be time enough for that later. Right now, I have thirsty patrons to serve.

Every table in the bar is full. There are a handful of unoccupied seats at the bar. It's already a busy night. That's good. It makes the shift go faster. Even though I enjoy the job, I can't wait to lock the doors and take Claude upstairs.

"Can you take this to table five?" Claude places a few drinks on a tray and gestures to the other side of the room.

"Got it." I take the tray, careful not to spill anything.

"Good girl," he whispers against my ear.

My body hums with need, and I'm even wetter than before. Why would he say that to me in public? I bite back a whimper and glare at him. His smirk tells me he knows *exactly* what those two words did to me.

I brush past him, confidently carrying the tray with one hand.

Weaving through the crowd proves a little tricky, but I make it without incident. With a smile, I dole out the drinks and ask if they need anything else.

The door opens and a gust of cold air breezes through the warm room.

I glance up, and my blood turns to ice in my veins.

Nick and two cronies stand at the entrance. They scan the crowd, searching for someone. For me.

Shit. He's back. I knew he would return, but I didn't think it would be so soon. I hoped to be long gone before it happened. That was before Claude and I—

Nick's gaze settles on me, and a thin, wicked smile curves his mouth. His nose is red and there's a bandage across the bridge, but he's still drawing attention. Most would call him handsome with his bright blue eyes, his thick black hair, and his custom suit. But he's a wolf in sheep's clothing. His looks, his charms…they're an act. A damn good act, but still bullshit. He's dangerous. I've heard him brag about the vile shit he's done. And when he tried to pull me into his twisted world, I drew the line.

My spine straightens as he approaches. I should run, but he'll chase me. It's no use. I don't want to cause a scene or for anyone to get hurt. Especially Claude.

"There you are, baby." He wraps his arm around my shoulders. "I was so worried about you."

I cringe at the overpowering scent of his cologne. *Obsession.* I'll never be able to smell it without immediately thinking of Nick. He pulls me closer to him, and I gag.

"What the hell do you want?" I snarl, fighting the nausea.

"Is that any way to talk to your fiancé?" He leads me toward the two goons standing near the door. "Your parents were worried. They offered a reward for your safe return."

"A reward?"

My gaze darts through the crowd and lands on Claude, watching from behind the bar, his eyes narrowed, his fist clenched around a towel. I want to call to him. Run to him. But I can't. Nick has me pinned to his side.

If I fight him, he'll hurt me. And if he does that, Claude will try to save me. Nick won't hesitate to shoot him. The gun he carries in a holster beneath his jacket digs into my shoulder. This could become a bloodbath if I fight. Instead, I keep him talking, distracted.

"Yeah." His laugh makes my skin crawl. "I should've known the bartender squirreled you away during that storm. Bet you fucked him in exchange for a job, didn't you?" His breath burns my neck as he murmurs his caustic words. "Whore."

I swallow the bile stinging my throat. "Please don't hurt him."

"Was it worth it?" he asks, his voice low.

I bite my lip. He's baiting me, trying to draw me into a reaction. As soon as he gets me alone, he'll unleash on me, so I keep my mouth clenched shut. I refuse to give him any ammunition against me. Or against Claude.

"How did you know I was here?" I breathe deeply, concentrating on not jerking away from his touch.

"Got a tip." He grins and turns his attention to Claude, whose countenance mirrors a thundercloud over a midnight sea. "Give him the reward." He nudges one of the goons and steps back. "I'm taking her home."

What? Disbelief fills me. My gaze flashes from Nick's self-satisfied smirk to Claude, leaning against the bar, watching us intently.

Tears fill my eyes. Did he call my parents? Tell them where I was? No. That can't be.

Panic chokes me. Claude's whiskey-brown eyes don't waver, even as Nick drags me to the door. He ignores the goon closing the distance between us. I shake my head, and he crumbles, finally dropping his gaze.

Nick opens the door and drags me into the cold December air. Goosebumps prickle my arms, and I shiver at the drastic shift in temperature. My legs shake, my heart wrenches in two.

Claude sold me out. I choke back a sob as the realization takes root in my soul.

Nick opens the car door and shoves me into a waiting Rolls Royce. I curl into a ball on the leather seat, keeping my distance from him as he slides in beside me.

The two goons get in the front, and the engine roars to life. Warmth fills the car's interior, but I can't stop trembling. After a few minutes, the cold wears off, but I'm still shaking. From fear. From rage. From disbelief. From pure heartbreak. From all of it.

"Did you enjoy your week of slumming, Gigi?" Nick asks, lighting a cigar. Smoke fills the car, making me cough.

I turn to watch the street outside, keeping quiet.

"Would you rather I torch the place? Burn the old heap to the ground?" He chuckles. "Might be an improvement."

I bite my tongue. He's doing it on purpose. Ignore him.

"I could buy the dump, turn it into my personal playground." He grips my chin and turns me to face him. "I'd fuck you on that bar in front of everyone. Then they'd know exactly who you belong to."

My jaw clenches. The image he paints leaves my stomach sour. I push his hand away. "I'd rather die than let you touch me."

"Is that so?" His dark eyes sparkle in the passing light from outside the car. "Too bad I have an agreement with your father. That contract is legally binding." He bares his teeth in an evil grin. "If you don't hold up your end of the deal, your whole family will pay the price, you selfish bitch."

"Go to hell."

"Been there, baby, and they love me." He leans back and runs his hand over his bulging cock. "Why don't you come over here, show me how much you missed me?"

"I'd rather die."

He grips the back of my head and drags me into his lap. "Your little adventure has made you a smart-mouthed cunt."

"Fuck you, Nick." I hold his gaze. "Unless you want another broken nose, I suggest you let me go."

His grip tightens on my neck, and I flinch.

"You got lucky." His voice is low, deceptively calm.

My blood runs cold.

"Once you're my wife, I'll make sure you know your place. If you cross me again, I will fucking kill you."

His threat pierces my soul. I swallow the lump in my throat as terror sinks into my bones. He means it.

When he releases me, I slink back to my side of the car and hug my knees to my chest. I should have run. Left the city. Burned every bridge behind me. Instead, I put Claude in danger. I've lost the only man who truly cared about me. The man I thought I could truly love.

The man who betrayed me like Judas for a sack of silver.

I stare blankly at the flickering lights outside the window as we make our way across the city. Hope fades with every passing block. My fate is sealed and stamped.

Legally, I am bound to Nick, but my heart will forever belong to the one-armed bartender from the Black Penny.

CHAPTER 17

Claude

She's gone. Fuck.

I stare at my reflection in the mirror behind the register. An open bottle of whiskey sits on the bar beside an empty glass. I haven't had a drink in years, but I'm close to drowning myself in whatever remains in the bottle, praying I never come up for air.

When they took her, I closed the bar, pushed everyone out. In all the years I've owned this place, I've never closed early. Not even for personal reasons.

There was always someone here. Someone to lend a listening ear, a comforting shoulder, a glass of their poison of choice. But tonight, I can't do it. I can't bear the crushing weight of my guilt. Or my pain.

A torrent of emotions swirls in my chest. I thought I had more time. When he came into the bar, my heart stopped. There was no way for me to get to her, to put myself between them before he spotted her. Once he did, it was too late.

For a weeknight, the bar was packed. If I had stepped in, someone would have been hurt. An innocent bystander caught in the crossfire. The DeLuca brothers have a reputation for being ruthless and single-minded. If they're involved, there are always casualties. I couldn't put anyone in danger.

And I sacrificed Gwen with my inaction.

My unfocused gaze blurs. I curse and swipe the tears away. Anger replaces the sadness, and I let the fire inside me rage out of control.

Someone called in her location. I knew better than to let her work at the bar. Putting her in full view of everyone left her vulnerable. I should have kept her hidden. Safe and sound. But I let her into my life, into my heart.

I rake my fingers through my hair and pull. My attention shifts to the bottle on the bar again. The writhing agony inside leaves me longing for the numbing embrace of liquor. It'll soothe the pain, even if only temporarily.

I pour a double and cradle the glass in my hand. Who did it? Who told DeLuca where to find her? It's possible he retraced his steps from the night she first came in, but I doubt he's smart enough to realize she'd stuck around.

No, with the promise of a reward, someone called in the tip

"You gonna drink that or just let it gather dust?"

"Go away." I ignore my brother's presence, keep my attention fixed on the glass.

Grant sighs, crossing the room and sitting on the stool beside me. He takes the glass and downs the contents.

I clench my fingers into a fist.

"You've been sober for years, Claude." He pours another. "Don't fall off the wagon now."

He's right. I haven't been tempted by a drink in a long time, but tonight pushed me to the edge of the abyss. I would have gladly tumbled into it if it would have granted me relief from the torment.

The soft hum of the cooler behind the bar and the occasional click of the jukebox in the far corner are the only noises filling the void. We embrace the silence. It's familiar, comforting. We've been here before.

The night of Pap's funeral.

The morning his ex filed for divorce.

The day I was turned away from the police academy.

But none of those nights held the same weight as this…except the night I gave up drinking. The night Grant found me with a gun in my mouth and an empty bottle of whiskey at my feet. Silence filled the space between us all of that night as he sat beside me until dawn. We never spoke about it, but Grant knows the darkness inside me. The darkness I've kept at bay for years.

"When I woke up in the hospital with my hand and nearly half my arm missing, the bloody stump wrapped in bandages, I panicked." My voice carries through the empty room. "I threw off three nurses and punched a doctor. They sedated me, strapped me to the bed. It wasn't until my commanding officer came in, shouting orders, that they eased the restrictions."

Grant sips the whiskey and turns to study my profile.

I keep my gaze fixed on the register, unable to face him. "I couldn't remember anything, but my body held onto every violent memory. My commander told me what happened. How I was injured. I'm glad that part is still a blank, but it left me in pieces, mentally, emotionally…physically.

"When I came home, no one cared. Ridiculed. Cursed. Ostracized for my service to my country. Literally spit on!" I grind my teeth. "For the first two weeks, I wanted to die. I crawled into a bottle and climbed to the roof with every intent to end it."

"I remember," Grant whispers, his voice cracking.

"You saved me." I face him. "I wouldn't be here if you hadn't sat with me that night until I sobered up. You reminded me I had a place here. With you. With Pap. You promised to help."

"I did."

"You believed in me."

"I still do."

"Why?"

His jaw clenches, and he pushes aside the empty glass. "Because you're the only family I have left. The only person I can trust. You have my back, and I have yours. That's what family does. We look out for each other, believe in each other."

I nod, swallowing the lump in my throat.

"I'm sorry about Gwen." He claps his hand on my shoulder. "Quinn told me what happened. You handled it well."

"I told her to speak to her family. Make a clean break. It was her choice to make. No one else's." My fist pounds the bar. "Whoever told them where to find her stole her choice."

"Did she really have a choice, Claude?"

Grant's question is soft, but it makes me flinch, coming at me like a knife from the darkness.

"Maybe." I shake my head. "Hell, I don't know anymore."

"What *do* you know?"

Visions of Gwen fill my mind. Her smiling at me when I showed her how to make a martini. Her laughter when I taught her how to flip pancakes. Her moaning when I drove deep inside her. Her snuggling against me after we both collapsed in orgasmic bliss. There's only her consuming me, stealing my heart and filling it with joy. With love.

Without her, I'm empty, a husk of the man I was when she came into my life.

"I love her."

Grant smiles. "That's obvious."

"I can't force her to stay. She chose to go back." My heart shatters at the thought of living without her.

"What if she doesn't have a choice?"

"Everyone has a choice." I look at Grant.

"Whatever you say." He stands and tucks the bottle under his arm. "Get some sleep. I'll talk to you tomorrow."

Staring after him, I turn his question over in my mind. She doesn't have a choice…does she? After what she told me about her family and their deal with the DeLucas, there may not be anything she can do to break free.

Defeated, I retreat to my apartment and collapse on the bed. The sheets smell like sex. Her floral scent clings to the pillow, and I bury my face in it. I inhale deeply, praying I have the strength to make it through the night.

Gwen has taken possession of me, and there's not a damn thing I can do about it. She's wedged herself under my skin, imprinted her glittering presence on every part of my existence. I can't go back to the man I was before her.

She has altered the structure of my world.

And I wouldn't have it any other way.

But how can I possibly go on, now that I've tasted such happiness, only to lose it without warning?

I wrestle with my demons until exhaustion pulls me into the darkness.

CHAPTER 18

Gwen

The prize bird has returned to her gilded cage.

A shiver that has nothing to do with the cold ripples through me when I step into the vaulted entryway of my parent's townhome. My shoes squeak on the marble floors, damp with slush dragged in from outside.

Nick follows close behind me. His presence is suffocating. The brief moments of freedom at the Black Penny with Claude allowed me to breathe. It was like I finally broke the surface of the water, only to welcome the warm sunshine on my face and take a few gasping breaths before being dragged into the cold, dark depths once more. My situation is almost more painful after that brief taste of what could have been.

Nick takes the lead, and I don't need a guide to know where we're headed. The staircase goes to the second floor, where my parents wait in the antiquated parlor they converted to a lounge. They receive guests and conduct business there.

That's all I am. A commodity to be traded. A business deal.

Squaring my shoulders, I open the mahogany door. My mother spins away from the window at the intrusion. Her silver-threaded dark hair catches the light, and the wrinkles near her eyes and mouth seem more prominent. She looks older, more tired than I remember.

"Gwendolyn." Her smile doesn't reach her eyes.

I bristle at the use of my given name. "Mother."

"We've been so worried." She crosses the room, and for a moment, I think she's going to embrace me, but she stops short, her eyes narrowing as she takes in my appearance. "What are you wearing?" Her distaste is clear in the simple question.

I tug at the secondhand shirt Quinn and I found at the thrift shop.

"Gwendolyn Monroe." My father's voice booms through the room.

My spine stiffens. I turn to see him enter from an adjoining door. He wears every year of his age. At fifty, my father was handsome with an air of sophistication; at sixty-two, he bears a strong resemblance to an overweight, nearsighted aristocrat with a penchant for port and tobacco. He exhales a plume of smoke, still clutching the cigar between his teeth.

"Father." I hold his gaze, willing myself to stand my ground. Neither of my parents seem pleased to see me, but there's an air of relief siphoning tension from the room, as though my presence has prevented a catastrophic implosion.

"Where in the devil have you been?" my father snaps.

"I needed some time for myself." My tone is borderline antagonistic, but I stand firm. He doesn't deserve an explanation. I'm under no compulsion to give one.

His gaze shifts to Nick behind me, blocking the door. "Where did you find her?"

"At a dive bar in Hell's Kitchen." Nick's mouth curves into a sadistic grin. "She was waiting tables and making eyes at the bartender."

A scandalized gasp escapes my mother's perfect mauve lips.

I don't turn my head in her direction. My focus remains solely on my father. His brow furrows, and he pulls the cigar from between his clenched teeth.

"Did you forget your responsibility to this family?" He raises his voice just enough to emphasize his disappointment.

Years ago, I would have cowered and groveled, begged for forgiveness. But I'm not the girl I once was. I'm stronger now. Wiser.

More determined than ever to break free of my parents' hold on my life.

When I don't respond, he blusters and pushes forward. "You have a duty, and I will be damned if you ruin the reputation of this family with your selfishness."

"You don't need my help there." The response leaves my lips before I think better of it. I'm prodding the monster beneath the bed, and it's only a matter of time before it devours me whole. Desperation has made me careless.

"What did you say?" My father stands toe to toe with me, his figure looming and imposing.

I choke on the stench of his cologne and the lingering cigar smoke. He glares down his bulbous nose, taking measure of the disappointment before him.

"I'm not the one who brought this family to ruin," I say, the words breaking free. I know I'm tempting fate by putting them out into the universe. "You did that all on your own."

Pain blooms across my cheek when the back of his hand connects with my face. I stumble sideways, clutching my jaw, staring at him in horror. My father has never struck me before. I take a few steps back to put some distance between us.

"You will not speak to me like that again. Do you understand?" He growls with barely contained rage. "You are my daughter. You will do as you are told. I have arranged for you to marry Nick. You will satisfy that agreement without argument."

"And if I don't?" Defiance pushes into recklessness.

My father's eyes narrow as he puffs his cigar. The tip glows red, and the color flickers in his dark pupils. He studies me for a long moment, assessing for weaknesses, securing the best, most injurious course of action. I keep my expression blank. His satisfied grin causes gooseflesh to prickle along my arms and neck.

"I will burn down the bar where they found you, with all of your new friends inside." He sneers. "Including the bastard who kept you hidden."

A lump forms in my throat. I should have known my father would punish the innocent for my presumed crimes. The pain in my jaw radiates across my face, and my watering eyes threaten to spill over. But I refuse to give him the satisfaction of bringing me to tears, of rendering me to the penitent child he thinks I should be.

When I don't respond, he nods. "You will marry Nick in one week, and I will wash my hands of you once and for all. Am I clear?"

I bite my tongue. A sarcastic retort would only burn bridges that are barely hanging on by rotting timber and decaying rope. I can't risk angering him further, having him follow through on his threat. He would order Nick to do it without a second thought, and Nick would laugh while striking the match.

I nod. Better to placate him now than give him ammunition to hurt me later.

Silence fills the room, and I take it as my dismissal. Spinning around, I sidestep Nick and exit. My heart pounds as I race up two flights of steps to my bedroom. I ignore the servants exiting the service elevator at the back of the hallway and duck through the door, slamming it behind me.

I curse my family and Nick.

Then I curse myself for being weak. For giving in to their demands. I should have fought harder. Pushed back. But unlike my family, I have morals. There are certain lines I refuse to cross.

That's not the case for my parents. They will do whatever it takes to ensure their survival and continued success. Even if it means selling their own blood to the devil in exchange for the financial stability to maintain the illusion of their status.

A scream lodges in my throat. There's no one to help me. Nothing I can do.

I'm their prized bird in a gilded cage. My fate has already been sealed, and nothing short of an act of God will free me from this prison.

What will I do? What *can* I do?

My father will hurt those who help me, those who show me kindness and compassion. If he discovers the truth of my relationship with Claude, he'll kill him…if only to solidify my commitment to his union with the DeLuca crime family.

I need to warn Claude. But how? If I call the bar, they'll know. And I can't go to the police.

He turned me in. I should be pissed at him. But I still care. Curse my heart. I don't want him to get hurt.

I flop down onto the overstuffed bed and stare at the ceiling. I could tear my hair out. Is there anyone who can help me? Anyone who can act as a messenger?

Chewing my fingernail, I ponder the possibilities. None of the servants will help me. I wouldn't put them at risk of my father's wrath anyway. No, it has to be someone outside of the staff. Someone who isn't connected to my family. Someone who can't be bought. Someone with connections and clout.

Do I even know anyone who would put themselves at risk in such a way?

I pull myself from the bed and pace the room. My mind dismisses possibilities as quickly as it provides them. Damn it.

My gaze lands on the open door to my closet. Inside, I see gowns glittering in the dim light. I smooth my hand over the secondhand top.

Then it hits me.

Of course.

Marcy Maxwell. Stylist to the stars.

She recognized me at the bar. If anyone can help me, it's her. No one knows of her connection to the Black Penny or Claude. She's got the perfect cover. While she and my parents run in very different circles, her status as a celebrity stylist gives her clout. And they would never question my desire to hire someone to overhaul my wardrobe.

Or better yet, design my wedding gown.

A light takes shape, bright at the end of a dark tunnel. My mind forms a plan, and all I need to do is convince my mother of the immediate need for Marcy to design my gown for the upcoming wedding. This shouldn't be difficult. My mother's penchant for perfection—or at least the illusion of it—leaves her desperate. She will hire anyone I request as long as they're the best.

And Marcy Maxwell is the best in the business.

Good thing she's on my side.

CHAPTER 19

Claude

I'm still in bed when Quinn shows up.

"What the hell is this?" She rips open the curtain, letting in sunlight and a gust of cold through the drafty windows.

I roll away from her and pull the blanket over my head. After the shit show last night, I struggled to fall asleep, but exhaustion finally overcame me around dawn. Even then, misery followed me into those few hours of sleep. I'm used to restless, sleepless nights, but this one was all in.

"Claude, get up. It's nearly noon." Quinn pokes my shoulder through the blankets.

"Go away."

"I'm not going anywhere until you get your ass out of bed and talk to me." The mattress gives under her weight as she sits beside me.

"I don't want to talk," I mumble beneath the layers of fabric.

My head hurts but less than my fucking heart. I don't want to think about Gwen or the asshole who took her away from me.

She sighs. "Are you hungry?"

"No."

"Come on." She tugs the blanket, pulling it away from my face. "You can't lay in bed all day, being a miserable wreck."

"I can and I will."

With a determined grunt, she rips the blanket off the bed. I'm fully clothed, but I shiver at the assault and her audacity. Glowering through my messy hair, I pin her with my most intimidating stare.

"Get up." She jabs my rib with her finger. "Your brother will be here any minute, and he won't be nearly as nice as me."

"Fine."

Quinn stands and smiles. "I'll go make some eggs."

I wave my hand in dismissal, anything to get her to leave me alone with my misery. When she retreats to the kitchen, I roll onto my back and stare at the ceiling.

What the hell am I doing? Moping and mooning over a woman I knew all of…what? A week? Two? I scoff. What did I think would happen? If her engagement hadn't been enough of a warning, the moment I realized who she was, I should have put a fucking electrical fence around her with a sign: *Danger. Don't sleep with her. Don't fall in love with her.*

But I didn't listen to any of the warning bells clanging in my brain. I followed my dick as it towed my heart headfirst into a fucking hurricane of heartache.

The sounds of pots clanging and running water remind me to get out of bed. Quinn won't resort to violence to get me moving, but Grant certainly will. He has before. He's worse than the boot camp sergeant who played reveille at four a.m. after we'd been running on only two hours of sleep for a week straight.

My head aches when I sit up. Part of me wishes it were a hangover, but I'm glad Grant stopped me from drowning my sorrows in that bottle of whiskey. This morning would have been worse otherwise.

I cringe at the mess I left when I crawled into bed. Clothes lay scattered around the room. For years, I kept my place neat, tidy, organized. Even when Gwen was here, I maintained order in my environment.

But now…I couldn't care less. None of it matters.

I stumble into the bathroom, turning away from the mirror. After I relieve myself and splash water on my face, I run my fingers through my hair. It sticks out, wild and relentless. There's no taming it. I give up and head to the living room.

Grant is leaning against the counter in the kitchen, speaking with Quinn. He pivots to face me when she looks up and smiles.

"Eggs are done." She scoops them from the skillet onto a plate. "Want some coffee?"

"Yeah."

Now that I'm moving, blood is flowing to my brain and my malfunctioning heart. It hurts, not having her here. How did I become so dependent on her presence in such a short period of time? I curse myself for allowing her to burrow into my life with so little effort.

Quinn hands me a cup of coffee. "No cream, two sugars."

"Thanks." I carry it to the table.

She follows, placing the plate on the mat before me and retrieving a fork. "Need anything else?"

I shake my head and sip the coffee. It warms me, but nothing can touch the regret constricting my soul. Damn it. Is this how life is going to be from now on? Memories and regrets haunting me?

"Did you get any sleep?" Grant sits across from me.

Quinn hands him a mug of coffee as she joins us, sipping her own. Her curious attention flickers from him to me, but she remains quiet.

"Not really."

I eat the eggs even though I'm not hungry. Quinn beams with pride when I shove a forkful in my mouth.

Grant taps his fingers on the worn mug advertising a popular restaurant chain. A holdover from Pap. My brother's expression shifts, but he doesn't say anything.

"Something wrong?" I ask between bites of egg.

"Got a call from Mickey this morning. He's been doing some digging for me."

"Digging?" I shove the empty plate away and wash everything down with bittersweet coffee.

"Yeah, into Gwen's family and their ties to the DeLucas." A shadow passes in his eyes when he meets my gaze. "It's not good."

My stomach twists. "What do you mean by 'not good'?"

"He confirmed the rumors I heard yesterday. Monroe's estate is in trouble. He's made some really bad investments over the last ten years, and they're coming back to bite him in the ass." Grant shifts uncomfortably. "He's deep in bed with the DeLucas, and they're calling in favors Monroe can't guarantee. It's a dicey game. And it looks like it's been going on for a while."

"Months?"

"Try years."

"Fuck." If her family is in this much trouble, Gwen is caught smack-dab in the middle of all of it. Especially if her father sold her off to Nick DeLuca.

"That's not the worst of it." Grant clears his throat and tugs at his collar. "Oliver Monroe is under investigation for embezzlement, tax evasion, blackmail, and fraud. If he goes down, the whole family will go with him."

I shoot to my feet. "What? But Gwen doesn't know about any of this. She's innocent."

Grant stands, holding his hands out like he's trying to calm a rabid dog.

I push away from the table to pace the length of the room. "She's caught in the middle of this. If the whole thing blows up, she'll end up on trial with the rest of them." Panic rips through my chest. I should have stopped Nick. I should have kept her safe. Resting my hand on the wall, I take a breath and close my eyes. "She's innocent, Grant. She doesn't deserve this."

"Did she say anything about any of it?" he calmly asks behind me.

"No. She just wanted to get away from them…from Nick and her family." I spin to face my brother, willing him to understand. "Gwen isn't like them. She could have gone back to them, but she didn't. Not until Nick came last night."

"You don't think she wanted to go back?"

"No."

"Neither do I."

"Then how the hell did they find her?"

Grant turns. A flush of red creeps up his throat. "I called in the tip."

I stare at the man I thought I knew. "You what?" Disbelief gives way to anger. "How the fuck could you do that?"

When I rush forward and grab his shirt, he doesn't react.

Quinn races across the room and rests her hand on my arm.

"Calm down, Claude." She grips my sleeve. "Let him explain."

"You ratted her out." I stumble back, feeling like the breath has been ripped from my chest. Dueling emotions rage within me. Fury easily overcomes fear. "Why? For the reward?"

"You know me better than that." Grant rounds on me, pain etched on his face.

"Then why did you do it?" My hand pulses in a steady rhythm—fist, relax, fist, relax.

"Mickey called me yesterday morning. Monroe is making a big move, and Vice wants to nab him before he can find a way to weasel out of the charges. They have enough on him to go to trial. All they needed was a witness willing to testify."

"They found a witness." The realization leaves me reeling. "When's the arrest?"

"Tonight during a fancy dinner party Monroe is having with the DeLucas. They plan on arresting both families at once."

"Fuck." I pinch my eyes closed and try to breathe. All I can see is Gwen caught in the chaos. It's going to be a clusterfuck, and shit can go sideways fast. "Why put her in the middle of it?"

"The whole family is under investigation, Claude. If she were absent, it would look suspicious." He rubs his hand across his jaw. "All the pieces need to be in position."

"But she could get hurt. Or die." I step closer and jab my finger in my brother's chest. "I swear, if anything happens to her, I will never fucking forgive you for putting her in that position."

"That's why I didn't tell you last night." Grant holds my gaze, his familiar face a comfort and a curse in the midst of the turmoil raging inside me. "I have a plan, but you're going to have to trust me."

"How can I trust you after what you did to her?"

Grant sighs. "I know you love her, Claude. But if you want a future with this woman, you're going to have to take this risk. Please, trust me."

"How can you possibly protect her when you're on a leave of absence, recovering from an injury you sustained during a shootout in *my* bar?" I jump when Quinn takes my hand.

"It'll work out." Her smile does nothing to ease the tension inside me.

"No." I shake my head and pull away from both of them. "I'm going after her. If anyone is going to protect Gwen, it'll be me."

I rip my coat off the rack behind me and put it on. Quinn takes Grant's hand and they watch me with concern.

"Where are you going?" Grant asks, his voice stern, like when he would boss me around as a kid.

"Down to the station." I button the coat, my fingers fumbling with the narrow loops. "Who's on the case?"

"McMasters."

My head snaps up at the name. This changes everything. "Good. I'll talk to him."

"What are you going to do?" Grant looks ready to stop me, but he refrains and clutches Quinn to his side instead.

"I'm going to do what I should have done last night." I pull on my cap and head out the door.

If anything happens to Gwen, I'll never forgive myself. I will put this right.

No one touches what belongs to me. No one.

Nick DeLuca might be a feared member of a mafia family, but if my experience has taught me anything, it's to never underestimate a veteran on the warpath.

CHAPTER 20

Gwen

Convincing my mother to hire Marcy proved easier than I had anticipated. Even with the current scandal surrounding the stylist, Mother recognized Marcy's work from an event five years ago. With one well-worded request, I had her blessing.

Thankfully, the napkin Marcy gave me was still in my pocket when Nick dragged me from the bar last night. It had been washed, but I could still read the faintf numbers. After a quick, impassioned phone call, Marcy agreed to come immediately.

I fidget with the hem of my shirt. It's softer than the ones I found at the thrift store. Cashmere, of course. My mother disliked the thought of me wearing hand-me-down rags for a moment longer than necessary. With a sour look at my open closet, I take a deep breath.

Marcy will arrive any minute, but I doubt we'll be left alone together. After I ran away from Nick, my father won't take any chances of me escaping again.

I spent all night staring at the ceiling, trying to come up with a plan. A way to get a message to Claude, to warn him. Somewhere between one and three, the planning became a desperate attempt to plot my escape. Even this morning, I am no closer to devising a realistic plan to evade my father's hired thugs and Nick's henchmen. Whatever freedom I had slipped through my fingers the moment Nick caught me at the Black Penny. The window of opportunity slammed closed in my face.

A knock at the door pulls me from my dark thoughts.

"Come in." I stand, clasping my hands together to keep them from shaking.

The door opens, and I frown at the man standing there. My mood sours further when Nick steps into my room.

"What do you want?" I brace myself, anticipating an antagonistic remark.

"Is that any way to address your future husband?" He clicks his tongue in disapproval. "Someone's here to see you." Nick steps aside to reveal another person.

"Marcy Maxwell. It's an honor." I rush forward and take her hands in mine.

She squeezes my hands, casting a glance in Nick's direction before fixing her smile on me. "It's so nice to finally meet you," Marcy gushes. "I'll admit, I was surprised when you called to ask me to design and style your wedding ensemble."

Picking up the subtle shift in her demeanor, I play along. "Well, if I'm going to get married, I should have the best stylist in the business."

She bats her lashes. "You flatter me."

I turn to Nick. "You can go."

His jaw twitches at my cool dismissal. "I'll be right outside the door." He lowers his voice and leans in close. It takes all my effort not to cringe. "In case you get any funny ideas."

Once he closes the door, I take Marcy by the hand and pull her to my closet. "Let me show you some of my ideas," I say loud enough for Nick to hear through the wall.

As soon as we reach the oversized closet, I cast one last look over her shoulder before playing my hand. "Thank you for coming."

"Of course." Her lowered tone matches mine.

"I need you to deliver a message."

Marcy snaps her gum and grins. "Good, 'cause I have one for you too."

"Wait, what?" I clap my hand over my mouth when it echoes through my room.

Marcy pulls me deeper into the closet, chattering about fabrics and popular styles to choose from. When she's sure there won't be an interruption from Nick, or anyone else, she drops her voice again.

"After we spoke this morning, I called Claude at the Black Penny. Grant answered." She thins her lips. "He told me what happened."

"Oh." The word sounds more like a squeak.

"I don't have time to explain everything, but when I told him I was coming here, he asked me to bring a message from Claude."

"Claude's the one who called in the tip." I shake my head, willing myself to remember he betrayed me. Even though I'm angry with him, I can't let my father or Nick hurt him.

Which is the whole purpose of this meeting, to send him a message. Looks like he beat me to it.

Marcy scoffs. "Not a chance, honey. Claude's more loyal than a hound dog."

"Then who?" Confusion swirls within me.

"Does it matter?" She takes me by the shoulders, and our gazes lock. "Listen, he wanted me to warn you. There's a warrant out for your parents' arrests."

I stumble back, my head drifting from side to side in slow motion. "No."

"They're coming, honey. Tonight. It'll be all over the news by morning."

Panic silences everything inside me. "What do I do?"

"Stay in your room. Keep your head down." Marcy hugs me. "They're working on a plan to get you out, but you have to stay here, in your room, for it to work."

Her whispered words do nothing to ease the fear churning in the pit of my gut.

"If they come, it'll get ugly." I stare at her in horror, knowing exactly how Nick will respond to a police raid. "People will die."

"I know, honey." She squeezes my hand. "That's why you need to lock your door and hide if you hear *anything*."

"We're having a huge dinner tonight," I stammer. "It was supposed to be a business thing, but now they want to celebrate the upcoming wedding."

"I suggest you find a way to miss it."

A million thoughts bombard me at once. I don't know how I'm going to get out of this, especially since I'm one of the guests of honor.

Shit. My parents are going to lose it if I bail.

A light forms at the end of the tunnel. This is my out. My opportunity to escape for good. With my parents arrested, I'll be free. A breath of pure relief escapes me before reality crashes down again. What if they arrest *me*? Just like that, the panic returns.

"This gown is lovely. A Versace? I'm totally jealous." Marcy laughs, and I mimic her. "I love your suggestions. Shall we take your measurements then? I can start the hunt for the perfect dress today."

My mind spins with information while Marcy pulls a measuring tape from a bag on her hip. She leads me back to the bedroom and takes my measurements, jotting them down on a small notepad. I follow her lead, all the while thinking about the implications of her message.

Claude didn't sell me out.

He's worried about me.

He wants me.

Does this mean he loves me?

I bite my lip as worry consumes me once more. How the hell am I going to avoid this dinner? I can't get caught in the middle of this disaster. I can't imagine how bad it would have been if she hadn't warned me.

"I've got everything I need to get started." She puts the notes and the tape back in her bag. Her voice lowers, carrying only between the two of us. "What's the message?"

"Huh?" I blink at her before I remember the whole purpose of having her come today. "Oh yeah. Tell Claude…" The original message I'd planned to send dies on my lips, replaced by a simpler one. "Tell him to be careful."

A grin splits Marcy's mauve lips. "Sugar, you don't have to worry about him. He can take care of himself just fine."

"Thanks, Marcy. I owe you one."

She laughs and crosses the room. Opening the door, she turns to face me, ignoring the imposing presence of Nick and his thugs behind her. She winks at me. "You be sure to tell everyone you were styled by Marcy Maxwell, and we'll call it even."

"Are you done?" Nick snaps.

"I've got everything I need to find the perfect wedding gown," she purrs. "You're a lucky man. Ciao!" With a wave, she walks down the hall.

"Escort her out," Nick growls to his goons. They rush forward and disappear down the hall, leaving us alone.

I fold my arms across my chest and hold his stare when he refuses to leave. "What?"

"Enjoy your freedom while it lasts." His grin borders on sadistic as he pulls the door closed.

What does he mean by that? *Freedom*? What freedom?

Then it hits me. The tiny strands of glittering freedom I have under my parents' roof will disappear completely when I'm his wife.

I stumble back and collapse on the bed. Grabbing the fluffy pillow in the center, I hug it to my chest like a shield.

There's nothing in this world that can protect me from my fate.

In the back of my mind, Marcy's message rings clear like a church bell on Christmas morning. *They're coming. Tonight. Keep your head down.*

Hope shines like a beacon in darkness. A flickering candle in a storm. If there's any possibility of escape, it will come in the midst of the chaos. I only hope I don't find myself trapped in an even worse position.

Married to Nick.

Arrested.

Dead.

CHAPTER 21

Claude

What the hell am I doing? It doesn't matter. I need to protect Gwen.

When I'm halfway out the door, Grant stops me. "Wait."

"What?" I turn, glaring at him. After what he did, I'm not sure I can trust his judgment. He wasn't wrong…but at the same time, I can't believe he let Gwen go back to that house knowing what awaited her.

"I'll come with you." He grabs the extra coat beside the door. "Maybe I can grease the wheels with McMasters."

Begrudgingly, I concede. If anyone can convince McMasters to let me tag along, it's my brother. They went to the academy together and have known each other for years. When I tried to join the force, McMasters tried to talk me out of it. After they denied my entrance to the academy, he never said, "I told you so." I haven't seen him in years.

Grant kisses Quinn, and I turn away, unable to bear a press of pain at the simple, loving gesture.

When I step into the hallway, my brother trails behind. Silence stretches between us like an old, weathered rubber band. Cold December air bites my skin, making me bundle deeper into the flannel-lined jacket.

The moment we fall into step outside, the tension snaps with a soft muttered curse from Grant.

"Why are you really coming?" I glance at him out of the corner of my eye. Grant has always been an overprotective older brother, but lately, he's been even more paternal than usual.

"Because you need someone in your corner."

I snort and turn my attention to the clustered groups of pedestrians in our path. "If you were really in my corner, you wouldn't have turned her in."

"You're right." He sighs and shoves his hands into his pockets. "I shouldn't have sent in the tip without telling you."

"Doesn't matter now." I focus on what's in front of me instead of dwelling on the past.

"It *does* matter."

We cross the street, and I'm too wrapped up in my own thoughts to respond.

"Claude." He reaches out and grabs the sleeve of my jacket.

I pull up short, stopping just before I collide with a tall man in a navy peacoat. "What?"

"It matters." He steps closer, and the foot traffic moves around us as we stand still at the corner. "You're the only family I have left. I can't…" His voice cracks.

I rest my hand on his shoulder. "I'm not going anywhere, Grant."

"I know but…" He takes a deep breath. "You love her, and if this shit goes sideways, I…"

The unspoken implication hangs in the air between us.

"I'm stronger now," I say. "I'm not the man I was then."

He nods, and the helpless fear in his eyes kicks me in the gut.

"I love her, and I'm going to do whatever I need to do to make sure she's safe." Quinn's face appears in my mind, and a flash of gunfire in my memory takes me back to August when I thought I lost my brother. He nearly sacrificed himself for the woman he loves. "You understand."

"I do." He releases me and sighs. "Let's go talk to McMasters."

Tension builds with every step.

When we reach the station, my brother turns to me. "Let me do the talking, okay?"

I shrug. There's no way I can make that promise.

With a shake of his head, Grant leads the way into the building, greeting everyone as he passes. By the time we step onto the fourth floor, he's spoken to half the building. I didn't realize how loved my brother was in the department, but I'm not surprised.

McMasters stands when we walk into the office, and he shakes Grant's hand. "Richards, what the hell are you doing here? I thought you were recovering."

"I am." Grant steps aside. "We needed to talk to you."

"McMasters." I offer my hand, which he takes without hesitation.

"Claude." He rests, half-seated on the edge of his desk. "What can I do for you?"

"You're working the Monroe case, right?" Grant lowers his voice, keeping the conversation between us.

"Yeah." His gaze shifts from me to Grant. "What about it?"

"You're planning to take him down tonight?"

McMasters narrows his eyes. "Yeah. Why?"

"I want in." I speak before I can second-guess myself.

He scoffs. "You're not a cop, Claude. You know I can't let you do that."

"I need to be there." I hold my ground. I don't waver. My hand clenches into a fist.

"Why?" McMasters crosses his arms.

"The daughter. She's innocent."

"She's not the target."

"Yes, but she's in the home. If shit goes sideways, she'll be caught in the crossfire."

McMasters scowls. "What makes you think this won't be a clean arrest?"

"Because Nick DeLuca is her fiancé. If there's a raid, he won't go down without a fight," I say.

If McMasters has done his research, he already knows this. But I can't take the chance he doesn't.

"And he'll take her down with him."

"Why would he do that?"

"Because he's a sadistic bastard who doesn't care who he hurts as long as he gets what he wants." I straighten, flexing my fingers, imagining them wrapped around DeLuca's throat.

"Why do you want to get involved?" McMasters's stare burns a hole straight through to my soul.

"She's mine."

McMasters's brows shoot into his hairline. "She's engaged to DeLuca."

"Not anymore." My voice rings with certainty and purpose. "Gwen is being held against her will."

"Do you have proof of that?" He rolls his shoulders and stands.

I quickly relay the events of that snowy night and the subsequent information she told me concerning her parents and Nick DeLuca. Most of it doesn't seem to surprise McMasters, but he's stunned to see me so impassioned.

"I love her, and if you don't let me protect her, you'd better not get in my way."

He chokes on his coffee. "I can't give you a badge and a gun for a day, Claude. That's not how this works."

"Then don't. But I'm going tonight, with or without your blessing."

"I don't want to arrest you for obstruction."

"I won't obstruct. I'll be in and out, five minutes." Purpose fills me.

"Gwen needs me."

"I can send in a team to make sure the girl is safe." McMasters strokes his jaw. "Make sure no harm comes to her."

"Put me on it."

"I *can't* do that, Claude."

"Then let me do it." Grant speaks up, and I turn, stunned. "I'll go with a small team. In and out. Ten minutes, tops. Let you focus on Monroe and DeLuca."

"I don't know, Richards." He shakes his head. "You're still recovering from a gunshot wound. You haven't been cleared for duty."

"I can handle it." Grant nods, pressing his lips together in a thin line.

McMasters's gaze passes from Grant to me and back again before he exhales sharply. "Fine. Come into the briefing room. I'll get you up to speed."

I move to follow them, but McMasters holds up his hand. "Not you, Claude. We can handle this."

I grit my teeth, let the irritation simmer into oblivion. "Fine."

A plan forms in my mind, but I keep it close, not willing to dwell on it yet.

Instead, I leave the station to head back home. The brisk chill steals some of my irritation, but I'm still smoldering when I reach the bar. Inside, I slam the door and head for the office. My head hurts. I rest it on the desk.

A volatile combination of emotions rages through me, each one warring for control. I'm two seconds from breaking every rule I've ever made for myself and storming across town to single-handedly bust down Monroe's door.

The phone rings.

"Hello?"

"Claude, thank God. It's Marcy."

"Marcy?" Confusion fills me. Why would she call me? "What's wrong?"

"Gwen called me. She hired me as her stylist. I just got back from seeing her."

"Is she okay?" Hope unfurls in my chest.

"She's fine." She sighs. "I gave her the message your brother asked me to deliver."

Grant spoke to Marcy? I close my eyes and shake my head.

"I called to talk to you, but he answered. Told me to warn her."

A slim thread of relief eases into my mind. "Good."

"She asked me to deliver a message to you."

My heart pounds. "What's the message?"

"Be careful and don't do anything stupid."

"Those are her exact words?"

"I added the last part." Marcy's tone softens. "You love her, Claude. Don't fuck this up."

"I won't. Thanks, Marcy."

A ragged sense of purpose fills me as I hang up the phone.

I have one shot at saving her, and it needs to count.

Carefully, I pull out the pistol I keep in the bottom drawer of my desk. The one Pap gave me when I came home from Vietnam.

The one I swore I would never touch again.

CHAPTER 22

Gwen

I'm going to puke.

It took me an hour to convince my mother I was too sick to attend the dinner. After my visit with Marcy, I concocted a plan to ensure I would remain in my bedroom for the duration of the evening. This might be the most reckless thing I've ever done, but I can't take any chances. Not when I know what my family, what Nick, is capable of. When the police arrive, all hell will break loose.

I have no idea when the police will arrive or what exactly will happen when they do. But I played my part. Wrapping myself under the blankets, I moaned and shivered.

Mother attempted to drag me from the bed, and I collapsed, clutched my stomach, writhed on the floor. She prodded my face and threatened to call a doctor. When I refused to budge, she threw her hands in the air and retreated to the bathroom for a bottle of aspirin.

She tapped her foot while I climbed back into bed, clutching the bottle in her perfectly manicured fingers and frowning at my sorry state. With a huff of impatience, she tossed the bottle onto the blanket and told me to come down by seven-thirty.

That was an hour ago. It's now seven.

Someone should give me an Oscar for my performance, but it won't be enough. My mother doesn't care if I'm at death's door. She wants me present. If I don't show up, she'll pull me from bed and drag me down the stairs to parade me in front of her guests. I'm the guest of honor, after all. Without me, who can my parents use as a glittering distraction? My stomach churns at the thought of being put on display. I'd rather die than be subjected to that torment for another moment. I can only pray the police arrive before my clock runs out.

I chew my fingernail and watch the clock beside my bed. Five minutes after seven. Cocktails started at six-thirty. If I don't dress and join them, my father will ensure Nick punishes me for disregarding their instructions.

And I know what kind of twisted asshole Nick really is.

My cuticle bleeds when I rip the nail too short. Shit. I grab a tissue to staunch the bleeding, then rush to the bathroom and wrap my finger in a bandage.

I catch a glimpse of myself in the mirror. What the hell am I doing? This isn't going to end well. Even if Claude finds a way to save me, it'll be too late. I'll be caught up in this mess, and they'll never be able to untangle me from the hell my parents have created.

It's over. I might as well embrace the inevitable. No matter what happens tonight, I'm fucked.

My cheeks are pale, and I look sick. Which helps my case, but it's not a stomach virus that has me in its clutches. It's my inevitable fate. Too bad Marcy couldn't smuggle me out of the house in her bag.

Nick's kept a close eye on me all day. Something that wouldn't have bothered me a few years ago, but now I know better. I want nothing to do with him. I'd be better off throwing myself from the fourth-floor window than following through with this farce of a marriage. He doesn't love me. He doesn't want me. I'm a commodity. A means to an end.

He's nothing like Claude. No one is.

A tear slips free, and I wipe it away with a sniff.

"He's not coming for you." My voice echoes off the bathroom tiles, as if I'm in a stone tomb, and a piece of my soul dies. "Stop dreaming."

Somehow, I manage to scrape together what remains of my sanity and take a breath. Maybe I can find a way out of the house while everyone is at dinner. No one will be watching my door, not with such prestigious guests in the house. I stash a few items in a bag and sling it over my shoulder. The sentimental tidbits hidden in a box under my sink are now tucked into an old bag on my hip.

I hope this works. It's my last chance to escape. With a deep breath, I stiffen my resolve. I can do this. I have to do this. Or I'll die trying.

I'm halfway across the room when the door bursts open, the wood splintering where the lock broke free under the force of the impact. It knocks me back, and I nearly lose my balance.

Bracing myself against the bedpost, I search for somewhere to hide. There's nowhere. I look again, and this time my gaze stops at the doorway.

Nick, eyes wild, hair standing on end, fills the space. The gun in his hand glints in the soft light. With a growl, he grips it tighter before leveling it at me.

My knees buckle, but I grip the post tighter to remain standing. I won't surrender to this bastard. Not now. Not ever.

"What are you doing?" I hate that my voice shakes, but the barrel of the gun aimed in my direction leaves my courage in a puddle on the floor.

"Shut the fuck up." He steps into my room, his aim steady. "If I'm going down, I'm taking you with me."

"I don't understand." I scramble backward, trying to keep some distance between us. He closes the gap, and I can make out the letters on the barrel of the gun when he stops.

"Come here," he growls and grabs my arm, pulling me against him and dragging me to the door. "Let's go."

"Where are you taking me?" My hands tremble as he hauls me down the hallway toward the back staircase.

He scoffs. "Where I should've taken you the night I pulled your ass from that bar."

"I don't understand what's going on."

He shoves me down the stairs, keeping a firm hold on my arm, the gun digging into my spine. "You'll figure it out soon enough. I need to get you out of here before the cops show up."

Fear trails its fingers over my heart. "What?"

"Got an inside tip. The cops are gonna crash our party. But they won't find either of us there." He chuckles, and the sound rips hope from my soul. "We'll be long gone."

Nick motions for me to open the door. I do it slowly, trying to find a way to break free from his hold, to escape. But there's no one in the street behind the house. Empty, frosted car windows stare back at me like vacant eyes from either side of the street.

The cold air bites my bare arms, and the padded slippers on my feet do nothing to stop the damp from seeping between my toes, numbing them.

A car appears at the end of the street. Hope flares in my chest. Maybe it's the cops!

When it comes to a stop in front of us, Nick shoves me forward. "Get in."

Damn it. I cast another panicked glance down the street, praying someone is there to see us.

"I said get in the fucking car!" He pushes me, and I stumble, pitching into the backseat.

By the time I right myself, he's seated beside me and the car is in motion.

I flop down into the seat and push my hair out of my face. "Why are you doing this?"

Nick turns, once again leveling the gun in my direction. Desperation glints in his eyes as he tightens his grip on the weapon. "You sold us out, you vicious little bitch."

"I…I didn't…"

"That's why you ran." He bares his teeth like a rabid dog, cornered and scared. "You knew they were coming for us and sold us out."

"No…I…" I shrink back, wishing I had run, had left the city when I had the chance.

"You fucking ran to the cops and spilled your guts." He presses the gun to my head.

The cold barrel digs into my scalp. Tears fill my eyes. Fear steals my breath. "I didn't say anything."

"You fucking lie. Don't fucking lie to me!"

"I'm not lying!" I choke on the sobs lodged in my throat. Part of me wants him to pull the trigger, to end my suffering. But if I relent—if I give in—he wins.

He's winning regardless. I'm trapped in this car, at gunpoint, with no possible means of escape. No one knows where I am.

No one.

Nick pulls back and the pressure of the cold barrel disappears. "It doesn't matter. Not anymore."

"Why are you doing this?" A sob breaks free, cracking the remaining fragments of my sanity.

"Your father and I had an agreement," he hisses. "You are mine, and I'm taking what I'm owed."

"You'll never get away with it. They'll look for me. They'll never stop searching for me."

His laughter makes my blood run cold.

"I've already taken care of it."

"What do you mean?" My voice catches.

"The cops won't find us at the little party your parents organized." His sadistic grin flashes beneath a passing street light. "They'll find our *remains*, barely recognizable, at my apartment uptown. *A desperate pair of star-crossed lovers take their lives.*"

I cringe at the reference to Romeo and Juliet. "No one will believe it."

"They will. Because they were well compensated to believe it." He rests the gun on his thigh, his finger still on the trigger. "Our new identities will be ready by the end of the month. All we need to do is lay low."

"And then what?" I snap, ignoring the weapon. If he wanted to kill me, he would have done so already. "You're delusional if you think I'll become your docile little wife."

"I'm sure you'll come around after a while." He relaxes against the leather seat.

"I'm not a dog to be housebroken." I stiffen at his glare. "You might as well kill me now and be done with it."

"What a waste that would be." He snickers. "Now that we're both officially dead, I can take my time, make sure you're properly trained to follow my instructions."

My empty stomach lurches at the implication of his words. I turn and stare out the window at the passing city. *Claude.* His name repeats in my mind, over and over. A silent prayer. A desperate plea. Tears spill free, and I pinch my eyes closed, finally caving to the reality of my situation. It's over. Nick won. There's no one coming to save me.

Thirty minutes later, we pull up to an abandoned warehouse, near the bay. It's hard to tell exactly where we are in the darkness. I don't recognize this part of the city. A lone light flickers in an upstairs window of the two-story brick building.

"Welcome home, sweetheart." Nick grabs my arm and pulls me from the car.

I trip over my feet when I finally break free of the car. He tightens his hold on my arm, leveling the gun at my chest.

The driver takes off without a word, leaving the two of us in a dark, narrow stretch between abandoned warehouses. I jerk my arm free and straighten my back.

"Don't even think about running." He sneers.

"Where the hell would I go, moron?"

He grabs my face in his hand and squeezes. "First lesson. Don't talk back."

His hand connects with my cheek.

The sting leaves me reeling.

I step out of his reach and cradle my face in my hand.

"Let's go." He gestures to the warehouse with the barrel of the gun. "Traitors first."

Keeping distance between us, I push open the door and step into a dark, open space. An overhead lamp flicks on, flooding the room with light. There's nothing but a table and a few chairs tucked in the corner.

Along the far wall, a staircase leads to the second floor, where I saw the light shining from outside.

"Upstairs. Move it." He nudges me with the pistol, and I spin, grabbing a chair and placing it between us.

"I'd rather die." Strength returns to my voice. This is my stand.

"Pity." He levels the gun at my head.

I close my eyes and take a deep breath. Peace fills me as I exhale. This is the end of the line.

"Put down the gun, DeLuca." The voice booms through the open space.

My eyes fly open, hope spears my heart. I turn toward the sound, mindful of Nick's gun still trained on me.

"Well, well." Nick licks his lips and turns, the gun still firm in his grip. He narrows his eyes at the intruder in the doorway. "What do we have here?"

"You're under arrest."

Nick's laughter echoes through the warehouse. "I don't think so."

"Let her go."

"What are you gonna do about it?"

The figure in the doorway steps into view, and I suck in a breath. Grant! The similarity in his features has me choking with emotion. For a moment, I thought it was Claude, but he's not a cop. He's not coming to save me.

Disappointment dilutes the adrenaline coursing through my body. I cling to the chair, wishing I could disappear into the darkness outside.

Grant's gaze remains solely on the man before him. "There's no way out of this, DeLuca. Put down the gun and come quietly."

"Or what? You'll shoot me?" He laughs, and I shiver at the cold, disturbing sound.

"Your only way out of here is in cuffs or a body bag." Grant's voice oozes confidence. "Pick one."

"You sure about that, pig?"

Grant's eye twitches, but he remains steadfast and only nods.

"If I'm going down, then this bitch goes first." Nick swings his arm wide, aiming the gun in my direction. He squeezes the trigger, a grin on his disgusting lips.

I hold my breath and close my eyes.

Gunfire echoes through the warehouse.

I brace for impact.

It never comes.

My eyes fly open to see Nick stumble toward me. The gun falls from his hand, clattering to the concrete. Red blooms across his chest as he staggers, blood seeping through his dark blue shirt. He lunges at me, catching me by the waist and dragging me to the floor as he collapses. His blood, warm and sticky, seeps through my cashmere shirt.

Panic seizes me, and I shove him away, scrambling backward. I'm filled with horror at the sight of Nick at my feet, his vacant eyes wide with surprise. I climb to my feet and spin around to find Grant, his gun at his side, his attention focused over his shoulder, a scowl on his face.

A second man steps into view with a pistol in his hand, smoke drifting from the barrel. The familiar curve of his profile mirrors Grant's.

"Claude?" Relief and disbelief pour through me.

He passes the gun to his brother and rushes to my side, dropping to his knees beside me. Without a word, he gathers me to his chest and holds me close.

"Are you all right?" he asks, his hand skimming over my bloodstained shirt.

I nod, unable to find my voice. Finally, I'm safe. He came for me. I close my eyes and rest in his embrace.

"Get her out of here." Grant's statement makes me look up. "I'll take care of this mess."

Claude slowly stands before offering me his hand. I take it and burrow myself into his side, wrapping my arm around his waist.

"Are you sure about this?" Claude asks, stopping beside his brother.

"Yeah." Grant sets his jaw. "Now go."

"Grant—"

His brother sighs. "Go. Now. Cyril will take you home, then come back for me."

With a nod, Claude leads me from the warehouse. Outside, I curl into his warmth. A black town car pulls up and the driver emerges.

He opens the back door. "Sir."

"Thanks, Cyril," Claude acknowledges the driver with a smile and helps me into the car. Safely inside, he closes the door, and moments later, we're speeding across town.

He pulls me into his lap and cradles me against his chest.

It's over. All of it. Nick is dead. My parents have been arrested. What the hell will happen to me now?

I sob, and Claude says nothing. He just holds me tighter.

CHAPTER 23

Claude

She's safe.

Safe.

The word repeats, over and over, in my mind. Even though she's cradled against me and I can feel every breath, the adrenaline won't recede.

Seeing her with a gun pressed to her head pushed me over the edge. I promised to remain out of sight, out of the way. But then I heard that manic edge to his voice, desperation in every word.

Grant's going to be pissed. I left a mess for him to clean up. Whatever happens, I'll take the heat for it. In my mind, it's worth sacrificing my own freedom to ensure Gwen's. Even if that means we can't be together.

She shivers against me, and I shove my thoughts aside. I'll worry about consequences later. Right now, I need to take care of her.

I gently stroke her hair and press soft kisses to the top of her head. She curls deeper into me. Her soft sobs cut through the silence. I close my eyes and hold her close. It's over.

Cyril turns a sharp corner with ease, and I look at him in the rearview mirror. He's focused on the road. I don't know what I would have done without him tonight. How I would have gotten her home. I'm forever in Arthur's debt for sending his driver to our aid.

When Grant returned from the station, he found me in the office with Pap's pistol in my hand. He confronted me in that irritating, older-brother-knows-best way. But I wasn't about to leave Gwen's life to the fickle wheel of fate. I was going to save the woman I love, with or without his help.

After five minutes of swearing and dredging up our past missteps, he conceded. While he agreed with McMasters that I shouldn't be a part of the raid, he wasn't going to say anything if I just showed up. But there was a catch.

I had to let him handle any problems.

An hour later, Rob and Arthur showed up, offering their support and whatever resources they could, including a car and driver, should we need them.

Our plan had been to get Gwen out while the rest of the party focused on the arrests. We hadn't counted on Nick DeLuca ducking out of the festivities and threatening to kill Gwen.

That isn't entirely true. I knew he would try to take her down. Possessive assholes like him love to show their cards, even while pretending they're bluffing.

Grant and I found the door ajar, but he made me stay back. Stay quiet. I could never do that while the woman I love is in danger.

Cyril passes the Black Penny and turns down a narrow street, stopping beside the side entrance. He climbs from the driver's seat and rounds the car.

"Come on, sweetheart." I nudge Gwen. "Let's go upstairs."

She pulls away and blinks up at me. Her eyes are bloodshot. Smears of blood stain her pale skin. She nods and follows when I step from the car.

I give Cyril a tight smile as I wrap my arm around Gwen. He tips his hat and closes the door before returning to the driver's seat.

Inside, the sound of music and conversation drifts from the bar. I ignore it and lead Gwen up the stairs to my apartment.

She doesn't cower or hide. She stands tall, tucked under my arm, as we climb the staircase. One hand clings to the front of my jacket while the other tightens around my waist.

I release her for a brief moment to unlock the door.

Gwen steps into my apartment and turns to face me. Questions swim in her eyes, but she doesn't voice them. She will when she's ready.

"Let's get you cleaned up." I take her hand and lead her to the bathroom.

"I can do it." She swats my hand away when I reach for the buttons of her blood-soaked sweater.

I lean against the counter and watch, my heart swelling at the sight of her, safe and whole. She's mine. I shouldn't react this way, not after what happened tonight. But I can't control how she makes me feel. How hungry I am for her. It feels like weeks since I've kissed her, since I've been inside her. When she pushes her pants down over her hips, I pivot away and turn on the shower.

Running water fills the silence. A gentle pressure surrounds me as Gwen wraps her arms around my waist and rests her face on my back. I freeze, hand braced against the wall beside the shower. She holds me, not moving for several moments.

When she shifts her weight, her hand drops to the top of my jeans. I hold my breath as she unfastens them and pushes the fabric down my hips.

"Gwen." I turn, but my brain stops functioning when I meet her luminous blue eyes.

"Join me."

She cups my balls, and all rational thought flies from my head.

I manage to push her away long enough to remove my clothes before ushering her into the shower. Under the warm spray, she embraces me, pressing her body into mine. Her hands roam over my skin.

I distract myself with the washcloth, soaping it up, washing the blood from her face and neck. She turns, letting me worship her with the suds.

The bloody memories disappear down the drain, leaving the two of us wet and clinging to each other.

"Claude," she whimpers, pressing back into me.

The cloth falls from my hand. I grip her thigh, letting my fingertips dance across her skin. When they brush the folds of her pussy, she arches into my hand.

"I want you," she gasps. "Please."

With a growl, I spin her around and hook my hand behind her knee. Pressing her against the wall, I lift her leg, and she opens for me. Her hand wraps around my cock, pushing the head to where she craves it.

I slide deep, and our mingled groans of pleasure echo off the tile.

She grips my arms, holding tight as I drive into her. Her sharp nails bite my skin. Her hips move in tandem with each thrust, meeting me with her own desperate need.

I grind against her, teasing her clit with every stroke.

She moans and throws her head back, biting her lip.

With all my effort, I pour myself into driving the demons from her mind. From her past. From my past.

Together, like this, there's nothing else. Just pure bliss. Utter abandon.

"Yes, more. More."

Her cries push me over the edge.

I wrangle myself under control long enough to feel her tighten around me. She buries her face against my chest as the orgasm ripples through her limbs. Shortly after, I come with a groan, letting our mingled mess rinse away under the shower.

It takes a minute before I can move again. She carefully disentangles herself from me and cleans us both before turning off the water.

Gwen stands on her tiptoes, kissing me softly. "Thank you."

I nod, unable to speak. My chest tightens. How can I love her so damn much it hurts?

Wrapped in a towel, she retreats to the bedroom. I follow and wrap my arm around her waist, pulling her onto the bed. I tug the blanket over us and inhale her sweet scent.

My hand rests on her heart, and slowly, the world fades into the background.

"Claude." Her voice cracks.

"Mm-hmm?" I tighten my hold on her.

"Thank you."

"For what?"

"Coming to my rescue."

"I'm sorry I didn't come sooner."

She shakes her head. "No. I'm sorry. I shouldn't have dragged you into this mess."

"Gwen, look at me." I tip her chin until she rolls over. Our eyes lock. "I will always come for you. I love you."

Tears form in her wide sapphire eyes. "I love you too."

I brush her damp hair back and smile. My heart expands at her simple confession.

"What happens now?" She chews on her lower lip.

"That's up to you." I stroke her jaw with my thumb.

"What do you mean?" Her brow furrows.

"Well, you can go to trial, testify against your family, or…" I pause, gauging her reaction. "We'll figure it out."

Gwen cups my cheek in her hand. "What if I just want *you*?"

"You have me either way."

She wraps her legs around me, rubbing herself against my thigh. I groan.

"Then let's start over," she says.

"You're willing to leave the past behind you?"

"Yes." With a sigh, she sinks into me. Our lips meet, and I'm lost in her once more.

This time I make love to her, savoring the moment, the woman I adore.

After she drifts off to sleep, sated from another orgasm, I slip from the bed and pull on my robe. I close the bedroom door behind me and pick up the phone.

"It's me. She's safe. What's the plan?" I lean against the wall and wait for Grant to fill me in. He tells me they caught Nick's goons, who confessed to his plan—them pretending to be dead, the new identities, the works.

A plan forms in my mind even as a weight lifts from my shoulders. When I hang up the phone, there's a renewed sense of peace. Of finality.

I climb back into bed, pulling her against me, locking her into place.

Nothing will take her from me again. She's right where she's meant to be.

CHAPTER 24

Gwen

I wake in an empty but familiar bed.

Slowly, the events of the night before filter to my consciousness. I shiver at the horrifying memories of Nick holding a gun to my head. His threats echo through my mind, like the haunting strains of a horror movie soundtrack.

Pulling the blanket around my bare shoulders, I scan the dim room. Where is Claude? It's morning, barely. He should be beside me, but the bed is empty and cold.

When he came to my rescue last night, everything else fell away. He saved me. He pulled the trigger on the one man who held my life in an iron fist. I shouldn't have doubted he would find a way. Not that I need a knight in shining armor, but last night, the presence of one certainly tipped the scales in my favor.

I had always known Nick was crazy, but I never dreamed he would take it to that extreme. I *should* have known. He was a ticking timebomb. I'm glad it's over.

But is it really?

Noise drifts through the door from the living room. I wrap myself in the blanket and creep across the floor. I crack open the bedroom door before sagging with relief.

Claude sits on the couch while the television flickers against the far wall. His furrowed brow and compressed lips tell me something's wrong. Quietly, I open the door and cross the room, dragging the blanket like a cape wrapped around my shoulders.

He glances at me when I flop on the couch beside him. His countenance brightens when I lean against him.

"Did the television wake you?" he asks, taking my hand in his.

"No." I shiver dramatically. "I got cold."

"Sorry, sweetheart." He wraps his arm around me and draws me closer. "Shall we go back to bed?"

"What are you watching?" I gesture to the television, barely registering the scrolling text at the bottom of the screen.

Claude sighs and turns up the volume.

"Veronica and Oliver Monroe were arrested in their home yesterday evening. Their ties to the DeLuca crime family have been under investigation for the last year." The blonde newswoman reads the script over images of the front steps of my family home, my parents being led away in cuffs bathed in flashing red-and-blue lights.

My stomach twists and I watch in horror as the scene unfolds on the screen. Claude holds me close, silent and supportive.

"Unfortunately, this has also been a tragic turn of events. Authorities have confirmed the daughter of Oliver Monroe, beloved socialite Gigi Monroe, has died at the age of twenty-nine. She was killed by Nick DeLuca before he took his own life."

My jaw drops open, and I turn to Claude, who seems unsurprised by the announcement. His attention shifts to me.

"Did she just say I *died*?"

"Yes."

"And that Nick killed himself after he killed me?"

"Mm-hmm." Claude nods thoughtfully.

"The bastard actually pulled it off." I study Claude's face. "You don't seem surprised."

"Grant told me last night. Nick's goons confessed his plan. Grant told the officials both you and Nick were found dead. End of story." A soft smile curves his lips. "You're a free woman."

I blink twice before it fully registers. I'm free. The pang of sadness over the loss of my past shifts into a grander spectrum, full of bright colors and unlimited possibilities. My heart soars.

"I'm free." I say the words in a reverent whisper, almost afraid to break the spell granting me the new beginning I've craved for years.

Claude kisses my temple.

"What does this mean?" I ask, looking up at him.

"It means you can do whatever you want. Be whoever you want."

Whoever I want? I shift and straddle his lap, the blanket tangling around us, pulling low to expose my shoulder. He meets me, eye to eye, his hand resting on my hip over the fabric.

I search his handsome face, admire the sharp angles and faded scars. When I walked into the bar that snowy night, I sought refuge, safety, escape. He came to my rescue when I needed him. He offered a bloody stranger a place to stay, a chance to escape. No questions asked, demanded nothing in return. Everything I gave him, I did out of gratitude…and out of love.

When I reach up to cup his cheek, the blanket slips, pooling around my waist. His jaw tightens under my touch. Warmth sinks into me, and the pieces fall into place.

I know what I want. And who.

"Claude." I lick my lips and lean into him. My breasts press against the soft fabric of his tee shirt. "Did you mean what you said last night?"

"What did I say?"

"You love me."

"Of course." He grins. "I fell in love with you the moment you walked into my bar."

Heat blooms in the pit of my stomach and radiates outward. "That fast, huh?"

"Yeah." Pink infuses his cheeks. "I guess that sounds crazy."

"Not crazy." I wrap my arms around his neck, resting my forearms on his shoulders. "I fell for you that night too."

"Did you really?" he asks, arching his brow.

"God's honest truth."

"Is that why you asked to stay with me?"

"Maybe." Heat singes my cheeks at the confession. "I thought you were handsome…and sweet."

"Sweet?" He chuckles. "Never heard that before."

"Well, you are."

Claude tosses aside the blanket, leaving me bare in his lap. I shiver at the glint of hunger in his eyes. He slides his hand over my hip, down to where my thigh meets my ass. His long fingers tease the seam of my pussy, nudging me closer.

I rock against him and moan. My fingers thread through his hair.

He slides two fingers into me, then removes them. When he brings the digits to his lips and tastes my arousal, I whimper.

"You're the sweet one." Claude grins and lays me on the couch. He drapes one of my legs over his shoulder while the other hangs off the side. I catch a flash of his teeth before he buries his face between my thighs.

The first swipe of his tongue against my clit is pure bliss. I roll my hips and bury my fingers in his hair. He fucks me with his tongue, devouring me, watching my reaction. I surrender completely and cry out when he sucks my clit, rolling it with his tongue.

"Claude, please," I beg as my body tenses.

He blows across my sensitive nub, and I buck in response. Before

I can catch my breath, he thrusts two fingers deep and covers me with his mouth. The flat of his tongue puts pressure on my clit as he thrusts, over and over, with his fingers. The climax hovering just out of reach slams into me with the force of a runaway train.

I scream his name. My panting whimpers drown out the television as waves of pleasure ebb through my limbs. I sink deeper into the couch, unable to move, let alone think.

Claude's soft laughter brings me back to reality. I open my eyes to find him kneeling between my legs, grinning at me.

"That's not fair." I pout.

"What?" He settles back against the couch as I slowly climb to my feet.

My body still humming from the orgasm he gave me, I kneel and palm him through his sweatpants. His head falls back against the sofa as I tug the fabric down.

"Gwen, you don't…" His protest dies with a moan as I take him deep into my mouth.

I fist the base of his cock with my hand. When I suck the head, I stroke. The sounds coming from deep in his throat spur me on.

I'm dripping wet, but I've never felt more powerful, more in control. So I keep going, letting him thrust, slow and steady, into my mouth.

God, his moans sound downright sinful.

When he pulls out, I pout, but he covers my hand with his, stroking until he comes. I lean into it, letting the warmth coat my chest.

Claude leans forward and kisses me, drawing me into his lap, careless of the mess I'm making of his clothes and his couch. He holds me against him and sighs.

A few moments pass in peaceful silence with the television still chattering in the background.

"I love you, Gwen."

"Good, 'cause I love you too," I murmur. "Can I stay here forever?"

"That's a stupid question." He kisses my forehead. "Of course you can."

"How will this work? Me being dead and all?"

Claude strokes my shoulder. "Don't worry. We've got this under control."

"We?"

"Shh." He squeezes me tight. "I'll explain later. Right now, I just want to enjoy the moment."

"Okay." I bite my lip. "Can we go back to bed now?"

His laugh rumbles through me. "You're insatiable."

"Is that a yes?"

"Yes."

He helps me to my feet and follows me into the bedroom, where he shows me just how much he loves me. Over and over again.

We're two lonely hearts who have finally found their place in a world without glitz and glamour, wrapped up in each other.

It's perfect, and I wouldn't have it any other way.

CHAPTER 25

Claude

After a day of uninterrupted bliss, reality sets in when my brother arrives before I've had my morning coffee, banging on the door with enough force to shake the building. Grumbling under my breath, I unlock the door and swing it open.

He hasn't shaved regularly in several months, but he looks especially rough this morning. I'm sure he caught hell from Quinn for tagging along on the raid and getting caught at the wrong end of DeLuca's rage.

"You look like hell."

"Thanks." He comes in, closing the door behind him. "Where is she?"

"Shower." I pick up my coffee mug and take a sip. "Want some?"

"Sure."

"Help yourself." I stifle a grin behind my mug when he bitches under his breath and turns to the cabinet where I keep the cups.

Grant pours some coffee into the biggest cup I own and cradles it in his massive hand before inhaling deeply. I sit at the table and motion for him to join me.

"Any problems at the station?" I ask as he settles in the chair near the wall.

"Nothing McMasters couldn't handle. It took a little paper shuffling, but I think we've come to a compromise."

"Good." Relief chases away my remaining uncertainty.

"What's going on in here?" Gwen's sweet voice interrupts us.

I pivot in my chair to drink in the sight of her wearing one of my flannel shirts and sweatpants. Her damp hair lays over her shoulder as she runs her fingers through it.

My pulse flutters at her presence. How has she consumed me so entirely in such a short period of time?

When she steps within reach, I pull her into my lap, uncaring of my brother's obvious discomfort at the display of affection. She wraps her arms around my neck and kisses me softly.

"Am I interrupting?" Her attention shifts to Grant who drops his gaze to the murky bottom of his coffee cup.

"Not at all," I say.

She shifts off my lap and into the chair beside me. "Good morning, detective."

"Grant." My brother finally joins the conversation. "Just call me Grant."

"Okay." She takes my coffee mug and sips the rich dark brew.

Grant reaches into his jacket pocket and pulls out a folded piece of paper. Gwen blinks when he offers it to her. She carefully unfolds it and reads the contents. Her full lips purse and her brow furrows in confusion as she skims the words.

"Is this…?" Her voice fades.

"Your official death certificate." Grant leans back in his chair with a smile. "As of today, you're no longer Gwendolyn Monroe."

She presses a hand to her throat. "Who am I?"

"Whoever you want to be."

My brother and I share a look.

He clears his throat and continues. "You'll need a new name, new look, new paperwork, the works. Just give me the details, and I'll have the documents made as soon as possible."

"How?" she asks.

"I know some people." Grant smirks.

"Is this legal?" Gwen bites her lip. Her luminous gaze shifts between us. She's worried, but there's relief in her eyes.

"Does it matter?"

I turn to stare at Grant. My brother—the rule follower and ace detective—stepping outside the confines of the law twice in one year. Will the surprises never cease?

"No, I guess it doesn't." Gwen's shoulders soften. "How did you manage to pull this off?"

"It was easier to get you away from your family if your fiancé murdered you before he killed himself. Saves you from a long, drawn-out trial." A sincere smile lights his face, and I'm reminded of my brother's soft side. "It all worked out."

"Thank you." Tears fill her eyes. "How can I ever repay this kindness?"

"Promise me one thing." Grant stands and shoves his hands in his pockets.

"Anything."

"Take good care of my brother." He winks at her, and I shake my head. "But seriously, use this opportunity to start fresh. You've got your freedom now. Embrace it."

"I will." Gwen rests her hand on my shoulder. "Thank you so much. For everything."

Grant gives us both a resolute nod before leaving the apartment. I follow Gwen to the door and wrap my arm around her waist after she slides the lock into place. She leans back against me and sighs in contentment.

"You're a free woman now," I whisper in her ear. "What do you want to do first?"

She turns around and rests her hand against my chest.

A million stray thoughts flash through my mind, but one lingers, strong and insistent, pulsing in my brain. I hold onto it, biting my tongue until she speaks.

"Seduce you."

I laugh, and the sound echoes around the room. My mood lightens at her mischievous smile. "I mean *aside* from that."

She slides her arms around me, embracing me tightly. I rest in her hug and hold my breath.

"I don't know."

"Have you thought about who you want to be now?"

She skews up her nose, as though pondering the possibilities. I want to kiss along the bridge of her nose and bury my face in her hair.

"What about a new name?" I ask, unable to bear the torment of impatience.

"Can I keep Gwen? Most people knew me by Gigi."

"We can ask Grant, but if we make a few other changes—dye your hair, change your wardrobe—I don't think anyone would notice your passing resemblance to a wealthy socialite's deceased daughter."

"You make it sound so illicit and suspicious."

"It is." I chuckle when she frowns at me. "What about a surname?"

"Richards has a nice ring to it." She stills against me and meets my gaze.

My heart pounds, and my breath catches in my chest. "You want to take my last name?"

"Can I?" She licks her lips.

"That's awfully presumptuous of you. Staying with me. Sharing my bed. Borrowing my name." The comment is made in jest, but it burrows beneath her skin.

"If you don't want me to, then I can pick something else." She steps back, and I regret my teasing comment. "I'll go if it's too much—"

I grab her wrist and pull her back. She tilts her chin up, tears in her eyes.

I'm making a mess of this, but I've lived alone for so long, I don't know how to share my life with anyone. How to care for anyone but myself. The one thing I've always wanted is finally within my grasp, and I'm floundering.

"Gwen." I manage to find the words, even though they terrify me with their implication. "I love you."

"But?" She sighs and tightens her grip on my flannel shirt.

"I want more." Losing myself in her eyes, it pours free. "I want you to marry me. The thought of living another moment without you in my life fucking terrifies me. Take my name as yours. Share your life with me. I promise I'll care for you until my final breath."

With a gasp, her tears break free. She jumps into my arms, pulling me down to her level, and kisses me soundly on the lips.

The taste of her consumes me. With a moan, she deepens the kiss, drawing me into her. When I finally break away, we're both panting and I'm desperate to be inside her again.

"Is that a yes?" My voice is breathless and hoarse.

"Yes." She cups my cheek in her warm palm. "I will marry you, Claude. That's what I want. To be yours. Forever."

"Then why didn't you just say that?"

"Why didn't you ask me?"

"Because I didn't think you'd want a broken man like me." I groan when she rubs against me.

"You're not broken. You're beautiful."

Gwen beams, and I swear I'm transported by her faith in me, even if I don't believe it myself.

"I think you need your eyes checked." I scoff.

She grips my jaw in her hand and forces me to look at her. "You listen to me, Claude Richards. You're the most beautiful soul I've ever met. You took me in when I had nowhere to go. You believed in me when no one else did. I love you. Do you understand?"

"I do."

"Good." She takes my hand. "Now, come with me."

"Where are we going?" I feign stupidity as she drags me to the bedroom.

"Where I should have taken you the first night we met."

"Wait." I stop outside the door and drop her hand.

"What now?" She props her hand on her hip.

"Are you telling me I slept on the sofa for no reason?"

A wicked smile curves her lips. "I wouldn't say *no* reason. You were being a gentleman, and that made me love you more."

"Mm-hmm." My mumbled grunt only makes her laugh.

"Thank you for being my knight in shining armor, Claude. It's nice to know chivalry isn't dead."

"Gwen."

"Yes."

"Stop talking and get into bed."

"With pleasure."

EPILOGUE

Gwen

I wake up at six a.m. on Christmas morning and squeal when I see the fresh dusting of snow on the rooftops and streets outside. Claude rolls over and pulls the blanket up, burying his face. No amount of cajoling will pull him from the warmth of our bed. Not even the promise of fresh coffee and chocolate chip cookies.

"Last Christmas" plays on the radio while I finish mixing the cookie dough. I take a bite before popping the first tray into the oven. The sweet fragrance fills the air in the apartment. I've never baked cookies before, so I hover near the oven in case I forget and burn the whole building down.

Singing along to holiday music, I bustle around the apartment, making sure everything is tidy before our guests arrive at noon. Claude insisted we host the celebration in the bar. More room, he claimed. I want to surprise him before the festivities start, and I don't need an audience.

"Smells good."

I whip around at the compliment. Claude's new flannel pajamas match my own, and his hair is sticking up at odd angles. He looks adorably messy, and part of me wants to drag him back to bed, cookies and Christmas be damned.

"Thanks." I pull myself together and manage to remove the last tray of cookies from the oven without incident. After I set them on the stovetop to cool, he wraps his arm around me.

His scent mingles with the sweet aroma of chocolate chip cookies. I close my eyes and lean into him. There's nothing outside of him, outside of us.

"Merry Christmas, wife." The deep rumble of his voice against my neck unleashes a flurry of butterflies in the pit of my stomach.

Only two days have passed since we stood before a minister to recite our vows, and I still get chills when Claude calls me *wife*. The title fills me with pride and desire. After years of being trapped in my parents' shadows, I'm no longer beholden to their demands. The woman I was is gone. Dead and buried. A new, stronger version of myself stands tall beside this man, who selflessly came to the aid of a stranger. A man I chose. I wouldn't be where I am without him. And although the journey was rough, I wouldn't trade it for anything. Claude has given me the future I always dreamed of. The freedom I've always longed for. I can never repay him for his kindness, but I can show him exactly how much it means to me.

"I got you a present." He goes still at my statement.

"A present? You didn't have to do that."

"I wanted to." I take his hand. "Come here."

He trudges behind me as I pull him to the couch. When he sits, I kneel beside the tree and reach as far back as I can until my fingers find a box tucked out of sight.

"What is it?" He eyes me suspiciously.

"Open it and find out." I hand him the brightly wrapped box. Anticipation pulses through me, and I bounce on my toes.

He pats the couch beside him, and I curl up in the spot. He slowly unwraps the gift, using his knees to hold it steady as he tears the paper. His brow rises at the sight of a plain box beneath the wrapping.

A grin spreads across my lips. I try to hide it behind my hands, but he chuckles and shakes his head at my excitement.

Claude sets the box in his lap and lifts the lid, his grip encompassing it with ease. Shifting the paper aside, he laughs.

"Stephen King." He pulls a pristine, first-print copy of *The Dark Tower* from the box.

"I know you already have a copy. But this one is special." I gesture to the cover. "Look inside."

He flips the first few pages. There, on the title page, is a note scrawled in blue ink with the author's signature.

"To Claude. Enjoy, Steve King," he reads aloud in a somber tone.

"Do you like it?" I bite my lip.

"I love it." He sets the book aside and pulls me into his lap. The brush of his lips against mine drives away any reservations. When it ends, he leans his forehead against mine. "How in the world did you get this?"

"I called in a favor."

"Marcy." Claude sighs when I nod. "How did you know this was my favorite book?"

"Quinn told me."

"Thank you." He cups my cheek in his hand. "I don't have your gift here."

My brow furrows. "What gift? I thought we weren't doing gifts."

"So did I."

My face warms at his pointed look. "Point taken." I clear my throat and redirect the conversation. "Maybe we should get ready for the party? I still have some things to set up downstairs."

"Can't we just call it off and go back to bed?" He squeezes my hip, and it takes all my effort not to succumb to those seductive brown eyes luring me in.

"No. It's too late to cancel now." I scramble off his lap before he kisses me again. "Let's go."

With a grumble, Claude retreats to the shower while I clean up the kitchen and put the cookies into a Tupperware container. I manage to trade places with him without being pulled into bed, and an hour later, we descend to the bar.

Quinn and Grant arrive shortly after us and help finalize the decorations. Rob and Marcy knock on the door promptly at noon. But at twelve-thirty, there's still no sign of Arthur and Kate.

"I wonder where they are," Rob says, glancing at his watch. "It's not like Arthur to be late."

By one, Rob's pacing the floor. "I'm calling him."

I place the phone on the bar in front of him beside the Crock-Pots keeping our Christmas meal warm.

The door bursts open with a gust of wind, reminding me of the first night I entered the Black Penny. Kate and Arthur step through, shaking off the cold.

"We were about to call in a missing person's report," Grant says as he closes the door behind them.

"You might have to." Arthur turns to him with a somber look.

"What's wrong?" I straighten up at the worry etching his handsome face.

"Cyril didn't show up this morning." He runs his fingers through his hair. "He was supposed to pick us up at ten thirty. I waited until eleven and tried to call him, but there was no answer. No one has seen him since late last night."

"Maybe he had a late night out?" I offer, hopeful.

"No, he drove us home last night and told us he was stopping to pick up the purse Kate left at the party." Arthur shakes his head. "This isn't like him. I've known him for years. He's worked for me for ten. He's never been late, let alone not shown up. Something's wrong."

Kate rests a hand on her husband's arm. "It'll be okay. We'll find him."

"I'll make some calls," Grant offers.

"Thanks." Arthur sighs. "I'm sorry. I didn't mean to ruin Christmas."

"You didn't ruin anything," I assure him. "I'm sure we'll hear something soon. Let's eat, keep our strength up."

Cyril's disappearance hangs heavy over the gathering, but we manage to grasp a few joyful moments.

"I'd like to propose a toast." Rob stands and holds his glass aloft. "To 1985, a year none of us will ever forget."

"To 1985," we all echo and drink.

"To finding our soulmates," Kate adds with a bashful smile.

I catch Claude staring at me as I drink to Kate's toast. He winks, and I warm from the end of my nose to the tips of my toes. If there's one thing this year has taught me, it's to expect the unexpected and make the most of every day.

Surrounded by my new family and friends, I'm finally where I'm meant to be.

Home.

"Come with me," Claude whispers in my ear and takes me by the hand.

I lace my fingers through his and follow him down the hall to his office.

"What are you up to?" I ask when he closes the door behind us.

He pins me against the door and kisses me. All my questions disappear into smoke and drift away. I run my fingers through his hair and deepen the kiss. God, I love this man.

With a curse, he takes a step back. "I wanted to…give you this." He reaches into his pocket and pulls out a small leather box.

My eyes fly wide, and my heart flutters.

"It's my grandmother's." He opens the lid and I gasp.

A round sapphire nestled on a simple gold band winks up at me. "Claude, it's lovely."

"Do you like it?"

"I love it." With reverence, I take the ring from the velvet and slip it on my finger. It fits perfectly. Tears fill my eyes.

"I would have given it to you sooner, but I had to get it resized and—"

"Claude." I place a finger over his lips. "Stop talking and kiss me."

Without hesitation, he does just that.

"Merry Christmas, wife."

"Merry Christmas, husband." I grin. "I love you."

He beams down at me. "I know."

Before I can say anything more, he kisses me again. All thoughts of our guests and Christmas dinner are forgotten.

There's only him and me.

And that's all I'll ever need.

PLAYLIST

"Sharp Dressed Man" - ZZ Top
"You Make My Dreams" - Daryl Hall & John Oates
"Get Outta My Dreams, Get Into My Car" - Billy Ocean
"Just What I Needed" - The Cars
"I Just Died in Your Arms" - Cutting Crew
"Unskinny Bop" - Poison
"Moving in Stereo" - The Cars
"More Than a Feeling" - Boston
"Drive" - The Cars
"I Was Made for Lovin' You" - KISS
"Paradise by the Dashboard Light" - Meatloaf

CHAPTER 1

Cyril

December 24, 1985

It's been a hell of a year.

Not that I'm complaining. Far from it. It's just...I've seen some crazy shit over the past twelve months. First, a girl from the future drops into my boss's lap, then I'm running all over town sticking my neck out for mafia busts, abuse allegations, and murder investigations. I'm not sure '86 can match the intensity of this year. Honestly, I'll be glad for a reprieve.

I turn up the heat and rest my elbow on the armrest. There's a line of cars in front of me, another line behind, my town car parked smack-dab in the middle. The Rolls is comfortable enough, but I can't ignore a pinch of jealousy at knowing my boss and his wife are enjoying a swanky holiday party in the Empire State Building.

Arthur Maxwell is the most prestigious architect in the city, and I've had the honor of being his driver for eleven years. Until this year, I've never thought of moving on, of trying my hand at something other than being a chauffeur. Don't get me wrong—it's a plush gig, and I get to do what I love, but it doesn't leave much time for anything else. Probably explains why I'm still single and haven't touched a wrench in ages.

With a sigh, I pull a pack of Doublemint from my pocket and stuff a stick in my mouth. My fingers tap the steering wheel in time with "More Than a Feeling" playing on the radio. Boston does their best to distract me, but the music doesn't touch my restlessness. I could go for a strong drink. Hell, even a cup of black coffee could do the trick.

Nodding along to the beat, I watch the entrance to the building, hoping the boss will decide to call it a night early. The air is cold and crisp with a few scattered snowflakes drifting in front of the windshield, glinting in the streetlight. Shit. The snow isn't supposed to accumulate, but I don't like the combination of icy drizzle and snow. Makes a slushy mess and turns people into assholes behind the wheel. There's already a dusting of snow on the roads. I grimace when a man steps off the curb and nearly slides into the front of my car. Great.

I check the clock on the dash. Nine thirty. I cave to the boredom and pull out a paperback stashed in my glove compartment. Claude recommended it. One of Stephen King's novels, *The Shining*. I typically read science fiction, but I'm willing to give it a shot.

Four chapters later, I snap to attention as a couple approaches. Shit. I toss the book to the passenger seat and step out of the car, pulling my hat down so it won't blow away. By the time I round the front of the vehicle, Arthur and Kate have reached the curb.

"Sir. Ma'am." I acknowledge them with a smile and open the back door.

Arthur nods and helps his wife into the car.

"Thank you, Cyril," Kate says from the interior.

"Just doing my job." Once he takes a seat beside her, I close the door.

When I return to the driver's seat, my demeanor shifts to pure business, and without prompting, I head for Arthur's apartment. A few blocks down the street, I steal a glimpse in the rearview mirror. Kate's leaning against Arthur with her eyes closed. He has his arm protectively wrapped around her shoulder, keeping her close. He kisses her forehead.

My heart softens at the tender display. I redirect my attention to the traffic and ignore an ache in my chest. It's been too long. With my unpredictable, random hours, it's difficult for me to find anyone to invest in long-term. Romantically, I mean.

There've been women. Scores of them. But none with the right combination of smarts and sexy to last beyond a brief fling. Fun distractions, nothing more. Seeing Kate and Arthur together makes me long for something I never before realized I wanted.

Maybe one day, I can open a shop and have my own fleet of cars with a little garage to tinker with my own restoration project. If I had that, it would give me more time to find someone to share my life with. I shove the dream aside and focus on the road.

Arthur and I have spoken about it at length. He knows how much I want to start my own business, have my own space. I can't be his driver indefinitely. He agrees, even offered to be a silent investor in my business. But that's as far as it's gone. I'll talk to him about it after New Year's to see if he's serious about the project.

When I pull up outside their building, Arthur nudges Kate. "We're home."

"Already?" She yawns.

I chuckle. With the holiday traffic, the normally short drive took an hour. I put the car in park and step out to open her door, offering my hand when she moves to exit the car.

"Thank you, Cyril." She takes my hand to steady herself on the slick pavement. Her brow furrows. "Wait." She pats her pockets. "Is my clutch in the car?"

Arthur turns to check the back seat. "Nothing here."

"Damn. I must have left it."

"We can get it tomorrow." Arthur takes her by the elbow and leads her toward the entrance.

"I can stop and grab it on my way home, if you want." I curse myself the moment I say it because it will put me thirty minutes out of my way.

"No, it should be fine." She stops midstride and taps her lower lip. "Unless I left it on the observation deck…" Kate grips Arthur's arm. "I did. When you took me up, I left it on the lower ledge near the elevator."

Arthur's jaw clenches before he exhales in defeat. "Fine. I'll call someone to retrieve it."

"No need, sir. I'll get it."

"Are you sure, Cyril? I wouldn't want you to use personal time running an errand for me."

"It's fine." I force a smile. It's not like I have a family, or anything, to rush home to.

"Okay." Arthur leads Kate to the front door and turns. "See you at nine tomorrow morning."

"Yes, sir."

Once they close the door, I return to the car. Why did I offer to do this? I groan as I put the car into drive and pull away. The clock reads eleven fourteen. By the time I reach the Empire State Building, it'll be close to midnight.

The return trip takes less time. I park the car outside the building and pocket the keys. Ten minutes tops, then I'll be on my way home.

Inside, I slip past the night guard, talking on the phone. The elevator takes me to the observation deck. I pull my coat tighter around me, but the cold, wet wind still bites my face. I walk around for a few moments, searching the ledges near the elevator, until I spot it. Kate's clutch. I tuck it into my pocket and turn around.

The night sky spreads over the horizon, snow drifting lazily through the air. I step close to the railing, wanting the full immersive experience of the skyline stretched out before me. I inhale deeply and let the chill sink into my lungs to purge the restlessness for a moment.

What if this is as good as it gets?

Stuck in the mud, tires spinning.

No legacy. No family. Nothing to show but some memories and a few laughs. Have I run out of time to make something of myself? To leave my mark on the world?

Would anyone miss me if I were gone?

I shiver at the thought and force out an uncomfortable chuckle. Guess I'm more tired than I realized. I should go home and rest.

Spinning on my heel, I step toward the elevator, only to feel the slick ground give way under me. My hands fly out, searching for something, anything, to break my fall.

But there's nothing. I fall in slow motion for an eternity until the snow flecked night consumes my vision. Pain radiates through my head as I hit the ground.

Everything goes dark.

Warmth brushes my face. I open my eyes and blink into a sun-filled sky.

What the hell? With a groan, I carefully sit up and look around.

It all rushes back in a wave.

Observation deck. Empire State Building. I pat my pocket. Kate's clutch is still there. Shit, is it morning already? How the hell did I survive a night outside? I shake my head and climb to my feet.

The elevator opens behind me, and a group of people step onto the platform. They keep their distance as they move to the railing. I follow them, trying to make sense of my situation, when I see something.

Well, it's what I *don't see* that scrambles my brain.

"Where the hell is the World Trade Center?" I squint, searching the horizon for the tell-tale twins, standing tall at the base of Manhattan.

There's a single skyscraper in their place. What the hell?

A small group of people stare at me for a moment before moving to the far side of the platform. I ignore their stares and head for the elevator.

As the car descends, I rub my scalp. Maybe I hit my head harder than I thought and I'm still unconscious. I wince when I pinch my arm. Nope. Not asleep. My brain is sifting through confusing possibilities when the elevator reaches the ground floor.

I step into the lobby. When I pass the directory, I pause, searching the company names. Confusion fills me again when I reach the end of the list and haven't recognized any of them.

"Where's Arthur Maxwell?" I read the list again, but he's not there. Another name is in the space once occupied by my boss. Strange.

"Is everything okay, sir?" A guard comes alongside me.

"Yes, of course." I play it off, but inside, I'm in a full-blown panic. "Do you happen to have the paper?"

"The newspaper?" The guard gives me an odd look, like I've sprouted horns or a third eye.

"Yeah. Any paper."

"No, but I can pull it up for you." He takes a small rectangular device from his pocket, like something Spock would have on *Star Trek*. "*New York Times*," he says and the device dings.

"Here are some results for the *New York Times*." A mechanical voice emits from the device.

My mouth drops open. "Did that just respond to you?"

"Yeah. So?" He scoffs. "You sure you're okay?"

Am I okay? No. No, I am not.

"Can you just tell me what day it is?" I manage to ask the question, even though my throat feels like it's constricting, cutting off my airway.

"December 21." He turns the device, showing me a narrow screen with a photo of a cat eating noodles.

Then I see the time. And the date.

It's December 21…three days ago. But why does the year read *2022*?

My head spins. I brace myself against the wall.

"I gotta go."

Without a thought, I race through the lobby, out into the cool morning.

This can't be.

It can't be true.

I remember the stories Kate told us about what happened that fateful New Year's Day, but I didn't think it was actually true…that she traveled back in time.

And yet, I'm standing in the year 2022. Just last night it was 1985. My knees buckle, and I stumble to the nearest bench. Slumping into it, I hang my head in my hands.

The hustle and bustle of the city surrounds me. Pedestrians walking with intent. Horns blaring. Engines purring. Exhaust perfuming the air.

It all fades into the background as reality settles like a nail in a tire, leaving me deflated.

"Hey, buddy, got a dollar?" asks a man in a tattered green coat and threadbare stocking cap.

My hand reaches for my wallet, if only to ensure it's there. But it's not. I close my eyes and shake my head.

Of course. It's still in the Rolls. I never keep it in my pocket while driving.

"Sorry," I mutter to the old man.

He ambles down the street, disappearing in the crowd.

A breeze ruffles my hair, and I reach up to pull down my hat, only to find air. Shit. What happened to my hat? It probably got sucked into the void that is the space-time continuum.

I scoff. Too much science fiction. Damn you, Doc Brown.

I can't sit here all day wondering what the hell happened. I need to find Arthur and Kate. The Black Penny is close. Maybe Claude and Grant can help me.

Halfway down the block, I freeze midstride.

It's 2022. It's been thirty-seven years. What if they're…dead? Panic grabs me by the throat and chokes me. What if everything, every*one* I've ever known, is gone? Fuck.

I pull my coat tight around my throat again and push forward. Does it matter? There's not a damn thing I can do about it. Life moved on without me, and that's the painful fucking truth.

Even without me…the world kept spinning.

With every block, the confusion deepens as the reality of my situation settles deep in the pit of my gut. I'm barely aware of the people and noise around me. In thirty-odd years, the city and her people haven't changed much. Though the styles have evolved some. And everywhere I look, people are using little devices like the one the guard showed me. What the hell are they anyway? A tricorder? Some kind of handheld computer? As long as it's not some strange *Terminator* shit…oh God, there I go again.

Several blocks from the Black Penny, I turn right out of habit, heading home. My apartment—well, my former apartment—isn't far from the Hell's Kitchen hangout Arthur and his friends frequent. It sits above a two-bay garage run by a Korean War veteran. Mac's Garage. He understands my need to have grease under my nails.

Is he gone?

Biting back my hesitation, I venture down the street leading straight to Mac's. To home. With every step, my heart pounds and my stomach lurches. I'm starving. I haven't eaten anything in….well, years. I feel like I'm going to puke.

I round the corner and the sign comes into view. I blink twice when I read it.

Cyril's Garage.

Wait. What happened to *Mac's* Garage? Why is my name on this building? I look up and down the quiet street. It's a small street and doesn't get much traffic. Today, I'm thankful for that. I stand in the middle of the road, staring at *my* name on the building where I lived thirty-seven years ago.

The sound of an air compressor echoes behind the large blue garage doors, drawing me closer. I pause outside the door, my hand resting on the knob. Muffled music hums through the air, vibrating the metal beneath my hand. When I push open the door, a familiar guitar solo lures me further inside. It's not a song I'm familiar with, but I know it's Aerosmith playing through the speakers. I'd recognize that screaming vocalist anywhere.

The clang of metal on concrete cuts through the music as the compressor cuts off. I venture deeper into the shop, taking in the familiar smell of grease and hydraulic fluid while noting the differences in the space. More organized, more colorful. More professional. Whoever owns this place knows their shit.

Then I see her—a 1974 green Dodge Dart Swinger.

I walk alongside the car, admiring the sleek lines. She's not finished, but I can see potential beneath the spotty rust and dinged rear quarter panel.

"Goddamn it." Another clang of metal strikes metal. "You miserable bitch. Why won't you cooperate?"

Is that a woman's voice? Curiosity pulls me around the car, and I see a curvy backside clad in denim bent over the front fender.

"Piece of shit! Just come off!" She jerks and pulls, continuing to swear under her breath.

I peer over her shoulder, glimpsing the engine beneath the hood. I whistle low, noting the 360 V8. Not stock but definitely not overkill. Someone has some taste.

"Need a hand?" I ask on impulse.

She drops the tool in her hand and spins around, hitting her head on the hood of the car. "Motherfucker!" She grips her head with a grease-covered hand and hisses.

"Who the fuck are you?" Her deep blue eyes narrow at me. "Better yet, why the fuck are you in *my* shop?"

I suck in a breath. Shit. She's even more glorious than the car.

CHAPTER 2

Jessica

Damn it! I rub the aching spot on the back of my head and lean against the bumper, eyeing the man who disturbed my peaceful morning.

I should have checked the door to make sure it was locked. Anyone could walk in while I'm working, and I would never hear them. Real smooth. Cursing myself, I tighten my grip on the screwdriver in case I need to use it as a weapon.

My gaze skims the intruder. He's tall, dark, and distractingly handsome. Judging by the sharp suit and pristine wool jacket, he's not a vagrant wandering the winter streets, looking for a place to warm up.

I narrow my eyes and point the tool in his direction. "Again, who are you and why are you in my shop?" I grit my teeth, irritated. "We're closed."

"Door was open." He shrugs in the general direction of the entrance.

"We're still closed."

His eyes sparkle with amusement. "Is that how you treat customers?"

"Are you a customer?"

"Depends on whether this is your typical customer service."

I roll my eyes. "Listen. We're closed for Christmas. All our services are booked for the holiday. But thanks for coming in. Don't let the door hit you on the way out."

I turn back to the engine, ignoring the way his perusal of my shop and my car makes me acutely aware of his presence.

He doesn't move as I reach down to adjust the carburetor.

"What are you doing?"

"Working." I ignore him and focus on my task.

"Why are you doing it the hard way?"

I sigh with exasperation, then glare at him. "What? You wrench?"

"A little." He shoves his hands in his pockets and shrugs. "Been a while though."

With a scoff, I turn back to the engine and continue my adjustments. Why does everyone assume I don't know my way around cars? Seriously. I've been doing this since I was eight. I don't need to be mansplained.

He steps closer, leaning over the bumper. There's six inches between us. I try to ignore him and focus on the carburetor. His warmth drifts to me, carrying the spicy, subtle aromas of cologne and leather. I refuse to react to the way it tickles my nose and weaves through my brain, short circuits sparking in its wake. My grip tightens on the screwdriver again, and I twist harder.

The tool gives under my hand and slips free, clanging against the compartment. My wrist nicks a sharp clamp edge near the radiator, and I curse as a spasm of pain radiates up my arm.

"Damn it." I jerk my hand free and pull a rag from my pocket to wrap around the cut. Biting back tears of frustration, I lean against the car and close my eyes.

"Let me see."

His soft voice pulls me from my pissy solitude. I open my eyes, and he's holding out his hand.

"It's just a scratch. I got it." The warmth seeping through the rag tells me it's more than just a scratch. Shit.

He huffs, like he can see through my tough act, and takes my hand. The moment his fingertips brush mine, the protest dies on my lips. I bite my tongue and watch in silence as he removes the dirty rag to examine the cut.

"Not deep enough for stitches, but we'll have to clean it up." He tosses the dirty rag aside and wraps a clean one around the wound, putting pressure on it. Where the hell did he get it? Must have grabbed it from the box on the shelf while I was bitching myself out for carelessness.

"I can take care of it." I jerk my hand out of his and head for the bathroom.

Inside, I close the door and lean against it. What the hell? Who is this guy? And why does he leave me off-kilter? I push the questions aside and wash the wound. Thank God I keep a first aid kit here. Once it's clean and wrapped in a sterilized bandage, I take a minute to compose myself.

I snort when I look in a small mirror on the door to find grease smeared across my forehead and cheek. How attractive. I shake myself. Why do I care? I'm working. I get dirty when I work. Any mechanic would know that. I use the damp rag to wipe the grease off.

Looks like I'm done for now. Just need to take the car out for a test drive before I make more adjustments.

Now to deal with the elephant in the room. I *wish* he were an elephant and not a tempting distraction with soulful eyes and a sinful smile. Nope, not going there.

Find out who he is and what he wants, then show him the door. Simple.

When I step back into the garage, I stop at the sight before me. He's bent over the front of my Swinger, the distinctive *click* and *tink* of metal against metal sounding from beneath the hood. What the hell is he doing to my car?

By the time I reach his side, he's pulled back and is wiping his hands on a rag.

I open my mouth to tell him he's a presumptuous ass for touching my baby.

"I made a little adjustment for you. Should start easier next time."

"That's bold, to barge into someone's garage and touch their goddamned car without permission." I glower at him before looking at the place he's indicating. He managed to adjust it just like I wanted, but I wouldn't be sure until I started the car. How the hell did he get the damn thing to cooperate?

Doesn't matter. I'm still irritated.

"Didn't mean to overstep. Just looked like you needed a helping hand." He smiles, and two identical dimples appear.

I brace my hand against the car. If he'd been handsome before, he was smoldering hot now. That alone pushes me from mildly irritated to pissed.

"All right, who the hell are you? Did my dad send you?" I cross my arms.

My dad's been on my case to find a partner to expand the business for years. But I'm not interested. This garage is *mine.* I've worked too damn hard to let some jackass come in here and steal it from me. It would be just like Dad to invite someone to come in as partner without my approval. Agitation itches beneath my skin.

"No one sent me." His brows draw together in confusion. "Is this your place?"

"Yes." Pride fills me as I look around the shop. "Why?"

"Your name is Cyril?"

That wicked smile curves his lips, and I'm momentarily distracted by the casual charm oozing off him.

"No." I shake my head and curse Dad, yet again, for being adamant about keeping the name he chose when he bought it years ago.

"Do I have to beg for it?"

His question leaves me stunned. My breath catches, and his eyes—green now that I see them up close—sparkle with mischief. "Beg…for what?"

"Your name." His voice, deep and even, feels like a distraction.

I bite my lip. Do I really want to tell him my name? There's something about him that feels off, but we've been alone together long enough for him to have hurt me if he really wanted to.

I exhale sharply in defeat. "Jessica."

"Jessica," he repeats, and I'm not turned off by the way my name rolls off his lips. "Pretty name."

"Thanks." I unruffle myself and prop a hand on my hip. "You gonna tell me your name and what the hell you want?"

He sets the rag aside and grins. "I'm Cyril. I'm looking for an old friend."

"Cyril?" Disbelief punches me in the chest, stealing the air in my lungs before laughter replaces it. I double over and slap my thigh. "That's a good one. Did my dad put you up to this?" I grumble under my breath, "I'm gonna strangle that old grump."

The humor in his eyes dims. "Who's your father?"

"That's it. He's gone too far. This is ridiculous." I pull my iPhone out of my back pocket. His gaze lingers on the device, and I swear there's a mix of curiosity and panic in his shifting facial expression. I ignore it and press the button. "Siri, call Dad."

"Who's Siri?" he mutters to himself more than to me.

The line rings, and I put the phone to my ear. "Pick up, Dad." My frown deepens with each unanswered ring. Finally, his voicemail kicks in. Screw it. I hang up.

Then I notice the time. It's nine thirty. Mom and Dad had an appointment this morning, uptown. They won't be back until noon. Shit. I glance at my wary companion.

His face is pale, his eyes fixed on a spot of oil on the concrete. My heart constricts at the way he looks like a lost puppy in the middle of Central Park. Damn it. None of this makes sense. Dad's up to something…but I'll be damned if I know what it is.

"Who's your father?" he asks again, his voice softer this time.

"Like you don't know."

"Please."

Whoever this guy is, he's not my problem...and yet, that one word echoes through the shop, fading into the music coming through the speakers. It breaks my resolve to stay detached.

"Arthur Maxwell."

His eyes pinch shut, and he sucks in a deep breath. When he turns away on his heel, I can almost feel the tension radiating from his dark form. He rakes both hands over his head, threading his fingers through his hair. After a few moments, he heads for the exit.

This guy is off his rocker. I should be happy he's leaving, but guilt claws at my gut. Damn it.

"Hey," I shout, jogging across the concrete to catch him before he reaches the door. I grab his sleeve and pull him to a stop. "Wanna grab something to eat? There's a place around the corner. My treat."

His shoulders relax. I brace myself as he turns. The strong jaw I admired earlier is clenched tight. Gone are the dimples, replaced with a somber demeanor.

"Thanks, but I don't want to take up any more of your time."

"Look, I'm sorry I was a dick earlier. Let me make it up to you." My hand tightens on his sleeve. "Please."

God, how desperate do I sound? Anything to quell the pressing guilt for being a complete asshole to a stranger.

When his green eyes meet mine, I smile, trying to show a little repentance.

One dimple appears as he responds. "Food sounds good." The second dimple appears. "I'm starving."

"Good. Great." I release his sleeve, suddenly overwhelmed with warmth. "I'll grab my coat and lock up."

He waits by the door while I run to the office for my things. I switch off the lights, leaving only one light on near the front door. He's leaning against the wall when I reach him. I finish tugging on my coat.

With one arm, he pushes open the door. "After you."

"Thanks." I step out onto the sidewalk and turn to lock the door after he comes alongside me.

There's a chill in the air. Feels like snow. I pull my jacket tighter and turn right, toward the diner. He falls into step beside me, and there's something weird about this whole encounter.

We walk in silence, a million questions burning a hole in my head. I bite them back, uncertain I want the answers. I shouldn't get involved. This guy isn't my problem.

And yet…

I study his profile. Strong and sharp, angular and regal. Why does he look familiar?

Something twists deep in my chest before breaking loose and nestling in my brain, tugging at a forgotten memory.

It's probably my guilty coincidence.

I just hope Dad's not trying to pull a fast one on me.

CHAPTER 3

Cyril

The diner apparently hasn't changed in thirty some years—chrome and glass, neon *Open* sign glowing in the window. Dirty, caked snow litters the sidewalk as we approach the door. Instinctively, I step around her, reach for the handle, and open it.

"After you." I gesture with a sweep of my arm, as I've done for years as her father's driver.

Her incredulous look sticks with me, even as she steps into the warm restaurant. I follow behind.

The aroma of fried, greasy food assails me. My stomach grumbles, pleading for attention. It's like I haven't eaten in years.

Wait…that's more true than I want to admit. As the reality of my situation sinks in, I square my shoulders and really take in my surroundings.

While the diner is largely the same, it's older, faded in spots. There are no familiar faces behind the counter. The restaurant is busy, but the conversation is muted. Then I see why. Most people are focused on the small devices in their hands rather than the people sitting across from them. It's not true in all the cases, but enough to make it noticeable. Sad and strange.

A waitress appears, wearing casual clothing instead of the blue-and-white uniform I'm used to. "How many?"

"Two," Jessica responds before I can.

The waitress snatches two menus and leads us to a booth tucked into a corner near the window.

"Sam will be right over." With a nod, she turns to leave.

"Wow," I mutter under my breath. Things have certainly changed. What happened to service with a smile?

"What?" Jessica asks, glancing up from the open menu in her hand.

"Nothing." I shake my head and skim the words on the menu. Then I see the prices. "Holy shit."

"Something wrong?" She folds the menu and sets it aside.

"When did breakfast get so expensive?" I rub my forehead trying to suppress an oncoming headache.

She scoffs. "It's gotten worse over the last two years. Trust me. The pandemic jacked up everything."

"The...pandemic?"

I bite my tongue at her exasperated look.

"Yeah, let's not talk about it, okay?"

"Okay." I have no idea what she's talking about, but I admit I'm curious. There will be time to catch up on the events of the past thirty-seven years later. Especially if I can get one of those distracting handheld devices—phones? computers?—everyone seems to have.

A waitress appears, her hair a bright neon pink. Sam, I assume. "What can I get ya?"

Jessica gives her order first. Coffee with cream, two eggs over easy, hashbrowns, and sausage. It sounds delicious.

"I'll have the same," I say when Sam looks at me. I hand her my menu. "Thanks."

After she retreats, Jessica leans back and pins me with those gorgeous blue eyes. Her dark hair is still pulled up in a messy heap on top of her head, but the grease stains are gone. Bummer. They were kind of sexy. Everything about her is sexy.

But she's Arthur's daughter.

The thought instantly sobers me. I clear my throat and wish I had coffee to distract my hands and my mouth. Shit.

"So...you gonna tell me how you know my dad?"

I clear my throat with a cough, covering my mouth. Sam appears with our coffee and creamer. I use the interruption to my advantage. While I pour cream into my steaming coffee, my mind spins. What the hell do I tell her? I can't tell her the truth. She'll never believe it.

As I scramble for a realistic response, she watches me, echoing my actions before taking a sip of her coffee. Her soft groan of satisfaction shoots through me, leaving goosebumps along my arms. Damn it.

I drink my coffee too fast and burn my tongue. Today is really not my day, is it?

"Well..." I set the cup aside. "It's complicated."

"How is it complicated? You met him *somewhere.*"

"He's an old friend. We met years ago." I hope she'll buy the vague response.

"Where?" She leans forward, resting her elbows on the table. The curve of her T-shirt dips low, and I catch a teasing glimpse of cleavage.

I look out the window to clear my head before finally meeting her intense gaze. "The Empire State Building."

"Dad hasn't worked there in thirty years." She scoffs. "How old are you?"

"Thirty-nine." At least, that's how old I *look*. Oh damn, this is complicated. I ignore the physics of time travel and the complications I'm compounding onto the space-time continuum. I pray I'm not irrevocably fucking something up in the universe or causing a rift in our timeline.

"You met him when you were young?" Her brows scrunch together as she digs deeper. "How?"

"I admired his work. Wanted to meet him." I sip my coffee. "He inspired me to work hard." I'm not lying, but if she asks more questions, I may have to spin some pretty creative tales.

"How old are you?" I ask, turning the tables, praying it will distract her from her current inquisition.

"Thirty-two. Why?"

"How long have you been turning wrenches?"

"Since I was eight." She points a finger at me. "Stop turning this around to me. I'm not stupid. I know what you're trying to do."

"What am I trying to do?"

"Distract me." Jessica glowers. "It won't work."

"I'm not trying to distract you," I lie with a placating smile. "I'm genuinely curious about how a gorgeous woman finds herself fixing vintage cars in a garage."

"It's *my* garage." Her eyes narrow. "Are you sure Dad didn't send you?"

"Nope. I was taking a walk and saw my name in lights. Had to check it out."

A small smile cracks her lips. "That's another thing. Your name. It's not common."

"No, it's not, but I'm partial to it."

"What are the odds of you passing by a garage with your name on it?"

"Pretty slim." My eyes widen. "Maybe it's a sign."

"A sign of what?"

"Fate."

Jessica scoffs. "You're as crazy as Dad."

"What do you mean?" I crave information about Arthur and Kate. Jessica is my only connection to them. If I can somehow convince her to take me to them, I can explain everything. They'll believe me. They're the only people who will understand.

"Dad always talked about fate bringing him and Mom together." Jessica rolls her eyes. "Sentimental ramblings of an old man."

Fate did bring them together. I saw it with my own two eyes. I remember the day like it was yesterday, vivid and fresh in my mind, how horror filled me when I saw Arthur exit the Empire State Building with an unconscious woman in his arms.

Who was I to question my employer? I bit my tongue and drove him home, even though my conscience told me to take her to an emergency room. Arthur convinced me he had it under control. It was the only time in my tenure as his driver when I questioned his judgment. In the end, he was right. It worked out.

Even though it had been difficult for me to believe Kate was from the future, there was always something about her that set her apart from everyone around. Something special. The way she spoke, her mannerisms. Hell, even her humor set her apart.

I miss them, Kate and Arthur. They were more than my employers; they were my family, my friends. Everything I had, I owed to their kindness. Did they mourn my loss? Questions burn, but I can't ask them. I need to see Arthur.

"I wouldn't be so quick to mock fate." My tone is soft between us. The spot between my ribs above my heart aches at the loss I've suffered…a gaping black hole of time I'll never get back.

"You sound just like him." She shakes her head.

The food arrives, giving us a reprieve. I pick up my fork and eat, not tasting the food I shovel into my mouth. I'm starving, but this hunger is for much more than sustenance. I quietly steal glances at Jessica between bites.

She devours her food with enthusiasm. Must have worked up an appetite arguing with me. I smile to myself and finish my breakfast.

I'm not sure if she trusts me, or even if she believes a word that has come out of my mouth, but I don't care. I'm at her mercy, even if she doesn't realize it. She's the easiest way to connect me to the only people who will understand the insane situation I'm in.

I'll survive, regardless of what happens, but right now, I need an anchor. Something to ground me. To hold me steady. To give me purpose and direction.

As I finish my eggs, I catch Jessica's eye. She offers the first sincere smile I've seen so far. Something inside my chest twists, rips open, and sinks to the pit of my stomach in a warm fizzle of resignation.

I thought Arthur and Kate could offer some solutions to my complicated situation. Maybe I've already found the answer.

Maybe Jessica is just what I need.

Thanks, Fate.

CHAPTER 4

Jessica

There's something weird about this guy. Not in a *I'm afraid he's a serial killer and I'll never see my family again* way. No, it's subtle…an undercurrent of electricity pulsing through my body. Familiarity nags at my brain, but I've never met him before. I know I haven't. I would remember a guy this hot.

He runs his fingers through his thick, dark hair and looks out the window. The way his eyes scan the world beyond the glass makes me think he's searching for something. For someone? He appeared out of the blue this morning—maybe he's wandering. Lost.

Damn it. I don't need this right now. Dad's put a lot of stress on me lately with his persistent suggestions to find a partner and expand the garage. We have a healthy clientele and a steady schedule that covers the bills. Why this sudden need to expand?

I mean, he and Mom are in their seventies now. They won't be around forever, but I don't need them to take care of me. I haven't needed it for a long time. After my divorce, I took control of my life and poured my heart and soul into the garage. And it's flourishing.

Is there room for expansion? Maybe. But why push when I'm content where I am? Besides, expansion means taking on a partner, and that's the *last* thing I want right now.

When the waitress returns with the check, I hand her my card.

"Thanks for breakfast," Cyril says, fidgeting with the edge of his placemat.

My heart softens at his tone. "You're welcome." A ding vibrates my phone in my pocket. I pull it out and read the text from Mom. *Dad and I are on our way home. Is something wrong?*

I quickly type out a reply. *Got a surprise visitor this morning. He wants to speak to Dad. I'm bringing him over.*

Mom replies with a thumbs-up emoji.

I shake my head and put the phone away.

"Everything okay?" He looks even more lost with that confused expression.

"Yeah, we're good." I take my card back from the waitress and sign the receipt, slapping a cash tip on top. "Ready to go?"

"I guess." He stands and pulls on his coat.

Once we're on the sidewalk, he tucks his hands in his pockets and falls into step beside me. Strange how comfortable I feel in his presence after our unusual meeting this morning.

We cover the short distance to the garage, and I unlock the door. The Swinger gleams beneath the shop lights. I grab the keys off a hook in the office.

"Let's go for a drive." I head to the driver's seat.

His brow arches when I open the Swinger's door. "You sure she's roadworthy?"

"Get in," I snarl. She's more than roadworthy. I had her running fine before. There are just a few kinks I want to work out with the carburetor. Once I get those fixed, I can finally take her to the body shop for a fresh coat of paint.

I look at him when he slides into the passenger seat. A teasing smile lingers on his lips, betraying a glimpse of those dimples. He's fucking with me. I jam my finger on the button to open the garage door. It slides up behind me, and I fire up the Swinger.

She purrs like a kitten. Nothing else sounds so good. Years of hard work and scrounging for parts has finally paid off. I slide my hand over the steering wheel and put her in reverse.

After slowly backing out, I close the garage door behind us. Once I'm sure it's down and locked, I shift into gear. She crawls forward with confidence. Most of the snow has melted from the roads, and the slick spots are dry. Should be clear all the way to Eighty-First Street.

I ease her down the narrow road and out onto the main street into traffic.

"Might be faster if you take Park Ave." He checks his watch. "We're past rush hour."

"I think I know the fastest way to get to my parents' house." I hazard a side-eye before refocusing on the traffic around me.

"Sorry." He throws his hands up. "Force of habit."

Silence envelops us. I turn on the radio and let a classic rock station fill the void. Bon Jovi drifts from the speakers, and I sing along under my breath as I weave through cars, around a truck parked on the curb with flashers on. Just another day in paradise.

Cyril stares out the window, searching the sidewalks and buildings.

His eyes widen, but his lips remain pressed firmly together.

I feel bad for him. I really do. He seems confused sometimes. Disoriented. But his eyes are clear, his tone steady. He's not on drugs, though he might need meds. Somehow, I don't think that's the case though. He just looks…out of place. Uncomfortable. It's strange.

Hopefully, Dad can help him. I know I can't. I have too much other shit on my plate to take care of this lost little puppy, no matter how attractive he is.

Forty-five minutes later, I pull up outside the brownstone on Eighty-First. Normally, I have to fight for parking, but there's a spot waiting today. I might want to play the lottery. I put the Swinger in park, turn off the engine, and pocket the key.

"Where are we?" he asks, stepping onto the sidewalk. A woman walks by with two toddlers, one clasped in each hand.

"Home," I reply, gesturing to the stone building, the only home I've ever known. It still looks exactly the same as when I was a kid.

"Your parents live here?" He turns to face the house. "Since when?"

"Late eighties, I think." I lock the car and come alongside him. "Come on, they're waiting for us."

I take the steps two at a time, careful not to slip on black ice. Cyril follows with measured steps.

I unlock the door and step inside, hanging my jacket and scarf on a hook by the door. "Hang up your coat here."

Dad has the gas fireplace on, warming the living room. I smile as memories surround me. Such a great home to grow up in.

Cyril stops at the doorway to take in the room. "Nice place."

"Thanks." I wave toward the couch. "Have a seat. I'll get my parents. I hear them upstairs." The floor creaks overhead, affirming my statement. "I'll be right back. Make yourself at home."

With a nod, Cyril wanders into the living room.

I make my way up the stairs. They knew I was coming over. Where are they?

At the top of the stairs, I knock on the first bedroom door. "Mom? Dad? You here?"

The door swings open. Mom blinks at me. Her hair is completely white, and she styles it to neatly frame her careworn, lined face. When did she get so old? I hug her.

"What's this about a visitor?" she asks, her eyes wide and sparkling. "I had to put new batteries in my hearing aids. Oh, how exciting."

"Where's Dad?" I glance behind her.

"I'm here. What's all the fuss?" Dad lumbers into view, leaning heavily on a cane. His gray hair is neatly combed, and his blue eyes flash.

"There's someone downstairs to see you."

"Who is it?"

"I don't know him. He showed up at the garage this morning claiming he knows you."

Dad taps his cane on the floor. "Does he have a name?"

"He says it's Cyril."

Mom gasps and turns to Dad. They share a long, knowing look. Tears prick at Mom's eyes. Dad takes her hand and pats it between his. Neither speaks.

I feel like I'm missing something important.

"What's going on?" I ask hesitantly, afraid the moment might burst like a soap bubble.

"Come on." Dad pulls Mom out of the bedroom.

I stare after my parents as they slowly make their way down the stairs. These two should live on the first floor, but nothing I say will convince them to change. They're set in their ways. I sigh and follow dutifully behind.

At least now I'll get some answers. I hope.

CHAPTER 5

Cyrid

The moment Jessica leaves the room, I steady myself against the back of the chair.

This is surreal.

I pinch my eyes closed and hope I'm dreaming. I'll wake up and find myself in 1985, running late to pick up Kate and Arthur. My gaze skims the furniture, worn in a lived-in way. This house has seen nothing but love and life for the past thirty-some years.

Jealousy rears its head, and I'm buffeted with the reminder of all the time I've lost. I manage to shake the thought free when I spy photographs hanging on the wall. As I drift closer, my heart warms at Kate's familiar smile and Arthur's halfhearted effort at one.

Some of the images feel like yesterday. Kate and Arthur at the Black Penny. Their wedding day at the top of the Empire State Building. A lovely shot of them in Rome, standing by the Trevi Fountain. I continue looking. In one photo, I can make out the grainy shape of my car in the background with me standing beside it, waiting. My face is impossible to see, but it's me. Always in the background. Always waiting.

I wander around the room, taking in moments I missed, moments held within the photographs. By the time I reach the mantel, they're family snapshots. Kate with her arms around three children, Arthur standing behind them. The photo captures pure joy. It lures me in and holds me captive.

As I study their faces, I can see the older two children, a boy and a girl, inherited Arthur's dark coloring and brilliant eyes. The youngest looks like Kate with her wild curls and bright, mischievous smile.

Jessica.

I laugh. It has to be her. The girl in the photo has the same spark in her eye. The same defiant stance I saw this morning when I stumbled into her workspace.

With every photograph, I find myself searching for her, trying to identify each person. Kate and Arthur poured their hearts and souls into their children, that much is evident in the images surrounding me. They seized each moment and made memories to last a lifetime.

Memories of a time I'll never experience.

I step back and put my hands in my pockets. Regret and disappointment creep in, wrapping around any hope of returning to the past. Kate was never able to get back to her time. She embraced the moment, the opportunity fate placed before her. She took a chance. Can I really do the same?

Uncertainty sinks like a brick in the pit of my stomach. It's barely been half a day and I'm already floundering.

I missed so much. Kate and Arthur. The crew from the Black Penny. They were my family. My circle. When I disappeared, what happened to them? Did they miss me?

I see the memories documented in film and shake my head. No. They went on. They embraced the moment and lived life to the fullest.

Life went on without me. It's selfish to think the world stopped revolving simply because I wasn't there.

Where was I? That's the question. One I'll never get an answer to, but it nags at me regardless.

"Cyril?" Arthur's voice, as familiar as my own, echoes behind me.

I turn, and Kate's gasp fills the air.

Arthur and Kate are old and gray. I was ready for it, thanks to the pictures around the room, but nothing could have prepared me for the shock of seeing them in person. It was just yesterday when they were young, vibrant, full of hope and life, brimming with love for each other.

"Arthur." I meet his gaze before shifting my own to his wife. "Kate."

She leans against her husband, one hand covering her mouth. A sob catches in her throat.

"Cyril." She crosses the room, reaching for me. I take her hands, feeling her wrinkles against my fingertips. My heart breaks at the passage of time and the mark it left on my friends.

"You look stunning, Kate." I grin at her.

She scoffs and wraps her arms around me, hugging me tight. "We were so worried about you."

I fold her into my embrace, unable to find words. She's so delicate, so frail. Goddamn it. I can't stop the tears pooling in my eyes. When I look up, Arthur steps closer.

"I'm glad you found us." Arthur claps his hand on my shoulder. The force of it startles me. For a man in his seventies, I wouldn't expect such a firm grip…but this is Arthur, so I'm not sure why I'm surprised by his strength.

"I wouldn't have found you if it weren't for your daughter." My attention shifts to the woman in the doorway.

Her stiff posture relaxes with my acknowledgment, and she drops her arms to her sides. "You weren't lying." The firm set of her lips softens to a hesitant smile, and she steps into the room. "But it doesn't explain anything. I still have questions."

"Oh yes. So do I." Kate releases me and guides me to sit beside her on the sofa.

Arthur settles into a recliner by the arched entryway, and Jessica leans against his chair, watching the scene with a skeptical eye.

"Where to start?" I laugh, trying to ease the tension in the room.

Kate takes my hand in hers and pats it the way my grandma used to when I was young. "Would you like something to drink? Coffee? Tea? Whiskey?"

"Nothing, thank you. I just had breakfast."

"What happened, Cyril?" Arthur's question cuts to the heart of the matter. "When you never showed up for work, we assumed the worst."

"Until I suggested you were transported like I was," Kate adds, nudging me with her elbow. Her luminous eyes search my face. I can see the woman she was all those years ago reflected in their depths.

"I returned to retrieve your purse…" I release her hand and reach into my jacket pocket. Her clutch is still there, tucked in the deep recesses of the fabric. I pull it out and hand it to her.

She gasps and runs her fingers over the beaded material. Tears fill her eyes. "I never should have sent you." Her voice cracks. "This is my fault."

"No, Kate. It isn't your fault." I pull her against me. "You couldn't have known this would happen."

"I knew that place had…has…this strange ability to transport people through time." She sniffs. "For years, I pushed it from my mind, thinking it was a freak accident. A coincidence. That what happened to me was a one-in-a million occurrence."

"Here I am." I smile and stroke her age-worn cheek. "Guess that makes us special, doesn't it?" At her smile, hope sparks in my chest. "Do you think we're the only two people to travel through time? We should start a support group, see if others come."

When she laughs, my heart bursts.

"So you got caught in the time portal, or whatever it is, and ended up here?" Arthur asks, stroking his jaw. "Why *now*?"

My gaze shifts from him to Jessica, leaning against the side of his recliner. Her green eyes burn through me. "I have no idea," I reply, keeping my focus firmly on his daughter.

"How did you meet Jessica?" Kate asks.

"When I woke at the top of the Empire State Building, I realized I wasn't in 1985 anymore."

"The towers," Kate says knowingly. "That was my first clue too."

"What happened to them?" The question slips out before I can stop it from derailing the conversation.

"Terrorists flew planes into them," Jessica replies. "September 11, 2001."

"Changed more than the skyline, that's for sure," Arthur mumbles.

"Dad." Jessica nudges his shoulder. "Don't start."

He throws his hands up but continues muttering under his breath.

My curiosity is piqued, but I force myself to stay on track. There's plenty of time to find out what I missed over the last thirty-seven years. From the sound of it, I missed a lot more than family vacations.

"Once I realized the date, I went to the only place I had any connection to."

"The garage." Arthur leans back, his hands steepled, fingertips tapping.

I nod, keeping Jessica in the corner of my vision, watching her reaction. I can't help it. It's like I need her to believe me, to understand this is the truth, no matter how crazy it sounds.

"You went inside?" Arthur's expression remains impassive.

"I did." I swallow and sneak a full peek at Jessica.

Her jaw clenches.

"I found your daughter working on the Swinger." I clear my throat. "Obviously, I didn't know she was your daughter, but when she asked if I knew her father...well, the missing pieces fell into place."

"I see."

"I need to know something." I chew the inside of my cheek, unsure how to ask, and decide to be blunt. "Rob and Marcy...are they..."

Kate takes my hand. "They're alive. Living upstate."

"And the crew from the Black Penny?" I look at Arthur and hold my breath.

"Still around. Retired, of course, but we see them all once a month when we get together for breakfast." Arthur's head wavers for a moment. "Grant had a heart attack a few months ago, but he's doing better after surgery."

Relief floods my body, and I sag back against the sofa. "Good to hear."

"Claude's daughter runs the Penny now." Arthur chuckles. "She's a piece of work. Don't cross her."

I blink twice before it registers. Of course they all have families. Children and grandchildren. I nod and swallow the lump in my throat.

"This is strange." I gesture to myself. "I haven't changed, but everything I know has."

"It does take some time to adapt," Kate assures me. "But you're a quick study. You'll figure it out."

What if I don't want to adapt? The question rises in my mind like a flashing neon sign. I quickly dismiss it. I don't have a choice. There's no going back to 1985. I'm stuck here. I'd better make the best of it before I get crushed.

"I'm glad you're still here." I look between Kate and Arthur before my gaze lingers on Jessica for a moment. "I don't know what I would have done without you."

Jessica's brow furrows. I redirect my attention to her father.

"You don't need a driver anymore, do you?" I ask hopefully.

"No, but I'm sure we can find something to keep you busy." Arthur exchanges a long look with Kate.

I shift at its intensity. Am I missing something?

"First, we need to get you caught up." She takes my hand and stands, leading me to the mantel with all the photographs. "These are our children. Sandra, Matthew, and Jessica." As she goes down the photographs, I take in every detail. She tells me where the photo was taken along with the story behind each one.

Slowly, she fills me in on thirty-seven years of Maxwell family adventure. Arthur fills in details when she asks for his input. Jessica remains silent, as still as a statue, poised beside her father. Watching. Listening. Waiting.

I can't help but feel she's taking my measure, weighing me against the stories her parents have told her…if they told her anything at all about me.

Curiosity burns hot as her cold stare follows where her mother leads me. She disappears, leaving me alone with Kate and Arthur. When she returns, she's bearing a tray of steaming coffee mugs.

She hands me a plain green cup. Why do I suspect she'd poison me if she had the opportunity?

Even though Kate and Arthur have welcomed me with open arms, my presence has the opposite effect on their daughter.

I have the distinct impression Jessica hates me, and I'm determined to unravel the mystery as to why.

CHAPTER 6

Jessica

My head is spinning.

When Mom dives into the story of our trip to the Grand Canyon, I decide I need a break. Escaping to the kitchen, I take a few moments of peace to rearrange my thoughts.

So this guy isn't crazy. He knew Dad, worked for Dad years ago. I remember hearing stories about his driver, but I never paid attention to his name or what happened to him. My parents are great storytellers, how was I to know *these* stories were true?

Agitated, I measure the coffee grounds into the antiquated Mr. Coffee and fill it with distilled water. Nothing about this makes sense. And yet, Mom always told us the story of how she and Dad met. How she traveled through time and wound up on the top of the Empire State Building.

It was just a bedtime story, right? Now I'm not so sure.

This guy, though. I don't trust him any further than I can throw him. He magically shows up, and he's Dad's long-lost driver? I scoff as I pull the mugs from a cabinet by the sink. Maybe he's trying to pull a fast one on Mom and Dad? He could be a swindler.

But then, how the hell would he know Uncle Rob and Aunt Marcy? How would he know the crew from the Black Penny?

Something about this doesn't add up.

It can't be a coincidence that this stranger's name is Cyril. Hell, I've never even met anyone with that name. I've always just associated it with the garage because that was its name when I was born in 1990. I wasn't even around when Dad bought the garage, but he always told me he did so for a friend.

What are the freaking odds that *friend* shows up on our doorstep? If I were a betting woman, I'd put money down it's impossible.

But the laughter in the living room tells me otherwise.

The fresh scent of brewed coffee drifts around me as I fill four mugs and place them on a tray. I add a container of cream to the tray before lifting it. Takes me back to the two weeks I tried my hand at waitressing in college but ended up dumping two plates of spaghetti on some guy's head. I definitely wasn't cut out for food service. With careful, measured steps, I return to the living room and place the tray on the coffee table.

Mom has moved on to stories of my nieces and nephews. I ignore the way Cyril's gaze follows me, handing him the green mug and picking up my own. It's hard to keep my expression impassive. I don't want to upset Mom and Dad, but this whole situation is hard to swallow.

"Sounds like you've had a great life." Cyril sips his coffee.

"We have," Mom says with a whimsical sigh. "We are very fortunate."

"It's good to finally have some closure though." Dad sets his mug aside. "We searched for you for months. Years. We never gave up hope that one day you'd return."

"You couldn't possibly know that." Cyril scoffs.

"You're right, but I held out hope it would all come full circle." My father leans back in his chair. Today, he looks every year of his age.

My heart aches when I realize I don't have much time left with my parents. I shove the thought aside and finish my drink.

"What will you do now?" Mom asks, her eyes shining with interest.

"Well…honestly, I don't know. Should I go to the DMV and renew my license? They'll never believe my age."

Dad waves his hand. "Don't worry about that. We had the same issue with Kate. There are ways around it."

"Not legal ones, Dad," I mutter under my breath. He shakes his head at me, but I persist. "You can't just expect him to pick up where he left off. It's been thirty-seven years."

"You're right." Dad strokes his jaw. "Things have certainly changed."

"I don't want to be a burden," Cyril assures us, breaking into the conversation. "I'll figure things out. It'll just take time, a little trial and error."

"It will be easier if you have someone to walk you through it."

I can feel Dad's attention shift to me, and I pinch my eyes closed. *Please don't. Don't drag me into this mess. I have my own shit.*

"Jessica could give you a hand. She's a whiz with computers. These millennials have knack for technology."

"Millennials?" Cyril asks.

"People born between the early eighties and the year 2000." I sigh at the explanation. "There's a whole generation thing now. Trust me, you're better off not knowing."

"What would I be?"

"Boomer." I mutter the word. "Can we move on?" I turn to Dad. "I have a lot going on at the garage. I can't do anything else right now."

"That's the genius to my plan." Dad's eyes sparkle, and I grit my teeth, bracing for it. "He can give you a hand at the garage."

"Dad…" I sputter. "I don't know…" Anger and frustration bubble inside me but I bite back the words, knowing how much they'll affect my parents. Instead, I just listen, helpless and raging inside.

"Cyril knows his way around cars. He was my driver for years, and he helped in the garage when it belonged to Mac. You'll make a great team." Dad grins like he's found the solution to all of life's problems.

"Team?" I bite the word and long to spit it in the trash.

"Yeah, partners. Bring him into the business, teach him the ropes. With both of you behind the wheel, you should be able to expand within the next year."

There it is. Even though my dad didn't send Cyril this morning, it's come full circle. The one thing I don't want has been dropped into my lap—a boomer dinosaur plunged into the twenty-first century. And I'm expected to play babysitter. Fan-fucking-tastic. What's next? Will Dad give him the garage and cut me out completely? The thought turns my blood to ice before it transforms to molten lava. My hand flexes against the couch, gripping the seam.

"Partners?" I shake my head and count to ten. "Dad, maybe we should talk about this…"

"There's nothing to talk about. Cyril's back." Dad beams. "He's practically family. The least we can do is help him get his bearings."

"But where is he going to live?"

"At the garage. Hell, his stuff is still in the attic."

I can't even bring myself to look at Cyril. None of this is his fault, not directly, but that doesn't mean I have to take it lying down.

"Dad, where am *I* supposed to live?"

"There's enough room for the two of you. You'll make it work. At least until he gets his feet under him."

"Sir, I…" Cyril tries to interject, but Dad cuts him off.

"It's settled then."

"Nothing is settled, Dad." I turn on him. "I've lived there for fifteen years. I've worked there since I was a kid. That garage is my life. It's my…"

"It's *my* investment." Dad fixes me with a stern look. "I hold the deed to the building and a controlling stake the business."

I bite my lip, stifling curses I want to hurl into the room. This isn't fair. I've worked so fucking hard to get to this point. Dad can't seriously give it all to some guy he hasn't seen in nearly forty years?

There's no way I can break. Not here. Not now.

Somehow, I manage to smother the tears and push up from the couch. I can't sit here another minute. Not when everything I've worked for hangs by a thread…a thread held by my father.

I won't do it. There's no way I will stand aside and let Dad give my dream to someone else.

"Jessica." Mom's voice follows me as I leave the room.

I keep walking, unable to bear the pressure of being in that room for a moment longer. I need to breathe.

At the back of the house, I pause near the side door in the kitchen. Panic overwhelms me, and the dam holding back my tears finally snaps. I swipe them away with the back of my hand.

This isn't fair. It's not *his* family. It's not *his* dream. *He* doesn't deserve to have it all handed to him on a silver platter.

And I shouldn't be expected to bend over backward to help my replacement.

Fuck. Is Dad trying to replace me? He's always been supportive of me, of my vision for the garage, for the business. Why now? Why *him*?

Inside my chest, my heart is being shredded, like an old tire beating on the highway. I thought I was stronger than this, but it seems today is full of disappointments.

I stare into the small garden beyond the back door. It's barren and cold. Hopeless, just like me.

If I want to keep the garage, I'll have to abide by my father's wishes.

I've never detested his obstinate nature more than I do at this moment.

I hate this.

CHAPTER 7

Cyrid

"It's *my* investment," Arthur says to Jessica, his expression stern. "I hold the deed to the building and a controlling stake in the business."

My body tenses at his statement. It wasn't my intention to stir up trouble. I didn't want to demand anything from Arthur or Kate. I just wanted to see my friends again, to make sure they were alive and well. To make sure my absence hadn't, in some way, left a scar.

While I'm confident they missed me, I'm glad it didn't stop them from living their lives. But fate has a funny sense of humor, dropping me into this decade unprepared and ill-equipped to deal with what I will find. What are the odds the first person I encounter, other than the guard, would be the daughter of my employer?

Jessica's eyes flash with unharnessed fury. If it were anyone else saying those words, I'm sure she'd rip them apart. But because it's her father, she bites her tongue and stuffs it down. Her body stiffens as she stands, her hands clenched in fists.

When she exits the room without another word, Arthur's stern expression falters. He closes his eyes and covers his face.

"Jessica!" Kate rushes after her daughter as fast as her elderly legs can carry her, casting a silent apology over her shoulder before leaving the room.

Several minutes pass, and I struggle with indecision. Part of me wants to leave. I can find my way on my own. I can make it work. There are jobs out there. Places to live. I don't want to burden anyone. I won't be a burden. It's clear Jessica feels strongly about the garage and her role there. I would never come between her and her father. I'd rather live on the street and beg for change.

"I'm sorry about that." Arthur's gruff voice cuts through the pensive silence.

"There's nothing to apologize for, sir." I fold my hands in my lap.

Arthur chuckles. "I think we're beyond 'sir,' don't you?"

"No, sir." I laugh softly. "But if you want me to call you something else, I will."

"Arthur. Please. We're beyond an employer-employee relationship now."

"If I take you up on your offer...technically, we're not." I gently broach the topic, knowing he offered but unsure how to negotiate around Jessica's unwillingness to take me on as a partner.

"She'll come around," he says, as if reading my thoughts.

"I don't want her to do something she doesn't want to do."

"Forcing a woman to do *any*thing is a surefire way to get nowhere fast." He sighs and nods. "Nearly forty years of marriage has taught me that."

"Then don't ask her to take this on. Don't make it her responsibility to teach me how to live in this time. I can figure it out on my own."

Arthur leans forward, groaning with the movement. He meets my gaze, and all I can see in his eyes is worry. "I know you can. No matter what, I'll help you get back on your feet. You did your job better than any driver I've ever had...and after you, I went through a lot of them. They could never live up to your standard."

"Thank you, sir." My heart warms at his kind words. "It was an honor to work for you."

"You were...*are* part of this family." He nods firmly. "Whatever you need, it's yours."

"I—"

"The garage is yours."

His words choke me. "What?"

"The garage. It's yours, been yours since I bought it in December 1985."

"You..." The implication of his words sinks into my brain. "You mean...Cyril's Garage is..."

"It's yours." He smiles at my obvious confusion. He can't be serious? But he is.

"You just..." I hazard a glance at the doorway and lower my voice. "But you told Jessica you are the owner."

"I know what I said." Arthur waves his hand. "But I bought that place for you. An investment in your business. I was going to transfer the deed to you on Christmas Day, but you disappeared."

"Sir, I can't..."

Words completely fail me. His belief in my abilities, his kindness, his generosity. It overwhelms me with emotions.

Then I remember the passion in Jessica's eyes at the mention of the garage. "Thank you. But don't you think circumstances have changed?"

"Have they?" Arthur leans on the arm of the recliner.

"Your daughter…"

"I'll take care of Jessica. She won't suffer. That I can promise you."

"But why would you demand she take me on as a partner and not tell her the truth?"

His blue eyes still hold the intense gleam I remember. Time hasn't stolen his fire and determination. I can see exactly where Jessica got her quick tongue and sharp mind.

"What are you up to?"

"Who says I'm up to anything?" Arthur reclines in his chair and kicks his feet up.

I study his smug expression, then it hits me. He's setting me up with his daughter. Forcing us to work together in the hopes something will happen. My God. He's playing matchmaker. I can't call him out on it. I'm not against spending time with Jessica to see if there's any chemistry between us that could spark a relationship. But there's no guarantee this plan will work. It could fall apart in spectacular fashion, and there would be a lot of carnage. This situation is strange, but what if I'm misreading the whole thing? I need to figure out his motive before I let this go further.

"You're playing with dynamite, putting her in a position like this."

"You think I don't know my daughter?" He scoffs. "She was my shadow for years. I thought she would be an architect like her dad, but when she showed more interest in cars than buildings…well, I couldn't deny her. She's my baby."

"All the more reason for me to *not* get involved." I clear my throat. "Whatever beef she's got with you is your problem. Don't put me in the middle of it."

"You're already in the middle of it, Cyril." His eyes gloss over, unfocused, as if he's lost in thought. "I won't be around forever."

"Sir?"

"I want to be sure she's taken care of—not financially, that's covered, and God knows, she can take care of things herself." The worry returns, making him pale. "She deserves to be happy. With someone who understands her."

"We barely know each other." But with one look at his face, I concede defeat. He won't listen to reason. "I can make sure she's taken care of, but there's no guarantee anything will happen between us."

"Do you know why I kept the garage? Why I kept your things in storage?" He reminisces with a grin. "Everyone thought I was crazy. Called me foolish. Even Kate."

I shake my head, unsure what to say. It seems his mind is made up, and everyone knows you don't argue with an old man. Nothing scares them anymore.

"I knew you'd be back." He presses his hand to his chest. "Every time I thought about selling, about giving up, something here stopped me."

"Sounds crazy."

"That's what Kate said." He chuckles. "But after finding her, after experiencing what we've experienced, I knew I had to continue on faith it would work out."

"There's no dissuading you from this, is there?"

"No."

"Just to be clear…" I pause, searching for the right words. "You want us to become partners in order to push us together as a couple?"

"Yes."

"This is weird."

"I know. Trust me. It was weird to see Kate as a baby while she stood right next to me." He shakes his head. "It was weird knowing the woman I was marrying hadn't even been born yet. Knowing there was an age gap a mile wide between us, even though we were technically peers if anyone saw us together."

"Okay, okay. I get your point." My brain hurts at the way he says it. "So you're okay with your daughter and me being in a romantic relationship?"

His smile fades. "I don't need the details, Cyril. Just make this work."

My mind replays my first meeting with Jessica. I was so busy lusting after the car, I'd barely registered a mechanic hiding on the other side. But the moment I saw her will be forever emblazoned on my brain.

"I don't think it will be a problem, sir."

"You're already half-smitten with her, aren't you?" His knowing smile spreads wider.

"Doesn't matter if I am. She hates me."

"She'll come around."

"And if she doesn't?"

"She will." Arthur shrugs. "All she needs is a little nudge."

"This is more like throwing her into the deep end of the pool."

"She can swim. I taught her."

The parallel isn't lost on me. Jessica is more than capable of taking care of a business and herself. I'm positive she learned everything from her old man. I just don't want to be on the receiving end of her fire.

"There's always a choice, Cyril."

"A choice?"

"If it doesn't work, you can walk away." He taps his fingers on the leather arm of the chair. "Start over. I'll help." His voice wavers. "Just give her a chance. That's all I ask."

I'm on my feet and across the room before he can react. When I offer my hand, he takes it.

"I'll do my best, sir."

Hope radiates from him as he pumps my hand. "I know you will."

The shuffle of feet in the hall pulls us from the moment. He releases my hand, and I gather the coffee mugs to put them on the tray.

I'm not sure how I'll be able to live up to his expectations. Or how he expects me to convince Jessica I'm not a monster who's taken the form of her father's former employee, sent to devour everyone. Maybe I've watched too many science fiction movies.

I take a deep breath. How the hell do you work with someone who trusts you about as far as they can throw you?

CHAPTER 8

Jessica

"Honey?" Mom's voice echoes behind me.

My body tenses, and I brace for the conversation. I saw the way Mom acted around Cyril, how she is with Dad. She always tries to smooth things over, to quell the conflict before it has a chance to start. She's good at it too.

But I won't relinquish the betrayal and fear racing through me. My hard work, my dream—they're too important to just throw aside like yesterday's newspaper.

She rests her hand on my shoulder. I close my eyes, unable to face her.

"Come on, let's sit in the kitchen." She tugs my sleeve.

There's no avoiding this. Begrudgingly, I follow my mother into the kitchen. She sets a tin of Christmas cookies on the table.

I snatch a snickerdoodle off the top before slumping into a chair opposite her. They're my favorite, and she knows it. Plying me with cookies is never a good sign. I stare at the cabinet while I nibble the sugary treat.

Mom grabs an oatmeal raisin cookie and sits patiently. Finally, she speaks. "What's going on in your head, honey?"

I sigh. "I don't want this."

"Want what?"

"I don't want to be in charge of bringing a fossil into the twenty-first century, Mom." I set the half-eaten cookie on the table.

"Cyril is hardly a fossil, sweetheart."

"I have enough to deal with. I don't need one more thing on my plate." I grind my teeth at the thought of him being in my space all the time. "I don't have the patience to coddle someone."

"He's not a child. You don't need to coddle him." She wipes her hand on a napkin. "I understand."

"Dad doesn't." I cross my arms. "He'll push until I snap, and then all hell will break loose."

"I think your father is worried about you running the business alone." Her voice is gentle, but I hear it in her tone. She agrees with Dad. "Maybe you should give it a try. A partner might not be a bad thing."

"I don't need a partner butting into *my* business, telling me how I should run things."

"I doubt he'll do that."

"You don't know what he'll do. That's the point." I throw my hands up. "You expect me to just take your word about this guy? You'll gladly give him a job and free access to whatever he wants. You're too trusting."

"He's never given us any reason not to trust him." Mom's brow furrows. "I know it's difficult to understand, but I've been where he is—lost in a time that isn't mine, without direction or resources."

I roll my eyes and mumble under my breath, *Here we go again.*

"He worked for your father for years without complaint." She studies my face. "The least we can do is help him get on his feet."

"By giving him *my* garage?"

"Ah. There it is."

"There *what* is?" I frown.

"The truth." She reaches over to take my hand. The warmth of her skin soothes my agitation, but I'm still pissed at this whole situation. "You think your father is going to give the garage to Cyril."

"It's *his* business. He can do what he wants." I throw Dad's words at her.

"You're right. It is. But do you really think your father would do something like that without discussing it with you first?" She squeezes my hand.

"I don't know. Would he? He doesn't seem to care what I want right now."

"That's not true."

"It is. He's not even willing to listen to me." I gesture toward the front of the house with a wave of my hand. "When Dad gets it into his head to do something, nothing I say, nothing I do will change his mind."

"Maybe you should give it a try." Mom cocks her head, her mismatched eyes carefully studying me. "What's the worst that could happen?"

"Dad giving away everything I've worked for." Passion laces my words. "I've busted my ass for years to get the garage to where it is now. I'll be damned if a stranger will come in and wreck all my hard work."

"No one is trying to ruin anything, honey."

"Yes, they are." My voice rises in pitch as my agitation grows. "That garage is my haven. My baby. I've dumped all my time and energy into it. It's *mine.*"

"You've worked hard—no one is saying you haven't—but you need help. At least give this partnership a try and see if it works out."

"And when it doesn't? Then what happens?"

"We'll cross that bridge when we get to it," Mom says diplomatically.

"I don't want to cross that bridge later. I want to address it now, before this whole mess implodes." I push my hair away from my face.

"Honey, don't you think you're being dramatic?"

"No. I'm not. This is my *life*, Mom. It's not a fad or a hobby." I take a deep breath. "I don't want a complete stranger coming in and telling me how to run my shop."

"I don't think Cyril will do that."

"Mom, he told me I was fixing a carburetor the 'hard way' before he even knew my name."

Mom chuckles. "That's men, sweetheart."

"That's exactly what I mean. Say I agree to this madness…he starts telling me all the things I'm doing the 'hard way.' He'll think his way is the only way to do anything, and I'll end up in prison for murder."

"Jessica." Mom's laugh echoes through the kitchen. "You really are my daughter with that flair for the dramatic."

"I'm serious, Mom. I won't let some guy from 1985 muscle his way into my life to mansplain things I've been doing for twenty years. I'll kill him."

"He's not the only man you've had to work with over the years, and you've yet to be charged with assault, let alone murder."

"There's always a first time," I grumble.

"It's not easy working with someone you don't know, but personal growth isn't supposed to be painless."

"You're dead set on this, aren't you?"

"I agree with your father."

"Why is Dad so determined to make this partnership happen?"

Mom shifts in her chair and exhales. "Before Cyril disappeared, he showed your father a business proposal."

"A business proposal for what?"

"A car service and garage."

Realization flashes like a light flickering to life in my mind. "Dad bought the garage as an investment, and Cyril was supposed to run it."

"Exactly."

"But then he disappeared, and Dad held onto the business in case Cyril returned."

Mom nods, a relieved smile on her lips.

"Now that he's here, Dad's trying to make good on his promise." My anger and frustration take a backseat to crushing disappointment. "So I've been keeping this business alive for years, just in case Cyril showed up?"

"No, honey. Your father let you run the business because he saw how much you love working on cars. How good you are at it."

"But now Cyril's back, I'm expendable."

"That's not true at all, and you know it."

I stare out the window, avoiding her gaze.

"Jessica, your father and I love you. We want you to be successful and happy." Mom rests a hand on mine, and I fight tears.

"Don't make me do this."

"You're the only one who *can* do this." Mom's eyes are brimming with tears too. "No one will understand his situation the way you do."

She's right. I hate that she's right. I don't have a mean bone in my body, but every cell is screaming at the injustice of what they're asking me to do. I pinch my eyes closed.

"Give it a few months. Help him get settled. If it doesn't work, we'll figure something else out."

I turn to face her. "Promise?"

"I promise."

Relief filters through me. Even though I'm not committed to this whole arrangement, knowing there's a light at the end of the tunnel makes it more manageable. I still have some stipulations before I agree to anything, but I nod.

Mom beams with joy. "Wonderful. Now, let's go back to the living room. I'm sure you'll want to discuss details with your father and Cyril."

She knows me so well. I wrap her in my arms and inhale. "Thank you, Mom."

"I love you, sweetheart." Her voice quavers. "Things will work out. They always do."

"I know." Uncertainty lingers in my mind, but I shake it off.

I can do this. I can show Dad and Cyril I don't need anyone holding my hand. I'm thirty-two, and I run a successful business on my own. The last thing I need is a man telling me how to do my job.

Mom squeezes me tight one more time and heads back to the living room.

I take a few deep, cleansing breaths, readying myself for the next round with my father. He's about to find out how well I paid attention to his lessons in negotiation. I'm his daughter, and I inherited more than just his blue eyes. Stubborn is our middle name.

CHAPTER 9

Cyril

Jessica walks into the room, and uncertainty punches me square in the chest. I'm not sure I can do this. She deserves to know her father's plan, but there's no way I can tell her. Or that she'll believe me.

No, I'm the enemy. I can tell from the way she glowers at me.

How the hell am I supposed to get her to work with me? From the daggers she's glaring in my direction, I'm pretty sure she'd shove me in front of the first train we come across or drown me in the Hudson if given the chance.

Learning to navigate the future with limited information and no resources was going to be hard enough, but having a grudging partner will make this ten times more difficult. I'm a quick study, and while it's hard to wrap my head around the fact that I just skipped nearly forty years of history and technological advancement, I'm not intimidated by it.

I grew up on science fiction. Nothing they have today will throw me for a loop. I guarantee it.

"Well?" Arthur asks Jessica, pulling me from my thoughts.

"Well, what?" She sniffs and ignores me even though we're standing only five feet apart.

"Are you willing to take Cyril on as a partner, show him the ropes?"

She turns to face me, and I'm stunned by how vivid blue her eyes are. Like a clear summer sky.

"I'll do it, but"—she holds up a hand to stop me from speaking—"I have a few conditions."

"Okay."

Jessica gapes. "Don't you want to hear what they are?"

"Do I get to counter?" I ask.

"No." Her brow arches, almost in challenge.

"Then no, I don't need to hear what they are." I shrug. "It doesn't matter. I'm not exactly in a position to negotiate."

She blinks twice and turns to her father. "He gets two months. If it doesn't work, we part ways, and I continue running the shop like I have for the last ten years."

Arthur's jaw tenses and his eyes narrow. "Six months."

"Three."

"Four," he counters.

I watch the volley between them. It's like I'm not even in the room. These two would make a formidable team. I can see why Arthur put her in charge of the garage. It's also apparent he needs someone to balance her. A strong temperament can stall business without someone to push them in unexpected ways.

"That's my final offer, Jessica. Take it or leave it."

"Fine, but he's not staying in my apartment."

"It's big enough for both of you." Arthur cocks his head. "Besides, all his stuff is already there. No reason to hunt down another place and move everything."

"He'll be moving in four months anyway," Jessica mutters under her breath.

I can't help but laugh. She side-eyes me, and it dies in my throat. With a cough, I look at Kate, who's wearing a knowing grin.

"Fine." Jessica throws her hands up. "Is that all?"

"For now." Arthur rises slowly to his feet, arching his back. "I'll call you if there's anything else."

Jessica stands and hugs her father.

"I love you, Jessie."

"Love you too, Dad." She squeezes him before stepping to the side and hugging Kate.

Keeping back, I watch the interaction, warm affection filling me. Kate and Arthur are my family, especially Arthur. When I had nothing but the clothes on my back and a hotwire kit in my pocket, he took a chance on me. Gave me a job and an opportunity to make something of myself.

Jessica steps into the hallway, leaving me to say goodbye to her parents.

Kate wraps her arms around me. "Take care of yourself, Cyril. You know where to find us if you need anything."

"Thanks. I will." I kiss the top of her head.

Arthur's expression is guarded, but I see a glimmer in his eyes, reminding me of our conversation. I offer my hand. He pulls me into a hug.

"Take care of her. She'll come around." His gruff whisper is low enough to stay between only us.

I nod when we pull apart, and he claps a hand on my shoulder. "Good to have you back."

"Thank you, sir."

Jessica's waiting for me in a small alcove by the front door, already wearing her jacket. I grab mine from the hook and pull it on. I reach behind her, and her eyes widen when I step into her space to grab the doorknob. She steps aside when I open the door.

"After you."

Her lips press into a thin line as she spins and heads into the cold December air. I admire the way she stomps down the front steps.

"Good luck," Kate says behind me. "You're gonna need it."

"Right." I give her a little salute and follow Jessica to the car.

We reach the dark green Swinger, and she pulls the keys from her pocket as she rounds the front end.

"Mind if I drive?" I ask, knowing I'm, yet again, tempting fate by even voicing the question.

"You want to drive *my* car?" She scoffs. "Want me to have Dad give you the deed to the shop while we're at it?"

Guilt settles around my shoulders, but I shrug it off. Nope. Not going there. "Just want to give her a spin, see how she handles."

Her hand rests on the driver's side door. I can almost see the gears spinning in her mind. She closes her eyes and sighs, her shoulders briefly slumping. When she looks up, I hold my breath.

A slight breeze catches her curly hair, and all I can see is the perfect blend of her parents in her features. Arthur's bright blue eyes and stubborn streak. Kate's delicate bone structure, curly hair, and dangerous curves. If someone had told me I'd be standing in the future, admiring my boss's daughter, I'd have thought they were smoking the good shit. How can this be real?

"Fine." She walks around the car and hands me the keys. "But if you hurt my baby, I'll snap your spine. Got it?"

"Got it." I clench the keys in my fist and head for the driver's seat.

I glance up at the brownstone before I climb into the car. Sure enough, Kate and Arthur stand at the picture window, watching with matching grins. I wave and climb into the Swinger.

Let's see how well she does with a master behind the wheel.

Kate grinds her teeth when I start the car but doesn't say anything.

"I got this." With a smirk, I put her in gear and pull out onto the street. "Trust me."

CHAPTER 10

Jessica

What the hell was I thinking, letting him drive my car?

I grip the armrest on the door as he maneuvers away from the curb. The roads are clear, but it still makes me nervous. He says he's a competent driver—and if he drove for Dad for years, he must be—but it does nothing to ease the knot occupying my stomach right now.

He eases the throttle up, taking to the streets with ease. Confidence ebbs through him as he rests his arm on the door and controls the wheel with one hand. His gaze flicks from the street to the mirrors and back again.

I should be disturbed by how good he looks sitting in the driver's seat of *my* car. Instead, I'm disturbed by a fluttering where my heart beats. Confidence is sexy, but when a man knows his way around a car, things can only go one of two ways—either I'm completely turned off by his arrogance, or I'm drawn to him. Right now, it's the latter.

Nope. We're gonna stop that right now. Dad might have slapped us together as partners for the next four months, but that's it. That will be the end of this whole…whatever's going on here.

It's bad enough I have this hurdle to overcome, but to have to babysit this dinosaur, attractive or not, only serves to agitate me further. Fuck. I don't like complications. And this is most certainly a massive complication. I should have known when I got up this morning and everything was going smoothly, that something bad would happen. It always goes sideways just when I'm starting to get my feet back underneath me.

It's been three months since I heard from Justin. Bastard dumped me in July when I refused to fix his piece-of-shit car for free. Dude, I'm not a charity organization. I have clients who pay me very well for my expertise. Just because I'm dating someone, it doesn't give him first dibs on my time or my knowledge. You wait, or you pay. He didn't like that, so he called off a three-year relationship. Buh-bye. Don't let the door hit your ass on the way out.

I should have learned from my failed one-year marriage at twenty-three, but I blame that on being young and dumb, smitten with lust.

"Mind if I turn on the radio?" Cyril asks, reaching for the knob.

"Knock your socks off." I nod to the stereo. "Driver picks the tunes, passenger shuts his cakehole."

His laugh curls through me like tendrils of warmth after drinking hot tea.

"Never heard it put like that, but I like it." He turns on the radio and cringes at the blast of music coming from the speakers.

"What's wrong?" I ask as he searches through stations.

"Is this music?" He looks physically pained with each passing song. He stops, and his expression relaxes at the sound of "Moving in Stereo" by the Cars. "Finally."

"A classic rock station?" I laugh, running my hand through my hair. "Of course you like the old stuff."

"It's not old stuff to me." He taps the steering wheel as we slow to a stop at a light. "I guess more than music has changed in thirty-seven years."

"Yeah, you got that right." I shift at the time that has elapsed for him. I'm nearly thirty-three, and I feel like an old lady some days. "So what do you want to know about the future?"

"Have they made another *Star Wars* movie?"

"Are you seriously asking me about *Star Wars* right now?" I blink at him. "Of all the things in the world that have changed, that's your first question?"

"I figure I need to know the most important information first." He glances at me, his eyes sparkling. "So…did they?"

"Yes."

"Really?" His excitement grows. "Come on, don't leave me hanging."

"They made three prequels in the early 2000s, and then some sequels in the mid-2010s."

"Yes!" He cheers. "What about *Star Trek*?"

"Oh God." Any grain of attraction I had for him vanishes into the exhaust outside. "Look, I'll let you look it up online when we get back to the garage. I'm not a nerd. I don't know anything about *Star Trek* or *Star Wars*. I haven't seen any of them."

"No way." His head whips around to face me, his mouth open in horror. "We'll have to fix that."

"I'm not watching nerd shows." I shake my head slowly, back and forth, emphasizing my point. "I had to suffer through my brother's obsession with *Star Trek: The Next Generation.* I'm not interested."

"What do you like then?" he asks, shifting the topic away from his nerd obsessions. "Horror? No…wait, don't tell me. You like cheesy romantic comedies?"

"I like a lot of things. But I just watch whatever's on Netflix or Hulu. Amazon has some decent shows, but I don't really watch a lot of television. The shop keeps me busy."

"I have no idea what you just said."

With a sigh, I explain the slow evolution of how we consume media and the concept of streaming services. He nods like he understands, but I've seen that look before. Glassy eyes and stiff posture. He's completely lost.

"I'll show you online."

"What the hell does *online* mean?"

"On the internet."

"The what?"

I cover my face with my hand. This is complicated. "I'll *show* you once we get to the garage."

He nods and makes a right, turning onto my street. The garage's neon sign lights the side of the building. I pull out my phone and open the garage with my app.

"Neat trick," he says, bringing the car to a stop outside the shop, watching the slowly rising door. "When do I get one of those…uh, pocket computer-phone-things?"

"It's a smart phone." I tuck it away. "We'll get you one tomorrow."

With a nod, he pulls the car into the garage perfectly. Not a dent or scratch. The ride passed quickly and without incident. Dad wasn't lying—Cyril is a fantastic driver. I can see why he kept him on for so long. My father is notoriously picky when it comes to his employees…well, when it comes to everything really. It's part of his charm.

Cyril turns off the car and hands me the keys. "She purrs like a kitten and handles better than any car I've ever driven." His green eyes meet mine; a flash of dimple compliments his smile. "And I've driven a lot of cars."

"I'm sure you have."

"Seriously though," he says as he opens the door, "you've done a great job with her. Did you do the restoration yourself?"

"Yeah, took me a few years between other projects, but I'm proud of her."

He runs his hand over the hood. "She got a name?"

"No, why?"

"All cars treated with this much love and attention should have a name."

"I don't know." My mind blanks, and I shake my head.

"Think about it. A name will come to you." He runs his hand across the front end, tracing the lines of the hood with his fingertips.

A thousand dirty thoughts run through my head, but I swallow them all.

"Come on, I'll show you where Dad put your stuff in the attic." When I'm sure the garage door is secured, I flip off the lights in the shop and go through a door at the back. It opens to a staircase leading to the apartment above the garage.

Cyril follows me up the stairs. "They look exactly the same."

"You lived here?"

"Yeah. It was two apartments back then, but rent was decent."

I unlock the door, chewing the inside of my cheek. When I took over the building, I combined the two apartments and moved in. It was easier than finding a place and commuting. Plus, I liked being close to my baby.

Inside, I toss my keys to the counter and head for the back of the apartment. There's a door leading to the attic where Dad stored all of Cyril's things, plus anything left behind when the last owner turned over the keys.

"It's all in here." I fiddle with the combination lock until it clicks open. "Have at it."

"Thanks." He leans against the wall and glances down the hallway. "So roommates, huh?"

Shit, I totally forgot about that. He quickly reads the expression on my face.

"If you're not comfortable with me staying here, I'll find somewhere else to crash."

"No. You're fine." I tie my hair up in a ponytail with an elastic band on my wrist. "I'll just clean the spare bedroom for you."

"You're sure?" His gaze holds mine, and his sincerity makes me pause.

"Yeah." I tap the attic door. "Grab what you need, and I'll get started on the spare room over here."

He acknowledges the room I point to. "Thanks again, Jessica. I know this isn't what you had planned."

"Story of my life." I shrug. "It's okay. We'll make it work."

Without waiting for a response, I head down the hall and flick on the light in the spare room. Just need to put some things away and then completely rearrange my life, but that's fine.

This isn't his fault. He didn't ask for this. I scold myself as I put loose clothes in a tote.

No one ever asks for it. But why am I always the one stuck cleaning up the mess?

CHAPTER 11

Cyrid

A chill wraps around me when I step into the attic. I flick the light switch inside the door to illuminate the space.

It's not huge, but I pause at the contents.

Boxes and tubs, stacked from floor to ceiling. Labeled with care and stowed away. My entire life reduced to the contents of this room.

My heart clenches, and I can't breathe.

Arthur could have thrown all of this away. But he didn't. He and Kate carefully packed every item and tucked it aside, just in case I came back. Their care and concern leave me overcome with emotion.

For Arthur to go so far as to give me the building...well, there aren't words to adequately capture the chaos inside me right now—hope, love, fear, desperation, and hovering over all of it, guilt.

Jessica is the reason all of this still exists. She brought my dream to fruition, even though she has no idea she did it. The woman has talent when it comes to business, I can tell that already. But her skill with cars? Incredible. I've never been more impressed by another motorhead in my life. What she's done with that Swinger takes time, patience, and dedication, on top of skill. Shit, it turns me on.

I push aside my blossoming attraction. There will be plenty of time to deal with it later. Right now, I need to sort through some stuff and get back to living. I start restacking boxes by type, searching for my clothes first.

Living with Jessica as roommates will create its own set of challenges. I've never been intimidated by a challenge before, but this one could be dangerous. I'm already attracted to her. And a soft spot in my heart is carved out just for her, because she's Arthur and Kate's daughter. I don't want to hurt her.

But I have a feeling it's going to be her doing the hurting.

She doesn't like me. I get it. It's a lot to take in over the course of a single day. I'm not sure I wouldn't be the same way if the shoe were on the other foot.

Reality is, I don't have a clue what I'm walking into in this new century, and I'm going to need all the help I can get. Jessica is the perfect person to show me, but doing so under direct order of her father probably wasn't the wisest course of action.

I don't know what game Arthur is playing, but if shit goes bad, this could blow up in all of our faces. Unease skates over me, but I shake it off. She deserves to know the truth about his plan. But there's no way in hell I can dump it on her today.

No. I need to get her to like me—or at the least, tolerate me. I'm on very thin ice here, and I'm not interested in seeing Jessica unleash her full fury.

If it were me, I'd be fucking pissed. This has to be handled with care, just like the bodywork on a vintage car. One small thing could completely fuck it all up.

A whoop of joy fills me when I uncover two boxes labeled *Cyril's Clothes*. I carry them to the bedroom and set them in the hallway next to the door. I find a few other items that might prove useful and add them to the stack.

At some point, I need to go through all of the boxes and decide what to do with everything. Right now, it's like I've found a time capsule. Maybe historians will want to be present for the unboxing of my personal possessions. Probably not. I didn't have much in '85, except a stash of *Star Wars* collector items. Wonder if they're worth anything now?

"Find everything?" Jessica asks from the other end of the hall.

"Yeah, I think so."

"Good. I'll let you get settled. Are you hungry?"

"I could eat."

"Pizza work?"

"Always." My stomach grumbles at the thought. "Thanks."

With a wave, she vanishes into the kitchen. I move the boxes into the bedroom.

The gray walls are bare, but there's a bed against the far wall, near the window, with a nightstand and a lamp. A tall dresser sits by the closet. On the other side of the room, there's a desk with a chair.

"What the hell is this?" I set the box on the bed and read the name on a black box sitting next to what looks like a small television screen on the desk. "Dell?" I make a note to ask Jessica about it later.

I unbox my clothes, wondering if I should wash everything before I put it away, considering how long it's been in storage. I check each item before deciding whether to wash it or put it away. By the time I make it through the three boxes, it's about even between a hamper behind the door and the dresser.

The last box holds an alarm clock, a few framed pictures, a Polaroid camera, and some books. Once I've emptied the boxes, I toss them in a pile to take out later.

"Pizza will be here in a few if you want to wash up." Jessica stands in my doorway.

I nod. "Where's the washer?"

"At the end of the hall, next to the bathroom. I'll show you."

I follow her with the overflowing basket. She gives me basic instructions, and I blink at the digital panel on the washing machine.

"Computers have taken over everything, huh?" I joke, tossing my clothes into the machine.

"You're in the digital age now." She grins. "Better get used to it."

"Let's just hope Skynet's not a thing," I mutter under my breath.

"Not yet, but there's still time."

"So you get a *Terminator* reference but want nothing to do with science fiction?" Damn it, this woman is a bundle of surprises.

Jessica rolls her eyes. "That's not what I said."

The urge to flirt is strong, but I bite back the instinct. Teasing flirtation can easily transform into button-pushing, and the last thing I want right now is to piss her off. It's weird though, knowing she's my boss's daughter and our ages are…yeah, it's a bit weird.

But is it?

Before I can dwell on it, Jessica leans close to press a button on the machine, and it whirrs to life. Her arm grazes mine. Warmth fizzles through me.

"Thanks." I move the basket out of the way to busy my hands.

"I'll give you a tour before the food gets here." She leaves the room before I can protest.

I know this place like the back of my hand. It might be renovated, but they didn't change the basic layout. I bite my tongue and follow her, admiring the soft curls lying against her sweatshirt, wishing I could see the curve of her backside again.

Her quick tour gets us only as far as the door by the time the doorbell rings.

"Shit. I'll be right back." She grabs some money off the counter and darts out the door, down the stairs to the side entrance.

When she disappears, I run my hand over my face. What the hell is wrong with me? I need to get my priorities straight. With thirty-seven years to catch up on, I shouldn't be thinking about Jessica and all of her delightful secrets and quirks I'd love to uncover.

The living room and kitchen sit directly over the shop floor. I lived here long enough to recognize the view through the wide windows overlooking the street below. The updated layout is spacious and welcoming.

I chuckle at a small cluster of plants making a jungle in the far corner of the room. What little direct sunlight there is will fill the space in the morning and afternoon. I used to have a chair in that corner. Never used it much, but I liked the way it perfectly caught the morning light.

Styles have certainly changed. Gone are the floral patterns, harvest golds and pea greens, replaced by neutral tones with pops of vibrant reds and blues. I pause at the gigantic monstrosity on the wall opposite me.

"That's not a television? It can't be." I step closer, admiring the sleek design and how much of the wall it takes up. It's massive. Like having my own personal movie theater! It looks like something straight out of *Star Trek*. Can you talk to people through it? See them? I search the sides for a switch or button, but if it's there, it's hidden.

"Alexa, turn on the television."

I'm surprised when Jessica reappears, but when the screen lights up, I stumble back, nearly tripping over the couch. My jaw drops. "How the hell did you do that?" I manage to right myself and clear my throat.

Jessica sets the pizza on the counter, her lips twisted in a half smile.

"Did you just talk to the television?" I stare at the screen, now filled with animated characters…no—animated children, cursing at each other. "What *is* this?"

"Alexa is a device linked to my network and the internet. Ask her anything, and she'll answer. Just use her name."

I glare at her. "And you told me Skynet wasn't real."

"The speaker is here." Jessica laughs and points to a box on the side table. "Or you can use the remote to turn on the TV, doesn't matter. That"—she points to the TV—"is *South Park*."

"*South Park*?" The words sound foreign in my mouth.

"Oh man, this is gonna be a long night. I need food." She opens the pizza box and fishes out a slice.

The smell hits me, and my mouth waters. "Giovanni's?"

She nods. "Been open for fifty years. Amazing."

I rush over and pull out a slice, letting the cheese slide and stretch. My eyes tear up. At least I have this. The first bite is exactly how I remember it. Perfection.

"Want a beer?"

"Yes, please," I say around a mouthful of pizza.

While she grabs two bottles from the fridge, I load my plate with two slices.

"Let's sit on the couch. I'll give you a crash course on entertainment evolution."

A shiver rolls through me, and I can't tell if it's fear or excitement. Either way, I'm committed. Maybe I can get her to put on one of the new *Star Wars* movies. I have a lot of catching up to do.

I take the beer from her and pop the top. She settles beside me on the couch, leaving a foot of space between us, even though there's more than enough room.

"Alexa, turn on Netflix." She turns to me with a glint in her eyes. "Hold on to your butt."

The screen loads, and then the clouds part while a chorus of angels break into song. It's fucking beautiful. I think I've died and gone to heaven.

CHAPTER 12

Jessica

Cyril looks like he's solved the ultimate question to life, the universe, and everything. His eyes are as round as vintage headlights.

I manage to stifle a laugh behind my beer bottle.

"So…" He sets aside the plate and stares at the screen. "This is Netflix?"

"Yeah. It's one of the first streaming services, although there are others."

"There are others?" He squints at me like he doesn't believe a word I'm saying.

"Paramount Plus, HBO, Amazon, Hulu…shit, the list goes on."

"You can just watch whatever you want? Whenever you want?"

I consider his question for a moment and shake my head. "Not really. It's complicated, but basically they need permission from the rights holder to showcase whatever they offer. Oh, and it changes all the time. Not a fan of that." I pout, remembering how they took *Friends* off Netflix a couple of years ago. Still kinda bitter about that.

"So I can watch *Star Wars* whenever I want?" His face practically glows.

"Well, you could for a while." I launch into a brief explanation of the evolution of entertainment since 1985. His expression is priceless.

"They don't make VHS tapes anymore?"

I shake my head.

"But they make…DVDs?"

"More Blu-ray, but that's a whole different thing. It's just easier to have a subscription to the streaming service and be done with it. Or you could buy a digital copy." Who knew forty years would have such big leaps in technological advancements for entertainment alone.

Cyril stuffs the last of his pizza in his mouth and chews thoughtfully while I skim through the selections. When I pass something familiar, he points, nearly bouncing with excitement. It's almost endearing.

"Can we watch a *Star Wars* movie now?" He wipes his hands on a paper towel before settling back against the cushions.

"I'll have to log in to Disney." I exit out of Netflix and choose the right app. I'm not interested, but honestly, it's worth seeing Cyril light up.

I can't imagine what it must be like for him, to wake up in the future, transported away from everything he knows. Everything he's worked for. I can sympathize with that. It's terrifying to think all your hard work could be wiped away without warning, to know you have to start all over again.

The screen loads, and I select the *Star Wars* icon. The selections fill the screen.

"Holy shit! What's the *Mandalorian*? *Rogue One*? *Boba Fett*?!"

"You really are a nerd." I hand him the remote. "Here, you can skim through everything. See what they're all about, although it might be easier to go online and do some research before you dive in."

"You keep saying *online*. What does that mean?"

With a deep sigh, I explain the birth and evolution of the internet as we know it, in the simplest way I can. No back history, no complicated threads, just my personal experience with the introduction of a personal computer in our home and the slow transition from analog to digital.

He soaks up every word like a goddamn sponge.

"So you're telling me, they use computers in cars now?"

"Yeah, it's a blessing and a curse. But I grew up with computers, so they make sense to me. We use them in the shop with the fleet."

"Fleet?" His eyes glow with interest. "How many cars?"

"A dozen. Keep them at a warehouse by the docks. Cheaper storage."

"How many drivers?"

"It changes, but we have a good team of fifteen drivers who rotate shifts and jobs."

"Damn." He whistles low. "That's not bad at all."

"We do most of the maintenance for the fleet at the warehouse. This shop is for custom jobs for high profile clientele."

"Spreading yourself too thin?"

I shake my head. "No, but the last two years have been a struggle. We're finally getting back on track."

"Is that why Arthur wants you to find a partner?"

My gaze fixes on him, even as a grumble of agitation builds in my chest. "That's why he *told* me I needed a partner. Then you dropped into my lap."

Putting Cyril and my lap in the same sentence should not have turned me on, but here we are. I shift uncomfortably and redirect the conversation.

"We can talk work tomorrow. I'll walk you through everything." My attention shifts to the television. "Tonight, let's just watch something and relax."

"Sounds like a plan." He swigs from his bottle, searching the screen again.

"What do you want to watch first?"

"Everything." He chuckles. "But honestly, I have all the time in the world to catch up. So pick something you think I'll enjoy."

A laugh escapes me. "I just met you this morning."

"True, but I trust your judgment."

His lopsided smile makes my stomach flip and my heart beat faster. Damn him and his charm. I take the remote from him, and my fingers brush his. Warm sparks crackle like fireworks, and I jerk my hand away.

"Static," I mutter under my breath. To my surprise, he says nothing.

Then it hits me. I know what movie he should watch first. With the unexpected thrill of introducing someone to something new, I scan through my accounts until I find it.

"What's this?" A grin forms when he sees the gigantic red lettering on the screen. "*Jurassic Park*? Is this a dinosaur movie?"

"Only the best dinosaur movie ever made." I hit play and grab the blanket beside me. "It's my brother's favorite. He made me watch it over and over when we were kids. Had to sleep in his room for months after the first time."

"That scary?" Cyril asks.

"To a five-year-old? Yeah, it's fucking terrifying." The introduction begins, setting the scene.

His soft laugh sinks into me with the comfort of a warm towel straight out of the dryer. Which reminds me…I shoot off the couch, blanket flying.

"Where are you going?" he asks with obvious concern.

"I need to switch your laundry to the dryer."

He moves to stand, but I shove him back down to the couch. His chest is firm beneath my hand. I will not look closely at that observation right now. "Stay here. I got this."

"But it's *my* laundry." He pouts. "And you'll miss the movie."

"I've seen it a million times," I assure him. "I'll be right back."

The screaming of pissed-off velociraptors echoes down the hall behind me, and I shiver at the memories it conjures in my mind. No wonder I couldn't sleep alone for months. That sound is fucking haunting. The echoing cry of Muldoon's order chases the noise. I can picture the scene, frame for frame, as I pull the wet clothes from the washer and toss them in the dryer.

I hit start and dash down the hall, just in time to see the dig site come on the screen, followed by Alan Grant. Every time I watch it, I find something new. A detail I missed. A line of dialogue that takes on new meaning. It's one thing I love about rewatching old favorites.

"That's a hell of a way to start a movie," Cyril murmurs when I sit beside him. He offers me the blanket he'd stolen when I discarded it.

I take it and drape it over both of us, knowing full well I have a trunk full of perfectly warm blankets next to the couch. This one is big enough to accommodate two people without being squished together. Besides, his warmth will help hold the temperature beneath the blanket.

He shoots me a quick look when I join him under the blanket but says nothing and refocuses on the story unfolding on the screen. Our elbows brush, and when I shift, it brings us thigh-to-thigh.

The movie fades into the background as my brain spins a hundred miles per hour. I struggle to get it under control, to get my thoughts back on the road, but they're determined to pull a *Thelma and Louise.*

I mentally shake myself. This is crazy. I just met this man. His past and the complication of our present make this whole situation very delicate. I spent all afternoon fighting with my parents, and my better judgment, about why I should not let this man into my business, into my life. I know almost nothing about him.

I hazard a glance at his profile. He's fully invested in the movie, but he notices the movement of my head.

"Something wrong?" he asks, his voice low.

He's not flirting, but I'll be damned if his tone isn't causing a riot of butterflies in my stomach.

"No." I swat them away with a shake. "You like it so far?"

He nods and turns back to the movie.

There's nothing but us and the action on the screen. After a few tense moments, I'm sucked into the story. Just like I always am. This movie never fails to amaze me. I've memorized every frame, every line, but I'm always entranced by it.

As we watch, the story twists and turns. I know the jumps are coming, but I flinch every time anyway. I'm not sure when, but at some point, Cyril's arm is around the back of the sofa, in an almost protective posture. But he removes it after a few moments.

Am I disappointed by that? Or relieved? Everything twists inside me, and I'm even more confused when the movie ends. The credits roll, and I seize the opportunity to fling the blanket back and stand, stretching my legs.

"You did good." Cyril also stands and arches his back.

Pride fills me, and I soak up his praise. "You liked it?"

"Loved it." He shrugs. "It's not *Star Wars*, but it's definitely a great movie."

I roll my eyes. "What is it about *Star Wars* that gets you all hot and bothered?"

"Have you seen Princess Leia in a bikini?" He laughs when I shove his arm. "I'm joking. Joking."

"Just for that, I should look up all the spoilers for the series and ruin the experience for you."

"Spoilers?" His eyes widen as he realizes the implication of my threat. "Don't you dare."

"Then don't be sexist."

"What? Han Solo is hot too. Should have given him his own shirtless scene, honestly."

I blink at him, twice, as his words sink into my brain. "Did you just say Han Solo is hot?"

"Yeah. Why?"

"Not many men would admit it." I straighten and smile. "I'm surprised, that's all."

"Guess I'm not like most modern men then." Cyril leans closer. His scent wraps around me, teasing me with a silent invitation. "And I'm full of surprises."

A strangled moan chokes me, but I manage to clear my throat and step away, snatching the blanket for something to do with my hands as I fold it.

"Well, I'll let you watch whatever you want. I'm going to take a shower and go to bed."

To his credit, he doesn't comment. When I walk past him, he gently touches my arm.

"What's that black box on the desk in my room?"

I think for a moment until my confusion fades. "A desktop computer. I can show you how to use it if you want."

"Please."

The simple word leaves me breathless.

After turning off the television and cleaning up the mess from dinner, I lead the way to his bedroom and power up the desktop. Once I give him a quick tutorial for how it works and how to access the internet, I let him take control of the mouse.

"If you have any questions, let me know."

"Thanks." He sits at the desk.

I pause in the doorway. "I'll set out a towel for you to take a shower."

"Sounds great." He turns to study me. "Thank you, Jessica."

His heartfelt gratitude sinks into my soul and chips away at the reservations I felt earlier at Mom and Dad's.

"You're welcome." I tap my fingers on the doorway. "I'm the last room on the left if you need me."

A sinful grin curves his lips, revealing those adorable dimples. "Got it."

Kicking myself, I retreat to the bathroom and take a long, hot shower. This man has turned my life inside out in only twelve hours. I can't imagine what tomorrow will bring.

CHAPTER 13

Cyril

My head hurts. No one warned me the internet is as addictive as cocaine.

I manage to drag myself out of bed, groaning at a quick glance at the clock on my nightstand. It's eleven a.m. I guess Jessica took pity on me. Either that, or she decided I wasn't worth the effort to wake. With a wary glance at the computer, I drag myself to the bathroom.

Last night, a half hour after Jessica introduced me to the glory of the internet, she returned to tell me the bathroom was free. I'm glad I seized the opportunity, because the moment I stepped under the hot water, everything crashed down on me.

The reality of my life. The situation I'm in. There is only one option. Embrace it.

Kate never found her way back to her time, so I'm willing to bet there's no way I can find my way back to 1985. It might not be what I want, but maybe it's exactly what I need.

When I returned to my room, I sat at the computer. After five hours on the internet, I've realized two things. One, this small piece of technology is a black hole; two, I need sleep to function as a human.

It's late morning, and the apartment is silent, but the hum of music and machinery pulses through the floor under my feet. She must be in the shop.

Grabbing an old pair of work pants and a dark T-shirt, I quickly dress. Thank God they didn't throw out my stuff. Arthur's forethought is saving me the hassle of having to hunt down clothes. With no credit cards, no driver's license, and no cash, I am at the mercy of my friend and his daughter. I tug on a pullover sweatshirt and snag a pair of work shoes from the bottom of a box I shoved aside last night.

When I step into the hallway, the haunting floral fragrance lingering in the air serves as a reminder of a woman I shouldn't be thinking about.

In the kitchen, I search for a coffee pot, but can't find anything even remotely resembling one. On the counter, there's a machine that says

Keurig and a small tree holding plastic cups. Dark Roast, Light Roast, Espresso…coffee. I struggle with the machine for a moment, but once I turn it on, I'm able to figure out the process pretty easily—the advantage of understanding basic mechanics. I place a clean mug from the cabinet in position and push a flashing blue button.

The warm, intoxicating scent of fresh brewed coffee fills the air. Ah, technology.

From the deluge of information I tried to absorb last night, I've come to realize the future is both as bleak and as fantastic as I imagined it would be. But I could be biased due to the unnatural amounts of science fiction I've consumed over the years.

And still, the future is *nothing* like we predicted.

Coffee in hand, I head for the stairs. Today, I'm putting both feet forward. No use dwelling on the past. I can do this. No sweat.

My mental pep talk does little to silence a screaming panic in the dark parts of my brain. But somehow, I manage to push it aside by the time I reach the door to the shop.

Warmth hits me when I open the door, followed by the blasting sound of rock music and the familiar scent of grease and gasoline.

I make sure the door closes behind me, keeping a firm grip on the mug. Weaving around the toolbox and past the Swinger, I follow the sounds of metal clinking against metal and swear words drowning in guitar solos. My smile widens.

When I round the front end of the car—a modern monstrosity sort with a Ford logo—I pause. Jessica's legs peek out from under the beast as she lays on a creeper.

"Need a hand?" I ask before sipping my coffee.

The creeper's wheels squeal in protest as she slides into view. Her brows rise in shock. "You're alive?"

"You didn't warn me the internet would suck my soul out and keep me awake all night."

A grin splits her plush lips. "We all had to learn the hard way."

"Thanks." I grumble the word, but I'm sure she hears the sarcasm.

Slowly, she climbs to her feet and wipes the back of her hand across her forehead, leaving a streak of grease. Her dark blue tank top gives me an eyeful of bountiful cleavage, and I drop my gaze to the coveralls tied in a knot around her waist. Guess she got too hot.

If I stare at her much longer, I might spontaneously combust.

"Whatcha working on?" I tug at the collar of my sweatshirt and step to the side when she picks up the creeper and sets it against the wall.

"Oil change. Nothing special."

"What is this?"

"2013 Ford Explorer."

"It's a beast." I admire its bulk.

"Suburbans were all the rage in the late nineties and early 2000s. Still popular, although not as fuel efficient as other options."

"I take it there *are* other options?"

"You name the company, they make one."

"Interesting." I make a mental note to look up more information about the evolution of vehicles over the last three decades. It can wait though. Right now, I want to spend more time with her. "So what can I do?"

Jessica wipes her hands on a rag and tosses it on the toolbox. "Dad wants me to get your feet wet, so let's cut the foreplay. I'll show you the office."

Her choice of words isn't lost on me. I follow, admiring the sway of her ponytail against her shoulders. Does she realize I'm not immune to the charms of a woman who isn't afraid to get her hands dirty and call me on my bullshit? Every moment, it's getting harder to find a reason not to stick around and see where this leads.

Maybe Arthur was onto something? Or maybe I'll get my face bashed in with a hammer? It's a toss-up.

After our truce last night, when she introduced me to the delights of *Jurassic Park*, streaming services, and the cursed internet, there must be some foundation…at least for her to *not* hate my guts. We were laughing, having fun. Relaxed. Like friends, right?

It's been one day. Let's not expect miracles.

She opens the door to a brightly lit office with several desks, a wall of filing cabinets, and framed pictures of different vehicles from over the years. Walking past two desks, she leads me to a third and gestures for me to sit.

I obey.

Jessica reaches over and turns on the computer screen, wiggling the mouse as she withdraws. Her floral scent drifts past me, almost hidden beneath the pungent aroma of oil. The screen flares to life.

"You're gonna distract me with the internet again?" I chuckle, drawing her attention.

Her gaze flickers from my eyes to my mouth before she clears her throat. "Actually, I was going to show you the programs the company uses for scheduling, billing, filing, and maintenance records."

"You can do all of that on a computer?" I'm stunned when she nods. "How convenient."

"It is, actually."

"Then what are those are for?" I point to filing cabinets along the wall.

"Old records we've archived from before the shop went digital." She sits on the edge of the desk and uses the mouse to open an application on the desktop. At least I learned *something* during her lesson last night.

My mind drifts into dangerous territory again, and I force myself to focus on the screen instead of her. "How many employees?"

"In the office, four including me. Six on maintenance at two locations, and fifteen drivers."

"How many vehicles in the fleet again?" I lean forward as numbers come into view on the screen.

"Twelve, but I'd like to expand both the fleet and the number of drivers by the end of next year."

"How many are you thinking?"

"Two dozen vehicles and ten more drivers."

I whistle low. "You're determined, aren't you?"

"Well, the last two years were hell with the pandemic and the recession. People cut back."

"You're a luxury they could do without." I nod, understanding her position. Quietly, I file away details of her statements to look up online. Asking a million questions won't keep us focused on the task at hand. *Pandemic* warrants a closer investigation.

"Dad thinks I should expand, try to find new clientele."

"What do you think?"

Her bright eyes lock with mine. "I think we need to rebrand. As a chauffeur service, we put ourselves in a higher class, and while I think there's still a market for it, we're not against only the cabs now but also Uber and Lyft."

"What?"

Jessica sighs and briefly explains the two companies. Interesting. I anticipated the cabs would throw a fit at the encroachment on their turf, but healthy competition improves service, right? This information gives me incentive to find a way to expand the company in a way that benefits and brings positive engagement.

"Show me what you're thinking?" I grab the nearest chair and pull it beside me. "Sit down. Run me through it."

"Really?" She blinks at me, surprised. It takes her a minute, but she shakes off the stunned look and grabs a notebook from a drawer before sliding into the chair. "Get me a pen over there."

I select a blue ballpoint from the cup of pens sitting near the computer screen and hand it to her.

Her fingers close over mine. Heat radiates through my body at the simple touch. But as fast as it sparked, it vanishes when she pulls away.

For the next two hours, she walks me through her thoughts for Cyril's Car Service. I agree with her—rebranding the garage might be in our best interest. Showcase our flexibility and unique service. Maybe add a vintage touch, since it seems what is old is new again.

When the phone rings at two o'clock, I grab it out of habit. "Cyril's, how may I help you?"

Jessica arches a brow but sits patiently silent beside me.

"Cyril? It's Arthur."

"Arthur, what can I do for you?" I glance at Jessica, who tenses.

"I'm gonna need you and Jessica to do me a favor."

"Whatever you need," I respond with a smile. Just like old times.

Jessica grabs the phone and presses a button on the receiver. Her father's voice fills the space.

"What's up, Dad?" she asks, her tone terse.

"Oh, hello, sweetheart." He clears his throat. "I need you both to go upstate. Rob has some things he needs us to pick up for Marcy's party next week."

"You want us to drive to Uncle Rob's? When?"

"Tomorrow. Should be able to make it up and back in a day if you leave early."

Jessica grumbles under her breath, and I jump in. "We can handle that, Arthur. No problem."

"Good. I'll let Rob know you'll be heading his way in the morning."

"Is that everything, Dad?" Jessica clenches her jaw. If she keeps it up, she'll break a tooth.

"That's all. How's everything at the shop?"

"It's good. We're fast friends," I say before Jessica can respond.

She glares at me and shakes her head, but there's a sparkle in her eyes and a lilt at the corner of her lips, belying a smile and giving me hope what I say is true.

"Glad to hear it. Keep up the good work you two."

"Tell Mom I said hi. Love you, Dad." She nudges her father to say goodbye. I've heard that tone a million times.

"Love you too. Bye."

With our goodbye, she ends the call with the press of a button.

"We should finish here and get some sleep. It'll be a long drive tomorrow."

"I drive…drove for a living. That part doesn't scare me."

"Then what does scare you?"

"Leaving the city."

"Seriously?" She laughs, and the sound ignites heat inside me, tingling through my limbs.

"I've never left."

"Ever?"

"Ever." I stand and shove my hands in my pockets. "The only forest I've ever seen is the one in Central Park, and I refuse to walk through it at night."

Jessica stares at me like I've just sprouted a horn in the middle of my head. "Maybe this is a good thing. Get you out of your element."

"I was transported thirty-seven years into the future. I'm firmly removed from my *element*."

"Noted." She presses her lips together. "Come on. You can help me finish this oil change, then we can grab some dinner."

"Good. I'm starving. All I had for breakfast was coffee."

"Serves you right for sleeping in."

"Won't happen again." I round the desk and head for the door. She follows me, wearing an expression I can't quite place.

"Something wrong?" I ask, opening the door and stepping aside for her to exit the office.

"Nope." She brushes past me, and I'm surrounded by the scent of *her* again.

Tomorrow's road trip is going to be torment in more ways than one. At least I have a pretty copilot to distract me.

I just hope she doesn't kill me and bury my ass in the woods somewhere along the way.

Chapter 14

Jessica

Nothing ever works out the easy way. When Dad offered to let me take his truck, I should have known something would go wrong.

It wouldn't start. Of course it wouldn't. Why would it when he only drives it twice a year?

Cyril and I spent the better part of the morning troubleshooting the problem. Then we finally found it. A mouse must have chewed through part of the wiring harness. An easy fix, but I wouldn't have even thought to check for it had Cyril not mentioned it.

I'm used to plugging in a computer diagnostic tool and letting it do the legwork. But that's the problem with Dad's old pickup. No computer in this early-generation Dodge. I don't know why he insists on keeping it, but why does any old man do anything? Because he can.

Once we fixed the broken wires, she fired right up.

Then the clutch gave out.

Making an executive decision, I leave Dad's truck in the garage and opt for the Ford Explorer. By the time we get on the road, it's after one in the afternoon. We'll never make it to Lake George and back tonight. It's a four-hour drive one way, and knowing Uncle Rob, he'll want us to stay and visit. Shit.

Cyril offers to drive, but since he's never been out of the city, I take the wheel. He grumbles and pouts until I plug in my phone and set the map directions to Bolton. His eyes widen as we weave through the city with an automated voice leading the way.

It takes until we reach the other side of the George Washington Bridge for him to stop gawking at the phone every time it issues a new direction. Around the time we hit Interstate 87, he seems more comfortable, both with the ride and being outside the city.

"Is it how you imagined it?" I ask as we cross the state line from Jersey back into New York.

His attention remains fixed on passing scenery. It's hard to get a good look from the interstate, but the expanse of trees stretching across the horizon are definitely a change from the narrow view between skyscrapers and buildings in the city.

"Nope." He turns with a smile. "It's worse. How can you find your way in this chaos?"

"A compass." I chuckle at the horrified look on his face.

"Just don't break down out here, Peggy," he purrs to the Ford, rubbing the dashboard with his long fingers.

My gaze follows the way he strokes the plastic with an encouraging caress. I will not be distracted by this man. My grip tightens on the wheel, and I stare straight ahead. "Did you just name my car?"

"Technically, it's a company car." He sits back and relaxes. "And I did. She looks like a Peggy."

"Really?" I scoff.

"What's wrong with Peggy?"

"Nothing, I guess." My mind wanders to the soft tone he used while speaking to the car. It was almost…loving. I shake my head. "What made you pick it?"

"It was my mom's name." He turns away. "She died when I was ten."

Guilt slams into me. "I'm sorry."

"Don't be." He turns back with a subdued smile. "It was a long time ago."

"We have a few hours on the road." I shift to something more neutral. "I'm sure you have a million questions."

"I do." He cracks open a Coke he grabbed from the refrigerator at the shop and takes a sip. "But I don't want to bore you. I can look them up online later."

"Well, you don't have to ask me *all* of them. Maybe just pick the burning ones."

"What did you mean by *pandemic* yesterday?"

A heavy sigh rips from my chest. It's not a topic I like to visit, too many conflicting emotions and disappointments. But he deserves to know. I try to keep it as unbiased as possible as I explain, but the wounds are still fresh.

He listens and interjects with questions. For the first time in a long time, I feel like someone is actually listening to me.

The conversation drifts to other world events and societal milestones. When I mention 9/11, his eyes widen.

"That explains the skyline," he says under his breath.

"What do you mean?"

"When I was at the top of the Empire State Building to retrieve your mom's purse in 1985 and I got sucked into the...time slip or portal or whatever, and woke up in the present." His voice wavers. "The skyline was the first thing I noticed. Without the Twin Towers in the distance, I knew I wasn't where I should be."

"Oh." What do I even say in response to that?

"How old were you?" he asks.

"Eleven." I ignore the flashes of memories from that day.

He winces. "I'm sure that was horrible for everyone. Especially for a kid."

"It was. A lot changed." I launch into a brief history of our post-9/11 world. The war on terror, the restructuring of travel. The conversation slowly spirals into a dark and depressing void.

"Life wasn't perfect in the eighties," he says, as though trying to reassure me. "Every era has its problems and life-altering moments. That's how the world works."

"What, are you an amateur historian?" The break in heavy topics gives me a chance to breathe.

"No, but I always kept three books in the car while on duty. Most of them were historical nonfiction or sci-fi."

"That's quite a shift in reading material."

"I like to change things up. It's always good to have balance, don't you think?"

"I guess."

We pass a large green sign for the Albany exit. Only an hour left.

"So how well do you know Uncle Rob and Aunt Marcy?" I ask, moving on to lighter topics.

"We're not close, but I spent a lot of time with them before I ended up here."

His laugh makes me shiver with awareness.

"Marcy was a wild thing back in the day."

"Really?" Aunt Marcy has always been my favorite. She would take me for the summers, let me run wild on the lake. I got into all kinds of trouble, but she always bailed me out. "Tell me about her."

Cyril recounts the spring of 1985, when Marcy and Rob finally stopped clawing each other long enough to see the mutual attraction simmering between them.

"It was clear to anyone with two eyes and half a brain they wanted each other." He laughs at the memory, and part of me wishes I could have seen it. "She got caught up in a huge scandal with an up-and-coming movie star. It was in all the papers and tabloids."

"You're kidding?" I gape at him. "She never told me."

"I'm sure she has her reasons for staying quiet, but it's out there. It's probably on the internet if you want to read about it."

Cherished childhood memories of summers with Aunt Marcy and Uncle Rob fill my head. Do I really want to tarnish them?

"Or you can always ask her." He studies my face, and I warm under his gaze. "It'll be nice to see them again."

Relief fills me as he nudges the conversation once more. We started this partnership under less-than-ideal circumstances, and I had my reservations. How was I supposed to relate to someone from a different decade? The thought of holding a conversation with him left me in a panic. I'd rather smash my thumb with a hammer than be forced into idle chitchat with a dinosaur.

But he's not a dinosaur.

He's smart and funny. Most of all, he's perceptive. I've never felt so relaxed with anyone. Whenever the topic gets too heavy, he steers the conversation to something manageable. His intuition makes me think he's hypersensitive to those around him. Not an empath, but in-tune with life.

Is it really possible that, within only two days, I'm actually *comfortable* with Cyril? It seems crazy. But even more crazy is this simmering attraction between us. The soft tension nudging us closer with every exchange.

I want to hate it, but I don't.

Mom was right. Cyril is a great guy. But what does that mean?

I stuff aside the nagging questions and focus on the remaining thirty miles. Instead of diving back into conversation, Cyril turns on the radio and searches for a station he likes.

"You don't have to do that." I hand him my phone. "Look for the Spotify app. It's green."

I keep my attention on the road while he messes with the phone. "Found it." He taps the screen. "What is it?"

I push the button on the console monitor, and my phone connects to the Bluetooth. "You can pick one of the playlists or search for whatever music you want by title, genre, artist. Try it."

"You're serious?" His excitement fills the car. After a few seconds, Bon Jovi's "Livin' on a Prayer" filters through the speakers.

"Had to go with the eighties, huh?"

"I have a lot of music to catch up on." He waves me off. "Just drive."

I laugh. "You can't commandeer my phone indefinitely."

"Watch me." He cackles.

"Tomorrow, we'll pick up a phone for you, okay?"

His eyes light up like my nephew's when he got a PlayStation from my parents last Christmas. His innocent delight shifts into something more acute. Hunger? No, desire.

The sign for the town pops into view, and I sigh with relief. "We've made it. And just before dark too."

I make my way through town and find a quaint motel at the edge of the lake.

"What are we doing here?" He looks up at the *Vacancy* sign.

"Staying the night. I don't like to drive in the dark." I turn off the engine. "I'll text Uncle Rob to tell him we'll be over in the morning to pick up the stuff for the party."

"Sounds good to me."

"You hungry?" I reach for my phone, and he places it in my palm.

"Starving." His green eyes glint in the fading light.

Don't read too much into it, Jess. I fidget with my phone for a moment until my brain clicks into gear. Within moments, I send off a text to Uncle Rob and we head inside.

Lucky us, there's one room left.

With one queen-size bed.

Lovely.

CHAPTER 15

Cyrid

I'm about to burst.

Between the information that's slowly been dumping into my brain and the delicious home-cooked meal from the diner down the street, I'm full to capacity. I can't possibly do anything but sleep at this point.

Jessica doesn't say much during dinner or on the short walk back to the motel. I kept my mouth closed when the clerk told us there was only one room left, with only one bed.

We're both adults. We'll figure it out. I thought about offering to sleep in the Ford, but with temperatures hovering around freezing, that would be stupid.

The town is quaint and homey. The shops have Christmas decorations in the windows, and lights strung across the main street cast a charming glow over the pedestrians. I glimpse an oversized Christmas tree in the town center with bright decorations and jewel-colored lights. It's not Rockefeller Center, but it's lovely and fits perfectly with the surrounding décor.

It's nice to be away from the city, but even if it weren't after dark, I'm not sure I'd be up for exploring. Maybe in the summer, but in winter, only a handful of days before Christmas, it doesn't sound like fun. I guess I can blame it on the lingering effects of time travel.

By the time we reach the room, I'm dragging. All I want is a shower and sleep.

"Are you sure this is okay?" I gesture to the queen-size bed dominating the room.

"It's fine." She shrugs. "I would call Uncle Rob and ask to stay there, but I don't think he wants Aunt Marcy to know we're here. He says it's a surprise."

"Won't she be home tomorrow when we pick the stuff up?"

"No, her quilting group meets at nine tomorrow morning. She'll be gone when we stop by."

Silence slowly fills the space between us.

"Mind if I take a shower?" I ask, moving toward the bathroom.

"Not at all." She pulls her phone from her pocket and flops down on the bed. "I'll take one after you're done."

I bite my tongue as an image of her joining me in the shower pops, fully formed, into my brain and expands like a hot-air balloon. Without replying, I turn and lock myself in the bathroom.

The narrow shower isn't built for two, which is a disappointment. I curse myself for allowing my brain to chase these details and cling to them for whatever twisted reason. Spending time with her has certainly increased my initial attraction, and I want nothing more than to sate my curiosity. What does she enjoy outside of cars? Does she read? The little things that are uncovered over time and with friendship—I want them now so I can better understand the woman in the other room.

Without lingering under the hot water longer than necessary, I wash and rinse. She's waiting to use the shower, and I don't want to be rude.

Once I step from the shower and dry off, I feel more comfortable. More relaxed. Wrapping the towel around my waist, I look at my reflection in the mirror. Damp hair hangs across my face, and there's nothing to block the expanse of my chest and arms from view. Shit. I forgot to grab my clothes before I came into the bathroom.

I double-check the towel secured around my waist. That's as good as it's going to get.

Opening the door, I peer around it to find her in the same spot, distracted by her phone. When I push it fully open, she looks up.

"I was worried you—" Her eyes shift from sky blue to midnight.

"Worried I what?" I ask, ignoring the hunger in her expression as her gaze rakes over me.

"Drowned." She finishes before dragging her attention back to her phone.

I chuckle. There's something here. Chemistry. I'd bet money on it. What will happen if I lean harder on that mutual attraction? I'm not the kind of guy to press my luck, but I *am* trying to win her over. Maybe there's hope. All I can do is try.

She stands as I reach for my bag and rifle through it. When she brushes past me, heat grazes my bare skin. It takes all my effort to remain still and not turn, not reach for her.

I wait, even though the tension is killing me.

"Mind if I borrow your phone? I want to search something on the internet." I hold my hand out.

"Sure." She places it in my palm. "If I get any texts, just ignore them." Pink spreads across her cheeks and down her throat. She's blushing.

I barely have a chance to enjoy it before she retreats into the bathroom, forgetting to take her bag of clothes with her. I chuckle and cross to the small duffle bag she left on the dresser. I grab it and knock on the bathroom door.

"What?" she asks through the plywood.

"Your bag."

"Shit."

The door cracks open and her arm sneaks out. I slide the loop over her hand, keeping my gaze firmly fixed on the door between us.

"Thanks."

The barrier goes back in place as the door closes. I lean against it and take several deep breaths. Had she still been dressed? Was she in just a bra and panties? Was she naked, wrapped in a towel like me? Fuck. The question drives me insane.

I'm a gentleman. I stopped myself from looking. My wild imagination made the whole interaction worse.

Shoving away from the door, I try to redirect my thoughts.

Get dressed. Yeah. Clothes.

Setting her phone on the bed beside my bag, I pull out a pair of gray sweatpants I'd found in one of the boxes. They need to be replaced, but I can worry about it when I get back to the city. I forgo underwear and pull on the sweatpants.

I'm already hard thanks to the thoughts spinning in my head. My cock protests when I tuck it out of sight. Even underwear wouldn't hide the insistent bulge it insists on making. Fuck. She's going to take one look at me and know exactly what's going on in my mind. There's no denim to hide it. No oversized coats or long shirts. It's there, and I can't do shit about it.

I move the bag to the floor and sit back against the headboard. I cradle her phone in one hand and open the internet application. After a few minutes, I hear her turn on the shower, and suddenly my mind is filled with thoughts of her wet and naked in the other room. Fuck.

Redirecting my thoughts again, I type in *boomer* and hit search. A few minutes into reading an article, the phone dings and a message appears on the screen.

Ah, this must be what she meant by *text*. I ignore it and keep reading.

Three more texts come up, one after the other in quick succession.

I try to ignore them, but when I try to swipe them out of the way, I accidentally open the notification. Shit.

Hey.

I miss you.

He misses you too.

A picture of an erection fills the screen.

"What the fuck?" I stare at the messages and the dimly lit image.

There's no denying it. That's a dick.

"Who would send something like this?"

The name at the top of the screen is Asshole Ex.

Ah. Well. That makes sense. But still, whatever happened to romance? Has it been reduced to impersonal messages and dick pictures? I shake my head in disappointment. Romance must be well and truly dead.

Another text comes through. This time, it's a photo of his dick with his hand wrapped around it.

Disgusted, I toss the phone aside at the same moment the bathroom door swings open. She sees her phone flying through the air, landing on the comforter at the foot of the bed.

"Not a fan of the internet?" she asks with a laugh.

"It wasn't the internet." I cross my arms, wishing I had put on a shirt.

She grabs the phone and reads the screen. "Goddamn it."

I snort-laugh. Guess she isn't a fan of it either.

"I'm sorry about that. I should block him." She shrugs a shoulder, which pulls her tank top tight against her body, revealing a patch of skin just above the waistband of her pants.

"Is that how men flirt now? They send suggestive guilt trips and pictures of their junk?" Anger filters up. It's irrational and overwhelming, but I can't ignore it simmering through me. "He shouldn't send shit like that if you don't want it."

"He's harmless." She laughs and waves her hand. "Most guys at least wait for an invitation to send pictures, but there are a handful who like to project their confidence with dick pics."

Her words don't carry confidence. I study her closely, noting the way she chews her lower lip and nervously looks everywhere but at me.

"Want me to take care of him?" The offer leaves my lips before I can think it through. Hell, I'm not even sure what I'm implying, but she smile regardless.

"No, I took care of it."

"He's your ex?"

"Yeah." She sets the phone on the bed. "We still hang out sometimes, but it's nothing serious."

"You're telling me romance is dead?"

I rise slowly to my feet, and her gaze skims down the length of me, widening as it drops lower.

"It's not dead." She licks her lips and meets my gaze. The midnight storm in her eyes is back. Pupils blown wide, swallowing the color completely.

"You're telling me these guys sending photos of their dicks know how to flirt?" I step closer.

"I guess." She sways but doesn't otherwise move as I approach.

"They know exactly how to seduce you with words, their actions playing a perfect harmony to bring you to your knees." My voice dips, softening, deepening as I step into her space.

We're a half inch from touching, but I refrain. If she wants it, she'll take the next step. I hold my breath, craving it more than anything I've ever wanted in my life.

"Some of them." Her response is hoarse, laced with uncertainty.

"Do they know what *you* want?" I exhale, letting my breath skim her shoulder in a delicate caress. "Do they know what you *need*?"

Jessica turns, her lips parted, her eyes brimming with desire. "What are you trying to say?"

"Those idiots know nothing of romance."

"And you do?" Challenge echoes in those three little words.

"Yes."

"Liar." Her tongue darts out to wet her lips.

I'm burning, and only she can quench this desire.

"Prove it."

The moment her words register, I swear and close the gap between us.

Her lips meet mine, and there's nothing but her, me, and this fucking kiss.

CHAPTER 16

Jessica

What the hell am I doing? Kissing Cyril might just be the stupidest thing I've done since I told my ex I'd go on one date with him three months after we broke up.

There's no resistance from Cyril. He slides his arms around me, like they're meant to be there. I've never been a slim girl, and no one has ever classified me as petite, and in his arms, I feel like I'm a puzzle piece sliding into place at the end of a long, stressful struggle.

As if sensing the wandering thoughts in my mind, he tilts his head to the side. His tongue slides against the seam of my lips, begging for more.

My mouth obliges before my brain registers the danger ahead.

Why the hell does he taste so good? Cinnamon and sugar with a hint of cloves. I barely remember what dessert he had at the diner, but I don't remember it being nearly as alluring on the plate as it is on his lips.

Fuck it. Reason completely vanishes in the cold December night. I thread my fingers through his hair, pulling him closer as he ravishes my mouth. He kisses me like he's savoring the moment, savoring me.

Gone is the petty challenge I issued with my snarky comeback. Cyril has replaced it with pure need. It's almost as if he knew it was there, simmering below the surface, waiting to erupt with the slightest nudge. The idle curiosity of the last few days transformed somewhere along the way.

I'm Alice, lost in Wonderland, tumbling down the rabbit hole, and I have no idea what the hell is happening to me.

Cyril breaks the kiss. Our breath mingles in a rush of lost thoughts and absent protests.

His eyes, ones I thought were simply green, transform into a kaleidoscope of storm gray, moss green, and sky blue. Flecks of amber swim in the background. His pupils widen as he studies me. A Cheshire grin forms on his lips and his dimples reappear.

We stare at each other for a long moment, and my sanity begins to unravel in the silence.

"That was..." I lick my lips, searching for words, but they never come.

"Fucking fantastic." He completes my thought.

He's right. It was amazing. More than amazing.

I nod and tease my fingers through his damp hair. "Cyril...I..." Again my brain fails me, and I curse.

"It's fine." He hooks his finger under my chin and strokes my jaw. "Whatever you need, Jessica. If you don't want this, I understand."

"That's not it." Frustration and arousal spin inside me, creating a vortex of need simple sex can't touch. But nothing about sex with Cyril will be simple. It will be complicated as fuck. I don't know if I'm ready for the emotional and logistical fallout should we go down in flames.

"What do you need?" Cyril's smile keeps me grounded. "Tonight, you can have whatever you want, no strings attached."

"You don't really believe that, do you?" I laugh and his smile falters.

"Believe what?"

"That you can compartmentalize whatever this is. No strings attached doesn't work. Trust me, I've tried."

"Are you talking about dick pic guy?" He holds me firmly, his hands on my hips, his fingertips stroking the skin of my lower back beneath the fabric of my top.

"Yes," I grumble. His casual mention of my ex only pisses me off. Whatever happened with him has no place in this conversation. In this relationship. Leave it to Justin to overshadow my life, even when he's no longer an active part of it. Fucker.

"I'm not him." Cyril pulls me a fraction of an inch closer, rocking his hips against mine. I'm hyperaware of his shirtless state and the bulge pressing hard against my thigh through his sweatpants.

"I know. But it doesn't work that way."

"It works however you want it to work. I promise." Cyril leans closer and presses soft kisses to my cheek, trailing them gently along my jaw. When his lips brush mine, I capture them in another desperate kiss.

Passion spills free. I have no reason or desire to restrain it. It's been months since I last had sex, and my vibrator doesn't live up to the real deal.

And Cyril is more real than I've seen...ever.

He spins me around, pressing my back to his front. The hard line of his cock presses against my ass, and I arch back, earning a groan from him. He wraps one hand around the base of my throat.

I close my eyes and whimper, resting all my weight against him.

"Ah, you like that?"

I nod.

"Use words. I want you to *tell* me what you like…and what you don't."

"Okay." My voice trembles as he glides his thumb along my throat.

"Good girl."

My knees buckle, and he catches me around the waist. His soft chuckle skims over my neck.

What exactly has he been looking up on the internet? The thought crosses my mind, but before I can ask, he rests both hands on my hips and hooks his thumbs in the top of the elastic band around my waist.

He pushes the fabric down. My face heats when he drops to his knees, eyes level with my ass, and urges me to step out of the pajama pants.

I look over my shoulder to find his gaze searching for mine. "Cyril."

"You want me to stop?" he asks.

"No."

"What do you need?"

The repeated question lingers in my mind, and I still don't have an answer. All I know is the heat building inside me needs release. And if he doesn't give it to me, I'll take it myself.

"You're thinking too much." He slowly rises to his feet. "Tell me what's rolling around in your lovely head."

"I need to come." In all the years I've dated, I've never felt comfortable voicing my sexual needs. I've always known what they were to an extent, but I've never had a partner I trusted to seriously consider them.

"How do you want to come?" He leans close, his words burning my mind, his breath teasing my flesh. "On my hand? My tongue? My cock?"

I take a deep breath. "Your tongue."

"Good answer." His eyes light up. "I've been dying to get my mouth on your pretty little cunt."

The harsh word throws me off for a moment, but I shake it off as he gently guides me to the bed. I settle in the middle of the mattress. He climbs between my thighs, lifting, spreading, feasting with his eyes.

A growl rises from deep in his throat as he settles into place. His hot breath teases my center before he drags his tongue over me. A moan rips from my throat, echoing off the walls. His eyes meet mine as he repeats the action. Shivers roll through me, and my legs fall wider on the bed. He smiles, and I lose all sense when his tongue descends once more.

My hands fist in his hair, twisting and pulling with every wicked pass of his tongue over my sensitive folds. He's a master, teasing my clit with gentle nips, suckling briefly before releasing pressure. I'm a writhing mess. He pins one hand on my stomach, keeping me still beneath him.

When he slides two fingers inside me, I buck off the mattress. "Fuck."

His laughter is drowned out by my panting curses. With every stroke of his fingers and lap of his tongue, my pleasure spirals higher. Just when I think I can't take any more, he adjusts his position, shifting his attention away from the oversensitive area.

He's teasing. Edging.

Fucking hell, I want to strangle him.

"May I…" The request comes in gasps from my lips. "Please."

"What?" he asks between licks. "I can't hear you."

"Let me come," I growl, desperation making me more agitated. "Please."

Pleasure spirals hotter and faster. I can't take much more of his torment. If I don't come soon, I might lose my mind.

Cyril takes my clit in his mouth, laving his tongue over the swollen bud. His fingers stroke deeper, harder, rubbing my inner walls, creating delicious friction. When he hums, the world shatters.

My climax overtakes me, dragging me under in waves of pleasure. He doesn't relent or release as I tremble beneath him. I rock my hips against his mouth, savoring the sensations slowly ebbing into the dull pulse of my retreating orgasm. My eyes close as my body shivers.

The bed shifts, and I rouse when he settles beside me, wrapping his arms around me. I snuggle into his warmth and note the hard length pressed to my thigh.

"Want some help with that?" I ask, reaching to palm him through the fabric.

He groans in my ear and thrusts his hips. "I won't say no."

I roll over, facing him and reach into the waistband of his sweats. His cock fills my hand, overflowing my grip. I stroke his length, noting the way he sucks in breath between his teeth, then groans when I squeeze the tip.

"Fuck, that feels good." He shifts to his back when I remove his pants and straddle his thighs. "Take off your top," he instructs me.

I strip the tank off, loving the way his eyes widen and those dimples appear when he sees my tits for the first time. I've always thought they were too big, but when he reaches up and takes them in his hands, I stand corrected. They fit perfectly.

His disappointed groan when I pull away is replaced by a satisfied grunt as I take him in my mouth. He's bigger than I'm used to, but I suck and tease, raking my teeth gently over the ridges.

"Fuck, Jess. I can't remember the last time…" He moans when I run my tongue over his head like a sucker. "It's been forty years."

His laughter disappears into the background of my mind when reality sinks in.

Forty years. Cyril is from 1985. He worked for my father. Dad's forcing us to work together. Forcing this partnership.

And here I am, choking on his dick like a good fucking girl. Oh, hell no.

I jerk back and climb off him.

"Where are you going?" Cyril sits up, confused, completely naked, his cock at full attention. "What's wrong?"

"This. It's…" I snatch my tank top and my pajama pants off the floor.

"It's what?" He rises, climbing slowly off the bed. "Did I do something? Say something?"

"No." I tug the top over my head, hiding my tits from his view, and struggle to pull on my pants. "I shouldn't have kissed you."

"Wait, what?" He grabs his sweatpants and pulls them on, grunting when they restrain his hard cock. I almost feel bad for him. Almost. "What just happened?"

"You don't belong here." I round on him. "You belong in 1985."

"Thanks for the reminder." He scoffs, a scowl marring his handsome face. "But there's nothing I can do about it. I don't have a time machine. I can't snap my fingers and go back to the life I knew. I'm here. Now. Whether I like it or not."

"That's not my problem," I snap.

"It is now." He steps closer, and I take the same steps back.

Fury pounds through me. Resentment for my father. Cyril. Mom. Life.

This isn't how it's supposed to go. All my hard work, gone in a flash. And wouldn't it just be the icing on the cake to fuck me while he fucks me over?

Cyril pauses and flexes his hands. "Look. I don't know what

happened or what I did, but I'm sorry. Okay."

"Are you sorry?"

"Of course. I never meant to hurt you."

"Really?" The dam slowly cracks, and I feel pressure pushing forward at an alarming rate. A rate I'll never be able to counter. Instead of biting it back, I embrace the flow as it bursts free from the depth of my soul.

"You walk in, and Dad welcomes you with open arms. He gives you a position in the company—in *my* company. A job. An apartment. Everything." I glare at him. "I worked my whole fucking life to make him proud of me. To get him to believe I could run the car service and the garage without his meddling. Without someone hovering over my shoulder, telling me what to do and how to do it."

Cyril straightens, his expression impassive. "Is that what you think I'm doing?"

"Aren't you?"

"No. I didn't ask for any of this, Jessica."

"You might not have asked for it, but you're in the middle of it."

"I'll walk away right now if it will make you feel better. But I think you should talk to your father first."

"Oh sure, make yourself a martyr. Poor Cyril." The hateful words spew from a dark place in my soul, and I cringe when he flinches.

"That's not what I meant." He sighs. "Or what I want."

"What do you want, Cyril? Do you want to steal everything from me? Including my shop?"

"I don't want to steal anything. I don't want the shop." His shoulders slump. "I just want you to be happy."

Fuck. I pull my hair in frustration. "Look, I'm sorry. It's been a long week. I'm obviously not in a great place, and pushing this into a physical relationship is probably the worst idea in the world."

"We can't deny the chemistry here."

"No." I agree with a nod. "But I can't act on it. I was wrong to kiss you. To put you in this situation and then pull away."

"Takes two." He shrugs. "I know what you mean, and I understand."

"Maybe we should just go to bed and start fresh tomorrow." My conscience takes a dive the moment the adrenaline wears off.

"Yeah. Okay." Cyril walks around me to the bathroom. "I'll give you some time alone."

"Thanks." I turn and watch him close the door behind him.

The moment the barrier seals between us, I collapse to the bed. Tears flow. What the hell just happened? What is wrong with me?

I like Cyril. I want him. Crave him. But he's a threat to everything I've worked so fucking hard for.

Can I trust him?

The shop is my baby. It's my dream. Where does he fit into this? Does he fit?

I grab a tissue and wipe my face before ripping back the blankets and climbing into bed. Once I'm nestled under the covers, staring at the wall, my mind races.

What happened between us? I wanted it. More than anything. Then why did I stop it? Why did these intrusive thoughts come barreling in at the worst possible time to ruin the moment?

I scream into the pillow before repositioning it under my head.

The faint sound of running water comes through the bathroom door. Is he showering again? Or is he taking care of the hard-on I gave him, so he won't have to sleep next to me with blue balls and a battered conscience?

I cringe. I'm the worst fucking person. I should apologize, talk it out with him. But shame has wrapped its claws around my neck. I can't do it.

Five minutes later, I hear the bathroom door open and pretend to be asleep. When the bed shifts, I hear his sigh as he lies down beside me.

My apology chokes me, and we fall asleep in strangled silence.

CHAPTER 17

Cyrid

I should have slept in the car. The cold and discomfort would have been equally matched to sharing this room with Jessica. I wake up before dawn, after struggling to sleep for most of the night. Finally, I give up, get dressed, and take a walk by the lake.

Jessica never moves.

The air is crisp and cold. There's a bite to it, like it wants to snow but can't. It's two days before Christmas, and I can almost imagine this place coated with a dusting of white, turning it into a winter wonderland.

With a sigh, I keep walking, soaking up this little paradise. For a moment, I forget I'm not in Central Park. It's almost freeing.

It's surreal. All of it. Being here, in this place, at this time.

But that's not what's eating me alive. It's her. The way she makes me feel. The way she's burrowed beneath my skin. The way I don't want anything as much as I want her. Not just sex. *Her.* Her company, her laugh, her sass. She's determined and smart, but there's so much more she's hiding, keeping firmly locked away.

I was so close to unwrapping those layers, to revealing her depth. Then she pulls away and closes herself off, snapping at me with such venom, it left me stunned. What the hell did I do? What happened?

Halfway down the trail around the lake, I turn around and slowly make my way back to the motel. A breeze pushes at my back, making me pick up my pace. I need a hot cup of coffee and something to eat.

What I truly crave is the woman who's got me twisted in knots.

She's afraid. That's obvious. This isn't only about the garage or who runs it. No, this runs deeper. I'm not a psychologist, but I know what it's like to have someone threaten to take away the one thing you love. It fucking sucks. When it's gone, the world feels hollow and empty. Life fails to have meaning. But there's always hope. If I found it, she can too.

How do I convince her I'm not going to take anything from her? What I want from her isn't the garage. It isn't tangible. It can't be bought, sold, or monetized. How the fuck do I convince her I want *her* and nothing else? That's the real question.

Frustration churns in my gut. By the time I reach the motel, I still haven't found a solution to my problem. All I can do is give her space, let her breathe.

My hand rests on the knob, and I pause. Fuck. I still remember how she tastes, the softness of her skin. I'm hard just thinking about her soft moans and whimpered curses. I spent thirty minutes in the bathroom trying to will my cock to relent. Finally, I caved, took myself in hand, and jerked off with the water running, hoping she was asleep and wouldn't hear me grunt when I came to thoughts of her. Goddamn it.

When I open the door, the scent of coffee hits me. I look for her, but the bed is empty and the bathroom door is open. Everything is packed, including my stuff. Shit. There's a coffee cup sitting on the table next to my bag. I pick it up and see my name on the side. I groan with the first sip. Warm and rich, it instantly soothes the caffeine craving.

The door opens and Jessica appears in the doorway.

"There you are. I thought you got lost in the wilderness." Her teasing comment alleviates some of my hesitancy.

"Just took a walk. Didn't want to bother you." I lift the cup in my hand. "Thanks for the coffee. I needed it."

"I picked up pastries too. They're in the car." She motions to the door. "Uncle Rob just called. He dropped off Marcy at the Senior Center, so we're in the clear to pick up the stuff."

"Right." Once I grab my bag, I do a quick scan of the room to make sure we didn't forget anything.

"I already double-checked the room. Your bag is the last thing to go." Jessica opens the door and holds it for me.

"Thanks," I say as I brush past her.

The sweet, tantalizing scent of her soap mixed with the heat of her skin leaves me aching. I'd give anything to pin her against the wall and taste her again. Make her cry out my name when she comes against my mouth.

Instead, I sip my coffee and make my way to the car.

The ride to Rob's place takes less than five minutes. We pull up to a quaint Victorian off the main street. Jessica parks in the short driveway behind the home.

I manage to stuff the remaining pastry in my mouth before getting out of the car.

Jessica leads the way to the house and knocks on the back door. A few moments pass before it swings open.

Holy shit. I expected it after seeing Kate and Arthur, but Rob's full head of gray hair and weathered squint behind bifocals stop me short. My heart breaks at seeing a man I admired so altered by time and life. I keep forgetting how many years have passed since I last saw him. Feels like yesterday to me, and yet, the man before me has lived a full life since then. I swallow a lump in my throat as Jessica greets him with a hug and a kiss on each cheek.

"Uncle Rob…" Jessica turns, but she stops when Rob steps down to the landing outside the door.

"Cyril." His eyes widen and fill with tears. "As I live and breathe." He claps me in a hug, squeezing me tight with a strength that belies his age.

"Rob." I bask in the warmth of his greeting. "It's so good to see you."

He pulls away and studies my face with an expression of awe. "When Arthur called and told me...well, I couldn't believe it." He grips my arm tighter. "I'm so glad you're here now. We were worried."

"Yeah, sorry about that." I run my hand through my hair.

"You're safe. That's all that matters." He steps back inside and motions for us to follow. "Come in. Would you like something to drink?"

"No, thanks." I follow Rob and Jessica into the hallway and close the door behind me.

The interior is not what you'd expect in a traditional Victorian home. The rooms have been altered to open the space. The kitchen and eat-in dining area are off to one side, the living room and office to the other, with a staircase and hallway bisecting the home neatly in half. The décor perfectly reflects its occupants. With Rob's background as a physician and Marcy's flair for fashion, the home represents them equally with a strange but fluid balance.

Rob steps into the living room and gestures to a sofa across from the oversized recliner he commandeers. "Sit. Relax. Take a moment to breathe before you get back on the road."

"We can't stay long, Uncle Rob."

He waves his hand. "You never visit me."

"You come to the city all the time," Jessica says before sticking out her tongue.

He mimics the action. "You've always been a brat."

"I learned it from you." Love sparkles in her eyes when she says the words. They truly have a unique bond.

Rob's knowing gaze drifts between the two of us, sitting beside each other. His lip twitches.

"So I take it Arthur filled you in on what happened?" I ask, diverting the conversation before it has a chance to take root.

"He did." Rob strokes his jaw. "I must say, I'm a bit surprised."

"Why?"

"For years, Kate has maintained her story. She traveled through time from 2020 to 1985." He scoffs. "It was a hard pill to swallow…the thought of time travel and all that."

"You believe her now?"

"I believed her then, only because there was no other explanation for the things she knew." He winks. "But now…now I'm positive it's true. Look at you! You haven't aged a day."

"Not sure if that's a good thing or not," I joke, unable to meet Jessica's curious stare. I feel it burning the side of my face as she studies me.

"The boys at the Black Penny aren't going to believe it's you next week at Marcy's birthday party." His bark of laughter echoes through the room, and I laugh with him.

"Do you have the stuff for the party?" Jessica asks.

"It's in the garage. You can grab it on the way out." He chuckles. "Marcy has no idea. We've been planning this for ages. Jackie reserved the whole bar for us."

"Does Claude still own it?"

"No. Retired years ago. His daughter, Jaqueline, runs it now." He leans back in the chair. "Yup. Claude and Gwen retired to a quiet place in the Poconos. Grant and Quinn bought a nice home in Brooklyn where they run a nonprofit for foster kids."

"That's great." Hearing these details pulls at my heartstrings. I've missed so damn much. "What about you and Marcy? Do you enjoy it up here?"

"We love it." He heaves a contented sigh. "We moved here in '86. I had a small practice for twenty years until Marcy told me to retire so we could travel. By that time, the kids were out of the house."

"You have kids?" I stare, gobsmacked.

"Two. Nicholas and James."

"Talk about brats," Jessica grumbles under her breath.

Rob laughs again. "You should've seen the five of them running around this place in the summer. It was pure chaos."

The conversation continues, and I slowly absorb the details of the family's lives. I missed so much. After an hour, Rob leads us to the garage and helps us load some boxes into the back of the Ford.

Jessica shuts the hatch. "We're ready to roll."

"Sounds good." I turn to Rob and offer my hand. "Thanks."

"You're family, Cyril." He wraps his arms around me and holds me tight. "If you need anything, give me a call."

"Yes, sir."

"Take care of my niece, would you?"

My gaze meets Jessica's. "Always."

There's a flash of pink in her cheeks before she spins around, heading for the driver's seat. "Love you, Uncle Rob," she calls as she opens the door.

"Love you!" Rob shouts back and nudges me with an elbow. "Be patient. She'll come around."

His whispered comment lingers in my brain as he retreats to the house. I climb into the Ford. "Want me to drive?"

"No, I got it." She puts the vehicle in gear without looking at me.

The ice wall between us has refrozen. Damn it. My mind spins as we drive out of town and back to the highway, heading south. I have four hours to break the wall down. But how?

Music plays through the speakers to dispel the silence between us. The phone periodically interrupts, giving us directions, but after two hours, I can't take the tension a moment longer.

I turn down the volume, and her grip tightens on the steering wheel.

"What's going on?" I ask.

"I don't know what you're talking about."

"Yes, you do." I exhale a half-exasperated sigh. "Last night—"

"What happened last night was a mistake. It won't happen again."

"Which part?" I pull at the fraying edges of the conversation, unraveling like a threadbare blanket.

"All of it."

"Ah. We're not going to discuss it like two mature adults?"

"What's to discuss?"

Her attention remains fixed on the road, and I'm relieved her hands are occupied because I'm pretty sure she'd throw something at me if it would shut me up. Judging from the tone of her voice and the rough edge to her words, she's not interested in discussing anything concerning *us*. I let the faint music fill the silence, creating a soothing reprieve from the tension.

"When I was a kid, I wanted to be a race car driver." The words spill free. Words I haven't voiced since I was young. Somehow, it feels right. I keep going. "Dirt track. No rules. No worries. Just the purr of the car and adrenaline coursing through my veins."

Jessica doesn't say anything, but she's listening. It's a start.

"My dad left when I was five. Mom worked three jobs to keep our apartment. When she died, I went to live with my Gram, but her place wasn't much nicer. There were rats, and bullies lived upstairs." My gaze fixes on the highway in the distance, losing focus and drifting back to those horrible years when we had nothing.

"I stole my first car when I was fourteen." The confession hovers in the car like an overfilled balloon, threatening to burst. "By the time I was eighteen, I'd been arrested four times. Gram had given up on me. Called me a lost cause."

"I was twenty when your father caught me trying to steal a car."

Her attention shifts to me for the briefest moment before returning to the road. She says nothing, but I can almost feel the gears churning in her mind.

"He just happened to walk past at the right moment. Caught me red-handed." I pause to let the words sink in.

"What did he do?" she asks.

"He gave me a choice." I smile as the memory appears in my mind, like a movie on the big television in her apartment. "Work for him or go to jail."

"He offered you a job?" She shakes her head. "How could he possibly trust a thief?"

"I don't know. Maybe he saw something in me. Maybe he felt bad for me." I shrug. "Who knows? I never asked him why he did what he did."

"Why are you telling me this?" she asks.

"I want you to know who I am."

"Why?"

"Because I want you to trust me."

She scoffs. "Why should I do that?"

He takes a deep breath. "I'm not here to take anything from you—not the garage, not your parents, your apartment, your life."

Silence meets my statement, so I continue. "I want to make this work. This partnership." My heart thunders in my chest. I hope she'll take the olive branch I'm offering. "You're a hell of a mechanic and a damn savvy businesswoman. I'm here to help, but you have to *trust* me."

"And if I don't?"

"Then it makes this ten times harder than it needs to be."

With a nod, she turns up the radio, and the conversation is over.

I shift, leaning against the door, staring at the passing landscape. I don't know how to get through to her. How to make her understand I'm on her side. I want her, *need* her to trust me. Otherwise, this is going to be miserable for everyone.

Fuck.

By the time we reach the city, the sun is setting. She pulls into the garage and turns off the ignition.

"Need help?" I ask, climbing from the car.

"Nope." She slams the door.

I get it. She needs space. Time to process everything. I leave her in the garage and retreat to the apartment upstairs to finish sorting through my past, still piled in boxes.

When she's ready, she'll talk. I hope.

All I can do is pray I didn't fuck this up beyond repair.

CHAPTER 18

Jessica

I can't avoid him forever. On Christmas Eve morning, I creep into the kitchen to make breakfast, careful not to wake Cyril. When we got home last night, I busied myself with work in the shop.

After the disastrous road trip to Uncle Rob's place—including the insanely hot encounter in the motel—I put distance between Cyril and me. I had to. There was too much going on in my head…and in my heart. I need time to think.

I'm stunned by his confession about his background. Revealing those vulnerable tidbits about his past left me wondering who he really is and how much my father truly knows about him. Why do I feel like there's something bigger at play here? It could just be my cynical nature.

I don't trust easily. I'm skeptical of everyone and their motives. I have to be. I'm a woman who owns her own business, living in the city. If I want to succeed, I can't be taken in by a handsome smile or flirty charm.

While the coffee brews, I make some oatmeal. It's not my typical breakfast, but it'll hold me over until we get to Mom and Dad's. Since before I was born, they've hosted a family holiday meal with all the trimmings. This year is no different.

Except for Cyril. They invited him to join the festivities as part of the family.

I'm dreading it. The first thing I'm going to have to field is my siblings' awkward questions and knowing winks. They're both happily married and have hounded me for years about my love life. Would it shut them up to think Cyril and I are dating? Probably not. They'll rip me apart the moment I walk into the house.

What's so wrong with Cyril? He's handsome, smart, and hardworking. His sense of humor is ten times better than any other guy I've ever met. All in all, he's not a bad choice. He's nearly everything I've ever wanted in a man.

Except he wants my shop for his own. He says he doesn't, but I can't stop this nagging suspicion he'll drop me once he gets what he wants from my father.

Why does the thought of his rejection sting so much?

His kiss lingers in my mind, tormenting me. The stolen moments of pleasure follow me like a thief in the shadows and invade my brain without warning. Was his confession sincere? Does he really care that much?

We've known each other less than a week, but being in his company is easy and relaxing. Even having to introduce him to the twenty-first century wasn't nearly as big a trial as I'd imagined it would be. He's taken everything in stride and assimilated into modern culture in a surprisingly quick period.

"Good morning," Cyril says from the doorway. His hair is rumpled, and he's wearing an gray eighties-style sweatshirt with matching pants.

For a moment, I'm back in that motel room with the tension crackling between us. *Girl, he's a thirst trap.* I shake the thought from my head and finish the last of my oatmeal.

"Morning." I jump down from the stool and carry my bowl to the sink. "Want some coffee?"

"I got it." He crosses the kitchen, brushing my elbow as he passes.

"You figured out the Keurig?"

He drops a pod into the chamber and closes it with a soft click. "Yeah, it's a clever little contraption."

"Hungry?" I ask, unable to replace the hard-won distance between us.

"Not really. Coffee should do the trick."

I glance at the microwave clock. Nine twenty-five. "Mom wants us at the house by eleven thirty. Gotta help her make Christmas Eve dinner."

"Oh. I wasn't sure if you wanted me to go or…"

"Mom and Dad requested your presence. You can't back out now." I put the excuse firmly on them. The last thing I want this morning is Cyril realizing I'm no longer angry with him. The truth is much more unnerving, something I'm not prepared to examine too closely.

A soft smile touches his lips as he lifts the coffee mug. "I don't want to impose."

"You're part of the family." I clear my throat and sip my warm drink. "According to them."

Fortunately, he says nothing. I watch as he crosses the kitchen and retreats down the hall. Damn him. I wanted to keep that wall between us, but without effort, he manages to chip away at it.

By eleven, we're ready to leave. I let him drive the Swinger. It's supposed to rain later, but there's no snow in the forecast, so we should be fine. We arrive a little before noon and have to fight for parking. Of course we're late. Hopefully, my siblings are keeping Mom and Dad distracted. I know the grandkids should be.

Cyril steps out of the car. He looks like a model selling a slice of the past in his eighties suit and coat, standing next to my '74 Swinger. I should take him to get an updated wardrobe.

Wait, why am I doing anything?

Because you want him.

My brain shorts. Goddamn it.

The moment I walk in the door, chaos descends around me. Christmas music drifts throughout the first floor. The thundering of feet overhead tells me the kids are playing in the spare bedroom. Overlapping voices drift through the hallway. The scent of spices lures me deeper into the house.

I pause to hang up my coat, and Cyril follows suit. I catch a grin on his lips as I turn. Ignoring the flutter in the pit of my stomach, I tighten my grip on the bag in my hand—gifts for my nieces and nephews. I never greet them empty-handed, even if it's only their favorite chocolate.

When I peer around the corner, I spy my brother and brother-in-law sitting on the couch. Dad sits in his chair opposite. The television is on, playing *It's a Wonderful Life*. A small Christmas tree glitters in the corner by the front window.

"Hi, Dad."

"Jess. I didn't hear you come in." He shifts forward, scrambling from his chair to stand. He hugs me, smiling when he sees Cyril. "Glad you both could make it."

"Thank you, sir." Cyril shakes his hand firmly.

My brother, Matthew, stands, as does Steve. They hug me and shake hands with Cyril after Dad introduces him.

"I'm gonna go help Mom in the kitchen."

"Sandra and April are in there already," Matthew says with a smirk. "They're cursing your name."

"Of course they are." I hand him the bag for the kids. "Put this under the tree."

When I reach the kitchen, Mom's laughter is filling the air. "There you are," she says when she spies me in the doorway. "Good. You're just in time to finish these pies."

I greet everyone with hugs and kisses.

"Where's Cyril?" Mom asks.

"He's with the boys in the living room."

"Who's Cyril?" My sister spins, spatula in hand.

"No one, Sandy."

"Wait…he's the guy Mom was telling us about. The time traveler." She sets the utensil aside and wipes her hands on her apron. "I need to see this guy."

"Me too." April follows her out the door.

I hang my head and start rolling out pie crust. Their questions will come in a flurry, and nothing will stop their curiosity.

Mom sets some pie pans down beside me and pats my arm. "Are you okay?"

"I'm fine." Forcing a smile, I meet her concerned gaze.

She squints like she doesn't believe me but sighs and waves her hand. "Your father had the house in a state this morning. Jimmy and Nate…" She chatters on about her two oldest grandchildren and a search for Grandpa's box of treasures.

Grateful for the distraction, I listen and work. Dad keeps a special box of mementos hidden in the house, adding to it occasionally with treasures he finds during his travels. The kids love hunting for it every time they come over, hoping something new appears.

The moment April and Sandra return, it's a flurry of questions. I fend them off easily enough, and Mom steps in, telling them to give me some space. I'm thankful for the reprieve, but I know they'll come at me again at some point today.

We fall into a familiar rhythm of making food. Rotating dishes through the oven with the precision of a well-run maintenance shop. By four o'clock, we've picked through the appetizers and drunk a huge bowl of sparkling punch. We set the table for dinner, then sit as a family precisely at five.

Cyril sits beside me, and I can feel my family's eyes on us both as we eat. My nieces and nephews are suspiciously quiet and well-behaved. I wonder if my sister and brother slipped their children chocolate this afternoon, hoping the sugar high would wear them out. I'm pretty sure it was grandma's fruit punch and chocolate chip cookies that pushed them over the edge into sugar coma though.

The meal flows without incident. It's nice to sit comfortably with my family and enjoy their company. I'm fortunate to live close to them all, to see my nieces and nephews growing up, to spend time with Mom and Dad. I'm a lucky woman.

Then there's Cyril. Sitting beside him, I'm reminded just how relaxing his presence is, like a warm blanket on a cold rainy day. Even without speaking, he puts me at ease. I *should* hate it. It's like I'm waiting for the rug to be pulled out from under me, and yet, there's nothing there but calm contentment.

Maybe he was telling me the truth and he just wants me to be happy. No strings attached.

After dinner, we open gifts and help clean up. Cyril and I are the last to leave. It's raining when we step out onto the stoop, and raindrops, splashing into puddles, reflect the streetlights around us.

Mom and Dad wave from the front window, and I smile as I get in the car. I was worried about today, but it ended up perfect.

Well, almost perfect.

Soft Christmas music plays through the speakers, filling the car's interior. I hum along, some of the lyrics slipping free. Cyril drives, his attention fixed on the road, hyperfocused on the conditions. Droplets spatter the windshield. Streetlights glow in the rain, creating halos of red and green light.

When he pulls up in front of the garage, I reach for the opener. He rests his hand on mine, nudging it away. He turns off the car.

The rain pelting the roof of the car and the thundering of my heart fill the silent void. I lick my lips, wondering what's going on inside his head. The neon light above the garage casts a surreal glow over the car. I track rain rivulets across the windshield.

"You really love this place, don't you?" His question startles me.

"I do." I focus on the building, but every ounce of my being is fixated on this man beside me.

"You've done well. Made something special."

I choke up.

"I'm not going to take anything you're not willing to give me, Jess." He takes my hand and turns it palm up. My body tingles, and warmth pools in the pit of my stomach. He places the keys in my palm. "I'll leave as soon as I can find a place."

I blink at him. What the hell is he saying? "You're leaving?"

"You've made it clear you don't want me here. And I won't stay if I make you uncomfortable."

"You don't make me uncomfortable."

I put my hand on his and draw him back. His gaze rests on me. The glass fogs from our warm breath in the cold and rain around us.

"I like having you here."

He threads his hand through my hair and pulls me to him. "Are you sure?" His lips hover over mine.

I'm desperate for him. "Yes. Please."

Then I'm drowning in his kiss beneath the patter of Christmas rain, and the last of my reservations wash away.

CHAPTER 19

Cyrid

Every uncertainty disintegrates under these pliant lips that cursed my existence.

I need her. Crave her. We're steps, moments, away from being upstairs in a warm, welcoming bed, but it's fitting to be here, in her car.

Breaking the kiss, I reach down and pull the lever. The bench seat slides all the way back. She chuckles at the sudden jerk as it locks into place.

Heat reflects in the depths of her blue eyes, drawing me closer, telling me she wants this as much as I do.

With as much grace as I can muster, I slide across the bench. She pivots, allowing me to sit in the passenger seat, and straddles my thighs. I curse the thick fabric hiding her body.

"I'm pretty sure this is illegal." Her heat sinks into me as she peels my coat open.

I push her heavy coat from her shoulders. "Does it matter?"

"No." She finally pulls my coat free and tosses it to the back seat. "But we could go inside."

My body is on fire with every movement. Her hips against mine. Her mouth against my jaw. Her fingers against my stomach as she fumbles to unbuckle the belt.

My hands come to a rest on her hips. I've managed to get her coat off, but if I don't contain the desire vibrating through me, this will be over before it starts.

Once I get her in a bed, I'll explore every inch of her. Right now, I just need to be inside her.

"Something wrong?" she asks, nipping my earlobe with her teeth.

"Not a goddamn thing."

"Then why are you shaking?" She hums, and I close my eyes. "You can touch me."

"It's been a while, Jess." I meet her gaze. "If I touch you, it won't be soft or gentle."

"Who says I want soft or gentle?" She reaches into my pants and strokes my cock.

"Fuck me," I mutter under my breath, and she laughs. "I won't last if you keep this up."

"We've got all night." She kisses me, and I'm lost.

The taste of sweet red wine lingers on her lips. I drink my fill, savoring the way she meets my hunger with her own, tangling her hands in my hair.

Hooking my thumbs into her waistband, I tug her soft leggings down, and she shimmies, maneuvering enough to get them to her ankles. She reaches back to pull them off with her boots, as though she's done this a million times.

My hand glides along her thigh until it brushes her damp panties. I press the fabric to her clit. The scent of her surrounds me. Her taste is still in the forefront of my mind from the night at the motel. I slide my fingers beneath the fabric and coat them in her arousal.

When I bring my finger to my lips, the action drags a moan from deep in her throat.

"You taste so good."

"Damn it, Cyril." Her eyes are dark midnight storms of need. "If you tease me—"

"I'm not going to tease you." I pull my cock out, rub the head across the heat burning between her thighs. "I'm going to fuck you."

"Then stop talking and do it."

She rocks her hips against me. I see stars as the pleasure sparks desperate desire.

"Condom?" I ask.

She shakes her head. "No. I want you like this."

"But—"

"Do you trust me?" She rests her hands on my shoulders. At my nod, she smiles. "Good. Now fuck me like you hate me."

I laugh. Her lips cover mine, swallowing the humor, converting it to pure heat. She nudges the panties aside and lowers herself onto my cock.

The moment her body closes around me, I nearly lose all restraint.

My body trembles at the force it takes not to go deeper. Then she rolls her hips.

I fucking lose it.

Clawing at her back, I grip her tight against me as I drive deep. Over and over, thrust after thrust.

She arches her back, gripping the door for stability. Our heavy breaths steam the windows.

It's only us. This car. This moment.

I love it. Treasure it.

Her hand slips, slides across the foggy glass. I press her hand flat against the window, letting the cold seep through our overlapped fingers. The only outward sign of what's happening inside the car.

She rides me, hard and fast, chasing her pleasure. I release her hand and press my cold fingers against her clit, rubbing slow circles.

Her movements turn frantic. She grips my shirt in her fists.

I barely glimpse the rush of pleasure on her face as her orgasm hits. Her head tips back, eyes closed, lower lip between her teeth, moan vibrating from deep within her.

She's fucking gorgeous.

I give in to my own release. It rushes me in waves until I'm completely spent.

Jessica rests against my chest. "That was a first."

"What do you mean?" I stroke her back with soft rhythmic movements.

"Never had sex in a car before." She leans back and studies my face. "Have you?"

"A few times." The memories refuse to come, but I know I have. Guess it never mattered before. "But never in a '74 Dodge Dart Swinger."

She scoffs and tries to move away. I hold her tighter.

"This is by far the best sex I've had. Let's leave it at that," I murmur.

"I'll agree with that."

We sit in silence for a moment. The rain slows to a gentle patter on the roof of the car.

"Maybe we should go inside."

"Sounds like a good idea. I'm getting a cramp in my calf." She rubs her leg as she climbs off my lap.

After we manage to somewhat cover ourselves, I hit the garage opener button and climb into the driver's seat. She fishes the keys off the floorboard and hands them to me.

After we park the car into the garage and secure the doors, Jessica grabs me by the arm and pulls me to the stairs.

"Ready for round two?"

I chuckle. "We haven't even recovered from round one."

Halfway up the staircase, she glances over her shoulder. "You too old for this?"

"I never said that."

Inside the apartment, she tosses the keys on the counter and spins to face me. Mischief dances in her eyes.

"What?"

"If you'd stayed in 1985, how old would you be right now?" she asks, resting her hands on my hips and pulling me closer.

Mental math was never my strong suit. "Mid-seventies."

"That's a hell of an age gap."

"I doubt you'd want an old man."

"Guess we'll never know." She grabs my ass and squeezes.

I cup her jaw and kiss her. Soft. A tender exploration I neglected when we were in the car. She melts against me.

Methodically, we pull off each other's clothes, a slow reveal of skin as we make our way down the hall. Articles of clothing litter the path we take. Our lips brush, our teeth clash with every tumbling movement.

Somehow, we manage to make it to her bedroom without breaking anything.

Jessica flicks the switch, and a lamp beside the bed comes on. Soft light floods the room. The only thing I see is her, naked, climbing onto the queen-size bed. The teal comforter is plush beneath my hands as I follow her.

She lies down, wrapping her arms around me while I cover her body with mine.

Finally. Skin to skin. She's a perfect complement of curves against me. We're like two puzzle pieces, strewn across different decades. How we found each other still amazes me.

Her kiss lingers between panting gasps as I explore her with my fingertips. She rakes her nails across my back, over my arms, down my hips. When she takes my cock in hand, I'm ready for her.

"Jess," I murmur against her mouth.

"What?" She strokes me twice. My head spins.

"I lo—"

She kisses me, stealing the words from my tongue.

Maybe it's too soon. Not the right moment. But those words linger in my mind. They've never felt more true than they do right now. I love her. Call me crazy, but I can't deny it. Whatever this is, it will always be love to me. Nothing else makes sense.

I wedge myself between her thighs and press into her. It's like coming home. She wraps her arms around me and locks her heels around my legs.

There's no hurry, no desperate need. Just a slow unfurling of pleasure as we move together.

If what we did in the car was fucking, then this is making love.

My hands glide over her smooth skin as I take my time with easy, measured thrusts. She meets me with equal hunger, her hands unable to stay in one place. Our lips explore every inch of flesh we can reach.

I roll her onto her stomach and pull her hips up. When I drive deep, her gasp of pleasure shakes the walls. She pushes back, meeting each movement with resistance. I grab her hips, her breasts, her thighs.

When I sink my teeth into her shoulder, she tightens around my cock.

Doing it again, I find her clit and stroke it, teasing to make her sputter curses.

"Damn you." She pants and grips the comforter.

"Do you want to come?" I ask. She's close. I can feel it.

"Yes."

"Ask me nicely."

Jessica glares at me over her shoulder.

"One word. That's it." I roll my hips, hitting the spot I know she likes because her breath catches every time.

"Please."

My pace quickens, and it doesn't take much to tip her over the edge. When the orgasm rips through her, she screams my name.

I've never heard a sound so goddamn sweet.

I follow her down, my climax tearing through me before she can pull away. She doesn't though.

We settle on the blanket, and she curls against me.

"Thank you," she murmurs into my chest.

"For what?"

"Staying."

I tighten my hold and kiss her head. "Thank you."

"For what?"

"Letting me stay."

She chuckles. "Merry Christmas to us."

CHAPTER 20

Jessica

Waking up next to Cyril on Christmas morning is the best present I never expected.

He curls tight around me, holding me close, burying his face in my hair. His hand cups my breast, kneading it like a kitten making biscuits. I can't tell if he's still asleep or in a weird, half-awake state of consciousness. I rock my hips back against him, and he returns the motion.

The sunlight through the window tells me it's later than I think it is. Not that it matters. I don't have anywhere to be today.

Honestly, there's nowhere else I'd rather be than in bed with Cyril, hungover from multiple orgasms and zero sleep.

It was totally worth it.

"You awake?" I ask softly, afraid to break the spell hovering in the room.

"Mm-hmm." He nuzzles closer and huffs in irritation. "Your hair is a nuisance."

Brushing my curls out of the way, he settles his lips beside my ear and takes the lobe between his teeth. The gentle tug leaves me aching for more.

"How are you still horny?" I chuckle when he grinds his cock against my ass.

"What can I say? It's all you, baby." He kisses my cheek.

"Sure." I wiggle against his hold, but he only tightens his grip and turns me to face him.

Those mesmerizing eyes hold me captive. There's teasing, but also an honesty that leaves me breathless. I cup his cheek.

"I'm sure this wasn't how you expected to spend Christmas," I tease.

"No, but I'm not complaining."

"Is there anything special you want to do today?"

"Aside from lying around naked with you? Nope." A flash of teeth and those matching dimples warm my heart.

"We can't lie around naked all day."

"Why not?" He grips my hip, stroking his thumb over my skin in gentle circles.

"We have to eat. And I don't think it's wise to cook without clothes on. Unhygienic and dangerous to…certain parts of your anatomy." I wrap my hand around his cock.

He sucks in a breath. "You have a point." His groan vibrates through me as I stroke his length. "What do you want from me?"

"Is that a rhetorical question?" I bite back a grin when he moans.

"I guess. Maybe. I don't know. It's hard to think when you're playing with my dick like that."

"Want me to stop?"

"Fuck no." He sighs. "But I'm gonna need food if you want to keep tormenting me."

I release him. "Let's go make something to eat."

He dramatically flops back on the bed when I climb out of reach. "Fine. You win."

Cyril watches me as I pull on some Snoopy Christmas pajama bottoms and a warm long-sleeved shirt.

"You covered all the good stuff."

"Exactly. Less distraction for you." I laugh and head for the bathroom.

Once I've taken care of the most demanding necessities, I return to find the bed empty. He's not in the bathroom or his bedroom. I venture further down the hall, following sounds of movement in the kitchen—the clinking of pots and pans, the slamming of cabinet doors. What in the world?

I round the corner to find Cyril wearing gray sweatpants and a dark blue short-sleeved shirt. He's got a carton of eggs in one hand.

"How do you feel about French toast?"

"I love it."

"Good." He beams as he sets the eggs next to a glass bowl. "Where's the cinnamon?"

I slide past him, resting my hand on his shoulder, and reach for the cabinet behind him. His gaze follows me as I retrieve the spice and put it next to the eggs.

"Do you want help?" I ask, leaning against the counter.

"I won't say no to a sexy companion in the kitchen." He lifts the fork and points it at me. "But no fondling while I work."

I lift my hands and smile. "I can't promise anything."

"You're saying we can't work together without you wanting to touch this?" He runs his fingers down his chest.

"I guess not."

He chuckles and cracks the first egg. "I thought so."

"At least let me put on some music." I turn toward the living room. "Alexa, play my Christmas playlist."

Cyril shakes his head when music fills the room. "That machine is witchcraft. I love it." He leans close and whispers, "Do you think she listens to *everything*?"

"Probably." I bite my lip to keep from laughing. I wonder if she did hear everything we did last night. Weird thoughts form in my mind…what would an AI do with that information? I shove the thought aside and focus on Cyril as he whisks the eggs and milk together.

I grab bread from the pantry and open the bag.

"The pan is hot. Go ahead and make the first couple. I'm gonna run to the bathroom."

"Okay." I turn when he heads for the hall. "Hey, can you grab my phone from the bedroom while you're back there?"

"No problem."

Alone with Christmas music and the sound of sizzling French toast, I relax. This is nice…whatever *this* is. I chew on my lip. What is this? Better question is, what do I *want* it to be?

My short marriage ended in flames, and my relationships after that weren't fantastic either. I'm not interested in diving into something else. Relationships didn't work in the past, why would one magically work with Cyril?

Because he's not like them. He's different.

That's what they all say.

Relationships are complicated…messy. I've finally got my life where I want it. Focused on me and my shop. Nothing else matters.

And yet, here we are.

I flip the toast as they reach the perfect golden-brown crisp. That's when my brain does a one-eighty.

What if Cyril is different? What if he's what I need to get this business to where it should be? What if he's exactly *the man* I need? Not just as a business partner, but as a romantic partner? I've never before had a connection this strong with anyone in any capacity. It's strange and wonderful…and absolutely terrifying.

I don't want to take a huge leap of faith only to land in a big pile of shitty disappointment. Damn it. I'm fucked either way. It's too late to turn back now.

After taking the crispy pieces of toast off the pan, I dip more bread in the egg mixture and start the process over again. Lost in my thoughts, I weigh my options.

Just ask Cyril. Talk to him.

It sounds so simple, and yet how the fuck do I bring this up without sounding like an absolute asshole?

Tell him how you feel.

And then watch him walk away.

The words linger in my mind longer than they should. When Cyril appears, bearing my phone in hand, I straighten and shake the uncertainty from my thoughts.

"Thanks." I take the phone and tuck it into my pocket.

"Your dad called. I answered it. He said he only had a minute but wanted to wish us a Merry Christmas."

"Oh. Yeah. He's taking Mom out for a special brunch today." I smile even though nerves twist in my stomach. "Did he say anything else?"

Like did he say anything about you answering my phone? Or ask if we finally hooked up? Just the thought of my father piecing it all together leaves me uncomfortable. I love my parents, but they don't need the details of my sex life.

"He said he'll call back later." Cyril takes the spatula from my hand and nudges me to the side. "These look great. Maybe I should let you finish cooking. I always burn them."

I take the spatula back and push him out of the way. "I'll finish this part. Why don't you get syrup and butter from the fridge?"

"Yes, ma'am."

His response leaves butterflies in the pit of my stomach. I watch him out of the corner of my eye as he works. I like this.

I like *him*. A lot.

Okay, more than a lot.

Fuck. Do I love him?

The question doesn't scare me like it would have a few months ago. What the hell is going on?

"Where are the plates?"

I point to the cabinet with the dishes.

"Cyril?" I ask, my voice hesitant.

"Yes?"

I bolster my courage and push on. "After last night, what's the plan?" I sigh. "What do we tell my parents?"

He pauses, his arms raised halfway to the shelf. "I haven't really thought about it."

"What do you want out of this? From us?"

He removes two plates and closes the cabinet before turning to face me. "I guess that depends."

"On?"

"On what you want." He steps closer, and his presence makes my body light up like a dashboard of error codes on the fritz.

"That's the problem. All my previous relationships, I thought I knew what I wanted, but I was wrong. I don't know if I can trust what my brain says I want."

"Then we take it slow. Double down on the partnership with the shop. Let it run its course, see where it leads in six months. Sound fair?"

"Yeah, it does. And this?" I rest my hand on his chest and meet his smoldering gaze. "Can we keep this part?"

"The roommates-who-fuck part?"

"Yes." I lick my lips. "Or am I asking too much?"

His sigh vibrates through me.

"I won't lie. I'm already half in love with you. Might break my heart in the end, but I'll agree to it, if that's what you want."

I can't tell if his tone is serious or teasing. His expression is guarded, but there's a mix of humor and honesty there.

"I don't want to make it awkward." I drop my hand. "We don't have to…"

"No, it's fine. We're beyond awkward at this point." He picks up the plates, one in each hand. "Can we eat now? I'm starving."

With a laugh, I put three pieces of toast on each plate and turn off the stove. We sit at my small table and enjoy lighter conversation as we eat. Even with the heaviness of unanswered questions between us, there's comfortable companionship.

After breakfast, he helps me clean up and we retreat to the living room. I retrieve a small package from under the tree and place it in his lap.

"I got you a present."

He stares at it in awe. "You didn't have to do that."

"I did. Open it."

When he unwraps the present, he laughs while he removes a familiar box with an Apple logo.

"You bought me a handheld computer-phone thingy."

"Close enough." I point to it when he pulls the phone out of the box. "It's already set up, and I've programmed our numbers into it. Everyone you know is in there."

His eyes glint with unshed tears. "Thank you."

When he presses the home button, he laughs at the image that pops on the screen. A rugged close up of old-school Han Solo. He holds the phone up and points to it. "Really?"

"It's your favorite series, and you told me how hot Han was." I sigh. "Harrison Ford is absolutely Daddy material."

Cyril chokes and bursts into laughter. "Oh God. No."

"What? Don't like me calling an older man who's not my father *Daddy*?" I jab him in the ribs.

"No."

"Should I call you *Daddy*?" I nudge him again.

"Absolutely not."

"Fine." I huff and reach for the remote. "But now you've asked for it."

"Asked for what?" He narrows his eyes.

"I'm going to introduce you to the Daddy of them all."

"Please no." But his curiosity gets the better of him. "Who are you talking about now?"

"Bruce Willis." My heart goes a little wobbly. "I've had a crush on him since I was twelve."

"The guy from *Moonlighting*?" Cyril scrunches his nose up. "And that's a highly inappropriate age difference. Twelve? Seriously?" He shivers. "Why were you drooling over older men at twelve?"

The pointed look I spear him with shuts him up immediately. "Considering the age gap between *us*, I wouldn't talk. I wasn't even *born* until 1990."

"Point taken." He gestures to the TV. "As long as you don't refer to him as *Daddy*, I think I can handle whatever you have to show me. What is it?"

"Only the best Christmas movie ever!" I turn on the TV and find *Die Hard* on one of the many streaming services I subscribe to.

"Wait? This is a Christmas movie?" He balks when he sees the movie poster on the screen. "This looks like an action flick. *Rambo* or something."

"Oh, it's something. That's for sure." I snuggle close to him, pulling the blanket over both our laps. "You're gonna love it."

I press play and bask in the comfort of a film I've seen a hundred times, mindful of the fact that Cyril has never seen it.

That doesn't stop me from grazing my hand over his cock.

Or slipping it free and taking it in my mouth.

His hand tightens in my hair as he watches the movie, his body responding to each stroke of my hand, of my tongue.

"Fuck." His breath hitches as McClane reaches the Christmas party.

Redoubling my efforts, I tip him over the edge and swallow every drop.

"Goddamn." He takes a minute to recover his breath. "That was amazing."

"The movie isn't over yet." I refocus on the pristine white tank top-wearing cop and grin. "We're just getting started."

Yippee ki yay, and Merry Christmas to us.

CHAPTER 21

Cyrid

The past two days have made the loss of thirty-seven years worth every stolen moment.

Jessica and I have reached a truce. Gone is the hesitancy, the uncertainty between us, replaced by something fragile and priceless. Over the course of Christmas and the following day, our tenuous relationship is transformed.

We spent most of the time in bed between movies and meals. I've never been so content in my life. She slowly revealed bits of herself between orgasms and laughter.

If I weren't already head over heels for her, I certainly am now. It solidifies the decision I made Christmas morning when I woke in her arms. I nearly told her, but there's no reason to rush. We have time.

Pulled from our domestic bliss, we finally relent to the demands of reality on the morning of the twenty-seventh. Marcy's party. Arthur called at seven a.m. to remind us to be at the bar by noon to decorate.

He didn't know was I was already awake with my head buried between his daughter's thighs. I mean, he *did* throw us together so we could come to an agreement. He might not have meant romantically, but part of me believes he hoped this would happen. Forcing two people to spend time together is a surefire way to ignite sparks already flying between them.

Outside the Black Penny, Jessica parks the Ford and pops the hatch. My gaze drifts over the familiar brick building. It looks mostly the same. The only difference is the neon lights have been replaced by a brighter, bolder sign hanging over the door.

"Carry this in." She places a box in my arms.

Stunned, I follow her into the bar. The lights are up, brighter than usual. I chuckle when I look around. The inside hasn't changed.

Well, the jukebox has been replaced with a digital replica. The floors have been refinished, as well as the bar. But otherwise, time hasn't touched the Black Penny. I'm grateful. It's like a little piece of home.

"Jess!" a woman shouts from behind the bar.

"Jackie!" Jessica slides her bags onto the nearest table. "God, it's been forever."

"It has." The woman rounds the bar, her short hair brushing the top of her shoulders. "How have you been?"

I watch as the two women embrace and fall into conversation. Hanging back, I listen, only taking in bits of information. Rob and Arthur said Claude's daughter runs the Penny now. Is this her?

Judging from the balance of her curves and height, her dark hair, bright blue eyes, and a healthy sprinkle of beauty marks across her skin, I'd say she's a perfect blend of Claude and Gwen. She's a knockout, but I'm distracted by Jess's laughter. Something in my chest does a little flip when I catch her glancing at me.

I smile.

"Who's this?" Jackie asks, turning to me.

"Cyril?" A deep voice echoes from the back of the room.

We all turn to find a small group slowly spilling into the bar. As with every reunion so far, my heart breaks to see the passage of time etched in every gray hair and wrinkle on those familiar faces.

Claude and his brother Grant step closer. Gwen and Quinn stand to the side, whispering to each other.

"Surprise." It's the only word I manage to say past the emotion choking me. I worried they were gone and I would never see them again. While this isn't the reunion I imagined, I embrace it.

"We thought you were dead," Grant says, shoving his hand into mine and shaking it before pulling me in to clap me on the back.

He releases me, and Claude mimics the action. "When Arthur told us, we couldn't believe it."

"Well, now you can see for yourself." I clear my throat when Gwen and Quinn shove their husbands aside and rush to embrace me.

I grin at their overlapping chatter. I missed them. All of them. I address their questions one at a time until I'm breathless.

"It's almost one." Jessica appears at my side and elbows me in the ribs. "Dad will be here soon. We need to finish setting up. Uncle Rob and Aunt Marcy will be here at two."

Everyone bursts into a flurry of activity. Claude and Grant help me hang streamers while Quinn and Gwen give Jackie a hand with the food. Jessica sets the tables, placing a favor on each plate. Uncle Rob had them made especially for her birthday.

As I work, I'm drawn to her. She lights up the room like sunshine on a summer day. I can't soak up enough of her energy.

Claude smiles when he catches me staring, but he doesn't say anything.

We've nearly finished when Arthur and Kate arrive. Jessica helps her mother retrieve a few more items from the car before offering to move it so it won't spoil the surprise.

I kiss Kate on the cheek, and Arthur nods a greeting. When his wife wanders off, he pulls me to a small nook beside the bar, out of earshot.

"Are you sure about this?"

"Absolutely." Confidence bolsters my tone.

"Okay." He hands me a sealed envelope. "It's all yours."

"Thanks, Arthur."

I look up when the door swings open and Jess steps inside. She's grinning. I suck in a breath.

"You're in love with my little girl." Arthur's quiet observation echoes between us. It's not a question. "I didn't think it would work, but I'm glad it did."

"You set us up?" I spin to face him.

"Of course I did." He claps his hand on my shoulder. "All those years I trusted you as my driver, my right-hand man. How could I not see the advantages of you officially joining my family?"

"Let's not jump the gun, Arthur." I scoff. "This is all new. It might not work out."

"It'll work out." He winks. "Trust me."

"I don't know. She gets a stubborn streak from her old man."

His laughter draws the attention of everyone in the room. I nearly hide my face, hoping they have no idea what we're discussing.

"It doesn't matter." Arthur waves his hand. "I know you'll treat her right, regardless of what happens down the road."

"Always, Arthur." I tuck the envelope into my sports jacket pocket.

"Grandpa!" A little girl shouts from the doorway and rushes Arthur for a bear hug.

Over the next thirty minutes, the bar fills with people. Kids. Grandkids. Friends, old and new. I'm surrounded by people and caught up in a flurry of introductions. I'm not sure I'll keep everyone's names straight, but I can't stop a grin from consuming my face. It's amazing, being swallowed alive by the love of family and friends, gathered to celebrate.

"They'll be here any minute!" Kate shouts, and the room falls quiet, except for the faint music playing over the speakers. "Positions."

Arthur comes beside Kate, Grant takes Quinn's hand, and Claude wraps his arm around Gwen's shoulders, pulling her to his side. These people—couples I admired and supported, standing as a unified front of strength and love—leave me speechless and a bit emotional. I clear my throat and look at the floor, willing myself to keep it together. This isn't about me or my miraculous return. I embrace this for the gift it is.

My found family reunited once more. Nothing could make me happier.

A warm hand takes mine. I look up to find Jessica beside me. Her fingers interlace with mine. I hold her deep blue gaze, and the air rushes from my lungs. This is what I'm here for. This is what I need.

Her.

That smile shatters my last thread of resolve.

"Jessica," I whisper. "I—"

The door swings open, and a chorused shout echoes through the bar. "Surprise! Happy birthday, Marcy!"

Jessica turns to greet her aunt, pulling me with her. My heart pounds in my chest at the gesture. She's claiming me. Showing them all there's something here. It gives me hope. A small spark. A tiny victory worth savoring.

Maybe she wants more. Wants me.

Marcy wraps me in a tight hug and showers my face with kisses. I'm pretty sure I have mauve lipstick all over my face, but I don't care. It feels great to be welcomed with open arms.

I shake Rob's hand, and he winks knowingly when Jessica comes beside me and rests her hand on my arm.

It's only natural when I wrap my arm around her waist, draw her to my side, and kiss her head.

Jessica spins and our eyes lock. She chuckles and shakes her head.

"What? You can't tell me they don't already know." I laugh.

She squeezes my hand. "You're right, but now we're the talk of the party."

I scan the crowd. No one's even looking at us. "I doubt that."

"The night is still young." Jessica cups my face in her hands and kisses me soundly.

With a groan, I pull her close and ensure she's thoroughly kissed. When we break apart, there's a smattering of applause in the background.

"Mission accomplished," she says with a breathy laugh.

Ignoring a pressing desire to take her home, party be damned, I pull away. “Come on. Let’s mingle.”

She drags me through the crowd, and Jackie hands us each a drink.

The envelope burns a hole in my chest, next to my thundering heart. I hope I don’t fuck this up.

CHAPTER 22

Jessica

Is this as good as it gets?

The thought strikes me as Cyril holds me close, swaying to the music. I balked at first when he took my hand and pulled me to him, but Bryan Adams's tantalizing lyrics are enough to make any hard-hearted girl swoon. I can still remember the first time I heard this song, long before I watched *Robin Hood: Prince of Thieves.*

Tonight, the lyrics hit differently. The tempo lulls me into a peace I haven't felt in years…but that could just be Cyril's presence. Heat builds between us with every rocking sway. I inhale deeply, memorizing the scent of spicy aftershave mixed with his unique aroma.

The clock on the wall reads eight fifteen. Everyone over the age of fifty has departed along with those with children. There are only a handful of us lingering at the Black Penny. Jaqueline hangs out behind the bar, indulging us because we're family, and a reunion like this doesn't happen often.

In the chaos, I forgot to ask her about the progress of her divorce. I can always text her later. Tonight isn't for that conversation.

Cyril's hand tightens on my hip.

I glance up at him, only to find him staring off into space.

"Penny for your thoughts?" I ask, curiosity nibbling at my conscience.

He startles and meets my gaze. "Just thinking."

"What about?"

"You." His dimpled smile makes my insides flip.

"What about me?"

He inhales, like he's bracing to go underwater. When he exhales, it *whooshes* out of him in a rush. "I was thinking, I like this…us."

"Me too." I link my fingers together behind his neck, drawing him closer. "I can't believe it's only been a week since you showed up in my shop."

"Feels like a lifetime." His confession resonates deep inside me, a long-forgotten melody.

"It does." My heart flutters as he shifts his grip, his fingers trailing over my sides.

"I'm sorry if it's been a lot of change in a short period of time." He licks his lips, and the movement leaves me distracted with wicked thoughts. "I never meant to come in and mess everything up."

"Sometimes, change is a good thing, although it might not feel like it at the time. You didn't mess anything up."

"You said I did."

"I said a lot of things those first few days." Regret fills me. "I'm sorry about that. It wasn't very helpful. I should have been more understanding of your situation."

"You don't have to apologize. I understand. If I were in your position, I'd have been pissed off too."

A laugh escapes me, lightening the tension. "Still, it couldn't have been easy, dropping four decades into the future without knowing what the hell was going on."

"It wasn't." He spins me with a little flourish. "But I was lucky. I found you."

"When you found me, I wasn't very nice or helpful. How is that lucky?"

"It was exactly what I needed at that moment. So thank you."

My face warms under his scrutiny. I lean my head against his shoulder as the song changes to REO Speedwagon's "Keep on Lovin' You." Mom always called these songs *classic rock* when we were kids. I didn't understand why until I was older. Until I learned the truth of her and Dad's first meeting.

Now I'm living my own surreal whirlwind romance, just like Mom and Dad did. I should be terrified of what this means, but there's no trace of hesitation or fear in my brain.

I close my eyes. This is comfortable. Safe. *Home.*

My final reservation leaves, and I embrace this for what it is. A miracle. Fate. Destiny.

"I love you, Jessica."

The soft words drift over me, a warm blanket settling around my shoulders. Then they take root in my mind.

"What did you say?" I pull back without breaking his hold.

"I love you." He braces like he's unsure of how I'll react.

A week ago, I would have called him crazy, but tonight, right now…his words unlock nothing but certainty.

I cling tighter to him, and his apprehension softens.

"I love you too."

"Really?" Joy blooms across his features, making him look ten years younger. "You sure?"

"Even though events of the past week make no sense, and your presence in this decade defies the laws of time and space, I've never been more sure of anything in my life."

He crushes me against him and kisses me. The taste of him ignites my ever present hunger. I'm tempted to cross Jackie and climb on top of him right here in the middle of her bar. But I manage to contain my desire, salvaging my relationship with the friend eyeing us suspiciously from behind the counter.

When he breaks the kiss, we cling to each other in a desperate attempt to regain our bearings. He presses a gentle kiss to my forehead before stepping away.

"Let's play darts."

I shake myself. The haze of lust slowly recedes, and I stare at him. "Darts?"

"Yeah. Do you know how to play?"

"Of course," I scoff.

"Then let's play." He moves to the rear of the bar where a dartboard hangs on the wall.

"What do I get if I win?" I ask, grabbing the darts.

"So confident." He laughs. "One of the reasons I love you. Set the terms."

"The garage."

His brow rises. "What about it?"

"If you win, it's yours. If I win, it's mine."

He rubs his jaw and groans.

"Too rich for your blood?" I tease. It's not like I'll hold him to these terms, but I'm curious. What will he do?

"Not at all." He takes off his jacket and drapes it over a chair. "I just don't want to upset you when I take it from you."

"Now who's being cocky?" I laugh and roll up my sleeves.

"Fine. It's a bet." He extends his hand; I shake it.

A thrill rolls through me at the impending challenge. I have the upper hand. When I was in college, I was unbeatable at darts. There's no way Cyril knows this. No way in hell.

He offers me the floor first. I throw. Bullseye. Fifteen. Ten.

Cyril nods before taking his turn. Six. Twenty. Bullseye.

"Jackie, keep score for us," I shout as Cyril tries to use the scorekeeper. "I want to make sure this is legit."

"You got it." Jackie rounds the bar and sits off to the side with a pad and pen.

Back and forth we go. By the third round, we've gathered a small crowd. Most of them cheer for me, but there are a few for Cyril. Jackie keeps score, meticulously counting and writing down every point.

The last round begins, and Cyril makes his final throws. It's close. So close.

Chatter flows through the crowd, and the noise hums in my head.

"Last chance, Jess." Jackie's announcement hushes the crowd. "Cyril's up by fifteen. One bullseye and you win."

I can't blow this.

Or can I?

Does it matter?

Cyril loves me. Would he really take my dream when he knows how much it means to me?

I take a deep breath and throw.

Bullseye.

Holy shit! I did it.

The crowd erupts into applause around us. I'm barraged with congratulations and celebratory hugs. By the time they all disperse, I'm drunk with relief.

Cyril closes the gap between us. "Good game." He pulls me into a hug. "The garage is yours."

I bury my face in his shoulder. "It doesn't matter. It's just a game."

He draws back and reaches for his jacket. "No. A deal's a deal."

"I…"

My voice trails off when he reaches into his pocket and pulls out an envelope. He hands it to me.

"What's this?"

"Open it." He bites his lower lip, letting it slide between his teeth.

I open the barely sealed envelope and pull out the papers inside. Skimming the contents, I freeze.

Deed. Jessica Maxwell.

Wait. It can't be.

"What is this?"

"The deed to the building." Cyril grins, shoving his hands in his pockets.

"How did you convince Dad to…"

My eyes widen when the realization strikes me. "Dad never owned the building, did he?" I stumble back and collapse into a chair.

Cyril inclines his head. "Technically, he did, but I was on the deed too."

"So all this time, *you* were the owner of Cyril's Garage?" Disbelief rips through me.

"That's what Arthur tells me." He takes the seat beside me. "He bought the building with the intent to give it to me after I got the business established. When I disappeared, he held onto it, always making sure my name was on the deed."

A sob chokes me as I stare at the paper in my hand. "Then why are you giving me this?"

"The garage wouldn't be what it is today without you." He takes my free hand. "It was your blood, sweat, and tears that made the garage so successful. I could never take that accomplishment away from you."

Tears slide down my face, and I swipe them away with the back of my hand, careful not to get the paper wet. He understands. My tears flow harder at the realization.

Cyril takes the deed and sets it aside. Then he gathers me, pulling me into a firm embrace. I wrap my arms around his chest. My soft sobs are lost in the fabric of his shirt and the warm skin beneath it. When I finally compose myself, I step back, just enough to face him.

"Thank you." They're the only words I can manage. Everything else is lost.

"Don't thank me." Those dimples flash again. "I fully intend to take advantage of the next six months. There's no way in hell I'm letting you go now."

My brows furrow. "Six months?"

"Our agreement. A partnership for six months. To see what happens between us. Remember?"

Heat radiates through me at the reminder. "Yeah."

His soft kiss leaves me wanting more.

"Let's go home and celebrate." The whispered words ignite an inferno deep inside me.

I nod, and we say our goodbyes. I let him drive home, not trusting myself behind the wheel. When I get him alone, all bets are off.

He's mine. It thrills me more than my name on the deed in my pocket.

CHAPTER 23

Cyril

Her face was priceless.

The moment she opened the envelope and recognized her name on the deed, my heart stopped beating. I was afraid I'd overplayed my hand.

When I answered Arthur's phone call on Christmas morning, I told him I didn't want the shop and asked him to put the deed in her name. Two days of patience led me to the perfect setup. Our little game of darts set the stage. It was always my intention to give her the shop, the business, the whole shebang.

It takes all my effort to focus on the road and not the woman in the passenger seat. I make a right, and the glow of the shop's sign comes into view.

The garage was hers, regardless of her win. It was never mine, even if Arthur had my name on the paperwork. It wasn't *my* effort, *my* life poured into making the business a success. Jessica did that. And her happiness is all that matters. Period.

She reaches over and presses the garage opener clipped to the sun visor. The sweet, heady scent of her soap weaves into my brain, causing a short circuit. My grip tightens on the steering wheel.

I pull into the garage and turn off the ignition. The door lowers behind us.

When I get out of the car, I take in the shop around us. Her influence is everywhere, from the decorative tin images along the upper part of the walls to the meticulous organization of the tools. Jessica deserves this. All of it.

If that means I take orders from her as we move forward, so be it. I'd rather run the business with her than have her fear the fate of her investment. To me, it's a double win. She gets the security of knowing it's hers to do with as she pleases while knowing I value her hard work and determination.

This place doesn't need me. It needs *her*. She's the lifeblood. The reason for its existence.

"You coming?" she asks from the doorway to the upstairs apartment.

"Yeah." I tap the front end of the Swinger as I walk by, like a good luck charm, and turn off the lights when I reach the door.

She's at the top of the stairs when I finally catch up to her. "Key?" Her hand sits palm up.

I lift her hand to my lips and press a kiss to her palm. She bites her lip, eyes darkening at the simple action. I place the keys in her hand.

Jessica fumbles with the lock for a few seconds until it finally clicks open. The moment we're inside, she spins around and pins me against the wall beside the door. Her hands hold firm against my chest. Her eyes the color of a midday summer storm.

"Before this goes any further, I need to know something." Her husky voice creates goosebumps along my skin.

"What's that?"

"Did you throw the game?"

I laugh. "What?"

"Did you let me win at darts?"

"Do you think I'm capable of that?" I study her face closely, noting the way her lip twitches and her nostrils flare when she's worked up. It's fucking adorable.

"I don't know what you're capable of, Cyril."

"You sure about that?" I tease my fingers under the hem of her shirt, finding her warm soft skin, stroking gently.

"Just tell me the truth."

"Why does it matter?" My fingers drift higher until they brush the delicate curve of her breast. I want my mouth there, but she won't relent. Not until she has her answer.

"You had the deed before we played, but there's no way you knew I could win." She steps closer, licking her lips and pushing her body into mine. "You threw the game so you could give me that deed."

Every delicious curve molds against me, and I'm desperate to be inside her. "If I tell you the truth, will you let me fuck you?"

"You're getting fucked either way."

A smirk steals onto her full lips. I imagine them wrapped around my cock like Christmas morning and groan.

"You're not giving me any incentive, love."

"That wasn't my intention." She trails her hand over my stomach and cups my erection through the material pulled tight over it.

"You're killing me."

"Did you throw the game?" She squeezes gently, increasing the pressure with each word.

"No." I gasp, unable to take it any longer. "I didn't throw the game."

My body nearly gives out when she releases her hold and steps back.

With a sultry glance over her shoulder, she pulls off her jacket and ventures into the living room, where she drops it to the floor. Then she pulls off her glittery top followed by her black lace bra. When they hit the floor, I push away from the wall and stumble after her.

My clothes follow, joining hers on the floor in a trail to the couch.

We're both naked, standing in the middle of the living room. I wrap my arms around her waist and pull her against me. My hand slides between her thighs.

"Shit. You're so wet."

She nods.

"For me?" I nip at her shoulder.

"Yes." Her gasp breaks on a moan when I bite harder and slide my fingers inside her.

"Can I play with your pussy?"

"Why does that sound hot when you say it?"

"Is that a yes?"

"Yes." She spins and pushes me down to the sofa.

I grab her wrist and pull her across my lap.

"Alexa, play the Cars." I grin at Jessica's startled reaction. "Moving In Stereo" drifts through the speakers.

"How did you…?"

"Shh." Her question dissipates when I part her thighs and stroke along her seam. "The only words I want to hear from your lips right now are *yes*, *please*, and *more*."

"Confident, are you?"

I press my thumb against her clit. She bucks her hips, arching her back.

"Damn it, Cyril." Her moan echoes through the room, harmonizing with the music.

With two fingers, I delve deep while my thumb works its magic. She writhes beneath my hand, and I use the other to gently squeeze her nipple. Her body hums as I stroke her higher and higher. Her desperation for release has my cock twitching, wanting to be included.

Jessica's cries echo off the walls when she comes. It hits her hard and fast, and I wring every last shuddering wave of pleasure from her body before I relent.

I gather her in my arms, cradle her to my chest. Her body trembles against me, still sensitive from her orgasm. After a few moments, she shifts to straddle my thighs. Her slick pussy rubs against my cock.

My body tenses as she slides down my hard length. I take several deep breaths once she's taken all of me. It's like Christmas Eve, when we fucked in the car. Only this time, there's no limit in any capacity. No physical restraints, no emotional barriers.

It's just us. Partners. Lovers. Friends. Nothing could be more perfect.

"Mine." I tighten my grip on her hips.

"Mine." She links her arms around my neck.

My restraint snaps, and I thrust up into her. She meets my motion with her own, rocking her hips in time with the music as the song switches to "Just What I Needed."

Delirious with want for her, I lose myself in the moment, taking every stroke and returning it with fervor. She clings to me and uses my shoulders as leverage to drive me deeper.

Her head tips back, her hair trailing down her spine. I wrap my hand in her curls, tighten the hair around my fist, and pull. She hisses and swears, but her pussy pulses around me as another orgasm builds.

"That's it, baby." I push her closer, letting her grind her hips into mine. The friction builds, and she flutters around my cock. Close. So damn close.

I kiss her hard, swallow her panting moans. My own release builds, but I want her there, spilling over the edge when I come.

She rips free and digs her nails into my shoulders when her climax finally hits. Her pace slows with the force of it, draining her.

I push her down onto the couch and fuck her into the cushions. Her pleasure-dazed eyes stare up at me, her lips parted. With every thrust, she grins wider, urging me on with soft moans, digging her nails into my ass.

When I come, she looks happy. A woman utterly sated with pleasure.

"Stay here." I climb off the couch and retreat to the bathroom. When I return with a warm cloth, I clean her, then myself before rejoining her on the couch. She snuggles against me, pulling a blanket over us.

"Shall we go to bed?" Her fingertips drift over my bare chest.

"I was hoping we could sit like this for a little while." I kiss her forehead.

"Okay." She turns her head. "Alexa, turn off music."

The music stops, and she reaches for the remote.

"What are you doing?"

"Turning something on." She presses the power button and finds the Disney app.

"Like what?"

"You'll see." Jessica scans through the selections until a title pops up on the screen.

"*The Force Awakens*?"

"Yeah."

I laugh. "I thought you didn't like *Star Wars*?"

"No, I said I've never *seen Star Wars*. There's a difference." She hits play.

"Maybe we should start with *A New Hope*."

"It doesn't matter. I'm sure you'll make me watch all of them multiple times."

I wrap my arm around her and pull her closer. "Have I told you before how much I love you?"

"Yes, but tell me again. It's been a while."

"I love you." The words spill out through laughter.

"Good, because I love you too." She props her feet on my legs beneath the blanket.

The movie starts, and I'm sucked into the story.

Later that night, as we're lying in bed, amid thoughts of betrayal and red light sabers, dreams of us take root in my mind. Possibilities and hope. The cogs click into place.

Being here, now, won't be easy, but I'll adapt and learn, especially with Jessica beside me. When she's ready, I'll ask the question slowly consuming my mind.

I'm not in a rush. I have a whole life ahead of me. Having Jessica in it will be the gilded trim on the sports car. She needs this time as much as I do to figure out what she wants.

I'm a patient man. I can wait. Victory will be that much sweeter.

Until then, I'm content. Truly.

CHAPTER 24

Jessica

Six Months Later

I pull up to the curb down the street from Mom and Dad's brownstone, basking in relief at finding some prime parking, and turn off the ignition.

Cyril casts a dimpled grin in my direction before getting out of the car.

"What?" I ask, climbing out of the driver's seat.

"Nothing." He closes the door and turns away from me.

The summer sunshine beams down, and I let it soak into my skin. I can't believe it's been six months since I first brought him here. A total stranger who upended my life for the better.

Since we joined forces, Cyril's Car Services has expanded to three locations across five boroughs, with plans for three more in the works. Between the two of us, we've made a name for the shop. His old-school ideas mixed with my new school technology. We rebranded Cyril's and cultivated a whole new clientele.

The two of us make a banging team.

Pun intended.

He takes my arm and nudges me. "What are you laughing about?"

"Nothing." I throw his response back in his face, and he scoffs. "Hey, what's good for the goose is good for the gander."

"Smart-ass."

We climb the stairs and knock before entering the house. My siblings have already arrived with their children. The younger ones gather around Cyril, begging him to play with them in the garden. He kisses my cheek and bounds behind them, heading for the narrow green space my parents have cultivated in the heart of the city.

"There you are." Mom wipes her hands on her apron when I enter the kitchen. She searches the hallway behind me when I come in alone. "Where's Cyril?"

"The kids dragged him to the backyard."

"Dad's out there. He'll make sure they behave." My sister winks and finishes prepping the sandwiches.

"So." Mom's voice lowers. "When are you two going to make it official?"

"Mom, you can't rush these things." I roll my eyes.

I love Cyril dearly, and I can't imagine my life without him. We've got a good thing going. Our partnership is blossoming, and so is our sex life. I'm content with what we have. It's comfortable. No pressure. Well, except from Mom and Dad, who claim they're not getting any younger. Like it really impacts them. Cyril and I are happy together, and that's fine with me. For now.

Mom huffs and tries to lift the tray of sandwiches.

"Let me get it." I shoo her away and pick up the over-burdened tray. "You shouldn't be carrying this heavy stuff anymore. Doctor's orders."

"As if." Mom waves her hand dismissively, but she leads the way, letting me carry the food to the backyard.

"Need help?" Cyril stands when I step onto the back patio.

"Sure." I gesture toward Mom with my elbow.

Ever the gentleman, he takes her arm and leads her to a chair beside Dad. I set the tray on the table. He follows me to the kitchen to help carry out the last of the food.

"I forgot the wine. It's in the car."

"I'll get it." Cyril offers, holding out his hand for the key.

"Thanks, babe." I kiss his cheek before he darts back inside.

"So when's the wedding?" Dad asks with a smirk.

"Why's everyone in such a hurry?"

"What? I can't want to see my daughter happily married before I die?" he grumbles.

"You're not going to die for another twenty years. At least. Hush." I make him a plate with two sandwiches.

The kids run around the small open space behind us. Their parents have set up a picnic table and chairs off to the side, careful of the renegade soccer ball.

It's perfect. I couldn't ask for a better summer day. Relaxing with my family, soaking up the sun. Cyril reappears in the doorway with a bottle of wine. My heart flutters when he meets my gaze and smiles.

Yup, it's perfect.

"Here's the wine." He sets it on the table in front of my parents.

"Keys?" I ask, holding out my hand. "I don't want to lose them."

Cyril turns to hand them to me but they fall to the grass. "Whoops." He drops down and picks them up.

But he doesn't stand.

He's on one knee.

Gasps echo around me, but I can't hear anything. I can't see anything but the man before me, kneeling like a knight in shining armor, my key ring dangling from his fingertips.

Beside it is a ring with a diamond glimmering in the sunlight.

"Jessica, when I showed up at the shop that morning, I didn't know what to expect from the future." He takes a deep breath. "But the moment I saw you working on that 1974 Swinger, I knew you were the woman for me."

Laughter bubbles around us, but I stay focused on him. My lip trembles.

"I'm sorry I caused you so much trouble," he continues. "It wasn't my intention. I didn't have a friend in the world…at least not one under seventy." More laughter. "You taught me how to survive modern technology. I showed you the value of being old school."

My heart beats wildly against my ribs, and joy chokes me.

"We make a fantastic team, and I don't want anyone else by my side. Will you be my wife? My partner for life?"

"That's so corny." I laugh, even though tears fill my eyes. "But it's so you."

"Is that a yes?" Hope glimmers in his eyes.

"Yes," I say with a laugh. "Of course it's a yes."

Cheers erupt around us. Cyril climbs to his feet and pulls me into his arms.

When he kisses me, the chaos fades to background noise. He pulls back and brushes a stray curl from my face.

Never in a million years would I have imagined this moment. This man. The universe knew what it was doing when it plucked him from the past and dropped him in my lap. I didn't appreciate it at the time, but I do now.

He is exactly what I need in my life.

"I love you."

"Love you too." I squeeze him tight.

"Finally! Took you long enough." Dad's voice rises over the noise, cutting through our tender moment. "Can we eat now?"

Cyril and I laugh.

He's right though. It's about damn time.

CHAPTER 25

Cyrid

"Are you sure you don't want to go somewhere fancy to celebrate?" I ask, pushing open the door to the Black Penny.

"What's wrong with the Penny?" Jessica scoffs and pushes past me.

"Nothing."

We step inside, and the door closes behind me. The familiar sights and smells surround me, both from the eighties and last December when I challenged her to darts for the deed to the garage.

"This is a great place to celebrate our engagement."

Jessica shoots me a look and shakes her head. "Come on." She tugs my hand, pulling me deeper into the bar.

There's a crowd. Typical for a Friday night, but not as busy as I've seen it. We've made the Penny one of our weekly dates—I buy her a few drinks, she challenges me to darts. Then we go home and fuck. It's a win-win all around.

"Hey!" Jackie calls from behind the bar. She whispers something to the other bartender before coming out to join us. "Congrats."

"Word travels fast," I mutter as she pulls me into a hug.

"You really think my dad wouldn't call his friends and tell them the good news?" Jessica laughs and hugs Jackie.

"He called my dad right after you left. Then Dad called me." Jackie shrugs. "I guess I'm glad he didn't call everyone to tell them when my divorce was finalized."

"Congrats!" Jessica hugs her again. "He was a dick. You're better off without him."

"I am." Jackie laughs and lowers her voice. "I just don't need it broadcast across the city. I have enough problems with men hitting on me without them knowing I'm single again."

"Not interested in trying for round two?" I ask, pulling Jessica close and resting my hand on her hip.

"No. Abso-fucking-lutely not." She grins. "I've got enough problems to deal with running this place. This girl is off the market."

"Well, I'm happy for you. You deserve to take some time for yourself," Jessica says.

"Why don't you guys have a seat? I'll send a waitress over." Jackie gestures to the bar. "I gotta get back to work."

"Thanks." I lead Jessica to a booth along the far wall.

We settle onto the pleather bench and pick up the menus, even though we know exactly what we want.

"The usual?" Jessica asks.

"Yup." I push aside the menu and scan the bar. "Good crowd tonight."

"Mm-hmm."

"He's back," I say, my voice low.

"No way." Jessica's head snaps up from the menu. She spies the man in question. "He's in the same spot as last week?"

"Yeah. The far end of the bar. Back against the wall."

"Who is he?"

"I don't have a clue. Never met the guy."

"What's he doing here all the time?"

I study the mysterious man, watching his movements for a few moments. He takes a drink. Glances at his phone. Then looks up, his gaze following someone behind the bar.

Jackie.

"Shit."

"What?" Jessica claws at my hand. "Don't leave me in suspense."

"He's watching Jackie."

"Should we tell her?"

Jackie's attention fixes on the man in question. She puts a hand on her hip and scowls.

"Nope. She's already aware of it."

"What do you think he wants?"

I'm too far away to accurately read his expression, but I've been around long enough to know when someone's thirsty…and the drink in their hand isn't what they want.

Mindy, our waitress, arrives and takes our order. When she leaves, we gravitate toward the drama brewing at the bar. Jackie approaches the man and takes his empty glass.

Shit, I wish I could hear what they were saying, but there's too much commotion to even try to read their lips.

When our drinks arrive, we give up. I make a mental note to ask Jackie about it later.

I lift my glass in salute. "To us. Partners for life."

"Cheers." She clinks her glass against mine and takes a sip.

"Movie tonight?" I ask, settling back against the booth.

She gives me a look that says, *Really?*

"What? I have years of catching up to do."

"Fine." Jessica sets her glass down. "But we're not watching *Star Wars* again."

"You're no fun."

"There are hundreds of other movies to watch."

"Fine." I tap my fingers on the table.

Her eyes brighten. "I know. We'll watch *Willow*. You haven't seen it yet."

"What's *Willow*? Sounds sappy."

She laughs, and the sound makes my whole body vibrate with need. "Trust me. You'll love it."

"Sounds like there's something in this for you?"

A wicked smile curves her lips. "There is." She sighs. "Madmartigan."

"It's a hot guy, isn't it?"

Her laughter breaks free, and she nods.

"Am I not hot enough?" I pat my chest and run my hands over my T-shirt.

Jessica bites her lip. "You're smoking hot, babe."

"You're teasing me?"

She nods again. "You make it so easy."

I fold my arms across my chest and grumble. "Who plays this Madmartigan?"

"Val Kilmer."

"I take it back. He's hot."

Jessica reaches across the table and takes my hand. "I love you."

"I love you too." I look at the waitress approaching with our food. "Think we can get it to go?"

"No. Let's enjoy our meal." She releases my hand and winks. "You can have dessert later."

I pick up a French fry and shove it in my mouth. "Tease."

She blows a kiss to me. "You love it."

You're goddamn right I do.

Whispering a prayer of thanks, I drink her in. There's nowhere I'd rather be.

About the Author Kirsten S. Blacketer

Kirsten S. Blacketer is a multi-published indie author of both historical and contemporary romance. When she's not writing, she homeschools her two children and enjoys time with her family. In those moments of freedom, she devours romance novels while sipping a glass of wine. Age has only shown her that writing villains can be just as fun as heroes. Her next life goals are to write a New York Times Bestseller and one day have Adam Driver play a starring role in a film version of one of her books. A girl can dream, right?

Read more at **https://KirstenSBlacketer.com**

Also Writes as Jen Bradlee

OTHER TITLES BY KIRSTEN S. BLACKETER

Thieves of Winter Series

Jewel of Winter
At Winter's Demand
Under Winter's Control
Seducing Winter's Gentleman
Stealing the Widow's Heart

Historical

An Irresistible Shadow
A Shadow's Kiss
Mississippi Moonshine
Deceiving the Earl
Seduction on the Alpine Express
Temptation on the Alpine Express

Contemporary

A Lockdown Love Affair
A Holiday Love Affair
Mistletoe and Mistakes
Confessions of a Fangirl
Confessions of a Gamer Girl
Confessions of a Glamour Girl
The Flight Before Christmas
The Cosplayer
The Artist
The Bodyguard
The Director
The Author

Fantasy/Fairytale

Curse of the Huntsman's Jewel
The Huntsman's Revenge

Pirate Romance

Queen Takes Hook

Paranormal Historical Monster Romance

Death and Desire

www.ingramcontent.com/pod-product-compliance
Lightning Source LLC
Chambersburg PA
CBHW030347310726
48979CB00001B/211

* 9 7 8 1 9 6 6 9 0 5 1 9 6 *